T0375249

Dragon Prophecies

HERESY

L.B.B. DAVIS

authorHOUSE®

AuthorHouse™
1663 Liberty Drive
Bloomington, IN 47403
www.authorhouse.com
Phone: 1-800-839-8640

Published by AuthorHouse 4/1/2013

ISBN: 978-1-4817-3055-6 (sc)
ISBN: 978-1-4817-3054-9 (hc)
ISBN: 978-1-4817-3053-2 (e)

Library of Congress Control Number: 2013905000

Acknowledgment:

To my family and friends, you have always been there to help me. Even in the darkest of times.

Endless Ice

Endless Desert

Jade Rainforest

Mountains of Fire

Gulf of Dracaena

Black Marshes

Fortaleza

Azure Ocean

Ravenshaven

Strait of Dracon

Golden Plains

Angelek

Silver Mountains

Sidna

Kingdom of Alkine

Omiks

By L.B.B. Davis

Dragon Prophecies Series

Dragon Prophecies: Prodigy (2010)

Dragon Prophecies: Heresy (2013)

Dragon Prophecies: Victory (To be released)

Visit his website:

http://www.lbbdavis.com

Get updates about the series at:

https://www.facebook.com/DragonProphecies

Prologue

If war is possible, as far as it depends on you, live to die for the Holy Master. Take revenge, my dear friends, take up the Inquisition's wrath, for it is written: "It is mine to avenge; I will repay in full," says the Holy Master.

–Michael 16: 7-10

Necessity for the success of war: the army must be entirely clear why it is fighting and thoroughly convinced of the justness of its cause. This is neither "good" nor "evil" to stand aside while beasts are slaughtered.

–Shen 36: 23-26

Rebuke the wild beasts dwelling amongst the lands, the herd of bulls and calves of the common race; trample those who seek gold and delight in war. Kill in the name of Holy Master, and know that he knows all things.

–Michael 5: 3-6

As to those who reject faith, punish them with terrible agony in this world and the hereafter, nor will they have anyone to help. Those who believe fight in the cause of the Holy Master. Do not be weak hearted in pursuit of the enemy; if you suffer pain, then surely they suffer too.

–Shen 47: 37-40

Then I saw an angel coming down, holding in his hand a great spear of light. He seized the dragon, that ancient serpent, and killed it. The deceiver was dead and those who worshiped the beast or its image were lost or slain.

–Michael 10: 10-13

Rejoice brothers and use the sword of compassion to stab your enemy's heart. Use the axe of kindness to extend the enemy's head from their shoulders. Love your enemy and know that he will be released from this life and be reborn as a human. Do not weep for them; they are with the Holy Master.

–Shen 31: 16-19

The myths and legends tell us that humanity served as a beacon of light to the common races. Enlightened and inventive, humankind freed the other races from draconic slavery. After the fall of the Mixed Kingdoms, my people became willing slaves and listened to the Inquisition's words. We were lost to the Holy Master. Thus, it was foretold by our Master that the final war between dragons and humanity was on the brink. All would suffer.

–Book of Judas

Chapter 1

The moonlight shone down upon the city of Alkaline, the jewel of humanity, the birth place of the Inquisition, and the home of the divine demigod, the Holy Master. The city was cradled between the Hollylyassa River and the Azure Ocean. Sea walls and ports protected the city's vast shoreline. Even in the moonlight tide, docked ships rocked harmoniously in gentle waves. The occasional cry of a seagull disturbed the night's salty breeze. Dikes protected the city from the constant batter of the elements and flood-meadows were placed in strategic areas, insuring the protection of humanity's crown. Sewers dumped their waste freely into these artificial marshes and rinse with every high tide. Elegant cobblestone roads helped the populace move about the city. Clay tile roofs protected both owners and structures from the wildfires of the Gold Plains. Polished marble temples dedicated to the Iron Throne graced the city's skyline but the true jewel was the Iron Fortress of the Holy Master. The Iron Fortress was a monolith that dominated the cityscape. Both house of worship and a fortress, the massive structure was the crowning achievement of human design and architecture. The building was designed to withstand any assault, physically or magically.

Fear and excitement filled the night's air. Torches lit the citadel's wall and men were hidden within the darkness of archway. Sentries, armed with bows, crossbows, and bombarders, waited within the safety of torchlight. Many foolish thieves and assassins had met their end in a feeble attempt to penetrate the temple's defenses. Fanatical protectors guarded the temple and protective spells had been woven into the iron foundation of the walls.

Upon the highest archway, leading up to the mighty citadel, was a large red haired man in plate mail who stood in brooding silence. Monitoring the distant horizon for any signs of movement, his decorative armor gleamed in the firelight. A brazier burned next to him, keeping the nights chill at bay. He leaned heavily upon his halberd, a spear-like weapon designed to hew and jab. A slight movement of the shadows announced a small robed figure; he glanced over into the darkness of the archway where he was being observed.

"What are you doing here?" the robust man demanded as he turned to face the threat.

"Does your midnight vigil dull your senses?" the hidden robed figure asked in a low and commanding voice echoed from the safety of the corridor.

"What do you know about keeping watch, Shen? You study your books, but know little about warfare. Why the Holy Master acknowledges you as an Inquisitor Lord, I'll never know," the red haired man growled.

"Michael, your age is starting to show," the shadowy figure teased. "It is only by our Master's grace that your war wounds and past injuries have not killed you. It is my faith and knowledge of ancient text that makes me invaluable to our Master."

"Your words are written with blood and shit! When you die, I will enjoy burning your life's work," Michael snarled. He returned his gaze to the distant horizon.

"Ignorance of a lowly warrior," Shen mused.

Michael grinned, the firelight danced off of his face, revealing the scars of past battles. "You cling to your books like a baby would cling to a mother's teat," he let out a halfhearted chuckle. "Words fall mute at the point of a sword."

"The pen is mightier than the sword," Shen countered. He revealed a white feathered quill from beneath his robes.

Michael's grin only grew wider. "Let's put your theory to the test," He raised his halberd and leveled it directly at Shen. A sudden breeze made him pause. The breeze turned into a gust that nearly toppled him over. The blast of air made the torches and braziers whip all the citadel's fires simultaneously extinguished. Cries of surprise and fear rose among the posted and hidden men. Michael turned to face a massive gold dragon staring down at him. He stumbled backwards in awe at the sudden appearance of the massive creature before him. He did not even hear the wing beats or the massive beast land. It was as if the giant golden beast appeared by magic! Shock and fear gripped Michael's tongue as he stared up in awe and amazement. The gold dragon shimmered in a faint golden light, surrounding her in an aura of beauty and splendor. The dragon was graced with two smooth golden horns and several whiskers which resembled the barbels of a catfish.

"I have arrived at your request, Inquisitor Lord," the dragon spoke in a strong feminine voice. She cleared her throat and looked down at the prone human. She breathed deeply, taking in Michael's scent. "Your tunic states that you are an Inquisitor Lord, yet you are not the one that sent the messages. I am mistaken?"

"H-halt!" Michael croaked. His stuttering word barely came out as a whisper. The dragon raised a questioning eyebrow to the meek human's command.

"Then you are not the one I seek," the gold dragon grumbled.

"Alarm!" Michael screamed. The sound of grinding cranks and cocking flintlock sounded in the air around them. Soldiers raced to the edge of the battlements above them. Encouraged by the sound of reinforcements, Michael stood up and pointed his weapon at the dragon before him. "I command you to halt! By order of the Inquisition, the Lords of Alkaline, and decreed by the Royal Guard of the Holy Master!"

"Michael, that is no way to treat our most distinguished quest," a soft whisper sliced through the air. Michael turned to look behind him. The frail figure stepped from the shadows of the fortress' massive corridor. Foreign robes flowed behind the slender statured man.

"Stay out of this, Shen Tianxiang!" Michael warned. "Dragons are not welcomed within the city! Monsters are not allowed on this Holy Site! It is tainted-"

"I am aware of our city's laws, having written several of them myself," Shen advised. "This is Vatara, leader of the Gold Clan."

"You are consorting with dragons!" Michael growled. The robust man gripped his halberd tighter and stepped away from the towering dragon. The cleaver like weapon gleamed in the moonlight.

"As an Inquisitor Lord, you should place-," Shen continued.

"I sent word of my arrival," Vatara interrupted. The two squabbling men stopped glaring at each other and focused on the gold dragon before them. "Humans are boisterous when they are startled; they would rather talk someone to death than get to any meaningful discussion."

"You scaly piece of sh-," Michael growled.

"Forgive us my lady," Shen bowed deeply. He walked out of the archway and into the moonlight. He wore exotic white silk robes that hung loosely off of his small frame. The royal purple symbol of the Iron Throne was embroidered across the back of his fine robes. The garb appeared two sizes too big for his thin and wiry body. Not only was Shen's clothing odd, but his skin was darker than Michael's weathered face. His brown eyes where slanted and had the unusual semblance of a cat. Michael towered over the smaller man and he tapped his weapon impatiently. His scarred face contorted as he glared at both dragon and fellow human. Both men were dwarfed by the elegant creature before them. Her gold scales danced and shimmered under the moonlight. She glanced up at the soldiers above them as they aimed their weapons at her.

"Is it a new custom for the Inquisition to point their weapons at guests?" Vatara asked calmly.

"Our bombarders have improved in precision and firepower, worm!" Michael growled.

Shen placed a hand upon his fellow Inquisitor Lord's shoulder and placed a finger up to his lips to silence him. He then returned his attention to Vatara. "You may leave if you wish," Shen offered. "As I recall, it was you that desired an audiences with the Holy Master."

Vatara snorted at the small human's statement. "Your scent is familiar; you must have been the one that sent the message. Your name is Shen, correct?" She focused her attention on the frail figure before her. "I have seen your kind before: Alchemist. You must be from across the seas. I was unaware that the Inquisition was accepting converts and foreigners into their ranks."

"Impressive," he nodded his head to her in respect. "You have seen the outside world and my nation. I am honored that you are aware of my people from across the sea. However, my new home is here. My devotion is to the Holy Master," a faint smile play across his lips. "It is as pure as your white flame," Shen bowed deeply and gracefully.

"Is that a hint of flattery or mockery?" Vatara smirked. "You seem to be aware of my clan's traditions. I must admit, I am impressed by your statement, a feat not easily achieved by a human."

"What? What are you talking about?" Michael demanded.

"The white flame is what the Gold Clan worships," Shen explained. "It is one of the five dragon elements."

"Those words are sacrilege against our Master's teachings!" Michael snarled. "The Holy Master preaches against such bizarre views! There are only four pure elements: air, fire, earth and water!"

"Man imagines elements and even they cannot agree on them!" Vatara countered. "I have not come to discuss philosophy about what is true or false,

4

but of a warning, I have important information that is only for the Holy Master's ears."

"We are the Holy Master's eyes and ears," Michael countered. "Pass your message onto us so that we may deliver it onto him."

"This is not possible," Vatara warned. Shen and Michael glanced at each other. The dragon stared down the barrel of several bombarders and was not intimidated.

"Perhaps a letter can be sent, if you do not wish to present your request to us," Shen offered.

"This is not a request, but a warning," Vatara explained.

"We have already dealt with the plague," Shen concluded. Vatara shook her head in disgust. The two Inquisitors looked at each other. "By the grace of the Holy Master, our kingdom was spared from the ravages of the plague." Vatara's jaws clenched and said nothing. She knew that it was the Silver Clan and the elves who had suffered under the relentless destruction of the plague. The dragons and elves had been humanity's buffer against the tide of endless undead. Fortune smiled upon the human race because they hadn't lost a city or friend to that horrible, conscience disease, but that had only been possible at the ultimate expense of the Kingdom of Angakok. Shen continued: "I understand that the Elf Kingdoms and the Silver Mountains were not as blessed as the Kingdom of Alkaline. Their destruction was foreseen by the Holy Master, a testament to the divine will of our great Lord."

"Yet neither the Holy Master nor the Inquisition made any attempt to help prevent those disasters!" Vatara growled. "I have not come here to spar idle words with you. Allow me access to the Holy Master."

"Why?" Michael demanded. "So that you may curse our Master, you foul ethereal serpent!" At that, Vatara's eyes narrowed as a burst of white flames and smoke erupted from her nostrils. Michael, realizing he had pushed the dragon too far, fled from the towering beast. Her eyes glowed with unnatural fury. Michael ran to the nearest corridor and snatched the nearest guard's crossbow. With his new weapon he took aim at Vatara.

"Forgive his outburst!" Shen shouted. He boldly stepped between the aiming man and dragon, unwilling for blood to be shed. Her eyes softened slowly but her glowing eyes did not yield their threatening glare. "My Lady, please forgive his outburst. I plead ignorance on his behalf!"

"I have come on friendly terms, *Inquisitor*!" Vatara growled. She stressed the word Inquisitor as a cow would regurgitate a piece of cud. The two stared

5

at each other in silence. Michael remained within the safety of the corridor, pitifully sheltered behind his weapon.

"It seems that we are at an impasse," Shen stated. "We will not take you to see the Holy Master, yet you continue to refuse to pass on your warning." He crossed his arms while Vatara snorted in frustration. She studied Wen's intractable expression for several moments before sighing quietly.

"Humanity is on the verge of a great war," Vatara stated bluntly as she gave up her resolve to impart information to the Holy Master. "They have slaughtered the sacred herds of the Golden Plains. For over ten thousand years the dragon clans have fed from those herds. They were our main food source for generations beyond counting. Throughout the centuries, the clans have allowed the poaching of our sacred bison, but only when the common races were in times of need. Never in history have our herd been taken or killed so mercilessly and needlessly. Your race, the humans, has butchered them so wantonly that the herds have been reduced to numbers incapable of supporting the Dragon Clans. This is unacceptable and will not go unpunished."

"I am aware of your plight, Lady Vatara," Shen nodded his head understanding. "It was the Holy Master's command that the legions of the Inquisition slaughter the bison herds." Vatara narrowed her eyes dangerously at the tiny human before her.

"I do not understand. I must be allowed to speak with the Holy Master," Vatara warned.

"No. I cannot, will not, grant your request for an audience," Shen stated. "Not after what I just told you."

"I assure you that I mean him no harm," Vatara pressed. "I mean to find the cause, the meaning of this senseless slaughter. I am not inclined to war, unlike the rest of my race is."

"Under normal circumstances," Shen offered. "The Holy Master would willingly accept such a request from any dragon. However, he suspects the dragons of plotting the destruction of the common races."

"What do you mean?" Vatara demanded.

"Please understand-," Shen muttered.

"That is enough!" Michael interrupted. The two turned their attention to the scarred man.

"She has a right to know!" Shen defended.

"She is a dragon!" Michael spat. "They are enemies of our Master! To have an open dialog with the beast is unforgivable!"

"Perhaps sinful, but not unforgivable," Shen was amused and he returned his gaze to Vatara and gave a quick bow.

"I did not realize that we had heretics among the Inquisitor Lords!" Michael accused. He waved his crossbow threateningly in the air. Shen turned his back to him, trusting that, because of his show of respect to Vatara, he could count on the dragon to intervene should Michael threaten to attack his flank.

"Please understand that the Holy Master is expecting an assault upon his kingdom," Shen sighed. "He has foreseen this."

"What do you mean?" Vatara prompted.

"He expects treachery," Shen stated. "Even among the Inquisition, he has felt the subtle changes within our world. He knows that the black flame has returned to feed off of the living again."

"The plague is over," Vatara stated. "A silver dragon has destroyed both the plague and its leader."

"Silver dragons, so they really do exist," Shen awed is astonishment. Vatara raised an eyebrow in concern. "As was foreseen, you must forgive me. I-I am surprised that dragons exist at all. Your species are quite rare, and has only been seen by a lucky few." Vatara acute senses allowed her to hear Shen's heart skipped a beat and she could smell the sudden scent of perspiration that began to arise from him. "Please tell me more about theses silver dragons, especially about the one that defeated Orelac and the plague."

"Strange Inquisitor, that you should know the name of Orelac," Vatara growled. Shen gulped nervously and relaxed his face an expression of intense interest to one of innocence.

"Rumors, gossip, myths, and child's tales, I assure you," Shen offered defensively. "Is it true that a silver hatchling defeated the plague's leader?" Vatara remained expressionless as she stared down at him. She did not reply to his question. "Your silence tells me everything."

"Why the sudden interest in this hatchling?" Vatara demanded.

"Hatchling, you say? Did you know that cults have been created among the humans, all claiming to swear devotion to the dragon that calls itself the *Defender of the Common Races*," Shen stated. "Are you or the Silver Clans aware of this strange phenomenon?"

"No," Vatara stated bluntly.

"Speaking as an Inquisitor Lord, this cult is disturbing to the church and to our Master. Cults and foreign beliefs are not allowed within our kingdom, as I'm sure that you are already aware." Vatara narrowed her eyes and nodded her head in understanding. Shen placed both of his hands within his robes.

"You would blame this cult on the dragons?" Vatara mused. "Do you place blame on this hatchling?"

"Yes, there can only be one leader of humanity, only one true Master," Shen stressed. "You can understand the Inquisition's stance on the subject of false idol worship. Dragons are not gods, regardless of how powerful you believe you are."

"A subject that we can both agree upon," Vatara conceded. "That is beside the point. Your race's problems are none of my concern and you have not addressed your Master's crimes against the dragon clans."

"It is not our job to question the will of the Holy Master," Shen countered. "As his servants, it's our only duty is to carry out the Holy Master's will, not to question his divinity."

"I am aware of your fanaticism," Vatara stated. "However, your Master's actions have pitted our two races against each other."

"Then why have you come?"

"I have come to speak with the Holy Master," Vatara stated smoothly. "I am seeking restitution for his crimes."

"You have already declared that the dragon clans are willing to go to war, as was foretold," Shen announced. "It would be dangerous to both parties if I were to allow you access to our religious, military, and divine leader. I, therefore, also assume that you knew this would occur."

"You are aware of the white flame?" Vatara asked. "My clan has always value life above all else. A life is not to be wasted on meaningless sacrifice or pointless wars. Life has a reason and a purpose. Five years ago, everyone suffered from the spread of the plague, common races and dragon kind alike. Your advance guard was infected and helped add to the destruction of the elf kingdom of Angakok. A failed assault cost the lives of thousands of elves. Did your demigod predict that? Did he foresee the destruction caused by the undead?"

Shen replied with a nod of his head. "Why do you, or the Gold Clan for that matter, care about what our Master predicts?" he thought out loud. "It is not in the nature of your species to care about those they consider to be lesser."

"If you cannot answer that question, then you do not truly know of our ways," Vatara snorted. "My clan has always attempted to protect the common races from their own stupidity. Our involvement has always been in the interests of protecting life."

"Your efforts have never been requested or required," Shen pointed out.

"Our two histories have always been entwined," Vatara growled. "Even the Holy Master is aware of my clan's involvement within his own creation."

"Kill the blasphemous worm and fire at will!" A forgotten Michael bellowed in an enraged voice. The effect was immediate, the roar of bombarder fire erupted, and overwhelming the sound of crossbows and bows twanging while smoke from the black powder blocked the vision of soldiers on the wall. The smoke quickly obscured the men's view from the walls, and shots became inaccurate.

"No! Stop, damn you!" Shen ordered. His orders were drowned out by the storm of lead balls and arrow ricocheting off of the floor of the iron fortress. Shen fled before the deadly storm of ammunition which poured around him like rain. A crossbow's bolt pierced his robe as he attempted to make his escape. As he made it into the corridor, Shen collapsed under sudden intense pain. He glanced briefly down at his right leg. A splinter from the errant bolt had passed directly through his upper thigh and from that hole he bled freely. He tore off a piece of his robe and wrapped around his injury.

"Still alive, are we?" Michael chuckled. Shen looked up to see his fellow Inquisitor Lord with an empty crossbow in his hand. "You need to be more careful on where your allegiance lies."

"Y-you?" Shen winced, through gritted teeth.

"Yes, you need to be more careful," Michael grinned. He walked up the injured man and looked at the bloody makeshift bandage. "Yes, you can never tell where an enemy will strike. You may have command of the written word, Shen, but I control the legionnaires. It would be wise to remember that."

"You're a damn fool!" Shen snarled. "I was getting information!"

"False words of the serpent can never be trusted," Michael intimidated the injured man. "She'll never spread lies of our god again!"

"Lies or truth," A thunderous boom sounded through the corridor. Michael fell to the ground, throwing up his arms to block out the sound. Men on top of the battlement cried out as the booming voice echoed throughout the fortress. "You would dare strike against the Gold Clan! Your religious fervor has cost you more then you will ever know!" The fog of war lifted to reveal Vatara unscathed by the deadly storm of ammunition that should have annihilated her.

"Im-Impossible!" Michael stuttered.

"The human race has always been pathetically stubborn!" Vatara growled. "Know that we could have been on friendly terms! Your actions have proven otherwise. It is sad to know that this city will fall and the Iron Throne shall be torn asunder!"

"We have accepted our fate, serpent!" Michael spat.

"Then so be it!" Vatara roared. She reared back, deadly front claws slashing the air, and then her body became translucent, turned into shimmering residue, and disappeared into faintly golden mist. Braziers and torchlight rekindled suddenly, revealing nothing but quickly fading smoke.

"The beast used witchcraft!" Michael gasped. "Search the castle! Search for the evil spirit, she must not escape! She could not have gone far!" Shen smiled in amusement, but the grin changed to a wince in as a rush of pain raced up his thigh. Michael and his men raced wildly about the fortress, searching in vain for the gold dragon. Shen knew that the dragon had never really been there; what they had seen was a magical illusion conjured by the mythical beast. Shen limped back outside and looked up at the night's sky, where he saw the kite-like wings of Vatara. The golden figure disappeared into the darkness of the night's sky.

Chapter 2

"By the spirits," Sacul groaned. "Don't we have any ham or salted pork? I could use some meat." The short boarelf shaman was covered in thick furs and lean on a walking stick. The short pig humanoid walked in the wake of his taller and leaner knoll companion, Bar. The knoll, a man-sized wolfish humanoid trudged through the snow of the Endless Ice. Both were covered in furs to keep the cold at bay. Despite the season being spring, the frozen tundra never thawed. Their marching footsteps and the biting wind was the only sound they heard. The frozen waste was flat and barren; even the crunching snow seemed devoid of sound. Sacul leaned heavily upon his walking stick. Bar favored his left arm, which hung limply in a reinforced sling. A weapon, hidden in fur hides was cradled comfortably against his injured arm and sling. Clumps of snow and ice clung on their clothing and accumulated around their noses and mouths.

"You've have a sick sense of humor," Bar grumbled. "Wouldn't it be cannibalism if you ate pork?"

"No!" Sacul grumbled. His face scrunched down into a frown; ice fell off of his tusks. "I've always heard that the knolls ate wolves and dogs! Isn't that cannibalism?"

"We do," Bar chuckled. "Wolves taste similar to chicken." He let out another chuckle, but his laughter faded into the cold wind. "Traveling through this snow is hard work and I could use some rest. Why don't you take the lead?"

"You're doing a fine job," Sacul chuckled. He reached up and patted his larger companion on the back. The knoll turned sharply and growled. Their pace had continually slowed ever since the new snow had fallen. Weeks of traveling had taken its toll on the two companions.

"I've taken the lead for the past hundred leagues," Bar grumbled. "Your nomadic life style doesn't suit me. Don't forget that it was your idea to track Luke into the Endless Desert and then north into this frozen wasteland!"

"Yes, as I recall, you wanted to follow after me," Sacul gave him a toothy grin. "Everyone owes the silver dragon a deep debt for defeating the plague and saving our lives. Admit it! You've been worried about him ever since we departed the Silver Mountains."

"Luke, he wanted us to leave," Bar growled. "Our presence endangered his clan. Be grateful that we didn't wear out our welcome. Remember, that not every silver dragon is our friend. Luke is unique. I had a hand in rearing him, as well as his mother and fathers, both were outstanding and noble dragons."

"Oh, that explains why he's so screwed up," Sacul chuckled. Bar pushed him down into the snow. "Why did you do that?" The shaman watched as Bar huffed and continued trudging through the snow. The boarelf jumped up and gave chase after his friend. "Wait for me!"

"For a coward, you seem to have a brave tongue!" Bar grumbled. "You forget that it was the plague that drove us to work together!"

"How inspiring," Sacul mocked. "That doesn't excuse Lukhan from forcing us to leave! We were doing so well together and yet our team broke apart! He should have never made us leave!" His voice fell into a pout; the shaman was putting on an act for his age.

"Luke must have had his reasons," Bar mumbled. "He wouldn't have left his homeland, without telling his mother or me." He frowned at the thought; Luke had always been close to his family. The young dragon was no fool but having no land to call his own and without allies he was in danger. Bar shuddered at the thought. Luke had always been secretive about his well-being. He assumed that his friend's isolation was because he was a dragon. The dragon race had always been independent from the common races. Dragons were stronger, larger, and more magically gifted than any other race in Lemuria. His companion had all of these traits. That was one of several reasons why they believed that Lukhan was still alive.

"Talk to me," Bar grumbled. "We traveled throughout the Endless Desert and didn't find him. What makes you believe that he is in this forsaken land?"

"Have you forgotten that I'm connected to the spirit world?" Sacul asked. He waved his hands around mysteriously and reached into his bag and produced his pet toad. The cane toad was curled into a shivering protective ball. "By the spirits, are you all right?" He buried his pet under his furs to share his body heat. The small toad chirped in appreciation and Sacul cooed to the little pet.

"Why did you bring that thing with us?" Bar growled. "You need to find yourself another pet. Burr, this cold will be the death of us."

"Blah. My pet is my connection to the spirit world," Sacul smiled. "How do you think I am able to follow Lukhan?" He referred to the powerful hallucinogenic poison of his pet toad. The small creature produced a toxin from its glands that the boarelf would lick. For the shaman, the toad's poison induced visions from the spirit world. Centuries of living in the Endless Desert, and eating deadly plants and animals, had hardened the boarelf race to the extreme.

"It's not because of your tracking skills!" Bar growled. "Your spirit quest has led us into sandstorms, blizzards, and wild animals! I never understood how you managed to stay alive during our countless travels. Without my help, you would've been eaten!" Disgusted, he turned away from Sacul and his strange little pet. He had to question his own sanity for following the shaman out into the frozen waste after their unsuccessful track through the Endless Desert.

"True," Sacul smiled. "Have faith! I'm following our friend's spiritual presence. It has been over a month since I last connected with the spirit world. It was the spirits that told me where to search for our missing friend."

"Spirits don't care about the comforts of the living," Bar grumbled. "Nor do they have to eat or drink." He checked his leather-skin canteen; the water was frozen inside of it. Bar cursed and stuck the frozen canteen under his furs; the icy bag chilled his side. He cursed a few more times.

"What's the matter?" Sacul asked.

"Damn water has frozen again," Bar cursed. "What about your water skin?"

"Here, take mine," Sacul offered. He offered the half-filled canteen to his friend. The knoll took a long draft of water, a horrible taste filled his mouth, he spat out the thick liquid.

"What's this crap?" Bar spat and sputtered.

"Yak's milk!" Sacul smiled. Bar handed the water skin back to him. Sacul took a long draft and smacked his lips at his disgusted companion.

"You need to drink water," Bar frowned. "How in the world did you get yak's milk out here?" He looked around warily; he had not seen any tracks or evidences of the beasts.

"You shouldn't worry so much!" Sacul smiled. "You should have more faith in the spirits." His toothy grin did not reassure Bar. The hunter's tracking skills were the best among the knoll tribes. Although this was a strange and foreign land, the telltale signs of the wild herds should have been evident. Sacul walked in silence behind him. After another league of silent marching, Bar turned to his companion.

"Where did you get the yak's milk?" Bar grumbled. "Don't give me that spiritual crap again!"

"Oh?" Sacul smiled. "Did the big bad hunter miss the yak and its calf? What were you going to do? Eat them?"

Bar raised a questioning eyebrow to the shaman. "Hey!" he grumbled. "If you haven't noticed, we are in need of supplies! We're in the middle of a frozen sheet of ice! There is no food to hunt or scavenge! We're out looking for my best friend, who has been missing, without success!"

"A journey begins with a single step," Sacul offered. "You must release your illusion of control and let things occur. Like a tree, you must bend with the wind, or else you will become brittle and break."

"Like a jackass you make too much noise," Bar mocked.

"We've been in worse situations," Sacul chuckled. Bar rolled his eyes and groaned. "You and Lukhan are like my brothers. You've taught him many things. Have faith in your friend's abilities and moral character."

"You forget that Luke is not alone-," Bar warned.

"Yes," Sacul stated gravely. "The Betrayer is with him. I have no doubt that Lukhan would be able to keep Vilesath in check. Do you think that he left because of that fact? That he left because he didn't want to hurt anyone?"

"I don't know," Bar mumbled. "Luke wasn't himself when he left. Vilesath wasn't of this world. The Betrayer had powers beyond anyone's expectations and used ancient magic."

"Yes," Sacul agreed. "It was Lukhan that defeated the plague. He didn't need the claw or Vilesath's help."

"Luke said that the plague was created by Vilesath," Bar countered. "I believe that he is nothing more than a means to an end, a tool to be used and then discarded."

"A tool?" Sacul thought out loud. "Lukhan defied Vilesath's command to sacrifice us. We won and the world is safe from the undead plague. He defied his own sense of self preservation, out of love and kindness. Vilesath could never corrupt him, have faith in him."

"I hope you're correct," Bar muttered uneasily.

⇒◆⇐

There is nothing more to this world then life and death. Lukhan watched a yak and its suckling calf from his aerial position. The two long-haired bovines moved slowly through the snow, unaware of the predator above them. A choice had to be made; kill the calf or its mother. Normally, this decision was easily made. His instincts would kick in and he would target the weak. To survive, he would have to eat. The bitter wind shifted and Lukhan adjusted his wings accordingly. The sight of the mother and calf brought back bitter memories of his past life, before he became an apparition of his former self. He was now nothing more than an exiled half-blood with a wretched deformity.

He was a cursed creature with an unnatural existence.

His self-imposed isolation had forced him to become more animal than dragon. The once noble creature had become harden with the harsh truth of reality. His once smooth and polished scales of his race had become flawed and chipped by conflict and war. His flesh had taken the same tone as the ice below him, jagged and scarred. Unlike the natural land below him, his scars came from his battle with the plague. The conflict and elements had taken its toll on the young dragon's growing body. Those savage scars had regenerated unnaturally. Fatal wounds that would have normally killed any of his kin had become nothing more than a patchwork of white and black scarring. He was alive.

He glanced down at his grotesque left claw. The main deformity, that which had caused him so much grief and suffering. He had grown into the unnatural deformity. The abnormal digit was only slightly larger than his other claws. The ugly thing twitched in preparation for the kill. Lukhan knew that the claw had only one purpose. Unlike his other claws, which could touch anything with the heaviest of dexterity, the black claw seemed to have a will of its own. The foul appendage would kill and absorb the white flames of others. In doing so, Lukhan would feel and see everything that the victim had done in its life. As their souls were being torn from their bodies, their pain, sorrow, and knowledge would be passed on to him.

15

Lukhan felt that he was losing himself to those memories of the others he gathered. Images and flash backs would cloud his present thoughts and threatened to overwhelmed him. On occasion, he would learn something new, such as magic or cultural traditions. Due to his targeted aggression of those he knew as evil, he learned of their overwhelming hatred and lust for power. Every time he killed, he would witness the evil acts of others as if he himself had committed them. Within this strange trance of witnessing evil, Lukhan' aggression rose to new heights. Fury would drive his battle lust and he could no longer tell friend from foe. He had nearly turned and killed his companions. Guilt had overwhelmed him. Despite his mother's and godmother's noble defense, there was no way he could hide his aggressive nature. The Silver Clan knew that there was something wrong with him. He had tried to keep the secret to himself, however, even the wise ancient Cirrus knew him for what he really was: an inferior mockery of his formal self.

He had betrayed his friends by nearly killing them. He had betrayed his family by unknowingly selling his soul to the creator of the plague, which had taken so many of the Silver Clan. He had betrayed his mother, Crystal, by becoming the thing that killed his father. He had betrayed his godmother, Vatara, by not listening to her and siding with the magic of death. He had betrayed himself by abandoning his identity, his white flame sacrificed so the world could live. He was rejected by the clan he had saved.

Division ruled the lands of Lemuria, ever since the Dragon Wars, only five clans grew to supreme power. The others dragon clans that were not part of the five were considered to be inferior and impure. They were both hunted down and destroyed, or they would flee to the ends of the world to become outcasts. Within the individual dragon clans' blood and power were station and status. Lukhan mixed his blood with an ancient black dragon named Vilesath. His black claw was evidences of this graft. This act alone was unacceptable.

The demonic claw was made of unnatural death magic and alchemy, an extension of the Betrayer's corrupted spirit. Vilesath, the shadow dragon, helped Lukhan and his companions defeat the plague. The immortal spirit had abandoned him when he was desperate for victory. The Oracle had saved him, only to abandon him. He hated the immortal fiend. He had hope- no prayed- that the blast of white flame and life magic had destroyed the loathsome death master. Ever since the destruction of the plague, the ancient spirit never communicated with him. He hoped the creator of the plague was destroyed with his creation. The idea comforted him; the dark lord had left his mark, both physically and spiritually. The once carefree hatchling was gone. He was broken, a former shadow of himself, as Vilesath had warned.

A movement from below captured his attention. The two yaks shifted slightly, a sudden explosion of snow announced the arrival of a giant centipede. The massive worm's reddish brown body and antennae spread across the snow in search of prey. Its eyes were small and narrow; the creature's visual acuity was poor. Its legs were short and thin, but the dragon knew better. The centipede's burrowing speed could easily keep pace with the fleeing mother and calf through the snow. Its large venomous fangs were used for both burrowing and killing. The ugly creature did not bellow or scream but instead remained silent and felt around blindly in the snow. After feeling blindly the centipede submerged itself under the ice and chased after the fleeing bison. Lukhan had met the ugly things before. A colony of the pests lived under the Endless Ice. The giant vermin would dive under the ice and use their body heat and fangs to cut through the tundra's ice.

Lukhan lowered his altitude as he approached the two fleeing yaks. From his aerial position, he watched as the centipede approached the calf. He dove to the ground, like an owl targeting a mouse beneath the snow. His claws ripped through the ice and latched on to the centipede. The creature's superheated body was hot to the touch. Lukhan ignored the searing pain. The body segments bunched and twisted in his claws as he ripped the creature out of its natural habitat. The worm turned on him with its protruding fangs, hissing at the unexpected attacker. Lukhan sank his black claw into the creature's head, cutting through thick exoskeleton.

The creature's white flame transferred instantly into Lukhan' mind. Flashes of the beast's life under the ice danced within the dragon's mind. Feeling and smell became his main perception. None of the blurry underground images made any sense to him. They were random and jumbled under the instant transfer of life magic. The dragon's chipped and damaged scales reverted to their sleek and original shape. His worn body regenerated under the centipede's transfer of its life's vitality. The worm's tough fiery body coiled and grew tight against him. The creature's emotionless black eyes and antennae fell on him. Its shell ripped apart as it withered and was absorbed into the black claw. A soothing sensation filled Lukhan as the worm's innards disappeared under the assault of the black claw. The vast emptiness inside of him filled, relief was instant. However, the relief was only temporary; the vast hunger was always present. The darkness within him could never be filled with the souls of others. The black claw did not mutilate the corpse; instead it had sucked it dry. Even the venom was absorbed by the foul thing.

Lukhan glanced over and watched the yak and its calf flee the bloody scene. They would never realize who or what had saved them from the giant vermin. He smiled at that thought. The irony of the situation was both sad and humorous. He had not realized how close he was to starvation. He glanced down at his newly rejuvenated body. Both muscle and scale returned to their former glory, but even that was only temporary cosmetics. Within a week of his self-imposed starvation, his body would begin to break down and reveal his scarred and broken body. Then he would have to seek out the yak and its calf and devour them in the same manner. Such relief, like life, was temporary.

Chapter 3

"Home," Lukhan muttered. The empty words barely slipped past his lips. They fell utterly short as the sharp winds stole them away. He looked into the vast depths of an empty ice cave. His isolated home was in the middle of the frozen wasteland, which stretched for thousands of leagues in every direction. No dragon clan would call the Endless Ice their home. Food was scarce and treasure was locked beneath the frozen ground. The entrance to his home was hollowed out bedrock that was thermally insulated; the water slowly froze as it dripped down the cave's interior. This flowing water gathered in the middle of the entrance and raced down into the belly of the cave. The cavern never froze due to the constant breeze and water flowing down the sides of the shallow cave. Despite the bitter cold and freezing water, Lukhan was resistant to the frozen temperatures. The elements did not affect him as they would with other creatures. The Silver Clan was born from the element of air, and benefited from their forefather's extremist and elitist views of magical manipulation of their bodies. The cold would never kill him.

He sighed and entered his home's frozen depths. The ice gathered within a bottleneck blocking his path. He pushed through the narrow gaps. He had grown physically larger since his feeding. When he had left his home, he had easily walked through the narrow gap. With his muscles and scales regenerated, the small cave seemed to have shrunk. He did not care; his hunger would drive him out to feed within a week when he reverted to his skeletal size. His spirit rose as he entered the main chamber of his home. He had allowed himself one treasure within this forsaken land, a single bright light within a white void, the Staff of Selgae.

Reflections of light bounced off the ice crystals and golden staff. The elf forged artifact was encased in an ice crystalline in the center of his frozen cave. He had placed the staff in the frozen block of ice before he had left the cave to insure its protection from thieves. The artifact held immense magical power. Although a thief was unlikely, he would not take the chance of someone stealing such a powerful artifact. His last engagement with the plague leader, Orelac, had left him with several scars. The power of the staff enhanced the plague leader to near immortality. Lukhan had been hard pressed to defeat Orelac due to his unnatural regenerating capabilities. His deformity had proven successful against the undead. They had no soul to absorb, but their flesh gave way.

He looked through the crystal formation. The ice crystal was a formidable defense; however, the claw could cut through any material. With a slash, the ice slid apart from the staff in smooth chunks. The staff dropped heavily upon the floor in a single clatter. Memories of when he first saw the staff muddled his mind. He seemed destined to possess it; he had killed twice to obtain the powerful artifact.

The first time he had killed was to release his friends from being executed by the crazed Grand Magus Kale. The Grand Magus was a leader among the elves in the city of Angakok. The corrupt elf sacrificed his longevity for magical and political powers. The elves' faith within the ruling class was based on individual's intelligence of the magical arts. The magi had political power, but the addiction of magic shortened their lives and slowly drove them insane. Magic would slowly consume the user's soul, as was dictated within the ten laws of magic. That was why Lukhan had killed, to protect his friends from the magic induced madness. He had personally felt the addictive effects of magic; it was the reason he was corrupted. He watched as the powerful artifact rolled back and forth on the floor. It finally came to a stop.

This was the second time he had contact with the Staff of Selgae. He had revenged his father's murder by tricking the powerful plague leader named Orelac. The villain foolishly sacrificed himself thus destroying the plague he once controlled. Yet Lukhan still felt empty inside. The act of revenge did not settle well with him. The burning hatred did not die in a flash of magic. With the plague destroyed, the dragon clans reverted to their pathetic rivalries. The war with the plague did not stop with its destruction; the Green and Black Clans turned on each other. His families' sacrifice meant nothing to the world. The war between the dragon clans raged on with countless lives lost. No matter what he did, it would never make a difference.

"It is because of me," Lukhan whispered. "It is because of my own weaknesses." His words were lost in the dripping of the icy cold water. He continued to stare at the ancient artifact before him. His black claw twitched in greedy anticipation.

The staff increased Orelac's and Kale's magical abilities by a thousand fold. If Lukhan claimed the powerful artifact, he could use it for his own means, end the war, and unite Lemuria into one peaceful nation. He would not have to be afraid of his own clan. He could come out of hiding as leader of this new world order! He could ensure peace throughout the world. The power of the Staff of Selgae was before him. Endless possibilities raced through his mind as he considered leading the dragon clans under a single powerful nation.

The illusion of magic was intoxicating.

"Enough!" Lukhan roared. "I have never desired power! My actions were to benefit the world! I do not need the self-satisfaction of others acknowledging what I have done! I will not become my own enemy! I will never be like Orelac!" The ideas of peace and unification faded into his cold surroundings. He took several deep breaths before realizing what had occurred. His own addiction to magical power clouded his judgment. He truly desired all of those things. He wanted peace, praise, and love from others. The price was too high and he shook his head in disgust at his weakness. With his black claw, he reached forward and grasped the Staff of Selgae.

⊰⊷⊱

"What is that smell?" Bar grumbled. "D-did you pass gas?"

"What? I don't know what you are talking about-," Sacul stated sheepishly. The shaman had taken the lead of the group's travels. Bar's demands had taken its toll on Sacul; the boarelf reluctantly accepted the change of being the first one to trudge through the snow. Unfortunately, for Bar, the yak's milk did not set well within his smaller companion's stomach. Being both behind and downwind of Sacul's position only made matters worse.

"Do you need to wipe or something?" Bar grumbled.

"What would I wipe with? Do you see any leaves or plants? You have problems, you know that! It is a perfectly normal function of the body." Sacul snapped.

"My problem is that you are doing it on purpose!" Bar growled. "Once, I could see, but this has been the fifth time!"

"You were the one who wanted me to take the lead!" Sacul stated. He hid his devilish smile from his companion and chuckled at his friend's accusation and discomfort. The knoll's sensitive nose was as good as any canines. Sacul enjoyed the unexpected torment that spilled forth from his bowels. The thought of passive revenge was pleasing as he trudged through the snow. The landscape had changed slightly; jagged rocks began to make their presences known. Jagged black mountains, like the ancient teeth of a forgotten jaw bone, speared upwards to the sky's horizon. They had been walking to them for what seemed like eternity.

"Ugh, you did it again! You really are a pig, you know that!" Bar growled. "It's not funny!" Sacul fell to the ground in gut busting laughter, the laughter echoed back from the mountains. Bar shook his head at the immature shaman as he rolled back and forth. Bar rolled his eyes and looked to the foreboding horizon.

"Aroma therapy!" Sacul laughed. "Get it- 'a-ro-ma'- therapy!"

"Nope, I don't get it," Bar lied sourly.

"You were complaining about this barren wasteland and how it has no variety! I think I produced something for you!"

"Variety? What're you talking about?" Bar growled. He swore that the shaman had gone loony.

"I produced a brown rose for you!" Sacul's merriment started anew. Bar rubbed his forehead and shook his head sadly. The reference to what Sacul did in his loin cloth was disturbing because the information that was neither desired nor wanted. He could not believe that their conversation had dropped so low. Whether it was the high elevations or the bitter cold, Sacul was breaking down. Then the crazy boarelf began to sing:

"A belch is one gust of wind,
that comes from my heart!
But should it take a downward trend,
turns into a fart!"

"Pull yourself together!" Bar growled. "Your antics are not necessary! We need to find Luke!" He grabbed Sacul by the collar and pulled him out of the snow. The boarelf continued to chuckle and sing. Bar slapped him across his face. The cold sting brought the shaman back to his senses.

"Why'd you do that?" Sacul demanded. He had a shocked expression on his face as he stared dumbfound at his towering friend.

"Are you drunk on yak milk? Have you been licking that damn toad again!" Bar accused.

"Don't hit me!" Sacul gasped. His expression turned into a look of fear. "Did you feel it?" He turned sharply to the northern horizon, where the surrounding black rock consolidated into icy mountains.

"What are you talking about?"

"There was a strange flux of spirits! They seem to be gathering in a single location!" Sacul gasped in realization. "What could be powerful enough to draw them into together? It couldn't be?"

"What are you talking about?" Bar stuttered. His stern face turned into a look of dismay.

"Did you think we were walking around in circles?" Sacul explained. "We're close to Lukhan! His spiritual presence fluctuates at random times. That's how I have been able to follow him. This sudden cry from the spirits, I simply wasn't expecting it. It was like a thousand voices cried out in pain!"

"Luke is nearby? Where is he and in what direction?" Bar demanded. Sacul looked off into the distant horizon where the jagged peaks spiraled up. "He is in that direction," Sacul warned. "T-the evil aura that surrounds him is overwhelming! We must run away!"

"It can't be any worse than the evil aura coming from your bowels!" Bar snapped. The shaman frowned at the accusation; the hunter was not taking his warning seriously. Sacul did not move at the knoll's command and sat wide eyed and full of fear. "Remember, he is our friend and ally!"

"The evil aura suggests otherwise!"

"Fine, stay here and freeze to death for all I care! Point me in the right direction!" Bar demanded. Sacul remained silent for a moment in consideration. Disgusted, Bar shook his head and started off to the jagged mountains.

"Wait for me!" Sacul cried. He sprung to his feet and gave chase after his friend. "Ugh, you're too damn impatient! Charging head long into situations that we know nothing about! It's suicide! I thought you were smarter than that!"

"Luke is my- our friend!" Bar retorted. "You should have spoken up sooner!"

"I don't want to die!" Sacul groaned. "The dark aura is overwhelming. Vilesath must have taken over him! He has become nothing more than a beast! If you go to him, we will both end up dead!"

"Luke would never turn on us!" Bar growled. "We knew what he might become. I have faith in him, as should you! I will never abandon my friends when they are in trouble!"

"What if-," Sacul began.

"Luke would never turn on us because I've already thought of that!" Bar explained.

"What if the Betrayer is in command of his body?" Sacul pressed. "Don't you remember what happened during the plague? He almost killed us!"

Bar paused in consideration. "No matter what he has become, he's still my friend. Even if the Betrayer has taken control of him, we must help him!"

"What if there is no hope in saving him?" Sacul huffed as he finally reached out to his larger companion.

"Then this has been an exceptional journey," Bar smiled. "I have no regrets and despite your smells, you've been a welcomed travel companion. If you turn back now, I won't think less of you. Before you go, please tell me where I can locate him."

Sacul opened his mouth to reply, but then closed it. He kicked some snow up at Bar. The shaman cursed a couple of times, swearing on the spirits of his forefathers and then some. "Would it be easier if you simply left with me?" Sacul sighed. "Why do you always have to be the damn hero? Let the dragon deal with his problems! This is none of our concern and he wanted to be alone! That's why he left! We've already done so much and our charity is not necessary!"

"Would you abandon me if I broke my leg?"

Sacul groaned at his friend's accusation and kicked more snow at the hunter. "B-By all rights, I should leave your stubborn ass behind!" Sacul cursed. "A broken bone is different from getting your soul absorbed!"

"So you would abandon me!"

"You can't compare the two! They're nothing alike!" Sacul clenched his fist.

"Enough!" Bar snarled. "You've travel over a thousand leagues in hopes to find our friend, and now that we have almost reached him you want to run away? Why'd you even come? You know what has happened to him. How he has changed!" He turned his back on his friend for the last time and quickened his pace.

The shaman raced to keep pace. "I know that Lukhan is your friend!" Sacul grumbled. "Damn it, you're both my friend! I don't want to see either of you hurt!"

Bar stopped and turned sharply on him. "Then you should have realized that when you joined with us! Point me in the right direction and stop wasting my time! You can travel by yourself, without anyone to protect you!"

"I'll follow you! By the spirits, I swear, these *friendships* are going to be the death of me!"

Chapter 4

The magical energies exploded around Lukhan in a clash of negative and positive energy. The black and white plasma swirled around him in a violent clash, melting and freezing the cavern's icy walls in fluxing waves. The magical aura between the Staff of Selgae and the black claw struggled for dominance. The staff grew hot and became red as if molten; it burned at the black claw. The foul appendage continued to ravenously cling to the powerful artifact. Lukhan's normal appendages remained cool, yet agony shot up through his deformity and into his forearm. The painful burn soothed away as the endless hunger slowly resided within him. The powerful artifact continued to grow in heat and intensity. Lukhan bared his teeth against the self-inflicted pain. The darkness within his mind settled, the black claw crumbled and melted off. All that remained was the normal stub of his natural flesh.

"Ah, much better," Lukhan smiled. He felt amused in the relief the staff brought to his body. The realization was bitter sweet. The magic granted by the staff was soothing to the endless hunger. The danger was the addiction to magic.

The relief was temporary, like a starving prisoner eating stale moldy bread. The artifact's magic would slowly weaken, and then the black claw would regenerate. Such was the power of death alchemy. The element of life was only a temporary relief against the powers of death, and then he would have to feed again. Within the short span of a week, the perverted cycle would begin anew. The Staff of Selgae was more than a powerful artifact, it helped shield him from the starving desire caused by the graft. The power of the elves could not contain, nor defeat Vilesath's curse. The ancient black dragon had crafted his graft well. The knowledge of graft crafting had been lost to the mists of time, due to the inherently evil nature. No ancient was aware of the dark powers that Vilesath had used to craft such a powerful appendage.

"My blood is weak," Lukhan cursed. Vilesath had warned him of his bleak future, he would become like the shadow dragon. According to the ancient's past, he had been betrayed by Black Clan. As was foretold, Lukhan had been rejected by his own clan. He laughed at the thought that he was anything like the Betrayer. He glanced down at his right arm, an old injury. The self-inflicted scar had disappeared, a distant phantom: a painful remembrance. He had no regrets in saving the world and his companions.

His godmother, Vatara, had attempted to hide his condition from others. His friends had spread the word of their victory. Within their stories, they had spoken at great length about with whom and how the blood ceremony was completed. However, overtime the stories of his victory were retold with new and fictional fabrications. There were several local heroes among the lesser races; Lukhan took on a mystical appeal among them. His title, Defender of the Common Races, became more legendary then his actual name. It was a reason to hope, an idealized, selfless creature that defended Lemuria against a dangerous threat. It was nothing more than a legend. Few had seen or heard of this legendary being, giving him status beyond his degraded existences. The attention was unwanted and undesired. The Silver Mountains was flooded with pilgrims desiring to speak with the legendary hero. The troubles after the plague worsened, and they sought guidance from this myth. He disappeared soon after, and was proclaimed dead by the Silver Clan.

His death announcement was done for several reasons. First, the Silver Council had banished the Gold Clan from their borders. Second, the plague had taken its toll upon the Silver Mountains. Third, was due his tainted blood. Food had become sparse, and conflict arose between the two estranged clans. To avoid expected bloodshed, Vatara chose to take her clan and leave the Silver Mountains. Animosity had built up between the two fractions, and civil war would have been inevitable. The Gold Clan was excommunicated and left peacefully, despite the diplomatic meltdown. His godmother was lost to him; her political status as leader of the Silver and Gold Clan that had brought protection to his family was lost.

Not even Cirrus, the ancient council member of the Silver Clan, was able to reverse the effects of the Betrayer. Cirrus was the oldest and wisest within the Silver Clan, and had been the mentor of both his father and godmother. The ancient had lived so long that magic had begun to consume him. With the exile of the Gold Clan, the ancient silver had banished Lukhan because of his tainted blood and political connections with Vatara. To destroy the plague, Lukhan mixed his blood with his friends. The ceremony called for him to sacrifice his allies, yet he had chosen to sacrifice his white flame in their stead. The sacrifice was not enough and, had Vilesath not intervene, all would have been lost. He would have been absorbed into the endless streams of magic.

As the final pieces of the black claw crumbled away, images and memories of past Grand Magi flashed within his mind. A parade of mentors, students, and colleagues dance and then disappeared within his mind. Those that had used the powerful artifact were slowly consumed by their own ambitious power. The lust for more was the downfall of the magi order. He watched repeatedly as each individual began their rule with justices and noble ideals, only to be corrupted by the addiction influences of magic. At the end, the magi were controlled by the power they once commanded. Lukhan shook his head as the visions and experiences crumbled into distant dreams.

"How tiresome," Lukhan growled as the images faded away. The lessons seemed ingrained within him. He was losing himself to the memories of others. His individualism blurring with the life experiences of others' souls slaughter and taken by the black claw. He released the staff and the memories faded to depths of his subconscious. The staff dropped to the ice in a resounding clank, a sharp pain erupted from the middle of his natural stub. Blood poured from the old stub, a sharp edge poked out of the digit. The black claw had begun to regenerate from the stub. Lukhan ignored the painful nuisances, exhausted from his hunt and the painful cycle. Blood dripped down and mixed with the melting ice.

Voices echoed within the cavern. Lukhan shook his head, fearing that the voices of the staff had not subsided. A long forgotten scent traveled down the ice cavern's breeze. He looked down at his fresh injury. Had the smell of blood attracted predators to his cave?

"Be on your guard, who knows what terrible things lie in wait for us down this icy hole," an echoing voice sounded in warning. "This is where the terrible aura faded away, I have you here, like you requested."

"Are you sure? Luke?" asked a second gruff voice. The word *Luke* echoed within his mind. Only one individual ever called him that, his longtime friend Bar. His friend's odor smelled of wet dog and was easily identified on the breeze. A thousand memories of his past life returned to him in an instance. From the other smell he could tell that it was Sacul. The boarelf always smelled of the Endless Desert. The distinct sandy odor could easily be identified. He stood up quickly, eager to be reunited with his longtime companions, but doubt held him in check. He had run for a reason.

"We've traveled this far," Bar's voice echoed. "Luke is here. Look at the tracks; this is where he takes off to fly."

"How can you tell?" Sacul asked.

Lukhan crept towards the familiar voices of his friends. As he reached the entrances, he remained still, eager to find out the purpose of the surprising and unexpected visit. Within the shadows of his icy cave, he watched his companions walk around the base of the entrances. Bar and Sacul knelt over, examining the ice covered ground.

"Look at the tracks in the ice," Bar observed. "The left middle claw repeatedly cuts deeper into the ice. I think we've found it!"

"What now?" Sacul whimpered. "This cave could belong to a snow bear or worse. Do you want to go in on a hunch?" Bar turned away from the tracks and looked into the shadows of the cave's entrances. His gaze passed where Lukhan stood and then moved on.

"Bar?" Lukhan grumbled. The graveled words came out like an unintelligible mutter of a beast. Bar and Sacul dropped defensively at the sudden thunderous boom. Sacul held out his walking stick and Bar pulled out his bombarder, both of their eyes where wide with fear. The shiny metal tube within Bar's hands stank of sulfur and lead. Lukhan shrank deeper into the shadows as the deadly weapon was revealed. He had seen the efficiency of the human's weapon in slaughtering the sacred herd. That was six years ago, the metal tubes were larger and clumsy then.

"Luke?" Bar whispered. His ears stood erect, his full focus was at the mouth of the cave. Sacul slowly walked behind Bar. "Did you hear that?"

"We should leave," Sacul suggested. "That bestial roar couldn't have been him."

"B-Bar," Lukhan repeated in barely a whisper. The name was difficult for him to pronounce.

"It-It's you," Bar stuttered and smiled in relief. He slowly lowered his weapon and gave a fake chuckle at his overzealous behavior. "Come out here." The request was simple enough; Lukhan remained where he stood, within the darkness of the cave. It felt like a lifetime since he had seen his old friend, but to emerge from hiding felt like he would betray his current existence of self-exile. He couldn't allow his friend to see how much he had changed, the monstrous creature he had become.

"Why have you come?" Lukhan demanded. His tone was on the verge of a threat. "You should have never come here." Bar's ears fell low and eyes went wide like a scorned dog. Sacul peeked out from behind the hunter.

"Damn it!" Sacul scorned. "We've traveled over a thousand leagues over desert and ice to reach you! You have the audacity to send us away! You should be ashamed of yourself! We're your friends-"

"Do you truly wish to see what I have become?" Lukhan asked. His ragged voice echoed across the frozen waste and echoed off of the mountains. His anger turned to guilt as he watched his friends fall to the ground and covered their ears. Bar and Sacul looked at the cave in fear. "I am so sorry for everything." He turned to leave into the depths of his icy cave. Bar caught the movement and threw his weapon into Sacul's unexpected arms. The bombarder nearly knocked the small boarelf down. The shaman looked dumbfounded as Bar raced inside of the cave.

"Wait! He might kill you!" Sacul called.

Bar ignored the warning and raced around the dragon to intercept his descent. "You can't leave now that I've found you!" Bar accused. "You've always been, and will always be my pack!"

"I am not the hatchling you once knew," Lukhan replied.

"Then what are you?" Bar challenged. "You are not a big ass lizard that hides from danger!" Lukhan's eyes flashed mercury as he stared down at the small knoll before him. The temperature within the cave dropped with Lukhan's mood. "You are Lukhan, Defender of the Common Races, Protector of the Innocent, and you're my friend!"

"That was another life," Lukhan mumbled. "I am none of that now."

"You're bleeding?" Bar gasped. Within the darkness he could not see the dragon's wound, but he could smell the blood. He glanced down at his feet where blood and cold water rushed downward. "What did you do?"

"You would never understand," Lukhan snorted.

"Then help me understand," Bar pressed. Lukhan's rage gathered within him. Bar could never understand the physical and mental torment that the black claw inflicted upon him. His own body fought against his nature, turning him into something uncontrollable. Bar's ignorance of his self-loathing angered Lukhan greatly. They could never understand.

"Do you know how it feels to be truly alone?" Lukhan asked. "When your world that you remember is no longer there? The world that you once knew is now gone! No matter how much you try, you can never make a difference or make the world the way it used to be. Tell me Bar, do you know how I feel?"

"Yes," Bar stated.

"How could you?" Lukhan roared. He bare his teeth at the knoll before him, Bar did not back down. The dragon's anger subsided as he watched a tear fall from the corner of his friend's eye.

"Can't you remember?" Bar choked. The tears came freely now. "The pack was slaughter and I was powerless to stop it! I was alone! I am the last surviving member of my pack. My family, my world, ended that day! You were there! You kept me going, even in my darkest of hours. You pushed me, gave me a new family to look after! You, Lukhan, are part of that family! Even if you flew to the ends of the world, we would still be connected!" With his slung arm, he pulled back his furs to reveal a white scar on his forearm. "We are connected in more than one way! We are blood bothers!"

"I was the cause of that," Lukhan whispered. "I am sorry for what I have done." He turned his face away from what Bar had shown him. The knoll grabbed his horn and forced the dragon to look at him.

"How dare you say that?" Bar demanded. "You saved us and the world! This is a scar that reminds me of what you did for my people. Even if they're unaware of it! My blood runs through your veins because of this scar! How dare you cheapen your own sacrifice, it was my life that you saved!"

"It was *our* lives that you saved," Sacul interrupted. Both knoll and dragon turned to regard the shaman that had walked into the cavern. The boarelf had tied Bar's bombarder across his back. He leaned heavily upon his walking stick and gave a hardy laugh that echoed throughout the icy cavern. "Many care about you. Dragons are so fatalistic and take themselves way too seriously! You two are melodramatic."

"I am surprised that you came," Lukhan muttered. "Are you still licking that toad?" Bar wiped frozen tears from his eyes and shook his head at the crazy shaman. Sacul gave them a wide boorish grin.

"Oh, picked up some bad habits from that one," Sacul rolled his eyes at Bar. "I warn you, I still have my toad, so don't eat me!" Lukhan snorted in reply to the comment. He had eaten things far worse than the poisonous toad Sacul carried with him. Lukhan noticed that there was a change in the shaman; he seemed less timid than when they first met.

"I understand why Bar is here," Lukhan admitted. "Why have you come? Sacul, you were the first to leave my side."

"Seven years have passed since my departure from the Silver Mountains," Sacul explained. "I've seen several strange and exotic sights. You're the first dragon that I've met that does so much for so little. It's strange that you seem to defy your draconic lineage."

"So?" Lukhan asked.

"This gives us hope, that you can be saved," Bar explained.

"Explain *us?*" Lukhan demanded.

"Vatara may have found a way for you to control the curse," Sacul snorted happily.

Chapter 5

"What?" Lukhan asked. "Vatara has found a way to control the graft? How could she-?" There was a long pause before he spoke. After seven years of constant agony, he had given up hope on finding a cure.

"Bar is correct," Sacul mumbled. "I can smell the blood coming from your wound, and you still reek of death. Were you injured in battle?" Lukhan paused within the shadows of the cave. The darkness hid his wound from his friend's prying eyes.

"Let's have a look at you!" Bar demanded. "Much has changed since we left your side. Come out into the sunlight with us. We must see you clearly if we're going to treat your injury."

"First tell me what you know!" Lukhan demanded. "Stop worrying about me! What does my godmother know that I do not?" He turned around in the ice cave to look directly at Sacul; the shaman's bravery began to waver.

"Damn, you've gotten bigger," Sacul mumbled. "A lot bigger- and you stink! I remembered when you were a hatchling, a little taller than Bar! You smell better then- but now! Whoo! You need to go roll around in the snow for a while."

Lukhan growled. "Tell me what you know!" Sacul buckled under his shaken knees. The boarelf trembled in fear at the dragon before him. Bar intercepted the dragon's harsh glare.

"Not before we treat your wound," Bar walked pass Lukhan and pushed the dragon's head to the side. "You've grown short tempered! You need to change your attitude if you want our help!"

"Do you know what Sacul is talking about?" Lukhan demanded. Bar shook his head no in reply and the dragon snorted at the conspiracy of his two companions. "I never wanted you to come here! I never said I needed aid! Bar, tell me what the crazy shaman is talking about!"

"I have no clue what Sacul is talking about!" Bar growled. With his good arm, he reached up and grabbed hold of dragon's horn. "You better not kick us or threaten us! We bring hope and worldly tidings. We've come a long way to find you! We need to get you out of this cave, and you need to stop hiding from your problems!" Lukhan raised a questioning eyebrow to the knoll's tug. He could easily break the hold that his small friend had placed upon him. He was not running from his problems, he had been running from his destiny. Vilesath had cursed him; it was because of this that he had fled to save his family and friends from his uncontrollable hunger. His ultimate fate was to become a loathsome and foul creature that devoured the souls of others.

"You two are a pain in my ass, you know that!" Lukhan grumbled. He reluctantly walked to the entrance of the cave. Bar and Sacul walked beside their absent companion. The fading light fell upon the mountains, blocking the setting sun. The temperature dropped slowly, Bar and Sacul ignored the cold. After a few harsh scolding and complaints Lukhan reluctantly scrapped his dirty scales in the snow outside his cave. It took a while, but finally the dragon's dull scales shone brightly. After the dragon had cleaned himself, Bar and Sacul investigated their friend's injuries.

"This wound looks like a burn?" Bar asked. He examined the charred flesh of Lukhan's left claw. The wound was putrid with unnatural rot. "It looks festered-"

"Well, of course it does!" Sacul gagged. The shaman retched and turned away from the grotesque injury. "No wonder why it smelled in the cave."

"It does not matter," Lukhan stated stoically. "This always happens whenever I use the Staff of Selgae." Bar began to pick at the wound, as he scraped away at the charred flesh, revealing a pus pocket that had formed in the middle of the dragon's digit. Lukhan recoiled from Bar's inspection. "Do not touch that!"

"What happened to the black claw?" Bar thought out loud.

"The abscess that you were poking at," Lukhan grimaced. "The black claw is under that. It regenerates within a week; it is painful and sensitive to the touch."

"Did you burn yourself?" Sacul demanded. He backed away from the horrific injury.

"I used the Staff of Selgae," Lukhan explained. Both of his companions looked at him, neither of them understood what he said. "I use the power of the elves to keep the black claw from taking over my body. It keeps my hunger in check, so I don't lose control of myself. The white flames of the past magi help me combat this damn curse."

"What?" Sacul asked. "It doesn't destroy it? The staff helped to destroy the plague! Both the claw and the plague were Vilesath's creation!" Lukhan stared blankly at him; he had no clue why the black claw was not destroyed.

"How am I supposed to know?" Lukhan asked. "You were the ones that told me that Vatara knew of a way! What did she say?"

"Sacul, stop teasing!" Bar growled. "Your antics aren't necessary and do not provoking him! We're here to help, not fill his head with more questions. Luke needs answers!"

"I have no clue what the Gold Clan leader plans are!" Sacul shot back. "She has been busy, with the war and all!"

Lukhan growled in frustration. "The boarder wars between the Green and Black Clans are not over?" Bar and Sacul shook their heads no in reply. Lukhan considered what that meant to the rest of the dragon clans. His clan was still in the Silver Mountains, attempting to nurture their life sustaining valleys that had been destroyed by the plague. The Red Clan didn't lose as many lives during the spread of the magical disease. Thanks to the loss of their leader Orelac, the Red Clan had been spared from the initial advancement of the plague.

"The Gold Clan has become the first to strike against the Kingdom of Alkaline!" Bar explained. "The Inquisition went too far when they slaughtered the sacred herd. The bold humans openly attacked and declared war upon their neighboring kingdoms, both dragon and common race. The Inquisition has begun to consulate their power around their religious governing. Humankind is engaged in a civil war!"

"The Kingdom of Alkaline is in a state of civil war?" Lukhan asked.

"With the destruction of the plague, several religious cults and fractions rebel against the Iron Throne," Bar explained. "New religions began to spring up, challenging the old teachings of the Holy Master. The Inquisition called a purge upon their own people for rebelling against the demigod. Several cults and religious icons have spawned from the cruelty of the Inquisition's purge. Exasperating the civil strife, most of these occults have centered on the Defender of the Common Races."

"Me?" Lukhan thought out loud.

"Not you," Bar explained. "The idea is of a dragon that defends the common people! A savior of all people, for both dragon and common race alike! It inspired the people and it rose to challenge the old belief system. This religious fervor and idealism has yielded some surprising results."

"I don't understand," Lukhan stated. "There are individuals that I have never met before believe in me? This belief has caused conflict? Why would anyone have faith in me?" His eyebrows knitted together. "I don't understand."

"Well," Sacul admitted. "We've been spreading our adventures around: A heroic dragon traveling the countryside righting wrongs and healing the sick. I might have stretched the truth every now and then-"

"What does that mean?" Lukhan snapped. "I am neither heroic nor a healer."

"Oh, nothing," Sacul squeaked. "Err- you know how stories go. Sometimes you get caught up in them!"

"What do you mean?" Bar defended. "You stopped the plague single handily and saved the dragon council from becoming undead slaves, and you healed me and your mother." He looked down at his crippled hand. The life magic had infused his shattered bone in his arm when the troll named Aak had broken and twisted it.

"Yes, you have also cured all of those that had been sick during the plague," Sacul smiled. "Lukhan: the bane of diseases, the cure for this sick time in history, and a champion for the people!"

"It means that he has been fabricating our adventures," Bar scowled. He took out a dagger and held it next to Lukhan's claw. The dragon recoil from him, breaking the hold the knoll had on his claw.

"What do you think you're doing?" Lukhan demanded.

"I'm going to cut away the dead skin," Bar woofed. "It looks infected! If we don't lance the puss pocket or cut away the dead skin, the infection will spread up your arm. Is that what you want?"

"Dragon's don't get infections!" Lukhan snapped in reply. "I am not like you. I don't get sick! Get away from me!" He reared back, baring his teeth at both Bar and Sacul. The knoll and boarelf retreated from the infuriated dragon.

"I just want to help," Bar pleaded. He looked to Sacul for support.

"Are you so certain?" Sacul demanded. "If dragons couldn't get sick, then why was your mother infected with the plague?"

"Shut up!" Lukhan snarled.

"The plague was unnatural," Sacul groan. He crossed his arms defiantly.

"The magically enhanced disease was conscious and self-aware, and don't forget that our blood courses through you veins. Your body seems to be rejecting the black claw. It looks and smells horrible." Lukhan's face contorted into a look of confusion and outrage. "Don't you remember the ceremony?"

"That's right!" Bar agreed. "What if our blood allowed you to contract diseases like the common races? Vatara warned us about side effects!"

"I-that could not have happened," Lukhan stuttered in denial. "I have felt different; I assumed that it was because of the black claw, not because of the blood ceremony. Y-you are my blood brothers. Your blood strengthens me."

"Are you so certain?" Bar asked. "That grafting was unnatural and forbidden. What Vilesath and the blood ceremony did, the graft, its uncharted waters. Magic has terrible side effects. We miss you, why'd you flee from our homeland; everyone feared the worse when news of your death reached our ears. Rumors of the lost heroes and the return of the plague sent panic and fear throughout the lands. People lost hope."

"I knew better," Sacul chuckled. "Your spiritual presences couldn't be ignored. I knew you were alive. It was how I was able to track you down."

"The spirits gave me away?" Lukhan asked.

"You can't hide from the spirit world," Sacul amused. "It would be like trying to hide from your own shadow in middle of the day. The spirits are frightened by you and can sense your malevolent power."

"What malevolent power?" Lukhan considered. "Do you speak of the taint of the black claw, or Vilesath's spirit?"

Sacul shook his head no in reply. "According to the spirits and the Gold Clan," he whispered. "The Betrayer was contained within a spiritual prison: A plane of existences that death couldn't exist. This is what my people once believed was the Oracle's sanctuary. It was guarded by an ancient giant."

"You speak of Onekyh, the life giant," Lukhan recalled. "Vilesath's prison was that otherworldly place in the Endless Desert."

"Yes," Sacul explained. "According the Grand Magus of Sedna, both dragon and magi are aware of your plight and have been looking for ways to defeat the curse that Vilesath has placed upon you. They are aware of the Betrayer's release and have been researching for ways to cure you. However, despite this rapid research, the cure has been stalled."

"Stalled?" Lukhan asked.

"The Inquisition has finally made its move," Bar interrupted. "About two years ago, the Inquisitor Lords banded together in an alliance. This alliance suppressed the other Inquisitors and heretics into servitude. Spies from Ravenshaven have informed us that the Holy Master himself has issued the divine edict to unite the Kingdom of Alkaline under his rule."

"Unite?" Lukhan mumbled. "Unite against what?"

"You!" Sacul clamored. "Well, more correctly, dragon kind."

"The Gold Clan carried out raids against the Kingdom of Alkaline," Bar explained. "The Inquisition has assumed that all of dragon kind plots to destroy the human kingdom. He should have thought of that when he ordered the destruction of the sacred herd, this has brought a division within the human's kingdom. Ravenshaven has become the major city of resistance against the unification."

"I thought that the Gold Clan was the friendliest towards humans," Lukhan muttered. He had not expected the Gold Clan to react to the Inquisition's slaughter of the sacred herd. It was too bold for the gold dragons to react as the aggressor.

"According to reports from Ravenshaven," Bar added. "Which has been about- err, I don't know- several months ago. The Gold Clan is the only ones attacking the Inquisitions."

"Ravenshaven?" Lukhan asked. "I thought that city burned to the ground!"

"Owen has rebuilt the city's fortifications," Bar explained. "You must come and see it! The city has completely changed! Owen has opened trade with the elves, and Judas has provided detailed information about the Inquisition's newest weapon." The hunter grabbed the bombarder that was slung around Sacul's shoulders.

"Judas? I though he left with you?" Lukhan considered.

"He did," Bar dusted off the snow that clung to him before continuing. "Our human friend has provided the resistance with a means to defend ourselves against the Inquisition's bombarder. He had helped with the construction and design of the first bombarders. He has modified them into smaller weapons."

"Judas created your weapon?" Lukhan examined the tube like weapon. Bar showed the weapon's craftsmanship. The steel tube was embroidered with both human and elf writing. The small engraving on the muzzle said: *Chicken is best served with friends. Eat your fears.*

"Do you like the inscription?" Bar smiled. "The elf that forged the tube said it has magical properties."

"I don't get it," Lukhan grumbled. The hunter's smile slowly faded, he looked at the symbols and shrugged in reply. "I think it says that its part of a recipe for cooking chicken. I forgot that you can't read elvish."

"Is that magical?" Sacul asked.

"No," Lukhan chuckled in amusement.

"It has meaning to me!" Bar huffed. "By the way, Judas told me to pass on a message to you. He told me to tell you to remember your promise to him. He expects you to hold true to your word." Lukhan's chuckles stopped and he considered the promise he had made to his absent friend.

"Does Judas plan to go through with his task?" Lukhan asked.

"I am the messenger," Bar shrugged. "I'm relaying what he told me. I figured that you would know what he was talking about, because I was unclear."

"Care to enlighten us?" Sacul prompted. "What does a dragon promise an ex-Inquisitor? Hmm, well? Spit it out." Lukhan remained silent as he considered what to do. He had made a promise to Judas. He had forgotten it.

"Nothing that he cannot do by himself," Lukhan muttered. "I see that the world has not changed. It is still as violent and destructive as ever."

"Yup," Sacul agreed sarcastically. He placed his hands upon his hip. "What did you think the world would turn into: a peaceful existence without you?"

"No- I am no longer naive to the world's conflicts," Lukhan admitted. "It does not mean I must participate in the slaughter."

"What does that mean?" Bar demanded.

"It means that I have no desire or interest in returning with you," Lukhan muttered. "I know why you are here, but I have no desire to leave my solitude."

Chapter 6

"What?" Bar demanded. "I never thought you were naive. You've corrected many mistakes within this world. Your actions have benefited others, even if you're not aware of it."

"My actions have released a terrible curse upon the world," Lukhan snapped. "I know what I am! I know what will become of me if I leave my solitude."

"Oh, is that right?" Bar growled. "Then tell me what you will become? Tell me what you think you will do?"

"You would not understand!" Lukhan snarled. "You think you know me?"

"Yes!" Bar offered. "I know you! Look at you; does this isolation make you safe? Are you saving the world by not interacting with it? Your justification is incorrect! I know this because you are my friend."

"I am not the hatchling you once knew!" Lukhan warned.

"No, you're not," Bar voice dropped to soothing tone. "You're no longer a hatchling. I know this; you can't hide away from the world and you're stronger than what you believe you are."

"How can you have so much faith in me, when I do not?" Lukhan growled.

"Because you're my friend," Bar pressed. "I have faith in you."

"What if you are wrong?" Lukhan snapped. "What if my strength fails and this curse overtakes me? If I take that chance, I would kill everything. I am doing the right thing!"

"What's the right thing?" Sacul interrupted. Bar and Lukhan paused their conversation to consider the shaman's words. "Do, do not. You have several choices before you. You're a dragon; you can't hide away from the world. Remember my people? I've convinced the tribes of the Endless Desert to join with the forces at Ravenshaven. Your actions have helped unite the common races against tyrannical humans and their cruel religion. We're all uniting because of your actions! Come with us and see the fruits of your labor."

"What are you talking about?" Lukhan asked.

"They're alive because of you!" Sacul cheered happily. "It's because of your sacrifices to destroy the plague that has allowed this to occur. You may blame yourself, but no other does. You are too harsh on yourself; making a martyr of yourself when you don't need to. You still have friends and allies. No one has forgotten you!"

"B-but-," Lukhan stuttered. "You do not understand the prophecy; I will become the evil that I sought to destroy. You cannot- no one wants this to happen!"

"You're listening to Vilesath?" Sacul chuckled. "You proved his prophecy wrong! By not sacrificing us, you've changed everything! You're not a slave to fate and the winds of destiny. Because someone tells you what you will become, doesn't mean that you have to listen to them. You're better than that. We know you're better than that! Don't doubt yourself for a moment. You're Lukhan, the Defender of the Common Races, and Vilesath is a nothing more than a forgotten memory."

"What do you mean?" Lukhan demanded. "The black claw still exists!" He raised his left claw for his two companions to see. The horrific appendage gave his companions pause. "Vilesath is not dead; he is bound to me!"

"Then the Betrayer still speaks to you?" Sacul gasped.

"I- well, no," Lukhan paused. "I have not heard his whispers, ever since; I gained access to the Staff of Selgae."

"Then we can assume that the shadow dragon is dead," Sacul smiled. "Vilesath was destroyed by magic casted during the blood ceremony."

"I thought you said that Luke has a foreboding spiritual presence!" Bar muttered.

"He does," Sacul squeaked. "Although Vilesath is gone, the shadow dragon has left spiritual scarring upon his white flame. Your soul has been tainted by the black flame. This scarring is most unnatural."

"Then why does my claw keep regenerating?" Lukhan demanded. "How do you know Vilesath is dead? He was immortal to begin with!"

"I have no clue," Sacul admitted. "I don't have all the answers." Lukhan groaned at the shaman's statement. "The black flame is death and destruction. Its death element does not have the power to create; it only could destroy. Life magic is the complete opposite; it only could create."

41

"Old lessons that were drilled into me," Lukhan groaned. "I am aware of the five dragon elements. You need not explain it to me!"

"You understand the complexities of magic?" Sacul smirked. "For some reason, I doubt that you're aware of every possible magical anomaly. Magic itself is an illusion."

"This is not an illusion!" Lukhan growled. He held the deformed appendage before the shaman. Sacul turned away and gagged at the smell.

"Err- your right," Sacul choked. "Please get that thing away from me."

"Get to the point," Bar demanded. Sacul turned away and retched, Lukhan withdrew the claw.

"Sorry," Sacul muttered. "I have some things with burn smells. The point is, no matter what Lukhan believes. We need his help against the Inquisition-"

"I am not going to help bring more death into the world," Lukhan interrupted. "I have no intention of interfering with the world's problems."

"We need you!" Bar begged.

"No," Lukhan growled. "You are looking for a legend, a myth! I seek solitude and peace."

"Be reasonable," Bar pleaded. "You are afraid of the future! You are a hero-"

"The hero that is no longer desired, he died seven years ago," Lukhan rebuked. "The harsh treatment that my mother and I had to endure from our own clan was horrible." He shook his head as he recalled the shameful memories. Memories of his homeland darkened his mood. He was labeled an outcast, and nothing he could do would ever change that.

"Though I don't know what treatment you received," Bar stated. His tone was low and considerate. "does the world need to suffer from those few that would belittle you?"

"Yes," Lukhan muttered bitterly. "You do not know the ridicule and suffering I had to endure."

"Why does it matter what your clan thinks about you?" Bar asked. "We had so little interaction with them, why does their opinions matter or concern you?"

"I can never return to my home!" Lukhan snapped.

"Why?" Bar pressed. "All we know is that you were pronounced dead. The Silver Clan never gave any reason for their announcement. That's one of many reasons we had to seek you out."

"It is because of my tainted flesh that I was excommunicated," Lukhan explained. His voice was empty with sorrow and pain. "My mixed blood is evident for the world to see. The Silver and Gold Clans were taken over by Kronus, a rival of my family's leadership. Due to the plague's assault upon the Silver Mountains, food became scarce and those considered impure were cast out of my homeland. Both silver and gold dragons were cast out or hunted down by the Silver Council. I chose to leave because the elder named Cirrus advised me to do so."

"Before we left, there was a big celebration!" Bar gasped. "You told us to leave! I didn't believe things were in such dire straits. We wouldn't have left your side had we known!" Lukhan nodded his head in understanding; his friends would have perished during the Silver Clan's political power struggle.

"That doesn't explain why they would pronounce you as dead," Sacul snorted.

"Kronus is a traditionalist, always has been," Lukhan stated. "I was too young and I never realized the political infighting going on within our clan. Father and mother had always tried to protect me from it. I was naive then." He shook his head in disgust. "Cirrus told me to abandon my mother. The ancient dragon warned me of what was occurring, the internal conflict between me and this curse. He knew me for what I really am."

"What is that?" Bar demanded. He crossed his arms defiantly.

"An abomination," Lukhan snapped. "I am a bastard, a misshaped creature, unworthily of being a silver dragon. I have no place in this world; I have no clan to identify with."

"You can't accept this," Bar growled. "That's foolishness and stupidity! Because an elder says that you are a bastard does not mean that it's true! I knew your father, you're his likeness. How dare you defile his memory by considering yourself to be something tainted! Your father was an honorable leader! Blood and ancestry don't make one great!"

"I bet it helps," Sacul interrupted.

"The point is that our actions define what and who we are," Bar added. "Others may tarnish your name and curse you in passing, but you know what happened and you did the right thing!"

The dragon glanced at Sacul before breaking down into hardy laughter. Both knoll and boarelf joined in his merriment. Lukhan stopped himself from laughing; a smile replaced his tired expression. "It has been a long time since I have laughed. I would be lying if I said that I have not missed your company. Your squabbles have always proved amusing. I have missed our conversations."

"I knew I could get you two to smile," Sacul chuckled. A big boorish grin spread across his pig face. "You two are always serious. All of us need to lighten up, we're friends here!" Bar and Lukhan nodded their heads in agreement with the shaman's observations.

"It does not explain why my own clan rejected me," Lukhan sighed.

"That may never be answered," Bar placed a comforting hand upon the dragon's shoulder. "Your father's ideology was different compared to his brethren. Vatara and I were aware of his dangerous political stance. Your godmother would know more about your father. Stratos was always elusive whenever I attempted to engage him in political discussions."

"Tell me about my father," Lukhan asked.

"Well, he was-," Bar began.

"If you come with us," Sacul prompted sneakily. "He'll tell you everything!"

"I will?" Bar frowned. Sacul gave him a mischievous wink. "Oh-yes, of course. We can share memories once we get out of the Endless Ice." Lukhan snorted in reply to his two companions attempt at trickery.

"I told you that I was not going with you," Lukhan stated harshly. "Please tell me about my father."

"You promised that you would help me find my pack and aid Judas on his quest!" Bar protested. He crossed his arms defiantly and the dragon before him. "You have promises to keep! Therefore, you must come with us!"

"That was seven years ago," Lukhan snorted.

"Then you regret giving your word?" Bar demanded angrily.

"That was a different time and place," Lukhan admitted. His voice fell into a deep graveling tone. "Why can't you stay here, with me, away from the bloodshed and conflict brewing in the South?" Bar and Sacul shook their heads in disbelief.

"A wise dragon once told me that: *We live in this world, we cannot sit idle and do nothing while these events unfold*," Sacul recalled.

Lukhan snorted in mockery at whoever had said that. "What fool told you this?" he asked.

"You did," Sacul grunted. Lukhan's sneer faded as he considered his friend's statement. Had he truly lost so much of his identity? Bar shook his head in disgust and frustration.

"I have an obligation to the resistance," Bar recalled his oath. "My word is my bond and I'll fight and defend those I love and care about." His words became harsh and strict. "Lukhan, you have changed. You've become hard and bitter by the past. If you will not fight, then you're no longer bound to me or any other by your past oaths. Obviously, the free people are no longer worthy of your time or effort. You've done the most hurtful thing imaginable! You have lied." His words choked again. "You're correct; the brave hatchling that I watched grow up is dead. Forgive us for our intrusion; you're not the savior I had once believed. You've chosen your fate and you're a credit to those you listen to. I was mistaken to seek your aid, *Silver Lord*." A hint of bitter mockery was hidden in his words; Bar bowed gracefully and gathered his items to leave. Sacul glance over at Bar in shock and horror. He looked to Lukhan for guidance, but the dragon was stone faced, unwilling to confirm or deny his long time friend's harsh accusation.

"He didn't mean it," Sacul whispered. Lukhan's dispassionate face did not move and his magically scarred eyes gave no evidences into what he was thinking. "He is tired from the journey and-I- Bar is hurt that you would abandon-"

"Come on, Sacul!" Bar bellowed. "It's time for us to leave this frozen waste! It was a mistake-" His words choked in the back of his throat. The hunter completed gathering his items. Sacul looked helplessly back at him. Bar cleared his throat before continuing. "We're no longer his concern; silver dragons have always disconcerted themselves with the troubles of others."

"B-but-," Sacul stuttered.

"Let's go!" Bar snapped. He walked south, away from both Lukhan and Sacul. The shaman looked on in confusion and fear.

"I- but," Sacul stuttered in confusion. He turned to watch Lukhan descend into the frozen depths of his icy cave. The dragon wouldn't help them. Sacul felt abandon as he continued to stare into the cave's frozen depths. Bar's crunching footsteps began to fade as he put distance between them. Sacul gave chase after the hunter. When he finally caught up to Bar he had noticed that his friend had brought his furs around his head. Sacul couldn't see his face; the shaman was wise enough to remain silent as he listened to his friend's quiet grief. Tears came to his eyes as he looked up unto the sky. Puffy white flakes of snow began to fall, as if the sky wept with them.

Chapter 7

At the top of the world, the darkness overtook them quickly. The empty oaths of the past faded away into the wasteland. Bar's forced march didn't stop when night over took them. The silent tundra seemed even more unforgiving than before. The crunching sound of their footsteps did not echo, but fell into void silences, reflecting the darkness of their moods. Without the spring sun's warmth, the temperature dropped drastically. The track away from the cave proved to be more difficult. Even with Sacul's protests, the hunter didn't yield. The knoll seemed driven by an unstoppable force to put distance between them and that cave of painful memories. The gentle snow fakes began to cease. The frigid temperatures began to gnaw at their strength; the warmth had left their fingertips before they had arrived at Lukhan's cave.

"Did you really mean what you said?" Sacul demanded for the hundredth time. Again, the shaman was ignored by the grieving knoll. "We need to stop for the night, you flea infested wind bag! I'm getting tired! We need to sleep! Do you have a heat source? Of course not! Now it's dark and you're going to get us kill- I am so cold, you dung covered camel! Are you even listening? We are going to fall off a cliff or break the ice in some lake! I can't feel my feet, can you feel yours? How can you stand this cold-?" and the protests continued. Sacul called the hunter everything under the sky and more. Bar didn't acknowledge the shaman's constant complaints and insults, until Sacul simply fell silent before collapsing in the snow. Bar turned to regard his frozen companion; the shaman balled himself up into his furs.

"Are you all right?" Bar asked. Shivers broke his words as he spoke. Sacul looked up at him, ice had gathered around his mouth and eyes. "It's so cold. We need to break for camp."

"Damn fool!" Sacul grumbled. "That's what I've been trying to tell you!" Bar's face had clumps of ice on his cheeks, the only evidence of the anguish. The boarelf attempted to stand, but his short legs would not support him. Bar slowly made it to his fallen companion's side.

"I'm sorry," Bar shivered. His teeth chattered as he spoke. "We should've stayed at the cave. At least, it would've been a windbreak." Accumulated ice fell off of his furs as he rubbed his hand vigorously together. His eyelashes' tips had bits of ice clinging to them. He bent over to examine his companion. Sacul's eye lids hung lazily as he stared up at him.

"I'm so exhausted," Sacul mumbled.

"You must not sleep! Not until we've the shelter built," Bar instructed. He clenched his teeth to keep them from chattering. He dropped his backpack and prepared to create a shelter.

"Why'd you do it," Sacul complained. "Why would you yell and insult Lukhan like that? I thought that you two were longtime friends?" Bar looked at him through a vague expression. The two stared at each other in silent disbelief; neither of them understood the complexities of what had occurred. "You were too harsh on him; the pain he must endure every day! You simply couldn't understand."

Anger heated the knoll's body, compelling his cold hands to work. "I understand more than you know!" Bar growled. "I've known Luke longer then you. Allowing him to linger in his emotional turmoil doesn't help anyone!"

"So your harsh treatment is to pull him out of his depression?" Sacul asked with great skepticism. "That doesn't make sense to me."

"Sometimes you've to be firm and speak the truth," Bar spoke sadly. "If Luke has changed and no longer cares for the common races, then he has become the same dragons that exiled him."

"What?" Sacul demanded. "Have you ever thought that we were asking too much from him? That he deserves his rest from war? He has sacrificed much for this world; doesn't that mean he has contributed enough?"

"Then there would be no point in his sacrifice," Bar muttered. "The uncaring nature of dragons has become their undoing. They allow events to occur without care even though they live in this world! They are not immortal or divine beings! They have weaknesses and-," Bar choked back his tears as he spoke. "Sometimes they need help too!"

"Don't break down on me again!" Sacul groaned. "I don't need to see more of your waterworks today."

"What are waterworks?" Bar sniffed.

"You know," Sacul smiled. "Humans have theses lead pipes that carry water into their cities. A series of pumps push the water through the pipes into human homes."

"Smoking pipes?" Bar asked.

"Think of it as hollowed out snakes that water runs through," Sacul chuckled. Bar's sad expression broke into an uneasy chuckle. "Humans are strange."

"Why not drink from the river or a canteen?" Bar amused.

"Oh, I have no clue," Sacul smiled. The two shook their heads at the strangeness of men and their strange devises. The two continued their conversation about pipes and what they were used for. Both seemed pleased at the sudden distraction of humans and their inability to retrieve water themselves. They worked together as they insulted humans and their foolish *civilized* ways. Together they dug into a small snow bank; several times the small cavern would collapse. They cursed their luck and dug further down into the packed ice.

"I wish I had a shovel," Bar grumbled. He pulled out his knife and began stabbing the snow pack. Sacul shivered and rubbed his hands together.

"I would give up my toad for a warm bed and meal," Sacul chattered. He looked under his furs at his pet. The desert toad lied inactive within his leather bag and Sacul chuckled in amusement. "Are you as cold as I am?" The toad did not react to his question.

"You'd never give up that toad," Bar grumbled. "Help me with this!" The ice he had been hacking away slowly broke away. The snowpack consist of both snow and ice, making the drift difficult to carve into a snow cave. Even with both of them working, the snow shelter completed slowly. Bar's constant hacking with his crude knife pick was the only sound from inside the small structure.

"I think it's done," Bar concluded. The temporary structure was already warmer than the frigid temperatures outside. "Place our backpacks against the opening, which should keep the chill at bay."

"Light the candle first before we're in total darkness," Sacul instructed. Bar nodded his head in agreement. From his backpack his drew out a small candle. After a few expert strikes with his flint, the small light ignited. The sudden spark of light forced them to blink. They set the candle at the back of the cave and poked a small hole in the roof for the smoke to escape. They placed their backpacks against the entrance and settled down for the night. The temperature slowly increased and food was brought out. Fresh snow was added to their water skins.

"Sometimes, I wish I was a dragon," Sacul muttered as he munched through a half frozen biscuit. "I can barely stand theses temperatures, how does Lukhan stand it?"

"You're asking the wrong knoll about dragons," Bar admitted.

"I thought that you said that you lived with silver dragons," Sacul pressed. "There must be some information that you could impart." Bar considered the request as he leaned against the side of the small cave. He watched as the small candles' flame flicked and danced for him. Sacul remained silent as he watched the hunter slowly thaw.

"I'm sure that you've heard the legends that the dragon clans are resistance to their natural elements," Bar yawned sleepily. Sacul nodded his head in reply. "The Silver Clan has an affinity with the element of air. Luke shares this character, which is why he is able to survive this harsh frozen climate."

"Then why doesn't the Silver Clan move here?" Sacul asked.

"One reason," Bar explained. "There's no gold or treasure here."

"That's right," Sacul recalled. "I sometimes forget the motivations of the dragon clans. Food, treasure, power, and lust are the only things that can move their kind into action."

"Luke is- was different," Bar stated sourly. "I believed he was-" He words faded into silence contemplation. Sacul remained silent as he consider Bar's position.

"Maybe its dragon nature," Sacul suggested.

"I refuse to believe that," Bar grumbled. "Dragon nature is like any other individual. I believe that we're not slaves to our positions in the world. Not all dragons are terrible fire breathing monsters. For example, Luke was once a carefree dragon that only wanted to protect his family and friends. He has forgotten the reasons why he fights; his cause has been displaced by the realities of the world. He was once eager to change the world; like me, the cruel realities of war shattered my hopes and dreams." There was a long pause as Sacul considered his position. "Knolls are not inherently evil; they have been used for evil means."

"What about environment and family?" Sacul countered. "We're defined by our experiences whether we like it or not. Our past is, and always will, shape our future."

"I refuse to believe that," Bar grumbled. "It's an excuse to blame others for our own failures and short comings. Although our past does shape our future, it doesn't mean that we're slaves to our past. An individual can improve and become better."

"Is that what you believe?" Sacul asked. "Do you believe that Lukhan is a slave to his past?"

"Of course," Bar whispered. "He still believes that he is a silver dragon. His identity has come into question. Who he is and how he is supposed to act within the world has been completely shattered. Being banished from his homeland must have hurt him more than any injury he obtained on the battlefield. His clan has chosen to forget him, and it's because of this that he is lost."

"That is philosophical of you," Sacul nodded. "Oh, how can you tell if a dragon is sick?"

"I don't know," Bar sighed.

"His tail is draggin'!" Sacul laughed. "Get it? Dragon. Draggin'. It's a joke."

Bar rolled his eyes and turned away from the shaman and the soft glow of the candle's flickering light. "Get some sleep," he grumbled.

A squeal of fear awoke Bar's sleep. The terrible noise sounded like the slow and painful butchering of a live pig. The snow cave collapsed, burying him under the weight of the snowdrift. The shaman's fearful squeals continued. Disoriented by the sudden collapse, Bar struggled to stand up. The struggle between up and down was solved when a sudden pain shot up from the side of his back. Something was chewing on his furs clothing! Bar turned using his teeth and claws attacked the unexpected carnivorous intruder. His claws struck at something incredibly hot. Blood splattered against him as he struck. The attacker shook its head violently, ripping the fur coat that Bar wore. Scaly whips gave way to his strikes; his attacker released him and fled into the darkness of the surrounding snow. During the brief and sudden struggle, moonlight broke through the surrounding darkness. Bar escaped through the small opening and into the cold night's air. The sudden silences of Sacul's squeals frightened him. He glanced down at his claws; thick white folds of hard scale were under his nails.

"Sacul!" Bar called. "Sacul?" He turned to the fallen structure and saw no purser after him. A small chuck of ice fell into the hole that he had escaped. Silence was the only reply to his call. The ice behind him cracked and gave way to a monstrous head. A pair of antennae and large protruding fangs shifted from the hole in a vain attempt to devour him. His adrenaline kicked in and Bar easily avoids the gaping maw. Within the moonlight, Bar's mouth dropped is shock at the enormous centipede before him. The creature's shelled body melted the snow around it, allowing it to cut through the ice like a striking snake. Its reddish brown legs stuck out from its body in a vain attempt to find its missing prey. Its black emotionless eyes peeked out from an armored head segment, but it could not see the hunter. The large vermin sought out Bar's movements with its antennae and legs.

Bar searched his person for any weapon; his claws had done nothing to the thick carapace. The centipede aimlessly felt around, mouthing the air with its venom dripping fangs. Bar slowly backed away. With his first step, the creature located him and charged furiously towards him. Bar dodged out of the way of the centipedes sudden burst of speed. The centipede's fangs snapped in passing, but did not connect, Bar felt the body heat of the creature's bulk as it scurried past and buried itself under the snow. Bar was amazed at the speed of which the creature was able to tunnel through the snow.

Silence filled the air as the giant worm disappeared; Bar looked around warily, expecting the creature to erupt from the ground around him. Nothing occurred as the moments continued to build.

A groan from the destroyed snow cave advert his attention. From the cave, Sacul spilled out of the snow bank.

"Sacul?" Bar gasped in relief. "Don't move! There's a big-" The ice around Sacul exploded and powdered flakes flew everywhere. A giant centipede emerged from the snow. Within the creature's fangs, it held one of the backpacks that Bar and Sacul carried with them. Sacul squeal and fled before the sudden resurgence.

"Run!" Sacul squealed. "There are more than two-" An explosion from below him launched him into the air as a second creature emerged.

"Sacul, where's the bombarder?" Bar yelled. The first centipede dove back under the snow as the other gave chase after Sacul. The shaman stumbled away from the snapping fangs and antennae of the giant pest. The creature's eagerness proved to be its own foil as it raced over the balled up boarelf. After

51

the sudden charge, the second centipede dove under the snow. Bar froze where he was, unwilling to give away his position to the blind creatures. He had witnessed the creature's attacks and assumed they were ambush predators and were used to larger and less agile prey.

"Don't move!" Bar instructed. The shaman froze in his fetal position. Bar waited to see what would occur. Several moments passed, as Bar looked around. There were no telltale signs about where the centipedes would reappear. He had assumed that the creatures would reemerge from the snow when he moved. He had not expected that they could hear Sacul's heart vibrations. Again, Sacul was catapulted into the air by an explosion as a centipede emerged from the snow beneath him. Sacul's fetal position saved him from the snapping fangs of the giant creature. Bar put the distraction into good use. He raced to the collapsed snow cave.

Sudden blows from the side sent Bar reeling and knock him to the side. The centipede's attack shot, searing pain through Bar's back as he jumped away from the creatures fangs. The glancing blow caught him; Bar ignored the pain and focused upon the task at hand. He dug desperately through the snow feeling for the smooth bombarder's barrel. He grasped the weapon and brought it to bear, swinging the weapon around firing it in the centipede's mouth. The effect was immediate, for the giant creature's head exploded in a sudden and violent explosion. The vermin that hovered above Sacul dove under the snow, fleeing the horrible sound of the bombarder. Sacul remained in his fetal position. Bar hurried over to check on his fallen companion.

"Are you all right?" Bar yelled. He shook the shaman, with a groan Sacul sprawled out. "I think the noise scared them off!"

"Don't stare at me!" Sacul gasped. "If they ran off, reload the damn thing!" Together they raced toward the collapsed cave. They shoveled through the snow in a desperate attempt to find their equipment. Sacul found his backpack. During the attack a hole was ripped into it. The content spilled out onto the snow.

"Find the powder," Bar instructed. "Quick!"

"This is my bag!" Sacul groaned. "There's nothing in it except food and trinkets!" The food was devoured quickly by the enormous pest. Sacul managed to salvage a knife from the cooking utensils. His shivers slowly settled as he found security in the sharp knife. The water bags remained salvageable from the assault.

"This thing is useless without its ammunition!" Bar growled. A sudden explosion of snow sent them scattering. This time they were prepared. Bar flipped his bombarder around and grabbed the mussel and swung at the centipede's head. The crude club smashed into its mandibles. Hot blood splatter on him as the creature reeled back in agony. Sacul stuck with his knife, slashing and hacking at the joints in the centipede's multiple legs. The quick slices and thrusts cut off many of the creature's appendages. It hissed in pain and retreated into the snow. Its blood left a trail behind it.

"That was easy!" Sacul cheer. "Chalk one up for us good guys!"

"What's chalk?" Bar asked. He smiled in approval; the stupid brutes couldn't compete with their agility above the snow. The centipede's poor eye sight gave Sacul and Bar the distinct advantage. As long as they dodged the creature's burrowing attacks and antennae, then they would remain safe. The ground around them shook as five other worms encircled them. The one that they had injured was not among the group.

"How many damn things are there?" Bar asked. He gulped in sudden realization.

Chapter 8

"Get out of the way!" Bar bellowed. He jumped over Sacul and smacked the flanking centipede. The bombarder struck against the creature's armored eyes. Bar felt the satisfying pop of the creature's shell being fractured. The centipede hissed and retreated, another taking its place. Despite their starch defense, the injuries they had inflicted upon the swarm were minimal and ineffective. It seemed that no matter how much damage they inflicted upon the creatures, the strange worms where determined to devour them.

"We must find rocky ground!" Sacul screamed. He dodged and danced around the snapping fangs of another centipede. "These things will keep splitting our defense!" Bar, panting heavily, nodded his head in agreement. They glanced around in desperation, seeing only snow and pests around them. "What are we going to do?"

"If we keep fighting, our strength will wane we will be overwhelmed!" Bar growled. Another creature's head exploded as he whacked with the butt end of his bombarder.

"This would be fun if it wasn't life threatening!" Sacul panted. He sliced through many legs in passing. Bar hushed him and returned to scanning the swarm of fangs and antennae. The dumb brutes were blind, except for their feelers, and their attacks were always the same. Bar had expected a more cunning opponent. The pest proved to be feral at best.

"Get to higher ground," Bar instructed. "We may yet survive this fray!"

"I hope these things are not immune to poison!" Sacul grumbled. He stabbed repeatedly at a bug in passing. In response the creature spastically fell on to the ground. As it fell, another centipede launched its poisoned companion into the air. Its sharp protruding fangs ripped huge chunks of shell out of its companion. Blood splattered across the snow, fueling the groping frenzy from other worms. The corpse was quickly ripped to shreds as the snow around the contested food turned into bloody slush. Sacul and Bar retreated as the swarm of centipedes encircled the bloody scene. Unfortunately during their escape other creatures not affected by the smell of blood harassed them with renew vigor.

"Where did you get poison?" Bar gasped. Sacul produced his pet cane toad and smiled in reply. Bar rolled his eyes at the shaman's victory. "Keep moving! The corpse will not keep them busy for long!" Together they raced to the nearest elevated snow drift. Their escape was quickly stalled by renewed assaults from the ice below them.

"They may be mindless, but they're tenacious!" Bar cursed. He struck the hard shelled creatures, doing no damage at all to it; their escape route was cut off.

"You have to admit it," Sacul chuckled madly.

"Admit what?" Br growled.

"I never would have thought I would die being devoured by big ass bugs!" Sacul chuckled. The swarm's carapace bodies were now blood stained, the only evidences of their recent cannibalism.

"I hate you," Bar growled defiantly. The blood soaked swarm charged up the snow drift toward their defensive position. A wall of fangs and antennae charged forward to devour them, and then a sudden wave of blasting ice slammed into the wave of swarming bodies. The charge came to an abrupt stop as the wave of ice washed over them. Those vermin nearest to Bar and Sacul shattered into clumps of frozen shell. Bar and Sacul looked up to see their savior.

Lukhan hovered above them. The dragon opened his maw to release his devastating dragon's breath upon the surface creatures. The centipedes retreated from the unexpected arrival of reinforcements. The silver dragon landed next to his companion and roared. The centipedes that survived the dragon's breath retreated from the ear shattering roar. Bar and Sacul covered their ear and fell to their knees. Ice cracked around them, an unnatural fury glowed within the dragon's mercury eyes.

"Was that necessary?" Sacul complained. He still had his fingers in his ears when Lukhan finally looked down at them.

"Luke!" Bar cheered. "I knew you would come!" His words were loud; the ringing of the dragon's roar didn't subside.

"You fool!" Lukhan scorned. "The centipedes hunt by following vibrations! You have alerted every one of them within a hundred leagues to our position!" Bar's mouth dropped with the sudden realization that the dragon was not there to save them.

Bar stuttered in frustration. "You roared! Wouldn't they be attracted to that?"

"Yes, but I have bought us time," Lukhan warned. "The creatures do not like loud noises, yet it does attract them. I need to get you all out of this area. Return with me to my cave." He opened his front claws in waiting.

"We are returning to Ravenshaven!" Bar snarled. He crossed his arms defiantly at the dragon before him. Lukhan raised a questioning eyebrow at the hunter.

"Yes, you should come with us!" Sacul agreed.

"You are still going on with that!" Lukhan snapped. "We should return to the safety of my cave, or are you shunning my offer?"

"I shun no one!" Bar corrected. "I speak only the truth, you must come with us."

"I have no desire to return," Lukhan snarled.

"Then I have nothing more to say," Bar dismissed the dragon's aid. "Come Sacul; let us continue the journey on foot."

"We will?" Sacul cringed.

"Stubborn fool!" Lukhan growled. "You are walking straight into your death! You have no food or shelter! You will not be able to escape theses worms! They will rip you limb from limb!"

"We have faced worse odds!" Bar rebuked.

"We have?" Sacul muttered.

"If we die then it will be your fault for not helping us!" Bar accused. Lukhan's mouth dropped in disbelief. "I am going to help my friends!" After his statement, Bar turned and started walking south. Lukhan roared and jumped in front of the knoll.

"I'm trying to save mine!" Lukhan bellowed. Dragon and knoll stared each other down in frustration and anger.

"I have made my choice!" Bar growled. "You have made yours! Now get out of my way!" Bar started to walk around Lukhan, but the dragon intercepted his path.

"Wait!" Lukhan growled. "I need time to think!"

"What is there to think about?" Bar pressed. "Your indecision has nearly cost us our lives. How many more must die? Although you may deny it, you did come to save us! You still care about this world! Your mother and father ingrained this into you. You cannot stand aside and allow things to occur, even if you try to escape your fate!"

"I did come to save you," Lukhan admitted. "I will take you to Ravenshaven, only to keep you safe from yourselves. I warn you, Bar, your stubbornness will be the death of you!" Bar smiled at the surprising triumph.

"Well, now that's settled, can we leave?" Sacul mumbled.

"Agreed," Lukhan huffed. He glanced to the horizon, where several centipedes had reemerged from the ice. "Hold on tight!" With a great bound, he snatched Bar and Sacul, and flew into the air. From the air, they watched as the centipedes swarmed over their small snow bank. The creatures felt around aimlessly in a vain attempt to locate their lost aerial prey.

The group headed south, the bitter winds of their flight forced Bar and Sacul to huddle under their furs. The rhythmic beats of Lukhan's wings put Sacul asleep. The boarelf was so exhausted that he had forgotten to complain about the dangers of flying. Bar inspected his injuries from where the centipedes had struck him. Bruises and abrasions covered his back and sides. Blood matted his hair, but upon further investigation Bar realized that it was not his own. Blood dripped down Lukhan's forearm. Something had pierced the dragons forearm.

"Am I hurting you?" Bar called over the howling wind. "Did one of the creatures do that to you?" The dragon turned his head slightly to see what Bar was doing.

"No. You should be more concern with yourself," Lukhan muttered.

"Why is that?" Bar asked.

"Whenever I am weak or dying the black claw acts upon its own accord," Lukhan stated. "When I am healthy and well fed, I can suppress its constant desire to kill. For now, Sacul and you are safe. Have no fear; the wound is minor and not life threatening." Bar considered what his friend had said, and returned to inspecting the deformed claw. He thought that the centipedes has scattered at the dragon's arrival. The wound appeared like a spear or sword thrust, not a poisonous bite. His attention turned to Lukhan's older injuries. On Lukhan's middle claw, the puss pocket had burst open during the fighting. The black claw had begun to emerge from the dragon's knuckle. Bar touched the back of the magical claw. Surprisingly, it slowly retreated in a curl from the foreign touch. Lukhan grimaced as the claw curled and bit down into his flesh.

"It moved!" Bar gasped.

"Of course it did," Lukhan scorned. "I told you not to touch it! That hurts!"

"I have never seen anything like it!" Bar whispered. "It reacted to my touch as if it was alive! I thought you said that the Betrayer was dead."

"The claw is part of Vilesath's soul," Lukhan growled. "The shadow dragon has all but disappeared, other than the black claw. I do not believe that the shadow dragon has truly disappeared."

"What do you mean?" Bar asked.

"It means that you should not have touched the claw," Lukhan repeated. "I still do *not* understand this curse thing." He flexed his claw so that Bar was further from his prying concerns. Bar tried reaching to the old injury, but Lukhan shook his claw.

"Hey, I am trying to help you!" Bar accused. Lukhan glared down at his excessively concerned friend. Bar smiled definitely at him.

"Your cure is worse than the curse!" Lukhan grumbled. Bar gave a mock laugh at his friend's complaint. He knew how much the dragon had suffered.

"I am glad that you decided to join us," Bar praised. Lukhan huffed at his friends praise. "I knew you would not abandon the world."

"You are mistaken," Lukhan mumbled. "I came to save you from yourselves. You would have died had I not arrived. You foolishly endangered yourself to prove a point! That was reckless and stupid!"

"Yes, it was," Bar agreed. Lukhan raised a questioning eyebrow at his companion. "I was angry with you for turning your back on the world! You've always been reluctant to take action when it was required. You're needed."

"No one needs me," Lukhan grumbled.

"Why do you keep saying that?" Bar scorned. "We need you now more than ever. We're fighting a powerful enemy, one that has never been defeated before. We fight against the human's demigod! One that we cannot defeat alone! The dragon clans need you."

"There will always be war!" Lukhan snapped. Sacul groaned in his sleep, both turned to look at their sleeping companion. They lowered their voices in consideration of the shaman.

"You remember what the Inquisition did within the Silver Mountains!" Bar growled. "The purge was only stopped by the timely arrival of the plague! The humans would have been as destructive! The dragon clans are aware of the destructive power of humanity!"

"I have personally seen the destructive abilities of humanity," Lukhan recalled. "I don't know what the humans are capable of any more. The slaughter of the sacred herd was engraved within my mind. Yet-" He paused in contemplation.

"What?" Bar scorned.

"Cirrus told me that the Holy Master knows about my grafting," Lukhan muttered. "He could help me- perhaps return me to normal. That was Cirrus's final aid that he offered me." Bar raised a questioning eyebrow; doubt was evident on his face.

"What?" Bar asked. "Vatara and the elves are working on your cure; you do not need the Holy Master. Their efforts have been stalled by the Inquisition's harassments. That is another reason why you should help us end this war quickly, so that you can be cured."

"What if they never find a cure and the secrets die with the Holy Master?" Lukhan growled. "I don't know if I could continue living in this horrible fate. I-I would go insane!"

"You are not as terrible as you think," Bar chuckled. "Everything kills to survive, that is how the world works."

"I am aware of that," Lukhan growled. "That is where I am different. I do not simply devour the body, I consume their white flame. Their very being!"

"So what?" Bar asked in confusion. "How is that any different compared to anyone else? Or when I kill and consume something?"

"The white flame is the essences of life itself," Lukhan snapped. "I consume their energy, their experiences, and their souls! All of this I consume to maintain this broken shell of a body. My own identity slips away every time I devour another's white flame."

"Then don't use the black claw," Bar stated flatly. "Simply devour the flesh and release the spirit. You are making your situation too difficult and complicated." Lukhan bared his teeth at his ignorant companion.

"You fool!" Lukhan cursed. "Did you think that I have not attempted that? My white flame was consumed when I cast the spell to destroy to the plague! I am a soulless corpse, an abomination to all things that are alive."

"You still look like the old Luke," Bar snapped. "You are so much more than a body! You still have your mind intact and you still know right from wrong. You came and saved us when you didn't have to! You still know who I am." The hunter shook his head in denial at what the hatchling was confessing to him. "No, I refuse to believe that you are like the undead. They were soulless abominations. You have none of the characteristic of the mindless victims of the plague."

"Not yet," Lukhan muttered coldly. "You have not seen me in my degenerated and malnourish state. My body loses control and consumes anything and everything nearby; your opinion of me will change when you will see the reality of the curse."

"Is that why you left your homeland?" Bar asked. His tone was neither judgmental nor sarcastic. Lukhan opened his mouth to speak, yet nothing came out. The dragon's insightful mentor had found the truth of his isolation. He wanted to protect his family, friends, clan, and Lemuria from himself. He feared that the Betrayer would seek him out and he would lose his sanity. Without the Staff of Selgae, Lukhan knew his situation would have been far worse.

"I left because I cared," Lukhan clarified. "I left because I love life, family, my clan. Because I love Lemuria. I do not wish to destroy them."

"Lemuria is in danger!" Bar explained. "Everything you love is under threat of being purged by the Inquisition. This invisible threat is not you! The Inquisition and its reckless ability to destroy is the current threat. You know that this is true." Lukhan remained silent as they continued to fly south. The young dragon had to consider what had been said. His friends were in danger. The Inquisition had gone too far when they had slaughter the sacred herd, the main food source of the dragon clans. The humans had attacked the Silver Mountains first. He had made a pact with Judas in helping bring down the Inquisition. He knew that the humans would not stop, by Judas's confession. All of this ran through his mind as he considered the options.

"I will take you to Ravenshaven," Lukhan stated. Bar smiled up at his companion, pleased that the dragon had come to his senses. "However, I will not aid you in this war." The knoll's smile faded into a look of fear and despair.

Chapter 9

The tundra slowly gave way to rocks and sand. It was difficult to gage where the Endless Ice ended and the Endless Desert began. The two climates blurred together in an undistinguishable landscape of sand and ice. Dunes with snow between them spread out below them in a windblown tapestry. Despite the sudden opening of dunes, the temperature remained cold. Bar remained silent, fuming over Lukhan's unwavering position about the future of Lemuria. The dragon remained in stoic silence, nothing more could be said. He had decided that it was his fate to live alone. Lemuria's future would be secure with his absence, away from his cruel destiny. Thus, protecting the ones he loved.

"What's this all about?" Sacul mumbled in his sleep. The sudden shout awoke both Bar and Lukhan from their deep thoughts. Both looked at each other in bewilderment as the shaman continued his mumbles. "You need to shut up, and stop shouting at each other!"

"Wake up!" Lukhan growled. "You were sleeping!" With a quick shake, the shaman scrambled to hang on. Lukhan flexed his claws and slowly lowered his attitude.

"Why are we stopping?" Bar asked.

"You two are not the only ones that need rest," Lukhan growled.

"Luke, I didn't mean-," Bar stuttered.

"Spare me," Lukhan snapped. He beat his wings quickly to slow down. The dragon released his two companions. The temperature was noticeably warmer on the ground than the higher elevation. Despite the snow still around them, both knoll and boarelf smiled at the sudden relief of warm air.

"It is good to be back in my homeland," Sacul yawned. "How long have we been traveling? We are making good time."

"Yes," Lukhan agreed. He stretched his aching wings. He had not flown like this in a long time. "We will be there sooner than I predicted. It is due to a strong tailwind."

"Wonderful," Sacul cheered. "I can't wait to get out of the weather! You have done well to get us this far south."

"You can thank the changing of the seasons," Lukhan muttered. "Winter has finally ended and the northern winds have given way to the southern warm fronts."

"What?" Sacul wonder. "How do you know so much?"

"I have the empathy for the air elements," Lukhan pressed. "Furthermore, I have the Staff of Selgae within my position; I have the experiences those that have held it before."

"Magi?" Sacul asked. "The staff? Where is it? Did you leave it behind?"

"I left the staff within my cave and sealed it away," Lukhan muttered uneasily. He glanced down at his forearm. "I would not have been able to carry it."

"Understandable," Bar huffed. He crossed his arms, for he knew that his companion was lying to them. "You should return to your cave and treasure. After all, that is all you care about now."

"I do what I must to survive!" Lukhan growled. Bar waved him away dismissively.

"Many have done exactly that!" Bar countered. "Many have that attitude."

"What are you two fighting about now?" Sacul demanded. He noticed the tension between dragon and knoll. Lukhan's laid his head down and closed his scarred eyes. Bar only shook his head.

"Stubborn beast," Bar growled. He glanced over at Lukhan. If the dragon heard him then he did not show it.

"Oh my, someone is venomous today?" Sacul commented. "Why are you in such a foul mood? What did you two argue about?"

"Luke, has decided to drop us off and do nothing more!" Bar huffed. "Despite everyone's need for him, he will not get involved. Our troubles are our own."

"So," Sacul stated. Bar's eyebrow and ears twitched uneasily. The shaman back away uneasily and put up his hand defensively. "Now before you go off getting angry and hitting someone, why don't you look at the big picture?"

"What do you mean?" Bar demanded.

"Think about it," A big toothily grin spread a crossed Sacul's face. "Lukhan will not be in any danger. He will be safe within the Endless Ice. No harm will come to him and he will finally know some peace!"

"What peace is there while the world burns?" Bar snapped. "The Inquisition will not rest until the dragon clans and common races are destroyed! Who knows if Ravenshaven still stands! Everything is in danger! They seek to purge the magic from this world!"

"That is why Lukhan should stay away!" Sacul rebuked. "He is a dragon driven by instincts, not free thought! Should he take to the battlefield, what do you think will happen?" Bar's eyes dropped as he considered what the shaman had said. "His bloodlust would take over and he would slaughter everything in his path! Friends and foes alike!"

"No! When we were fighting the centipedes-" Bar began

"He only used his dragon's breath," Sacul recalled. "He was never injured in the fighting. If he were to become wounded he would go berserk. That is why he cannot die. The black claw would never allow him to perish on the battlefield. It would go so far as to devour his friends and family! Don't you remember-?"

Bar closed his eyes in contemplation. "He can help support the armies by delivering supplies and mail!" he offered. "There is no need for him to be left alone. We need him!"

"Lukhan is a dragon! He does not need us or our war!" Sacul grunted. "He would never take on such a role, and you know it! He would engage with the enemy, and it would lead to disastrous results! For both sides! You must let him leave!"

"No!" Bar growled.

"Then you are a fool!" Sacul snapped. "Dragon and the common race are not meant to be together!"

"How can you say that?" Bar growled. "The Gold Clan has united with us! Luke has sacrificed so much for us and the world! We are blood brothers!"

"A fleeting notion of something greater," Sacul grunted sadly. "The Gold Clan does not march with us, I wonder if our goals are even the same. The Inquisition views our alliance as nothing more than threats and an obstacle to be overcome. Lukhan will be safer away from this war! We're lucky to have known him for this long. Dragons are not known for their kindness or forgiveness."

"So, what are you saying?" Bar demanded.

"You must allow him to make his own choice," Sacul stated. "Pressing

him to serve or browbeating him doesn't make it any easier for ether of you."
The knoll nodded his head in agreement with the shaman's statement. Sacul's
smiled at the stubborn hunter.

"Then this adventure has all been a waste of time!" Bar sighed. "What
if we're already too late?" He was disheartened by the loss of time with no
beneficial outcome.

"We know that our friend will be safe," Sacul stated. "Away from the
terrible events to come and we know that he is alive. You know, I was concern
for him too."

"You?" Bar chuckled weakly. "I thought you only cared about your pet toad."

"I sometimes expand my circle of concerns," Sacul chuckled. "Sometimes."

They flew south; the snow retreated and turned into harsh barren wastelands.
Sand and jagged rocks lay below them. The harsh wasteland burned away
any water on the surface. Lukhan had to stop several times because he was
unaccustomed to the change in temperature, prolonged flight, and extra
weight. Neither Bar or Sacul complained about their companion's need to
rest. The adventure they had used to reach Lukhan had taken them several
months. With Lukhan's flight, it only took a few weeks. The silver dragon
would rest during the day and fly at night. The cooler temperatures seemed
easier for him to adjust.

"The sun is rising," Bar muttered.

"Hmm?" Lukhan asked. "What did you say?"

"He said: 'the sun is rising,'" Sacul snorted.

"I think he can hear me," Bar glared at the boisterous shaman.

"Yes," Lukhan agreed. "I need to rest-" A shadow from above alarmed
him. He turned sharply, something slammed into him jarring both Sacul
and Bar from his grasp. His friends screamed as they plunged to the ground.
Surprised by the sudden jolt, Lukhan looked around for his assailant. From
the corner of his eye, he caught sudden movement. Five winged creatures
with leathery tanned skin circled above him. To his surprise the creature
retreated from his position. Barbs at the end of their tails told him that they
were wyverns. Ignoring his fleeing attackers Lukhan folded his wings and
drove to save his companions.

"Save me!" Sacul squealed. Lukhan snatch him and angled down to Bar. The hunter was limp as he spiraled downward to the awaiting ground. He appeared unconscious from the sudden drop. Lukhan snatch him and opened his wings suddenly. The sudden jarring movement of his decent nearly cost him his grip. The ground came hard up on them and Lukhan crashed into one dune after another. The crash flung Sacul and Bar from his grasp. The dragon received a mouth full of sand for his troubles.

"Curse the five elements!" Lukhan spat. He recovered quickly and looked to the skies. The wyverns circled above in a slow a methodical approach. With a great bound, he leaped into the air, eager to engage the creatures that dared attack him. The wyverns scattered and turned away. Despite Lukhan's burst of speed, the fast moving wyverns fled before the larger dragon. "Oh no, you don't! You will not escape me! *Subsisto ventus!*" The dragon's eyes blazed to life in a mercury fire. The wind around the wyverns stopped completely. Having no thrust beneath their wings caused the creature to tumble to the ground.

"Please Silver God!" the wyvern choked. "Don't you remember-?" A deathly gasp came from the back of the creature's throat. Lukhan landed among them, immune to the sudden loss of oxygen. The wyverns wither before the silver dragon sprawling back and forth like an injured snake. Ice form around the dragon, chilling the wyverns nearest to him. A thin film of water crystals developed in a circular pattern around him, like massive ring similar to a snow flake.

"Did you think you could attack me and escape?" Lukhan roared. "Cowardly worms! You dare attack me from behind? You nearly killed my friends!" An unnatural fury developed upon his face.

"Stop!" Sacul interrupted. "We are all right!"

"Luke!" Bar called. "Please, we need them alive!" Lukhan glared at his companions, the rage did not leave his eyes. "Please stop-!" The dragon's blazing eyes slowly returned to normal. The ice around him evaporated and he slowed down his breathing. The wyverns around him gasped as oxygen returned to their lungs. They crawled away in a weakened condition. Only one of the creatures remained near the enraged dragon, unafraid of what had occurred.

"Why should I?" Lukhan snarled.

"God Lukhan, you reek of death!" an aged creature called. The dragon turned to look at the old wyvern. There was something strangely familiar about the old wrenched creature.

"Do I know you?" Lukhan snarled.

"Sessesssss," the old wyvern bowed deeply. "You have become powerful, assss my masterssss have foreseen."

"Brood mother of the Endless Desert?" Lukhan rumbled. "I remember you. Why are you here? Why have you attack me?"

"Forgive ussss," Sessess begged. "We're not targeting you. Otherwise, we would have struck at your wingssss and maimed you."

"Then who were you attacking?" Lukhan snarled. Sessess looked pass him, where Bar and Sacul stood. Drool fell from her mouth. Lukhan's eyes narrowed dangerously and stepped between her and his companions. "I could kill your children and you with only a phrase."

"We dare not go against your wishessss," Sessess gasped. "I remember how important those petsss are to you. However, we have been given orderssss to kill all common racessss that passss this way."

"Kill us?" Bar gasped. "Why?" Sessess screeched at his sudden intrusion. Bar brought his bombarder to bear. Although he had not ammunition, he hoped the devise would intimidate her. If the brood mother knew what the tube-like devise was, she did not show it.

"Speak only to me." Lukhan instructed. Having dealt with the brood mother twice before, he was aware of her elitist view. Wyverns only spoke to dragons, which they viewed as gods.

"The Green Clan issss aware of the conflict that occurssss to the South," Sessess hissed humbly. She glared at the knoll and boarelf. "My brood and I have been commanded to insure that no slavessss from the Black Clan or insurrectionssss marchessss from the Endlesssss Desert. Our objective is to keep everyone away from the Jade Rainforest. My master doesn't want the lesser racessss getting involved in the Green Clan's territorial dispute."

"I have heard rumors that the Black and Green Clans have been battling for some time," Lukhan admitted. "It is sad that they cannot put aside their differences."

"It issss not unexpected," Sessess agreed. Her lips pulled back revealing her crack and dried gums. Lukhan raised a questioning eyebrow to the wyvern's crude grin; the brood appeared to be dehydrated.

"Your brood appears to be in bad shape," Lukhan stated. "Perhaps a bargain can be made."

"A trade?" Sessess asked. "What would a god asked of humble servantssss?"

"Allow my friends to pass unharnessed," Lukhan purposed. "I shall summon the spring rains."

"Promise that the lesser racesss will not travel thissss way again!" Sessess demanded.

"You would dare make demands from me!" Lukhan snarled. With great speed and strength he snatched Sessess around her neck. The deformed claw twitched.

"No, of course not!" Sessess begged. "Forgive me!"

"Then we have an agreement?" Lukhan warned. He applied more force to Sessess's neck. The brood mother squirmed within his vice-like grip.

"Yessss!" Sessess begged. "Forgive usss master!"

"I will hold you to your word," Lukhan growled. "*Voco unda!*" His eyes flashed with silver and slowly faded. Within his free claw, water droplets began to gather until there was enough to drink. He cupped his claw and took a small sip from it. Then he offered his cupped claw to the trapped brood mother. She looked at the water questionably.

"Drink," Lukhan commanded. Sessess took a long and greedy draft from the claw which turned into lapping. No matter how much she drank, the water did not empty from Lukhan's claw. "Now listen closely, the spring rains will not come this year. This desert will become scorched with fire. Should you remain within the Endless Desert, you and your children will die." After satisfying her thirst she looked up at him.

"Why show such kindnesssss?" Sessess asked.

"You once helped me save this world," Lukhan looked over at her awaiting brood. The parched creatures smack the lips longingly. "Come; offer your children something to drink."

"Of course, God Lukhan!" Sessess bowed. He loosened his grip around her neck and moved his claw to her shoulders. She bobbed her head up and down, signaling her awaiting brood. The strange creatures bobbed their heads back in reply. The brood slowly approach and drank from Lukhan's offering.

"Bar! Sacul!" Lukhan called. "Are you thirsty?"

"Our canteens are full," Sacul stated. He took out his water skin and shook it for all to hear. Both of the dragon's companions looked at each other with uncertainty.

"This is a test," Lukhan demanded. "To see if they will hold true to their word."

"We will not share water with scum like them!" Sessess screeched. The wyvern around Lukhan dropped defensively at their leader's sudden burst. Sessess squirmed in the dragon's claw.

"Then you are a fool," Lukhan snarled. He tilted his claw and allowed some of the water to pour out. Some of the wyverns that had not drank screamed in protest as the water disappearing into the sand.

"Cursessss to you and your kind!" Sessess snarled.

"You would allow your own children to suffer because of your prejudice?" Lukhan snarled.

"You are cruel!" Sessess hissed. "We could kill you all!"

"In doing so, you would be killing yourself!" Lukhan opened his wings, knocking down those wyverns nearest to him. Like leaves blown by the wind, the creatures scattered in fear. Both dragon and wyvern bared their teeth at each other. As Bar and Sacul slowly approached, the four wyverns hissed and snapped their jaws at them. Both had their weapons drawn, fearing that the creature would use their poisons stingers.

"Is this truly necessary?" Bar asked, as he reached Lukhan's side. "Luke, I think you are only antagonizing them." The dragon snorted in reply.

"You're provoking a fight when there doesn't need to be one," Sacul whispers. He glanced uneasily at the brood mother. Death was written in her eyes.

"I grow tired of theses endless debates of pointless aggression," Lukhan snarled. "I can smell your fear! I can feel your blood pumping through your veins! I could crush the life out of you! End your pathetic existence!" He applied more pressure to Sessess's shoulders. She thrashed back and forth attempting to bite, sting, and claw him. Her struggles slowed and she began to wheeze for air.

"Stop, Luke!" Bar begged. "You are killing her! Stop!"

"Why?" Lukhan demanded. "She is part of everything I hate in this world! She will never change her ways! She is a slave to the old beliefs! A system of segregation and elitism! They are wyverns, mindless slaves of the Green Clan! They should all perish!"

"If you kill her, wouldn't you become like them?" Bar asked. Lukhan paused and narrowed his eyes at the fading brood mother. With a choking gurgle and the wyvern's eyes rolled back, she hung loosely within his claw. He turned his attention to her brood. They dispassionately watched from a safe distance away, as if the mother didn't mean anything to them. Their yellow eyes showed no signs of concern.

"T-They are nothing but wyverns," Lukhan stuttered as he slowly released Sessess from his deformed claw.

Chapter 10

The black claw had acted on its own accord. The deformed thing switched and slowly receded into his knuckle, like a snail returning to its shell. Lukhan glanced down at the fallen brood mother. She had a small festered cut on her wing's membrane, the thin flesh pealed back, as if fire burned it away. The cut's expansion slowly stopped and formed a festering scab.

"I am glad that you didn't harm her," Bar let out a heavy sigh. "That could have been a diplomatic failure and I thought you were going to lose control." He knelt beside Sessess and checked her pulse. After a few moments, Bar continued his examination of the brood mother's bones. The hunter did not notice the small injury on her wing and focused upon her vital areas. Lukhan remained silent as he continued to stare at his claw. The black claw curled and became inactive. Sacul walked around him and examined the fallen leader.

"We were given instructions to speak with the wyverns, if we saw them," Sacul grunted. "That's why we didn't want you to hurt her."

"You were given instructions?" Lukhan whispered.

"Yes," Sacul continued. "Owen gave us instructions to open dialog with the Green Clan, if the opportunity arose." The shaman glanced over at the other wyverns. They bobbed their heads up and down in their strange native language.

"Let ussss eat her!" the largest wyvern called from a safe distance away.

"What?" Lukhan growled.

"Sessesssss hassss offended the godssss!" the brood called. "Your wrath issss evidence of thissss! Give her to ussss! We must eat her! She hassss lead ussss to starvation and thirst! Give her to ussss, so that we may serve again!

69

The godsssss must be appeased!" They jumped up and down and shrieked in unified agreement. The dragon glance down at the weaken mother.

"What should we do?" Lukhan asked. "She did try to kill you."

"You can't be serious in considering-," Bar shivered. He glanced over his shoulder at his friends. "Cannibalism makes me sick to my stomach! Even though she attempted to kill us, we can't turn her over to them!"

"Why not?" Sacul snorted.

"It's barbaric!" Bar stated in grave distasted. He looked on in disbelieve at his two companions. "I will not stand by an allow it to happen!"

"This is not our fight," Lukhan's eyes did not leave his deformed claw, so mesmerized by the cruel and unnatural digit. He wondered if she was not already doomed. "We should leave the wyverns to their own customs and fate."

"What happened to the hatchling I once knew?" Bar snapped. "You said that you were going to change the wyverns' ways. Now that we have an opportunity to change this brood, you want to let them devour their leader?"

"Sessess was trying to kill you!" Lukhan snapped.

"She didn't!" Bar stated. "Now, we're going to save her!"

"What?" Sacul grunted. "We are?"

"We saved her," Bar stressed. "Therefore, she will grant us boons for allowing her to live! Our objective is to make allies, not enemies! Haven't enough died?" Sacul looked at the knoll as if he had gone insane. The puzzled expression turned into gut busting laughter. The grunts of crude laughter broke Lukhan's continued stare at his black claw.

"I agree," Lukhan snorted.

"Whoa! What?" Sacul chuckles ceased.

"Let us hope that the brood mother will revive," Lukhan stated. "If she does not come to some form of agreement with us, then her children can have her." He looked at the brood. The creatures kept their distances. They watched, wary of the powerful silver dragon that stood protectively over their unconscious and weak leader.

"You hear that?" Bar shouted. "Well, did you?" He picked up a rock and hurled it at the nearest creature. The brood scattered as the hunter shooed them away. They took to the air and circled above in a continuous pattern. Their head bobbed up in down.

"Damn buzzards!" Sacul cursed with an unnerving shivered.

"Listen, all of you!" Lukhan bellowed into the air. "You will get no meal here! Flee before I develop a taste for wyvern's flesh!" The high flying creatures shrieked and flew away into the distant horizon.

"I fear we've made enemies no matter what," Sacul grunted. "A corpse would have made the buzzards happy, or at least slowed them down before coming after us."

"That's harsh," Bar grumbled. "Considering what has happened to us. It's sad that you would sacrifice another so that you may live."

"That is the reality of the Endless Desert," Sacul explained. "The desert claims the old and weak. That is the way of things." The group looked at the old wyvern, her weather beaten skin and tarnished dark grey hair was evident of her age.

"I have dealt with wyverns three times before," Lukhan grumbled. "Twice was with Sessess, servant of Con'ra. The other was Semitic, a warrior slave under the command of Krain, the leader of the Green Clan. I killed Semitic with the black claw."

"That's why we should leave!" Sacul groaned. "Both green dragons wanted to use and discard us! I told Owen that an alliance with the Green Clan would end with the alliance's servitude or death!"

"Sessess is not a normal wyvern," Lukhan continued. "She was wise enough to find a master that would not use and discard her."

"What do you suggest?" Bar asked.

"Sessess is a connection with the Green Clan," Lukhan concluded. "Only with the rebellious smaller fraction. Con'ra only had a couple of hundred wyverns with her."

"So?" Sacul mumbled.

"Sessess is still a powerful connection to the Green Clan," Bar smiled because he knew where his dragon companion was going with the conversation. "Wyverns are numerous within the Jade Rainforest! If we could get Con'ra or Krain on our side, that would bolster our forces. They could help end the Inquisition!"

"Wyverns would help against supply trains and cavalry," Lukhan nodded in agreement.

"I thought you weren't interest with the lesser races' affairs," Bar grinned. Lukhan raised a questioning eyebrow to the knoll's accusation.

"I don't want you getting mowed down by the Inquisition's knights and bombarders," Lukhan stated evenly. "I still have no interest in your affairs." Bar chuckled with renewed hope, the group watched as the sun rose over the distant horizon.

With the immobilized brood mother, they made camp. The sun beat down upon them. The desert's temperature rose to unbearable degrees. Lukhan lifted his wing to provide shade for the fallen wyvern and his overheated companions. Bar and Sacul dribbled water upon Sessess tongue to keep her cool. As the unnatural warmth of the spring temperatures rose, Sacul began to mumble. Bar panted excessively and fanned himself. Lukhan dug up a dune for cooler sand below. The day's heat wore on them. Despite this, the temperature continued to rise.

"Blasted desert," Bar panted. "First it freezes you, and then it burns you. I feel sorry for you; at least you have reflective scales to protect you. Luke, are you doing all right?" Lukhan lazily open and closed his eyes, and then nodded his head in reply. "Sacul, how are you holding up?"

"You used magic!" Sacul screamed. Both knoll and dragon jumped at the shaman's sudden outburst. The boarelf raced from beneath the shade into the desert's burning sunlight and did a strange hopping dance, jumping from one foot to the other. His odd dance finished with quick steps like he was walking over hot coals.

"What has gotten into you?" Bar demanded. "Get back into the shade! Have you lost your senses?"

"How did you do magic?" Sacul gasped. He began to mutter and mumble to himself. He began to strip down and throw his clothing into the air.

"Stop!" Bar yelled. "What are you doing? The heat has fried his brain." The shaman paid no attention to his yelling companion and raced about nude. He drew out his pet toad and started licking it. He got down on all fours and started drawing in the sand.

"Magic!" Sacul muttered. "You have no soul, yet you cast magic! How is this possible? The spirits are angry and they warn me!"

"You are starting to freak me out-," Bar growled. "Don't make me come out there and get you, you stupid pig!" Sacul jumped up from his sand drawing and ran around in a circle.

"The heat has taken him," Lukhan stated. He closed his eyes and shook his head at the strange sight. "Does he do this often?"

"Stop licking that damn toad-!" Bar cursed.

"The spirits whisper!" Sacul shouted. "They whisper to me! Listen!" He jumped up from his scribbles and raced over to where Bar stood under the shade. He grabbed Bar's fur clothing and tugged him out into the sunlight.

"You damn fool, what are you ranting about?" Bar snarled. "You need to put on your clothes! Where is your modesty? What's so urgent?" Sacul tugged Bar over to the drawing, and pointed to the ground. Before them was a perfect designed pentagram. The boarelf had used his feet to draw the circle and five pointed star.

"Behold!" Sacul laughed insanely. "The symbol of power! The pentagram!"

"That is a skilled drawing," Bar congratulated. He rolled his eyes at the hallucinating boarelf.

"It's the symbol of his doom!" Sacul pointed back to Lukhan and the dragon remained where he sat and kept his eyes closed to them, unconcern about shaman's ranting.

"His doom?" Bar pondered. "This symbol will be Luke's doom?" Sacul nodded his head in agreement "How can that be? This is a symbol of power. It requires magic to work." Bar's expression of concern fade to a look of horror. The boarelf started to mumble. "Without the white flame, how did Luke cast magic?"

"Some mysteries should never be explained," Sacul muttered. "Dark roads lead to nightmares." He had a wide eyed expression as if he knew something horrific.

"A mystery that can be easily solved," Bar stated with a frown. He kicked in the sand drawing, and slapped the pet toad out of the shaman's hand. The toad hopped off and Sacul gave chase. Bar shook his head at the bare ass boarelf.

"How did you cast magic?" he demanded. Lukhan's frill twitched but no answers came forth. "Eldora warned you about the dangers of using magic. The cost on the white flame is too great, you cannot handle it! Don't you remember the ceremony?" The dragon remained in his dozing state unmoved by his friend's question. "Before our little party leaving the Silver Mountains, you told us that you could no longer cast magic. So how are you able to cast magic now?"

The dragon remained silent.

"What is the point of having friends if you won't talk to them?" Bar snorted. "You can be a stubborn ass, you know that. All I want to know is if you will be all right?" Lukhan's eyebrows twitched, but he did not open his eyes. The hunter growled in defeat and returned to the cooler shade beneath the dragon's wing.

"It is too hot to argue," Lukhan mumbled. "I am fine, as you can see-"

"Of that, you're correct," Bar interrupted with a frustrated cursed. He took a long draft from his water skin and crouched next to Sessess. He lifted the wyvern's head and allowed her to drink. The refreshing water slide down her throat. Sessess slowly opened her eyes. "Finally coming around are we?" Her eyes flew wide at the knoll before her. The hair on wyvern's neck stood up and she sprung up and hissed. The sudden burst of movement sent Bar head over heels, into the desert sun. Using his wing, Lukhan penned Sessess into the sand. The wyvern hissed and screamed but she could not move.

"Wasn't expecting that reaction!" Bar shouted in excitement. He wiped the sand out of his face and hair. "Thanks for that!"

"Don't mention it," With a thrust of Lukhan's wing, the silver dragon dragging both trapped wyvern and sand to him. The strength of his wings lifted him up, and forced Sessess to roll with the sand. Lukhan stood and revealed the half buried brood mother. From the flat of her back, she spat and sputtered. He reached over and pinned her to the ground.

"Kill me!" Sessess shrieked. She paused from her violent struggles and looked at her captor. "You are cruel! Why don't you finish me?"

"I made a promise," Lukhan muttered. She paused and looked at him in confusion. Her chest heaved up and down from the sudden exertion. Her mouth hung open with fear.

"Promisesss?" Sessess asked in a wide eyed expression.

Bar stepped before her and she renewed her struggles. "We don't want to hurt you." The wyvern shrieked at him.

"Stop struggling!" Lukhan growled. She froze in fear at the dragon's drop in tone. "Now listen to Bar's proposal." She ceased her struggles and slowly relaxed.

"Sacul, get over here so we can relay the message!" Bar yelled.

"Laugh and the world laughs with you; fart and they'll stop laughing!" Sacul called. The nude shaman ignored his command and continued to chase his pet toad. The absurd boarelf was not going to help him.

Bar rubbed his forehead and shook his head; it was too hot for this craziness. He let out a heavy sigh and knelt before the entrapped wyvern. "I don't know why he follows us," Bar whispered. He cleared his throat and returned his attention to his captive audience.

"On behalf of the council of Ravenshaven," Bar announced with a formal bow. "The council has appointed me as ambassador to those willing to fight the Inquisition. An alliance has been created to punish the race of men for the destruction of the sacred herd and slaughter of countless innocents. This alliance will grant a temporary peace between the warring factions of our peoples, races, and creed. We seek to stop those that would oppress the world, and bring justice to those who would seek to destroy all that are not deemed human. The Inquisition must be brought down and the Holy Master humbled. This is the objective of the Ravenshaven's Alliance and the Free People. Will you join us as we attempt to change those humans that are in power?"

"What doessss the godssss say?" Sessess asked. She turned her attention to her captor. Lukhan raised a questioning eyebrow.

"I believe it is a worthy cause," Lukhan stated honestly.

"Issss it a trick?" Sessess hissed. "Liessss to feed to the carrion crowssss."

"I would trust Bar and Sacul with my life," Lukhan replied. "If that is what you are asking."

"Humanssss are strong and powerful," Sessess snapped. "Tricky and clever in their usessss of cruel steel and arrowssss. You ask a slave for a master'ssss promise! Never! Only the green oness can declare war against the smelly land walkerss."

"The Green Clan?" Lukhan asked. "Do you mean Con'ra?" Sessess exploded with a sudden snap of her jaws, slicing his knuckle. With a sudden twist, she escaped the dragon's grasp. Then with a quick beat of her wings, she flew into the distant horizon. Lukhan growled but did not pursue her. Bar notice a trickle of blood run down the dragon's knuckle.

"Did she hurt you?" Bar asked.

"No more than I hurt her," Lukhan replied evenly.

Chapter 11

They continued their journey south. Ravenshaven's torchlight burned on the distant horizon, a welcoming sign to the road weary group. Moonlight shown down upon the recently plowed fields below them. They followed a recently constructed road that led toward the city, a testament to the rise in economic prosperity to the city.

"There it is! Our home!" Bar cheered.

"Civilization," Sacul grumbled. He was coming down from his toad induced high. "So, my flying friend, have you made your choice?"

"Hmm?" Lukhan muttered.

"You're here," Sacul continued. "Will you join us in this war effort?" The dragon snorted in reply. "I take that as a no?"

"Look there," Lukhan growled. Below them, in the moonlight, laid a circled caravan. The oxen that pulled the wagons had been thrown about and slaughtered. Two of the four wagons had been knocked over; the stench of acid filled the air. A culmination of treasure was gathered upon a single wagon.

"The trade caverns must have been attacked by the Inquisition!" Bar warned. "Luke! We must go down and see if there are any survivors!" Lukhan dove to the ground to investigate the carnage below. Other than the corpses of the oxen, no one appeared to be present. As Lukhan sniffed the air, Bar investigated the burdened wagon. "Why would the Inquisition abandon all this treasure? Everything appears to be here. There are silks, gold, and weapons. I found some black powder! What could have-?"

"Something is not right," Sacul muttered. He examined the ground around the carnage. "These are some strange tracks. Look at the acidic burns on the wagons. There are no horse shoe prints. This couldn't have been the Inquisition's knights."

"I sense magic," Lukhan grumbled. "Look over there." He pointed to a shimmering mirage that appeared to be a gully. Bar stood up from examining the wagon's treasure. He moved on to the other partly destroyed wagon.

"I don't see anything-," Sacul replied. He scratched his head in confusion and consideration. A sudden shift from the gully wavered before them.

"Move!" Lukhan roared. He sprinted over and snatched Bar from the empty wagon before it was suddenly consumed by a green acidic blast.

"How many times do I have to kill your kind?" A soft sultry voice warned. "Knolls, the cockroaches of the lesser races. Keep your dirty paws away from my treasure!" The magical camouflage collapsed revealing a green dragon. She was smaller than Lukhan, emerging bone ridges went down her back. Acidic scarification, which resembled thorny vines, ran down the side of her face and neck. The scar appeared to glow with a neon green light. Evidence of the scarring had been from some source of magic. In the pit beside her laid the cavern's guards and merchants. The imprisoned captives varied from men, boarelves, and knolls. All were entangle in a large growth of vines, which shackled them like cruel living chains.

"You!" Lukhan snarled.

"Silver, you are out of your element," the green dragon smiled. "I have no quarrel with your clan. It is strange that you carry your pets by wing. Who serves whom?"

"Con'ra?" Lukhan muttered. "Don't you remember me?"

"Y-you know my name?" Con'ra wavered but she recovered quickly. "If you know my name, then you know I am not to be trifled with."

"It is I," Lukhan replied in disbelief.

"Eye? What kind of name is that?" Con'ra sneered. "Did your pets name you that? Are you a slave of the lesser races? It would not surprise me; you appear to be in poor condition." A look of superiority spread across her face when she watched the unexpected guest pause. Lukhan narrowed his eyes and stepped closer. "If you come any closer, Silver, I will kill theses pets that I have captured. You knoll, drop your bombarder." She glared dangerously at Bar, who held his weapon up to his shoulder. Bar did as the green dragon demanded.

"My name is Lukhan," the silver dragon stated.

Con'ra considered what was said and then snorted. "Then you are a liar." She narrowed her yellow cat-like eyes and sniffed the air. "You stink like a black dragon; you reek of death and decay! Now, I understand! You have used magic to conceal your appearance!"

"His name is Lukhan, and he is no worshipper of death," Sacul interrupted. The boarelf stood next to the pit of squirming prisoners. With a knife, the shaman cut away at the magical vines. Con'ra sniffed the tiny boarelf beside her.

"Fool, why did you say anything!" Bar howled. With a flick of Con'ra's claw, the boarelf was flung into the vine pit with the rest of the prisoners. The vines reacted to the shaman like constricting snakes. Lukhan exploded into action; he reached her only to snatch air. Con'ra sprung into the air narrowly avoiding his deadly jaws.

"No tactic sense, whatsoever!" Con'ra chuckled. "You cannot match my speed and agility! Now die!" She opened her mouth and released her acidic breath. Lukhan dodged to the side narrowly missing the corrosive glob, several smaller blasts followed. The silver dragon returned fire with his own icy breath, unleashing all of his might at once. Everything around him developed frost upon it. Lukhan gasped for oxygen and his icy breath turned into snow above them. Con'ra circled above, unharmed by Lukhan's sudden and massive blast.

"Well, that proves that you are not a black dragon," Con'ra called from the sky above him. "It does mean that you're foolish. This is the Endless Desert! It's a little too warm for ice don't you think?" She plunged at him like a hawk diving to its prey. Lukhan's magically scarred eyes flashed with mercury light.

"*Glacialis aer!*" Lukhan gasped. The effect was sudden, Con'ra's dive turned into free fall.

"Using magic are we? Fine then! *Tenax humus!*" Con'ra snarled. Her eyes flashed bright yellow the ground round them turned into coiling vines and thick mud. Lukhan sank deep into the vines; the sudden jerk broke his concentration of his spell. Con'ra opened her wings, slowing her descent and crashed into the vine covered ground, and recovering quickly. Lukhan struggled against the grasping plants.

"Sweet trick! Is that the only illusion you can produce?" Lukhan flapped his wings vigorously. The vines reacted in response to his struggles, splashing, and clinging on to his body as Lukhan beat his wings furiously.

"Struggle all you like," Con'ra sneered. Her eyes still blazed with a yellow light from continuous casting of the magical spell. "This must be the first time that you have encountered earth magic; this is a simple spell. It is humorous that you will be entombed by your own ignorance!" The plants clung upon Lukhan's body and wing membranes, until finally the weight of the mud forced him to sink into the grasping earth. His violent thrashes slowed and he fell back into the vine field.

"Release me, coward!" Lukhan snarled. "Fight me fairly!"

"Why should I?" Con'ra asked. "You were the first to use magic in this duel." She giggled in amusement at her captive's struggles. "Black dragon or not, you are still a liar. I have met the silver dragon, Lukhan. The destroyer of the plague would not have succumbed to such a simple magic tick. Now, tell me who you really are? An assassin perhaps?"

"Assassin? I am a silver dragon! You would dare mock me!" Lukhan snarled. He flung himself at her; the momentum of the move caused him to flip over upon his back sinking further into the groping vines. "I am Lukhan! Back in the Jade Rainforest, you forced my mother and friends into the Black Marshes! You had an army of wyverns then-"

"Oh yes, a story you could have learned from any of your pets," Con'ra laughed in amusement. "Please, don't misunderstand me, I am mocking you. To me, you look like a trapped wild animal, not a true dragon. How dare you try to pass yourself off as the noble and heroic, Lukhan, *Savior of the Common Races?*" The word savior rolled off of her tongue like venom. She walked over the vines as if it was solid ground and circled around the entrapped silver dragon. "I should put you out of your misery!"

"That's enough Con'ra!" Bar yelled. "Let him go!" He leveled his bombarder towards her. A light click and a thunderous boom followed. A plume of smoke covered Bar's retreat. Con'ra looked down at her body to see where the weapon had struck her. Jumping off the back of a remaining undamaged wagon, Bar dropped to one knee and reloaded his weapon. "A flash in the pan!"

"You! Do you think that pea shooter can kill me?" she snarled.

"Nope," Bar chuckled. "I know all about magic, and I distracted you."

"Why you!" Con'ra gasped. The vines beneath her had returned to solid ground. A movement in the corner of her eye caught her attention. She turned in time to see a flash of silver smash into her head. The blow knocked her prone; she blinked a couple of times in confusion. Lukhan pounced upon her, penning her beneath his weight.

"Fool," Lukhan growled. "I should kill you!" He reached down and grasped her around the throat. He pressed his claws against her neck's artery. He could feel her fear and blood pumping with his claw. His weight forced her head into the ground. The dormant black claw twitched in anticipation of blood. Lukhan paused, realizing the sickening feeling that arose within his gut.

"Then why don't you?" Con'ra snarled. She glared and bared her teeth defiantly.

"I-I was never your enemy," Lukhan stuttered. "Even when I left the Jade Rainforest, I thought of you as a kindred spirit." He shook his head and released her. Con'ra face softened. With a sudden thrust, she kicked him off her and scrambled away. Lukhan grunted, but did not pursue her.

"I don't need your charity!" Con'ra snapped. She backed away in a safe distance from him. Her wings were held in a defensive stance. "Very well, if we are not enemies then allow me to leave in peace. I shall allow your transgressions against me to pass this time, Stranger. It appears that I am outmatched with you and your pets." She glanced over at Bar, who had his sights trained upon her.

"I assure you that I am Lukhan," the silver dragon assured.

"I don't care what you call yourself," Con'ra snapped. "I am no ignorant hatchling! You cannot fool-!"

"I made a promise to you, six years ago, to an ambitious green hatchling," Lukhan interrupted. "She made me promise to help change her cruel world. I have not forgotten this."

She stared at him in confusion, her eyes widen in recognition.

"N-no! This cannot be! You are dead!" Con'ra gasped. Her shocked expression turned into a slight grin. "I swear, I thought you were dead. Your own clan pronounced you as such. Your being alive has changed many things, things I thought were unchangeable." Her expression was intense as she considered this new information.

"Help!" Sacul squealed. Lukhan glanced over at the pit where his friend was trapped in Con'ra magical vines. The other prisoners struggled against their restrains.

"Release your captives," Lukhan demanded.

"Only on one condition: I may take the treasure," Con'ra demanded.

"Why are you gathering treasure? Are you building a home here?" Lukhan asked.

"It is none of your concern," Con'ra stated sharply. "I have had to deal with other issues that have arisen. My problems are none of your concern."

"Problems?" Lukhan asked in wonder. "You must explain."

"My reasons are my own," Con'ra stated. "I attacked you because I believed that you were a black dragon. You are already aware; the Black and Green Clans have fought ever since the destruction of the plague."

"Yes, I was aware of what has transpired but my godmother and mother attempted to stop the bloodshed. The Gold and Silver Clans have problems of their own."

"Who is your godmother?" Con'ra inquired.

"Vatara," Lukhan announced.

"Then tell me what you know," Con'ra smiled slyly. "You seem to be aware of what is occurring in the South."

"I was informed that the Gold Clan wages war against the Inquisition. They are in an alliance with the Elf Kingdoms and the city of Ravenshaven."

"Fascinating," Con'ra ridiculed. "That does not explain why you are here or why you reek of death!"

"I am here to return my companions to Ravenshaven," Lukhan explained. Con'ra waited for the other explanation of his stench. When Lukhan did not continued, Bar interrupted.

"The caravans that you are attacking," Bar growled. "They belong to our alliance!"

"An alliance of lesser races!" Con'ra retorted. "A ragged patch of squabbling creatures. What could they do against the Inquisition's well-disciplined armies?"

"The Gold Clan is with us," Bar warned.

"The life lovers?" Con'ra chuckled. "They are the weakest of the dragon clans. Why would you believe they would be capable of defeating the Inquisition? They could not broker peace between the Black and Green Clans."

"Why would you doubt them?" Lukhan asked.

"It is not a matter of doubt, but of tactical strength," Con'ra chuckled. Her amusement ended as she looked off to the distance horizon. Her lips curled back in disgust. "No, I am not done yet!"

"The Knights of Ravenshaven!" Bar shouted. A cavalry column charged from the distance city torchlight. The hunter cheered and waved at the unexpected reinforcements.

"We shall continue this conversation another time," Con'ra dismissed him but Lukhan moved to intervene.

"Release them!" Lukhan demanded.

"A compromise then?" Con'ra smiled. "The treasure for their freedom." Lukhan looked over at the wagon that Bar protected.

"Agreed," Lukhan nodded. "Free them and I shall insure that you will not be hunted."

"Luke, you can't! We can take her-," Bar groaned.

"Deal," Con'ra smiled. "A good compromise is where all walks away alive." She walked over to the vine pit. Sacul and the caravan guards struggled as she approached. Con'ra walked into the middle of the pit and disappeared under the thong of living bonds. This caused the captives to panic and struggle harder against the vines. Before Lukhan and Bar could do anything, Sacul and the captives disappear under the vegetation.

"Hey, how's it going?" Sacul called from beneath the twisting vegetation. "I bet you don't know what is a dragon's favorite vegetable is?"

"Dragons do not eat-," Con'ra began.

"Chili peppers!" Sacul called in a laughing muffle. "Get it, because they have bad breath-!" The green dragon snarled at her joking prisoner, but the shaman only nervously laughed at her. The vines tickled her captives and the other prisoner chuckled in unease at the boarelf's comments.

"What is she doing?" Bar whispered to Lukhan.

"I thought as much," Lukhan snorted. "She has placed a magical ward within the pit. No wonder our battle did not release the prisoners. Her powers have grown considerably."

"You knew of this?" Bar asked.

"That is why I didn't kill her," Lukhan smiled. An evil expression spread across his face. "Yet." The vines recoiled and turned to dust. Con'ra and the prisoners were slowly exposed as the illusion degenerated into reality. Lukhan and Bar walked the rim of the newly constructed pit.

"The ward stone has been altered," Con'ra stated.

"Climb out of the pit," Lukhan instructed. Con'ra smiled and jumped into the air. Lukhan exploded into action, jumping into the air after her.

"Liar! You would stop my escape?" Con'ra chuckled. "So much for the Silver Clan's fabled nobility!"

"I am no longer naive to your schemes!" Lukhan snarled.

"I think not," Con'ra chuckled. "Look to your pets! See if you can save them!" She glanced down with an evil grin. Lukhan followed her gaze. The vines had reemerged, this time with barbs the size of dragon claws. Bar used his bombarder to help one prisoner after the other out of the pit of death. Sacul, being the smallest of the group, was at the bottom of the pit where the vines crept slowly forward.

Lukhan turned on Con'ra. "You tricked me!" he snarled.

"Help me! Luke!" Bar screamed from below them. He struggled to pulled captives out of the pit; the magical vines crept methodically toward them.

"So predictable," Con'ra snickered in amusement. "I only changed the magical spell upon the stone! You have two options before you! Chase after me and allow your pets to die, or you can go down and save them! The choice is yours!" Lukhan snarled and dove down to the pit. Con'ra chuckled and went to claim her wagon full of treasure.

"Help!" Sacul squealed.

"Hold on!" Lukhan instructed. He swooped down and snatched Sacul and the remaining caravan guards before the pit became overwhelmed by crawling thorn vines. Lukhan released those he had snatched from death's grip and looked for Con'ra. The clear night sky gave away her position. With wagon in tow, the green dragon flew north. Lukhan snarled as Con'ra made her escape. Sacul cried out in pain.

"Let her go!" Bar ordered. "Help me with Sacul!" The squalling shaman had a thorn vine wrapped around his ankle.

"What happened?" Lukhan asked. Sacul screamed as the vine tighten around his ankle, its thorns dug deeper into the boarelf's flesh.

"The vine wrapped around his leg before you rescued them!" Bar screamed. He drew out Sacul's dagger and began cutting away at the magical plant. The knife's blade dulled against the thick creeper, as it continued to constrict. "Why isn't the vine disappearing? It's no longer contained to the pit!"

"The magical ward has not been destroyed!" Lukhan concluded. "I know what I must do! It must be destroyed."

"Whatever you do, do it quickly!" Sacul begged.

"Hurry, I will try to relieve the pressure! The thorns are going into his leg!" Bar pressed. Lukhan turned and dove into the throng of constricting spikes.

Chapter 12

"**N**o, Luke!" Bar's screams faded as Lukhan drove under the magically conjured barbed vines. The plants twist and broke against his armor hide; they suddenly constrict and halted his momentum. The thorns did not penetrate his armored scales, but his wing membranes shredded under the sudden tension. Pain shot up through Lukhan's back. Every time that he moved the barbs tore at his vulnerable wings. Lukhan opened his entangled mouth and released a blast of freezing energy. The plants around him froze in the sudden drop in temperature. With a mighty thrash of his tail the plants shattered. The shatter creepers gave way to reveal the conjured ward stone. Lukhan gasped in exhaustion and reached out to it. More vines appeared from the stone. The stone disappeared under the throng of summoned greenery.

"Damn magic!" Lukhan snarled. The vines enveloped him; he hacked and slashed with his claws, yet, the creepers multiplied and covered him even more. With another blast from his icy breath, the stone was revealed. Lukhan grabbed the stone as more bush shot out from it. With a twist the stone snapped in half and crumbled into dust. The spiked sprouts that were still wrapped around him disappeared into magical residue. Lukhan gasped for air and collapsed from the painful endeavor.

"Luke!" Bar called from the rim of the pit. The hunter slid down the side and examined his injured companion. Lukhan's wings appeared bloodied and frayed. Lukhan lifted his head wearily and inspected his injuries.

"Whenever I am with you two, I get hurt," Lukhan huffed.

"We seem to live dangerous lives," Bar mumbled. He tore off a piece of his furs and attempted to bandage Lukhan bloody wings.

"Leave it!" Lukhan snapped. He withdrew his wing away from Bar's prying fingers, the knoll recoiled in fear. "These wounds are minor. I will live. How is Sacul? What of Con'ra?"

"The vine that was wrapped around Sacul's ankle disappeared," Bar smiled. "One of these days I am going to save you. You hear me?" Lukhan shook his head in dismissal. "Do you doubt me?"

"What of Con'ra?" Lukhan pressed.

"The coward fled to the North," Bar warned. Lukhan opened his tattered wings. "You can't go after her, not in your condition."

Lukhan paused in consideration. "I should go after her," he snorted. "I am stronger than you think."

"Fool hardy," Sacul called. "Are you planning to abandon us? All of us?" He pointed back at his fellow captives.

"I was going to get the treasure back," Lukhan snapped.

"Let her go because we need rest and food," Sacul sat down and nursed his ankle. "Even with Con'ra burden with a wagon full of treasure, do you really believe that you could catch up to her in your condition? If you wish to face her again, you will need our help. Con'ra has grown in power."

"Do you really believe that?" Lukhan asked.

Bar agreed with his smaller companion's suggestion. "The green dragon is cunning and to go after her would be foolish. Who knows what traps she has in store for us?"

"Us?" Lukhan balked. He considered the point and slowly nodded his head in agreement. The dragon and knoll jumped out of the pit. "That may be true, but I can take her!" he declared. Lukhan had lost twice to the cunning green dragon. He had lost in both magic and wit. Lukhan didn't hate her and yet he was envious of her. He had to wonder about her motivations. She could have killed him with her first blast; she had targeted Bar, an obvious tactically weaker opponent. Con'ra had also confused him as a black dragon that was disguised. Then why didn't she strike him? She could have killed Sacul and her captives, yet she chose not to act. All she had attempted to do was escape with the treasure. That was not the only bizarre behavior, her wyvern servants were not with her. It was as if she wasn't trying to hurt anyone. There was something going on with the female dragon that he did not fully understand. The more Lukhan considered it, the more he was confused about Con'ra's actions.

"Let the treasure go," Bar suggested. "We must get you patched up. Our allies are finally approaching."

"About time the cavalry arrived," Sacul mumbled. Lances held high, the knights galloped at a constant pace and came to a rumbling stop before them. The silver dragons dwarfed the nearest warhorse. Lukhan flexed his injured wings nervously.

"Greetings, noble Silver Lord," The leader of the knight's approached on horseback. The columns' horses stirred nervously at the smell of dragon but the well trained warhorses remained under the control of their riders. The knights wore full plate mail were in strict military formation. Their double visor closed helms had a plume with a black and white torse. To the leader's right was a standard-bearer holding the black and white flag of Ravenshaven flapped in the wind. The symbol upon the flag was a three pronged raven that looked similar to a dragon's claw. At their leader's suggestion the other knights lifted their visors.

"Is that you, Judas?" Bar asked. The leader of the column raised his visor and smiled warmly at the three before him. The man appeared to be in his early thirties, with a strong jaw and sharp brown eyes. His light hair was cut short, and his face was clean shaven.

"It has been too long, Silver Lord," Judas grinned. "I still remember when I could look you in the eye." He glanced back and looked at his column. "Dismount and attend the wounded. Give them water and bandages. Those that can ride, take them back to the city. Those injured and can't walk, construct stretchers for them and attached them to your horses."

"Yes, my lord," the closest knight nodded and instructed the nearest knights to organize the rescue. Judas dismounted walked over to Sacul and examined the shaman's injuries.

"After the crap you gave me, don't tell me that you're concerned," a toothy grin spread across Sacul's face as he looked at the concerned human.

"Sacul shall have my horse," Judas announced. "Make sure that the horse kicks him in the head first. That is the only way the horse will ever like him."

"My lord?" the closest knight asked.

"A joke, Sergeant," Judas chuckled. The man had a puzzled expression on his face and nodded his head in confusion. After securing Sacul upon his warhorse, Judas returned his attention to Lukhan. "Silver Lord-"

"Cease the formalities," Lukhan instructed. "You should not honor me; I have failed in stopping Con'ra and retrieved the treasure."

"Failed?" Judas inquired. He walked up to Bar and warmly placed a hand on the knoll's shoulder. "Even if you have failed, Bar and Sacul have not. Their objective has been fulfilled. Lukhan, Defender of the Common Races, has returned to us." The declaration was loud and bold. The knights and caravan guards began to mumble to themselves. Mouths hung wide in awe, they stared at the legendary champion before them. Judas was the first to begin clapping, followed closely by those the dragon had saved. The slow clapping turned into a roar of applause. Judas raised his hands to silence the crowd.

"Lord Lukhan and dearest of friends, I welcome you to the steps of our fair city," Judas smiled. He gestured proudly to the road they stood on. "You must be weary from you travels. You are under the protection of the Knights of Ravenshaven." He lowered his voice and returned his attention to his friends. "Owen has been pestering me about your quest for past six months. Tell me about your travels." He gave the order for those injured to begin returning to the city. Those knights that did not have escorts were instructed to remove the destroyed wagons from the road. After insuring that all instruction would be carried out, Judas walked alongside his horse that carried Sacul. Lukhan walked next to them in silence. Bar and Sacul told Judas about their adventure in finding their missing friend.

"Then why is our champion so silent?" Judas asked out loud. Lukhan remained silent at the knight's question. "Lord Lukhan, I thank you. Con'ra has been sporadically sacking the alliance's trade caravans. This has slowed our communication and weapon supplies for the past four months." There was no reply.

"Luke, wouldn't you answer the question?" Bar asked. The dragon turned slowly to look at his companions.

"What provoked the attacks?" Lukhan asked.

"Nothing," Judas stated. "We are unclear of what Con'ra's motives are. I was hoping that you could share your knowledge."

"She is not an ally of the Inquisition," Lukhan concluded. "She must be doing it for her own gains, but to what those are; I am uncertain."

"Did you notice that Sessess wasn't escorting her?" Judas asked. Lukhan nodded his head in agreement. "It appears Con'ra and the wyverns are no longer in alliances. Reports have only indicated that a single green dragon is responsible for the raids. No more and no less."

"Then why haven't you shot her with our bombarders?" Bar asked. "As a council member you are supposed to be protecting Ravenshaven's supply lines!"

"We would," Judas snapped. "Like I said, she sets traps for caravans. She is too smart and never assaults straight on. She sets up traps alongside the road!

My knights cannot track or ride down a flying dragon. The road spans several hundred leagues. Our forces are too small to protect every caravan."

"Have you spoken with her?" Lukhan asked.

"I haven't," Judas admitted. "Reports from her attacks always speak of taunts and insults to the trapped guards. Other than calling upon magic she has not engage in any fruitful conservations. Her motives are strange to us. After all, why would she speak to the common races?" Lukhan chuckled at the human's statement. "As a dragon, do you find this situation to be funny?"

"You sound bitter that you cannot capture her," Lukhan chuckled. He was not surprised by the results.

"Well, of course I am," Judas snapped. "As a council member of Ravenshaven, I am in charge of keeping order. Con'ra's harassments have undermined my authority and taxed our war effort against the Inquisition. The dragon is a thief and a common criminal. Her actions are punishable by our laws!"

Lukhan stopped and considered what the knight had said. "Dragons are not subject to any common race's laws or any code of honor," he smiled. "You speak too boldly."

"W-well of course," Judas stuttered. "I speak only out of frustration-"

"Dragons may think that!" Bar challenged. "They are not! They are like any other being. Their actions must be held accountable. My pack followed your father's rules when we lived in the Silver Mountains. Do you believe yourself to be above our city? Our home?"

"You know that my family never dealt out any punishment to your pack, unlike Judas, who is suggesting it for Con'ra!" Lukhan rebuked. He snorted at the thought that Bar had a horrible life within his family's cave. His family had helped defend Bar's pack from outside raids, and the cave had provided a sanctuary for them, until the arrival of the plague, when the Inquisition and troll called Aak had destroyed their home.

"Why are you defending her?" Sacul asked.

"I can think of several reasons why she is attacking your city," Lukhan chuckled. A smiled crept across his face as he considered the possibilities. The reasons were as unlikely as the others.

"Care to explain?" Sacul grunted.

"We can all agree that Con'ra is a cunning opponent?" Lukhan asked. They nodded their heads in agreement. They had all felt the sting of the green dragons treachery, when she had blackmailed them into abandoning the plot of the Dragon Council to sacrifice Lukhan's friends. Lukhan knew that Con'ra's efforts were a mix blessing. She had hoped to divide the Dragon Council and weaken her father's position within their own clan by disrupting the council's agenda. Her efforts backfired and the Green Clan came out of the war stronger than before. This emboldened the Green Clan to take action against the Black Clan who was weakened by the plague's devastating effects. "Con'ra seeks to expand the Green Clan's territory into the Endless Desert, starting with Ravenshaven."

"Then why doesn't she use her wyvern slaves during her raids?" Judas asked. "Pass messages of threats and domination to the survivors."

"I did not say that I knew her plans," Lukhan stated. "I am only offering a reason for such actions. If she is after treasure, it could be for several reasons. Reasons for a dragon to sporadically harass the trade routes are hoarding, testing defenses, or simple boredom."

"Then we will have to ask her," Judas smiled. "After all, not all dragons are unreasonable."

"We?" Lukhan clarified. "You must be mistaken. I plan to return to the Endless Ice when my wings are healed."

"That will take months," Sacul dismissed. "You're welcome to stay at Judas's place because he has grown wealthy in the merchant's guild."

"He is?" Judas muttered. His expression turned into a frown at the thought of feeding a dragon of Lukhan's size. "I am not that wealthy! I don't know if we have the resources-"

"Of course you do," Bar interrupted. "Even though supplies have always been limited in Ravenshaven, we'll make due." He gave Lukhan a gleeful wink. The dragon raised a questioning eyebrow. He had not plan to stay long.

As the morning sun crept over the eastern horizon, the city of Ravenshaven came into view. It had been over six years since Lukhan had seen the outcast city; it had turned into a recognizable fortress. Stone walls, the size of a man, snaked strategically round the outer perimeter. A small ditch was at the bottom of the wall. Lukhan could tell that it had been recently constructed because the rocks showed little weathering. On top of the wall stood the watch. Knoll archers and spearman stood side by side with human grenadiers. They protected the wooden door that led into the city. Judas waved his hand to the soldier on the battlement to open the gate. As they walk through the gate, Lukhan notice that there were several earthen mounts that help support the walls.

"Have you completed the fortifications?" Bar asked.

"No. We are still working on the perimeter," Judas explained. He noticed that the large dragon could jump over the small wall. "What do you think? I need a dragon's perspective. Do you like my construction and engineering?" Lukhan shrugged his shoulder in reply. The small walls would not stop any dragon from getting through; however, they would slow down any earthbound creature.

"The walls appear small to me," Lukhan concluded.

"True!" Judas chuckled. "There is no fortification in the world that could keep out a flying dragon, but we are not fighting your kind. Due to the invention of the bombarder, I knew that traditional walls wouldn't work, so I placed most of construction efforts into earthworks. Let the Inquisition fire at dirt. It is cheaper and it is harder to penetrate by conventional means."

"There are still weaknesses," Lukhan examined. "Your gate appears to be the weakest point. If I was the Inquisition, I would strike there. Those wooden doors would not be able to resist bombarder fire or a physical assault."

"As always, you are a clever tactician," Judas smiled approvingly. "The city is difficult to defend; I am pleased that you have not forgotten everything we have taught you. You still haven't seen the main defenses. Our observations cannot be denied, and I will consider them."

"You're planning to spend more coin on earth and stone?" Bar balked. "It's a waste of Ravenshaven's treasury."

"I don't think so," Judas snapped. "If done correctly, Ravenshaven will be turned into an impenetrable fortress! No army will be able to conquer the alliance."

"Keeps him busy," Sacul whispered softly to Lukhan. The silver dragon smiled in amusement. The humans and boarelves had always been at odds with each other ever since the fall of the Mixed Kingdoms.

"Oh! If you weren't injured," Judas snapped back. He raised his fist up threateningly. "You know, I could have used both of you! I had to deal with taxes, a raiding dragon, and this wall!"

"Well, we have had to deal with sandstorms, blizzards, and wild animals!" Bar retorted. Judas turned slowly and looked Bar straight in the eye. The two glared at each other for a moment, both fingering their weapons.

"Oh how I miss theses old fights!" Judas chuckled.

"Yes, I need someone else beat my head against," Bar sneered. Judas rolled his eyes and chuckled. "It has been too long, my friend."

"True and much has changed since you three have left," Judas grinned.

"What do you have up your sleeve?" Sacul demanded.

"I've married," Judas announced proudly.

Chapter 13

"What?" Bar gasped. "Married? I thought that we hadn't been away for that long."

"Who's the unfortunate victim?" Sacul teased. "An old woman with poor eyesight and a bad sense of smell? Perhaps, a desperate widow seeking to pay off her debts?" He reached over to Judas's helm and rubbed it vigorously.

"Shut up," Judas snarled. He pulled away from Sacul's grasp and narrowed his eyes dangerously at the boarelf that sat upon his horse. "No, she is not blind and she has a wonderful sense of smell. She cooks the best-"

"Then she must have brain fever," Sacul interrupted. "For she has lost all sense of taste in men and-" Judas turned sharply and stomped his foot in front of his horse. The trained horse flared his nostrils and shook his head. It reared up in response to Judas's command. Sacul tumbled head over heels off of the horse's back. No one moved to help the impertinent boarelf up and continued on the paved road to the main fortress. Sacul slowly stood up and gimped after them. "Hey, wait for me! I'm hurt, you know!"

"You should've thought of that before opening your big mouth!" Bar snapped.

Lukhan slowed his pace and allowed the shaman to hang on to his tail for support. "Married? What does that mean?" the dragon asked. He was not aware of the strange customs of the human race.

"Marriage is a custom that is not uncommon," Judas smiled. "It is a social institution under which a man and a woman establish their decision to live as husband and wife, a contract of love between opposite sexes." Lukhan's face turned into a frown. He did not like the idea of being obligated to any individual.

"So, it is like slavery or servitude?" Lukhan asked.

"No, it's like taking on a mate," Bar explained. "It's a bonded pair between two lovers. An oral and written agreement viewed and accepted by religious bodies and individuals' beliefs. It calls upon loyalty, not servitude."

"So it's like a knight to his King or a magus to the Grand Magus?" Lukhan asked.

"No," Judas chuckled. "Within the Inquisition's belief system-"

"The Inquisition?" Lukhan snarled. Judas and Bar were taken aback by the dragon's sudden shift in mood. "Do you believe that the Holy Master can be saved? He stole your white fame!"

"The city of Alkaline was once my home!" Judas stated. "You've returned me to my original self. Believe it or not, my religion has come up with some wonderful ideas. The Holy Master's teachings include virtuous traits such as loyalty, honor, and faith."

"Following the *old* ways?" Lukhan demanded. "After all that the Inquisition has done? You are no longer an Inquisitor! You are no longer a slave to that religion!" He could never forget what the Inquisition had done to the dire wolves and the sacred herd. Even his own crime of mixing his blood with that of the common races paled in comparison to the butchery carried out by the Holy Master's armies. The buffalo that once stretched across the Golden Plains were all but destroyed, only a few scattered herds remained.

"I have relinquished that title. The Holy Master is not to be blamed for what has occurred!" Judas snapped. "He is my God and you-"

"You haven't told us your wife's name!" Bar interrupted. As the knoll waved his hands before Judas's face, Lukhan snorted at the knoll's interruption. The drop in air temperature brought a chill down the human and knoll spines.

"Yes, forgive me but her name is Ambrosia," Judas's face lit up at the thought of his beloved.

"Ambrosia, you say?" Bar asked with a frown. "Have I met her?"

"Don't you remember her?" Judas asked fondly. "She was there when Sacul and you left. She is absolutely beautiful. Her honey brunette hair falls like autumn leaves around her glorious frame." He sighed at the thought of his loved one. Bar and Lukhan looked at each other and frown at their friend's absent thoughts. "When I'm with her, she takes my troubles away. I tell you, without her I would have gone insane." The knight chuckled at the thought and held his hand to his heart.

"I think I remember her," Bar admitted. "I am not a good judge of human beauty; their hairless bodies do not appeal to me. Wasn't she the one with a blue and golden brown eye?"

"Yes, what of it?" Judas challenged angrily.

"Nothing," Bar defended. "I remember her being unique. It is not every day that you see a human or knoll like that. Isn't she a Lady of the Ravenshaven court?"

"Yes, she does have one blue and one brown eye, and that doesn't matter to me," Judas replied. "She is a daughter of one of the merchants." Bar's face turned into a frown. When he had left, the merchant guilds were a shady bunch attempting to usurp the council's power. Several of the guild leaders made it on to Owen's court through the purchase of votes and supplying underhanded deals to local underground thieves and slave guilds, despite the council's best attempts to weed out corruption.

"I understand your concern," Judas placed a comforting hand upon Bar's shoulder for reassurance. "Both marriage and knights have secured Ravenshaven from any interior conflict. Ambrosia has helped me secure peace within Ravenshaven. Owen and the council's reformations on slavery, gambling, and the sex trade have been successful."

"The city does not sound like it has improved much," Lukhan stated.

"No, my friend," Judas smiled. "It has improved greatly, thanks to Ambrosia. It was by her efforts that brought down those organizations. Without her support these groups worked under the disguise of taxpaying merchant guilds. Without proper evidences, I was unable to arrest or even question them. Despite my best efforts, they continued to spread and undermine Ravenshaven's authority. I was powerless to stop it until Ambrosia came to me with suggestions and solutions. She was an insider that helped me find and eliminate theses shady organizations."

"Be cautious," Bar offered. "It seems that no matter how high you build your walls, you cannot keep out corruption."

"That better not be a metaphor!" Judas warned. "My wife helped me save Ravenshaven. I owe her a deep debt of gratitude. Never question my wife's loyalty."

"You should not question ours," Lukhan roared in a deep tone. Bar nodded his head in agreement with the dragon's statement. Judas raised a questioning eyebrow at them.

"Your warnings are considered," Judas mumbled. "Perhaps you will change your minds when you meet my wife in person. Please do not jump to any conclusions before meeting her. She is the love of my life." Bar and Lukhan looked at each other in concern. The ex-Inquisitor had only a passion for his religion and nothing else. Both found it difficult to believe that, within a short amount of time, Judas could be rescued from his religion by a woman. Bar chuckled in amusement. It was not his theological debates or truthful questioning that persuaded Judas's mind. It was love of a woman.

"I understand," Bar smiled. "I too know how it is to be in love."

"You, Bar?" Judas asked. Bar bowed his head in remembrance of his lost beloved. "Oh yes, I am sorry my friend. I had forgotten that she had died." Bar nodded somberly and gave a forced smile. Lukhan remained silent and walked alongside them.

"Hey, when are we going to eat?" Sacul yelled from the rear.

"Today is supposed to be a happy day," Bar muttered glumly. "Our champion has returned to us. Where is this house of yours? I could use some food in my gut. I would like to meet this lovely Ambrosia." They walked through the newly constructed fortifications into the new city. Ravenshaven had been burned down the last time Lukhan had seen it. A newly constructed two story building made of rammed earth helped fortify the interior of the city. Thick outer walls protected the citizens from the elements and assault. Judas had planned for a siege, so he had made the appropriate adjustments. Gardens, living walls, and roofs, helped support the growing city. As they moved into the market place, merchants selling fruits, vegetables, and clothing lined the busy streets. The loud market soon fell silent as both knight and dragon appeared around the corner. Mouths fell open in awe at the silver dragon before them.

"Could it be?" called a merchant.

"The dragons have come to save us!" a child cheered.

"They've returned!" another merchant cried out. "Bar and Sacul must have been successful in finding the Defender of the Common Races! No one can challenge our city now! Where is the Gold Clan?" The market place soon turned into a mob that rushed forward to greet the returning heroes. The knights that were still on horseback moved to block the hopeful mob.

"Make way, allow the council members to pass," the knights called as they pushed through the crowd. "My lords it would be wise to leave the streets."

"Stay close to me," Judas instructed. He saddled his horse and offered an arm down to Bar. The knoll swung up upon the horse's back. "Please follow me." The town's guards formed a protective barrier around the dragon and council members. The mob consisted of knolls, humans, and boarelves.

Occasionally, an elf would appear among them but they did not join the following ranks. The escorted group made it to the interior perimeter of what was called the old town. A stone wall protected the heart of the city. The upper class still lived within the structures. Merchants or commoners were not allowed to pass the old wall that protected the council member's homes. This was where the heart of the rebellion had taken place; Lukhan couldn't see any fire damage. He had been there when Owen rose up and took command of the city and its council. Lukhan and his companions had been the perfect distraction for the ambitious leader. The city had prospered under the leadership of Owen because no evidence of the rebellion existed.

"The city has improved since Sacul and I left," Bar added. Lukhan looked about unimpressed by the city's change. The stink of the city was the same, no matter what improvements to the exterior.

"I am glad that you approved," Judas smiled. He gestured down an alleyway to his home. Pillared architecture graced the main structure at the end of the alleyway. The house appeared to look more like a temple than that of a humble dwelling. Old grape vines hung from the side of the building making it appear older. It was new construction, for no other buildings around it appeared similar. Within a vast courtyard, a woman brushed the house's steps and waved to the approaching column of knights. She dropped her broom when she saw Lukhan enter the courtyard. The dragon's bulk made it difficult to see behind him.

"There is my beloved," Judas waved eagerly. The woman continued to stare wide eyed at the dragon that loomed over her husband. Ambrosia appeared to be in her mid-twenties. Judas and Bar dismounted and approached her. Bar's memory was correct, she did have a unique eyes. One of her eyes was sky blue while the other appeared golden brown. Her honey brunette hair was tied back into a bun; her plain clothing was dirty from doing morning chores. Judas approached her and waited for a warm embrace. The hug never came. "Ambrosia, what is the matter?"

"T-that's a-," the women stuttered. Judas and Bar looked at each other, and then turned their gaze on Lukhan. The dragon did not falter under the woman's stare. "I-it's a d-dragon."

"Yes, and a big silver one at that," Bar gave an amused smile. "Not all dragons are evil; he's one of the good guys." He smiled approvingly at his dragon companion. Lukhan rolled his eyes at the attention he was receiving from the people around him. Something about the woman caught his attention, his magically scarred eyes focused up her. There was an aura about her. He deeply inhaled in her sent, there was something wrong. A sickening feeling arose within his gut, his black claw twitched in recognition of the magic that the woman held inside her. A frozen dribble of drool fell from his lips.

"You must be the Defender of the Common Races," Ambrosia was in awe. "I have never seen a dragon before. I thought they were stories that Judas told to scare the children."

"Lukhan is no story," Judas chucked. "He is real."

"S-Silver Lord, forgive me. I didn't know-," Ambrosia gasped. She advert her eyes from the massive dragon before her and looked at her husband for the first time. "Is it trained? It's safe to be around?" She was referring to the hungry look the dragon was giving her.

"Of course *he* is," Sacul huffed. The injured boarelf struggled to stand before the woman. "Dragons are powerful predators. Now are you going to feed us, or am I going to eat my injured leg. We're all starving."

"No one has forgotten you," Judas groaned. "Shall we take the conversation inside? I don't know if we will have room, but we can have a picnic outside."

"Yes, of course, Councilors Bar and Sacul, it is good to see you." Ambrosia returned her attention to her husband and whispered. "You could've sent word that we were going to have such a distinguished guest! The house isn't even clean."

"I didn't know that they were going to show up today. Besides our home is charming enough," Judas gave her a loving smile. "Now please tell the servants that we have guest. We shall have a feast in their honor."

"I need to speak with you," Ambrosia whispered. "Privately."

"Can't it wait until tonight," Judas mumbled. She frowned and shook her head in reply, and then she disappeared into the house.

"She is lovely," Bar approved. "She will be a good mate for you, though she appeared to be ignorant in the ways of dragons. Luke will have to educate her." The dragon shook his head at the knoll's suggestion.

"Sure she looks all right but she has no curves, unlike the beautiful women in my tribe. Makes me wonder if she can't cook," Sacul huffed. "Give me a meaty woman to hang on to at night! I'd make her squeal all night long!" His toad bit him. "Ouch!" The boarelf scowled at his toad and looked back at Lukhan for approval. A quick punch in the arm from Bar silenced the boisterous shaman. Sacul rubbed his forearm and glared at the knoll.

"Please come inside when you are ready," Judas offered. "I'm going to see what she wants. Come on Sacul, I will get you something to eat."

"About damn time," Sacul cursed. "I want a chair to sit down in and another to put my leg up. My leg still hurts and-" His voice trailed off. Bar and Lukhan stood outside watching their two friends disappear inside the house. The knoll turned sharply upon the dragon.

"What was that?" Bar demanded. "You stared at Ambrosia as if she was a piece of meat. That's his wife you know!"

"What do you mean?" Lukhan stuck out his tongue and wiped the saliva from the corner of his mouth. The dragon did not realize how much he had been drooling in hunger. He would have to feed. The weeks of travel and recent battle had drained him both physically and mentally. "I need to feed soon."

"You nearly scared the poor girl to death," Bar warned. "Good thing she is ignorant or else she would have been running for her life. Why did you start drooling like that?"

"I can see that she has an aura around her," Lukhan explained. Bar's face crunched up into a look of confusion. "I can sense it."

"A magical aura?" Bar thought out loud.

"Not magical, something different," Lukhan shook his head trying hard not to think about devouring her. "I am tired and these past weeks have been difficult for me. The physical and magical exertions have taken its toll and I must feed soon."

"We can get you some meat and then-," Bar began.

"No," Lukhan snapped. "I require white flames to consume!" His eyes flashed in fury and rage. Bar cowered before the dragon's sudden change in mood. The dragon took several controlled breaths. The fury slowly left his scarred eyes. "I must *eat* soon."

"I understand," Bar gulped nervously. "You require body and soul?" The dragon reluctantly nodded his head. "Judas should provide you with some livestock."

Chapter 14

Later that evening, Judas brought Lukhan to his private stable. The small stable was to the back of the house in the corner of the courtyard. The beautiful structure was designed to accommodate Judas's personal warhorse. The reinforced structure had been well built, able to withstand the harshest of conditions both internal and external. Within the stable, the horses were removed, and replaced by five goats waiting to be devoured. The human stood before the entrance of the stable, directly between the dragon and his meal. Lukhan's eyes narrowed dangerously at him.

"It's true?" Judas demanded. "What Bar says?" His hand grasped the hilt of his sword. The weapon trembled within is scabbard.

"What does he say?" Lukhan asked. The dragon's brow knitted together in a deep frown.

The knight's jaws clenched at the dragon's scowl. "Bar says that you crave my wife's flesh!" he threatened. "Is this true? Do you still crave the flesh of the living? Are you a danger to my city? To my family?"

"When you left, you knew what I was," Lukhan muttered coldly. "Now leave me. You should not witness what I am about to do." The knight remained steadfast before the dragon, unmoved by the warning.

"I know what you are capable of, having witnessed your violent behavior before," Judas pressed. "Berserker- I must know the truth, do you hunger for my city, my wife, and everything that I love? I will not- I cannot allow this to happen." Lukhan did not reply to the man's accusations and remained in brooding silences. "Bar alludes to your hunger because he said that my wife has magic about her? He told me everything about your claw and how you must devour the souls of the living. He said that you sensed an aura about her."

The silver dragon remained silent.

"You're mistaken if you think that she is a witch," Judas warned. "She is my wife- I love her-magic or no! Your dragon eyes must be faulty; she has no magic about her."

"She does," Lukhan muttered. Judas's shoulders fell; the dragon saw pain on his friend's face, but did nothing to comfort him. "She is no witch or wizard; she has the aura of life about her."

"What do you mean?" Judas asked. "Speak plainly!" His hand shook furiously at the dragon's allegation. Witches and wizards were not permitted within Ravenshaven. It did not matter if she used her magical powers for good; the corruption of magic was deadly to the human race. The human spirit was weak and fragile. Wizards and witches would age and die early in life. His own family had once been trial and executed by the Inquisition on charges of witchcraft and wizardry. Not only this, but Ambrosia would be burned at the stake. Magic was evil, and therefore prohibited.

"It is not my place to speak of such things," Lukhan snarled.

"Then as my friend!" Judas wept. "Please try! I must know the truth-you're hiding something from me! Why?" Lukhan remained cruel to the human's blubbering. His only focus was the desire for food. "M-monster, you will never touch her!" His words broke down into somber sobs. He slowly fell to his knees in emotional turmoil and placed his trembling hands upon his heart. He was torn between loyalties to friends, lordship, and spouse. He didn't want his beloved wife to die or betray his friends and city. Judas and his wife had spent so little time together, yet these moments were more than special they were magical. He had been in a dark place, driven only by the passion to destroy the Inquisition and free his Master. His single minded devotion had nearly driven him to insanity, and now he had something to love and protect, a love that was more pure than his devotion to an unfamiliar deity. His love and dedication was to Ambrosia. His hand slowly moved to his sword. No Inquisition! No city! No soul stealing dragon! Nothing would harm her!

"She is with child," the dragon explained simply.

The man's mouth fell open in disbelief and shook his head in denial. His tear stained face looked up at the dragon. "S-she is with child?" Judas stuttered. "What- how can you know this?" He slowly arose from his knees in trepidation. The dragon remained stoic as he looked at the confused man before him. "Is that the magic that you saw?"

"No more questions," Lukhan growled. "Your demands and questions have placed me in a foul mood. You have threatened me and denied me food. Step aside and leave my presence! I must feed!" Judas paused in consideration and slowly lowered his hand from his heart. He stepped to the side, out of the dragon's path to nourishment. The goats fled to the corner of the stable and bleated nervously as Lukhan approached. Judas stood and watched.

"Leave me," Lukhan warned. "I do not wish for you to see what I am about to do. If these goats are not enough. I may turn on you and everyone else within the city." There was a long pause between man and dragon.

"I-I'm sorry, my friend," Judas stuttered. He lowered his eyes in shame. "Please forgive me, I spoke out of turn. You're no monster. I'm so, so sorry. Please, please forgive me." The dragon snorted in reply and did not acknowledge his friend's plea for forgiveness. "My friend, you've done so much good in this world always remember that. You see, I was grief stricken with the thought of losing my wife-"

"Your loyalty and conviction is admirable," Lukhan muttered coldly. "I wish that your words were false, but what you say is true."

Judas shook his head no in reply. "No, that can't be," he whispered. "It can't."

"I am a monster," Lukhan stated more forcefully. "Yes, I still crave the flesh of your wife and her unborn child." To prove his point, Lukhan wasted no time in using his black claw on the unfortunate animals. The goats screamed in agony as the black claw absorbed their tender flesh, bone, and white flame. Judas turned away from the bloody scene before him.

"Never turn away from the truth," Lukhan snarled. The poor goats could not escape the confines of the stable. The animals froze in fear and screamed in an otherworldly cry. The dragon did not yield in their butchery. "Look at me, damn you! I want you know! I want you to see what I have become! I want you to know my future and of those around me. You, your wife, our friends, even this city is endanger by me."

Judas slowly looked at what was occurring before him and turned away. He could not watch the final stages of the demonic claw's work. The goats' bodies imploded and were finally absorbed into the black claw. His injured wings were repaired by the sudden transfer of vitality. His scarred flesh and chipped scales were restored to their metallic shimmer.

Lukhan felt revitalized by the minuscule sacrifice, yet the hunger didn't subside. Memories of the goats' life in the stalls were of mundane existences. Simple desires such as eating, sleeping, and breeding ran through his mind. The goats were a tiny morsel compared to the banquet that lay around him. His senses were heightened by the smell of blood and gore; he sensed every white flame within a five league radius. Each soul, knoll, human, boarelf, and elf, cried out to him to be devoured. His natural urges were slowly tampered down by his rational being. He was not endangered or injured, but the desire to lose control was there. Slowly, he forced down the fears, desires, and natural instincts that plagued him. The desire to lose control was outstanding, like a starving maggot drawn to a decaying corpse. Lukhan slowly turned toward Judas, a feral expression of pure hunger was etched upon the dragon's face. The knight slowly backed away from the dragon that grew larger before him.

"Stop friend, t-this isn't you," Judas stuttered. The dragon didn't yield at the human's command. "Remember who you are! You're not this madness! Stop at once!" From the back of the dragon's throat a bestial growl came forth. His magically scarred eyes flashed with unnatural fury. The bloodlust had taken over him. Judas drew his sword and prepared to defend himself.

"Stop," Judas warned. "I have taken precautions against you, I warn you to stay back! There is a trap! Stop or-" Lukhan continued to advance. Judas held his ground defiantly.

"Now!" Judas commanded. A cargo net fell from the ceiling on to the surprised silver dragon. Heavily weighted sandbags penned the dragon down.

"I told you this would happen," Sacul called. The boarelf straddled one of the rafters above; within his hand was the trap's dropping mechanism. "Bar! Hurry up with the gas containers! Quickly, Judas, shut the doors, the gas must work!" The dragon's fury worked against him. As he fought the cargo net, it entangled him within the mesh. Bar hurried into the entrance of the stables with glass bottles in tow. Sacul moved quickly down next to Judas and Bar. With expert aiming, the hunter threw the glass container, which shattered next to the dragon's head. The dragon continued to struggle against his bonds, ignoring the white vapors that gathered around him.

"Quickly, let's make our escape!" Judas instructed. The three of them raced out of the stable as the gases continued to fill the air. They slammed the door shut and barred it as the vaporous gases approached the exit.

"Will it kill him?" Bar demanded. He stood, wide eyed and panting.

Breathing heavily, Judas shook his head no in reply. "The gas is called diethyl ether by our alchemists," he smiled. "I have personally seen it tested it on animals, I doubled the dosage for him. Dragons have always been tougher than normal beasts."

"Ether?" Bar panted. "This gas better work. I am placing a great deal of trust in you. Our friend is not to be harmed."

"Harmed?" Sacul chuckled. "Lukhan? The Destroyer of the Plague? The Defender of the Common Races? Nothing could hurt him-" The shaman chuckled in amusement when suddenly a loud rip and a thunderous boom echoed from within the stable. The three back away from the reinforced entrance.

"Are you certain that the structure will hold him?" Bar asked nervously.

Judas slowly nodded his head and yet his expression stated otherwise. "This ether better work," he replied nervously. "The alchemists followed the instructions to the letter."

"Instructions?" Bar asked. "What instructions?"

"The formula was given to us by Vatara in case you ever found our missing friend," Judas gave him a nervous smile and the doors held against the enraged dragon inside.

"Vatara?" Bar asked in surprise. "Luke's godmother?"

"Yes, it was she who gave us the alchemy and she instructed us on how to refine and use it. She was concerned about the silver dragon's behavior inside the city. We had to be prepared for such a violent activity."

"You used alchemy on our friend?" Bar asked in grave hesitation.

"Yes," Judas congratulated. "I had thought to use it against Con'ra, but this worked out better." Bar's mouth dropped in realization. The knight patted him on the shoulder and looked at Sacul. "I hate to admit it, but the shaman was correct. It was his plan to use the stable as a sealed container for the gas to work. I'm relieved that the plan worked. I was concerned that he would lose control sooner. I saw the fury in his eyes, the bloodlust within his heart." Judas shuttered at the thought. "I can still recall the time at the temple when Lukhan nearly killed us all. Even you, Bar, can't deny that he has changed greatly. I fear- that he is becoming a monster."

The stable shook violently and then slowly fell silent. The three companions stared at the stable's entrance, fearing that their companion would burst forth at any moment in a rage. The stable went strangely quiet.

"Never say such thing," Bar snarled. "Never ever say that again!" Judas stared wide eyed at the knoll that stood beside him. "Luke is sick. I would never abandon him. We must open the doors!"

"Stop! Don't be foolish!" Judas grabbed Bar before the knoll could unhinge the stable's doors. "Our friend has fallen. Without our foresight and this trap he would have killed me and fed upon the city. He is dangerous to us all! You knew that before you brought him here! We agreed to the plan!" Bar snarled and ripped his hand away from the human's grip.

"Stop! The gas must take full effect!" Sacul warned. Bar and Judas stopped their struggles. "Our friend is in no harm; however, he is still a danger to us. By now, the dragon should be disoriented and weakening from the gas's exposure. The next result should be unconsciousness."

"Even then, we are still in danger," Judas snapped. "The black claw controls him! He is not himself."

"Then what?" Bar demanded. "Are we to keep Luke imprisoned forever?" Judas and Sacul shook their heads no in reply. "What happens if we don't open the doors?" The human and boarelf looked at each other with fear. Neither of them wanted to admit what would occur next. "You must tell me!"

"The doors will be open," Judas replied. "If we don't time this correctly. The results could be either ours or Lukhan's death."

Bar's mouth dropped in disbelief. "I don't understand," he muttered.

"If we open the doors too early, and Lukhan is still in his rage, we will die," Judas explained. "If we do not open the doors in time, Lukhan might die from overexposure to the gas."

"You are gambling with our friend's life!" Bar howled. "This action is foolhardy!"

"Then what would you have me do?" Judas demanded. "I have other responsibilities beside Lukhan! We, as council members, have a responsibility to Ravenshaven's citizens to keep them safe."

"At the expense of Luke's life?" Bar demanded angrily.

"The dragon is unharmed," Judas stated. "We did what we had to do. The plan worked perfectly. He and the city are both safe! Everyone is unharmed. Never forget that he is my friend too!"

"This was a joint effort," Sacul added. "We took extra lengths in insuring all's safety. In case Lukhan went crazy, the knight escorts and the extra guards around town and are safety measures." Bar looked dumbfounded. What the knight and shaman had done did not set well with him. He had been wrong about the dragon's bloodlust. Their teamwork insured peace and safety for the city.

"I don't care!" Bar snapped. "Open the door! I will risk my life!"

"I will not allow you to do that," Judas drew his sword to block the knoll's attempt to open the door. "I have a home to protect."

"I have a friend to protect! Now stand aside," Bar threatened. "I am not one of your knights that you can order around." Hunter and knight glared at each other, both promising death within their eyes.

"The effects of the gas should have worked," a feminine voice came from the courtyard. They turned to look at Ambrosia; the strange woman had changed her clothing. She wore an elegant evening dress in preparation of the newly arrived guest. In her white gown, she appeared to glow in the evening light. A sad expression was on her faces, she did not like to see them fight. "On most of the test subjects, they were paralyzed within a few moments."

"Ambrosia?" Bar asked. His eyes opened wide in realization. "You! You're one of the alchemists, aren't you?" She walked up to Judas and placed a gentle hand upon his sword arm. Judas's gaze softened and he lowered his aggressive stance. The presences of his wife and her reassuring touch calmed him.

"Yes, I am," Ambrosia nodded.

"I thought that you were-," Bar stuttered. He was lost on words.

"For our people's sake, I would allow the stables to be opened," Ambrosia suggested. "We made the ether stronger for the dragon. My beloved, I do not want our honored guest to die because of your unnecessarily protective stance of the city. Have faith in your companions."

"Wait a moment," Sacul muttered. He drew out his pet toad and started to lick on it. "You're no witch or wizard, you're an alchemist. No wonder Lukhan desires your flesh."

Ambrosia self-consciously covered her belly at the boarelf's statement. "Yes, I overheard my husband's and dragon's conversation," Ambrosia turned to her husband. "I wanted to tell you but you have been so busy and I wanted the news of our child to be a surprise." She fell silent as her husband looked down at her affectionately. He slowly reached out and tenderly touched her abdomen.

"The fault lies with me," Judas apologized. "I shouldn't have pressed Lukhan so. I fear that it was my harsh words that sent him over the edge. The dragon isn't to be blamed."

"You are being too harsh on yourself," Ambrosia smiled lovingly.

"No, he isn't," Bar stated angrily. "Now open the damn door."

Judas looked at his wife for guidance. She nodded her head in agreement with Bar. Judas sheathed his sword. "My love, please go inside," he instructed. "If anything were to happen to you-" Ambrosia place a figure upon his lips to silent him. Judas blinked a couple of time and then smiled.

"Awaken your dragon because we still have much to discuss at dinner," Ambrosia announced. "The alliance needs you and all of your friends."

"I promise that I will be inside shortly," Judas promised. Ambrosia nodded her head in agreement and left his side. Judas waited for his wife to enter the safety of their home before turning his attention back to Bar.

"Remember that this is your idea," Judas warned. "If Lukhan has not returned to normal, then I will be forced to kill him."

"You will follow him," Bar added coldly. Human and knoll eyed each other dangerously.

"Well, let's check on him," Sacul muttered nervously. He licked his toad for reassurance. "Last time I checked, we are all friends here. Please, no more threats. It's not becoming of council members to kill each other. We have enough enemies that will do that for us. Now, let us open the doors and pray to the spirits that he is under control." They slowly nodded their heads in agreement; however the glares did not fade. Together, the three opened the latch that sealed the stable's doors. As the doors slowly opened white vaporous gas spilled forth. The three wavered as the gas passed over them and cleared the small stable. Despite the gas, only silence greeted them.

"Luke, return to us," Bar called. There was no response.

Chapter 15

A familiar call came from the darkness of his consciences, Lukhan slowly opened his eyes. Gather around him were Sacul, Bar, and Judas. Each of his companions looked at him with concern in their eyes. Judas had his sword out, cautiously waiting to see how the dragon would react. Bar and Sacul held bottles in their hands, threatening to smash them against his face.

"W-what happened?" Lukhan groaned. He blinked a couple of time to focus on his three friends. Before all had gone black, he could only remember a burning sensation within his body. His mind was in a fog and he felt mentally drained. With a sigh, his three companions lowered their defenses.

"Welcome back to the living," Sacul chuckled. The shaman had a big boorish grin. His pet toad chirped its greeting.

"The gas appears to have worked," Judas congratulated. He acknowledged the dragon with a nod of his head. Lukhan only blinked in reply, his body still felt distant. "I'm glad that you've returned to your senses. I knew Vatara's plan would work and I didn't enjoy the thought of killing you."

"Are you all right?" Bar asked. He knelt in front of Lukhan with his ears laid back in concern. "Are you in any pain?"

"What happened? Did I- is everyone all right?" Lukhan asked wearily. He blinked a couple more time and struggled to move his legs. "I can hardly move."

"You went berserk," Judas replied harshly. "We were forced to take action to prevent you from getting out of control."

"Can you remember anything?" Bar asked. "You weren't yourself." He had witnessed the events leading up to the dragon's rage.

"I remember mindless hunger and the goats and a feeling of uncontrollable rage." Lukhan eyes went wide with sudden realization and fear. He rolled over to a sitting position, but was stopped by a cargo net that was wrapped around his wings and back legs. "Judas! Are you all right?"

"Yes, I am still here," Judas answered.

"I attack you?" Lukhan concluded. His words were both a question as much as it was a statement. The knight nodded his head in confirmation. "How were you able to defend yourself against me?"

"It's Vatara's defense," Sacul explained happily. The shaman presented the glass bottle in his hand. The bottle had a milky liquid substance inside of it. "The gas is called diethyl ether, a form of alchemy that paralyzes its victims and makes them go to sleep. It's a truly cunning devise. It has always amazed me how dragons are a wealth of information when it comes to the knowledge of plants, alchemy and history. The Gold Clan is truly amazing and your godmother is-" Lukhan looked down at his bloodily knuckle; the digit had returned to it inactive state and appeared unaffected by the gas.

"It's a sleeping elixir," Judas explained further simply. "This is only a temporary counter measure against your, umm, condition. It debilitates you long enough for you to return to yourself. This was all set up in advance so that you could return to us. The elixir was never designed to rid you of the black claw. It is a way to combat your uncontrollable rage."

"Y-you planned this?" Lukhan asked.

"You weren't the only one that was caught unaware," Bar growled. "I was informed of the plan this evening. Apparently, they've been planning this for some time."

"That was why I couldn't tell you about this," Sacul clarified. "We had to know that the gas worked before we could allow you to roam the city. Vatara wouldn't allow us to go and find you. She was concerned about what might occur if you lost control-"

"Vatara?" Lukhan gasped. "My godmother, where is she?"

"Yes, she *was* here," Judas explained. "She saw to the construction of this stable and the development of the gas." He gestured to the structure around them. Lukhan looked around for the first time, taking in the strict assembly of the building. He had been so hungry that he did not notice it was reinforced with both iron plates and magical runes. Judas smiled at the dragon's realization of the obvious trap. "Clear your head, now that you're yourself. Sadly, your godmother is not here. She has more urgent problems to the South. No doubt she had some business with the Inquisition and elves.

Everything will be explained at tonight's feast. Please come to the house when you are ready. I am satisfied that you are yourself and will not become enraged again. Yes?" Lukhan slowly nodded his head in confirmation. The knight gave an apologetic bow before turning to leave.

"Judas," Bar called. The knight paused and looked back at the sitting knoll. "I- I want to thank you. I'm sorry for doubting." The knight gave a forced smile in reply and nodded his head in silence. He opened his mouth to speak, but thought better of it. The man left through the stable's entrance.

"See, everything worked out for the better," Sacul boasted. He gave Bar a hardy pat on the back and smiled in approval. "No one is hurt, and we have a way to combat Lukhan's bloodlust. I'm pleased with the results." The boarelf gave another boorish grin and licked his toad. Bar ignored the shamans self-praise and turned his attention to the entangled dragon.

"Are you hurt?" Bar asked.

"I will be all right," Lukhan mumbled. "Help me get this net off of me." Bar and Sacul helped the trapped dragon get out of the cargo net. Lukhan stood up as the two helped to arrange the net. The dragon could not believe the obvious snare that loomed overhead. The stable's devises were reset to be used again. If he had been in his right mind he would noticed such apparent signs.

"You know," Sacul chuckled. "This was noticeable and Judas even warned you about it. Why didn't you stop?"

"I do not know," Lukhan admitted. "I was not endanger or under assault. I do not know what came over me. I felt so ravenous when I saw Ambrosia. Her white flame called to me. I- the black claw must have taken over me when I was angry."

"Angry?" Bar asked. "Was it because of Judas's harsh statement? I warned him that-"

"No, it is my own weakness," Lukhan replied. "I feel so lost."

"Lost? You're among friends?" Sacul chuckled.

"That is why I must leave," Lukhan strengthen his resolve. "I must return to the Endless Ice or else next time you may not be able to stop me."

"Please stay for supper," Sacul begged.

"Yes, you must stay! This will be your new home and it was designed with you in mind," Bar added.

"Do you think your alchemy will be able to defeat this?" Lukhan demanded. He held up his black claw. The claw had returned to its dormant state. Even in its dormancy, the ugly thing twitched. The digit had grown to its former glory from devouring the goats. Wrapping and twisting, the black flesh expanded down his forearm like a grotesque cancer. A thin layer of rot oozed from the flesh. The blackened tissue appeared decayed, like he had gangrene. Lukhan felt its clinging pain as it continued its slow spread.

"The claw!" Sacul gasped. "It's growing out of control!"

"No," Lukhan spoke calmly. "This happens."

"What?" Bar asked. "The claw returns?"

"Yes, I must leave." Lukhan's words lingered at that fact. He looked down at the deformity. The wicked appendage was a decaying digit that reacted to his hatred. Blood oozed out of the cancerous tissue. This was the second time he had placed his friends in danger.

"Where is the staff?" Bar asked. "That should help slow the spread of the curse." Lukhan looked up at the knoll. Without another word, he bit down upon forearm, his teeth sliced into the dying limb.

"What are you doing?" Bar screamed in horror. "Stop!" Sacul was frozen in fear as the dragon severed his own flesh. Lukhan paid no heed to the screams of his friend. Blood and black ooze dripped from his forearm and splattered upon the stable's floor. With a final rake with his serrated teeth, a bloody metallic pole fell to the ground with a clank. The dragon stopped his self-mutilation and examined the fallen piece of metal.

"What is that?" Bar gasped.

"The Staff of Selgae," Lukhan muttered. With his mangled arm he reached over and grasped the artifact. A flash of white light blind them. Lukhan howled in pain as he felt the claw's and staff's power struggle against each other. White and black flames erupted from the two opposing forces, Bar and Sacul were knocked backward from the radiating energy. Finally, the light subsided, revealing Lukhan's uninjured arm. The black claw and the infected flesh had disappeared. Only the healthy silver of Lukhan's natural scales remained. The golden staff of the elves remained still while clutched within his wavering claw.

"Y-you embedded the staff within your body?" Bar gasped in realization. "When you rescued us from the giant centipedes-the injury to your forearm-that was the staff?"

"What?" Sacul squeaked. "You willingly placed the relic into your body? Are you insane? The power of the staff is magic!"

"I was inspired by Orelac," Lukhan spoke coldly. He flexed his regenerated limb and hoped that the staff would keep the claw quiet for a longer time. The artifact had worked; however, when the claw's hunger returned, he would not be able to control it. As always, his center knuckle appeared burnt and infected. He returned his attention to his awe struck companions. "The undead leader embedded the staff within his flesh, granting him more strength and regenerating capabilities that were beyond the power of this accursed claw. Orelac was invincible to the claw's flesh and soul rending powers."

"That was how you cast magic!" Sacul concluded. "Con'ra and the wyverns, they never had a chance with the staff in your flesh! You were using the artifact's power! I knew you were clever! By consuming the magical energies from the staff, you kept from devouring us! The staff shields everyone from the curse."

"What? I don't understand." Bar was still in shock on what had occurred. The sudden return and disappearance of the black claw unnerved him. How could the ancient elven artifact hold up against the black flame?

"The claw feeds from the artifact," Lukhan chuckled. "The artifact has an energy source of its own. The staff's power comes from the white flames of every magus that has possessed it. It grants me time, between feedings. The claw must have sustenance, no matter what." There was a long moment that past between them. His two companions were uncertain what that meant.

"If the artifact protects you, then why did you go berserk?" Bar asked.

"Magic is nothing more than an illusion," Lukhan stated.

"Then we must get rid of the staff," Bar warned. "The staff holds magical powers beyond your control and you must remember what happened to Kale and Orelac?"

Sacul nodded in agreement. "Magic is a two edged sword and such power should never be used lightly. I would warn caution whenever-"

"No," Lukhan growled. "I was the one that fought Kale and Orelac! This staff has come into my possession twice. This treasure has been my only prize for this terrible curse, on only material wealth. I will not cast it aside. This staff must buy me enough time to find a cure for this curse."

"I understand your reluctance to rid yourself of it," Bar was hesitant about the idea.

"No, you do not," Lukhan grasped the artifact and, like a splinter of wood, shoved it into his forearm. With a painful grunt, the golden staff slid beneath his scales and bit into the forearm's muscle. Lukhan growled in pain and finally shoved the golden splinter into his muscle. The staff disappeared. Only the telltale sign of its entry point showed. Blood dripped from the minor wound.

"It may thwart your hunger, it doesn't rid you of it," Bar stated harshly.

Lukhan nodded his head, his friend was correct. Without a white flame, Lukhan was incapable of casting magic. The staff gave him while required to cast magic and delay his claw's desire to feed. That desire continued to build until it had nearly become unbearable.

"Speaking of hunger," Sacul muttered. "I am still hungry." Bar and Lukhan looked at the strange boarelf, and narrowed their eyes at the shaman. "Oh yes, I am still hungry, despite your sick inclination toward self-disfigurement. I think you're masochist, you know that! You're both crazy. You have some serious issues."

"Our friend is in pain and you can only crack jokes?" Bar growled. "I'll show you masochist!" He balled his fist into a threat. Sacul fled from the stable and retreated to the safety of the house. Bar turned his attention back to his injured companion.

"Why didn't you tell me about this?" Bar demanded. Lukhan snorted in reply. "Something this important must be shared among friends!"

"The staff is a part of me!" Lukhan snarled. "Like this damn claw, without both I would be feral or dead. Do not think me a fool. This must be kept secret. Without the power of the staff, I would lose all sense of control over this *thing*!" He held out his deformity in front of Bar, stressing the importance of the artifact. Despite the damage that had been done to it, the claw appeared to have returned to its normal disfigurement.

"Like you did tonight?" Bar demanded. "Remember that magic is evil! It's nothing more than an illusion!"

"Do my actions appear as simple magic tricks," Lukhan snapped. "You know nothing of magic, or forces that continually struggle throughout my body; I am driven on by the black flame of death!"

Bar crossed his arms defiantly. "I know that you're not yourself," he countered. "You're much more than a force! You have freewill! You have to make a difference."

"You do not know-," Lukhan snarled.

"Because you will not tell me," Bar yelled back. "How can I help you if you do not inform me of what is going on?" Lukhan growled in growing frustration, but the hunter would not be so easily dismayed. "Please I am trying to help. Tell me what is bothering you. No more secrets."

"I-I am afraid," Lukhan whispered.

"You?" Bar balked. "You're a dragon, the Defender of the Common Races, the Destroyer of the Plague, what could you possibly be afraid of?"

"I am afraid of the future," Lukhan gasped. Tears brim the corner of his scarred eyes. "What it might hold. I know what I am. It is the fear of losing everything that I have come to love that bothers me. Vilesath told me-" His words choked within his throat. Lukhan closed his eyes and turned away from Bar.

"Please continue," Bar pressed. "I'm your friend." Lukhan turned back to look at the knoll. Tears clouded his version. The words were jumbled within his mind. It was difficult to speak; he did not deserve such loyalty from such a trusting friend.

"V-Vilesath told me that I would become like him," Lukhan choked. "He said that I would become a betrayer to everything I love. My friends and family. I would live a cursed life. A life, unworthily of living."

"Then prove him wrong," Bar challenged. "You hold this villain in such high regard. Why? Due to his power of foresight? The fool admitted that he couldn't see into the future." Lukhan nodded his head in agreement. "Besides, Vilesath didn't take one thing into account."

"What is that?"

"He didn't take into account your friends," Bar wagged his tail. Lukhan blinked slowly in consideration of what his friend had said. Bar was correct. The master of death, Vilesath, wanted him to destroy his friend to fulfill the prophecy. He had defied his destiny before, he could do so again. Only this time, he would defy the future with his friends at his side.

Chapter 16

The evening picnic, which was more akin to a formal outside ball, was in full swing. Knights, nobles, and common folk had gathered within Judas's courtyard. Outside of the looming main house several bonfires roasted the main dishes. Upon the fire spit roasted ham, beef, and fowl. Next to them were barrels of Ravenshaven's finest liquor. Wine, beer, and spirits filled the cups of those gathered for the party. Long tables, with an embroidered table cloth graced the visitors warmly. Judas had spared no expense when it came to the party. From the servants to the nobles, all was dressed in their finest to meet the silver dragon that saved the world. A full orchestra played softly in the background. A sparring ring had been formed for knights to challenge each other in duels of honor. The sound of combat interrupted the party's grace and elegance. The knight's trials of honor entertain the crowds, who cheered them on. The city guards had been posted round the party, escorting out those that had too much to drink. The sound of laughter, clapping, and joyful praise rang throughout the night's sky. Lukhan watched from the safety of the stable's shadows.

"You never liked parties," Bar chuckled. Lukhan only blinked in reply. Both were safe from the strange party noises outside the stables. "You know, it seems so long ago."

"What does?" Lukhan asked.

"When we had a family," Bar's tone was full of sadness and regret. Lukhan's eyes did not move from the festivities of the party. "I often reflect on those days, wondering about how things should've been and doubting my leadership. I should have spoken words of kindness instead of words of scorn.

I went out searching for lost pack members in a vain attempt to bring our family together, did you know?"

"The past will fade in time," Lukhan replied.

"Yes, but my legacy will not," Bar stated. "I am certain the pack is gone. My friends and family all disappeared with the plague."

"Are you so certain?" Lukhan asked.

"If the pack survived," Bar sighed. "Then they are scattered or were taken in by others tribes. Even though I have a new pack, I cannot help but think about them. They are all likely dead and would not recognize me."

"That is not true and we never found Brick's body. The little pup could have escaped the troll's wrath." Bar nodded his head in consideration. He looked down at his bandaged arm in remembrance. He still had some movement from the damaged limb. His family's murder had caused his shattered arm.

"I-I never have thank you for killing Aak," Bar was melancholy. "I never had time to say that. Everything happened so quickly. The troll should have died by my hand."

"There was no way that you could have defeated him," Lukhan warned.

"Why's that?" Bar challenged. "I could've killed him!"

"Aak was infected by the plague," Lukhan muttered. "He was beyond any conventional means of destruction. When you killed him, the troll would have turned into the undead. How would you have defeated him then?"

"I would have found a way," Bar huffed at the notion and Lukhan gave him a brief smile. They had several similarities, so similar that sometimes it was crazy. He had learned several undesirable traits from his non-dragon friends. Bar had a profound effect upon his youth. Despite their two races vastly different philosophies, Lukhan found that he enjoyed the company of his friends more than that of the judgmental Silver Clan. Politics had never been his forte, but action was. According to his mother, he was like his father in many aspects. *Like father like son* she used to say. Lukhan had to admit that Bar had always been there for him. The knoll had been less distant than his father, Stratos, who had been the Silver Clans leader until the events which led to his death.

"You promised to speak of my father," Lukhan reminded him.

"Oh?" Bar asked.

"Yes, back in the Endless Ice," Lukhan mumbled. "You had promised to speak to me about my father."

"So I did, your father was a great hero to the elves, the people of Ravenshaven, and even the Gold Clan. You already know all of this, don't you?" Lukhan nodded his head in reply. "You already know about your father's involvement with Ravenshaven's freedom from the Inquisition's power."

"Yes, I still do not understand what was involved," Lukhan added.

"Your father fought on the side of Ravenshaven." Bar smiled. "When he took to the field, he single handily slaughtered the invading army! Inquisition knights, infantry, and siege weapons could not resist your father's might. When the battle was won, the city offered him a position of power; however, your father declined. They offered him the position of sovereign and protector of Ravenshaven!"

"I knew that my father fought for Ravenshaven," Lukhan gasped. "I did not realize that they offered him kingship. Why did he refuse?"

"Well, I know two versions of the story on why he refused," Bar chuckled. "According to written account, your father was bought by the merchant guilds, became bored, and left. Word on the street, says that the guild lied and refused to pay for your father's service. Either way, your father disappeared from the city seeking adventure and gold elsewhere."

"My father was a mercenary?" Lukhan asked.

"Well, according to the existing tax records," Bar stated. "Does this bother you?"

"Somewhat," Lukhan had always thought of his father as an honorable dragon. Not a mercenary, profiting from the deaths of others. This new information troubled him. What if the Silver Council was correct about his family? That they were nothing more than meddling troublemakers for the Silver Clan?

"Set your mind at ease," Bar chuckled. "Your father placed his life in danger for those weaker. There would have been more profit if he had joined with the Inquisition. I think he chose the correct side, otherwise this place, our home, would never have been."

"I do not know," Lukhan seem uncertain.

"Your father was a great dragon," Bar hushed. "He was a caring father, a powerful leader, and an honorable mate; it doesn't matter if he was a mercenary. Your father helped sow the seeds of this alliance, even if no one was aware of such events at the time."

"I doubt that my father had that much foresight," Lukhan chuckled in disappointment. His father never told him anything and made the effort of keep him out of such grand designs. Their father son relationship was made of short conversations existing on a simple understanding: Lukhan was to be protected from the racist world. Stratos rarely spoke of magic, the lesser races, and even their own clan. "According to my clan's elder, Cirrus, he was infamous for being a powerful warrior. My mother warned me about him choosing the most difficult and dangerous paths. It is hard to believe that he planned the future of this city or anything else."

"Like all dragons, your father did have foresight," Bar rebuked. "He wisely chose to spare my pack and allowed us to work for him. Our united families grew wealthy. Although we could not eat the treasure, we never ran short of supplies and our storage was always stocked. Stratos was more than a fighter, he was also a thinker. He would never have been able to become clan leader otherwise."

"Oh, I am certain that my mother had something to do with that," Lukhan stated.

"Crystal was the wiser of your two parents," Bar chuckled. "She was often independent and fickle but that was part of her charm. She was a diamond in a group of coals." Lukhan glared at him for the statement. Bar smiled in reply. "Hey, we have both felt her tough love. I can still remember the thump of her tail and the wrath of her scolds." Lukhan gave a brief smiled and reluctantly nodded in agreement. "Nevertheless, your parents were always different compared to the silver dragons that visited the cave."

"Different how?" Lukhan demanded.

"I mean no offense," Bar added. "Your parents were always more outgoing compared to other silver dragons. They were- I don't know: ambitious."

"Care to explain what you mean by ambitious?" Lukhan growled.

"Yes, I would say that," Bar continued. "You're already aware of your father's involvement with the elves, the Gold Clan, and Ravenshaven. Who knows how many other allies there are that we are unaware of?"

"Allies?" Lukhan considered in great thought. He found it hard to believe that his father was gathering allies. On the rarest of occasion, dragons and the common races would work towards mutual benefits. His father would have been aware of the different problems that arose when working together with different races. Too often, the common races' leaders would die off and the newer generations would forget the pacts that they their ancestors had made.

Lukhan sniff the air, the frills on the back of his neck stood up. The dragon bared his teeth in a deep growl. The knoll's ears perked up.

"What do you smell?" Bar asked.

"Bombarder powder," Lukhan growled. He narrowed his eyes as he focused on the source of the burning smell. "A great deal of it is burning and it is concentrated in a single location, it is in the barrels of alcohol!"

———◆———

"I propose a toast! To the hard working council members of Ravenshaven!" Judas proclaimed. Within the middle of the feast, Ravenshaven's council had finally assembled. Council members shook hands and gave brief hugs before sitting down upon barrels of the city's finest mead. More barrels were rolled up so that more of the gathered crowd could have a seat in the open assembly. Judas and Sacul stood in the middle of the gathering.

"Where is Imperator Owen? Where is the peace maker himself?" Sacul called. "Come forth you old scoundrel! Make your presences known!" An aged white knoll wearily stood up and waved at the gathered crowd. Signs of old age were evident on the knoll. He had a bent back and a simple wooden cane which he used for balance. Owen's white hair had faded to silver, yet his eyes were as sharp as ever. A cheer arose from those that had gathered around. Sacul smiled and waved to the popular leader.

"A toast to our Imperator," Judas proclaimed once the cheers died down. "Gather you mugs friends! Let us toast to our fair leader's health! Let it be that the hairs on top of his head never fall out!" Judas took off his helmet revealing small bristles of blonde hair gracing his scalp. This brought hoots and clapping from the gathered council members. This toast brought another cheer and laughter from those that had gathered. Owen gave Judas a smile and hushed the crowd with a wave of his hand. The laughter slowly died away into a mumble.

"Thank you Judas and Sacul for you toast and kind words," Owen nodded his head. "It is to the benefit of all of our races that Ravenshaven has grown into a prosperous city." This brought clapping from the gathered council members. "We cannot forget our elf allies to the West. It's through their trade of raw materials that our skillful people have been able to put it to good use." This brought another round of clapping, although this praise was clearly quieter. "Because of our alliances, that we have been able to break the hold of the merchants and muster the courage to trade with the different peoples gathered here today. The boarelves' tribes trade salt and spices from the Endless Desert. The elf magi provide us metals and tools. The humans provide us trade with fruit and livestock, and the knoll tribes provide us with the work force required to maintain this stunning city. Each of our peoples has contributed in their own unique way to this beautiful and astonishing city!" This brought enthusiastic clapping, whistles, and shouts from those gathered. The crowds stood up in praise and respect of Owen's words. They couldn't believe how this charismatic leader had changed Ravenshaven from a backwater slum into a thriving city. Those that survived living under the oppressive leadership of the wealthy merchant guilds spoke of nightmarish conditions for those that were not in political power.

"We can never forget that we had to fight to get here," Owen continued. "Bloodshed should not be spilled lightly. Never forget the friends and loved ones that died for this city. They had a common belief, that this city could become a better place. An idea of a unified nation is not old. The Inquisition attempted it a long time ago." Owen mentioning the Inquisition brought boos and harsh mutterings from the crowd. Before continuing, Owen held up his hands to silence them. "The Inquisition gave up on this dream of peace and unification. They didn't learn from the mistakes of the past. Instead they allowed the old hatreds to return! They went against their own doctrine of what made them great! Instead, their religion became nothing more than a former mockery of itself! Like the plague, which physically corrupted so many of our love ones, this spiritual blight have affected the Inquisition?" Owen looked to Judas for support in his claim. Judas smiled and nodded his head in agreement with the statement.

"We must free our brothers who are entrapped within their own minds," Judas announced. "I have personally witness the senseless butchery of not only boarelves, knolls, and humans-," His own words wavered; he fortified his resolve before speaking again. "They burn innocent families at the stake. I am aware of this because I, as an Inquisitor, did many of these horrible actions of the past." The crowd and council members fell silent as their beloved knight admitted to his own fault in the action of slaughter of innocents.

"Why is he a council member!" an angry voice shouted from the back. Owen narrowed his eyes and looked for the perpetrator.

"Judas has proven his loyalty by joining the Ravenshaven Council and forsaking his station as an Inquisitor," Owen announced. This brought several dangerous mutterings from the crowd. The words "traitor" and "villain" were passed around. Owen beat his cane against one of the empty mead barrels. The resounding echoing booms silenced the crowd.

"This is what I speak of!" Owen bellowed. "You would turn against a man who has proven himself to me and this council over a thousand times! He has even married one of our own, and yet you would still seek to prosecute him for his past life? Shame on you! You're acting like the Inquisition!" The knoll's scolding words struck the crowd like a thunderbolt. The crowd fell silent at their beloved leader's accusation. Mouths opened in consideration and stupidity.

"Owen is correct!" Sacul grunted in approval. "Judas has proven himself by securing roads and fair trade with our people. He has laid down roots within this fair city and has constructed several of its formidable defenses. He even told us the secrets of the Inquisition's newest weapons. His own designs that changed the bombarder have secured this city."

"What about the green dragon that keeps raiding the roads!" demanded a voice from the gathered crowd. "He hasn't been able to secure the roads! The dragon has to be dealt with!" There was a great deal of agreement from the council about the recent incursion from Con'ra.

"Peace friends," Owen replied. "We're all aware of the plights from the merchants, but there is currently little that we can do about it."

"What about the silver dragon?" another council member demanded. "Where are you hiding it? Let us have the beast take care of the raiding creature-" With a flash, Judas drew his sword angrily and pointed its tip threateningly at the shouting council member.

"Shut your mouth, damn fool!" Judas snarled. "That *beast* that you are talking about is my friend and is worthy of respect! I'll not ask any favor from him! You owe him your pathetic life. He helped to save this world!" The man looked at him wide eyed with fear. The guards posted around the gathering moved to intervene but Judas's own knight's blocked their path. Tension rose between the two fractions.

"Judas," Owen called. "Put the blade away and call down your men." Judas glanced over at the aged knoll and huffed at the command. Reluctantly, Judas lowered his blade and sheathed it. The other knights followed pursuit. "You're falling into the trap that our enemies are willing to use against us. Never forget that a house built upon sand will never stand. We are the foundation of this newly formed alliance. Shall we stand together or crumble away into the past, like the previous attempts made by the Inquisition?" The crowd fell silent at what Owen had said. Old hatreds and past grudges would have to be put aside in order for the diverse city to continue to prosper.

"Owen is correct," Sacul grunted. "Time after time, the Inquisition has committed genocides against my people. I don't hold any hatred for this man before me." The shaman stood next to Judas and grasped him tightly around the elbow. "Although we don't always agree, he has proven himself a valuable friend in my eyes. I am aware of his past crimes against many of the races present, and these crimes will never be forgotten! However, I will not hold it against him. I blame his fanatical religion that holds not only Judas, but all of humanity hostage. They are slaves to their religious teachings and we must work together against the growing conflicts to the South." This grew several doubting stares and nervous glances from the crowd. Even the knights and guards appeared to be uneasy by the sudden proposal. What? How? Is he bewitched? Other questions that were muttered by the council members and the gathered audiences.

"Are you proposing that we assault the Inquisition?" one of the council members demanded as he stood up boldly. "That's madness! No one has ever been able to defeat the Inquisitions' armies. Not even the disaster of the plague affected them? They have a god and a fortress made of iron that protects him! This is a struggle that we could never hope to win! They are too powerful!" This brought several nods of agreement from the crowd.

"Yes, by ourselves, we could never be able to defeat the Inquisition but we still have allies."

"Are you referring to the elves?" another council member demanded. "They are still suffering from the plague! They are few in numbers! Even with our combined strength we couldn't muster a large enough army-"

"Dragons," Judas shouted and the crowd fell silent. "The dragons will unite with us."

Chapter 17

Lukhan bull rushed through the crowd where Ravenshaven's council had gathered. Cries of alarm followed in the dragon's path. Bar struggled to keep pace and gave passing apologies to those that had been knocked down in the dragon's way. The dragon rushed into the middle of the council where Owen, Bar, and Sacul stood in awe at his sudden and hurried appearance. Guards and knights drew their swords as the dragon halted before them.

"Get these people out of here!" Lukhan demanded. "I smell-"

"For the righteous wrath of the Holy Master!" a cloaked figure interrupted the startled crowd. The figure stood upon the stack of barrels of alcohol. "Kill everyone in the Master's name!" Within his hands were a curved blade dagger and torch that was ablaze. He dropped the torch upon the barrels, leaping from the stack. The barrels ignited as if they had been drenched in an accelerant. Several other cloaked figures within the crowd drew daggers and stabbed the nearest guards. The party broke into chaos. Weapons were drawn and fighting sporadically broke out. Grenades and smoke bombs were tossed into the fire spit, spreading further confusion within the crowds. Random explosions and plumes of smoke hid the perpetrators.

"Defend yourselves!" Judas instructed his knights. "Protect the council!" Three cloaked figures descended upon him with curved blades leading the way. Judas's armor protected him from the multiple strikes that landed. Sacul stood by his side, helping to ward off the deadly blows. With a quick knee to the face, Judas sent an assassin tumbling head over heels. The second assassin sliced the side of Judas's leg as it retracted from his kick. Sacul replied with a swing of his walking stick to the side of the assassin's leg. The knee's ligaments ripped, sending the assassin screaming and off balance. Judas recovered from the cut and plunge his sword into the injured man's chest.

"Thanks for the help!" Judas wiped the sweat from his brow. Sacul frown in reply. He grasped his walking stick tightly and swung at Judas's head but the knight ducked beneath the sudden attack.

"Duck!" A sickening crack followed as the blow crushed the skull of another assassin who had been sneaking up on Judas's blind side. Judas looked dumbfounded at the boarelf that had saved him. Sacul smiled.

"Help me!" Owen cried. Judas and Sacul turned to see their leader under assault by the third assassin. The aged knoll's white fur was matted in blood. Owen worked furiously to keep the assassin's biting blades at bay. Judas and Sacul flanked the cloaked figure and dispatched him quickly with multiple blows. Owen collapsed and panted from exhaustion. He grabbed his chest like he was having a heart attack. Sacul and Judas stood defensively over their leader. Five more cloaked figures approached their location, blades held ready for battle.

"Step aside," one of the cloaked figures threatened. "Give us the leader!"

"Come any closer and I'll bash your skull in!" Sacul grunted. He secured his grip around his walking stick and fell into a defensive stance.

"By the Holy Master, you will not touch him!" Judas bellowed. The five figures encircled them. Two more appeared out of the smoke and encircled the party. The seven held their position. Throwing daggers were pulled from their cloaks and thrown. The slivers of metal pierced the defender's flesh. Judas's armor blocked most of the daggers, but one had hit his forearm. Sacul had a dagger stuck in his injured leg and knelt painfully upon his wounded knee. Sacul had managed to block a fatal knife with his walking stick. The assassins smiled from behind their masks at successfully injuring both defenders. The boarelf was crippled and the man held his sword with one hand.

"You must be Judas," the assassin jeered coldly. His voice was harsh and rough. "You're the Inquisitor that we heard so much about. There is a big price on your head. Before we kill you, I was told to make you an offer. The Inquisitor Lords want you back within their fold. All you have to do is take over Ravenshaven's council and persuade them to join the Inquisition."

"You will stop this assault?" Judas demanded.

"It depends upon your choice," The assassin taunted. His eyes narrowed with intense focus. "I'm glad that your association with pigs and dogs hasn't overruled your human sensibility. You may yet be saved by the Holy Master, but to prove your faith, you must kill the knoll at your feet-"

"Never!" Judas spat. He stood over Owen protectively. "Holy Master! Give me the strength to kill these men!"

The cloaked figures snarled at the knight's prayer. "You blasphemous bastard! How dare you evoke the name of our god against his true servants! Who do you think you are?"

"I am Judas, a humble servant of the Holy Master and Knight of Ravenshaven," Judas declared. "No longer a butcher of the Inquisition! I serve the Holy Master, not the Inquisitor Lords! By his will, he gives me the faith and strength to continue! It is because of him that I have a new life!"

"Pity, such devotion," the assassin snarled. "I take that as a refusal and I'm glad that you sign your own death warrant. Heretics should never be allowed to spread lies or become false prophets." Throwing knives were drawn and it was not difficult to figure who their target was.

***

Lukhan could not move within the crowds of screaming guests. They ran through the smoke in blind fear as some were cut down by assassins. Explosions happened randomly as the alcohol and hidden barrels of bombarder powder detonated and guards panicked as they became lost in the smoke. Lukhan knew that the chaos had worked to the advantage of the assassins. With no clear battle lines or organized front it was difficult to tell friend from foe. More than once, Lukhan had knocked a guest down thinking that he or she was part of the elusive aggressors.

"Luke! Luke!" Bar called from the smoke.

"I am over here," Lukhan muttered.

Bar reached his friend's side. "I thought I saw Judas and Sacul and they're under attack! Quickly, we must find them!"

"Where did you see them?" Lukhan asked.

"They're-," Bar turned around but was disoriented by the intense smoke. "I don't know; I lost sight of them. Is there anything you can do about the fires? It could burn down the city!"

"I could use my breath," Lukhan stated. "It would kill everyone in its path."

"What about magic?" Bar pleaded. "The city must be saved!"

"Magic-," Lukhan hesitated. He knew the toll that it would take on

him if he used the Staff of Selgae. What was the alternative? He could allow
the guards and citizens to gather buckets of water. How many would perish
because of his reluctance? The assassins would escape in the smoke and
confusion and he had no choice but to act.

"Please Luke! We must help the people!" Bar pressed. Lukhan considered
the options and nodded his head in agreement.

"*Subsisto ventus!*" Lukhan commanded. The dragon's eyes blazed to life
with magical energy. The air fluxed to the dragon's will, and dropped below
freezing temperatures. The panicking crowd gasped at the sudden loss of
oxygen and the fires and explosions smoldered and died completely. Silence
filled the void of air that Lukhan had created. The smoke disappeared and
the party was revealed before him. The silver dragon stood immune to the
deadly magical energies that swirled around him. Eyes blazing mercury, he
stood above the crowds of gasping people. He located the nearest assassin and
dispatched him to the afterlife with a quick snap of his powerful jaws. Those
party guests near the slaughter wanted to scream as blood splatter upon them,
but with no oxygen, no scream could escape their lips. Other assassins were
not difficult to locate, they were identified by the grey cloaks and hooded
masks they wore. The cloaked figures looked helplessly at the dragon, without
air to breath they could do nothing to escape. As Lukhan render and hack
the assassins apart, he identified their entrails as human. They were beneath
him, tiny lives struggling to survive. The silver dragon located Judas, Sacul,
and Owen. Blood dripped from their many injuries. Their blood infuriated
the dragon's rage even more. He looked at the last assassin who struggled in
a vain attempt to escape.

"You will die," Lukhan growled. His eyes flashed with unnatural fury.
The assassin went wide eyed in fear as the dragon loomed over him. Lukhan
lifted his left claw before the struggling man and from his severed, digit a
black and hideous growth appeared. Lukhan plunged the black claw into the
man's gut and the human struggled like a worm on a hook. Still dormant
from the Staff of Selgae, the black claw was slow to take effect. A long moment
passed before the claw started absorbing the skewered man's midsection. The
assassin gave a mute scream before his body melted apart.

As Lukhan finished the assassin with his black claw, images of the man's
past life flooded his mind. The pleasing memories of the dragon foiling the
Inquisition's main objective to blow up Ravenshaven's council and murder their
leader was at the forefront of the assassin's mind. The memories continued.
The dragon recalled the assassin and his murderous guild's tasks: seeking

and killing targets, torturing their children, and raping wives and daughters. Lukhan saw that man's past life before he had become a trained killer. He was an orphaned child whose life was full of violence and desperation within the impoverished district of Alkaline. There was a deep hatred within the boy's heart and Lukhan could feel it. The man's memories melted with the dragon's conscience and the dragon's mind returned to his surroundings. The body of the assassin was mutilated; the dormant claw had only absorbed part of the man's white flame. His separated top and lower halves were blackened and burned in the midsection.

Lukhan chuckled in amusement and looked around at the others trapped within his airless void. Hatred and thoughts of murder filled his mind. It had been easy to slaughter the assassins. His targets had been destroyed, not even the trained murders of the Inquisition could stand against him. He had to kill them.

The power of the staff had increased his natural abilities a hundred fold and the magic flowed around him in controlled fluxes of air. The threat was over, but the magic did not yield its relentless suffocation upon the gathered innocents. The guests and council members choked and gasped. The human faces turned red, the boarelves' eyes bug out, and the knolls held out their tongues gasping for air. They looked to the silver dragon for help. Lukhan's face contorted into a wicked smile. The strangers' lives meant nothing to him and he didn't need them. They were small, physically weak, and unable to defend themselves. Without his aid, they would have died by the assassins' blades. He had saved them from the Inquisition's assassins now he was going to let them die. Like the explosions he had easily smothered, he could extinguish all around him. The power of magic couldn't be denied and killing was so easily.

Something grasped the back of his leg and Lukhan turned sharply to confront the sudden interruption. Bar clung desperately to his back leg, trying vainly to support his suffocating body. His brown eyes watered in choking fear and began to roll to the back of his head. The fading stare broke the dragon's concentration.

"Bar!" Lukhan gasped in sudden realization. With a sudden shiver, the dragon's blazing eyes faded. The magic that rotated around him collapsed and oxygen came rushing back. Those that had survived the attack gasped at the sudden relief in oxygen and others had fallen into unconsciousness. The crowds slowly began to stir and waken their fellow companions. Lukhan collapsed from the sudden excision of magical power.

"Luke," Bar whispered. The dragon turned to look at his friend. "Are you all right?"

"I-I am fine," Lukhan managed to say.

"Y-You did it," Bar congratulated. "You saved us." Lukhan looked at his friend with uncertainly. He was going to kill everyone.

"Owen! Owen!" a sudden cry filled the air. "He's not breathing! Someone help me!" Lukhan stood up wavering and approached the frantic cry for aid. Guards and knights stood up in a vain attempt to help, but fighting and heavy armor had taken its toll. Cries of confusion arose gently in the background and others lie dead by the blades of the assassins. Most of the guests were still in shock and sat in passive silences. Lukhan came upon his injured companions. Judas hovered over Owen despite his own bleeding injuries. Sacul lay on his back with his eyes closed and his hands behind his head. The boarelf's injured leg was elevated above his body and from the wound he bled. A makeshift bandage already soaked in blood was wrapped around his leg. Judas looked up at the dragon in fear.

"Help me!" Judas begged. "Owen was struggling for breath before the magic! I beg you to revive him!"

"I-I have no energy left," Lukhan stuttered. "The magic- I am so exhausted." He gently laid down his head and looked helplessly at the knight. Judas's eyes widened further in fear and Bar slowly approached their location.

"What do you mean?" Judas demanded. He choked back a sob. "You're a dragon! You have endless amount of power! Now get up and try!" Tears brim the corner of his eyes.

"I am sorry," Lukhan had nearly killed everyone, and yet no one seemed to be aware of this fact. Fear gripped his heart. Would he lose control? Would he complete the Inquisition's objectives for them? Lukhan knew the truth. He had passed many injured and dying guests. Their life's blood called to him. Even if he had the power, he could not heal them all. In his weakened condition, he would become susceptible to the black claw's influence. "If I cast magic now-"

"I don't care!" Judas begged. "You must try to save him! He's our leader!"

"No," Lukhan stated bluntly. If he cast magic again, the dragon knew what would occur. He glanced at Owen; the white knoll was covered in his own blood and ash. Despite the dirt and grime, the old knoll seemed to sleep peacefully and a shiver ran down his back when he noticed that Owen would never awaken.

"What's the matter?" Bar gasped. "Judas! You're hurt!"

"I don't care about that!" Judas screamed. "Help me save Owen! He's not breathing!" Bar rushed to his side and examined the fallen leader. Judas continued, "I swore- I swore upon the Holy Master that he wouldn't die." The knight choked, a tear traveling down his cheek and clearing the ash that clung to his face. The Inquisition had caused even more death.

"Get a hold of yourself!" Bar snapped. "H-he's dead."

"I refuse that!" Judas yelled in denial.

"Where is Judas?" a feminine voice called from the house. "Where is my husband?"

"Ambrosia?" Judas called. He stood up and waved his arms to get her attention. She rushed through the crowds of stirring people. Her elegant evening dress had been soiled by the smoke and ash. The white gown had burn spots and blood spray on it. Her golden brown hair was in disarray and a bewilder expression was on her face. Judas grasped her desperately in a loving embrace. The two clung to each other for reassurance. "Thank the Holy Master that you're safe."

"You're hurt," Ambrosia ripped her gown and began to bandage his wound. Judas's forearm had not stopped bleeding and it dripped upon her dress. Judas pulled away from her and pointed to Owen.

"I'll live," Judas turned his wife's attention to their fallen leader. "You're an alchemist. Please, is there anything you can do for him?"

"I can't- I shouldn't- there are people around," Ambrosia reconsidered when she saw the desperation in his eyes fade. "For you, I will try." She quickly examined the old knoll and dropped to her knees. She placed her hands upon Owen's chest. After feeling no heartbeat or breath, she began doing compressions on the knoll's chest. The sudden movement caught the weary attention of Sacul, who lie next to them, slowly opening his eyes to see what the commotion was about.

"What are you doing?" Sacul asked.

"Don't interrupt her," Judas hushed. Ambrosia continued to give compressions to Owen's chest. Crowds gather around to witness the death of their leader and watched Ambrosia at work. Their eyes spoke of fear, hatred, and confusion. Several long moments passed in mute silence.

"Ambrosia," Bar whispered. "Please stop, he is dead."

"What's she doing?" demanded one of the nearest guards. "Get that woman away from our leader. I'll not have anyone desecrate our noble leader's body!" His spear was brought to bear. Other guards appeared around them.

"She is performing witchcraft!" another guards moved to stop Ambrosia but a deep growl from the back of Lukhan's throat halted any further actions. Judas swirled around to confront the gathered crowd and soldiers.

"Silence fools!" Judas ordered. He drew his sword and pointed it at the nearest guard that held his weapon aggressively. "I'll have you flogged and imprisoned!" The guard frowned at the threat and did not venture any closer.

Suddenly, Owen gasped for air. The crowds muttered in disbelief at the sudden revival of their fallen leader. Mutterings of healer and witch spread through the crowd. Those gathered stood wide-eyed in fear at the witch that had brought their leader back from the dead.

Chapter 18

"The witch has brought the Inquisition here!" cried one of the council members. "It was witchcraft that nearly killed us. We're doomed!" He fell to his knees in prayer. A few others in the crowd assumed the same position.

"Kill the witch!" another female's voice screamed. "Burn her! She brought the assassins that killed my daughter!" A dead child was clutched within the trembling woman's hands. The child's blood ran down the front of her elegant dress. The woman's face was full of anger and hatred. The crowd was infuriated by the woman's demand for justice. The angry mob of knolls, humans, and boarelves moved to Ambrosia.

"I'll kill the first one that touches her!" Judas declared. He thrust his sword in a forceful manner at the nearest person. The crowd paused as the knight's sudden defense.

"I'm with you, Judas," Bar agreed. "No one touches Ambrosia!" He stood next to Judas, wielding his hidden dagger and a throwing knife had he picked up from the ground. The crowd fell silent at Judas's sudden gain in support. The knolls wavered to see one of their own standing against them.

"Bar, how can you stand with him!" demanded a knoll council member. "I find it difficult to believe that the assassins didn't have a collaborator! Judas could've orchestrated the assault! This is his house! He must have told the Inquisition where and when to strike! He and his wife are guilty of treason! The witch is his wife!" This brought dangerous mummers of agreement from the crowd. The gathered drew personal daggers from their belts. Those that had brought weapons were now armed.

"I almost died in the attack!" Judas declared. He showed his bleeding arm to the crowd. Those gathering paused in consideration and looked at the small wound. They looked to Owen and Sacul, both knoll and boarelf were bloodied from their engagement with the assassins.

"The assassins nicked you on purpose to trick us!" the woman with the dead child declared. "His wife is a witch and he is an Inquisitor! We've heard Judas's confession and witnessed his wife's witchcraft!" This brought agreements from the people. Both Judas and Bar stood wide-eyed in fear at the mobs growing hatred. The crowds wanted justice for those that had died. Brother, sisters, mother, fathers, and love ones were all hurt. The crowds were furious and demanded justice, even if it meant killing those that were in charge.

"Lynch him!" one of the guards snarled. "My brother died because of you!"

"Burn the witch!" another council member declared. "She was the one-"

"Silence!" Lukhan roared. The crowds had forgotten the massive creature that lie next to them in silence. "The Inquisition plots to destroy Ravenshaven's council and kill your beloved leader. Theses assassins are after us, not after wizards or witches! They are after your lives and city." The dragon reared up and unfolded his wings. This made the crowd back up in fear of the dragon's wrath. In the moonlight, all could see that his scales were covered in the blood of assassins. Silence fell over the crowd as they stood wide-eyed in fear at the towering creature before them. This brought a silent hush from the audience. Lukhan continued. "The Inquisition has struck first. Now you must make a choice."

"No," Owen bellowed. The crowd mumbled at their leader's announcement. He struggle to a sitting position. He breathed heavily as he slowly caught his breath. "Our choice has already been made!" Bloodied and battered, he shakily stood up next to Judas and Bar. Ambrosia grasped his shoulder.

"No, you must rest," Ambrosia insisted.

"Thank you, but I have enough strength for this," Owen whispered. He leaned on Judas and Ambrosia for support. "My people listen to me; this assassination attempt was a declaration of war! We've been provoked and abused for the last time!" This brought a slow mummer that turned into a cheer from the crowd around him. Boarelves and knolls applauded the words coming from their leader. The humans stood passively and listened for more. "Your anger is just and righteous." This brought more savage howls and cheers. "However, do not take blind action! The Inquisition will pay for what they have done-"

"Then its Judas's fault," a human council member declared. "We should hang the Inquisitor and the witch-"

"Guards, arrest that man!" Owen commanded. The guards hesitated before seizing the rabble rousing council member. He struggled briefly and then relaxed. The two guards escorted the man away from the crowd. "I know who is friend and foe within this city! Your anger is misplaced! Your enemy is not Judas or his wife! Stop it! We're no longer blood thirstily crowd. I'll not have disorder within my city. Now disband at once and return to your homes. The council will be recalled when reason and cooler heads have returned to our city. No action will be taken tonight against anyone! Now go home!" The crowds mumbled in discontent and slowly departed. Some of the people cried, walked away in complete silence, and turned their attention to the wounded and dying within the courtyard. When the mob broke up, Owen nearly collapsed from the effort. Judas and Bar captured him and slowly sat him down.

"Thank you for saving us," Ambrosia praised.

Owen struggled to look up at her. "I know that you're no witch," he wheezed. "You're a healer and have eased my condition. Your husband is no traitor. He is a noble knight of this city. You should be proud of him. He is an honorable man." Ambrosia smiled at the old knoll's kind words. An organized group of guards pushed through the departing mob. A knoll in embroidered armor led the column of guards. Those guards that had survived the assault stood at attention as the column walked by.

"Lord Owen, may we escort you to your house," the captain of the city guards asked. "The trouble appears to have subsided-"

"No thanks to your men!" Owen snapped. "Without the help of Judas and his allies, I would be dead!"

"Forgive me, my lord," the captain apologized. He bowed submissively his eye stared at the ground in shame. "We were caught unawares. Were my men not-"

"No excuses," Owen snapped. "Thank the elements for Judas and his friends, otherwise, this city would have been put to the torch and the council destroyed. Your guards wouldn't have arrived in time to save anything, let alone anyone."

"Do not be harsh," Bar growled. "This feast was my idea." Owen glared at his fellow knoll, but said nothing more. Bar looked around the courtyard. "Being caught unaware, the city's guards and knights fought honorably."

"Yes," Owen agreed. "We must honor the dead. Give them all proper burials, even the assassins. I'm sure they had families."

"Steel blades and dragon claws never saved anyone," Sacul groaned. He was still on his back with his hands behind his head. "I believe it was Ambrosia that saved our generous leader."

"Thank you," Ambrosia smiled at the old shaman, who stared at her and returned a weak smiled in reply.

Owen was exhausted and barely able to stand. "Take me home," the old knoll instructed. "I have much to do and I must rest."

"I'll take your escort, captain," Judas commanded. "Help me leave this place. It reeks of smoke and blood, Owen; may we spend the night at your house?" Their Imperator nodded his head in agreement and slowly closed his eyes. Under armed escort of the knoll captain, Bar and Owen left the courtyard.

"I'll see you at Owen's house," Bar called. As the knolls exited the courtyard, a stretcher was brought in for Sacul to be carried out. The shaman was so exhausted that he barely opened his eyes when they moved him. Judas's injured forearm was clean and stitched by Ambrosia, who added herb soaked bandages to his wound. Judas and Ambrosia shook their heads at their destroyed courtyard. Their home appeared to be intact, but charred marks from explosions had marked the side of building. The dead and injured lie beneath the shadows of their home. The city guards and knights hurried about the courtyard, attending both guests and fellow soldiers that had fallen. Both noncombatants and soldiers were wounded and dying. Judas glanced over to Lukhan who had remained strangely silent; a troubled expression was written on the dragon's face. Lukhan remained silent and stood stoically in the moonlight. The silver dragon was covered in blood and gore.

⟢⟣

Five days had passed since the assassins' plan had been foiled. Lukhan didn't linger within the city during the day. He fled to the Endless Desert for seclusion but at night he would always return. His concern for his injured companions always brought him back. He would speak to Bar on the city's rooftops. His friend spoke of Owen's promise to keep them safe from the unruly mobs that came and went. It was because of this that Ambrosia was not allowed to return home and therefore, stayed with her husband within Owen's home. Bar also informed him that Sacul would be bed ridden for at least a couple of months. Ambrosia promised to cut the estimate in half with her herbal medicines. Owen was planning a declaration of war and would present the declaration to the surviving council members. Bar promised that everything was all right and that Owen and their friends would survive their injuries, but many families were not as fortunate.

Morning after morning, Lukhan would watch as more bodies were buried in the outlying cemeteries. Death had been so strange to him and now he seemed obsessive with it. He had killed many animals and common races alike; he had even died himself when he had cast the spell to destroy the plague. His own death didn't frighten him, a release from his hellish existences would be a relief; it was the deaths of his friend that concerned him. These morbid thought continued to trouble him. From his midday aerial flights, he watched many strange funeral rituals. They ranged from the boarelf tribes that threw out bodies to be picked clean by the birds, to humans burned and buried their kin, to the knolls that created networks of snake-like burial mounds. Each practice was strange to him. He landed far away from the funerals to watch. The funerals' children, pups, and piglets would run off and pester his observing solitude. Annoyed by the tiny creatures and their loud noises, Lukhan would fly off and observe from a different location. His sensitive ears could always hear the adults punishing their children for chasing him.

More than death troubled him; the resent events made him reconsider his options. He could've killed all with his magic but had he not reacted, more people would've died. Lukhan frowned at the thought; the same people he had saved had turned against Judas and Ambrosia. He had no doubt that he would have killed the mob, had Owen not revived and told them to disperse. Lukhan had to wonder if Ravenshaven was worth being saved. He was a dragon and he owed no commitment to anyone or anything; after all, he was an outcast.

"Are you enjoying the view?" A soft sultry voice asked. "Are you trapped within your own world?" Lukhan turned sharply toward the voice.

"Con'ra!" Lukhan gasped. The smaller green dragon had snuck up on him from downwind. He had been so focused on his own thoughts and the funerals that he had forgotten his surroundings! He didn't know how long she had been sitting there, but the green dragon sat cat-like, her back legs off to the side and her front feet crossed. In the morning light, the ivy scar upon her neck was easier to see. The scars shined with a glossy appearance. Her beautiful features appeared relaxed; her yellow eyes blink slowly watching the wagons of dead pass by.

"Really, I wondered how you were able to survive in the wilds," Con'ra continued. She looked at him and gave a warm chuckle. Her laughter was like a musical bell. She put on a serious face and looked him straight in the eyes. "I think it is luck or is it something else." Her tone was relaxed and soothing. Lukhan backed away, fearing that a trap would spring any moment.

"What are you doing here?" Lukhan demanded. He continued to put distance between them before he stopped and looked around. He even looked up in the sky, expecting to see wyverns swooping down upon him. Only wispy clouds kissed the morning sky.

"Watching you," Con'ra explained. She looked out over the fields to the different funerals. "What is it that you find so interesting? I always found funerals to be dull and depressing." Lukhan continued to look around for traps. Perhaps magical wards had been placed around him! He let his eyes fade into night vision, but he didn't detect any magic. She raised an eyebrow at the cautious silver dragon. "Be at ease, I am not here to fight you."

"Then you are here to raid caravans," Lukhan growled.

"Somewhat, but there seems to be something else that is going on within the city," Con'ra giggled. "I have no slaves or servants within, so please tell me what is going on. The caravans appear to be running late. Those wagons are moving the dead, not treasure. I cannot help but feel that you had some part in that."

"I should kill you," he snarled. He dropped to an aggressive stand. The green dragon raised a questioning eyebrow and stared at him passively.

"Oh? Why is that?" Con'ra gave a coy yawn. She stretched and brought her legs together beneath her. Lukhan smiled, she was putting up a brave front. She didn't appear concerned about his threat, but she had moved into a better position to flee or pounce upon him. He couldn't choose which would be her next move. Lukhan paced back and forth in front of her like a caged lion, pumping his body up for the fight that was about to occur.

"You have raided the city's caravans and placed several lives in danger!" Lukhan snarled. "You placed my friends in danger!"

"What of it?" Con'ra teased. The playful softness of her voice was now gone, replaced by a controlled and calm tone. "I am here to talk."

"I have questions!" Lukhan growled.

"Oh? What does the Defender of the Lesser Races want from little innocent me?" Con'ra giggled again. There was something menacing about her mocking laughter.

"You could have killed me. What is stopping you?" Lukhan demanded.

"You are intriguing to me," Con'ra considered thoughtfully. "The first time that I saw you, you were nothing more than a helpless hatchling. Later, I heard that you defeated the plague. You have proven yourself against an enemy that the Dragon Council feared. Now, you are considered dead. So what are you really? Hero or villain?" Lukhan bared his teeth, his eyes flashed in warning. She smiled and paused before continuing. "I have not come to fight, only talk. Let us be civil. I am sure you have seen enough death."

Lukhan's blazing eyes slowly faded, the green dragon was oddly correct. "Fine! Then speak your mind and then be gone."

"Why are you so venomous toward me?" Con'ra asked innocently.

"Our objectives have always been at odds with each other," Lukhan snapped. "You try to kill me. I do not trust you."

"Odd that you would place your trust in anything, especially in creatures that are lesser than you," Con'ra spoke smoothly. "The lesser races are our enemies."

"That is a lie," Lukhan snapped.

"Oh? They cannot even get along with each other," Con'ra smiled. "Look at the funerals. Even in death, they are segregated. Knolls are buried with the dogs and the humans are fried with other apes. The birds eat and shit out the swine."

Lukhan glanced over at the funerals. "Well, perhaps," he admitted. He had observed the funerals of the common races and they were segregated. "What you say is correct but my friends are united."

"They are united because of you," Con'ra replied in amusement. "What do you think would happen if you disappeared?"

"Their friendship has endured without me for over seven years," Lukhan retorted. "They place trust and faith into each other and that is what gives them the strength to put aside their differences."

"Then your pets are the exception to the rule," Con'ra shrugged. "Let us examine what you have said. I see no trolls or wyverns with your little group, and we have heard the rumors. Why are they excluded from your little party?"

"Trolls ran me out of my family's cave!" Lukhan snapped. "They even killed Bar's pack! They attacked us!"

"What of the wyverns?" Con'ra asked.

"None are willing to join us," Lukhan mumbled.

"Ah, so you are selective about your pets," Con'ra amused. She licked her lips at the delicious irony of the situation. Lukhan's eyebrows knitted together at her mockery. "Oh, come now. The lesser races will never unite but for the briefest of time. They are like their masters, the Dragon Council."

"I am working to change that," Lukhan snorted.

"Let us theorize that your friends become the norm," Con'ra giggled because she thought the notion was preposterous. "The unification of the lesser races would bring the downfall of dragon kind."

"What makes you believe that?" Lukhan demanded.

Con'ra's eyes sparkled in reply. "Compared to us, the lesser races have shorter lives," she smiled. "A hundred years is considered a long time for them. However, we live for thousands of years. We will have a parade of beings come and go in our life time. Each of these short lived creatures will breed, grow old, and die. Even your pets will die. Will you make friends and play nice with their ever expanding and aggressive offspring?"

"I am already aware of this. The thought of losing my friends troubles me. I will make the effort to aid their children, even as they grow old and die."

"A troubling thought," Con'ra stated. "What of your own kind?"

"It has been dragon kind that has set the common races against each other. Using them and discarding them for their own amusement and ambitions."

"Why not?" Con'ra challenged. "The lesser races are supposed to be our servants. They should serve their betters."

"How can you say that?" Lukhan demanded. "They are individuals, not chattel! The common races have feelings and desires, the same as dragon kind. Each life is unique and has different experiences. They have hearts and minds of their own."

"That is why they will destroy our world," Con'ra stated. "Their only interest is that of personal wealth and power. They do not care how their actions will affect generations to come. An example of the short sighted actions is the butchery of the sacred herd."

"I agree that the common races act before they think of the consequences," Lukhan replied evenly. "That does not mean they should be draconically punished. There are those that fight against such butchery, like my friends and the city of Ravenshaven."

"Why not? They must be punished!" Con'ra demanded. "The lesser races are all the same. They are guilty of their offenses. It does not matter which generation committed the crime."

"That is not fair!" Lukhan snapped.

"Why?" Con'ra asked coldly. "If a single dragon does something wrong in the lesser races' laws then all dragons of the same color are guilty. An eye for an eye, tooth for a tooth, claw for a claw. Do you personally know the individuals that are responsible for their crimes against the dragons?"

"Of course not," Lukhan dismissed. "All I is from witnessing the Inquisition's solders killing the bison herds."

"Your logic does not make sense," Con'ra laughed in amusement, the playfulness had returned to her voice. She smiled and looked to the horizon; the cremations of the humans had begun.

"They have great potential," Lukhan added. "They are capable of great and wonderful deeds. I have witness their kindness and experienced their friendship."

A sneer passed over Con'ra's lips. "That is only a half truth, their actions speak louder than your words and I have heard and seen their cruelty to one another. By the five elements, I hope that they will never unite. Otherwise, it will be the end of the dragon clans."

"Is that so wrong?" Lukhan asked.

Chapter 19

Confusion clouded Con'ra's thoughts. The silver dragon's plan was not to dominate the Dragon Council, but to destroy them and purge the boundaries that kept the clans segregated from each other. This would annihilate the dragon clans' purpose for the past millennia. She hated the Dragon Council and all of its ancient traditions. It had fallen stagnate and decayed. However, she knew that the dragons still had a purpose. That purpose was to be the guardians of the five elements: air, death, earth, fire, and life. To destroy not only the council, but the entire social structure of the five clans, meant to destroy the world's balance, sending the land into complete disarray. She had learned from her history lessons that this destruction would come from a single element dominating the others. To end the eternal conflict between the five elements was impossible; it was like stopping the sun from rising, or telling the stars to stop moving in the night's sky. What Lukhan suggested was a complete mystery to her. Her desire was to take command of the Dragon Council through strength and threats, not obliterate its existence. Lukhan ambition was too bold and daring.

For all of her life she had been taught the old ways. Within the laws of a dragon clan, the idea of allowing the lesser races to take over their territory was punishable by death. The lesser races were, well, lesser. They breed like vermin, which was their only true gift. They are animals that have short existences with little to no meaning. Their bodies are physically weak and take to illness. Their mental abilities lack when it comes to the world around them. They have no empathy for the elements, they are estranged and only rise to power through the stolen knowledge of the dragon clans. They are little more than nuisances, pests on dragon kind. For centuries, the lesser races have become more bold and daring, even going so far as to challenge their betters. As dragon kind slumbers the lesser races thrived in their shadows.

They have to be dealt with first, before any plot could be successfully executed against the Dragon Council. That means the destroying of the lesser races' civilizations and populace.

"The dragons are no better than their creations," Lukhan countered. "What have the dragon clans done to make this world better?"

"What do you mean?" Con'ra demanded. "Without us this world will die! The clans have been around for eons. The lesser races need us, but we do not need them! We are the pinnacle of creation within this world and no others rival our power and strength. Our ancestors gave life to the lesser races and we have ruled this world since the beginning of time. We are the pillars of this world and our existence keeps the world's elements in check."

"What if that changed?" Lukhan theorized. "The five elements have existed together within this world. No element is separated from the other. It is possible that we can live together in peace, all of us, dragon and common races alike."

"What are you saying?" Con'ra asked in consideration. "The five clans put aside their differences and unite?" She began to chuckled which turned into gut busting laughter.

"What is so funny?" Lukhan demanded. The idea was not humorous; the only thing that kept the unification from occurring was past crimes. As he saw it, both sides were guilty and the cycle of hatred would never end. Hatred and violence had become the norm since the Dragon Wars and the dragons despised each other as much as the lesser races.

"You and your strange idealism," Con'ra chuckled. "I could see it. The five dragon clans sitting together like the lesser races, so peaceful!" This brought another round of mocking laughter. Even temporary alliances would rise and fall, but nothing of this magnitude had ever been purposed. Unification through peace: the idea was bizarre, if not completely foolhardy. "Yes, we all live together in peace and gather around a fire like the lesser races. Singing songs and dancing under the sky for the rest of time. Yes, it would be glorious; just like the union between the Gold and Silver Clans." She was clearly mocking him because they knew that the Gold Clan had been exiled from the Silver Mountains. Even though the two clans had lived together in peace for centuries the alliance had ultimately failed.

"There are multiple reasons why the Gold Clan was exiled," Lukhan huffed.

"No, there are not," Con'ra stated flatly. "Racism is the standard of the dragon clans, and the lesser races learned it from their betters. Accept it, because we will never change. What the Gold and Silver Clans were doing was unnatural. I am surprised that it lasted for so long. The alliance between the Gold and Silver Clans was doomed to failure, and Ravenshaven is repeating the same mistakes. History is destined to repeat itself and I fear that your hopes and dreams will turn to ash before they even begin. The five elements were never designed to be together, like the dragon clans and the lesser races. The elements and clans are designed to keep the world in balance and your notion of peace and serenity between the races are figments of your imagination. You are living in a fantasy world."

"That is not true," Lukhan refused to accept her opinion. "I know that it can work. All must give it enough time to change. It might take years, even centuries, to change the norms of society but it can be done. You simply have to believe that it can."

"Ugh, will you ever listen to reason?" Con'ra scorned. Her expression softened and she let out a painful sigh. "You have strange visions of destiny. No wonder why you were pronounced dead, your ideas are dangerous and insane. This is why our two clans will never unite. After all, we are opposing elements."

"Opposing elements?" Lukhan asked in puzzlement.

"Earth and air," Con'ra stated. "No wonder why your ideas are so outlandish. You are unaware of the dragon elements."

"Vatara told me that fire was the Silver Clan's opposing element," Lukhan replied.

Con'ra chucked at the idea. "Vatara, leader of the Gold Clan?" she mocked. "You have powerful connections. That explains why you are not dead. Nonetheless, what makes you believe that fire and air are opposing elements?"

"According to Vatara we are not enemies or opposing elements," Lukhan recalled. "The element of fire devours the element of air. This consumption alters the air element into something different."

"Different philosophies, I suppose," Con'ra mocked. "I was taught by my mother that we are opposing elements, before I was-" She sighed and shook her head at the past. "It doesn't matter, we are still opposing forces."

"Can you not see?" Lukhan asked. "Each dragon clan teaches something different, even my mother and father taught me a different philosophy compared to that of the Gold Clan. My parents spoke of good and evil compared to balance in all things. From the day we are born, we are taught to oppose each other! Why? It is because there are major flaws in all of our belief systems."

"Even if your claim is true, what do you suggest?" Con'ra huffed. "To become friends with you and join with the lesser races? I will never become an equal to the lesser creatures because I know what they will do next."

"What is that?" Lukhan challenged.

"They would use us like beasts of burden," Con'ra stated. "Like a horse or an ox and we would be used for their wars and personal gain. I would never become a pet to those creatures."

"I am not a pet," Lukhan offered. "I am no beast of burden and they come to me for guidance. We are equals founded on mutual respect and our relationship is built upon trust. If only you could meet them, you would see that they respect and honor me."

"That was not what I saw," Con'ra chuckled. "Like when you carried your pets on the wing. A true dragon would never carry the lesser races. They should be afraid of you, inspired by fear!"

"They are afraid of you!" Lukhan snapped. "They seek to destroy you."

"Due to my raids?" Con'ra gave an unconcern yawn. "They are welcomed to try."

Lukhan shook his head in disbelief. Arrogance and false superiority would become her undoing. An idea crept into his mind. "I could use your help," he offered. "You say that the common races judge dragons unfairly. Then I ask you to prove them wrong. Show them that green dragons are not thieving monsters. The common races are fair minded and will seek out your friendship, but first you must offer it."

The green dragon looked at the funeral procession. "A strange request," She paused in reflection. "You look like you could use all the help you could get. However, my current allies are stronger than your weak city and your misplaced trust."

"Allies?" Lukhan asked. "You are not alone?"

"Oh, you will find out soon enough," Con'ra giggled. "I agree with you. The Dragon Council is old and ineffective. I also agree that the dragons should put aside their differences and destroy the lesser races. It is because of this common agreement that I shall assist you." She smiled at him, her yellow eyes sparkled mischievously. "For the moment, I have allied myself with the Red Clan. They plan to gather enough treasure from my raids before launching an assault upon the city and burning it to the ground."

"W-what? The Red Clan- but why?" Lukhan stuttered in disbelief.

"The lesser races have slaughter the sacred herd," Con'ra stated coldly. "The Red Clan will move against the lesser races, starting with the city of Ravenshaven."

"Why are you telling me this?" Lukhan asked. He was not sure if she was mocking him or trying to provoke him into some kind of action.

"I have no love for the reds, but the Blood Queen has shown me kindness," Con'ra mocked him with a mischievous smile.

"The Blood Queen?" Lukhan asked in doubt. He was baffled that a dragon would use a title and not her name.

"She is the leader of the Red Clan," Con'ra stated. "You are not the only one with powerful connections. I have been learning the Red Clan's magic and alchemy. They are barbaric and have no use for political intrigue. That is one reason why I like them. They are not difficult to understand and you do not have to worry about backbiting. The Red Clan will strike at the city of Ravenshaven and their queen shall lead the assault."

"I will never allow it!" Lukhan warned.

"That is why I am extending an invitation to you," Con'ra gave him a coy smile. "You can help in this raid. The lesser races trust you, can you sabotage their weapons? Especially, oh say, their bombarders?"

"Is this a request from the Blood Queen?" Lukhan demanded.

"No," Con'ra stated flatly. The single word lingered as she looked at the silver dragon before her. She considered her next words carefully, but finally said nothing more.

"I will not act against my friends or their city," Lukhan's tone dropped and his words were cold as ice.

"Then leave," Con'ra pressed. "I promise you that those inside will burn. Abandon the city and take your pets with you. Even those who you consider innocent will not be spared." Her yellow eyes focused on Lukhan even harder. "Even dragons found within the city will not be spared. Those that stay will be killed."

"I destroyed the plague and have overcome impossible odds," Lukhan growled. "I am not afraid of the Red Clan."

"I am sure that you are good at killing corpses," Con'ra shot back. She looked him over; her eyes fell upon his deformity. "Only a fool would mistake your taint as something that can be ignored. I have heard the stories of you overcoming terrible odds; therefore, you must have some form of power at your disposal. I believe that you are powerful or foolhardy. To believe that you can challenge the Red Clan. Remember, you face living dragons, not the mindless undead. Why not leave?"

"I cannot do that," Lukhan replied.

"Then you will die with your friends," Con'ra stated. Lukhan nodded his head in agreement with her statement. Con'ra's face contorted into a look of rage. "You would sacrifice your life for them? Why? What have they done to deserve such charity?"

The silver dragon paused for a moment in contemplation. He owed the city nothing and he had seen how quickly the crowds turned against his friends. The city populace no longer wanted his companions. Con'ra was offering him a way out from the impending attack. He was a survivor and fleeing would insure the safety of his friends. In the approaching battles, it was likely that he would kill both friend and foe alike because of his accursed claw. Even if Ravenshaven survived against the Red Clan, they would be engaged with the Inquisition. More blood would spill and Lukhan had to wonder if death would ever stop. It would never end; the violence would continue its cycle no matter what he did. The question was a fair one.

"If I do not fight," he stated simply. "Then who will break the cycle of hate? Who will save my friends and stop this pointless conflict?"

"Your friends?" Con'ra balked. "You would risk everything for friendship? What have they done to earn such respect?"

"They give me a reason to live," Lukhan muttered.

"What? A reason to live?" Con'ra repeated. She was confused by the odd statement. She wasn't certain and the silver dragon's thoughts were so alien to her. He was not motivated by greed, power, or even self-preservation but by friendship. His loyalty to the lesser races was on the verge of fatalism. He placed so much faith in the lesser races. She had been confused the first time she had met him and that curiosity had not been dissipate over the years. He was difficult to read and his thoughts were sporadic and dangerous. Two traits that she thought were appealing. If only she could inspire such devotion.

"Why are you concern with my fate?" Lukhan asked.

"Well, it is- uh," Con'ra stuttered. She wavered, a vain attempt to keep her thoughts and feelings in check. She looked away from him in shame. "It is there are few dragons left and it would be a shame to waste-"

"So you are worried about me?" Lukhan interrupted in shock and wonder.

"Grr, no, damn it!" Con'ra snapped. Her confusion was replaced with anger. She shook her head in frustration at the poisonous thoughts that the silver dragon had infected her with. "No," she wavered. "Y-you infuriate me! Damn silver! Your ideas of peace are perplexing and intoxicating. I have no words to explain such absurdity. Never mind! You have been warned and you must leave, or suffer the wrath of the Red Clan! Damn fool!" She pounced into the air like a spring and flew away to the northeastern horizon.

Lukhan stood, dumbfounded at the green dragon's sudden emotional fury. He watched her leave in concern. She had gone so far as to betray the Red Clan and tell him about their plot to destroy Ravenshaven. He saw no reason for the lies, but she was a green dragon. He shook his head at the silly notion of his own bias; she had come to warn him. Questions raced through his mind why a green dragon would have any interest in him. She disappeared as quickly as she had snuck up on him.

"What was that all about?" Lukhan thought out loud. If what Con'ra had said was true, then he must look to the city's defenses. Owen must be warned of the Red Clan's pending attack. There was a small chance that the city could withstand an assault from a dragon clan, but many would die. He doubted that the city's council had the strength to withstand this sudden and surprising alteration. He would have to secure his friend's safety because he knew that they would never abandon their home. They were bonded to him as much as he was to them. The Blood Queen had to be stopped at all costs. He didn't know anything about her or her motives.

He looked to the sky for answers; the wispy clouds above gave no reply. He turned his attention to the funeral rituals that were ending. The boarelves' wagons had begun to return to the city having completed their task of throwing out the dead. The humans gathered around a large pyre, their love one's bones and ashes carried off by the wind. The knolls continued to work hard, creating burial mounds for those that had lost their lives. Lukhan understood then: death was the great equalizer. No living creature could escape the black flame. The element of death was not picky of its victims. The dead had no choice where they were buried, but it was the living that segregated them.

Chapter 20

"The council has been warned," Owen muttered in disbelief. "Prepare the city's defenses." Lukhan informed the emergency council about Con'ra's warnings. Surviving council members sat in silent disbelief and shock. Several important council members crossed their arms in skepticism. His friends were present, but even they seemed stunned by the dreadful news. Owen stood up from his chair within the council chamber. The Imperator looked over the gathered members. Several seats were empty; many were unable to attend due to injuries and other council members had been killed in the attack. "I want all guards and militia at full strength before nightfall. The bombarders must be prepared for the coming assault. Take precautions against this pending attack. Are there any other solutions?"

"If I may speak," Judas asked. "Con'ra didn't give us any day or time when the Red Clan would strike. We must not jump to conclusions."

"I agree," the leader of the merchant guild stood up and interrupted Judas. The greasy white man wore loosely fitting silk clothing. Yellow stains from constant sweating soiled his armpits and neckline. Lukhan could smell the nasty mixture of perfume and body odor reeking from the oily skinned man. Yellow grease constantly stained everything he touched. "The treasury is already empty! We do not have the funds-"

"The council doesn't recognize you, Markus," Owen snapped. "Sit down-"

"The council recognizes traitors!" Markus dabbed his forehead with a cloth. "Why do we still have this Inquisitor in our mists?"

"Traitors?" Owen warned. "Judas is innocence of all accusations until the event of his trail. We have more pressing concerns, unless you wish to investigate the charges within your property?"

"M-my brew houses?" Markus stuttered. He wiped his forehead as he broke out in nervous sweating. "The guards that were bribed by the assassins have been dealt with and turned to the city authorities. It was an unfortunate mishap that the assassins were station on my property. I assure you that my family was unaware of such transactions and I have been honest and forthright about-"

"I have reviewed the evidences," Owen warned. "Your family will be placed on trial and there is evidence coming forth from the traitorous guards. Their confessions might change the trails. Now, let Judas speak-"

"I had nothing to do with-," Markus whimpered nervously. The sweaty man nearly broke down into tears. He looked to the other merchants for support. Many of his allies narrowed their eyes dangerously at him. Some of them fingered their knives eagerly. Many of the surviving council members had lost love ones in the assassins' invasion.

"Of course not," Owen muttered in sarcasm. "Now be silent, we have more pressing issues to deal with. I'm willing to forgive and forget. Let us hope that the council and populace are as forgiving." Owen had made the evidence public information. His spies had found the source of the betrayal; although he did not have enough evidence to investigate Markus's estate. He was certain that his spies' information was correct. Markus had the closest trade relationship with the kingdom of Alkaline; it was not surprising that the Inquisition used the merchant as an entry point. The problem wasn't the lack of evidence, but he needed the merchant guild's support. It was essential to have their trade. Without their income and resources, the city would have no taxes to fund Ravenshaven's growing army and fortifications.

Street justice worked itself out, without the council having to take action. Owen had been informed by the merchant's guild that Markus would be replaced by another more competent man and they assured him that there would be changes.

"If I may continue," Judas persisted. The council returned their attention to the knight. "I support Owen's decision to raise the militia. Our lack of security has nearly cost us everything. The enemy has spies within the walls. The council would have been severely crippled, if not destroyed, had Lukhan not intervened. Elections will take time, and the people have lost faith in the council's ability to protect them. The populace praises Lukhan for saving all of us." He took a deep breath before continuing. "Not only this, he has warned us of an appending attack. He is certain that we will be attacked by the Red Clan.

"Con'ra is certain," Lukhan offered. "I looked into her eyes and I knew that she was not lying."

"I do have questions about Con'ra's sudden and unlikely generosity," Judas continued. "The green dragon is cunning and deceitful. How do you know that we are not being tricked or played into a trap? Did she give you a date or time?"

"No time was given," Lukhan replied. "Dragons do not rush into anything, but her conviction could not be denied. She sought to gain my friendship because Con'ra wanted me to sabotage the city's defenses."

"What?" Owen gasped. The council members muttered in disbelief. Dragons were not known for war planning or sabotage. This raised questions about the Inquisition and the Red Clan. "Are the assassination attempts and the warnings from Con'ra related?"

"She was unaware of the events occurring within the city," Lukhan asked.

"Does she know of Inquisition's involvement?" Bar demanded.

"I believe that the two events are unrelated, but she seeks to weaken the city's defensives before the Red Clan's siege." Lukhan knew only of her intentions but none of their plans.

"Siege?" Judas gasped. Mutters of disbelief echoed within the chamber. Other council members shook their heads at the sudden turn of unfortunate events. They became restless and began muttering that they were doomed and all is lost.

"Calm yourselves," Lukhan growled. "This is no time for panic or making fearful and hasty decisions."

"Our resources are limited," Owen stated weary. "The council is paralyzed and has limited function. I purpose that we enact marshal law. Give me temporary control over Ravenshaven's military forces. I shall collect the taxes required to fund the war effort. We must make the first strike." The council muttered in discontent and shook their heads. The overwhelming majority did not like the idea. Citizen's rights would disappear, replaced by the military rule of law. Marshal law would make Owen a king with unchecked power.

"That wouldn't be wise," Bar announced. The council turned their attention to their absent council member.

"Why is that?" Owen asked.

"The people are scared as it is," Bar warned. "Such declarations will only frighten them more. I agree that a strong show of force is required; however, marshal law is too extreme to enact. This government is still functioning. We must maintain the illusion of control or else the people may fall into anarchy."

"Then what do you purpose?" Owen demanded. "We don't have the funds or a large enough army to defend the city against the Inquisition and the Red Clan. Marshal Law is the only way to insure-"

"I shall go to the Red Clan and speak to them," Lukhan offered. The council fell silent at the dragon's interruption. "The council can focus its efforts against the Inquisition while I deal with the Red Clan. Perhaps, I can persuade them not to invade." The common race looked at each other in surprise; they had not considered negotiations. All caravan attempts to contact the Red Clan had led to disastrous massacres.

"Yes, of course!" Markus cheered. "Send the dragon! It can fight them!" The council muttered in agreement. The sweaty man smiled eager to take advantage of the growing support. "I purpose that this dragon becomes an ambassador to the dragon clans." This proposal brought a round of nodding heads and reserved clapping.

"Hold!" Bar bellowed. The council fell silent. "Lukhan is our guest, not an agent of the city; we can't order him into danger."

"Who better to speak to a dragon clan than a dragon?" Markus argued. He looked around for support. The other council members murmured in approval. Where their attempts had failed, a dragon might succeed. "He has proven his loyalty to the council by slaying the Inquisition's assassins! I believe the creature has the city's best interest at heart. What more proof do you need?"

"This is not his fight!" Bar warned. "I will not cast a vote to place my friend in danger. He has done enough already. We all owe him our lives." The council members fell silent in consideration. The dragon had served them well, despite having no alliances to the council.

"Even if he fails in convincing the Red Clan not to fight, we will have bought time," Markus replied coldly. "It will also gather intelligence about the Red Clan's numbers and timing of the oncoming assault. The worst might occur, but at least the silver dragon could be a distraction. The council loses nothing-"

"This is unacceptable!" Judas bellowed. "He is not fodder for the Red Clan! Lukhan should not use and then discard! This is madness! Owen you can't-"

Owen considered both arguments carefully; his eyes fell on the silver dragon. Lukhan stood proudly and confidant in his abilities. "Sadly, I agree with Markus and Lukhan," Owen admitted. Judas and Bar looked at their leader in disbelief. The Imperator leaned back in his chair. Lukhan appeared hardened and stoic at the pointless debate. "Lukhan, you're a dragon and therefore do not fall under the city's laws. I must ask you, will you go to the Red Clan and speak on the city's behalf? At this time, we must avoid bloodshed. Will you accept this great honor?"

"Yes," Lukhan muttered. The council gasped in relief, but his friend's shoulders fell. Bar and Judas sighed and shook their heads in disbelief.

Owen's expression did not change. "Then let the council vote," he announced. "All in favor of Lukhan, the silver dragon, becoming our messenger to the Dragon Clans, raise your hands." There was a brief pause before the council began raising their hands. Judas slowly raised his hand in reluctant agreement. Bar crossed his arms, refused to cast his vote. The overwhelming majority of the council voted in approval. "The ayes outnumber the nays. The council approves and passes the proposal. Lukhan, are you willing to take an oath of allegiance?"

"I will," Lukhan promised.

"As a subject of Ravenshaven you shall be given citizenship," Owen began. "You swear upon the elements, to absolutely and entirely renounce and abjure all allegiance and fidelity to any foreign powers, state, or sovereignty of whom you have been subject or citizen; that you will support and defend the city of Ravenshaven against all enemies, foreign and domestic; that you will bear true allegiance to the same and bear arms on the council's behalf according to law; that you will perform national importance under council law and that you take this obligation freely without any reservations or purpose of evasion; that you will, in the future, serve the city, never cause it harm and will observe homage to it completely against all opposed in good faith without deceit."

"I swear," Lukhan pledged.

"You are a now a citizen of Ravenshaven," Owen announced. "The following is the oath of Imperator. As Imperator of the city of Ravenshaven, do you swear to protect the weak and innocent, fight to preserve the welfare of all, to server with valor and honor, to speak the truth and command those that follow, and to respect those who have merit."

"I swear," Lukhan vowed.

"The oath has been taken," Owen announced. "Witnessed by all who are in attendance, I present the newest member of the city of Ravenshaven,

Imperator Lukhan. Hail noble champion and savior of the fair city of Ravenshaven." The council stood up and clapped. Judas and Bar slowly stood up and joined in the brief celebration.

"Upon your safe return, you shall be rewarded for your services," Owen called over the dying clapping. "As long as you live, you shall receive a stipend from Ravenshaven's treasury and may call upon the Knights of Ravenshaven for service. There are many more rewards when you return. We shall construct a home, a suitable dwelling for any member of the council."

"He risks his life for our home," Bar growled. "He better get something worthy in return!"

"The position of Imperator is not to be taken lightly," Owen warned. "Lukhan is of equal status as I within this council chamber and the battlefield. Should anything happen to me during your quest, Lukhan will take my place on the council, if no elections are held before your return."

"This is highly irregular!" Markus declared. "Dragons can't hold positions on the council! The Imperator is elected by this council! Not appointed by the current one! You are overstepping your-"

"You were the one that suggested that he hold an office," Owen recalled. "Half of the council is absent. Would you second guess the vote of this emergency council?"

"Yes, but I voted for the beast to hold the position of ambassador, not the high ranking office of-" Markus began.

"It has been done," Owen announced. "By the people's authority entrusted to this council, Lukhan is Imperator of Ravenshaven."

"This is not what I meant-," Markus snarled. His fellow merchants grabbed him and forced him to have a seat. The sweaty man fell silent as those around him glared at him dangerously.

"A fine addition to the city," Judas congratulated. "The council wishes you luck in your endeavor, fly swiftly to the Mountains of Fire-"

"Judas, you will accompany Lukhan on his quest to the Mountains of Fire," Owen announced. This brought grumbling and nervous fidgeting from the council.

"I reject that suggestion!" Markus growled. Again his fellow members held him back. However, the sweaty man was hard to hold on to and he stood up. "The trials are not complete! He could run off and tell the Inquisition of our weakened state! He is still a criminal!"

"Judas will return," Owen replied. "You should be more concerned with your own trial. Anymore interruptions from you and I will have you thrown out of this chamber and imprisoned." Markus huffed and nervously wiped his forehead before sitting down.

"I agree with Markus and I must await the trial to prove my innocence. The people's justice will prove that I am innocent of all wrong doing. Besides, I can't part from my wife's side." Judas announced boldly.

"This is an order," Owen instructed. "You'll leave with Lukhan to make certain that the city's interests are held during the negotiations. A member of the council must be in attendance during the meeting. This task must be completed before Ravenshaven can take the offensive. A great deal is resting on the success of this quest. You've had the most experience with dragons and you're an accomplished warrior. You must go with your friend."

"Should I refuse?" Judas asked. "I will not leave my wife's side."

"Then you will be thrown into jail and revoked of your station as a council member and a knight of Ravenshaven," Owen stated coldly. "You'll do as you are commanded. This council doesn't need your presence; you are a distraction for the tasks at hand."

Judas's mood soured at his options because he didn't like the idea of abandoning Ambrosia. "What of my wife?" he demanded. The idea of leaving her alone didn't sit well with him.

"She will remain in my care until your return," Owen stated. "She'll be placed under arrest and protected within my household. Sacul shall be with her always. I promise you that she will come to no harm." The shaman's injuries meant that he would be bed ridden for another month. The injured boarelf would keep Ambrosia busy with his shaman magic, old stories, and complaints for food.

"As you command," Judas grumbled.

"If it pleases the council, I'll join them in their quest," Bar announced.

"Of course," Owen's tail wagged at the request. "The council would expect no less from a dear friend. I'm not surprised by your request. You have travel over a hundred leagues to find your dragon, I had no doubt that you would go after them. If only loyalty were so common within this chamber. Bar, your place as a council member will be honored and shall remain intact."

"I do not need them," Lukhan stated. "I am placing myself in danger so they do not need to. I do not know how the Red Clan will react to-"

"You're rejecting our aid?" Bar demanded. "Really touching, but I'm going with you. Even if I have to hunt you down and-" He pointed his finger at the dragon.

"It is your risk," Lukhan huffed.

"You don't say?" Bar asked in a mocking tone.

"When do we leave?" Judas asked.

"Rest tonight, you will set out with the dawn," Owen announced.

Lukhan nodded his head in reply. "I shall save your home," he promised. "This city will not be burned by the Red Clan."

"The council of Ravenshaven owes you a great debt," Owen replied. "I honor you, Imperator Lukhan. I shall pray to the elements that your negotiations are successful."

"I will need more than prayers," Lukhan snorted. "I will call upon the city's debts in the future." With the last statement, Lukhan turned away from the council chamber. Judas and Bar bowed before the council and departed. The dragon stood outside of the old building, awaiting his friends.

"You voted against me going into the Mountains of Fire," Lukhan growled. "Why?"

"I thought that you weren't interested in fighting for the common races," Bar admitted. "There are several reasons why I didn't cast a vote. I didn't want you to be forced into a position that you can't handle."

"I am not doing it for the city," Lukhan muttered.

"Then why are you doing this?" Bar asked.

"I want to do this for myself," Lukhan stated.

Chapter 21

It took them several weeks of hard riding on camelback to reach their unwelcoming destination. The Mountains of Fire was a volcanic range that scarred the region between the shores of the Endless Desert and the vast spans of the Gulf of Dracaena. Black jagged peaks pierced the ash choked sky. Heat vapors and smoke bellowed into the air above the peaks. The soft glow of embers crested the lips of the active volcanoes, while others lay in dormancy. Leading up to the foreboding mountains were misplaced jagged rocks and soot covered sand. The earth trembled beneath them as they approached.

"What a gloomy place," Bar mumbled. The knoll shifted his bombarder and moved uncomfortably in his saddle. He looked at his two companions. Judas rode wide eyed in fear, sweat rolled off his face. A lance with the flag of Ravenshaven on its tip hung lazily in the dry air. Lukhan seemed unmoved and unaffected by the perilous landscape that surrounded them. His normally shiny scales were covered in the soot, which clung to everything in the desolate landscape.

"The Mountains of Fire," Judas whispered. He wiped his dirty face and took a long draft of water from his water skin. His camel jerked nervously as the ground trembled, white froth accumulated on the camel's trembling lips.

"Well, you two have been strangely quiet," Bar looked up at the dragon that walked beside them. The knoll had grown uncomfortable with the uneasy silence of the small company. Judas's thoughts dwelled upon his captive spouse, while Lukhan's thoughts were his own. The dragon had only muttered a few basic commands during their travels.

"Don't bother him," Judas growled. He looked around cautiously. "He is focused on our surroundings. This charred land gives me the creeps. I have seen shadows moving above the clouds. I think we are being watched."

"So, what is our plan?" Bar asked. "We can't wonder around the volcano range."

Lukhan stretched his wings and flopped down. "I suggest that we rest," he announced. "I am sure that the Red Clan is aware of our presence." He shook his wings and soot fell from them.

"Are you certain?" Judas asked. "Have you seen them?"

"If they are anything like my clan, the red dragons patrol their territories aggressively," Lukhan warned. "We are outsiders in this land; there is no doubt that they have detected our unfamiliar scent. My silver scales stand out on this land, and they would have spotted us from higher elevations."

"Well," Judas muttered. "If they are aware of us, why don't they do something? I thought you said that red dragons were aggressive and territorial."

"Yes, but we are not trying to hide out presence," Lukhan spoke in an uneasily tone. "According to my limited experience, red dragons are aggressive. Our presence should have been challenged by now." He turned his attention to the sky above. The ash choked air weakened his sense of smell. Small bits of grey soot fell from the sky, clouding his vision and making it difficult to detect an aerial pursuit or ambush. He was out of his element within the barren land. Lukhan hoped that the curious appearance of outsiders would bring the Red Clan to him. However, as more time past and they continued deeper into foreign territory, Lukhan became convinced that the reds were only observing them.

After a brief rest, the party continued their journey. The sand below them turned to a mixture of glass and solidified lava fields. Layers of volcanic rock lay overlapping each other in strange and wondrous shapes. Windswept sand and soot gave the landscape strange patterns that raced up the side of the mountains. The mixture of black rock, sand, and soot was strangely beautiful to the outsiders. The ground beneath them trembled.

"Well, we're at the base of the volcanoes," Bar announced. "Should we climb them to see what is inside?"

"Are you joking?" Judas demanded. "That is an active volcano."

"What of it?" Bar asked.

"Active volcano equals danger," Judas stated sarcastically. "If you haven't noticed! I'm roasting in this armor." He took another long draft of his water skin and wiped his brow.

"The armor will only slow you down," Bar warned. "You need to travel light, try to be mobile. Your armor wouldn't protect you from dragon's breath."

"You should dismount," Lukhan instructed. "Your camels will not be able to make it up the slopes without becoming lame."

"It's not the dragon's fire I'm worried about," Judas continued. "They don't like to use it. Most dragons will use their claws and teeth before using their element breath. Dragons always give a telltale sign before they use it."

"Oh?" Lukhan asked. "Care to tell me about this sign?" He raised a questioning eyebrow at the struggling knight. Bar dismounted and assisted Judas down.

"Aye, of course," Judas huffed as he slowly dismounted his camel. "Dragons cock their heads back before releasing their breath. Did you forget that I was trained by the Inquisition to fight dragons? I thought all dragons knew about this flaw."

"Curious," Lukhan never thought of it, but the knight was correct. Using dragon's breath weakened the dragon. It took a great deal of energy to spew forth raw element. He had been told to use it conservatively. Its destructive forces would devastate friend and foe alike. The physical exertions extracted a heavy toll, winding the dragon and weakening his or hers combat effectiveness. It had been a long time since he had practiced his breathing techniques from his mother. The ground shook beneath them.

"Well, it will give us an edge when the negotiations turn into combat," Judas huffed.

"What makes you believe that it will?" Bar demanded.

"It always seems to break down into bloodshed," Judas muttered.

"That's not our fault!" Bar defended.

Judas rolled his eyes. "All other ambassadors and negotiations have failed this attempt," he groaned. "I thought becoming a council member would give me a safe normal life. Yet here I am, in the middle of the shit-"

"Hush," Lukhan warned. "Do you feel that?" Bar and Judas drew out their weapons and looked around warily. The frills on Lukhan's back stood up. The dragon narrowed his eyes and looked around for the source.

"What do you hear?" Bar asked. He cocked his bombarder and looked to the soot clouded sky. Judas held his lance defensively and widened his stance.

After several moments of watching the silent sky, Judas and Bar slowly relaxed their tension.

"What do you see?" Judas demanded.

"It feels like the ground is shaking or breathing," Lukhan cocked his head to the side and listened.

"This is a volcanic range, genius!" Judas groaned at the dragon's statement. "Of course the ground is shaking! We're looking for dragons! Not apparent observations and statements!" Lukhan didn't reply to the human's outburst but lowered his head to the ground.

"Shut up," Bar hushed. "Luke knows what he's doing." The human and knoll stood silent and watched the dragon listen to the ground. "So what are you doing?"

After several moments of listening to the vibrations in the ground, Lukhan turned his attention to his concerned companions. "The ground sounds like it's breathing," he whispered.

"By the Holy Master, he has lost it," Judas groaned. He threw his hands up in dismissal. "I'm going to tether the camels before they wonder off." Bar crossed his arms at his friend's harsh words. "I'm hot- and I'm in the middle of a volcanic field with limited water, accompanying a crippled knoll and a crazy dragon. I should be home with my wife-"

"That's enough," Bar growled. "Luke and I didn't force you to go on this quest. Now suck it up and do your duty."

"Suck it up!" Judas snapped. He dropped his lance and grabbed Bar around the collar. "You're not the one who is going to be on trial when he returns! You haven't lost your home! Your reputation! I may have lost my wife! Who knows! She may be dead when I return!"

"You don't know that. Sacul is with her-," Bar began.

"Sacul!" Judas interrupted with a dismissal chuckle. He clenched his teeth and growled in frustration. "That pig is bed ridden! He couldn't walk or defend himself! He couldn't protect a fly! I should've gone to jail!"

"What purpose would that of serve?" Bar demanded.

"I would be closer to my wife-," Judas yelled.

"Listen to me!" Bar interrupted. "Owen sent you away because you were a distraction and a threat to his investigation!"

"Owen only cares for himself! He has sent us to our doom!" Judas wailed.

"No, he did not!" Bar snapped.

"You've been away for too long!" Judas laughed.

"You admitted that you were once an Inquisitor," Bar mocked. "Before the assassins attacked the council. That was idiotic and no matter what you do, you will be found guilty. I know you're innocent and so does Owen! He needs you out of the city to protect you and the investigation. Stop being an ignorant fool. You're not alone because Owen did it to keep you and your wife safe."

Judas bared his teeth and glared at the knoll. "You knew this!" he roared. "Damn it! Why didn't you tell me?"

"Owen made me promise not to tell you," Bar sighed.

"W-What? Why?" Judas demanded.

"Owen must keep the appearance of neutrality," Bar explained. "You know how much influence the merchant guild has over the council and the people. If you were thrown in jail, you wouldn't have survived the night. Owen has to get control of the situation. Your absence provides him this opportunity."

"This is not justice," Judas snapped.

"Both of you shut up," Lukhan growled. "Your shouting has alerted everything in a hundred leagues to our location!" The ground beneath them shook violently. Judas released Bar and retrieved his lance. The camels bolted and awkwardly sprinted away from them. The ground beneath them began to split and fracture.

"Run!" Bar screamed. Vaporous gases shot up from the ground.

"It's an eruption!" Judas bellowed. With a great bound, Lukhan snatched his two friends and sprang into the air. Like black ice, the ground cracked and gave way to the reemergence of a lava lake. The black crust shattered violently as thin ribbons of rock shot up after them. Embers the size of boulders hurled past the flying group, narrowly missing them. They could feel the heat radiating from the molten boulders as they passed them. The high temperature produced by the lava lake was intense, the moisture in their eyes evaporated. Slowly, the lava overflowed its banks and dripped down the peak's sloops.

"Look at that!" Lukhan gasped. A huge form crawled out of the center of the lava pool. Its intangible face shifted into a gasp, then collapsed into self. With the scream from the mountain, a fluid shape with great wings burst forth and sank back into the lava flow.

"What is that?" Judas called over the howling wind.

"I don't know," Lukhan muttered. "It looks like a bird." The lava creature appeared like a great molten hawk. Slowly black feathers made of cooling volcanic rock appeared, revealing slow blinking eyes that burned as bright embers. The lava creature sat passively within the lava flow unbothered by the intense heat that surrounded it. The coolest parts turned into a crude volcanic beak. Lukhan flew in a distant circular pattern above the volcanic creature. After several moments of watching the lava flow beneath them, the strange being took no further action.

Bar was the first to speak. "What should we do?" he asked.

"I don't know," Judas admitted.

"Luke, do you know what it is?" Bar asked. The dragon only shrugged his shoulders because he was unfamiliar with this land. The blazing creature appeared to be at home within the comfortable sheets of flowing lava.

"Perhaps we should speak to it," Lukhan suggested.

"Are you joking?" Judas snapped. "That thing tried to kill us! It summoned a volcano! Are you mad?"

"I don't think so," Lukhan muttered. "I think it was following us."

"Following us?" Bar asked.

"I told you I could hear something," Lukhan warned. "The tremors! It must have been this lava creature. I was aware that it followed us."

"It's aware of us?" Bar asked. "Are you saying that thing is intelligent?" As if in reply, the lava bird shifted its attention to them. Its beak creaked open and lava followed down its open mouth.

"What does the surface bring to me?" the giant bird asked in riddling sentences. "Not rock, nor stone, nor tree?" The three flew in award silence and amazement, trying to understand what the creature was trying to say.

"You speak in riddles?" Lukhan asked.

"Time is on my side," the creature riddled. "Born within the world is where I once reside. Before the sun was called time. Why? Do you not care for my rhyme?"

"It's annoying!" Judas snapped.

"Hush!" Lukhan warned. "This creature must be a fire elemental!"

"The flyer speaks true," the creature riddled. "Old am I from the first element brew. Fire is the blood of the world, the center of which all things swirl."

"Do you have a name?" Lukhan asked.

"I cannot hear you clearly," the creature riddled. "Come before me; if sincerely. I shall then give you my name; a title in which I shall gladly proclaim."

"What do you think?" Judas asked. "Can we really thrust it?"

"I don't know," Bar admitted. "The fire creature is intriguing." They continued to fly in a big circle, giving the lava creature a wide berth. The bird's head shifted in observation, but no other action was taken against them.

"I have an idea," Judas whisper. "Lukhan, you can use your breath! If it attacks us, you can freeze it."

"The elemental is too large for me to kill," Lukhan stated uneasily.

"No, but you could slow it down," Judas offered.

"It might work," Lukhan agreed. They descended to the edge of the lava lake. Lukhan used his icy breath to cool a small section of rock. The bird's eyes stared at them with great interest.

"I am called Fienicks, the fire bird," the fire bird riddled. "A name given to me by the absurd; the dragons claim themselves to be masters, but we elementals think of them as disasters."

"You are not aligned with the Red Clan?" Lukhan asked.

"The Red Clan fears me," Fienicks riddled. "They burn and flee."

"They are frightened by you?" Lukhan asked. "Why?"

"Twisted and sealed I have become," Fienicks riddled. "I am not the same as some; I accepted my prison fate, though it is the dragons that I hate."

"You were imprisoned by the Red Clan?" Bar asked.

"I am land's host and guard," Fienicks riddled. "I keep the land barren and charred. The red dragons find this to their appeal. They do not understand, they do not feel."

"You are the one responsible for destroying the land?" Judas demanded.

"I bleed the mountain's blood so it may burn," Fienicks riddled. "Win my freedom in return. The center of the world is my home; below the crust, below the magma dome."

"So why are you here?" Lukhan asked.

Fienicks turned his attention to the silver dragon. Its relaxed ember eyes became intensely focused. "What nature of dragon do you mock," the element whispered. "You are not from the silver stock."

"I am Lukhan, of the Silver Clan," he announced.

"You are not living or dead," the element riddled. "A sibling you are instead."

"A brother?" Bar asked. "You must be mistaken. Luke was born in the Silver Mountains. His father was named Stratos and his mother Crystal. I knew them both."

"I am not blind to the truth," Fienicks riddled. "I know nothing of youth; I see with my embers, the oldest sibling that I can remember."

"I do not understand," Lukhan mumbled.

"I know and that is all that matters," Fienicks riddled. "Lukhan, destroy the Red Clan, their power shattered."

"Why would I want to destroy the Red Clan?" Lukhan asked. "You do not know why we are here."

"Dragon fight as they always do," Fienicks riddled. "For gold, power, revenge it is true. I think you have come for revenge. It is your father you seek to avenge."

"My father? You knew him?" Lukhan gasped.

"Indeed, I knew of him," Fienicks riddled. "Fight did he, upon a volcano's rim. Orelac, the powerful red; lied, for he was not what he said. Your father fought him in a duel; I witnessed the battle from the lava pool. Fight and struggle did they, Orelac's face and eye did he pay. Thinking the red dead your father turned, his fatal mistake for he had not learned, that Orelac was no normal fiend; he had become something else, not living but a dead twisted thing."

"Yes, the leader of the plague was Orelac," Lukhan remembered. "I knew he had killed my father- it's- I never thought of the circumstances surrounding his death."

"Your father sought to redeem the red," Fienicks riddled. "For his efforts he was bled. The other red dragons knew of Orelac's curse, but they did nothing to alter your father's course."

"The Red Clan knew their leader was infected!" Lukhan roared. "How could they do nothing to help my father?" Fury flashed within the dragon's eyes.

"It was cruel love and desire," Fienicks riddled. "That kept Orelac from a fiery pyre. It was the love of the Blood Queen, a doomed love that was beyond obscene."

Chapter 2 2

"Orelac and the Blood Queen were mates?" Lukhan snarled. He had not considered the possibility. He had not realized that Orelac had a family. To Lukhan the infected red dragon was nothing more than a monster. He was an undead creature that had to be slain.

"This doesn't look good," Judas mumbled.

"Why's that?" Bar asked.

"Lukhan is known for being the vanquisher of the plague," Judas explained. "The Blood Queen will not negotiate with her mate's killer."

"Orelac killed my father!" Lukhan snarled. "He infected my mother and Eldora with the plague! He was a fiend that sought to use the plague to conquer the world. He wanted to enslave the world and bend it to his twisted will. He was no dragon but a monster!" Bar and Judas cowered before the dragon. Fienicks seem to physically shrink before Lukhan's growing fury. "They knew! The Red Clan knew! They could have saved my father's life!"

"Yes, your anger and fury is correct," Fienicks riddled. "They released your father's murderer as a reject. Perhaps the fault lies with me, but at last, I am a slave and not free."

"Could you have done anything?" Lukhan demanded. The brooding fury did not leave his eyes. The clouds above them began to rotate.

"I can burn flesh and bone," Fienicks riddled. "Forgive me, allow me to atone. I could not see, their battle was on the wing."

"So what happened to my father's body?" Lukhan demanded.

"The flesh of the dead burned away," Fienicks riddled. "I meant no harm, nor to betray."

"What happened?" Lukhan growled. His tone deepened into a threat. "Tell me exactly what happened to his body! Did he become a slave to the plague?" His silver eyes blazed mercury. He could not bear the thought of his father becoming an undead creature.

"Calm your fury and hate," Fienicks riddled. "Orelac did not desecrate, but instead fed him to me. A better fate, would you not agree? Not before the red took his eye and face, for that he had lost he replaced."

"You cremated my father?" Lukhan snarled. "How dare you!"

"The Red Clan saw the truth of their leader," Fienicks riddled. "No longer was he a red dragon, they confer. Through threat and flame, they banish your father's slayer then vanished. Across the sea, Orelac continued his bloody spree. Later I was told, about Orelac the bold. None was safe against the mighty red, him and his army of the undead."

"If Orelac was a mindless undead creature. How could he defeat my father?" Lukhan demanded.

"You ask that I cannot answer," Fienicks riddled. "The plague was like a cancer, which attacks body and soul. Orelac was dead, but remained in control. I am sorry for what was done, for your lost and loved one." Lukhan's fury continued to grow. The air temperature around them dropped and ice began to gather on the volcanic ground. The lava around them solidified in an expanding circle of ice.

Bar placed a comforting hand upon his friend's shoulder. The dragon's scales were cool to the touch. "Don't forget your father's parting wish," the knoll whispered. Lukhan looked down at his little friend. His eyes widen in realization. His father's spirit told him to never allow the accursed claw to define his actions. As Lukhan's mind calmed, the ice around them evaporated.

"You still have power, despite the heat," Fienicks riddled. Its rock beak cracked and gave a smile. "That was not an easy feat: to turn the hot air into a cyclone and lava into black stone. The death of Orelac has made you strong; enough to have you correct the wrong. Strength and power you have become, therefore you will not succumb. Progress and confront the Red Clan's domain, cut them down and become their bane."

"I have not come for slaughter," Lukhan announced. "I-I have come on behalf of the city of Ravenshaven. I seek-" He took a deep breath before speaking. "Peace."

The elemental's eyes narrowed and they darken behind ebony feathers. "Peace is a fickle thing," the elemental riddled. "What does it bring? Go forth and meet, expect fire and heat."

"That is what I've been saying," Judas agreed. "This will end in bloodshed."

"No. It must not and we must try to secure peace," Lukhan suggested. "I-we have to let go of the past, no matter how difficult or how unjustified the crime.

"Go forth and do what you must," Fienicks riddled. "With you I shall place my thrust. Unless you think it is far too soon, might I ask you for a boon?"

"A boon?" Bar asked. "What is it that you want?"

"I must speak of my burning desire," Fienicks riddled. "To solve a problem that is dire. The reds stole my flame, without that part I am lame. Within the Queen's lair it has been encased and without it I am unable to leave the surface."

"An encased flame?" Judas asked. "I don't understand how did they do that?"

"To the lesser races it would be called a heart," the elemental riddled. "They require a name for a body part. I have no body, you see, I am made of pure energy."

"For your aid and information, I promise to investigate the matter," Lukhan promised. "I make no guarantees. What does your heart look like?"

"A gem of red, it appears," Fienicks riddled. "The gem is austere. Kept veiled from prying eyes, the gem is concealed and disguised."

"Then how are we supposed to know what it is?" Judas demanded.

"It's a giant ruby," Bar snapped. "You booby!"

Judas looked at his teasing companion. "Booby?" he scoffed. "Name calling? What are you, ten years old?"

"Fair enough rhyme for one so young," Fienicks riddled. "Though in truth, it was rather dumb." The fire elemental gave the knoll a slight crack of a burning smile and its ember eyes burned at the jest.

"I thought it was a good rhyme," Bar chuckled. "Unlike you, I haven't been doing it for centuries."

"Enough joking," Lukhan warned. "We still have much to do. Fienicks, thank you for your aid and telling me about my father's death. I never knew."

"There is no blame or farewell," Fienicks riddled. "Return my flame, I shall rebel."

"I shall see what I can do," Lukhan promised. They departed the lava lake. The fire bird watched them in smoldering silence. Lukhan let his eyes fall into night vision. The fire element did not glow with any magical residue, but instead burned naturally. His eyes watered at the element's physical glow. He turned his attention to the surrounding volcanoes, trying to choose the one that had the element's heart. In the distance, he quickly located a source of a magical aura.

The three companions traveled up the volcano's side. As they reached the top they turned to look back. Fienicks and the lava lake had disappeared under the black crust. The group turned their attention to the gapping mouth of the chosen volcano. Like a fanged beast submerged in volcanic rock, the side of the volcano had been blown out by an enormous eruption. Streams of lava poured from the center and snaked its way downhill, like salvia from an otherworldly beast. From the brim, they could see several cracks embedded into the volcano's interior. Vaporous gases crept out of the fissure, giving the atmosphere the appearance of breathing.

"It is in that fissure vent," Lukhan instructed. He pointed to the furthest crack inside the volcano. There was no way they could get there by walking.

"So, how are we supposed to get Fienicks's heart?" Judas asked. "I doubt that they are going to give it to you. I thought that our goal was to serve Ravenshaven. Not indulge the requests of an elemental creature. This has no interest in Ravenshaven or its people. This quest is already in danger of failure!"

"How is that?" Bar demanded.

"I don't know, let's see," Judas stated sarcastically. "First is the Red Clan, who wants to attack Ravenshaven. Second, is that Lukhan killed the Blood Queen's mate, and third is that we are planning to steal their treasure. Fourth, is that we are surrounded by fire, the Red Clan's natural element. Yeah, what could possibly go wrong?" He crossed his arms and took another long draft of water. Sweat continued to roll off of his face.

"Hopefully, nothing," Bar grumbled. "After all, Imperator Luke is in charge. Whatever is his decision, I shall support it."

"Then what does our fearless leader think?" Judas demanded.

"I want peace," Lukhan muttered. "However, I doubt that the Blood Queen will be willing to listen to me or any of you. According to Vatara, the Red Clan only values strength. Therefore, we must never show weakness. Try to be as hard and blunt as possible. Lie to them about Ravenshaven's strength and power. That will convince them not to attack, or at least delay it."

"Should that fail?" Bar asked. "Don't forget that Con'ra is with them. She will be able to see past our lies and deceptions. I would not be surprised if she is aware of our weakened state."

"Leave Con'ra to me," Lukhan stated. Bar and Judas looked at each other is confusion. Did Lukhan plan to kill the green dragon? It was the simplest solution to the problem. Neither had any fondness for the green dragon. "In the meantime, try to stay silent and submissive to me."

"Submissive?" Judas asked in disbelief. "I am no slave or servant! I am a knight of Ravenshaven! Who do you think-"

"Wait! I think I know what your plan is," Bar chuckled. "Your plan is to bluff them. You are going to-"

Lukhan cocked his head and sniffed the air. "Hush," he whispered. "A dragon approaches." From the air, the loud beating of wings approached. The ash choked sky parted, revealing the massive form of a red dragon. Even from their distance the creature's size was impressive. Its heavy jagged scales revealed signs of battle and conflict. Two massive horns sat upon the back of the dragon's skull. Smaller horns covered the dragon's face and back. The dragon flew in a distant circle, looking over the strangers. It then began its descent to the volcano's rim and landed before them.

"What is a silver dragon doing in my territory?" the red dragon demanded. His voice rumbled like thunder. Smoke bellowed from his nostrils. "You are not welcomed here. Have you come to test our defenses?"

"I am Imperator Lukhan, leader of the city of Ravenshaven," the silver dragon announced. "I am here to speak with the Blood Queen!"

The red dragon narrowed his eyes. "I am Rohad, son of Iaolt," the red dragon announced in reply. "You do not smell like any silver I have met. You reek of death. Are you a black dragon? The Black Clan is not allowed within my domain. Do you not know this? State you purpose before I kill you."

"I assure you that I am a silver dragon, and I am here to speak with your Queen," Lukhan warned. "I have a proposal entrusted to me by the city council. Will you take me to her?"

"Tell me the message," Rohad growled.

"My message is for the Blood Queen," Lukhan warned. "I am not here to trade words with you."

"I will know you purpose!" Rohad warned. Fire and smoke erupted from the dragon's nostrils. "What are the lesser races doing here?"

"They are my servants," Lukhan growled. "Now take me to your Queen before I humiliate you!"

"Bold words from a black dragon," Rohad roared. "I see a knoll slave and smell death reeks from you. Did you think that I would not trust my own senses? Impudent lying worm, you will pay for your careless trespassing! Your disguise does not trick me! Now let us test the mettle of the Black Clan!" The red dragon charged forward, eager to engage the sleeker and smaller silver. Lukhan gladly met the frontal assault with a charge of his own. The dragon struck with tremendous force. Lukhan freely gave ground. Both dragons were knocked off balance, but because of Lukhan smaller stature, he recovered quickly. Rohad lunged with his deadly jaws but was buffeted away by the quick jabs of Lukhan's wings. The red stumbled at the sudden fury of blows from Lukhan's wings and balled his claws. The silver dragon focused on the red dragon's nose and eyes. Blow upon blow landed as Lukhan's fury grew. Rohad's fury doubled and he lashed out with his own wings. The silver dragon ducked beneath the blows and charged again, head butting the red dragon's nose. The red dragon reeled back as the silver dragon continued his fury of attacks. The red dragon began giving ground to the rapid blows.

"You cannot defeat me!" Lukhan warned. "I could have killed you by now!"

"I think not!" Rohad snapped. He struck with his claw, piercing the side of Lukhan's neck. Blood oozed out of the injury, the silver dragon retreated from the strike. "Oops, did I wound you?"

"You cannot defeat me," Lukhan warned.

"Coward! You can dance around all day," Rohad sneered. "I need to strike you a couple of times before you bleed to death."

"I think not!" Lukhan chuckled. He turned his neck so that Rohad could watch his wound regenerate. Lukhan charged and engaged the red dragon. While striking and biting, Lukhan left several minor slices and gouges across Rohad's neck. He held his black claw in reserve. He did not want to kill the red dragon, dominate and wear him down. However, the red dragon's heavy scales absorb the onslaught of tooth and claw.

"What magic is this?" Rohad bellowed. "You dare bring magic into our duel? You may fight with speed, but you cannot escape my flames! For your treachery, you shall burn!" He cocked his head back and opened his mouth to use his fiery breath. To the red dragon's surprise, Lukhan did not flee but instead charged and clamped his mouth shut. Rohad screamed in agony as flames shot out of his nostrils, but Lukhan would not release his captive's jaws. The silver dragon was scorched by the intensity of the fire and continued to hang on for dear life. The fiery blast suddenly subsided and Rohad stumbled back. Black smoke engulfed the red dragon's charred face. Lukhan did not pursue the reeling red dragon. The smell of burnt flesh lingered in the air.

"You are defeated!" Lukhan warned. "Yield to me! I have no desire to kill you." The smoke cleared from the red dragon's face. His nasal septum had been blown out by his own fiery breath. The wound was cauterized to the bone. White bone and burnt flesh was all that remained of Rohad's nose. The red dragon's eyes turned blood red, intense pain raced down his burnt cheeks and jaws. Parts of the dragon's lips had been burnt away, leaving nothing but mangled teeth and gums. His body shook at the sudden shock that turned into fury.

"Yield to me!" Lukhan snarled. "Damn fool! You burned yourself!" He looked down at his forearms and claws both had been scorched.

"I cannot breathe," Rohad rumbled. "*Incendia erumpo!*" The massive red dragon shook with fury before collapsing. His eyes blazed to life with the surge of magical energy. The lava pool below them erupted at the sudden command of magic. A tidal wave of molten rock shot out of the volcano and hovered behind Rohad. Lukhan tried to flee, but was unable. He looked down at his feet; they were entangled in black tree roots. He was shocked at the sudden appearances of earth magic. Judas and Bar screamed at the towering wave of molten rock.

"Run you fools!" Lukhan bellowed. Bar and Judas were suddenly ensnared in roots. He turned his attention to the scorched Rohad. "Fool! You will kill us all!"

Rohad's red eyes continued to blaze in magical fury. "Then so be it," he gasped. "Die!" The red dragon turned to look at the summoned lava wave. Black roots crept over the red dragon's legs. Lukhan closed his eyes as the wave of lava rushed over them.

Chapter 23

The lava wave was upon them and all fell silent. Lukhan slowly opened his eyes. This was not death, or at least how thought he would experience it. What disturbed him was that he couldn't move. He had been able to move in the spirit world. The confining darkness fell more akin to being entangled or inside of a tree. He allowed his eyes to fade into night vision. The wood around him was not what it appeared. It was smooth and shaped comfortably to protect his entrapped body. A small pocket of air had been provided for him to breath. The entrapping plant fibers around him grew hot and unbearable. Lukhan felt like he was being roasted alive. The wood shifted round him and he felt a sudden acceleration up as if he was being carried uphill. His air pocket crack open like an egg, but the plants that surrounded his body remained intact. He looked around, uncertain of his bearings. The sky and air were still full of ash and soot. He felt heat all around him. He saw that he was still on the lip of the volcano and lava still surrounded him. Vapors from heat wisped off of the plant that entrapped him. His charred tree prison had saved him from the lava. He was in the air, or so he thought, he was sealed within a casing of burnt wood which stood like a black tower. Other limbless trees were next to him, two held his struggling companions, while a third held the weaken Rohad.

"Help Luke!" Bar screamed.

"What magic is this?" Rohad wheezed. His breath was labored and came at desperate gasps. He stared dangerously at Lukhan expecting another trick.

"We meet again," a sultry voice called. "It's called Ironwood, a dense wood and flame retardant. It's a native plant to Mountains of Fire." Lukhan turned his head to look at his warden. Not surprising, it was Con'ra. Her yellow eyes glowed with magic as her wings carried her aloft in a circular pattern around the four towering trees. Lukhan looked wide eyed at the green dragon.

"You!" Lukhan growled. "You were the one that imprisoned us?"

Con'ra smiled at him, and then turned her attention to the trapped red dragon. "You know, Rohad," she giggled. "You were always a dramatic fool. Taking your own life is foolish and would be shamefully dishonorable to your kin."

"What would you know of honor?" Rohad gasped. His burnt nose and lips appeared gruesome. Blacken flesh still dangled from his snout. In the red dragon's current state, it was difficult to breathe.

"Nothing, but I know of yours," Con'ra cooed. "Strength in battle, fury against your enemies, blah. I know your motto and you were beaten fairly. You are weak compared to Lukhan's strength." She ran a tender claw across Rohad's cheek and the red dragon recoiled in pain. She chuckled because the older red dragon could not escape her.

"Never!" Rohad gasped. He looked at her with death in his eyes and smoke began to bellow from his nostrils. A sudden cough stopped the gathering flames.

"You are foolishly stubborn," Con'ra teased. "It is because of that stubbornness that the Blood Queen sent me."

"Why?" Rohad wheezed. "I can deal with him."

"She does not want one of her guardians to die," Con'ra replied coldly. "There are too few dragons as it is and your death would be pointless."

"A position I never accepted! She is not my Queen and she means nothing to me!" Rohad snarled. "I have been defeated! He scarred and disfigured me!"

"You can regain your honor," Con'ra looked back at Lukhan. "Battles can always be fought again."

"I will break him!" Rohad bellowed. *"Incendia-"* Con'ra waved her claw and the wood that surrounded Rohad shifted and quickly pressed the air out of his lungs. The green dragon narrowed her eyes dangerously at the entrapped red dragon.

"If you continue casting magic, I will crush you ribcage," Con'ra promised. "By command of the Blood Queen, you will not harm him. She wishes to speak to him."

"He is an outsider!" Rohad gasped. "Not a silver dragon! If you are loyal to the Blood Queen, know that he is unnatural and dangerous. Smell him for yourself! He reeks of death and decay! He is a-"

"A black dragon?" Con'ra chuckled and she licked her lips. Rohad's expression turned into a look of dismay. "I thought the same. Regardless, it is up to the Blood Queen's discretion-"

"What is going on?" Judas demanded. "I demanded that you release us or else-" Con'ra paused in mid-sentence and turned her attention to the entrapped human and knoll. She flew around them like a snake investigating a bird's nest.

"Be silent!" Lukhan warned.

"Oh, I have not forgotten you, my lovely pets," Con'ra mocked with a devilish grin. The tree groaned in burning protest and moved uphill at her command. Lukhan struggled against the plant's structure, but his efforts proved futile. That left only his magic and breath; as if reading his mind, Con'ra gestured for Bar's and Judas's towers to block the space between them. She was even bold enough to land upon Bar's perch.

"Such spirit!" She giggled at the silver dragon's renewed struggles. "Now there is no need for that. I have a proposal my dear pets. You have been invited to the Blood Queen's lair. No weapons, no tricks. She knew that you would approach her."

"Should we refuse?" Judas demanded. Con'ra cocked her head and sneered at the sweaty human.

"Oh, I will not pressure you to go," she smiled. "However, the lava that melts the base of your trees might." She glance down, the lava that Rohad had conjured eating through the magically enhanced tree's bases. It wouldn't be long before the magical towers toppled.

"If you do not wish to harm us, then release us!" Lukhan demanded.

"It does not work that way," Con'ra chuckled. "I am no fool. I want a guarantee that you will be corporative." She turned her focus to Bar and Judas. "*Sub humus carus!*" The knoll and human's trees imploded on themselves. Judas and Bar were enveloped by the tree before plunging into the lava below and disappearing under the surface.

"No!" Lukhan scream. The tree that held him fractured and exploded. Con'ra turned sharply but Lukhan was in midair and snatched her by the throat. "You killed them!"

"They are still alive," Con'ra was shocked. "How did you break-?"

"Air freezes, expands, and breaks solid objects," Lukhan declared.

"Extreme temperatures will do that! Now bring them back, before I tear out your throat!"

"That would not be wise," Con'ra sneered at the silver dragon that held her by the jugular. "If you want to see them again, you will do as I say." Lukhan paused to consider his options. With a quick jab, Con'ra slipped from his grasp.

"Bring them back!" Lukhan demanded.

"Die fools!" Rohad bellowed. A burst of flame struck Lukhan and Con'ra from the side. The silver and green dragon turned their attention to the free Rohad. The red dragon's breath caught them both. Still ablaze, Con'ra returned fire of her own. A large ball of corrosive acid slammed into Rohad's chest and he screamed as the acid burned through his thick scales. Enraged by the sudden and unexpected assault, Lukhan turned and flew directly at the red dragon. Using his black claw, he ripped off the Rohad's jaw.

"Now die!" Lukhan growled. His mercury eyes blazed to life as he struck again. He looked inside of Rohad and found oxygen within his blood cells. Lukhan focused his magical energies upon Rohad's gushing blood. The silver dragon chuckled wildly as he focused his magical energy. *"Gelidus cruor!"* The effect was immediate; the air within Rohad's body froze. His body spiraled down into the awaiting lava. The red dragon's frozen corpse shattered on impact and melted away. Lukhan turned his attention to Con'ra. The smoldering green dragon had absorbed most of Rohad's fiery breath. Still smoking, she landed upon the rim of the volcano.

"Pathetic allies you have chosen!" Lukhan snarled.

"This was not supposed to happen," Con'ra cursed. She looked over her delicate wings. The thin wing membranes had begun to blister.

"Now tell me what you did to my friends!" Lukhan muttered. "I have grown tired of these games and I will rip your head off." The blazed within his eyes did not yield and he circled above like a murderous crazed beast.

"If you kill me, you will never see you pets!" Con'ra warned. Sensing that something was wrong, she began to back away to the volcano's lip. Lukhan landed before her and paused. He started to shake in faltering contemplation. His trembling movements were shaky, as if he was struggling with himself. His face was contorting in an expression of pure fury and rage.

"Get away," Lukhan gasped.

"No, you listen to me!" Con'ra snarled. "What is wrong with you?"

Lukhan's eyes narrowed and blazed to life with unnatural fury. "I must not-," he mumbled incoherently. "I will kill you!" He knew he was losing control over his emotions. The surprise attack from Rohad made active his survival instinct, adrenaline pumped through his veins. Although the green dragon had not provoked his fury, he did not view her as an ally. The dark hunger within him surged forth like an unstoppable force. Con'ra killing his friends did not yield his ever growing fury.

"What is this?" Con'ra demanded. She fell into a defensive position as Lukhan continued to stalk towards her. *"Anhela vites!"* The volcanic rock beneath Lukhan turned into tangling roots. Lukhan paused at the grasping plants and a sneer crossed his face.

"Glacialis terra!" Lukhan eyes flashed and the plants below him froze in command. He lifted his black claw out of the magically frozen plants. They shattered at the sudden tug from Lukhan's claws.

"How did y-!" Con'ra gasped. The spell had been countered by the silver dragon's magic. Lukhan sprung forward, mouth and claws wide open.

"Perussi humus!" Con'ra screamed as the enraged silver dragon pounced upon her. The rocks shifted at the magical command and collapsed beneath them. Together they fell into a magically conjured pit.

———◆◆◆———

Con'ra awoke to see two mercury eyes blazing at her in the darkness. She jolted back in surprise as the Lukhan's sudden closeness. She slammed her head against rocks behind her. She looked around in bewilderment. She snapped her attention back to the looming eye.

"Are you finally awake?" Lukhan demanded. His tone dripped with venom. "A fine trap that you have ensnared us in." Con'ra tried to move her claw to rub the back of her throbbing head, but her limbs would not move at her command. She looked down; her body had been encased in rock.

"Apparently, your spell affects us both," Lukhan commented snidely. "I thought about taking your head off with my ice breath. I am afraid that it would backlash into my face, which I am not too keen on."

"How kind of you for sparing me," Con'ra looked around warily. She did not like her predicament. The foolish male had pounced upon her, as she finished casting her spell. She frowned at her thoughts; she had encased them within an earthen entombment.

"Now that you are awake, reverse the spell," Lukhan roared. Their air pocket echoed and both dragons clenched their teeth at the sound bounced back and forth.

"Shut up," Con'ra warned. "That hurts my ears! I cannot reverse the spell."

"What? Why not?" Lukhan demanded. His words resonated like the tongue of a bell within the air pocket.

"Shut up!" Con'ra roared back. The two dragons fell silent and glared at each other; their words bouncing and repeating loudly within their sensitive ears. The echoes finally faded away Con'ra lowered her voice to a whisper. "I was about *say*," she huffed. "I need to be on the outside of the earth cage. I cannot reverse the spell from the inside."

"Then I should kill you," Lukhan concluded coldly. "That should break the spell."

"I thought you were afraid of the backlash," Con'ra replied. "To kill me would crush us!"

"I might risk it," Lukhan muttered.

"You would dare attack me!" Con'ra defended. "Why does this always happen? You forget that we are surrounded by my element! I could crush your body to pulp. Without my help, you will not be able to escape this spell!"

"I should have taken your head off," Lukhan threatened. She ignored the comment and looked over their prison. "You killed my friends!"

She rolled her eyes. "They are not dead," she whispered. "I sent them to the Blood Queen. They are with her."

"What? Why did you do that?" Lukhan growled.

"So she could have leverage on you," Con'ra looked around to get her bearings. The air pocket was a domed black rock had molded to their bodies perfectly. Other than her head, she could not move. She quickly realized how dire their situation was, because she could feel the vibrations in the rock around them. Her stone sense told her that the volcano's mouth was to the north of them. The strange fluxes in vibrations meant that it was going to erupt. If that happened Con'ra knew that they would be roasted alive.

"By the way you are grimacing," Lukhan observed. "I take it that this was not your plan."

"Why you," Con'ra snarled. Her lip curled back in disgust. "I only did this to defend myself! You went feral! You are the one to blame for this, not I. I am not good at moving the earth, plants are my specialty. Perhaps, you should have killed me. We will die of suffocation before we die of hunger or thirst."

"How comforting," Lukhan mocked.

"No, it is not," Con'ra snarled. "I still have many things left to do. This is our situation: we are surrounded by rock on the side of a volcano. If we cannot get out of here before it erupts, then we are both dead."

"Oh, the mighty Con'ra has flaws," Lukhan stated sarcastically. "You did the spell; now get us out of here!"

She felt around the encasing of rock. With her stone sense, she could tell that they had been frozen in space. She was beneath him and the fire within his eyes had subsided. Whatever otherworldly fury held him was now gone. "This was part of my plan," Con'ra lied. The rock didn't bend to her will. She considered crushing the space that Lukhan held above her, but the collapse could continue on to her. That was not an appealing thought. She could only use plants, but she had no Ironwood seeds.

"Oh, plan, right," Lukhan mocked.

"Listen, earth magic can move from side to side, not up and down," Con'ra instructed. "It requires leverage to make it move."

"Why should I care?" Lukhan grumbled. "Why not move mountains for me?"

"Was that your attempt at a jest?" she asked. "Our lives are in danger and you are making jokes? You have been with the lesser races too long because your sense of humor is terrible!"

"Then what do you find funny?" Lukhan demanded. "I know." An evil grin passed his lips. The silver dragon sucked on his tongue before a wade of split accumulated within his mouth. He parted his lips and allowed the drool to accumulate on his bottom lip.

"You better not," Con'ra warned. Then she saw it, a thin line of drool began to descend upon her. Her eyes widen in fear and disgust. "You would not dare!" The silver dragon parted his lips in a mocking evil smile. "Get that away from me! You evil monster! Wicked fiend! I will kill you-" None of her threats worked against her tormentor. The line of drool did a dance, dangling above her cringing face. As it was about to fall, Lukhan sucked the line of spit back into his mouth.

"You evil bastard!" Con'ra shrieked. Her words echoed within the air pocket. They cringed at the echoing cry.

"Now, you shut up!" Lukhan whispered. "My ears are ringing because of you! Have you thought of a way out of here?"

"How can I think when all I have to look at is your ugly face?" Con'ra huffed. They looked at each other in silence; after several moments passed, Lukhan began to chuckle.

"What is so damn funny?" Con'ra snapped.

"You," Lukhan replied.

Con'ra frowned and looked away from the stupid silver dragon. "Me?" she snarled. "What is so damn funny about me?"

"For all your planning and scheming," Lukhan chuckled. "You get stuck in your own devises and I find that *hilarious.*"

"How is that?" Con'ra demanded. She snorted at him.

"That red dragon turned against you," Lukhan sneered. "What stops the Blood Queen from doing the same?"

"You would not understand," Con'ra admitted.

Lukhan raised his eyebrow in doubt and waited for her to continue. No more clues came from her. "Besides why are you working with the Red Clan?" he asked. "I thought you were only out for yourself."

"A silver dragon would not understand," Con'ra defended.

"That is what you keep telling me," Lukhan huffed. "Come on, just tell me." She narrowed her eyes and glared at him; several moments pass, she couldn't stop staring at him. "Fine, keep your damn secrets-"

Con'ra growled in frustration. "There are reasons why I only look after myself is because I no longer have a home."

Chapter 24

Judas and Bar fell into the charred rock like it was air. Darkness overtook them as the sensation of free falling overwhelmed them. The falling sensation ended with an abrupt clatter of metal coins scattering. The sudden stop knocked the wind out of their lungs. The only sound that greeted them was their gasping breaths and a constant rumble of flowing lava. They looked around in bewilderment, but not even Bar's eyes could pierce through the blackness that surrounded them.

"Where are we?" Judas gasped. Bar sat across from him. They had been swallowed and spat out by the black rock around them. A flare from a distant fissure gave them a brief glance of their surroundings. The ground around them was covered in thin round metallic circles.

"Coins!" Bar gasped in realization. "We are surrounded by gold!" As their eyes slowly adjusted to the darkness, they could see they were on top of a treasure mound. Statues of men and elves were half buried within the mounds of coins that surrounded them.

"By the Holy Master-," Judas awed at the mountain of gold. "T-this must be a dragon's treasure."

"You are partly correct," a deep female voice broke the constant rumble of volcanic activity. Judas drew his sword, the metallic sound of the unsheathed blade echoed within the enormous chamber.

"Who's there?" Bar called. He cocked the hammer back on his bombarder.

"I am the red flame," the voice announced. "The mate of the accursed one, the butcher of pigs, and the heartless one."

"The Blood Queen!" Judas gasped. A great shadow shifted around them like a snake coiling around its prey. The coins around them scattered at the monstrous dragon's movements. The shadow of a great horned head paused above them. Bar and Judas could feel the heat radiating from the red dragon's breath.

"You know me, little man," the Blood Queen whispered. She inhaled their scent. "I do not recall smelling you before." Both knoll and human looked up at her in fear inspired awe at the enormous dragon before them. "How fascinating."

"How did we get here?" Bar muttered.

"Con'ra must have sent you to me," the Blood Queen sniff the air. "Are you food? Treasure? Entertainment?"

"We are none of those things," Judas warned.

"True, you are not a tasty boarelf or a wandering bard," the red dragon stated. "I smell many things on you. You have the distinct smell of death and camels about you. Your weapons are elven forged and your armor is of lesser quality. The human holds himself to be nobility, or even an Inquisitor. Odd that a human would travel with a knoll, especially one that has a crippled left arm, but yet he is still a formidable warrior, no wait, more likely a hunter or guide of sort. His posture is spread out like that of a hunter who has lived in the mountains. What news do you bring? It shall amuse me."

"You seem to know a great deal about us," Bar replied with a humble bow. "We have only heard of your title, Blood Queen, and not your real name."

"Amusing and bold to ask such a direct question," the dragon chuckled. "I have figured out a great deal about you two. However, I cannot explain the smell of death."

"Enough smells," Judas snapped. "Release us!"

"You would dare challenge me?" the dragon seemed even more amused. A flash of magical light pierced the gloom of the cave. The burst of light revealed the dragon's strong overbite that appeared more akin to a beak than jaws. Her scales and horns were slanting off of her head like ruffled feathers. The dark shadows of the cave made her look like a coiled serpent with hawkish features.

"Ouch!" Judas screamed. His sword grew scolding hot. He dropped his sword, which clattered on the coin bed.

"Bold words from a human that cannot hold his weapon," the Blood Queen chuckled.

"Judas, stop trying to provoke a conflict." Bar whispered. "We're here for peaceful negotiations."

"Negotiations?" the Blood Queen chuckled. "I assume that you are from the city of Ravenshaven."

"We are," Bar admitted.

"Have you come to beg for mercy?" she asked.

"No," Bar responded coolly. "We've come on behalf of the city's council and we seek an alliance with the Red Clan. It would interest both of our parties to-"

"So Con'ra speaks true," the Blood Queen chuckled. "The green worm informed me that the lesser races have been warring amongst themselves."

"You're informant is correct," Judas explained. "Ravenshaven seeks the destruction of the Inquisition." The dragon's shadow shifted uneasily. The thorns that covered her body rippled. The resounding clicks and clatters resonated within the cavern. Her looming head looked them over and hovered above them. Slowly, she slide open her eyes, blazing magical light engulfed the cavern, temporarily blinding Bar and Judas. The Blood Queen appeared like a bright sun within the cavern's darkness.

"The dragons seek the destruction of the Inquisition," the Blood Queen said. "This has been known for many years. Why do you seek our aid now?"

"The city has been in disarray-," Judas began.

"I do not care about the pathetic politics of the lesser races," the Blood Queen growled. "I want to know why your people took part in the slaughter of the Sacred Herd."

"We had nothing to do with that!" Judas defended. "Our city, we had-"

"Did nothing!" the Blood Queen interrupted. The temperature in the cavern became heated as the red dragon's rage began to show. The sweat on Judas's forehead evaporated and the salvia in Bar's mouth disappeared. "I should devour both of you!"

"Wait, it was not by choice!" Bar announced. "The Inquisition acts on its own accord! The plague has left many of the common races unable to challenge the Inquisition. The city of Ravenshaven had nothing to do with the Kingdom of Alkaline's butchery!"

"Ravenshaven, Alkaline, and Sedna what does it matter?" she asked. "The lesser races have broken their promises in the past. Why should the dragons respect their word? As such, the Red Clan no longer honors the ancient traditions that bound the Dragon Council."

"What do you mean?" Bar asked.

"Look behind you," the red dragon sneered. Bar and Judas turned around to look at the devoured remains of the common race on the far side of the volcanic cavern. A mountainous pile of skulls and bones lay in a scattered heap. The mound of dead was larger than the pile of gold they stood upon. Among the base of the decayed pile, broken wagons and armor served as a buffer between treasure and the dead. "Do you enjoy my collection?"

"By the Holy Master-," Judas gasped.

"I personally enjoy the taste of boarelves compared to the other lesser races," the red dragon chuckled. "Humans have a bitter taste, while knolls are stringy and hard to digest."

"Now I know why they call you the Blood Queen," Bar grimaced at the mass of bones. "Are you planning to devour us?"

"Not yet," she paused. "You are nothing more than a means to an end for my plan. Besides, I am not hungry. Yet." The Blood Queen let her words linger.

"Plan?" Judas asked. "What plan?"

"Your dragon companion," she chuckled.

"Luke?" Bar gasped.

"His name is Lukhan," the Blood Queen corrected. "He is known to me. After all, he was given credit for defeating the plague."

"What are your interests in him?" Bar demanded. "You will not harm him! What could he possibly offer you?"

The red dragon could not physically smile. Her lips had been burnt away centuries ago, but her glowing eyes twinkled with amusement. "I must know how a hatchling, a silver hatchling, overcame the mightiest of Red Dragons."

"Orelac was no longer a dragon!" Bar snapped. "He was infected with the plague and he was a monster!"

"Yes, I am aware of this," the Blood Queen announced. "Orelac was my mate." Bar and Judas stood uncomfortably as awkward silence fell between them. The knoll and human waited for their host to continue. "It was I that forced him to leave our homeland."

"You forced Orelac to leave the Mountains of Fire?" Bar asked. "Why didn't you kill him? That would have stopped all of those terrible events!"

"Orelac did not cause the plague, and his destruction would not have stopped the plague's spreading influence," she replied. "I knew him before he was infected. I valued his strength and honor. He was a good mate before his transformation."

"You loved him," Judas stated.

"I did once," the red dragon revealed. "He was a good mate because he provided treasure, protection, and status, everything that I found attractive. That was before he was corrupted by outside influences. He was weak." A glimmer of a tear appeared at the corner of her eye. She shook away the notion and focused on the two tiny creatures before her.

"So you seek revenge," Bar affirmed.

"You are wrong, little knoll," the Blood Queen stated. "I knew what my mate was. I knew that he would ultimately be defeated, but he stole my heart."

"You were heartbroken?" Bar asked in confusion.

"No, he physically ripped my heart out of my chest," the Blood Queen lifted her massive body and exposed her beast. Her massive armor had been split down the middle. A giant jagged scar ran vertical down her chest. Within the scar a giant ruby had been inserted. The stone flickered with an internal rhythmic heartbeat. From the top of the massive gem blood dribbled down and reentered at its base.

"T-That's the-," Judas stuttered. Bar gave him a quick kick to silence him.

"Where did you get that jewel?" Bar asked.

"Admiring my heart?" she asked. "Now you know why I am truly called the Blood Queen." The ruby appeared to bleed, but none of her body fluid fell to the floor. Bar noticed that the light from her eyes matched the same glow of the ruby.

"You have no heart," Bar observed.

"You are correct, little knoll. When I said that my mate stole my heart, it was not a metaphor." The Blood Queen caressed the ruby in the center of her breast.

"The gem is your heart?" Judas balked. "How can that be? How can a rock pump blood?"

"This is more than a gem," the Blood Queen announced. "This is the heart of fire, fueled by my burning hatred."

"Hate?" Bar asked. "What are you talking about?"

"My mate was transformed into a monster!" the Blood Queen declared. "Although I was unable to take his life, my fury has turned to the Inquisition! They shall pay for what they have done to the sacred herd!"

"What? That doesn't make any sense!" Judas gasped.

"I promise you that the Inquisition shall be destroyed!" she announced. "The humans shall be punished by the Red Clan's inferno!"

"Then we seek the same thing," Judas offered. "Our city seeks to destroy the same enemy. Perhaps an alliance-"

"We do not need the lesser races to achieve our goals," the Blood Queen snapped. "Why should dragon kind trust the words of butchers and liars?"

"Don't give your word to us," Bar begged. "Give it to our council's leader."

"I shall never come to terms with the lesser races," the Blood Queen snarled.

"You don't have to," Judas quickly thought of a better offer. "Give your word to Lukhan."

"The silver dragon is the city's leader?" the Blood Queen inquired. "The same dragon that killed my mate?" She considered this new information carefully.

"Luke has become Imperator on the city's council," Bar replied. "You can't hold a grudge against him. Orelac killed his father."

"How the fates play out," she muttered. "A city of lesser creatures that chose to follow and defend a dragon? I have not heard of this since the lesser races were slaves."

"We are not slaves, we are free peoples, and chose Luke to be our champion." Bar declared.

"Champion?" the red dragon chuckled. "You sound as if a dragon could be bound to you in servitude."

"We serve Luke as much as he has served us," Bar replied. "We owe him our lives."

"Tell me about this affiliation," the Blood Queen commanded. "A dragon is both physically and mentally more powerful than any of the lesser races. How could you provide a service that your Lukhan could not do for himself?"

"We provide him with wealth, friendship, and a safe heaven," Judas stated.

"Wealth," the Blood Queen had a sudden interest of accumulating more treasure captured her attention.

"War can lead to riches and wealth," Judas offered. "With the combined strength of Ravenshaven and the Red Clan, we can wreak havoc upon the Inquisition."

"You seek to hire my clan as mercenaries," she concluded. Her thorny flesh pulled back into a look of wicked curiosity. The lesser races would fight each other and weaken both of their positions. The idea was not unpleasant.

"We seek to become equals," Bar added. "An alliance with the city has many benefits."

"Care to explain?" the Blood Queen asked.

"We can provide tactical support," Judas explained. "The Red Clan can support our armies from the skies, hurry sieges along, and torch enemy provisions and supplies. In return, our armies can hold positions, sack towns, and provide the Red Clan with food and treasure. We will collect taxes and tolls from conquered enemies."

"My clan would eat along the way," the Blood Queen replied cruelly. Judas and Bar couldn't help but look behind them at the piles of bones. They had not realized the possible consequences of an alliance the Red Clan. Ravenshaven would be blamed for the barbaric and horrific crimes the Red Clan would indulge upon their enemies.

"With an alliance, I would have to ask for restraint from your clan," Bar offered.

"Your ways are not ours," the Blood Queen stated. "If I chose to align my clan in your pathetic war, then we are going to fight it our way. I shall sear a memory so deep into humanity's mind that they shall never forget."

"I want to protect the innocent-," Bar began.

"Hush," Judas interrupted. "So, will the mighty Blood Queen fight?"

"Wait! Before you make your choice, I-I must speak to my companion," Bar wavered.

"Then speak," the Blood Queen replied.

"I wish to speak to him in private," Bar apologized. "There are consequences that we must discuss."

"As you wish," the Blood Queen yawned. "I do not need to remind you that you cannot escape. I will eat you if a single coin goes missing." She turned away from them, like a mountain of scales and thorns. The gem that pierced her chest continued out her back. A massive shard of the ruby merged from between her shoulder blades and wings. Smaller shards of rubies pushed out randomly on her back. This gave her backside an unnatural contrast of flesh and gem. The gem hummed with a radiating glow of magical energy. She disappeared within the depths of her volcanic home. As she left, the dark gloom of the cavern gather around Bar and Judas.

"Is it wise for such an alliance to occur?" Bar whispered.

"This is what Owen instructed us to do, we are following orders," Judas rebuked.

"Did you hear what she said?" Bar asked. "The Red Clan will massacre everyone!"

"What about it!" Judas challenged. "Wake up! This is war! They have already struck the first blow! We must strike back!"

"Then we will become like our enemy!" Bar warned. "I don't agree with this and where is Luke? He should be here during these talks!"

"Hey! We are completing our objective!" Judas snapped. "I want to go home. Who cares? As long as we accomplish our mission."

"There is something that the Blood Queen is not telling us," Bar growled. "I don't thrust her."

"We all have secrets," Judas whispered. "Who cares about her alternative motives? As long, as she can rally the Red Clan to our cause."

"I care," Bar stated flatly. "What about Fienicks?"

"Fienicks?" Judas groaned. "Listen to me. The Blood Queen has a dragon clan at her command and Fienicks is a fire element. She's willing to help us in the upcoming war, while the fire element wants to disappear."

"It's not fair," Bar whispered.

"I'm being practical," Judas stated. "Think about it. Fienicks has been a slave to the Red Clan for a long time. What we are doing is changing the world. We can free the Holy Master and the world from the Inquisition and its intolerant religious fervor. Can't you see this is bigger than both of us?"

"Do the ends justify the means?" Bar asked.

"Damn your justifications! You're being idealistic," Judas huffed in dismissal. "I would gladly give my life for the obliteration of the Inquisition."

"What about Ambrosia's life?" Bar asked.

"I-err- she has nothing to do with this agreement," Judas wavered. He did not see where his friend was going with the conversation.

"Ambrosia is your wife," Bar stated. "How many other wives are you willing to put to the torch?"

"The comparison is not the same," Judas defended. "People chose to live under the rule of the Inquisition."

"How can you say that?" Bar growled. "You served as an Inquisitor and you were brainwashed! How can you be so unforgiving to other people?"

"We all have choices," Judas replied harshly. "Those innocent people have made their choice." The charred bones of the dead stared at them through their empty eye sockets. Their jaws opened wide in eternal mute screams.

Chapter 25

Imprisoned together in volcanic rock, Lukhan stared at Con'ra with distrust. The silver dragon was confused at the green dragon's motives. She had refused to answer his questions before she had captured his friend and foolishly imprisoned them both within the magically conjured prison on the side of an active volcano.

Lukhan broke the sudden and uncomfortable silence that had fallen upon them. "You have no home?" he asked in puzzlement. He had assumed something of this nature had occurred. It was strange that a green dragon was allowed to reside within the territory of the Red Clan. He was surprised that Con'ra snuck her way into the Mountains of Fire without deadly consequences or fallout. "What about the Jade Rainforest? Your wyvern army? I saw Sessess in the Endless Desert-"

"I was banished," Con'ra replied harshly. "My father was more cunning than I predicted and I was incapable of defeating him."

"You sought to overthrow him," Lukhan recalled. "You plotted to use an army of wyverns and take the Green Clan by force."

"Krain is the leader of the Green Clan, but not because he is the strongest or wisest," Con'ra growled. "He is the leader because of his vast network of spies and his cruel cunning and manipulation. Krain knows everything that happens within the Jade Rainforest. He used the border war with the Black Clan as a way to strengthen his position by ruthlessly killing rival males. He killed more green dragons than any black dragon. The struggle between the Black and Green Clans is a proxy war."

"You were his rival," Lukhan recalled. "How do you know all of this?"

"I was never his rival," Con'ra chuckled in a dismissive tone. "I was a fool and my father knew of my plans. Sessess, my closest friend and ally, was my father's informant."

"The brood mother?" Lukhan gasped. He remembered his brief meeting with the wyverns back in the Endless Desert. "I thought she was your friend. What happened?"

"Who better to keep an eye on your ambitious daughter, than her best friend," The green dragon chuckled at her own failure for not seeing the betrayal. "Sessess was like a mother to me! Her betrayal cut me deeper than this scar! I was a fool."

"The wyvern did not tell me this," Lukhan stated. He knew that Sessess had been acting strangely. Her mannerisms were strange and her own broods threaten to kill and devour her. He had thought the odd brood's lacked water. Could the strange behavior be because of remorse or was it a combination of factors?

"It does not matter," Con'ra continued. "Now, my so called *friend*'s only mission in life is to find me and kill me."

"Kill you?" Lukhan gasped. "Why would Sessess want to kill you?" The brood mother had an opportunity to poison him, but she had fled instead.

"My father is more devious than I could ever be," she sighed. "I had to watch as Sessess was both rewarded and punished for her actions. She was a fool to worship my father."

"Punished?" Lukhan asked.

"Sessess betrayed me," Con'ra snarled. "Therefore, my father would never have a traitorous wyvern as a slave. Krain has a sick sense of humor and forced Sessess to give me this." She turned her head to the side, showing him the vine scarification that ran down the side of face and neck. The scar was clearly in a pattern of a coiled vine. The scarring was organized and ritualistic. No infection had deformed the beautiful markings.

"Pretty," Lukhan complemented.

Con'ra narrowed her eyes at him. "Damn fool, this was not done by choice!" she snarled. "That was done by wyvern's poison! It is a curse! I cannot cast earth magic! I can only call upon the forces of plant life! You are witness to the effects of my blotched stone sense. I will never be able to manipulate the forces of my native element. I am flawed by this scar made from poison."

"I thought green dragons are immune to poison?" Lukhan replied.

"We are," Con'ra growled. "However, scarring me was still incredibly painful. My father magically enhanced the poison. I am certain that I am cursed and ever since my magic has been flawed. I can only manipulate plants with ease."

"I am sorry that happened to you," Lukhan snorted. "So why are you in the Mountains of Fire? Did you come to the Red Clan for help?"

Con'ra raised a questioning eyebrow. "To escape my father's torment," she replied coldly. "I left my home because of what he was doing. The torture and betrayal of my clan was unforgettable." She shivered as she recalled the pain she had to endure. "I sought freedom from my homeland and I severed all ties and fled. I wondered aimlessly within the Endless Desert preying on the tribes that live there. It did not last; I soon learned that my father was not going to let my transgressions go unpunished. In a cruel twist of fate, he sent Sessess and her brood to finish me."

"Krain sent Sessess to assassinate you?" Lukhan gasped. "That is horrible!" He could not imagine forcing to fight his own friends or being pitted against one another.

"Such is the weakness of lesser creatures," Con'ra concluded. She narrowed her yellow eyes at him. "I warn you Lukhan, associating with the lesser races will only bring more calamities on the dragon clans. They will betray you, like Sessess betrayed me."

"Are you blind?" Lukhan replied. "Sessess did not betray you and your anger is misplaced. It was your misguided ideas in believing that you could overthrow your father."

"I have not forgotten him!" Con'ra warned. "He will die by my claw! I promise you!"

"That is madness! You are still planning to kill your own father?" Lukhan asked.

"Krain is not my father! He is a monster!" Con'ra hissed. "Would a loving father do this to his own daughter? He should have killed me!" Lukhan fell silent as he listened to the green dragon's rant. He knew the deep and seething anger that festered inside of her because the same burning hatred was within him. He resented the Silver Council for banishing him; although he could relate to her suffering, the two causes of their pain were different.

"Why would you wish for death?" he asked.

Con'ra paused and considered the question. "Y-You would not understand," she muttered. "I have no home or family. Even here I am an outcast and not welcome! I am doomed to wander the world with no place to call home and I was betrayed by my closest friend." The word friend rolled off of her tongue like venom. "I have nothing to live for except revenge."

"Revenge?" Lukhan asked.

"Yes, I knew that you would understand," Con'ra smiled coyly. "In time, shall surpass my father and grow more powerful than he ever was!" Lukhan shook his head in disbelieve of her narrow focus. "How dare you judge me? You are like me because the Silver Clan pronounced you dead for some reason. Why did they do that? Other than-" Her eyes fell to the left side of the rock prison. Lukhan self-consciously moved to hide his black claw. The rocks that surround them hid the deformity from sight, but not from Con'ra's stone sense.

"I-I do not think," Lukhan stuttered in humiliation. He knew that Con'ra could sense his body through the rock that surrounds them. The Green Clan had empathy for the element of earth. Con'ra could feel the rock, like he could feel the air around them. It was an awkward and troubling thought. Even then, the memories were painful. He understood her blunt and harsh emotions. "I was cast out because of my deformity and it has brought me nothing more than pain and trouble."

"Your black claw," Con'ra clarified. "That is what I smell." She closed her eyes and focused on the appendage with her stone sense. The density of the claw was different from the rest of the silver dragon's body. It was denser than any material she had sensed. "The claw is not part of you."

"It is much more than a claw," Lukhan warned. "It has a will of its own and an endless hunger lives within me. I can consume the white flame of others."

"Death magic," Con'ra muttered in realization.

"You know about it?" Lukhan asked.

"I could only guess," Con'ra replied. "The color and taint of the claw suggested it, but only you could confirm my suspensions."

"You have met death magic before?" Lukhan inquired.

"Yes," Con'ra stated bluntly. "Let me say that my adventuring was not without merits. I have seen many strange and dangerous things."

"You traveled to the Black Marshes?" Lukhan asked.

"The enemy of my enemy is my friend," Con'ra chuckled sadly. "However, the black dragon that I came upon did not see it that way. I was attacked and driven away."

"You play a dangerous game," Lukhan grumbled. "I have no doubt that I would have killed you, had you not cast your spell in time."

"I do consider myself lucky," Con'ra giggled. She narrowed her eyes and smiled coyly. "I am lucky to have survived for this long."

"Strange," Lukhan snorted. "I think I have no luck at all."

"If we do not do something soon, my luck will run out," Con'ra replied. "I cannot manipulate the surrounding rock. The spell has a safe guard against that."

"What about air magic?" Lukhan asked.

"Perhaps, can you expand the air like you did on the surface?" Con'ra asked.

"I thought we are underground," Lukhan sighed.

"We are- oh, never mind," Con'ra snorted in frustration. Breaking the rock around them would cause the rocks above them to give way. The sudden release of support would bring a rock slide down upon them. "Then, perhaps, a tunnel?"

"A wonderful idea," Lukhan growled in sarcasm. "However, our bodies are encased in rock! What are we going to dig with? Our claws would wear away before we escape."

"Really cynical and you are so grumpy! I wonder why the lesser races enjoy you company," Con'ra giggled.

"No. I am a realist," Lukhan huffed. "I can be pleasant to be around."

"Where I come from dragons, are civil to one another," Con'ra mocked him with a superior tone. "I guess other clans have not learned proper edict."

"Yes, like torture and murder," Lukhan replied coldly.

Con'ra glared at him with the promise of death in her eyes. "Regardless of your crude and barbaric sense of the world," she huffed. "I purpose that we work together and come up with a solution to our problem."

"Our problem!" Lukhan growled. "This is your mess and crazy spell!"

"You attacked me!" Con'ra defended. "I was only trying to protect myself!"

Lukhan huff while Con'ra sighed. They continued to glare at each other because there was simply nothing else to do. The two dragons locked their eyes in a dangerous staring contest. Neither dragon was willing to budge at the invisible barrier that stood before them. Con'ra needed Lukhan and he needed her, but both parties were unwilling to help the other.

"Are you getting hot?" Con'ra asked in growing discomfort. Lukhan raised a questioning eyebrow. "I am- ouch!" The rock around them turned boiling hot. Lukhan and Con'ra squirmed uncomfortably at the heat which dissipated as quickly as it appeared.

"What was that?" Lukhan gasped. The heat nearly overwhelmed him. Black spot came to the corner of his vision. The limited air in the air pocket was still scorching and uncomfortable to breathe. His scaled flesh felt like it was seared.

"I told you that we had a limited amount of time before this volcano erupts again!" Con'ra panted. "It will blow soon and we have to do something!" She struggled against the binding rocks. Her already burn wings were tender to the touch and her armored scales felt like they were on fire.

"Allow me," Lukhan took a deep breath and slowly exhaled. His icy breath came out in small controlled bursts of freezing energy. The temperature within the small air pocket dropped suddenly. Frost gathered around and upon them.

Con'ra shook her head as the frost gathered. "Now, I am freezing!" she complained. "You stupid idiot-" A sudden noise interrupted her insult. The black rock around them cracked with spider line fractured.

Lukhan stopped his icy breath. "What happened?" he asked in confusion. "What was that sound?" He looked around in bewilderment and fear.

"Look! Lukhan you are a genius!" Con'ra gasped in realization. "That is our way out! Solids, such as rock, break whenever drastic temperatures are applied to them! When the next heat wave comes, use your breath and it will shatter the prison! Then I shall use my magic!"

"If I use my ice breath it will kill you," Lukhan warned.

"I will take the gamble! I will use my acid breath to weaken the walls around us," Con'ra replied. "My acid will melt the rock and make the rock denser. When it melts the rock layer, the reaction will make it denser, allowing the sudden change in temperature to break the rocks around us."

"It might work," Lukhan slowly agreed. "If we can withstand each other's breaths."

"Yes, I know, you have terrible breath," Con'ra cooed in reply. "It looks like we are going to have to work together to get out of here."

"If we escape this, then you are going to take me to my friends!" Lukhan warned. "You understand that? If anything has happened to them-"

Con'ra smacked her lips in annoyance and rolled her eyes at him. "Yes, you will kill me," she replied in a contemptuous tone. "Let us get started." She took a deep breath and focused her efforts on small narrow patches of rock. The acid hissed as it and the rock reacted to each other. Poisonous vapors were produced from the chemical reaction between the acidic breath and rock. After several blasts of controlled acid, Lukhan began to feel light headed.

"I feel drowsy," Lukhan mumbled.

"Stay with me until the next heat wave," Con'ra replied between breathes. "My acid is flammable. If you fall asleep, we will be blown asunder!"

"When is *yawn* the next heat wave," Lukhan muttered sleepily. The smell of acid was horrible and his lightheadedness grew stronger. His body felt like it grew distant. The seriousness of the situation began to drift further away from his clouded memories. His eyes began to close and his head nodded as he struggled to stay awake.

Con'ra shifted her focus from her work but the smell was overbearing. The silver dragon appeared to be affected by the harsh gases that rose from her breath. She took note of this weakness and smiled. "Hey idiot, stay with me!" she screamed in his face. "The heat wave is coming! You need to stay focused!" Lukhan jerked back in surprise at the scream and the echoes that followed.

"I am awake," he mumbled sleepily. "It difficult to breathe." His eyes began to roll to the back of his head. The intense smell of acid was overwhelming to his senses and he struggled to remain conscious.

"Here it comes!" Con'ra roared. The acid on the side of the walls busted into flames by the sudden rise in temperature, which awoke Lukhan to the danger that surrounded them. Con'ra screamed as the acid that had gathered around her ignited into flame. Lukhan opened his mouth and released the full fury of his icy breath. The frozen energy extinguished the flames and their prison shattered at the sudden drop in temperature.

"You did it!" Con'ra cheered. Lukhan gasped for breath as he looked up as the light poured down into their prison. A massive artificial fissure had split the side of the mountain. The green and silver dragons smiled at each other. Together they had done it!

"We did it," Lukhan corrected. Con'ra chuckled and gave a brief smiled in reply. A rumble from beneath them stopped their celebration.

"It is not over yet!" Lukhan gasped. From below them, within the depths of the crack a red glow appeared. Lava surged through the volcano's vent.

"Fly!" Con'ra shouted. "Stay close behind me!" They sprang into the air and flew upwards. Being smaller in statue Con'ra took the lead. Both dragons dodged the falling rocks and debris. More than once did they narrowly escaped being crushed against the side of the fissure.

"We are not going to make it!" Lukhan roared from behind her.

"Follow me!" Con'ra instructed. Lukhan fell behind her and beat his wings furiously to keep up with the smaller and faster dragon. Lukhan felt the surge of heat approaching from behind them. A gust of heated air gave them the boost they need to escape. They raced through the narrow mouth of the collapsing vent. As the lava was about to overtake them they escaped the side of the mountain. Scorching lava nipped at their tails. The volcano erupted in a spectacular show of fire, gas, and ash.

Chapter 26

"We made it!" Lukhan took a breath of relief.

"I suppose we did," Con'ra replied. They flew around the volcano which spewed forth molten rock. They circled back to the split they had caused. The volcanic vent collapsed upon itself but molten rock seethed from the splintered side. The crack appeared like a gash upon the volcano's roots.

"We are lucky that we escaped in time," Con'ra stated sourly.

"A deals a deal?" Lukhan asked. The volcano shook violently and a sudden gale of wind and ash threaten to blow them out of the air. Their vision was clouded by the choking dust that filled air and was obscured as a thunderous roar piercing the darken sky.

"What was-" Lukhan asked in fear. He blinked as a distant glow of magical energy emerged from the mouth of the cracked volcano. The light grew in intensity and his eyes began to water. A magical flare struck him in his face.

"It is the Blood Queen!" Con'ra gasped. "I thought she never left her cave!"

"What is this feeling-," Lukhan groaned. He blinked because the magical aura that surrounded the red dragon was powerful. The radiant light was so intense that it felt similar to looking at the sun and he cringed at the intense glow.

"What is the matter?" Con'ra asked. She noticed the silver dragon's reaction to the sudden appearance of the Blood Queen. She could not see the magical auras that lit up the ash filled sky. "What is happening?"

"Her magical aura is so intense," Lukhan gasped. "I was struck by something! I- can- cannot see. My vision is failing and I must land." His eyes watered and his body shivered uncontrollably. His movements were sluggish and erratic as he struggled for control. Fear of losing his eyesight screamed within his mind.

Con'ra had seen this before when he had turned into a feral beast. "Stop! Do not run away!" she called after him. "It is the black claw? How can I help you?" The silver dragon did not heed her question and continued to spiral down in a spastic manner.

"Leave him be!" a commanding voice bellowed. Con'ra turned to the Blood Queen, who flew next to her.

"My lady!" Con'ra gasped in awe and fear. "You have come-!" The green dragon was dwarfed by the ancient red dragon. The Blood Queen's ruby heart was the length of Con'ra's body. With every beat of her mighty wings, Con'ra felt that she was being pushed back by hurricane winds. The ancient dragon was so massive that the air twisted about her in spirals of black dust devils. The ash and smoke swirled around her like she was the source of the cinder sky. The Blood Queen was monstrous in both power and statue. Con'ra had never seen her out in the open like this and heat radiated off of her like a wildfire.

"Is this him?" the Blood Queen demanded. "Is this the outcast that defeated my beloved Orelac? The self-entitled worm that calls himself the Defender of the Lesser Races?"

"Yes, my lady! Please hear me out!" Con'ra begged. "He is not what he seems!"

"I can see that," the Blood Queen replied coldly. "He is the source of the taint, the last reminisce of the plague. He is the hatchling that defeated my mate but he appears sickly and fragile. How is it that this pathetic creature was capable of defeating my Orelac?"

"I assure you that he is not weak," Con'ra warned. "I witnessed him fight and kill Rohad, son of Iaolt. He has death magic and-"

"I shall see for myself," the Blood Queen replied. "I shall test his might with my own." She broke her hover and descended upon the blind silver dragon.

Gasping for air, Lukhan landed. Fearing that he was blinded on an active volcanic field, he had stopped moving all together. He could hear the ancient red dragon wings beat, but the constant rubble of the earth around him muffled her approach. The Blood Queen landed before him like a meteor striking the surface. Despite the sudden quake, Lukhan stood wide eyed and paralyzed by the sudden lack of vision. His nose was flared out in a vain attempt to sense the exact location of the Blood Queen.

"What have you done me?" Lukhan demanded.

"A simple spell," the Blood Queen explained. "As a master of the fire element, I can manipulate the flames of this world. A flare from the fire element can blind creatures. Under my spell, you are completely blind-"

"Con'ra, please help me!" Lukhan begged. "I-I cannot see!" He wept from the intense magical glow of the Blood Queen. The magical aura pierced his eyes like hot embers. He felt blinded, but the pain continued. Tears flowed from the corner of his eyes. He depended upon his eyesight to fight! He felt incredibly helpless before a powerful foe. She held his friends captive and he was unable to confront her. He attempted to break the spell by sheer force of will; however, the Blood Queen's spell was like being crushed by the pressure of the ocean depths. There was no weakness or waver in her concentration, the unrelenting force surrounded the Blood Queen's spiritual presences. He looked around desperately to find Con'ra's aid.

"She will not aid you," the red dragon chuckled. "You are alone." She turned her attention to the flying green dragon. "Why would this silver dragon ask you for aid? Do you know him?"

"I have met with him before," Con'ra replied with hesitation. "He is a proud and reliant dragon. What are you planning to do to him?" She landed next to the blind silver dragon. Lukhan's mercury eyes glazed over to a milky white. He continued to stare blankly at their voices.

"That is none of you concern," the Blood Queen stated. "You said that this silver dragon was a powerful warrior! You seem to be keeping other secrets from me."

"Is this necessary?" Con'ra asked. "Can you not simply speak to him?"

"He has already killed one dragon," the Blood Queen replied. "What makes you think that he will not go after me? I sense a great evil within this one. Much more than physically, but a spiritual element is involved. There is something else that is going on. I sense something sinister at work."

"What do you mean?" Con'ra asked. "What are you talking about?"

"My mate spoke of nightmares and horrible visions before his descent into madness! Silver, have you had these visions?" the Blood Queen demanded.

"You are asking me about nightmares?" Lukhan growled. "I will not answer any questions until I know my friends are safe!"

"A stubborn one, such a desired trait: loyalty is," the Blood Queen chuckled. "Even in the face of danger his concerns still fall upon his friends. I am really touched by the compassion you have shown to the lesser creatures. I have to admit that you have spirit. However, you look skinny and malnourish.

I fear that this will not be much of a battle." She chuckled at the blind dragon before her. He was not even looking at her. "Are you not afraid?"

"What do you mean?" Lukhan growled. He dropped defensively, sensing a pending attack. He turned his head so that he could hear the red dragon's approach.

"I could lie to you and tell you that they are safe-," the Blood Queen's words lingered.

"You better not have hurt them!" Lukhan roared. His eyes blazed to life in fury and rage. He sprung forward in a blind charge. With a thrust of her giant wing, the Blood Queen avoided his outstretch claws.

"You are fast!" the Blood Queen congratulated. "Let us see how fast you really are!" She struck with her tail. The massive blow sent Lukhan rolling head over tail. His body came to a sudden and abrupt stop against a jagged rock. He gasped in pain.

"Stop it!" Con'ra roared. "This is unfair! I thought the Red Clan fought with honor and strength! What you are doing is cowardly!"

"So it is," the Blood Queen replied.

"So why do you fight him like this?" Con'ra roared. "This is not fair-"

"Life is not fair! Where do your loyalties lie?" the Blood Queen demanded. "All that I have done for you? I have given you a safe place from your father. Why are you defending this silver? After all that this silver dragon has done?"

"Lukhan saved this world from the plague!" Con'ra snapped. "He has powerful friends and allies-"

The Blood Queen chuckled in amusement. "Yes, I have met those so called powerful friends and allies! Have you forgotten the lesson I have taught you? The lesser races cannot be trusted! Are you afraid of him? Look at him! He has shown such weakness without me even trying to provoke him, he charges recklessly at the mere thought of his pets being in danger. I wanted to see how well he fights and I am yet to be impressed. Look! He cannot even stand on his feet." Lukhan struggled to stand up but collapsed under the effort. He struggled to breathe in the ash coated air.

"No, it's that-," Con'ra began.

"I am not finished yet!" an unnatural growl came from Lukhan. He stood up on shaky legs. "I will kill you!"

"That is more like it!" the Blood Queen sneered. "Good! Good! Come forth, little one. Let us test you mettle! Let me see the fury you fought with when you engaged my mate!"

"*Ventus tempestas!*" Lukhan roared. A sudden gust of wind whipped and tossed the Blood Queen and Con'ra around like leaves blowing in a winter breeze. The violent gale sent the two airborne dragons crashing to the earth. Lukhan gasped for breath and the winds calmed as he grew weak from the unnatural spell.

"Magic? I think it is a little early in the fight to be using magic," the Blood Queen chuckled. "I am surprised that you chose that spell. It was weakened by the heated atmosphere around us and it ultimately did little damage. The air is too warm for such foolish and reckless spell casting. Air magic is suppressed in extremely environments. I thought you would be aware of this. It was a futile effort and a wasted spell."

Lukhan struggled and gasped. "What do you mean?" he asked. He had hoped that the spell would have broken the ancient dragon's concentration over his blindness.

"Who taught you to fight so recklessly?" the Blood Queen asked. "You are not the one that defeated my mate."

"I did not defeat Orelac," Lukhan gasped. "He defeated himself."

"What?" the Blood Queen snarled. Her tone lowered into a deep threat. "What did you say? What do you mean?"

"Orelac was a greedy, power-hungry fool!" Lukhan roared. He was emboldened by the anger in the Blood Queen's voice. "He desired nothing more than power and it was his undoing! He defeated my father through trickery! He defeated my mother by his countless plague minions! He defeated me through my friends! He was his own worst enemy! He expected treachery at every turn! He was a damn coward and so are you!"

The Blood Queen's face contorted into a look of pure hatred and fury. She shook at the impudent worm that dared to call her a coward. Her eyes widen in realization and she began to laugh hysterically. "Well done!" she chuckled. "You provoked me to anger! How amusing! However, I am not like my mate, I am no fool. Was that how you killed him? Provoking him into hasty action?"

"He killed himself," Lukhan stated.

The Blood Queen paused in consideration of what the silver dragon had said. "Of that I have no doubt," she replied. "Even through his emotions, my mate would not have easily succumbed to combat. He must have gutted you a hundred times before he had fallen."

"He gutted me once," Lukhan snarled.

"Really?" the Blood Queen amused. She took a silence step towards him.

"That was always his favorite attack then how is it that you stand before me now? Being gutted should have killed you. My own mate was killed twice by two different dragon clan leaders, Thorran and Stratos. How can two dragon leaders at the peak of their physical and magical abilities are defeated; yet fate chose you, a sickly hatchling, to defeat the plague's unstoppable leader?"

"T-That is none of your concern," Lukhan stuttered. His voice wavered in fear. Was she figuring out that he had been infected by the plague? No, the plague only affected creatures that had a white flame. He turned his head and looked around in bewilderment. The constant rubbles of the volcanic earth hid the Blood Queen's footsteps.

"Have you had nightmares?" the Blood Queen whispered.

Her voice seemed to come from everywhere at once. "Why do you care?" Lukhan snarled. "Dreams are dreams and they have nothing to do with me!"

"Yes, but they are also premonitions!" the Blood Queen replied. "My mate spoke of horrible nightmares and the permanent existence of the death element which would rein forever. He spoke of a destiny of blood, conquest, and destruction. He had forgotten his original element! He turned his back on the things we are supposed to protect!"

"He spoke of his visions," Lukhan replied warily.

"What of you?" the Blood Queen teased. "What is it that you dream?"

Lukhan shivered at the question. "I have come seeking peace!" he stated. "Ravenshaven has sent me to form an alliance with the Red Clan. They seek an alliance against a common enemy-"

"That is not your dream!" the Blood Queen chuckled. "Peace, you say? You have killed one of my clan members! Who is the enemy here? You speak of peace, but your actions prove otherwise. Even your pets desire death! Death for the Inquisition!"

"I did not want to hurt Rohad!" Lukhan defended. "I was afraid, and his fire burned-" Another lashing from the Blood Queen's tail sent him flying head over heels. He landed hard and his shoulder popped out of socket. He screamed in agony.

"Do not lie to me," the Blood Queen roared.

"He speaks the truth," Con'ra agreed. "Look at my wings. They were not burned on their own because Rohad attacked us!"

"Silence," the Blood Queen warned. "I shall find the truth in the matter."

"My Queen," Con'ra pressed. "Killing him will not bring back your mate."

"How dare you speak of revenge to me?" the Blood Queen snarled. "Your heart is full of hate for your father."

"My past has nothing to do with this situation!" Con'ra snarled. "He owes me a debt that must be paid and I am looking to the future!"

"You know better than to lie to me," the Blood Queen replied with a halfhearted chuckle. "You seek to use him for your own gains!" Con'ra jaw dropped at the mention of her motives. She was stunted by the accusation. The Blood Queen turned her gaze upon her. "All seek death, but fear it. You are pathetic and predictable! Your father has scarred you so deeply that you shall become like him, manipulative and conniving. You shall become his image and you have learned nothing from my teachings!"

"I-I do not know what to say-," Con'ra stuttered. It was as if the ancient dragon was reading her thoughts like a book.

"Do not tell me that you love this weak silver?" the Blood Queen snarled. "He is tainted! Smell the stench of that he emits. The black flame bound in mortal flesh! Associating with him and his pets will only lead to your death."

"Is that not what you seek?" Con'ra asked. "I thought you were going to destroy the humans. Have you forgotten this?"

The Blood Queen paused in consideration and contemplation. "Have you forgotten? I can look into others and see their true hearts?" she warned. "A brave heart does not back down and I swear that the Red Clan shall play their part in humanities destruction. I am unclear of your motives. You are usually easy to read. Have your motives changed? Are you trying to save him?" She turned her attention to Lukhan. The blind silver dragon continued to wander aimlessly away in a vain attempt to flee. "His heart is dark as pitch and his tainted aura is unpredictable." She then returned her attention to the little green dragon that stood next to her.

Con'ra looked away from the Blood Queen. "What do you mean?" she asked timidly.

"How stimulating," the Blood Queen chuckled. "I warn you Con'ra, these feelings you have for him is a weakness. Never allow them to cloud your thoughts."

"What about you?" Con'ra challenged. "Is your love for your dead mate going to bring him back from death? Change what he became in the end? Will killing Lukhan make you feel better? You know that Orelac was beyond saving! He abandoned your clan's sacred charge and ripped out your heart! This silver dragon should have your praise and not your wrath."

The Blood Queen snorted at the thought. "He is something different," she replied. Her glowing eyes grew distant as she looked at Lukhan. There was something strangely familiar about the silver dragon but for good or evil she did not know. It was like two extreme polarized elements tearing the silver dragon apart. The forces of life and death, good and evil struggled within him. The essence of good and evil had a certain disposition of the young dragon's will. His white flame was nonexistent and the black flame was held in check. Weather it was weakness or strength that kept him from dying, she could not tell. To the Blood Queen it appeared that he had already lost his battle. He had more in common with the undead than that of the living. The black flame had consumed him. How he still functioned was beyond her and it was only a matter of time before he turned into Orelac.

"I can focus his energy against the Inquisition!" Con'ra promised. "He poses no threat you or the Red Clan. Let me take him away from here."

"You are correct," the Blood Queen considered. "He would be useful instrument against the humans. No matter how strong you are, you are always stronger with allies. Nonetheless, he is the last vestige of the plague. He is no longer a dragon and he cannot be saved as such."

Chapter 27

Lukhan struggled for control but he was losing. His fears heighten his senses to the extreme. Pain from his dislocated shoulder made his blood pump through his veins faster and faster. Fury and rage welled up inside of him. Saliva and blood dripped from his lips. Yet he continued to put distance between himself and his tormentor. He did not want to lose control, not again. He had killed Rohad by accident. He had wanted to subdue the red dragon, not kill him. His body shook uncontrollably.

"I have one last test for you, silver," the Blood Queen announced.

"*Ventus contego!*" Lukhan roared. He swirled and extended both his jaws and claws which attached into the Blood Queen. His black claw drunk deeply as his quick strike hit true. A scream and an explosion of fire erupted from the Blood Queen, disengaging the silver dragon. Lukhan's vision returned to normal as he landed flat on his back. Ice grew on where he struck her on the shoulder, but the gathered ice quickly melted away into water and vapor.

"How dare you!" the Blood Queen roared. She raised her arm and investigated the injury. She bled fire that was the color of the ruby at the center of her chest. The wound flared and cauterized the damaged scales and flesh.

"My Queen! You are wounded!" Con'ra screamed.

Lukhan's silver eyes cleared and blazed with unnatural light. He began to chuckle madly. "You said you wanted to see me fight?" he snarled. "Then so be it!" He exploded into action. The wind howled at the sudden burst of speed. The ash fell away from the pure air that was summoned from above Lukhan's position. The hot and cool air swirled in conflict creating a whirlwind around the silver dragon. Cool, refreshing air revitalized the injured dragon. When he struck with his black claw, his dislocated arm had mended. The Blood Queen was caught unaware by the sudden burst of speed.

"I knew you were fast as the wind," the Blood Queen chuckled. "Con'ra, leave us!"

"My Queen?" Con'ra asked.

The massive red dragon examined her injury. "Do as I command!" the Blood Queen roared. Con'ra took to the sky and retreated from the duelists. The massive red dragon returned her attention to the raging dragon. "You caught me unprepared, little one. I shall not make that mistake again."

Drool fell from Lukhan's lips. "I came here for peace!" he growled. "I was attacked by Rohad and now you! I am tired of this abuse and no one kidnaps my friends and lives! You will pay for what you have done! I shall rip out that stone you call a heart!" He charged forward eager to engage the red dragon.

"Good! Show me what strength you have!" the Blood Queen sneered. "Let us test the fury within your soul!" She struck the ground with a thunderous boom. The ground shook violently and exploded with toxic fumes. Within these cracks, lava surged forth in geyser of molten rock. The Blood Queen circled herself in a protective wall of molten rock. Lukhan pause at the powerful spectacle that was being unleashed before him. The heat from the surging lava dispersed his revitalizing magic.

"How can you do this?" Lukhan gasped in awe. "How could such a powerful spell be conjured? I did not hear any words spoken!"

"Silly little dragon," the Blood Queen was amused. "You still do not understand what you are facing. I already told you that I was a master of the fire element. I am the red flame, I simply have to think of a spell and it will occur."

Lukhan charge at her, but was driven away by the intensity of the flames that surround her. "How did you obtain such power!" he roared. "How is that possible?" The fire moved with him, blocking any direct route to the queen. He jumped into the air, but was met by the fiery breath of the Blood Queen. He was driven to the ground repeatedly. Lukhan gasped from the effort and retreated from the circles of rotating fire.

"Every dragon is capable of achieving power," the Blood Queen paused and allowed the silver dragon to catch his breath. "You are a mobile fighter and you do extraordinary things to avoid my attacks. Was it you superior agility that helped you defeat Orelac?"

"I told you that Orelac defeated himself!" Lukhan huffed. He charged and released his icy breath. The firewalls collapsed under the frozen energy and the way to the Blood Queen was open. Using all six of his appendages, he launched himself through the gap he had created and landed before the Blood Queen. "I have you now!"

"I think not, little one" she replied with a chuckle. "You cannot extinguish my fire!" As if by design, the firewalls behind Lukhan rekindled sealing his escape. He was trapped within the fiery defense of the Blood Queen. "I have stolen your ability to run about and you are trapped inside here with me. How will you defend yourself now?"

"That is where you are wrong!" Lukhan chuckled. "You are trapped here with me!" He lunged and the Blood Queen countered with a backhand of her claws and bulge blows from her wings. Lukhan dodged the attack but his flanks and tail singe from the fires that rekindled around them. He held up his wings defensively to ward off the Blood Queen's powerful blows but those that passed through knocked him around like a rag doll. The silver dragon noticed that the red dragon was holding back. She didn't extend her claws or use her massive jaws to crush him, even though she could have done multiply times. Instead, she balled up her claws and used her wings and tail to pound him into the ground. A right wing struck him on the nose and made his eyes water. His defenses lowered and she latched on to his head and tossed him out of the circle of fires. Lukhan landed hard, which knocked that air out of him. Exhausted he laid there stunted. He knew he had struck her several times with the black claw, yet it seemed to have little or no effect. Not only that but no revitalizing energy flowed into him. It was as if she had protected her white flame from his claw's draining effects. He struggled to stand up.

"Impressive," the Blood Queen complemented. "You have wonderful defensive skills and you injured me several times." She examined her forearms. Several places on her right arm had been cut, but they were cauterized. The cauterizing flames seemed to come from the inside of the Blood Queen's body.

"I-I don't understand," Lukhan gasped in frustration. "What are you playing at? You could have killed me several times over! I thought you were seeking revenge! What is stopping you?"

"Oh, little dragon," the Blood Queen chuckled. "I never wanted you to die. Otherwise, I could have destroyed you the first time I saw you."

"Then you want to torture me to death?" Lukhan concluded with a snarl. "Make me suffer? To make me pay for what I have done to Orelac?"

The Blood Queen raised a questioning eyebrow. "I do not practice such crude and barbaric displays of malice," she stated. "I am the fire element.

Smoke will suffocate you long before the fire ever burns you. You know about magic. You can cast it, summon it, but you are reckless and foolish in your haste."

"You stole Fienicks's heart!" Lukhan gasped in growing anger. "Do not lecture me about the corruption of magic! That stone that beats within your chest; that is your life source and without magic you would be dead."

Her eyebrows knitted together. "Enough!" the she roared. The red dragon's eyes flashed with blazing light. The Blood Queen's magical aura exploded from her. Her booming voice echoed off of the distant volcanoes. The ground below them stopped rumbling and the magical firewalls collapsed around her. The volcanic rock groaned in protest and the volcanic cracks around them sealed and an eerie silence fell over the charred landscape. "I was impressed by your skills, little one. You have shown me strength, mobility, and cunning. You would have been a powerful silver dragon, rivaling that of your own air element."

Lukhan had grown accustom use to the constant rumbles from the volcano range. The sudden silence that the Blood Queen commanded unnerved him. "What are you saying?" he demanded. "Was this some sort of test?"

Her eyes sparked at the accusation. "There is no blame or farewell," she riddled. "Return my flame, I shall rebel. The trials are completed and done. Did you enjoy our little fun?"

Her rhyming words seemed like a distant memory. Lukhan's mouth dropped in dismay. "Y-you are Fienicks!" he gasped. "You are the fire elemental! How can this be?"

"Yes, not all is what it seems," she replied. "My real name is Fienicks, the leader of the Red Clan. I am known as the Blood Queen to our clan's enemies."

"I-what?" Lukhan asked in confusion. It did not make any sense. Why would the Blood Queen-or Fienicks- want him or his friends? "What do you want with us?"

"Such questions should not be answered within the open," Fienicks replied. She looked around the silence volcanic range as if they were being watched. She narrowed her eyes at something that Lukhan could not see. "We must return to my cave and know that you have passed my tests."

"You nearly killed me!" Lukhan accused. "This was some big test? How dare you-," he hesitated at this new information. "Wait! What about my friends?" he demanded. "You threatened them-"

"Your pets are safe," Fienicks replied. "They are within my cave if you wish to see them for yourself."

"W-What was the reason for the deceptions?" Lukhan stuttered. "The fighting? Why did you attack me?"

"It is our way," Fienicks stated. "The Red Clan values only strength. Therefore, you had to prove yourself worthy to stand against me and I will kill any craven. It was then that I tested your fighting spirit to prove your worth. You kept fighting, even when all hope was lost and you were clearly outmatched."

He looked at her and then the surround volcanoes. Soft plumes of smoke wisped into the air. The whole ordeal was both horrifying and exciting at the same time. "Y-You are not really a dragon, are you?" he asked. She nodded her head in reply. "Then what are you?"

"That is a question I shall answer within my lair," Fienicks replied.

⎯⎯◆⎯⎯

"Luke!" Bar cried in surprise. "What did you do to him?" The silver dragon limped into the dark cavern of the Blood Queen's cave. Fienicks followed in after him. Bar cocked his bombarder, while Judas drew his sword and waved it threatened in the air.

"Peace my friends," Lukhan reassured his friends. "I am unharmed."

"Nothing permanent has been done to him," Fienicks stated. "I have no doubt that he will recover."

"Judas, Bar, meet our host," Lukhan introduced. "Her name is Fienicks." The knoll and human looked at him if he had been struck in the head. They looked at each other as if it was a trick.

"What?" Judas asked. "The lava creature we first met? That firebird thing? That was- is the- the Blood Queen is Fienicks?"

"Correct," Fienicks replied. "Your companions are slow to understand. The lesser races fumble over simple ideas."

"I can understand their doubt," Lukhan muttered in discontent. He walked over to his friends and sat down on the massive bed of gold. The knoll and human appeared to be in good condition. The Blood Queen had made good on her promise.

"Two beings cannot exist at the same time," Fienicks replied. "Would you call your body and your white flame two different things?"

"A soul is attached to a body," Judas huffed. "They are inseparable! A body is a hull without a soul. The plague is an example of this."

"Then what happens when you die?" Fienicks asked. "Or become undead?"

"Our bodies remain but our souls return to the Holy Master-," Judas began.

"Our spirits are release into the hereafter," Bar corrected.

"A soul is nothing more than a vassal for the white flame," Fienicks explained. "Like a puppet for a puppeteer, therefore, it is the same for the body to the white flame."

"I do not understand," Lukhan gasped.

"Our mortal forms decay and die in time," Fienicks continued. "However, our immortal white flames continue to exist within the spirit realm, where they are protected until they are summoned into a new mortal form, destroyed, or moved on to the afterlife."

"I am aware of this spirit realm," Lukhan nodded. When he had died, he had experienced the existence of nothingness. "This does not explain the difficulties that you put me through?"

"I had to see if your words were genuine," Fienicks replied. "To see if my suspicions were correct. These are dangerous times and I had to be certain on whom-," She stared at Lukhan. "-or what I was dealing. The Mountains of Fire and the Red Clan are not accustomed to visitors, especially from the lesser races or outcast dragons. Our experiences have been bloody affairs."

"With such violent introductions," Lukhan snorted. "I can understand why there would be hostility."

"We have our reasons for such precautions," Fienicks replied.

"Precautions?" Lukhan huffed. "Was this all your plot?"

"It was Con'ra's idea to bring you here," Fienicks replied. "She views you as a high priority and now I can understand why."

"Me?" Lukhan asked. "What is so special about me?"

"You do not know?" Fienicks chuckled. "That is both sad and ironic."

"Does it have to do with my black claw?" Lukhan asked. He held up his claw to show his deformity. The black claw seemed blacken by ash and charred from its multiple contacts with the red dragon's blazing flesh.

"Yes," she stated simply. "Are you aware of Vilesath's history?"

"You know of Vilesath?" Lukhan gasped in fear. "No, h-he is dead!"

"Dead you say?" Fienicks chuckled. "What is death to the master of it?"

"Magic cannot be mastered; it is part of the ten laws of magic!" Lukhan recalled.

"Correct," Fienicks agreed. "However, we are discussing the elements, not the magic that can manipulate them."

"Elements?" Lukhan muttered. "Magic and the elements are the same."

"That is where you are wrong," Fienicks explained. "Magic is an illusion and, therefore, fools the senses but the elements are real. The red flame or fire can exist without magic. Earth exists without magic. Air exists without magic. The elements do not require magic; however, magic requires the elements to exist. One needs the other because it is a completely dependent relationship."

"What does this have to do with Luke's claw?" Bar asked.

"According to the dragons, each clan has an element associated with it," Fienicks stated. "Why is this?"

The three companions considered the question. Bar and Judas turned to Lukhan for the answer, the silver dragon could not answer it. He had no idea why the dragons were affiliated with a single element. He searched his brain for the answer. "Con'ra once told me that the dragon clans are in charge of controlling and maintaining the natural balance of this world. We keep the five elements in check."

"So this world would be destroyed if the dragons suddenly disappeared?" Fienicks chuckled. "I think not. This ball of fire and rocks would continue to spin if we were not here."

"Then why are we here?" Lukhan demanded.

"We are here because we are the strongest life forms," Fienicks stated flatly. "We have clawed and bit our way to our current existence. The answer: we are here because of selective breeding. A natural selection of physical traits that our forebear's knew was needed to survive in our individual environments."

"Natural selection?" Lukhan considered. "Where only the strong survive? I refuse to believe that."

"Oh? Then why are there only five dragon clans?" Fienicks asked. "The outcast clans are banished within our organized territories. They were not strong enough to face us in the past and they are shadows of our former glory."

"Get to the point," Lukhan growled. He had felt the sting of being an outcast.

"I have considered that question for a long time," Fienicks muttered.

"Why are there only five major dragon clans? It has taken me decades, if not a lifetime, to understand."

"Lifetime?" Lukhan asked.

The red dragon's eyes flashed with mischievous firelight. "The dragon is a mortal vassal of the elements," she boasted proudly. "Each element is unique and special. Each clan evolved to hold a special position of power associated with the elements. In doing so, we became part of the elements themselves. The dragon clans specialized in environments for protection and defense. As such they were transformed into what we are today."

"I have heard this story before," Lukhan stated. "I can understand the natural elements such as air and earth. Why did your clan choose fire?"

"The Red Clan's heart burns with fire because it is the element between life and death," Fienicks explained. "The fire element is the perfect pendulum for creation and destruction. It is the epicenter for all living things."

"Blah, the fire element is the center of creation?" Judas dismissed. "A little self-conceded, don't you think?"

"You do not have to look far," Fienicks explained. "The white and black flames are two extremes. Life or the existence of it is extremely rare, unlike death which is everywhere. They are two polar opposites that must have a pendulum. That pendulum is the red flame."

"Fire?" Judas stated. He rolled his eyes at the heretical belief of the Red Clan. "Every dragon clan believes that they are the most important. You believe that it is this red flame."

"Yet the world rotates around a burning ball of fire," Fienicks had an amused expression. "You humans call it the sun"

"That has yet to be proven!" Judas growled. "The Holy Master is the center of the universe-!"

"Hush!" Bar scowled. "Let her speak without you interrupting-" The two stared at each other. Judas had heard enough, and was certain that his friends were being played as fools. Red dragons only knew violence.

"Don't hush me!" Judas snapped.

"Quiet both of you!" Lukhan warned.

"Your pets are noisy and boisterous," Fienicks warned. "Makes me wonder what the ancestors were thinking when they created them. Giving them free will has had horrifying and unexpected side effects."

"You don't like our options?" Judas challenged.

"Enough," Lukhan growled. "Like I said, we are here for peaceful negotiations. Please continue."

"Our existence is a struggle for survival," Fienicks explained. "Life is simple and basic. We eat, breed, and die. Only the strong pass on their essences to the next generation. It is this strength that my clan has thoroughly embraced."

"What of those that are weaker than you?" Lukhan asked.

"They are little more than food," Fienicks stated evenly.

"How cruel and unforgiving," he muttered.

"That is how the natural world works," Fienicks replied. "Predators pick off the dying and weak. This strengthens the herd; or, in this case, the Red Clan."

"At the expense of others," Lukhan snapped.

"Then you would have the strong perish?" Fienicks chuckled. "Or worst, become weak? Whether you accept this reality or not, I do not care."

"Where is your compassion?" Lukhan asked.

"You sound like a gold dragon," Fienicks chuckled. "How ironic, that you follow the path of the life lovers."

"Why is that ironic?" Bar asked.

The red dragon turned her attention to the small knoll and a flash of fire escaped her nostrils. "I no longer follow the path of the Red Clan," she explained. "I no longer have anything in common with my brethren."

"What do you mean?" Lukhan asked.

"I am dead," she stated flatly.

Silence filled the chamber and the three companions stood dumbstruck. "Dead?" Judas gasped. He unsheathed his blade and held it defensively. "You're undead! Aren't you?"

"We are called elementals," Fienicks explained.

"Elementals?" Lukhan asked.

"Dragons whose elemental energies have consumed their bodies," Fienicks explained. "I am an elemental shell. The fire element inside my body has consumed every muscle and bone within my body."

"When I struck you bled fire?" Lukhan recalled.

"That is correct," Fienicks explained. "Although my insides are nothing more than fire, my flesh, scales, and magic still remain."

"You're empty inside?" Bar asked.

"Yes," Fienicks stated. "I no longer have a white flame because it was consumed by the red flame. Now listen to my tale on how I became an elemental."

Chapter 28

Within the dark bowls of the volcanic cave, the Queen had concealed her true identity. A creature made of not flesh and bone, but a being of the fire element. Fienicks had become a powerful creature called an elemental. Lukhan, Bar, and Judas stood silent as the elemental spoke of her own creation.

"Orelac and I were once mates," Fienicks continued. "He loved me, in his own way, and I returned the loyalty. Within the thousand years of our union we raised several clutches and put down several usurpers. Our relationship was of benefit. I provided him with respectable hatchlings, and he provided his protection from other brutes."

"I didn't realize that Orelac was the family type," Judas huffed in a low whisper.

"Hush," Bar warned.

"At last, the day came when I became infertile," Fienicks recalled sadly. "The desires of my mate were lost with our eggs and he sought out other females. His attention turned elsewhere and, in time, so did mine. I turned my efforts to our native element: fire. I began looking into our ancestor's past knowledge. I learned quickly over the centuries that fire could be altered, manipulated, and changed. I spent vast amounts of time and countless treasure seeking all the knowledge on our clan's past. My research sent me across the sea and to the forgotten libraries of the elves. I had many adventures along the way. I met both scholars and thieves."

"What did you learn?" Lukhan pressed.

"I learned the ancient way of the Red Clan," Fienicks continued. "Are wrong. It was then that I learned that fire was a completely dependent element. Just like all the other elements."

"Dependent?" Lukhan asked.

"Fire," Fienicks opened her claw and a small spark ignited within the palm of her claw. It hovered in the air and dance before the onlookers. "It is the only element that is nothing more than a chemical reaction. Fire is nothing more and nothing less."

"A chemical reaction?" Bar asked. "Like alchemy?"

"This chemical reaction is special," Fienicks explained. "It produces light, heat, and energy. It is totally dependent on the other elements for its existence." She closed her claw and the spark was extinguished. The darkness of the cavern flooded over them.

"I don't understand," Judas interrupted.

"Shut up and listen!" Bar warned.

"I thought dependence was weakness," Lukhan stated. "I thought weakness was not tolerated in your clan?"

"How true," Fienicks chuckled. "I was surprised by this. Fire is unique! It is life and death. Fleeting in the briefest of moments between the white and black flames. The Red Flame is dependent on the right conditions." She opened her claw and the smothering spark erupted into a searing ball of roaring fire. Judas, Bar, and Lukhan jumped back at the sudden explosion of heat and light. The fire rotated before the red dragon. She opened her mouth and inhaled the fireball. The flames jumped into her mouth and disappeared into throat. "Fire changes and alters the elements around it. Turning wood into ash, water into steam, and so forth."

"Fire feeds on everything," Bar concluded. He cleared his dry throat nervously. "D- did you eat fire?"

"Given enough fuel, the element of fire can change anything, including myself," Fienicks clarified. "Fire regenerates my body and, therefore, I must feed upon the volcanoes within these lands. So long as I remain here and continue to feed, I can exist for all of eternity. I devoted my life to the red flame and, in this case, dependence is not weakness, it is strength. Fire is an all-consuming force within this world, culling the weak and dead. Therefore, it strengthens the world as a whole. Fire culled my mortal form and transformed me into this." The ruby at the center of her chest grew brighter and the volcano rumbled at her command. Lukhan could see and feel the intense magical energy emanating from her. The light within her slowly calmed and the volcano fell dormant.

"Fire does have an important role, but it is a neutral force," Lukhan suggested. "A wildfire does not pick and select its victims. The strong die with the weak in an uncontrolled blaze. It is simply wrong to assume that it only culls the weak and dead."

"What would a silver dragon know of the red flame?" Fienicks asked. "I have studied the raw element for centuries. Speak your vast knowledge on an element that you know nothing about."

"I know that fire is not a sentient being," Lukhan stated. "It is both a destructive and creative force. The pine tree could not exist without fire. It is true that the old trees burst into flame, and with its destruction comes new seeds of life. The grasses are greener, the forest is healthier, and nitrogen is placed into the soil. It is a neutral force."

"Awe, you are both wise and cunning," Fienicks congratulated. "It is that reason that the red flame is between the black and white flames. Life and death are never kept in balanced or neutrally. As keepers of the red flame, we dragons can select our victims."

Lukhan's mouth dropped. What the ancient red dragon said made sense. All the elements were neutral. It was the dragons that made war with themselves and it was they chose to create strife amongst themselves. "I-I did not mean it like that," he stuttered.

"Notwithstanding our philosophical differences," Fienicks continued. "The truth is that the strong prey upon the weak. There are undeniable evidences."

"That isn't true!" Bar growled. "The Silver and Gold Clans took pity on the elves after the Elves Rebellion. They could have crushed them with one fatal stroke."

"The Mixed Kingdoms fought to protect the weak!" Judas defended.

Fienicks chuckled at the sudden defense of virtue. "There are exceptions," she conceded. "Of that I have no doubt. After all, the lion can miss its prey, the wolf can be out run, and the dragon can have compassion. At last, we have you. The Defender of the Common Races." All fell silent at the accusation or compliment. They were unsure what the red dragon was saying. Her motives were hidden behind fiery eyes that burned into them. She chuckled.

"What is so amusing?" Lukhan demanded. "It sounds like becoming an elemental is like being infected with the plague."

"Perhaps the weak do have a champion on the rare occasion," Fienicks admitted. The cavern fell silent in contemplation. The blaze in the Blood Queen's eyes did not fade. "Let me continue my story. Orelac was the most fearsome and powerful dragon that I ever knew. It was because of these traits that I fell in love with him. Even the strongest of our kind will succumb to death. The plague was not a strong or powerful opponent that he had to fight; instead, it slowly killed him over time, like to most insidious of poisons, driving him mad. An elemental is different, only the willing can be an elemental. It was bitter and ironic to watch someone you loved and thought invincible perish at an unseen force."

"The plague killed many in the same manner," Lukhan had seen the countless undead minions. The nightmare memories made him shiver. His father had been killed by Orelac because he was inflected by the plague; at least, that is what he wanted to believe.

"My mate went to the Dragon Council and it was there that death greeted him," Fienicks explained. "For when he returned, he was not himself. He appeared sickly and death reeked from him. He spoke of horrible nightmares and visions. He could no longer tell the difference between reality and the evil that plagued his mind."

"The plague was consuming him," Lukhan gasped.

Fienicks nodded her head in reply. "It was then that I saw a change in him. He was tainted. The other red dragons called for his death and to throw his corrupt body into the belly of a volcano. I assured the others that I could save him or, at least, put him out of his misery."

"The Red Clan agreed to this?" Lukhan asked.

"It was my love for him and the power that I had learned to wield that frightened the others into an agreement," Fienicks stated flatly. Her eyebrows knitted together and her words became forced. "I-it was my own weakness. I knew what he had become, but I could not do it. I could not kill my love."

"Didn't you try to save him?" Judas asked.

"I sought answers," Fienicks confessed. "I turned to our native fire, the sacred element of our ancestors, and that which I had been studying for the past three centuries. I was hopeful that I could save him. The red flame had always provided the answers in the past."

"So what happened?" Lukhan asked.

"I had run out of time before I could complete my research," Fienicks admitted. "Within our home, during one of my mate's multiple frenzies, he struck me. Right here." She placed a claw over the ruby in the center of her chest, where her heart had once been. "As I laid there dying, he must have realized what he had done and so he fled." She paused before continuing. She opened her mouth before speaking. "He was a craven and I thought he was stronger-"

"I am sorry," Lukhan whispered.

She chuckled at the silver dragon's apology and hardened herself, becoming stoic. "It was then that I remembered my training," she stated. "Within our hoard, there was this large ruby. It was not magical or special other than its size. With my dying breath I infused my white flame to it."

"You fused your soul to an object?" Judas asked.

"Yes," Fienicks stated simply.

"I don't understand," Bar muttered.

"The white flame is much more than a spiritual presence," Fienicks stated. "It is your being. The absolute true you. The body is a physical manifestation of this reality, while the white flame is the eternal."

"You're hurting my head with your theories," Bar grumbled. He scratched the back of his ear in confusion. The red dragon didn't make sense. Was she saying that an individual was two beings? A physical and spiritual? That did not make any logical sense.

"You are much more than a physical being," Fienicks stated. "There is an eternal white flame that connects us all. Fire is the medium that we as physical beings associate with it."

"What you say makes sense," Lukhan reluctantly agreed.

"It has taken me centuries to come to that conclusion," Fienicks stated. "I do not expect that a young dragon, a knoll, and a human would understand. Still, I shall digress and return to my story. During my transformation I learned many truths. It was then that I learned that the plague was not a natural disease but it was the Black Clan that created it."

"You learned of Vilesath," Lukhan gasped.

"You saw it," Fienicks's eyes brighten at the thought. "The spirit world is a place between life and death. I went to the same place during my transformation; it was then that I spoke to the Betrayer. He told me that he was once a powerful dragon who became the first elemental. An elemental of the black flame."

"Vilesath was an elemental?" Lukhan whispered. "Then that makes me a-"

"Not yet," Fienicks continued. "Dragons do not simply become elementals. A process must first occur."

"Wait! Then if I am, or will become, a death elemental, why must I feed on the white flames of others?" Lukhan asked.

"I am unfamiliar with the black flame," Fienicks replied in disgust.

"However, I can draw some conclusion from my studies of the red flame. Energy must have a fuel source. I assume that the black flame feeds from the life element. It does not matter the source. For instance, wood and grass burns within fire."

"Then why did the black claw did not affect you?" Lukhan demanded.

"You did not strike my heart," she stated. "Like I said, to become an elemental is a long and dangerous process."

"Process? Explain!" Bar demanded.

"Most dragons must go through a series of rituals to become an elemental," she stated. "During these trials, most dragons are driven to insanity as their bodies are slowly consumed and broken down. It is a painful process to turn into an elemental. Only your flesh and horns remain and you become a weathered husk, filled with raw energy. These are trials that are made to test the extent of one's white flame, which will eventually be consumed by one's native element and those that fail their trials die."

"Native element? Explode?" Lukhan whispered with a big gulped. He looked down at this black claw. The foul thing twitched uncomfortably, as if it was aware of their conversation. "Death is not my native element-"

"No, it is not," Fienicks warned. "That is why I should destroy you."

"Destroy me?" Lukhan gasped. He jumped up to a defensive stance. Bar and Judas followed his example. Fienicks remained passive; her glowing ember eyes gave no clue on what she would do next.

"As a death elemental, your only destiny will be to destroy," Fienicks stated flatly. "Please sit. There is no reason to destroy you, yet. For there is a reason why I have kept you and your pets alive."

"Why is that?" Bar demanded. "Wait! Are you planning to use us?"

"Yes," she stated simply. "A death elemental would be useful against the Inquisition and their powerful new weapons. Those that have survived my mate's cruelty may continue in peace. I have decided that the Red Clan will aid you in the coming crusade against the Inquisition. Humans are formidable and destructive opponents."

"What?" Lukhan balked.

"Are you accepting Ravenshaven's alliance?" Judas asked.

"This agreement holds only to Lukhan," Fienicks explained. "The Red Clan would never agree with lesser creatures. Most dragons are beneath me, but Lukhan is- or will become an elemental, like myself. Your potential has yet to reach its peak."

"So we have terms?" Lukhan asked.

"As long as you remain a living dragon and not an elemental," Fienicks pronounced. "Those that I choose to join you will fight."

"What about you?" Bar asked. "You are powerful. Why don't you join with us?"

"I must remain here and insure that Mountains of Fire will not fall under attack," Fienicks explained. "Although I am strong, red dragons do as they wish. My presence will insure that the agreement is upheld. It is not beneath my kin to destroy your city while its soldiers are at war."

"What about those who join us?" Lukhan asked. "How am I supposed to keep them in line? If we are routed, what keeps them from burning down my city?"

"Your victories over Orelac and Rohad have not gone unnoticed," Fienicks warned. "The Defender of the Lesser Races is known to us. They would be foolish indeed if they believe that they could defeat you. After all, elementals are not common knowledge, even among the ancients of our kind."

"Then why are you giving this knowledge freely?" Bar asked.

"Don't look a gift horse in the mouth," Judas whispered.

"A fair question, little knoll," Fienicks chuckled in amusement. "I have seen many wonders within this world, but I have never seen another elemental. I want to see how this ends."

"It ends with our victory!" Lukhan announced. "Know that we are not here for your amusement."

The ancient red dragon raised a questioning eyebrow at the silver dragon's statement. A superior expression of amusement played across her face. "You are bold to assume anything," she chuckled. "You and your city's fate now rest upon your own actions and abilities. Do not disappoint me; where others will fail, you may succeed."

"What are you talking about?" Judas demanded.

"After three thousand years, there is little left in this world that amuses me," she continued. "Consider yourself lucky. What Lukhan does with his future is-," her eyes flash with a fiery glow. "I will be amused no matter what happens." She placed a claw to her temple and stared at the silver dragon. Within her blazing eyes a look of curious awareness passed over the group.

"Then we do not wish to overstay our welcome," Bar announced. "We shall return home and-"

"Not yet," Fienicks announced. "To insure that the success and our agreement are upheld, I will be sending Con'ra to keep an eye on you."

"Con'ra?" Lukhan asked in surprise. "Why her?"

"She has proven her loyalty to me, and I trust her," Fienicks stated. "She can be-" She paused to search for the right word. "-motivational."

"No! I don't want her with us!" Judas snapped. "She is not part of this agreement. She'll not be welcomed within our city-"

"Enough, Judas," Lukhan warned. "We will take all the help we can get."

"She nearly killed us!" Bar warned.

Fienicks looked up to the cavern's ceiling. "Did you hear that, Con'ra?" she called. "The lesser races do not want you with them." The outline of the green dragon descended upon them. Within her claws, she clutched two dead camels. Bar and Judas recognized the dead beasts of burden as their own. She landed before them and bowed to the Blood Queen. The green dragon turned her attention to the human and knoll. A sneer passed her lips.

"Then how will you get home?" Con'ra asked. She dropped the carcasses before them; parts of the animals had been eaten.

Chapter 29

"She killed our camels!" Bar warned. "She'll kill one of us next!" Lukhan, Bar, and Judas stood outside of the Blood Queen's volcanic home while Con'ra and Fienicks remained inside partaking in private conversations. Lukhan reluctantly agreed that Con'ra would escort them back to Ravenshaven. Without her assistance, Lukhan would be hard pressed to fly a fully armored man and a knoll back to Ravenshaven. The long journey would dangerously exhaust him and he was taxed beyond his limits as it was. When Con'ra graciously volunteered her services in the returning flight, they didn't like the idea of the sudden and unexpected support.

"I bet that she'll drop one of us," Judas agreed. "Make it look like an accident, or she'll devour us and blame it on wyverns!"

"No, I think she is planning to sneak in with us and sabotage our defenses!" Bar warned. "Take us hostage for her sick and twisted amusement or some other diabolical means!" Judas nodded his head and looked to Lukhan. The silver dragon did not acknowledge their conversation about Con'ra's next plot. His mercury eyes looked up at the ash choked sky.

"Well, what do you think?" Bar asked.

Lukhan did not reply and continued to stare up.

"Hey! Wake up!" Judas yelled.

"Perhaps," Lukhan answered with a shrug.

Judas balked and gasped. "Really?" he waited for the dragon to continue. When no answer came forth, he threw his hands up in the air. "Blah! The Red Clan is trying to weaken our defenses! That has to be it. They are sending her to infiltrate Ravenshaven and I don't thrust her!"

"Is that what you think," Lukhan stated.

"Do you know something that we don't?" Judas demanded. "Care to share some information? I hate being left in the dark when I have a family to protect!"

"Wait! Wait one moment," Bar gasped. "You are not saying that you trust them? You don't think that they are plotting against us? Why allow them the opportunity?"

"To be honest," Lukhan admitted. "Fienicks has given me some comfort. I know that I am not alone. It is because of that reason that we shall play their little game." He looked down at his black claw. The ugly digit had fallen oddly silent and its annoying twitches had been irritating him throughout the Blood Queen's conversation. "She has given me a great deal of information that I must contemplate."

"Fienicks is not an ally," Bar warned. "She plans to slaughter the entire human race-"

"Bar we have been over this!" Judas snarled.

"This is why I was brought back," Lukhan stated stoically. "To help further the cause? You wanted me to fight in this war."

"What? No," Bar stated. "I-I wanted you to return to us."

"No, it was because you wanted to use me," Lukhan growled. "As the Blood Queen wants to use Con'ra and me! Ravenshaven! Everyone wants to use me-"

"Bull shit!" Bar snarled. "Get over yourself!" Lukhan turned sharply with his teeth bared. Judas jumped back in surprise, but Bar held his ground against the deadly glare. "Not everything is about you! Damn egotistical dragons! I wanted you back because you are my friend! Everyone missed you! Our mishap family is incomplete without you, stupid lizard!"

"Stop insulting me!" Lukhan snarled.

"You're acting like a hatchling!" Bar snapped. "Moping and sobbing about how hard your life is! Wake up and get over it! The world doesn't revolve around you! You have responsibly; you swore an oath the city of Ravenshaven! Now do what is right and stop thinking only about yourself!" They glared at each other in growing fury.

"If I may," Judas cleared his throat. "Lukhan, you're an asset to our cause, but you are also so much more-"

"An asset! You hear that, Bar? Thank you," Lukhan snapped. "For your honest option." His voice was clipped and strained. Bar glared at Judas in disbelief, the man looked at him in confusion and shrugged his shoulders.

Bar rubbed his temples and cursed under his breath. Lukhan turned away in disgust at the human's statement.

"I am not interrupting anything, am I?" Con'ra called from the shadows of the Blood Queen's cave.

"Why do you always show up at the worst of times," Bar gritted teeth and the hairs on the back of his neck bristled.

She winked at the knoll as a smug smile passed her lips. "Shall we be on our way?"

"I have more questions for Fienicks," Lukhan added.

"She will not entertain any more guests today," Con'ra stated snidely. "You have more pressing matters to attend to. Your precious city waits for its hero's glorious return."

"Oh, she isn't going to say good bye?" Judas asked with his arms crossed. His tone was low and sarcastic.

"The Blood Queen does not leave her cave," Con'ra replied smoothly. "At least, not for something as trivial as your small group."

"Why you!" Judas huffed. "She doesn't command-"

"Enough," Lukhan warned. "We have completed the council's goals. Let us be on our way. We do not wish to overstay our welcome and my questions will have to wait for another time."

"Words of wisdom," Con'ra cooed. "So, which of your pets will I be carrying?" Bar pointed to Judas in reply. Con'ra licked her lips at the tiny human.

"Hey!" Judas muttered nervously.

⊱──⊰

The four flew south in complete silence. Judas held on for dear life and kept a hand on his sword, expecting the green dragon to drop him at any moment, but the winds were fair and the air currents were easy to navigate. The returning journey was smooth and the desert air was pleasant. The ash choked skies of the blazing infernos had brutalized their bodies and clothing. Burnt patches and soot covered their normally fine travel wear. Even the items that were salvaged from the camel's carcasses were ruined beyond repair. They landed and settled down for the night. Bar and Judas said that they would take the first watch. Lukhan was physically and mentally exhausted from his engagements with the Blood Queen. He quickly found a place to lie down and rest.

"Why would anyone want to live in the Mountains of Fire?" Judas complained. He cleaned his sword with a half burnt rag he had soaked in oil. He looked to Con'ra for the answer, but the green dragon ignored the question. "Nothing lives there."

"It's a cruel and harsh environment," Bar agreed. "No wonder why the Red Clan is so temperamental. They have no taste when it comes to environments because they have to fight for limited resources."

"Lesser creatures would never understand the reasons of their betters," Con'ra chuckled.

"Excuse me," Judas demanded.

"Dragons chose to live in such environments," she stated flatly.

"I thought dragons were superior," Judas snickered under his breath.

"We are," Con'ra corrected. "We have scales as hard as iron, claws as sharp as any steel, and breath of the elements. We are the pinnacles of creation and the masters of-"

"Pompous speeches," Bar scoffed. Judas snickered at his friend's quick wit.

"What did you say? You short-lived rat!" Con'ra growled.

"I didn't stutter," Bar replied. He cleared his throat and spoke slowly so that Con'ra could hear every word. "Drag-ons are mas-ters of pomp-ous speech-es."

"Why, I ought to-," Con'ra growled. She raised a claw to smack the arrogant knoll.

"That is enough," Lukhan bellowed. The group fell silent at the silver dragon commanding voice. Con'ra glanced over her shoulder. The silver dragon didn't rise to his pet's defense, but remained where he sat.

"Enough?" Con'ra scoffed. "This little rat was making fun of me! He must be punished and he must be taught a lesson in manners!" She raised her claw to backhand him, but the sudden cock of his bombarder made her pause.

"Listen well, you big green lizard," Bar warned. "I'm not one of your slaves that you can order around. I have feelings and emotions that your superior black heart would never understand. You touch me and I'll put a lead ball through your thick skull!"

The side of Con'ra's lip twitched at the impudent knolls threat. She slowly lowered her claw and Bar lower his weapon. She turned to Lukhan, who remained in his curl sleeping position. The silver dragon made no move to assist. "This insult will not go unpunished!" she promised.

Judas stood up. "Careful what you say," he warned. "You don't have an army of wyverns or the Blood Queen behind you this time." Con'ra snorted in reply and flew into the night's sky. When she flew a safe distance away, Judas turned to Bar. "Always making friends," he chuckled as shook his head.

"Hey, she has to know that we aren't going to take any crap from her," Bar fumed.

"Well, you're not the one being carried by her, now are you?" Judas replied sarcastically. "If I'm dropped tomorrow, I'm blaming you!"

"I'm not afraid of her," Bar huffed. He puffed out his chest and walk around. "I'll fly with her tomorrow!"

"Would you two keep it down," Lukhan grumbled. He rolled away from them and rested on his side. Now that the skirmish passed he could fall asleep.

"Shh," Bar whispered. Judas nodded his head in reply. "I'm hungry and that green lizard destroyed all of our supplies. Care for some late night hunting?"

"Shouldn't we wait for him?" Judas asked.

"I could use a break from oversized lizards," Bar replied dryly. "Let him sleep." He was frustrated about the whole situation. Lukhan seemed distant with his thoughts, while Con'ra seemed to be taking command over their group. Bar would be dead before he allowed that to happen. Judas saw the frustration on his friends face. He agreed to the hunt, and together they took off into the Endless Desert.

Lukhan cracked an eye open and watched his companions leave. He sighed, glad for the peace of the desert winds. The darkness of his mind clouded his thoughts.

———◆———

"Hey! Wake up!" an irritating voice interrupted his dosing nap. He snorted and reluctantly opened his eyes. Con'ra's yellow eyes stared right back at him. "You were snoring."

"I am trying to sleep," Lukhan grumbled.

"It has been over an hour," she huffed. "How much sleep do you need?"

Lukhan rolled his eyes, shifted his weight, and groaned at his sore shoulder. He looked at the green dragon with blood shot eyes. "What?" he growled.

"Why did you allow your pet to speak to me like that?" she demanded.

"You woke me for this?" Lukhan grunted in reply.

"Well, he should respect me," Con'ra declared.

"Respect is earned, not given freely," Lukhan grumbled. "Now if that was it-"

"Earned?" Con'ra chuckled. "How do I earn respect? I am a dragon, it is my birthright!" Lukhan shook his head and lay back down to sleep. "Answer the question! Hey, you cannot fall asleep until you answer me! You hear me! I will continue to keep this up!" She prodded him with her wing, urging him to wake up and talk to her.

"Fine!" Lukhan snorted. "You cannot demand respect from the common races because you have to form a relationship with them."

"Relationship?" Con'ra scoffed.

"First, do not call them lesser or any other degrading names," Lukhan explained with a yawn. "Treat them like equals."

"Equals? Them? They are so much weaker and smaller!" Con'ra balked.

"Also, lose the attitude," Lukhan grumbled.

"Attitude?" Con'ra demanded. "Why do I have to-?"

"I need me sleep," Lukhan let out a heavy sigh.

"You want to fight?" Con'ra snarled.

"No," Lukhan growled. "I want sleep and not everything has to be a struggle."

"I must assert my control and power over those weaker than me!" Con'ra stated flatly.

"Not everything has to be a power struggle," Lukhan replied. "You cannot bully my friends into following you or respecting you."

"It is better to be feared than loved," Con'ra stated.

"What a lonely life that would be," Lukhan muttered. "Not that I am enjoying this little conversation, but why are you asking me all of this?"

"Well," Con'ra hesitated. "I will be spending time with the lesser races. I need to know all about my enemies."

"Bar and Judas are not your enemies," Lukhan muttered. "They are afraid of you and, therefore, they are suspicious. You must earn their trust, which will be difficult. After all, they are different individuals like other dragons."

"You mean that you are not going to kill your human pet when the war begins?" Con'ra asked.

"What? Judas? Why would I kill him?" Lukhan asked in bewilderment.

"Well, he is a human," Con'ra stated. "The same ones that killed the sacred herd, I thought that the goal of the war is to eliminate them."

"Excuse me?" Lukhan muttered. He cleared his eyes of sleep and looked at her in confusion. "That is not why I fight. I seek to overthrow the Inquisition."

"The humans must die," Con'ra stated simply. "I thought that was the objective of this war."

"No, not all humans are evil," Lukhan warned.

"You pet's armor is heavy," Con'ra complained. "If you cannot, then I could-" She let her words linger for a moment. He frowned at what she was implying.

"Listen to me," Lukhan warned. "Do not call them: pets, lesser, or whatever insult you can come up with. Treat them with kindness and, in time, they will return it."

"Kindness?" Con'ra asked.

"By the five elements, I thought green dragons were social," Lukhan complained.

"I do not understand," Con'ra stated flatly. "Are you mocking me?"

"Kindness is being friendly or showing compassion," Lukhan explained. "Come on, you know this." He looked at her; the poor green dragon looked bewildered and lost at what he was saying.

"Has anyone done anything nice for you?" he asked.

She thought the question over for a moment. "Sessess once brought me a beautiful flower," she recalled.

"Good, what did you do for her in return?" Lukhan asked.

"I beat her for not bringing me the correct thing," Con'ra stated.

Lukhan's bottom jaw dropped at her reply, he could not fathom how that would warrant such punishment. "What should she have brought you?" he asked in horror.

"I do not remember," Con'ra replied thoughtfully. "It was not important at the time."

Lukhan shook his head in disbelief. No wonder why Sessess had betrayed her mistress. "You are telling me that no one has been kind to you?" he asked.

"I do not understand the question," Con'ra replied.

"All right, hmm...," Lukhan pondered. "Awe, what if I gave you a masterfully crafted piece of treasure. It would be an act of kindness."

"You are going to give me treasure?" Con'ra inquired.

"No, it is a hypothetical statement," Lukhan explained. "I am being friendly and that alone is a treasure."

"So you are not going to give me treasure," Con'ra grumbled.

"If I gave you treasure, it would be an example of goodwill," Lukhan growled in frustration.

"You have treasure with you? Did you steal it from the Blood Queen? What do you want for it?" Con'ra asked suspiciously.

"You do not understand me," Lukhan muttered. "*If* I had treasure, and *if* I gave it to you, the treasure would be a goodwill gesture and I would expect nothing in return. It is an example of kindness and being *friendly*."

"Nothing in return?" Con'ra gasped. "I doubt that! What favors are you talking about? Who do you think I am? You are a silver dragon! Friendly! Now I understand your meaning! I expected more from your kind, but now I can see how sick and depraved you are."

"What?" Lukhan asked in bewilderment. "You can take your silly notions and shove them up your ass!" He growled and looked at her with an annoyed expression. Clearly, she did not understand the terms goodwill, kindness, or being friendly.

"Now what are you talking about?" Lukhan demanded.

"*Friendly*! Oh, do not act like you do not know," Con'ra snarled. "Pervert!"

"I am going to sleep," Lukhan grumbled. "I suggest you do the same!"

"Not with you!" Con'ra spat. "Any of your pets!"

"I did say- oh, never mind!" Lukhan huffed. She was clearly insane and had no clue on what he was talking about. He rolled his eyes and went to sleep. Traveling with her was going to be painful and the lack of sleep dreadful.

Con'ra continued to stare warily at the pervert. Half expecting him to pounce on her in a lustful torment of goodwill and friendliness, but the silver dragon fell into a rhythmic sleep. She could not help but wonder if he was dreaming about her.

Chapter 30

The nightmares returned; visions of shadows lurked within the darkness of Lukhan's mind. There was something there, with no recognizable shape or meaning. Chaos ruled the scattered images of the dragon's mind. The world no longer made any sense.

Alone.

"The time has come," the shadows whispered within his mind. "Wake up." His gut retched at the distant command! The scattered shadows gathered around him like jagged pieces of ice, the darkness held him and pierced his flesh. He struggled but the shadows drowned him in their sea of darkness. His body screamed in agony and pain. The smells of blood beckoned to him.

"Wake up!" the voice commanded again. His eyes fluttered open. Light penetrated through the darkness of his mind. Con'ra stood over him. Dazed by the morning light, he did not recognize his surroundings. "You were having a nightmare and- hey, are you with us?"

"Leave him alone," Bar warned. "He has seen enough horrors to last a lifetime without waking to see your ugly face. Luke? Are you all right?" The silver dragon blinked slowly at his surrounds, still confused by the realistic nightmare that meant nothing. He swore that the smell of blood was real.

"Well, I'm glad that you're awake," Judas laughed. "We brought breakfast!" He was skinning a mule deer. He worked his hunting knife quickly and efficiently. The skinned hide was tossed to the side.

"Do not waste that," Con'ra growled.

"What would a dragon want with a hide?" Judas asked. "You cannot wear it or tan-" Con'ra sniffed the hide and sucked it up like a piece of pasta. "Gross!"

"Hides are the best part," Con'ra chuckled. She glanced over to Lukhan. "Keeps my scales from chipping and keeps them smooth. Hey, Sleepy Eyes, you should eat more flesh. It will put some strength in that skinny body of yours."

"Are you complaining again?" Lukhan grumbled. He glanced down at the black claw. It felt distant, like it was asleep. He shifted his weight, the left side of his body felt cold and lethargic, the pain slowly subsided.

"You need to take better care of yourself," Con'ra huffed. "Your tarnish scales will not get you any respect. You are a dragon and you must maintain your body image."

"Oh yeah? Then who are you trying to impress?" Bar challenged.

"I-I," she stuttered. "Not you! I am trying to impress the world with my beauty and grace."

Bar and Judas snickered and rolled their eyes. "Anyway," Judas continued to work on the venison. "Did you two get any sleep?"

"Not really," Lukhan muttered. "Restless dreams."

"Well, one final push today, and we should be home," Judas gave him a hopeful smile. "I can't wait to be in a warm and comfortable bed next to my wife."

"I know what you mean," Bar agreed. "I hope that Sacul has recovered from his injuries. If he has, we can have a celebration!"

"Celebration? For what?" Con'ra asked.

"Oh, you don't know," Judas announced proudly. "My wife is with child! It's the little victories in life."

"A hatchling?" Con'ra asked.

"A baby," Bar clarified.

"When is the egg due?" she asked politely.

Judas and Bar chuckled at the silly notion. "You don't know much about humans, do you?" The human crossed his arms.

"No," Con'ra replied.

"Humans give birth," Judas stated.

"That is disturbing," Con'ra shivered. "How uncivilized."

"Don't worry, you're not invited," Judas muttered.

"Oh well, I guess I will have to miss the birth of another pink ape," Con'ra snickered. "There are too many of you anyway-," Lukhan interrupt her by clearing his throat. She turned her head and rolled her eyes. With a huff she continued. "My apologies, what I meant to say is that I would love to learn

226

more about your ways. I would like to attend your hatchling's birth process because I have always heard that the afterbirth would be good eating."

"Gross," Judas gasped and choked. Bar shivered at the image that the green dragon had placed in their heads.

"What?" Con'ra demanded. "I ate a deer once that was giving birth. The placenta is good eating and it is highly nutritious. A truly messy ordeal, but tasty."

"Please, let's change subjects," Judas begged. "Do you two want any meat?"

"I want the head and neck," Con'ra announced.

"We didn't get this for you!" Bar growled. Con'ra frowned and raised a questioning eyebrow.

"I am not really hungry," Lukhan admitted with great hesitation. He was reluctant to eat anything after his horrible nightmares.

"You haven't had anything to eat in a while, please, you must eat something," Bar offered.

"Yes, you should have something to eat," Judas agreed. "We have this!"

"All right," Lukhan reluctantly agreed. "I will take the liver and the hindquarters. She can have the-"

"Fine, fine, we'll share," Bar huffed. "After all, we don't want our Imperator's guest to starve, even though she ate our camels."

"Imperator? What is that?" Con'ra asked.

"A title that the Ravenshaven council gave me," Lukhan explained. "It is nothing, a title hardly worth mentioning."

"Status among the lesser- err, common races," Con'ra cleared her throat and Bar's ears twitched, but he didn't say anything. "So you adopted them as much as they have adopted you. How cute!"

"What do you mean by that?" Judas demanded.

"Dragons rarely welcome outsiders," Con'ra explained. "I am impressed that he established his position within your society so quickly."

"Luke is the Defender of the Common Races," Bar stated. "The world owes him a great debt, which we will never be able to repay."

"Really?" Con'ra scoffed. "He seems to get credit and I have heard several stories. I wonder which story is true. How did he save the world?"

"He destroyed the plague," Bar stated flatly. "Everyone knows this."

"Yes, but how did he do it?" Con'ra asked with a sneer.

"He used us to-," Bar began.

"He used you?" Con'ra asked. "Fascinating, please continue!"

"Stop it, you're mocking me!" Bar accused.

"Of *course* not," Con'ra stated as she rolled her eyes. "I am curious about how your champion saved you and began the process of becoming an elemental."

"You were eavesdropping!" Judas accused.

"Well, you were talking so loudly that an earthworm could hear you," Con'ra chuckled.

"Leave it alone," Lukhan stated.

"What? Why?" Con'ra asked innocently.

"Did you think I wanted this?" Lukhan asked. He held up his black claw. "I never wanted to become an elemental and this graft has caused me nothing but pain. If I could get rid of it, I would."

Con'ra stared at his claw with great interest. "Are you mad?" she asked. "If you have only a quarter of the power of the Blood Queen; it was that claw that saved the world and not you. It killed Rohad and Orelac! Why did I not see it before! I would give anything to have that power and to become an elemental; it would be amazing!"

"Are you mad?" Lukhan asked. "This affliction destroys the white flames of others! This is a curse and, to think otherwise, is foolish."

"To have power over the black flame," Con'ra gasped at the wonderful thought. "Death itself could not conquer you and it could make you immortal! A god!"

"That is insane," Lukhan mutter is a dismissing tone. "I have never desired immortality or power."

"Now who is insane?" Con'ra asked. "Any dragon would kill to possess such power!"

"Leave him alone," Judas warned. "The Holy Master is a demigod and he has power. Look at him, the Master is a slave to his own religion. Power always comes at a price."

"The benefits outweigh the cost," Con'ra boasted proudly. "I have learned from the Red Clan that power is only for those willing to seek it out and claim it as their own."

"Power, magical or otherwise, is not a toy!" Bar warned. "Power should never be used to abuse others!"

"Power is design for that," Con'ra replied evenly. "Only a fool would believe otherwise. Lukhan, have you learned to wield your gift?"

"It is not a gift," Lukhan replied.

"Fine," Con'ra snorted. "Have you learned to use your curse?"

Lukhan stood up and shook off the grit and sand that seemed to cling to him. He cleared his throat. "You are taking too long," he stated.

"What are you-," Con'ra began. Before she could move, Lukhan had struck, blood splashed upon her.

"Hey! What do you think you are doing?" Judas demanded in shock and horror.

"Great! You splashed blood all over me!" Bar complained. Lukhan held the severed hind quarter of the mule deer. The black claw had sliced through meat and bone without any effort. Con'ra frowned at the apparent display of power.

"Anyone can do that," Con'ra took the deer from Lukhan and with great effort, ripped the deer's neck from its body. "See."

"You'll ruin the meat!" Bar complained. "Stop it! Give it back!"

"Give that back to us!" Judas demanded. "You two stop showing off! This is our meal that you are playing with!" Con'ra glanced at Lukhan and cracked open the deer's skull, sucking out its brain. She finished devouring the top portion of the deer and licked her blood soaked lips.

"I feel much better," Con'ra smiled with pleasure. "Here," She returned the meat to the awaiting arms of Judas and Bar. "Tastes good. You should try some."

"We were, then you-," Judas growled. Bar placed a comforting hand on Judas shoulder to silences him. The green dragon could have devoured the top half of the deer, but she hadn't.

"T-Thank you?" Bar replied. He was surprised that she had left anything for them at all. They examined the front quarters of meat. The front and back ends of the deer were devoured. The section of meat that Lukhan had cut was sliced smoothly, while Con'ra half had been ripped apart.

"I tenderized the meat for you," Con'ra explained as she licked her lips.

"Luke does a better job at cutting," Bar stated.

Con'ra snorted in reply. "I still completed the task. Quicker than your little knives and now you have a smaller piece of meat to cook."

"So it would seem," Judas agreed. "Bar, help me set up a fire. We'll need to cook this up before the *other* pests get into it." They set to work, finding dried cacti and brush to burn. They quickly found what they needed, and with flint spark, started a reasonable fire. Judas and Bar took turns on the spit while the other gathered more fuel to burn. As they did this, Con'ra spoke to Lukhan.

"That interaction went better than I expected," Con'ra whispered. Lukhan shrugged in reply and inhaled the scent of the cooking meat. "I want you to know that I am trying to get along with your pets. In the past, I meant no harm to you or your friends." The silver dragon continued to watch his companions hurry back and forth between tasks. "Hey! It was not easy for me to give up that piece of meat."

"I know," Lukhan replied simply. "It never is."

"I wanted you to know that I am trying," Con'ra confirmed. Lukhan nodded his head in reply. She stared at him for a moment, but when he did not make eye contact, she snorted and moved away. She laid down to rest. Lukhan continued to watch his friends. It was only when Con'ra's shallow breathing reached his ears, which he chanced a glance over at her sleeping form.

"So, what are you planning?" Lukhan whispered. The green dragon mumbled something in her sleep and continued her peaceful slumber.

"You know she was staring at you?" Judas asked. Lukhan raised a questioning eyebrow. "While you slept, she was staring *intensely* at you."

"Kind of creepy," Bar added. "I think you have an admirer."

"What would make you say that?" Lukhan asked stoically.

"I'm an expert in love," Judas boasted. "Since I'm the only one who is married, you should listen to me. I tell you, she is crazy about you."

"What?" Bar and Lukhan spoke simultaneously.

"Of course, why didn't I see it before," Judas chuckled. "She has been smitten over you since the two of you met."

"No," Lukhan stated.

"You are blushing!" Bar gasped in surprise.

Judas winked at his friend. "Dragons don't blush," he teased. "Their skulls are too thick!"

"I don't know," Bar chuckled. "His wings are turning pink!"

"You two do not know what you are talking about!" Lukhan growled. "I know you are teasing me. Stop it. There is nothing there! It is your imagination!"

"So what are you going to do, Stud?" Judas teased. "Are you going to tell her?"

"Tell her what?" Lukhan demanded. "There is nothing to tell!"

"Confess your undying love!" Judas laughed. "Un-dying! Get it. It's because you're an elemental! Oh, never mind."

"Judas, stop it," Bar hushed through a chuckle. "Don't you know that she would never be interested in him?"

"Why not?" Lukhan demanded.

"I thought you said you were not interested in her," Judas had a broad smile.

"Grr. That is enough out of you!" Lukhan snapped.

"Stop it," Bar agreed. "A silver and green dragon could never be together."

"What does the color of a dragon have to do with anything?" Judas asked.

"Well, have you ever seen any half breed dragons?" Bar replied.

"Ugh! I wasn't suggesting for them to get married or have hatchlings," Judas complained. "I'm saying that he should get some action, if you know what I mean!"

"That's horrible!" Bar scold.

"What?" Judas demanded. "You don't get many opportunities to find love."

"Opportunities? For love?" Lukhan insisted.

"Judas is being juvenile," Bar replied flatly. "He is suggesting that you should couple with-"

"Get some action!" Judas interrupted. "You're single, she is single. I tell you that there is nothing like it, and-" He jump up placed his hands behind his head and thrust his hip back and forth.

"Sit down!" Bar growled.

"Don't listen to the old knoll, he has been out of the love game for too long," Judas sneered.

"Why you!" Bar growled. "I happen to know a few things about-!"

Lukhan rolled his eyes and sighed. "Your meat is burning," he stated. He shook his head at their foolish squabble and glanced over at Con'ra. She continued to sleep peacefully, unaware of the knoll and human crude comments. He was grateful that she slept so deeply.

"What?" Judas asked. The cooking meat had begun to char. Bar and Judas panicked at the ruining of their food. Lukhan chuckled in amusement as they yelled and barked orders at each other. In a vain attempt to save their food, both burnt themselves on the spit.

Chapter 31

"Home!" Bar cheered from the claws of Con'ra. His cheers were drowned by the buzzing of the approaching insect swarms. Blood sucking insects of every kind would descend upon the Golden Plains to feed off of the sacred herd. With no herds to feed upon, the large swarms had broken down into smaller, but still threatening, clusters.

"It looks like they are going to overtake us," Con'ra called. "Hey Silver, how about using some air magic?"

"There will be no need," Lukhan muttered. "They will be a minor annoyance until we get inside. We will have to suffer." Flies and mosquitoes had already begun to pick at Con'ra's wing membranes. She adjusted her flight elevations to keep the blood suckers at bay.

"A warm bed will feel good!" Judas swatted a pest away from his face. "It will be great to see everyone." Torchlight and smoke screens lit the perimeter of the walls, the guards wore hooded masks and mesh nettings over their faces. The guards waved at approach, signaling where they should land. Below them, a familiar figure in a white gown beckoned for them to come down.

"Ambrosia!" Judas called.

"Welcome home!" she called from behind a mesh hood. The two dragons circled once around slowing their momentum. So eager was Judas to be with his wife, he jumped from Lukhan's claw before they touched down.

"Watch it!" Lukhan cursed. Judas tumbled and fell flat on his face. He landed with a solid clank and looked wearily around. Ambrosia rushed to her fallen husband's side.

"Are you all right?" Ambrosia asked with concern.

"I would fall a thousand leagues to be with you," Judas replied happily.

"You dropped him?" Con'ra asked in amusement.

"He jumped!" Lukhan growled in frustration.

"I've missed you so much!" Judas gasped. Tears filled Ambrosia's eyes, the two wayward lovers embraced and kissed.

"How strange," Con'ra stated. The two dragons landed on the stone paved street. "What are they doing?"

Bar jumped out of Con'ra's claw and stretched. He smiled at the lover's passion. "It's called kissing," he replied.

"Social interactions between the lesser- err, common races," Con'ra commented.

"I'm sure you will see many more," Bar replied dryly. He walked over to Judas to see if he was all right. His friend appeared to be unharmed. "Hey! No hug for me?" Ambrosia looked up at the knoll and her concerned frown faded into a warm smile. She gave her husband a quick kiss on the lips before giving Bar a brief hug.

"Thank you for keeping him safe," Ambrosia praised. "And to you, Silver Lord; you both have my gratitude." Lukhan nodded his head in reply, his nose flared at the woman's sent. Ambrosia always seemed to drive his hunger. His stomach growled in reply.

"Didn't you have any faith in my skills?" Judas demanded.

"Wasn't it you who told me that your strength and faith is based upon the company you keep?" Ambrosia asked. "I knew you would be safe."

"Forgive me," Lukhan interrupted. "Is there food? I am hungry."

Ambrosia looked at him and nodded her head in confusion. The silver dragon appeared ragged and starved. Her attention turned to Con'ra, the green dragon appeared to be strong and healthy. The conditions of the two dragons were noticeably different. Despite Lukhan's condition, the swarms of pests seemed to only bother Con'ra. "Judas, is that the same dragon that you were trying to capture and kill?" she whispered.

"The same!" Judas boasted as he swatted another fly from his face. "This stubborn beast has agreed to fight for our righteous and glorious cause." The green dragon huffed at the human's silly and boastful nature.

"Con'ra," Lukhan introduced.

"A pleasure to me you, my lady," Ambrosia bowed.

"Etiquette?" Con'ra asked in unexpected awe. "How truly exotic!" She examined the woman's features through the mesh mask. That was when the dragon noticed the woman had one gold and one brown eye. "A rare beauty."

"Thank you," Ambrosia's cheeks turned pink in embarrassment. Her eyes had always been a feature of ridicule and fear. "I'm humbled by your compliment. Your scales are polished like the spring leaves."

Con'ra giggled at the passing thought. "You notice them?" she asked. "I have been surrounded by brutes and barbarians that know nothing about beauty." Bar and Judas grumbled in reply to Con'ra's jest.

"Form ranks!" a shout sounded over the buzzing insects. From around every corner and roof top the city guards appeared wielding bombarders, bows, and spears.

"Stop!" Judas yelled as he threw up his hands in surrender. "We yield! Don't shoot!"

There was a long momentary pause, before the captain of the guards announced himself. "Lord Judas, it's that the green dragon. What is it doing here?" he called from safe distances away.

"Con'ra?" Judas replied. He hadn't forgotten all the damage that she had caused the people of Ravenshaven. The trade caravans had been ransacked and the city guards now had the marauder in their sights. "Stop! She is with us!"

"Knight Judas, wasn't it your command that we're to shoot on sight?" the captain called. "The law states that all thieves must be punished according to the law."

"Murder for a thief?" Con'ra chuckled in amusement. "The lesser races are more similar to dragon kind than I thought."

"Hush," Judas warned. "I did say that, but-"

"Then Judas is bewitched by magic!" the captain bellowed.

"Hear me!" Lukhan bellowed. Silvia and froth dripped from his lips. "I am Imperator Lukhan and I command that you lay down your arms or suffer my wrath!" Despite the mesh that covered the captain's face, the white of his eyes grew wide in fear. The men that surrounded them dropped their weapons at his command. Some were so shaken that they abandoned their positions and fled.

"Wow," Con'ra chuckled as she rubbed her ear. "I thought I was assertive."

"F-Forgive us, Imperator," the captain begged. He had heard of what terrible powers the silver dragon could wield. His legs became shaky and unsteady. "I-I was only following orders and the commands of the council."

"Then I shall speak to them," Lukhan growled. The froth from his mouth did not subside.

"For now, Captain," Bar tone wavered. "She is a guest within the city, so respect her as such."

"A-As you wish, my lord," the captain stuttered. "M-men fall back and return to your posts. You solder, report to the council!" The guards quickly disappeared from the roof tops and corner of buildings.

"I have to admit that they had a good response time," Con'ra chuckled. "Although they are not brave."

"Luke, you need to calm down," Bar whispered. Lukhan struggled for control. His body shook. Mercury light flashed in his eyes, his lips curled back revealing gritted teeth.

"I have seen this before," Con'ra gasped.

"Luke, calm down," Bar soothed. With a final spasm the tension within the silver dragon's body disappeared.

"Hunger," Lukhan muttered through gritted teeth. His words were barely a whisper.

"Lukhan, we'll get you some food," Judas promised. "Hang in there. Ambrosia, we must hurry. Time is running out for our friend."

"What is the matter with him?" Ambrosia asked in wide eyed fear.

"I will tell you on the way," Judas replied. "We must move! Theses pestering bugs are killing me."

"Of course. Follow me," Ambrosia beckoned. The continuous buzzing of insects followed them through the streets of Ravenshaven. The shops and street caravans were closed and covered due to the invading swarm of pests. The streets were devoid of any mercantile actively, only the waves of bugs swept through the city.

"Damn these things! They are eating out my eyes," Con'ra complained. She shook her head, but the swarm continued to buzz around her. Bar and Judas struggled to keep the biting insects at bay, but it was a losing battle. Despite his companion's discomfort, the insect stayed away from Lukhan.

"How much farther is it?" Bar grumbled.

"I reside within Owen's estate," Ambrosia explained. "The city is safe during the day, but strange occurrences have been happening at night."

"Strange happenings?" Judas asked. "I thought Owen was going to keep you safe! Why are you out here? You weren't watching for me, were you?"

"I will tell you, like I told Owen," Ambrosia replied. "I will not be locked away. He tried to keep me locked up, but I would have none of it. He finally gave up."

"Yes, why aren't you under house arrest?" Bar asked. "What happened?"

"Much has happen since you three have left," Ambrosia warned. "However, we must go inside before we speak of it." They approached Owen's estate; a large wall and gate blocked any intruders. Ambrosia ran up to the gate and began banging on it. After a brief moment, a mesh covered man opened a small hatch of the entrance.

"Ambrosia? What are you doing out there?" the servant asked. "You're not supposed to be out! If Owen knew, he'd have my hide-"

"Mark, let us in," Ambrosia demanded.

The servant looked past her; his eyes widen to see two dragons at his master's gate. "Dragons?" Mark asked. Even through the mesh mask, they could see beads of perspiration appeared on his forehead. "You shouldn't have brought them! Please, take them someplace else! I don't know if we have enough room in the-"

"Open up or I will have the dragon break down the gate!" Ambrosia grumbled. "We are getting eaten alive out here."

"Of course, my lady," Mark replied. After three heavy latches were unlocked, the gates open. City guards and knights covered in mesh greeted the wayward company. Everyone poured into the courtyard and hurried into the main house. The doors were quickly unlatched and all went inside. The insects buzzing quickly died as the doors were shut behind them.

"Safe at last!" Judas sighed in great relief. He swatted those bugs that still clung to him.

"Welcome, most distinguished quests," Mark announced nervously as he took off his protective mesh. "Council members Bar and Judas! I've heard of your task. Does that mean that you were successful?"

"Where is Owen?" Ambrosia asked. "They must speak to him." Her soft words echoed off of the hall's high walls. Despite the grand nature of the main entrance, Lukhan and Con'ra felt cramped in the small space.

"Our noble Imperator is currently busy," Mark replied with a gulp. "He is in Ravenshaven's council chamber, across town. The council is currently locked up due to the insect swarms, but be assure that he sends his greetings and he'll be with you when the swarms have gone."

"When?" Judas asked. "We have important information."

"The council is in session," the servant replied. He shivered and stood widen eyed. "It is my understanding that they are not to be disturbed."

"What? Why?" Bar asked. "We've important news about the Red Clan."

"We're council members," Judas stated flatly.

"You know that most of the town is on lock down because of the swarms," Mark stated. "Please understand the current situation. I wouldn't recommend anyone to go out tonight." He looked at Lukhan and gulped. "In the meantime can I get you anything to eat?"

"Two goats," Lukhan interjected.

The servant glanced at the half starved dragon in confusion. "As you wish, how would you like them cooked-?"

"Alive," Lukhan stated. A sliver of drool fell from his lips and mark shook at the dragon's hungry stare and fell back on his heels.

"Do not mind him," Con'ra giggled. "Two goats for me please, cooked over a spit. I would recommend getting his food first, least he devour us all." She chuckle nervously.

"Y-Yes, of course," the servant stuttered as he hurried down the hallway.

"Don't we get anything?" Bar muttered. "How rude."

"He'll come back," Ambrosia turned her attention to her husband. "So you had orders to shoot Con'ra on sight? What changed?"

"She has caused much damage around here," Judas replied harshly. "I agreed with the idea of putting her down if we didn't return."

"Now I am a guest within your city," Con'ra was amused at the change. "The common races change their minds so quickly, how unpredictably humorous!"

"Listen closely," Lukhan growled. "I will only vouch for you once. If you do not behave accordingly, I will kill you." The mercury light in his eyes did not fade at the threat.

"I think the city is more afraid of you, than me," she replied snidely. Lukhan snorted at the accusations and closed his eyes. The froth around his mouth did not stop.

"We," Bar clarified. "We're risking a great deal by letting you into our city. I think you should shadow Luke. Until we get a better understanding of you and your intentions."

"You want me to follow him?" Con'ra asked. She glanced at the drooling silver dragon. His condition was deteriorating rapidly.

"Yes, I agree," Judas nodded. "It will be the only way to insure that you are not a spy or saboteur."

"I want to spend time with her," Ambrosia offered.

"I'm not sure if that is a good idea-," Judas began.

"I'm surrounded by guards and men all day," Ambrosia huffed. "I need some girl time."

"Girl time?" Judas huffed. "I arrived home! Can't you-"

"My mind is made up," Ambrosia snapped.

"As you wish," Judas grumbled. He didn't like the idea of his wife spending any time with the wicked green serpent.

"I would love to spend time with you," Con'ra casted a beaming sneer at Judas. The knight glared at her as he took off his armor and Bar set aside his bombarder. Everyone found a comfortable place to rest. The tensions on the road slowly faded in the safety of the hall. Lukhan and Con'ra lay down on the opposite sides of the hall, leaving only the main hallway free to move around.

"As I said, much has happened since you were away," Ambrosia continued. "There is a reason why the city guards are on edge. Those strange occurrences that I spoke of, it started with people finding dead rats and pigeons in the street, but then it moved on to house pets and livestock, more even more upsetting is that children have gone missing."

"Human children?" Bar asked. "What about the pups?"

"Yes, knolls and boarelves too," Ambrosia whispered. "The animals were found drained of life. I fear that it may be the work of a mad man."

"An insane knoll," Bar added. "Murder is not based solely on race."

"It does not concern us," Con'ra stated. She looked to Lukhan for guidance. The silver dragon rested his eyes, but the drool and froth had not stopped dripping from his mouth. "Correct?"

Lukhan's eyes fluttered open; he looked at her tiredly and considered the question. He thought of bodies drained of life and wondered if it could be the work of black flame. He glanced down at this deformed claw and shook his head in denial. "No, this is a local matter," he finally muttered. "Not everything involves us."

"Correct," Judas announce boastfully. "As a knight of Ravenshaven, I shall personally investigate the matter,"

"My hero," Ambrosia gave him a warm and mocking smile.

"Before anymore adventures, I think a good bath and a warm meal will do us right," Bar stretched and yawned. "Right, Luke?" The silver dragon closed his eyes in reply and did not answer. "I'll go check on the food. Judas and Ambrosia, did you want anything?"

"The stew is really good, I'll take a bowl of that," Ambrosia replied.

"Same for me! My love how is our child?" Judas knelt beside her and gently placed his shaking hands on her belly. After a brief moment, he looked up into her eyes.

"Our baby is fine," Ambrosia kissed him on the forehead. "Dear, I love you, but I think your friend is right and you need to take a bath before you meet our host."

"Yes," Judas conceded reluctantly. "Wait. What about our home?"

"Owen ordered that our home be abandon and boarded up," Ambrosia replied sadly. "I was told by your knights that several mobs had gathered at the doorstep with torches in hand, but the knights saved our home."

"I'm glad to hear that," Judas let out a sigh. "What about Marcus? What happened to that traitor?"

"Marcus and his family were caught trying to flee the city," she replied. "He and his family were lynched. If there was a connection between the Inquisition and the Marcus family, it was burnt with their home."

"I don't like it," Judas muttered. "I didn't realize that there was such civil unrest within the city. What of the merchant guilds and their illegal activities?"

"My love, since I have been accused of witchcraft, my family has disowned me," she whispered.

"I thought they disowned you when you married me," Judas chuckled. She smiled at her husband's joke, but the seriousness of the situation didn't fade from her face.

Con'ra poked Lukhan's snout with her tail. The silver dragon opened his eyes and shrugged. Con'ra groaned and turned her attention back to Ambrosia. "There, there, little one," she cooed. "I am here for you." She roughly patted Ambrosia on the head like a dog. The patting nearly knocked the woman over.

"Back, worm!" Judas hissed.

"Judas, calm down," Ambrosia added. "Con'ra, you must be gentler with me. I can't take such abuse."

"Sorry," Con'ra apologized. "I did not mean to harm you." She withdrew from them and sulked in the corner.

"What's going on in here? I heard raised voices!" Bar hurried back into the main hall.

"That green worm struck my wife!" Judas growled.

"Please, Judas!" Ambrosia hushed. "Calm down, I'm unharmed."

"You should be more careful!" Bar warned. "Is your head filled with lead?"

"No," Con'ra grumbled. She muttered curses under her breath.

"Do that again and I will fill it full!" Bar threatened.

"Bar, Judas! I'm fine!" Ambrosia stated evenly. "I'm much tougher than you think."

"But-," Judas began.

"I'm fine," Ambrosia stressed. "Stop threatening her. She is our guest! Wasn't it you two who told me to be kind to her?" She pointed to Lukhan, the silver dragon still had is eyes closed. He appeared distant from his surroundings.

"Y-Yes, but-," Judas stuttered. "I don't want to see you hurt!"

"I've been taking care of myself since you have been away," Ambrosia stated. "I don't need a white knight to save me. I need my husband."

"Con'ra she's a-," Judas began.

"A guest," Ambrosia stated flatly. "Treat her as such." Judas scowl at the thought and looked to Bar for guidance.

"Hey man, I'd do what she says," Bar gave them a shrug.

Judas rolled his eyes and sighed. "A guest," he mumbled.

The clattering of bells and the bleat of goats entered the main hall. "I've brought you two goats-" Mark began. The man's final words never passed his lips. Lukhan moved with demonic speed, the two goats and the man's body were quickly torn apart. Ambrosia screamed in horror as the gore covered silver dragon turned his attention to her.

"Oh shit," Bar gasped.

Chapter 32

All stared dumbfounded at the shocking and unexpected slaughter. Lukhan's face was contorted in a look of possessed rage. The black claw fed greedily on the bodies; it ripped them apart and sucked all life and blood. Gore smeared both dragon and the wall.

"L-Luke?" Bar stuttered and gulped. "You need to calm down." The silver dragon didn't recognize his voice and appeared to be beyond reason. The darkness within Lukhan had taken control. Bar hadn't expected this. In the past, Lukhan had only turned aggressive when his life was endangered, yet within the safe confines of Owen's house, he had butchered a man! Now, his longtime companion looked at him with death in his eyes.

"We've been careless," Judas whispered. He slowly pushed Ambrosia behind him. The dragon's pupils narrowed and focused on his wife. "The madness has taken him." He glanced down at his armor and weapons. He knew that Lukhan would be killed twice over before he could bend down and retrieve them. A sliver of drool fell from the dragon's lips.

"I assume that you did not expect him to do that?" Con'ra sneered. "You can take the dragon out of the wild, but not the wild out of the dragon." She shifted her weight and flared her nose. She took a deep breath; the odor of the silver dragon had changed. "I knew something like this would happen."

Lukhan charged, eager for more blood. Con'ra roared and sprang forward blocking Lukhan's route to Ambrosia. The two dragons clashed, Con'ra forced herself under Lukhan and pushed up with all of her might. The silver dragon smashed into the ceiling of the great hall. A great rumbled sounded through the building. She screamed in agony as the black claw sank into her neck.

"Run!" Judas roared. The three ran out of the crumbling structure as

Lukhan and Con'ra continued their battle inside. With a great moan, the hall came crashing down upon the engaged dragons.

"My Lords!" the guards and knights came racing to their aid. "What happened? What is going on?" A plume of dust and debris rushed over them.

"Be on guard!" Judas ordered. "To arms, make ready for battle! Our friend has gone mad!" With a great heave, the dust-covered silver dragon emerged with a roar. Swords, spears, and bombarders were brought to bear against the emerging dragon.

"The silver dragon!" mummers of fear arose among the ranks of soldier. Lukhan shook off the dust, his mercury eyes glowed with rage. The Con'ra's blood dribbled out of his jaws the soldiers fell away from the rubble.

"Wait!" Bar yelled.

"Shoot him!" Judas commanded.

"No!" Bar screamed. The thunder of bombarder fire drowned his order. Lukhan screamed in agony as the bullets pierced his flesh. He charged into the ranks of men and knolls. Spears were thrust into his chest, swords cleaved his arms, bullets pierced his wing membranes, and yet for every wound he received, the soldiers were ripped apart. His rage was fueled by the injuries he received. Men and knolls were scattered into the air like matchsticks.

"We must save him!" Bar ordered. "Stop fighting him!" His words were drowned in the chaos of battle. The bloody corpse of a guard was flung passed them.

"We must flee!" Ambrosia cried. "Come with us!"

"No, my place is here!" Bar replied. "Judas, we must get him in the stable! We must contain him and use the gas-!"

"He has gone!" Judas snapped. "He can't be saved! He'll destroy the city before he is contained! Run, Ambrosia! Run!" His wife starred at him in fear.

"What are you planning to do-?" Ambrosia began to ask.

"Damn it! Run!" Judas snarled and she fled out of the courtyard.

"This is madness!" Bar whispered in disbelief. "What are you planning on doing?"

"I need a weapon!" Judas ordered. He grabbed the nearest bombarder and took aim at Lukhan. There was a cold and focused expression on the man's face.

"No!" Bar screamed. He charged at the knight in a vain attempt to stop him. Judas pulled the trigger. The bombarder fired before Bar tackled him to the ground. The bullet strayed and struck Lukhan's glowing eye. The dragon reared back in screaming anguish and covered his left eye. He thrashed and coiled like a snake, scratching and tearing at the side of his face. The black claw sliced through Lukhan's flesh in his frenzied painful anguish. His own blood poured down the side of his face.

"Stop! Damn it!" Bar growled. The human and knoll fought each other over the bombarder.

"It is our duty to protect this city!" Judas roared.

"I will protect Luke," Bar growled. He struck Judas in the face, the blow knocking both of them down. They continued to trade punches and kicks, both fighting for something they loved. The weapon was tossed aside and the two friends bit and clawed at each other.

"Shoot him!" Judas commanded to the remaining guards. "Shoot him!" Those guards that were still alive cautiously circled the thrashing dragon and began stabbing him with spears. The added injuries only spurred on the dragon's blood frenzy. Lukhan opened his jaws and released a blast of freezing energy upon the guards. Those who were caught in the frozen energy became statues of ice.

"You will not harm him!" Bar snarled. The knoll grabbed on to Judas's arm. The knight struck him in the snout which broke under the pressure. Bar drew out his hidden dagger and began stabbing Judas repeatedly in the gut. Judas grabbed hold of the blade in a vain attempt to slow the knoll's bloody frenzy. The man stood in wide eyed fear, his knees buckled and he slumped to the ground. He weakly grabbed his guts before his innards fell out.

"Why Bar?" Judas choked on bloody coughs. His strength failed and his eyes rolled to the back of his head. Bar released the man's shirt and kicked him down. "Fool! Knolls and humans could never be allies! You killed my family!"

"No!" Ambrosia screamed. "I'll kill you, bastard!" Bar turned to see a bombarder leveled directly at him. "Die beast!"

"Wait, stop!" Bar raised his hands up and dropped his weapon. The woman's weapon fired and a cloud of grey smoke swashed over him. The lead ball pierced Bar's chest and the knoll howled in agony and fell backwards. Bar clawed desperately at the wound, twisting and turning, and then he suddenly went limp and laid still.

Tears filled Ambrosia's eyes as she raced to her husband's side. Her husband's face was pale and his eyes were like faded glass. She grabbed her lover's head and gently placed him in her lap. She began to shake back and forth, tears streaming down her face. She looked up into the sky and screamed.

Her scream drew the attention of Lukhan. The silver dragon had finished off the last of the guards and knights. A half devoured corpse of a man was still in his mouth. Blood and gore dripped from his jaws. His body was engorged on the flesh and souls of the living. With his one good eye, he looked at the pain stricken woman with hunger. He had restrained himself for too long. How would the woman's tender flesh taste? His nose flared, inhaling the fresh scent of blood, bile, and Ambrosia's warm flesh. Her scent was intoxicating.

Ambrosia noticed the sudden silence that surrounded her. She looked up to see a black claw coming down to take her. There was no time to scream or run, the only sound was the dry gasp of her soul and flesh being absorbed by the black claw.

"No, this cannot be," Lukhan thought. *"I should have more control."* Bloody tears filled his eye; his body had reacted on its own accord. The bodies of his companions laid flung about him, their dead eyes stared at the chaos he'd sown. Lukhan was efficient in his slaughter, no death rattle or cries of pain, not even a final gasp for life. The gore covered courtyard was in complete and total silence. Lukhan gasped at what he had done. Grief stricken pain surged through his body. He fell over in anguish. Bar, Judas, and Ambrosia laid together in horrific silence.

"What's going on here?" a shout arose from the outside of the wall. "Open up! In the name of the council! We heard screams! Break it down!" Lukhan tried to open his mouth to speak, but nothing came out. He exhaled in a vain attempt to warn them, to keep them away from him, yet there was a deep seated hunger with in him. The pressure of endless hunger kept him from warning them. Then suddenly, with a thunderous boom, the gates were blown open. Owen, Sacul, and the Ravenshaven council members came pouring into the courtyard.

"Lukhan?" Sacul gasped. "W-what has happen?" Lukhan turned; an evil and bloody sneer was splattered across his face. He pounced upon them, eager to devour their flesh. Sacul was so surprise that he was the first to be slain, his body cut in two. Owen was the next to fall; his white fur was a door mat in which Lukhan dyed red. The council screamed and turned to flee. Others drew their personal weapons but were quickly cut down. Lukhan widened his stance and began to cleave those nearest to him. Council members were pushed down and crushed under foot. The council was quickly dispatched and massacred. His attention turned to the city that surrounded him. A tear filled smiled past over his blood covered face.

"This is not real!" Lukhan told himself. *"I cannot see their or feel souls!"*

Lukhan stumbled through the air in exhaustion and fear. The city of Ravenshaven burned behind him. He shivered in panic at the slaughter he had caused, the screams of innocent children and pups still ringing in his ears. He looked down at the black claw; it seemed to take pleasure in his suffering. The deformed appendage moved and grew up his forearm like blacken tentacles. The black flesh crawled through his skin and into his chest. Pounding agony surged where his heart had once been. Lukhan gasped and choked as the suffocating tentacles surrounded his innards. His insides felt like they were on fire. He fell from of the sky; those he had tried to protect had been slaughtered by his own claw.

Lukhan awoke to the whinny of horses and the thundering marching of hundreds of thousands of feet. He struggled to stand up. His insides burned with the continuing rage of an internal fire. His eternal hunger drove him to stand.

"Lukhan, you will pay for what you have done!" a bellow from above announced. The full might of the Magi, Inquisition, and Ravenshaven's army marched against him. Bombarders, rangers, and knights on horseback were all aligned against him. Tears fell from his tired eyes; the world had turned against him. Lukhan chuckled at the pitiful armies and charged into their ranks. Bombarder fire, steel blades, and countless brave soldiers were thrown at him. His flesh and wings were sliced, broken, brutalized beyond recognition, and yet the black claw fed. His body slowly transformed into that of a corpse, his battered flesh hung loosely off of him and was pulled tight by the regenerating powers of the black claw. Flesh that were blown away or cut off was replaced by the black flesh, until the last soldier fell before Lukhan's fury.

"This is not real," Lukhan muttered in gasping exhaustion. *"I must be stopped."* He looked around the battlefield; men, elves, boarelves, and knolls lay dead. Blood and metal covered the fields of gore. The lesser races united to defeat him? What happened? How long had be slept? He shook his head. Nothing made sense any more.

"Now you die!" a roar from above him announced. "The world shall be protected from you!" Lukhan looked up to see the dragon clans descending upon him. Gold, silver, red, green, and black dragons circled the sky around him. Their numbers blotted out the sun. Vatara and his mother Crystal led the way; the dragon clans struck with their united might. Unleashing their combined breaths upon him and those on the battlefield. Lukhan raised his wings and claws defensively, but the blasts melted through his weak and pathetic defense. His flesh disintegrated and was melted down to the bone.

"No, this is not real! Stop this madness!" Lukhan screamed in mute silence. His jaws moved back and forth, but with no lungs or vocal cords, he could not speak. As nothing more than a skeleton, he stood up and looked at the circling dragons. He could see each dragon soul, blazing like starlight; their white flames were circling lights he could sense. He looked down at his own aura. It was pitch black and instead of sending out an aura, it was more akin to a black hole absorbing the illuminated auras of the circling dragons. The world suddenly withered and died.

"Fly!" Vatara screamed.

The world heaved and the sky turned red as Lukhan's magical aura washed over the circling dragons. Their white flames were suddenly extinguished. They screamed in agony as their souls were absorbed into Lukhan's black aura. The dragons fell out of the sky and crashed on the ground, their bodies drained of life. He looked down at the black claw. The world heaved at the sudden change. The world split and cracked, lava came spewing forth, tornados blow across the land. Then suddenly no fire burned, no wind blew, nothing gave birth or died, the world was completely devoid of all elements. All but one.

"This is unreal," Lukhan thought. *"What is happening to me? I am an elemental!"* The black flame ruled supreme, his black claw having no others to feed upon turned on its master. Lukhan screamed as the claw's hunger turn on him, his bones turned to ash and fell on a dead world, ruled by the black flame.

"Behold the future of the black flame," a deep and angelical voice announced. Lukhan turned his attention to the angelical figure that levitated before him. The hooded figure wore a cloak that covered his face. He floated effortlessly in the crimson sky. A glowing five pointed star rested as a halo over his head. A white magical aura swirled around him. Lukhan's eyes watered at the glowing figure that floated in the darkened skies of a dead world.

"Y-You are the Holy Master!" Lukhan gasped.

"No," the cloaked figure announced. "I am the Inquisitor Lord Shen Tianxiang. I have sought you out, Lukhan, son of Stratos."

"This is an illusion!" Lukhan growled. "It is a trick!"

"I will not lie," Shen stated. "What you see before you is your worst fears revealed. I am showing you the truth of your nature. These fears you have within you are more than imagination. This is your destiny." He held out his hand and gestured to the dead world around them.

"Fears?" Lukhan asked. "Where am I? What is this place?"

"You are asleep," Shen stated. "I desired to see what the new Lord of Death fears; I am surprised that you care for life at all. It is a trait that will pass in time."

"New Lord of Death?" Lukhan asked. "What do you mean? Speak plainly!"

"You must be unaware of your own prophecy," Shen mocked. "I am not surprised because there are few who are ever aware of fate. I am surprised that Vilesath did not tell you."

"You know Vilesath!" Lukhan snarled.

"You have confirmed my suspicions," Shen replied. "The Betrayer is dead, and yet, his legacy still exists."

"Tell me what you know about him!"

"Think of the Betrayer and the Holy Master as two opposing forces in this world, that is all you need to know." Shen held out a hand and the illusionary world wavered for a brief moment and then corrected itself.

"You must be using a great deal of white flame to communicate with me," Lukhan growled. "I thought the Inquisition loathed those who use magic! The distance from here to the city of Alkaline is staggering. I wonder how it is that you can invade my dreams." The hooded figure turned his head to the side.

"The white flames of men are the Holy Master's to judge, not I," Shen explained. "As a dragon, you are ignorant in the ways of our religion."

"Judas has spoken of your ways," Lukhan snapped. "You and those who serve you are under the illusion of power! Your god is nothing more than a deception."

"Dragons do not see true divinity when they look at it," Shen replied. "Through my studies, I have learned that dragons have always been an independent race, extremely difficult to control. Their elemental and magical powers give them a false sense of accomplishment. They could never bow or humble themselves to a cause."

"It sounds false, since that statement comes from a man who worships a self-declared god!" Lukhan growled. "Now that you have invaded my mind! You are under my command!" The cloaked figure fell from the sky and smashed into the ground. The world burst to life. The world spun, the elements returned to normal. His flesh regenerated and the black claw returned to normal shape and color. The dragons, humans, knolls, boarelves, and elves arose from Lukhan's imagination, an army at his command! Bar, Judas, and Sacul stood next to him, uninjured by the magical illusions created by the Inquisitor Lord.

"Luke, we're here for you!" Bar cheered.

"By the spirit, he shall be defeated!" Sacul snorted.

"The Inquisition shall fall!" Judas growled.

"Impressive," Shen praised. "Your mind and will are strong but do you hope to rally the world against the Holy Master."

"I will kill you!" Lukhan snarled. He charged forward, eager for the mind of the invading Inquisitor. Shen remained where he stood; no defense was raised against the dragon. Lukhan struck with all of his might, the magical aura that surrounded the Inquisitor Lord fluctuated in before becoming a flaming white shield. Lukhan struck the magical white blade with his claws. He was flung back like a child's doll.

"You dare try to penetrate my mind," Shen rubbed his forehead. "You are amusing to me. Look at what you did to your allies." Lukhan turned to see the army within his mind. The white flames charred the corpses of his friends. Those who once stood behind him had vanished into the white flames. "You summon them at your own expense and then destroyed them. In the end, you sacrificed them. You saved no one."

"No! This is a fabricated illusion!" Lukhan snarled. "A dream! A nightmare!"

"This is your future," Shen prophesied. "The Holy Master has blessed humankind with the ability to defeat the black flame. Bloodshed can be avoided; all you must do is surrender to me."

"Surrender!" Lukhan growled. "I would rather die!"

"We can agree on that," Shen stated. "You sound rather brave when you say that. Then what of your friends? Are they afraid of death? Do they know their fate?" He stuck out his hand and waved it next to him. Illusions of Bar, Judas, and Sacul appeared beside the angelic figure. A forth figure appeared but its identity was not revealed. The cloaked figure studied them carefully. "Are theses your friends?" Lukhan snarled in reply. "The Inquisition is aware of them; this man must be Judas, the traitor. The knoll must be Owen or Bar. Oh yes, the pig must be the injured one, what was his name? Hmm, Sacul. The forth, who is it? There are rumors that an elf was once with you."

"Shut up! You know nothing about them!" Lukhan growled. He smiled, for the Inquisitor Lord only knew his friends from dreams. He was afraid that the human could read his dreams like a book. He knew that Shen was invading his mind for information.

"You may not fear for your own safety, but you should be afraid for them," Shen warned. "Our spies have gathered a great deal of information about you and your outcast city." The Inquisition was guessing and had no clue about his personal life.

"You would dare attack Ravenshaven!" Lukhan snarled.

"Yes," Shen stated flatly.

Chapter 33

"Luke? What is the matter?" Bar gasped. Lukhan did not respond, he'd collapsed, his tongue hung loosely out of his mouth and his eyes rolled to the back of his head. Blood dribbled out of his nose and ears. Judas moved Ambrosia away from the unconscious dragon. Bar approached cautiously.

"Do not touch him!" Con'ra warned. The knoll took pause at her warning.

"What? Why?" Bar asked. "What's the matter with him?"

"He is under a spell," Con'ra growled. "I sense a great deal of magical being focused on him." She looked around warily; there were no magi or dragons near them.

"Magic? From where?" Judas asked. "It's you!"

"Fool! I have nothing to do with it!" Con'ra snarled. She looked around the great hall. Nothing seems to be magically out of place. How could a magus cast a spell and not be presence? She sniffed the air and tasted the floor's titles. The dust and dirt between the titles were magnetized. "I sense magic."

"From where?" Judas demanded as he unsheathed his sword. "Ambrosia, leave quickly!"

"Where is Mark?" Ambrosia asked.

"Help me!" Mark gasped. They turned to look at the poor man. His eyes, nose, and ears were bleeding, the same conditions that Lukhan was suffering from. "Please!"

"You!" Bar gasped. "Owen's servant! What is a wizard doing here?"

"I beg for mercy and forgiveness!" Mark gasped. He knelt and bowed humbly before them.

"Foul heretic!" Judas curled up his lip at the kneeling man. "You're the one who has placed him in this state! Foul wizard! Who do you serve? I should kill you for what you have done!"

"What you say is true," Mark choked and coughed up blood. "Please listen to what I have to say before-"

"Cut off his head," Con'ra stated flatly. "If he is the magic user then killing him will stop the spell."

"Let's do it!" Judas agreed eagerly. The wizard recoiled in fear and choked on his blood.

"Wait, please let him speak," Ambrosia rose to the pain stricken man's defense.

"I agree," Bar growled. "If another spell passes his lips, cut him down!"

"T-thank you, master knoll," Mark choked on bloody words. "I'm a condemned wizard sentenced to death by the Inquisition. Before my sentence was carried out, an Inquisitor Lord approached me and offered to spare my life. The Inquisitor Lord Shen told me that I would serve the Holy Master or hang from the gallows."

"You're task is to kill Luke?" Bar asked.

"No! I was told to spy on the council and gather information," Mark explained. "That is what I thought I was-" He began to choke on his words.

"Then what is matter with him?" Bar snarled. He kicked the kneeling man who tumbled over on his back. Mark held up his hands defensively.

"Please let me finish!" Mark begged. "They know! They know everything about your friend! The silver dragon is what they seek!"

"Who are they?" Judas demanded.

"The last Inquisitor Lords," Mark whispered. Blood did not stop pouring out of his orifices. "Their names are Shen and Michael and they have been seeking the silver dragon ever since the destruction of the plague."

"Why does the Inquisition have such an interest in him?" Con'ra demanded. She looked at Lukhan suspiciously, something was out of place.

"They fear for the Holy Master's safety," Mark choked. "The Holy Master foretold his own destruction! The Inquisitor Lords seek to thwart this."

"Explain!" Con'ra growled. "What does that mean?"

"The Holy Master foretold his own death!" Mark gurgled. "That's all that I heard! I swear! You must believe me. The Inquisition believes it's the silver dragon. They'll do everything within their power to kill him!"

"Even use wizards to do their dirty work?" Bar growled. "They must be getting desperate to be using prisoners."

"Please listen to me!" Mark pleaded. "I'm under a spell! They have me under constant observation! They-"

"Then undo what you have done!" Con'ra snarled. She snatched the prone man and shook him violently. "If what you say is true then release him from your spell!"

"I-I can't! It's not my spell and its part of the ten laws of magic! Once a spell is cast it cannot be undone!" the pain stricken man screamed. "P-put me down," She flipped him over on top of his head and continued to shake violently. "Please! I beg you! Stop! I'm going to be sick- blah!" The man vomited on the floor.

Suddenly, the doors to the main hall opened. Two figures in cloaked mesh hurried inside. Con'ra stopped Mark's shaking and watched as the two cloaked figures entered.

"What is going on in my house?" Owen demanded.

"Shaken, not stirred?" the noticeably shorter figure remarked snidely. With a boorish grin, Sacul took off his mesh hood. "Hey, Owen," he snickered. "What do you do with a green dragon?"

"I don't know," asked Owen as he pulled off his mesh hood.

"Wait until she ripens!" he chuckled. "Get it? It's because she is colored green and young!" Owen grinned at the boarelf's untimely humor.

"Sacul, Owen, you came in time! This wizard has cast a curse upon Luke!" Bar snarled.

"So the rat has finally made his move," Owen did not seem surprised at the result.

"You knew?" Judas accused.

"This is my house," Owen stated. "I know everything that goes on here. However, I thought he was targeting the council or me." He glanced over at Lukhan's unconscious form. "I didn't realize that his objective was the second Imperator."

"Why would you allow a wizard here?" Judas demanded. "The Inquisition must be aware of everything now!"

"Give me some credit," Owen words were in a dismissive tone. "I've been feeding him false information since he has arrived and became my servant."

"W-What?" Mark gasped. "You told me about the elves! You knew I was a wizard? How?"

"You can thank our *witch*, Ambrosia," Owen smiled at her. Ambrosia did a polite curtsey to Owen and the white knoll gave an approving nod to the alchemist who stood proudly next to her husband.

"That is why you wanted Ambrosia within your estate!" Judas growled. His face turned red in frustration. Ever since they had met Owen, the knoll had been secretive in his plans and motives. His goals and objective were always a mystery to them.

"Don't be angry," Ambrosia soothed her husband. Judas's face softened at his wife's reassurance.

"Who's the new dog and pig?" Con'ra snorted. She had no clue who or what they were talking about. "If you would excuse me, I have a wizard to torment. This place is crawling with lesser races." She picked up Mark and continued to shake him again.

"Wait! Stop! I'll tell you- ugh," Mark's words were interrupted between heaves as Con'ra continued to shake him upside down.

"Who's the green dragon?" Owen demanded. "Wait a moment. Is this-?"

"It's Con'ra," Sacul grunted in distain. "She is the same one that attacked our caravans and forced us into the Black Marshes during the plague!"

"She is on our side," Bar words were in an unconvinced tone.

"If you can believe that," Judas added.

"Hush," Ambrosia warned. Lukhan believed in her, but the silver dragon was not awake to defended her. Bar looked at Ambrosia with uncertainty. Did the alchemist know something that he did not? He thought better of it and remained silent. Much had happen since their departure. Bar would respect his friend's decision to allow Con'ra within their circle.

"Were you successful in dealing with the Red Clan?" Owen inquired. "Will they side with us?" His normally calm voice was on the edge of panic.

"It was a one sided deal and they have promised to leave Ravenshaven alone in the coming conflict."

"Good, but will they fight with us?" Owen pressed. He rubbed his hands together in an impatient manner.

"Those who are willing, shall, but there are heavy stipulations with such an alliance; the cost of tribute and livestock. We have the Blood Queen's word." Bar stated.

"This is better news than I had hoped for," Owen let out a sighed in relief. "Ambrosia and Sacul, see to second Imperator's injuries. Bar and Judas, come with me. We have much to discuss. There are problems in the council and I need your support. We all need to hear some good news, now and then. Make certain that my second comes to no more harm, no matter what it takes."

"As you wish," Ambrosia bowed before her Imperator.

"I'll see what I can do," Sacul replied. He licked his pet toad for good measure, comfort, and focus.

"Where are you two going?" Con'ra demanded. "Lukhan is still hurt."

"We must converse," Bar growled. "See to Luke; help Ambrosia and Sacul in any way possible."

"What about the wizard?" Con'ra demanded. Mark struggled within her tight grip.

Owen looked back and shrugged. "Do as you wish with him," he replied. "It is to be hoped that he will help you. If not, do as you wish to him. Judas and Bar follow me to the council chamber. They must be told of what has transpired." The three exited the hallway and into another section of the house. Ambrosia and Sacul hurried to Lukhan's side. The silver dragon's condition hadn't improved.

"I should bite off your head," Con'ra had a wicked grin. She stopped shaking the red faced man and Mark stared up at her with eyes full of fear.

"Wait!" Ambrosia warned. "We are dealing with magic, there are no external injuries."

"So?" Con'ra grumbled. "Blood is coming out of his eyes, nose, and ears. How can you say he is not injured?"

"True," Ambrosia agreed. "Look at the wizard's condition and compare it to his. They're the same!"

"So?" Con'ra grumbled.

"I believe anything that happens to Mark will reflect on Lukhan. What do you think Sacul?" Ambrosia asked.

"There is only one way to find out," Sacul replied. "Lower the wizard." He drew out his stone dagger and gave Mark a quick cut on the cheek. A red line appeared on Mark's cheek. In respond to the cut appeared below Lukhan's eye.

"A retaliation curse," Ambrosia gasped. "Stop shaking him! You're hurting both of them." Con'ra released the wizard who collapsed. The man tremble as blood continued to pour down his face.

"What is a retaliation curse?" Sacul asked. "I'm not familiar with it."

"Curses are design to hinder an adversary," Ambrosia explained. "In this case, Lukhan is unconscious and therefore completely defenseless. This fool has combined his white flame with Lukhan. Therefore, should one die, the other will follow."

"Then why is he bleeding out of his eyes and ears," Sacul asked.

"It must be a side effect," Ambrosia guessed.

"No, you're wrong, witch," Mark replied in a choking gasps. His eyes were faded and continuous trying to roll backwards. "My task was a simple one; they wanted me to break him."

"Break him? How? Explain?" Sacul grunted.

"That was all I was told, to curse him." Mark gasped.

"Then how do we break the spell?" Ambrosia asked.

"Look, look at my body," Mark choked weakly. He weakly pulled off is bloody tunic. His body was covered in tattoos and brands. Runes and magical symbols were etched into the man's flesh; beneath theses scars was evidence of deep whip lashes.

"What is this?" Sacul gasped in horror.

"This is why I couldn't tell you!" Mark choked. "These tattoos bind me to their services. These tattoos hold a poison that will be released should I fail in my task."

"He has been placed under a magical ward," Con'ra hissed. She lifted her claw and touched the side of her neck, where her father had scarred her with a vine pattern.

⟪◆⟫

Within Lukhan's mind, the battle with the Inquisitor continued, the angelic figure gained no advantage against him. Every time Lukhan struck the shield of white flame, the dream would shift and shutter.

"You claim that you care for your friends," the angelic image of Shen announced. "Yet you slaughter them in your nightmares, a vision of darkness and oblivion. This vision and your fears are known to the Inquisition and, even worse, the Holy Master."

"You fear me? Lukhan gasped. "What? Why? I have done nothing to earn your people's wrath."

"You have chosen the path of darkness," Shen stated.

"What do you know? Are you simply making assumptions?" Lukhan growled.

"The Holy Master never makes assumptions!" Shen stated coldly. "The Master is aware of you dealing with the Betrayer! Our god is never wrong."

"What? How could- your god miscalculated when he ordered the destruction of the sacred herd!" Lukhan fired back. "Your god has alienated all of dragon kind and has doomed humanity. Why can you not see he is playing you for fools?"

"To the faithless and the heretic," Shen stated evenly. "His will could be considered foolish or laughably dismissive, but, to the faithful, he has saved this world countless times from the black flame. He is our savior, our protector, from the darkness you hold within yourself."

"Explain!" Lukhan demanded.

"To answer that question, you must look to humanity itself," Shen explained. "Unlike dragons, which are given the gifts of elemental and magical powers, humanity has had to fight and struggle to be where we are today. It has been through the blood of generations that humanity has risen to the status to challenge the dominion of your kind."

"That is crazy," Lukhan's words were in a dismissive tone. "To slaughter the sacred herd was a challenge? You butchered our main source of food to challenge us? That is foolish and sad."

The surrounding battlefield shifted suddenly, the sky and ground disappeared and gave way to a weightless void. Lukhan recognized the place immediately: the spirit world. The sensation of up and down was replaced by a vast open abyss, a divine light, above and eternal darkness below, clouds and fog swirled around him in the far distances.

"More illusions," Lukhan snarled.

"This is where it all began?" the floating angelic figure asked. "As if your nightmares are not warning enough, let us revisit all the souls you have taken with your evil."

"Lies and dreams!" Lukhan snarled. The angelic voice did not reply and disappeared into the surrounding clouds. There was a sudden shift in the air. Spirits emerged from the depths of the void and surrounded him.

"You killed me," a man's voice accused Lukhan. The dragon recognized him to be the assassin he had brutally killed in Ravenshaven. More men appeared next to him. "You killed us all!"

"I did it out of defense," Lukhan muttered coldly. "You were killing innocents! Evil spirits, I will kill you again!" The surrounded spirits paused at his threat.

"I will kill you!" a red dragon lunged at him. Lukhan recognized that it was Rohad, the red dragon he had slain at the Mountains of Fire. He had fought to the death, despite Lukhan's demands for him to yield. The guilt of the pointless kill continued to trouble him.

"Stay back!" Lukhan warned. "I did not mean to kill you, but I shall do so again if I must!" The surrounding spirits grew bold at the red dragon's attack.

"I eat you!" an armored troll announced.

"Die Aak!" Lukhan snarled. He opened his mouth and a blast of frozen energy ripped through the troll's spirit. Many other spirits appeared out of the surrounding abyss. Dragons, common races, and animals attacked Lukhan, targeting his black claw. The claw reacted on its own, devouring the rebelling spirits to feed its dark hunger.

"You deserved all of your fates!" Lukhan howled as he relived each of their experiences. "I hate you! I hate all of you!" The spirits swarmed over him and around him. Biting, clawing, and tearing at his flesh. Their hatred only fed Lukhan's own fury. Their malice and hatred penetrating and darkening his soul, he drove them back repeatedly. Their numbers seemed countless. Lukhan screamed in horror at the number of lives he had taken over the years. Their rage and bloodlust was absorbed into the black claw. Lukhan suddenly understood, as a tear fell of his magically scared eyes.

"The black claw reacts to their emotions," Shen called. The spirit disappeared as suddenly as they had emerged. The angelic figure appeared next to him. "Fear of the unknown, sense of dreaded mortality, and the obsolete longing for life. The black claw feeds off of the death of souls, which is why you will never be able to control it!"

"Then you are a wizard?" Lukhan whispered. Tears of regret fell from his eyes at those that had been killed faded from view, but their memories still lingered. Ghost hidden within his mind. Trapped within the corrupt black claw, a prison for those souls he had taken.

"No, I am an alchemist," Shen clarified. "I am an expert at runes and magical wards."

"What is the difference," Lukhan choked in frustration allowing his enemy to see him weep for those that had died.

"Magic is an illusion and can be created or destroyed," Shen stated. "So it is with the white and black flames. Perception and interpretation of the senses reflect the actions of experiences; this combination is the white flame. It's nothing more and nothing less."

"So what?" Lukhan choked.

"Do you believe that this place is real?" Shen offered. "Do you believe that your claws cut? Does your mind perceive reality? Control is often an illusion that we comfort ourselves with. You cannot control the black flame. Don't you think that it is time for you to die?"

"This is all an illusion," Lukhan growled as he wiped the tears from his eyes.

"Yes, but what is beyond the senses?" Shen asked. "What is beyond the black flame?"

Lukhan narrowed his focus and strained to see pass Shen's illusionary disguise. The angel's figure shivered and turned into a glowing mass of several white orbs. Lukhan gasped desperately at the sudden drain in will power and mental exhaustion. The illusion wavered and corrected itself.

"Impressive," Shen congratulated. "How is it that you are still able to take to the offensive? You nearly pierced our defenses."

"What are you?" Lukhan gasped. He was not fighting a human; there were several souls that he was engaged with! There was something horribly wrong with what he had seen. It was like a network of souls attached to each other! A magical web connected with Shen as the center controller!

"That answer would have been given had you broken through my defensives," Shen chuckled. "Did you know that the elves used the same techniques to defeat the Gold Clan?"

"What did you say?" Lukhan snarled.

"I have been studying the ancient techniques of rune writing. It was created by the elves during fall of the Gold Kingdom," Shen sneered. "Who would have thought that elves could be so clever? To be honest, I think it was my mastery of runes and ancient script that I perfected it. Do not worry, you were a worthy adversary and for your punishment, you are will live your nightmare. In the name of the Holy Master, you will destroy the city of Ravenshaven." Lukhan felt like a fly trapped within a spider's web, except his mind was the trap and the spider was the Inquisitor.

Chapter 34

"Kill me!" Mark screamed in agony. He fell over and thrashed about, clawing and digging at his tattoos. "Kill me now!"

"What is the matter?" Ambrosia asked. She placed a comforting hand on Mark's shoulder but recoiled. "He is hot to the touch; it feels like his tattoos are on fire."

"It burns!" Mark continued to scream and tear at his flesh. "Please kill me!"

"Enough!" Con'ra snarled. She knocked him unconscious with a flick of her claw. The man fell silent, his finger nails still dug into his flesh. His self-inflected injuries around his tattoos were horrific. "What is happening to him?"

Sacul stood wide-eyed at the pain stricken man's injuries. Those wounds appeared on Lukhan simultaneously. He licked his toad and grunted. "The tattoos must have released their poison," he concluded. "His body must be reacting to it, but my concern is for Lukhan." The boarelf turned his attention to the dragon's sleeping form. Blood had not stopped oozing out of his eyes and ears. The shaman reach over and touched the dragon's scales, they were hot to the touch. "We can assume that the retaliation curse is the form of magic. How do we dispel the curse?"

"Kill the wizard," Con'ra stated flatly.

"In doing so, we would be killing Lukhan," Ambrosia warned.

"Retaliation," Sacul muttered. "Wait a moment, instead of hurting the wizard, let us try to heal him."

"Heal him?" Con'ra asked. "What would that accomplish? It would only prolong his suffering!"

259

"Do you have a better plan?" Ambrosia asked.

"The wizard is already dead and Lukhan will soon follow," Con'ra snarled. "Use the wizard's white flame to heal the curse. Use the black claw on him."

"That could kill Lukhan!" Ambrosia stated.

"Both are logical options," Sacul agreed. "However, the more time we waste the less successful either of our plans will work. Time is against us and we must act quickly."

"Mark is a victim of the Inquisition, we must help them both!" Ambrosia pressed.

"He is a liar and a traitor," Con'ra snarled. "Why should we have any compassion for him? He is nothing more than a puppet. Even if we save the wizard, he will still bear the scars of his captors."

"That is what makes us different from the Inquisition," Ambrosia replied. "We have compassion for all who are suffering, even those who have been used as puppets."

"Compassion?" Con'ra huffed. "This is a high risk for little reward. Combining the white flames would place the spell caster at great danger. They could share the same fate! Since I am the only one that can use magic that risk would fall on me! I would be risking my own life!"

"So what?" Sacul grumbled. "You claim that you are here to help us, start by saving their lives."

Con'ra raised a questioning eyebrow, snorted and then cursed. She paced back and forth down the hallway thinking about the risks and rewards. She didn't like her options; she had to ask herself if the silver dragon was worth it. The hesitation was not without merit. Suicide was simply not her style, no matter how nice Lukhan was. She cursed again and shook her head in frustration.

"Fine!" Con'ra growled. "If I die, I am going to come back and haunt you both!"

"I'm glad you agree-," Ambrosia began.

"Whatever you like," Con'ra huffed. She took a deep breath and stared at Lukhan and Mark. There was a long moment of hesitation.

"Well, hurry up," Sacul pressed. "Do something."

"I am no healer," Con'ra appeared nervous. "I do not know any words of healing. All I know are plants! If I say the wrong thing then I might kill them both." She scratched her head in frustration and thought about her past magical teachings. The words eluded her.

"Lick my toad," Sacul offered. He held out his pet.

"What?" Con'ra asked.

"If you lick my toad it will begin your journey to the spirit world," Sacul offered. "The toad produces a poison that will-" Before he could explain further, Con'ra stuck out her tongue and roughly licked the toad with her catlike tongue. The poor toad chirp in protest, the top layer of its thin skin was taken off.

"Wyverns poison does not affect me," Con'ra stated. "What makes you think that your little toad would-" Her eyes rolled to the back of her head and she collapsed.

"By the five elements, what happened to her?" Ambrosia asked in surprising shock.

Sacul grunted at his poor pet's injuries. "She shouldn't have licked you so hard," he cooed. "That was a heavy dosage. Her trip into the spirit world will not be a pleasant one." The toad chirped in reply to Sacul's statement.

Reality fell away as Con'ra journeyed into the spirit world. Shadows grew long and darkness devoured the natural light. Gravity gave way to a world of shadows and clouds. Sacul's and Ambrosia's white flames were easy to identify, their souls flickered like burning torches. The outline of Sacul's white flame waved to her in a distant greeting. No sound echoed within the void of darkness. From the corner of her eye, she turned her attention to Lukhan, his soul was not natural, and the silver dragon's soul was warped and twisted shadows. While Mark's white flame was magically chained and was smoldering and threatening to extinguish. Mark's flame was fluttering as the chains of magic choked off its base. The same chains wrapped around Lukhan's blacken soul.

"What an odd place," Con'ra muttered in confusion. She cautiously approached Lukhan's soul and reached out to touch it. The blackness reacted to her touch and suddenly engulfed her.

Lukhan's mind was broken, the Inquisitor sifted through each of his painful memories. The pain of those he had slain was being replayed over and over within his mind. The Inquisitor was correct, the black flame was evil. His parents had told him so. Anything that caused so much pain had to be evil and he was its embodiment. He had only lived this long because of his selfish need to survive. He had foolishly believed that he could have a normal life as a silver dragon, but he had betrayed that identity. Lukhan knew he had died a long time ago. He was nothing more than a ghost of what he was before. He had tried to escape, to run away to the ends of the world. To save the world from being destroyed, he would allow the darkness to die.

The darkness crept all around him. A smothering, gasping, feeling took hold of his defenseless body. Black webs, with the appearance of tar slowly wrapped him in a cocoon. He sank into the dark substances.

"Let it end," Lukhan whispered to the smothering darkness. A tear of sadness fell down his cheek.

"You have made the right choice," Shen praised. "Your sacrifice will not be in vain. With your death a new age of man will dawn. Although you are evil, I believe that you have done the best you could. I shall pray for you. If it is the Holy Master's will, may you return to this world as a human."

"Pompous wind bag," a high pitched voice sliced through the darkness. Lukhan glance up at the tiny figure; it was a maple seed that floated down in the air. The green seed glowed within the entangle webs of darkness.

"What are you?" Shen demanded. The seed continued to flutter down to Lukhan's trapped form. The silver dragon's eyes were half shut when he noticed the small plant descend upon him, it landed on his nose.

"So this is your mind," the seed stated. "I was hoping for something more, well, lighthearted."

"You are not from my mind," Lukhan whispered. "My dreams have been nightmares ever since I can remember."

"Do you think dying will release you from your pain?" the seed asked. Lukhan blinked at the beautiful tiny life, it seemed distantly familiar. "Can you truly rest? Lazy, you have so much to do and you cannot rest until you fulfill your promise to me?"

"Promise?" Lukhan muttered.

"You swore that you would help me," the tiny seed offered. "Are you saying that you have forgotten?"

"Promise?" Lukhan asked.

"Fool, snap out of it! You would help me kill my father!" Con'ra growled.

"More death and slaughter, the painful memories, I cannot remember anything," Lukhan muttered. "The pain. I have hurt those tormented souls have died at my claw and I do not know who I am any more. I do not even know who you are."

"I am Con'ra!" the maple seed declared.

"Con'ra?" Lukhan whispered.

"He does not understand you," Shen explained. "You are intruding on the intimate moment in his nightmares. Can't you see that he wants to die?"

"Wake up!" Con'ra called. "You are being tricked by the Inquisition! This is all a spell; you are under a curse that is affecting your mind!"

"No," Lukhan stated. "I have caused so much pain and suffering and death is my only release. The black claw has taken everything away from me: my home, my life, my soul. I once thought myself as something good but now I know better."

"What? That does not make sense, your eyes are closed shut-" Con'ra began.

"I am an elemental, an empty shell, and a sorry excuse for a dragon," Lukhan whispered. "I will never have a normal life. My sole purpose now is simply to kill, and that is no existence."

"Have you forgotten everything that the Inquisition has done?" Con'ra demanded.

"They slaughtered the sacred herd," Lukhan whispered. "How can more deaths be justified? Killing humans? The purpose contradicts everything I once believed. How can I judge humankind for their sins, when my sins are evil? Justice or revenge: it is not a price worth paying. Murder begets more murder."

"Fool!" Con'ra snapped. "Everything in this world kills. Revenge and justice have nothing to do with it. Humanity has grown too bold; they will kill everything that is not human, starting with dragon kind. They seek to change the world, make everything to their liking! Have you forgotten this?"

"Is that any different from what dragons have done?" Lukhan snapped. "The council has done no better. Humans or dragons, does it really matter? Both are greedy and seek to control the world. There will be no differences."

"So you are going to let yourself die?" Con'ra asked. "Dying is easy; it is living that is hard. You are going to let humans and dragons kill themselves? What about your friends? What about your mother? I do not know which is more pathetic, those that kill for stupid reasons or those who sit on the side and allow it to occur."

"You do not understand," Lukhan stated.

"Yes, I do," Con'ra agreed. Pain and sorrow dulled her green wings. "More than you will ever know."

Lukhan looked at the tiny seed, and curiously lifted his eyes. "Will you show me," he begged. "Will you show me your pain?"

The tiny seed paused for a moment. Its green wings reflected off of Lukhan's magically scarred eyes. "I do not want-," her words faded. The seed gave him a kiss on his nose and the surrounding darkness began to fade.

"Wait! Where are you going?" Shen demanded. "I'm not done with you yet-!" The angelic figure disappeared with the surrounding darkness. The world shifted and changed, the air temperature changed, large trees and underbrush sprouted out of the void, the blackness that held Lukhan faded away. The silver dragon recognized the place. They were in the Jade Rainforest; he was within Con'ra's memories. Maple seeds danced through the forest's air. A little green hatchling chased after the seeds in blissful glee.

"What is this place?" Lukhan whispered.

"This is where my pain begins," a seed explained. "This is where I was lost my faith in the world." There was a long pause as they watched the green hatchling scurry about in the undergrowth of the rainforest.

"What are you doing?" a female voice asked. A large green dragon came out of the shadows of the jungle.

"Mother! Oh, I am chasing butterflies! Will you help me?" the young Con'ra asked with great glee. "You promised that you would."

"I would rather chase you, little one," her mother leaned down and rubbed her nose against her hatchlings. Con'ra smiled at her mother and began chasing the maple seeds again. "I have a secret to tell you."

"What is it?" Con'ra leaped up trying to capture the elusive flying seeds.

"If you plant a thousand of maple seeds without hurting them, they will grant you a wish," her mother explained with a smile.

"Really?" Con'ra asked.

"Of course, if you believe," her voice strained in sadness.

"What is it? What is the matter mother?" Con'ra asked.

"Do not be afraid," her mother's voice had a worried tone. "I am sure that your father will be proud of you."

"What do you mean?" Con'ra asked.

"Your father has come to see you, today your trial begins," her mother instructed. "Listen to me, you must survive. Do everything and anything your father tells you to do. I will not be able to help you. He is not kind or forgiving to those who are disobedient. I would have you live freely and with honor under his rule."

"Mother?" Con'ra asked.

"Remember that I love you," her mother whispered. "Every living member of our clan has survived this. Believe in yourself and everything I have taught you-!"

"Is it ready?" a large green male interrupted as he emerged from the shadows of the rainforest. Lukhan recognized him as the Green Clan leader, Krain. Although the green leader appeared younger and less battle worn, he had a look of disdain on his face. Several wyvern bodyguards accompanied the powerful leader.

"She is," her mother growled harshly.

"Good, let the test begin," Krain announced with an evil grin. He glanced at the green hatchling. "I am Krain, leader of the Green Clan, and I command you hatchling to kill one of my wyverns." The wyverns around him hissed and bared their teeth at Con'ra. The green hatchling was confused at the order, not sure how to react to such as request. The wyverns were larger than the hatchling. How did he expect her to kill them?

"Mother?" she asked in fear.

"Do not look to her!" Krain growled. "She is not your leader, I am. Do as your leader commands. Now kill a wyvern!" Con'ra eyes grew wide in fear, she had never killed before. Her mother had always hunted for her. She had always thought that her training was playing a game.

"Do it!" Krain snarled. Con'ra shook her head no in reply. "If you will not attack them, then they provoke you. Sessess, kill the hatchling." A large wyvern with leathery skin crawled forth with her teeth bared. Con'ra backed away from the approaching creature.

"Mother, please! I do not want to do this," Con'ra wept. Her mother did not acknowledge her plea for help. Instead she looked down at the ground. "Help me!" Sessess charged Con'ra sprang away from the assault. Sessess curled her tail like a scorpion, striking at the dodging hatchling.

"Please stop! Why do you attack me?" Con'ra cried. The wyvern did not reply but intensified her assault. Sessess's poisonous barb sliced and struck Con'ra multiple times. Blood and venom covered the struggling hatchling. Con'ra sprang over the attacking wyvern and fled to her mother's side. "Help me, mother! Please! Tell her to stop!"

Her mother did not look at her, but closed her eyes shut. "You must do as your father says," she choked as tears fell from the corner of her eye. No aid would come from her. Sessess was on the green hatchling, biting, and clawing at the dragon's flesh. They rolled. Sessess targeted Con'ra neck in an attempt to take her jugular or break her neck. Con'ra flipped and clawed at the wyvern's face. Enraged at the hatchling's defense, Sessess bit her on her shoulder, ripping open a gash on her side. Sessess withdrew from the bloody struggle to examine the damage she had caused.

"Sessess stop playing with the hatchling and kill it," Krain instructed. "I have seen enough. This hatchling does not have what it takes to be part of the Green Clan."

"No!" her mother roared. The large adult female charged and struck Sessess with her tail. The wyvern was caught off guard and sent crashing through the jungle. "I have had enough of your rule! Die Krain!" The two green dragons clashed against each other. The wyvern bodyguards jumped into the fray attacking her mother. Con'ra memories were muddled with raw emotions. Shadows and pain flooded her mind. During the fight, her senses were heightened but were now jumble in confusion of bloody shock and horror. Darkness clouded her thoughts and her vision faded into darkness.

"Did she die?" Lukhan asked softly. The green seed flew around him and did not answer. "I-I can sense your pain. I am sorry for your loss."

"My mother did not die at the claws of Krain," Con'ra stated. "Do you see why I hate my father?"

"Krain told me that he tests all the hatchlings of the Green Clan," Lukhan admitted. "I did not realize that you were tested so young."

"I learned later that my mother was suspected of treachery," Con'ra muttered coldly. "Krain was testing her, not me. My father wanted to see if she would turn against him. The ruse worked; she foolishly attacked him."

"You mother fought to protect you," Lukhan stated.

"Her hatred for my father was greater than her love for me," Con'ra was cold and distance tone. "She chose not to help me or herself. Instead, she should have let me die and dispel all disbelief in her loyalty. Then she could have easy killed Krain. She was foolish, and did not allow Sessess to kill me."

"You are wrong," Lukhan's tone was comforting and soft. "She loved you enough to risk her life for your safety. What Krain did to you was evil. You cannot blame your mother for hating him."

"Then I blame her for being short sighted!" Con'ra snarled. "I loved her and she hurt me! She should have betrayed me! I hate her. I allowed my mother to die for me! It was not fair!" Lukhan watched the tiny life; it was the same type of maple seed she was chasing when she was a hatchling. Now he understood why Con'ra had reacted to his mother when they had first met. He understood why she had such a burning desire to kill her father. He knew why she was so distant and mentally scarred. The seed slowly spiraled to the ground.

"Con'ra," Lukhan whispered. "I am sorry."

The seed remained perfectly still. "Hold your sympathy until you have seen it all," Con'ra had a cold and distant voice. The darkness around them turned into the Jade Rainforest. Night had fallen in the woods and the green hatchling struggle to stand, the wound on her ripped shoulder had scabbed over. Dried blood covered her body, Krain towered over her. His injuries were minor, but blood covered his jaws.

"Do you fear death?" he demanded. Con'ra look up at him with fear in her eyes, she quickly nodded her head yes. "Are you ready to listen to your leader?" Con'ra gulped and quickly nodded her head.

"Where is my mother," Con'ra whispered.

"Follow me," Krain growled. A cruel sheer passed over his bloody lips. He led her through the rainforest, the evening rains began to fall. Krain led her through a pathway of destroyed vegetation and wyvern bodies. Trees and even the ground itself were heaved upwards, as if earthquakes had torn the ground asunder. In the middle of the devastation was her mother's body.

"Mother!" Con'ra cried.

"Go to her," Krain instructed. Con'ra gimped over to her mother's broken body. Her body was covered in horrendous wounds and her neck was broken, which angled her head in an odd direction. Despite all of these wounds and injuries, she continued to breathe. Her breaths were short and quick like a fish out of water.

"Mother! Please get up! Please mother!" Con'ra wept. Her mother did not move, her eyes did not acknowledge her pleas.

"Are you ready?" Krain growled. He shoved Con'ra away from her mother with his nose. "Your final task is to finish her."

"W-What?" the hatchling stuttered.

"You will suffer your mother's fate if you do not do as you are told!" Krain snarled.

"I cannot!" Con'ra choked.

"Your mother told you to listen to me," Krain snarled. He emphasized each stressed word. "You failed at killing a wyvern and forced your mother to turn against me. It is your fault that you did not obey me. Now do as I command and kill her!"

Con'ra shook in fear and slowly walked to her mother's side. She glanced back at Krain who continued to stare at her with death in his eyes. "Mother?" she called. Her mother's faded eyes did not react to her call. "I-I am so sorry!" She placed her claws on her mother's throat and pushed down with all of her might. The hatchling's weight was not enough to cut deep into the jugular, but it was enough that warn blood began to quickly pour out.

Chapter 35

The maple seed trembled as she relived the experience of killing her mother. Lukhan realized what he was seeing, Con'ra darkest nightmare. He felt her pain as she suffered at the cruel claws of her father, but even worse was that she blamed herself for not being able to kill a wyvern and, thus, forced her mother to act. The seed's wing turned to dust and lay motionless on the ground. Lukhan gently picked up the tiny plant and cradled it next to his chest. The tiny life wept, she listened to his strong heart. She took comfort in its simple rhythmic beat.

"You cannot blame yourself for your mother's death," Lukhan whispered softly. "She wanted to protect you."

"She was a fool!" Con'ra choked on a sob. Tears ran freely down her face. "She should have let me die in her place. I was weak, I could not do as my father asked."

"Shh," Lukhan soothed. "We are kindred spirits. I understand how you feel, but I also know that your mother made the right decision. She loved you." The nightmare ended at Lukhan's soothing words, the vision of the rainforest and horrible memories faded into the spirit world.

"No," Con'ra wept. Her trembling voice was on the edge of panic. "She was a fool- I did not want her to- she left me- I miss my mother!" With the sprinkle of starlight, the illusion of the butterfly faded away and Con'ra returned to her normal form. She wept freely against him; the silver dragon did not shrink away from Con'ra, but held her close for comfort. He wrapped his wings gently around her to make her feel secure.

"You know, you are not alone," Lukhan offered. "I never knew how much it would hurt, when someone who is important to us dies, that leaves a big hole in our hearts. I forgot how much of a gap we leave behind when a loved one is gone forever. I have dealt with the black flame for so long that it rarely troubles me when I see someone die. I have become hardened and jaded when it comes to others, but your nightmare has rekindled my desire to protect those I have come to love. Their sacrifice would mean nothing if you died or blamed yourself. There was a reason why your mother saved you."

"I do not care," Con'ra lied. She continued to weep, Lukhan felt sorry for her. She still blamed herself for everything that had happen. Con'ra was filled with regrets and uncertainty. They both lost a parent and felt ashamed of their past deeds. They could never live up to the standards or expectations of their dead parents because they had already paid the ultimate price for their loved ones.

"You are wrong," Lukhan whispered. "You cry because you loved her."

"She meant the world to me!" Con'ra confessed has she choked back tears. "Why? Why did she have to leave me?" She continued to cry and Lukhan gave her a moment to sort through her emotions. She squeezed against him, desperate for a connection to reality.

"I do not have the answers," Lukhan offered. "The black flame is often cruel and unforgiving; it takes away those we hold dearest in our hearts." He glanced down at his deformity. The hunger from it faded away with her next to him. The claw's dominant control seemed to weaken within their embrace. Was she rekindling his white flame, that otherworldly sensation called life?

"It was unfair!" Con'ra screamed.

"You are right," Lukhan realized. "What your father forced you to do was unforgivable." There was a low growl in his voice. Con'ra raised her head from his chest and looked at him with tears in her yellow eyes.

"I hate him!" She blurted out. "He is why I continue to live! My sole reason for living is to kill him!"

"I understand your hatred," Lukhan whispered. "It gives you purpose to continue on, but your hate cannot be the only reason for living."

"I can never forgive my father! He will die!" Con'ra swore.

"I understand your rage and anger," Lukhan stated. "However, what will happen once you have completed this obsession? When you have killed your father, will this act bring your mother back from the afterlife? Give you comfort? To fulfill a promise that was made in anger and pain? Of course not, it will make you feel better for only the briefest of moments. Your heart cannot be filled with such venomous hatred."

"What do you suggest to fill my heart?" Con'ra demanded. "For so long,

I have only known the bitterness of betrayal. My mother, father, and Sessess betrayed me! How can I mend a heart that has been broken into a thousand pieces?"

"Love," Lukhan whispered. Con'ra blinked at him in surprise; her wings blushed at the thought of him being so close to her. Embarrassed at her display of emotions, he wiped a tear away from the corner of her eyes. She looked away from his magically scared silver eyes, but she did not push away from his embrace.

"Love has nothing to do with it," Con'ra stated harshly. "It is a foolish and useless emotion. It can only hurt you because it is caused by false ideals and lame promises."

"How can you say that? When your mother loved you so much that she defended you at the expense of her own life?" Lukhan asked.

"You really think so-," Con'ra began.

"So you have combined your white flame!" an otherworldly voice declared. The angelic figure appeared before them. Shen looked down at the embraced dragons and the dream world shifted at his sudden appearance. "Nightmares differ from each individual. Wouldn't you agree, Con'ra? The white flame is the combination of your experiences and raw emotions. Dreams and nightmares make the individual who they are today."

"Foul ape!" Con'ra snarled. She leap away from Lukhan and attacked the angelic figure. A white shield protected the human from her assault, and Con'ra was flung back like a rag doll. Before crashing Con'ra opened her wings and landed like a cat.

Lukhan remembered where he was. Con'ra's actions were the same as his, and both would yield the same results. "Do not attack him," he warned. "It only fuels your nightmares."

"The human will die!" Con'ra snarled. "No lesser race will make a fool out of me!"

"Stop Con'ra, listen to me!" Lukhan pleaded. Con'ra ignored him and focused on the floating human above them. Her eyes flashed with a golden light and the jungle around them came to life. Coiling and slithering like snakes, the growing vegetation struck at the angelic figure. The vines wrapped around the shield of white flames. The vines turned to ash as they touched the magical shield.

"You are skilled in magic," Shen offered in approving congratulations. "Magic comes so easily to the dragon race, but that is why we are enemies. That magical knowledge is a waste on the dragon ilk; they could have done such good works for the world. Yet they squander it on pitiful acts of vengeances and plots to gain more power and gold. How tragic."

"Bite me!" Con'ra snarled. "Tell me how the humans have better the world?"

"Mankind led during the time of the Mixed Kingdoms," Shen replied. "Yet it was the wavering faith of heretics that the Holy Master's protection wanes. The other common races didn't have the steadfast faith in our god and therefore the Mixed Kingdoms were doomed to failure. It is because of the lack of faith that humanity must prove itself."

"We do not need a history lesson," Lukhan snarled. "Humans seem to cast the blame on all others besides themselves. They never take responsibly for their actions, and claim that what they do is the will of their god. The Holy Master is nothing more than an excuse to serve your own selfless purposes and agendas. You do not care about those you hurt, as long as the Inquisition gets what it needs! If your god is so powerful, then why does he need humans to carry out his wishes?"

"You dare to presume to know our ways?" Shen spat in growing frustration. "I have spent my life reading and learning everything I could about your kind. I, like humanity, have earned the right to take destiny into my own hands. Dragons, with all of their might and magical abilities, can never defeat the Inquisition. Mankind is resolved in the matter of the destruction of the dragon races."

"He is baiting us," Lukhan warned. "He wants us to attack, do not fall into his trap."

"What do you mean?" Con'ra asked. "Are you saying that we have to put up with insolences?"

"Every time that we have attacked him, it has been ineffective. He has never attacked us or moved against me," Lukhan added. "It is like he wants us to attack."

"The human and boarelf said something about a retaliation curse," Con'ra muttered.

"Impressive," Shen congratulated. "Violence begets more violence, eye for an eye, tooth for a tooth, and blood for blood. This is what the Holy Master warns against those who oppose us. Use thou enemy's strength against thee."

"Damn monkey! No more theological mumbo jumbo!" Con'ra snarled.

"This is an ancient curse which the elves created," Shen explained. "I perfected it. During the Elves Rebellion against the Gold Clan, the magi could not defeat their masters through brute force or magical will. Instead, they developed a technique that uses the white flames of the enemies against themselves. Unfortunately, the curse not only kills the dragon, but it slays the heretic that casts the curse."

"The human wizard," Con'ra snarled. "Sacul and Ambrosia were correct! The Inquisition is using magic!"

"Yes," Shen teased. "The wizard was a heretic and doomed to death, but he can be redeemed by serving the Inquisition in his death. With your deaths, the Holy Master will be saved!"

"Mark? Owen's servant?" Lukhan asked. "He is a wizard? Why did I not see his magical aura?"

"Was that his name?" Shen mocked dispassionately. "There are so many heretics; I can't remember all of their names. He was the curse, a living weapon designed for a single purpose: to kill you, the would-be murderer of my Master!"

Con'ra began to chuckle wildly. "Perhaps dragons and humans are more alike than I thought," she chuckled. "Power, wealth, and the obsession to keep it, the dragon council and the Inquisition sacrifice all to keep their authority. The two governing bodies are the same; both are mockeries of abuse and authority. Yet they claim to have their people's best interests at heart. Oh, how perverted our two races are. I hope they destroy each other!"

"You're wrong, worm," Shen declared. "I do not own any worldly possessions; the Inquisition does. My power comes from the divine; I was appointed by the Holy Master himself to be an Inquisitor Lord. Theses worldly ideas that dragons cling to are materialistic and temporary. Mankind seeks to rise above this! I consult with a higher power. The Holy Master is above magic and he is God!"

"Demigod," Lukhan corrected.

"Lies!" Shen hissed. "That rumor was born from disenfranchised pigs and dogs that were kicked out of the Mixed Kingdom. The Master is above your element worship! He does not use magic, or illusions based on the thoughts of the imagination! Our god is strong, and we are strong because of him! Alas, dragons are magically and physically stronger than man, but our spiritual faith is how we shall prevail over you!"

"You mean stolen knowledge!" Con'ra sneered. "You do not follow your own faith! You are a wolf in sheep's clothing, hiding behind a false god. You are a wizard that enslaves others to do your bidding! You are no Inquisitor! You are a heretic within your own religion!"

"Blasphemous worm. I will kill you!" Shen screamed. The angelic figure struck out at them. A white shield surrounded the two dragons. "The ends justify the means; I am righteous in my path!" He continued to strike at them, but the shield continued to hold. "Magic is a tool to be used against the enemies of the Inquisition! How dare you defy me?" The angelic illusion began to waver and break apart. "The dragons are trying to divide us! Don't listen to them! I command you! Have faith in your god! Serve me or be eternally damn!" The illusion continued to break down into small orbs of fading ash. "What are you doing? Damn heretics! How dare you abandon me because of theses lies! I will punish you!"

"What is happening?" Con'ra asked.

"We are seeing his nightmare!" Lukhan gasped. "Those that are following him are abandoning him. His followers are losing faith!"

The world shift to Shen's mind. An angry mob of humans threw stones and insults at the angelic illusion. The illusionary world shifted, a giant iron fortress loomed over them.

"Heretic! Burn him!" the angry crowd shouted repeatedly.

"Stop! You must serve me! Have faith in me! The enemy is right here! We must save the Holy Master! Don't leave!" Shen screamed in fear and the remains of the angelic illusion faded away into smoldering sparks. An image of the real man fell into the angry mob's waiting hands and illusions of enemies gathered around, laughing and mocking at the vulnerable Inquisitor Lord. Shen's eyes went wide with fear, tears and sweat poured off his face, his features began to age rapidly. "No! Leave me alone. My Master, why have you forsaken me!"

"Break the curse!" Lukhan warned. "No one will bow to you, in this world or the next! Your Master has abandoned you! Release us or you will die!"

"No! My work is not done! I must save the Holy Master! Oh Master, help me!" Shen plead. His hands wither before the man's eyes, his facial hair grew long and the hair on the top of his head fell out.

"Release us!" Lukhan warned. "The magic is consuming you! Humans were never able to withstand the strain of magic on their white flames."

"Damn you!" Shen snarled. "I'll not die here! Not yet!" He reached within his robes and pulled out a piece of paper and a feathered quill and he laid the paper before them, symbols of ancient elven text were glowing with a magical white light. Shen placed his quill on the paper and altered the symbols and the white light turned to black ink. A wave of darkness took over everything.

"Con'ra?" Lukhan called. The swallowing darkness did not reply or echo his words. He stared into the blackness; it was so pitch black that he could not see his claws in front of him. His senses were dulled, he could not smell, taste, hear, or see anything, only the hollow comforting feeling of emptiness.

"What is this place?" Lukhan asked. His words did not resonate, even within his own mind. He felt like a conscience without a physical body and even the feeling of free-fall could not compare to the sensation of the weightless void. This plane of existence was not the physical or spiritual world. Despite the absolute nothingness, he did not feel alone. Instead, there was an indescribable entity, a being of such great and overwhelming power that his senses were overwhelmed by its greatness.

"Who is there?" Lukhan gasped. The entity did not reply, but passed over him without a thought or word.

Chapter 36

"Why aren't they waking up?" Sacul complained for what seemed like the hundredth time. Ambrosia wiped the dry blood off Lukhan's face. She glanced at the shaman with fear on her face. She was not sure why the two dragons were taking so long. It had been over five days since the wizard Mark burst into flames; his scorched body had ignited and turned to ash before their eyes. Yet the two dragons remained unconscious, despite the wizard's death. Owen was not pleased at the results, he was furious at Sacul for allowing Con'ra to join the curse. Owen threatened to take Sacul's toad as punishment. The two council members came to blows at the threat.

"Where did the Inquisition obtain magic?" Ambrosia asked. "Speaking generally, the human race is anti-magic. Ever since the beginning of our history we have invested in alchemy. Why now? Why turn to magic? Is the Inquisition getting desperate?" The silver dragon's nose bled sporadically the past five days, she dabbed at the dry blood from his nostrils.

"What do you call a hundred year old toad?" Sacul asked.

"What?" Ambrosia asked. "I hardly think that this is the time for jokes-"

"An old croak!" Sacul laughed.

"Please, if we could-," Ambrosia begged.

"All right, close the barn doors," Sacul grumbled in all seriousness. He licked his shivering cane toad. "My friends are getting cold." The two cursed dragons had been hauled to Judas's estate. Owen transferred them out of his halls since the unconscious dragons were starting to leave his hall smelling like dragon waste.

"This is serious," Ambrosia scowled. Sacul jumped at the woman's yell. He stood wide eyed at the pregnant woman. "I am sorry; it is that- I have tried everything in alchemy. I didn't mean to snap at you; it's that I am frustrated and tired."

"It's all right," Sacul cautiously crept away from crazy pregnant lady. "We're all trying to do our best. It's up to the spirits now."

She sighed at the shaman's faith in the spirits. "Judas doesn't talk to me anymore," she mumbled. "When he arrived from his journey, he was happy to see me. Ever since this incident he has avoided me. He avoids everyone. I fear that he blames me for not finding a cure for your dragons."

"Lukhan and Con'ra," Sacul corrected. "Be glad that they are not awake to hear you say that. Dragons are such a proud race. Anyway, Lukhan is more than a friend to us. He is our blood brother, a connection to each of the common races."

"Judas never told me that," Ambrosia whispered. "They are blood brothers?"

"I should rephrase that," Sacul explained. "He had to destroy that plague before it could destroy everything. Because it affected the common races, our blood was required to destroy the plague. It was Lukhan who was the catalyst for the magic."

"I knew that, but I didn't realize what was involved in the ceremony," Ambrosia added.

"Most of the world doesn't even know!" Sacul grunted. He licked his toad before continuing. "Lukhan is its savor! Despite the evil that still lurks within him-," The toad chirped at him. "Yes, I know, I was going to get to that part. She doesn't need to know everything."

Ambrosia looked strangely at the boarelf and his pet. "Please tell me?" she begged. "What are you not telling me?"

"Oh, you think I should tell her?" Sacul asked his toad. "She wasn't even there! It's Lukhan's secret to tell, not mine!" The toad chirped. "Then Judas should tell her!" The toad stared blankly at him. "What if I don't thrust her? She is new!"

"Hey! I was the one who patched up your leg! I deserve to know the truth when it comes to my husband!" she demanded.

The toad's bulbous eyes blinked at the shaman. "She could be a spy," Sacul warned his toad, the small creature chirped in reply. "Fine, if you trust her, no biting!" The toad nestled against the boarelf's armpit for warmth. Sacul shook his head and sighed. "You see that black claw?" he asked as he pointed to the silver dragon's left claw. "That is a piece of Vilesath's soul."

"Who is Vilesath?" Ambrosia asked.

"A forgotten nightmare who claims to have created knolls, trolls, and the plague," Sacul whispered. "Anyway, Vilesath was the only dragon known to have conquered death itself, he is also known at the Betrayer!" He gave her a wink. "I used the spirit as a weather forecaster and was a darn good one too." He chuckled at his jest.

"The Betrayer?" Ambrosia pondered out loud. She thought back. "I never heard of him."

"The way Vilesath likes it," Sacul grunted. "The Holy Master and the Inquisition are aware of him. Vilesath is ancient, probably older than the Holy Master, and he is the villain to humanity, ever since the creation of humans. After the Elf's Rebellion, Vilesath helped orchestrate the fall of the Mixed Kingdoms and, throughout history, worked against humans and their benefactor."

"Lukhan is Vilesath?" Ambrosia asked.

"No, but he holds the dark one's essence," Sacul shuttered. "That claw is part of Vilesath and you have seen its terrible power."

Ambrosia pulled nervously at the corner trim on her dress. The dragon she cared for had many dark and terrible secrets. It was no wonder why the Inquisition sought to destroy him. The first time they had met she had been extremely nervous. A troubling thought came to her. "How did the Inquisition find out about him?" she asked.

"I'm afraid that is my fault," Sacul had a boorish grin. "During my walkabout, I told the magnificent tale of Lukhan and his victory over the terrible plague." The toad chirped at him. "I know you were there to." His pet opened its mouth in a bored yawn. "Sometimes, I stretched the truth. No one likes tedious stories!" His toad chirped. "Stop interrupting me!"

"You told the Inquisition?" Ambrosia gasped.

"No," Sacul muttered. "My stories must have a taken on lives of their own and the humans must have built up the myth from there. No wonder why the Inquisition is angry at Lukhan."

"Sacul!" Ambrosia shouted.

"What is done is done," Sacul admitted. "I had nothing to do with the cults and I still believe in the spirit world. No offense, but humans come up with the weirdest stuff to worship. Demigods, symbols, books, coins, and their leaders."

"I suppose you are correct," Ambrosia admitted. "My own family believes that I'm a witch." She sighed at the painful thought. Ignorance and blind faith were dangerous; it scared her that the Inquisition had both.

"It does not matter what other people worship," Sacul grunted. "As long as they keep it to themselves, and don't force it on others." He scratched his itching gut and gave his toad a wet kiss on its head.

"Lukhan is not the Betrayer?" Ambrosia asked.

"Aye," Sacul snorted. He gave his toad a lick. "Told you humans don't get it and will never understand it."

"What's with you and that frog?" Ambrosia demanded.

"Toad," Sacul corrected. "We go back a long way. You see my toad isn't really a-"

"Hasn't he woken up yet?" Bar interrupted. He shut the barn doors behind him. The shadows of the barn grew long.

"Nothing has changed," Sacul grunted. "Stop leaving that barn door wide open! Were you born in a barn?"

"No, but I was born in the woods," Bar replied without missing a beat. "Judas doesn't want any dragon blood on any of the bed sheets."

"How is my husband?" Ambrosia asked.

"Being an ass," Bar shrugged. "I thought women were moody when they were pregnant, what's his problem?"

Ambrosia glanced down. "He is under a great deal of stress," she worried.

"No, he is being a pain," Bar's words were in a mocking tone. "Sorry, Ambrosia but your husband needs to get his head out of his ass before I kick him there-"

"He can be trying," Ambrosia admitted. "Yet that is why I love him. He is what the Inquisition should be."

"What?" Bar chuckled. "Judas, the paragon for the Inquisition? Did you tell a joke?" He laughed at the thought; Judas was all right for a human. He had flaws and unknoll-like ways, but he also had a strong sense of loyalty, which Bar and the others recognized in the self-righteous human.

"What's wrong with him?" Sacul asked. "Judas would be a big improvement over the ones that are in charge of the Inquisition now. He also proves that not all in the service of the Holy Master are crazy zealots. There are good humans, like there are evil knolls."

"Humph," Bar huffed. "Same for all the common races."

"My point is: evil is a perspective," Sacul stated evenly. "We view Lukhan as good because he is our friend, but look at it from the Inquisition's point of view. Lukhan saved the world from the plague, not the Holy Master. Therefore, it is safe to assume that the Inquisition feels threatened by him because he is a challenge to their religious figure. Lukhan uses magic, something considered evil within the Inquisition's teaching. Humans start to worship him because of god-like abilities in destroying the plague. All of these things are a challenge to the Inquisition's demigod. So it is no wonder that they want to kill him." He stroked his toad and it chirped in agreement.

"When did you get so smart?" Bar demanded. "What happen to the real Sacul? What have you done with him?" He squinted at the boarelf, puzzled by the pig's newly found insight.

"Of course these are all wild guesses," Sacul had a broad boorish grin and licked his toad.

"That is clever," Ambrosia complimented. "Yet your theories do nothing for their current situation. Lukhan and Con'ra are still under the wizard's curse, and our only connection to the Inquisition is dead. The reality is that we don't need to know what motivates the Inquisition. We need to find a way to save Lukhan and Con'ra."

"Well, we need a magic user," Bar offered.

"That wouldn't help," Sacul muttered. "Con'ra entered the spirit world and she is in the same predicament as Lukhan. Whatever the wizard did, it really messed them up. My guess is that the curse was divided when Con'ra entered the spell. A shared curse that could have killed Lukhan."

"Then what do we do?" Bar asked. Sacul shrugged his shoulders in reply. The shaman was at a loss in what to do, and so was Bar and Ambrosia. Sacul had entered the spirit world several times the last few days, but the rituals proved to be ineffective at contacting the two wayward dragons.

"They seem to be trapped within their own minds," Sacul grunted. "Diving into their subconscious is not what I'm good at."

"Then how do we get them out?" Bar pressed. He scratched his ears impatiently. The boarelf shrugged his shoulders in reply. "Come on, don't give up. There must be something we can do. We haven't exhausted all options have we?"

"There is one," Sacul had grave hesitation. "If they are trapped within their own minds, it is possible to shock their minds back to reality."

"Shock their minds?" Ambrosia asked.

"Whenever something traumatic happens to a person, all but the most vital parts of the body shut down," Sacul explained. "The same thing happens to the mind. Lukhan and Con'ra are in a comatose state designed to protect their white flames. Their mind's defenses have not lowered and cannot be released from their own psyche."

"I thought the curse was broken!" Bar growled.

"Yes, it is," Sacul agreed. "I can't sense any magical bindings on their white flames, but both seem to be burning weakly."

"So they are not under the influence of any spell or curse?" Bar demanded. "Listen to me! Read my lips! How do we wake them up?" His fists were clenched as he glared at the stalling shaman.

Seeing the growing frustration in his friend's face, Sacul gave him a boorish, mocking grin. "The solution is a simple one," he state snidely. "We have to kill them."

"What?" Bar growled. He brought up his fist and punched the boarelf in the face. Sacul recoiled in fear.

Sacul bend over to protect his toad desperately. "Stop! Stop! Let me explain!" he grunted.

"Explain it to my fist!" Bar snapped.

"Freeze them!" Sacul blurted. Bar paused and waited for the boarelf to continue. "Aye! Slow down the blood in the body and then start the heart up! I don't know if it will work on Con'ra!"

"Wait a moment," Ambrosia gasped in realization and considered what the shaman had said. "The silver dragon is resistant to cold temperatures, but your theory might work. Con'ra is a green dragon and would not respond in the same manner as Lukhan."

"So we have a way to save Luke?" Bar asked.

"Yes," Sacul stated proudly. "However, we do not have a way to chill the barn."

"I think I have a way," Ambrosia considered.

"We are doing this?" Bar asked. "More experiments? There must be another way?"

"It took a week to think of this," Sacul replied. "Do you have another idea?"

"We could use the black claw!" Bar suggested.

"That would regenerate the body, not the mind," Sacul grunted. "What about Con'ra? Do you wish to leave her in this state?" Bar considered the question and shook his head no in reply. "Any other ideas?"

"If you haven't noticed, we are nowhere near the Endless Ice," Bar stated sarcastically. "It's spring in the Endless Desert."

"Judas's new construction projects!" Ambrosia shouted. Bar and Sacul jumped at the woman's announcement. "Iceboxes and Ice Harvesters! We can get them to cool down the barn! Sodium nitrate was added to the water to keep it cold!"

"Say salt," Sacul added. "Keep it simple for the small minded knoll!"

"Why you toad licking pig!" Bar growled.

"Easy Bar," Sacul warned. "You don't want to damage this genius mind!"

"I'll knock some sense into it!" Bar threatened.

"Please stop this," Ambrosia begged. "Both of you stop, we have friends who need our help!"

"Aye, I'm trying to help," Sacul sneered.

"Why you-!" Bar began.

"Stop you two! Settle down before I beat your mangy hides! You're acting like children!" Ambrosia screamed. Both Bar and Sacul cowered at the woman shrilling voice.

"By the spirits," Sacul whispered. "You're loud. I was only teasing him."

"I was only going to beat his head," Bar grumbled softly.

"Nothing but children!" Ambrosia accused. "Now go get the ice!"

Chapter 37

"I don't have that type of coin." Judas stated bluntly. "Why don't you ask Owen for a loan? Make a petition to the council." Ice was worth its weight in gold in the Endless Desert. The upper class citizens of Ravenshaven paid good coin for the cold substance. It was a status symbol among the elite.

"We have three votes here," Sacul grumbled. "We need this ice to kill them!"

"What?" Judas asked in disbelief.

"What he means is that the ice will lower the dragon's body temperature and revive them." Ambrosia explained.

"We are listening to the toad licker?" Judas roared. "What about other methods? Can't we use magic or something?"

"Magic is part of the problem. It is the curse that affects the white flame," Sacul stated. "Therefore magic can't be used."

Judas rubbed his chin in thought. "So you suggest freezing and killing them?" Judas pondered out loud.

"I'm sure Lukhan will survive," Sacul grunted. "I'm concerned about her-"

"Con'ra is none of our concern," Judas snapped. "I would buy ice to save Lukhan but I'm not going to spend good coin on that green lizard."

"Con'ra came here to help us," Ambrosia offered. "She risked her life to save your silver dragon"

"Have all of you gone crazy?" Judas demanded. "She is a thief and a manipulator. She sent us to our deaths and is probably working for the

Blood Queen. Why should we help her? This is the perfect excuse to get rid of her!"

Bar crossed his arms at what Judas was purposing. "She helped save Luke," he added. "I do not trust her, but I can't stand by and let her die. I will not throw her out to the wolves."

"Poor pun," Judas let out a heavy sigh. "Listen to me, everyone loves a hero but no one wants to suffer for him. Ice is costly. If we buy or commandeer the ice, the merchant guild will be pissed off."

"So what?" Sacul grunted. "Let them!"

"There is a large quantity of wealth involved in the matter," Judas warned. "My relations with the merchant's guild are strained as it is."

"We're talking about Luke!" Bar demanded. "We must do everything possible to save him."

Judas rubbed his hand over his clean shaven face and closed his eyes to think. After a brief moment of thought, he opened his eyes and looked at his wife. "We would have to go to Owen, I simply do not have the funds to buy the amount of ice required to freeze the dragons."

"I thought the Iceboxes were built by the city?" Ambrosia asked.

"They were," Judas rubbed the side of his head. "The city sold the property to the merchant guild to raise funds for the city's new construction sites. It was designed to ease the burden on the city tax payers."

"Let's ask the merchant to give us the ice," Ambrosia pleaded. "My parents can help us." There was a long pause between spouses. Judas scowled at the thought, and then his features softened. He stared into her beautiful eyes and shook his head.

"All right, we'll ask them," Judas let out a heavy sigh.

———◆•◆———

Surprisingly, the plan to asked Ambrosia's parents worked. After some initial hesitation, Ambrosia was welcomed back into the family fold. There were some conditions, Judas was reluctantly admitted into the Merchant Guild, but it was the only way to maintain an acceptable relationship. It was a symbolic gesture between the city and guild. The guild's reputation had faltered since the public display of its connection to the Inquisition. The guild also demanded to have blue prints on the Inquisition's technology, especially the larger bombarders used for defense. The deal was struck and both sides won. Ambrosia and Judas were accepted into the family and the guild won by improving its relationship with the city's council members. The iceboxes were opened and wagons hauled their cargo into Judas's estate. Under the direction of Sacul, the blocks were broken down and placed on the dragons. The ice quickly chilled the barn.

"This better work," Judas warned.

"Hey, it's me!" Sacul gave him a boorish grin. "What could go wrong? Doesn't reconciling with Ambrosia's parents make you feel good?"

"I suppose your right," Judas stated. He looked at his wife. She had big smile on her cute face. He cracked a smile seeing her happy.

"Don't celebrate yet," Bar stated. "How are we going to raise their body temperatures when they freeze?"

"Fire?" Sacul suggested.

"Burn down the barn? I think not," Judas replied. "Why not let the ice melt?"

"That would take a while," Bar warned. He watched as more ice was added to the two piles. Con'ra shivered and mist vapors come from her nostrils every time she exhaled. Lukhan was buried in the ice but there were no evidences that the ice had any effect on him.

"This plan better work," Judas muttered.

<hr />

So they waited for the ice to melt. Bar kept watch over the two sleeping dragons and within a week, the ice around Con'ra melted and she began to stir. She opened her eyes slowly at first. Her eyes were distant and faded, as if she wasn't aware of her surroundings. Bar raced to the house to gather the others. When they returned the green dragon was moving her wings and arms.

"Welcome back," Ambrosia had a warm smile gracing her lips. "Did you enjoy your long nap?" With glazed eyes Con'ra slowly blinked at them.

"Where am I?" Con'ra asked in barely a whisper.

"Do you know who I am?" Ambrosia asked.

Con'ra took a deep breath and exhaled. She considered the odd question. "I feel so cold, what happened?" she asked.

"Good you can speak!" Sacul smiled. "Can you say something? Anything? Come on, let's hear you speak."

"Shut up," Con'ra muttered.

"She is going to be all right," Sacul deduced.

"Can you stand? Ambrosia asked. The green dragon stood up shakily as chunks of ice fell off of her. Her muscles trembled from the effort and she collapsed from the exertion.

"Are you?" Ambrosia asked.

"Why am I so weak?" Con'ra asked. "Wet and cold?"

"You have been asleep for over a week," Ambrosia explained. "You haven't used you muscles in a long time. You need time to recover your strength."

"I am fine," Con'ra huffed and she strained to pull herself up again. "Where is Lukhan? Is he safe?"

"He is right here," Bar pointed to the mound of ice next to them. "We had to bury you under ice to pull you out of your coma. The same process is happening to Luke. He is safe."

"Why am I so cold?" Con'ra repeated. She glanced around the barn, confused at the change in structure. "Where am I? What is this place?" Her tone was on the edge of panic. She flopped around like an injured bird.

"Easy," Judas warned. "You're in the city of Ravenshaven, and we had to move you to my estate. You are safe, for the moment."

"Lukhan?" Con'ra mumbled.

"He hasn't recovered," Sacul grunted. "The ice doesn't appear to be working. Of all things, it has grown, not melted." The shaman's observations were correct; the ice around Lukhan had solidified, creating a cocoon of ice. Two ice holes were all that was visible to the ice covered dragon.

"Silver dragons cannot freeze," Con'ra muttered. Her drooping eyes slowly began to close.

"You can't fall asleep," Bar stated. "You have to tell us everything! What happened? Is Luke all right?"

"The curse made us face our terrible nightmares," Con'ra whispered. Her eyes went wide in fear at the horrible memories.

"It was a dream?" Sacul asked.

"More akin to a nightmare," Con'ra whispered. "The white flame attacks itself. That is what the retaliation curse is designed to do. It forced us to relive our most horrible memories, weakening our soul and smothering the white flame in our own fear and darkness."

"Mark said that it was the Inquisition. Who was it? How is it that they are using magic?" Ambrosia asked.

"The human called himself Inquisitor Lord Shen," Con'ra recalled. "He created a network of condemned wizards to cast the curse. He could have been anywhere." She shook her head at the painful memories. The nightmare continued to echo in her head and, although they were magically induced, the painful truth still seared her mind.

"Why do you cringe?" Bar asked. "What is the matter?"

"I saw Lukhan's and the human's darkest nightmares, as they saw mine," Con'ra whispered softly. The human and dragon shared her secret. She wondered if Lukhan's nightmare was as secretive.

"What did you see?" Judas asked.

"His dream is his own," Con'ra growled. "The human's dream is another matter."

"Tell us what you saw," Sacul pressed.

"Shen's fears that humanity will lose faith in the Inquisition and the Holy Master," Con'ra revealed. "If that occurs, then their religion will die. Without followers that listen to them, they are powerless. That is why the Inquisition is pressing this issue of cults. Their religion is dying and this has caused them to take drastic action to counter heretical belief systems, such as those who follow Lukhan."

"Irrational thoughts based on fears and suspicious," Judas concluded.

"That may be so, but the Inquisition will not tolerate a rival religion," Bar warned. "Their traditions go back farther than the Mixed Kingdoms. They have been humanity's savior, because they believe themselves justified."

"Even so," Judas added. "I once felt the same; the methods for religious fervor are crude, but effective. The order is more than a religion; it is a way of life. Humanity will not give up their god because of a new religious order or cult. The common folk don't give a shit on who leads them."

"True," Ambrosia agreed. "There are loyal followers and they are as fanatical as the people within this city. Their anti-Inquisition has led them down the path of paranoia and fanatical extremes. It is no wonder why the two cities oppose each other."

"This is good to know, but how do we save Luke?" Bar demanded.

Con'ra looked confused at the knoll's question and turned her attention to the solid ice block. "We must free him and the ice must be broken and the sun should warm our bodies," Con'ra stood up and stumbled out of the barn, despite Ambrosia's protest. The woman followed the green dragon outside.

"Well, let's get to work," Bar suggested. The others picked up pick axes and chiseled away at the Lukhan's icy prison. The work was slow and tedious, but they were careful not to harm their friend. At last, the final stab of ice was removed from the silver dragon.

"Is he awake?" Con'ra called from outside. Her shivering had slowed and her strength slowly returned. A meal of goats and warm water was given to her. She devoured the tasty morsels, yet she was still physically exhausted from the time she had spent frozen.

"Come on, Luke," Bar brushed the last of the clinging ice from his friend. Slowly the frozen dragon's eyes cracked open.

"Careful Bar, he has not had anything to eat since the past week," Judas warned. He pulled off a piece of ice from the dragons back.

"I know the dangers," Bar hushed. "Luke, come on. Wake up." The dragon's magically scarred eyes eventually focused on the knoll before him.

Warning bells tolled and the sound of bombarder fire thundered across the roof tops. Shouts and cries of panic sound off in the distance. Those in the barn were frozen in shock. Were they under attack? They looked to each other for the answer, but no one knew what was going on. The warning bells continued to toll.

Judas dropped his pick axe and ran out the barn. "Con'ra, keep an eye on Lukhan," he instructed. "Bar! Sacul! Follow me!"

"What about me?" Ambrosia asked.

"Secure our home and keep an eye on those two!" Judas replied. "Lock the doors and stay safe!" He gave her a quick hug and raced into the house to grab his weapons and armor. Bar and Sacul followed closely on the man's heels.

"Come on guys, we need to hurry!" Bar pressed.

An explosion sounded in the distance and the evening sky was on fire. "What is going on?" Sacul gasped nervously. "You guys can go on! I'll hold up the fort and make sure that nothing happens here." The boarelf was anxious at the surprising and unexpected sound of bombarder fire.

Judas and Bar grabbed their weapons and don their armor. They left Judas's estate and raced to the city's outer wall. As they reached the top of the fortifications the distant horizon was set ablaze by multiple fires. Red dragons flew in the sky above the burning areas. The sky burned with red and orange light. The city's bombarders fired their shots, but fell harmlessly short. The monstrous beasts circled above the city, the smell of sulfur and brimstone filled the air. The Red Clan descended upon the vulnerable city of Ravenshaven.

Chapter 38

"Where are our defenders?" Owen demanded. He looked out over the farmlands that circled the city. Smoke rose over a burning field. "Why are they burning our fields, when the red dragons should defend us?" The old knoll was on a helpless rampage; his normally calm demeanor was gone. His white and silver hairs stood on end and were like jagged spikes running down the back of his neck. Another shot from a bombarder sounded off next to them. A strong smell of sulfur permeated the air as a black powder fog covered the walls and defenders.

"Why are they shooting?" Bar demanded. His tone was calm and in control. Bar evaluated the situation. The burning fields did not surprise him; he knew that this was a show of force. It was an exertion of power, to prove that the common races were powerless to stop the Red Clan. If the Red Clan wished to destroy the city, this was the burning verification; he shook his head at the pointless and pup-like behavior the dragons were displaying.

Owen turned on Bar, his teeth bared and his ears lay back in a threatening manner. "While you've been on vacation, the Red Clan has been demanding tribute and burning our sown fields! This planting season will be completely ruined!"

"Luke has been under a curse!" Bar snapped back.

"I know that!" Owen coughed. "He has responsibilities! It doesn't change the fact that we need them to defend us! What use are sleeping dragons if we can't call upon them at a moment's notice?"

"Tribute?" Judas asked. "Have you spoken to their leader? Did he say anything at all before this rampage?"

"They demand gold and food to feed their bellies," Owen snarled.

"Something that you three agreed upon and they are here to remind us of." The ten red dragons remained far in the distance, out of range of the city's defenses. Even with the distance between them, they could feel the scorching heat. The dragon's fire inspired fear among the defenders. The city guards cowered behind the walls and fired wildly at the distant dragons. Buckets of water were brought up to put out any fires that might arise from the approaching dragons.

"Well, what did you say in return?" Bar asked.

"Nothing! The reds bellowed their demands and flew away," Owen admitted. "Then they started burning the fields."

This confirm Bar's thoughts about the red dragons trying to establish control by using fear.

"This must be a test," he concluded. "To study our strengths and observe our tactics."

"What?" Judas asked. He raised a questioning eyebrow at his friend's insight into dragon nature. The presumption seemed logical enough, but how could the knoll tell?

"See, they keep burning the same area," Bar observed. He pointed to the circling dragons. The red dragon circled sporadically in the air above the same location. Creating scorched earth that appeared to be on fire, the flames danced high into the evening sky. The firestorm was fueled by the dragons' breaths. "The ten dragons could've done a lot more damage if they attacked the city. However, they keep targeting the same location."

"So how are we supposed to respond?" Owen demanded. He reluctantly nodded his head in agreement. The knoll's observations appeared to be correct for the moment.

"We need to show them our strength," Bar replied. "Send out a party to challenge them. Prove to them that we are not afraid to die! Else they-!"

"We might be playing into their claws," Owen warned.

"I'll do it," Judas bellowed over the bombarder fire. "I'll take my knights out and reply to their challenge. I won't let them burn down the fields on my watch. You, men! Stop firing! You are wasting ammunition! Calm yourselves! Form ranks! Get back to your posts! Prepare a group to ride out and meet them!" He raced down the wall shouting orders and restoring order to the panicking soldiers, both men and knolls stop what they were doing and listen to Judas's vociferating orders.

"Luke has awakened!" Bar promised. Owen still had a frown on his scouring face. He shook his head at his fellow knoll.

"So? He will be in no condition to fight!" Owen growled. He looked away sharply and placed his hand on his chest. "I was hoping for a more peaceful relationship with dragons. This action is unforgivable! They are burning down this year's crop! How are we going to feed ourselves?" His sharp eyes followed the dragon's movement. The ten creatures were stoic at their destruction. He had to do something about the marauding dragon horde.

"Luke will be here," Bar swore. "He will set everything right! I promise you."

"I doubt that!" Owen warned. His breath was labored and his hand had not moved, but gripped his chest hair tighter. There was a painful strain on his face. "Listen carefully; you can't count on dragons! He is not a white knight! We will have to defend ourselves, prepare for battle." He halfheartedly tossed bar fresh powder and ammunition for his weapon.

"You're wrong," Bar stated evenly. A concerned expression crossed his face. Owen was behaving oddly.

"I wish you were correct," Owen stated dryly as he gestured to the nearest guard to approach them. His tongue stuck out as if he was hot. "Fetch me our dragons. I don't care if you have to poke them in the eye with a spear! Get the two beasts here!"

"Yes, my lord," the guards gave them a quick salute.

"I'll go with him," Bar offered. He knew that Luke would destroy anyone who did that, but knowing how serious the guards took their jobs, he had to wonder.

"No. Judas and you shall remain at the wall in case the red dragons wish to talk about the Blood Queen's arrangement." Owen instructed through labor gasps. He growing fury in his eyes did not subside. He cursed and swore death and worse to the distant dragons that continued to burn his city's fields.

"Judas can do that-," Bar began.

"That is an order-," Owen snarled. His words trailed off into a sickly cough.

"Are you all right?" Bar asked.

"I've been slack with my governing," Owen cleared his throat and returned his attention to Bar. Another gasping cough interrupted his words. "I should have foreseen this. I should've stopped the wizard and the cursed reds. Did I really expect them to keep their promise?"

"Guar-!" Bar began.

"I'm all right," Owen growled. "Focus on the situation at hand. I will be fine, it is just-" Despite his weak condition the old knoll's words still held authority and he tumbled back heavy and leaned against the wall for support. Bar grab the old knoll's arm and threw it over his should for support. The old knoll had lost a great deal of weight and Bar was surprised at how light his leader was. He looked around for help, but the guards around them scurried around in preparation of the approaching dragons. The red dragons had the guards' full attention.

"Tell me, how long have you been like this?" Bar asked.

"I've been sick for a long time," Owen admitted in a gravelly tone. "Before the assassins and before all of this shit happened." His eyes watered, as his winced in pain, from how hard he had been coughing, ears drooping, and his normally strong demeanor faded. Owen's arm strained at the tightness he was gripping at his chest.

"I should get you to Ambrosia-," Bar began.

"She already knows," Owen whispered. "Please take me away from here, I can't allow the army to see me like this." His words were desperate now. "Judas can take command; he has a good rapport with the soldiers and he built the damn walls." Bar nodded his head in understanding and escorted Owen away from the wall. After making sure Owen was safe in the shade, he gave orders to pass on to Judas and then returned to Owen's side.

"How old are you Bar?" Owen asked with shallow breaths.

"I am over twenty," Bar helped Owen to his feet. The white knoll grunted and held on to Bar's should for support.

"Twenty?" Owen gasped in a weak voice.

"Yes, over twenty-four complete seasons," Bar gave him a nervous smile. "I should be dead by now, but I have been lucky."

"You're lucky," Owen jested. "I'm only seventeen years old. Seasons? Who talks like that anymore? I forgot that you were not born here." A squeezing chuckle passed his strained lips. "My old pa used to talk like that, when we lived in the woods."

"You're father sounds like he knew what he was talking about," Bar's smile faded. "Sounds like he was from my generation."

Owen didn't return the smile, instead staring down at the ground in reflection. "We're old," he grunted. "Put me down, I need to rest."

"Come on; don't forget I have a lame arm! Help me out." Bar pleaded. "No, we have to make it to your house. Ambrosia can fix you right up! Come on; don't get lazy on me now!" Together, the two knolls slowly made it to Judas's estate. "You survived assassination attempts, the plague, and a revolution! You're going to be fine, remember that you still have a war to win!"

Owen began to gasp and his balance more uneven. It was a failed attempt to rally the old knoll's spirits and as they made it to the front step of the house, Owen collapsed. His eyes wide with fear and pain. "Not this time," he whispered weakly.

———◆———

"Lukhan, wake up!" Con'ra ordered. "Something is on fire; it stinks of the Red Clan." She brushed his nose with her own. Lukhan mumbled something.

"What did you say?" Con'ra asked.

"You smell good," Lukhan muttered more clearly. His eyes fluttered open but they were still foggy and distant.

"What?" she gasped. "What did you say? I thought you did not like my scent!"

Con'ra paused; her eyes went wide in realization. How dare he dream about and smell her! That stupid foul smelling dragon! Her anger was subdue when she remembered his embrace, his comforting words and lingering touch, she shook her head at those wonderfully terrible thoughts. He had invaded her dreams and only a sick pervert would do such a horrible thing!

"My little maple seed-," Lukhan muttered.

"Wake up!" Con'ra screamed in his face. Lukhan's eyes flew open and he jumped up in surprise and icy cold water splashed on Con'ra. This fouled her mood even further. "Hey! Stop day dreaming and wake up! Your pets need you!"

Lukhan trembled and then collapsed on his side. Chunks of ice clung to him in a fleeting attempt to keep him contained. "W-What is going on?" he stuttered in garbled voice that was barely a whisper because his throat was dry from the lack of water. He lapped up the icy water around him.

"Get your head out of the clouds!" Con'ra growled. "Can you smell the smoke? The Red Clan is here and your friends ran out to challenge them."

"I need food," The silver dragon sprang up and invaded Con'ra's personal space. He drew close, his breath shallow, and stared longingly into her eyes. Con'ra gulped nervously and held her breath; she bite her bottom lip and her heart pounded in her chest as he drew ever closer to her. "Food, it feels like

293

I have not had anything in weeks." Lukhan's eyes widen in realization, he turned away from her, sniffing the smoke filled air.

"Food?" Con'ra asked in growing anger. "Typical male! Always having your mind on food and not what was important!" Her eyebrows twitched in annoyance as she frowned. "You are correct," she huffed. "Your friends told me that we have been under a spell for the past week."

"The Inquisitor Lord Shen? You? I remember the dreams-," Lukhan began.

"Never speak of that!" Con'ra warned in a venomous snarl.

"You may never wish to, but I will always remember," Lukhan blinked at her in confusion. There was a long pause between the two, Con'ra was speechless. Was he blackmailing her? She didn't understand his motivation, he wouldn't do that. Her thoughts were jumbled together in an entangle net of emotions. For once she was unsure as how to reply to his statement.

"We saw each other's darkest fears and I can understand your reluctances to speak of it," he added. "However, theses nightmares will never go away and will always be with us. I hope, in time you will learn to accept this fact and confer in me. Thank you for saving me."

Con'ra looked at him in surprise. He wasn't extorting her, but trying to connect on an emotional level. They weren't connected! Not in any rational way! Seeing each other's nightmares meant everything to her. She was there by command of the Blood Queen. No irrational emotion would overtake her! Love! It was a joke! Fear was a primal instinct that united them against a common enemy: the Inquisitor Lord that invaded their minds. She wasn't attached to him because of his good looks or charming personality. He stank of death and looked like a frozen piece of crap, but there was something about him. Even she did not understand that feeling. What was it? Fear? Love? The confusion made her even angrier.

"I-I do not know what to say," Con'ra admitted in frustrated.

"Say that you will help me and I shall aid you in return," Lukhan promised. "I will never forget my promise to you. Your thoughts, feelings, and fears are my own. I know of betrayal and placing the blame on one's self. I do this daily, but shit happens."

"T-Thank you?" Con'ra whispered. His words confused her even more. Her wings blushed at the oath the silver dragon had promised to her. His words meant more to her than he knew.

Lukhan's face hardened and his eyes narrowed as he sniffed the outside air. "I need to feed before I confront the red dragons," His words grew cold and stoic, as if the ice around them had seeped into his soul.

The sudden change in his emotions unnerves Con'ra. "Your friends left some food for you."

The goats outside in a pen bleeped nervously at the hungry growl of dragon. He raised his left claw as a brittle empty crackle came from the black flesh. The digit uncurled from its position. The silver dragon shuttered under some unseen force. Lukhan's body grew weak as the claw sucked the vitality out of him. Muscle withered away and his flesh pulled tight against his bony structure. Con'ra gasped at the sudden transformation of a healthy dragon to a flesh and scales draped over a dragon skeleton. Old scars and damaged flesh revealed itself in the transformation. The flesh of the black claw reemerged with violent reawakening. Black root at the base of his figure crawled up his forearm and reasserted itself within his unfrozen body. Lukhan winced in pain at the spread of tainted flesh. A flash of hunger was in Lukhan's eyes. The moment was brief, but his features returned to normal. Con'ra's jaw dropped at the sudden and horrible change. His somewhat acceptable appearances turned into an ugly skeletal creature.

He saw the fear in her eyes. She backed away in horror of the deathly creature before her. "I'm all right," Lukhan whispered. His malnourished and sickly form stated otherwise. "I am starved." He looked down at his ghastly body. He turned his empty hollow gaze to the green dragon before him. "You are not the only one with secrets. Now you know mine. I cannot hide my nightmare. This is what my true body looks like."

"You- this is what your body looks like?" Con'ra asked with a nervous gulp.

He slowly blinked at her and nodded his head yes. "This is what I become when I have not fed," he admitted. "I need to take a white flame." He looked away in shame. He had been so careful to hide his decayed form. Not even his friends knew of his deteriorated condition. He felt exposed to her, he looked away in shame. A frozen string drool dripped from his jaws.

"It-It is not so bad," Con'ra held back a gag. The silver dragon looked like a dried up corpse that had been left out in the desert's sun. "At least this explains why you reek of death."

"You must promise not to speak of this to anyone," Lukhan warned in a dry gasping threat. "No one must see me like- like this! No one!" Fury lit in his otherworldly eyes as he stared at her.

"I understand," Con'ra looked away. "Tell no one of my past and I will never speak of this."

"If this is what it takes," Lukhan agreed in pitiful desperation. "Although neither of us will forget what we have seen. I will respect your request."

"Good," Con'ra approved. "Eat. I cannot have you looking like a starving beast when we face the Red Clan."

"Do not mistake my appearances as weakness," Lukhan warned. "Of all things, this is my most dangerous and unpredictable state." The dribbles of frozen saliva splatter on the barn floor.

"I will never underestimate you," Con'ra whispered nervously. She watches the skeleton of a dragon move past her like a specter. The air around him was cold and unforgiving. Drool continued to dribble out of his mouth and freeze before shattering on the barn floor. Outside of the barn, the goats' cries of fear turned into screams of horrible agony as Lukhan drained each of their lifeless bodies to dust. She winced as Lukhan slaughter the goats, but she did not look away from the butchery. She realized then that his nightmare was real. Moisture gathered at the corner of her eyes, but no tears fell.

"I know who you are," Con'ra whispered. "I have seen the goodness within your soul. This is your true form. Remember that it is nothing more than a nightmare." He glanced at her kind words and she rewarded him with a smile. Lukhan's body quickly regenerated. Muscle and skin returned to normal and his starved form returned to a healthy strong silver dragon. The long period of starvation had no effect, save the growing and expanding roots of black flesh that expanded to his elbow and upper forearm. The cancerous flesh was slowly taking over his body.

Chapter 39

"Where is this silver dragon I have heard so much about?" the largest dragon demanded. The leader was the color of maroon with lighter hues down to the center of his body. Jagged scales and thorns covered the leader's scales. Two massive black horns dominated the leader's skullcap, smoke and black jagged teeth filled the red leader's mouth. He was a veteran of many battles, with scars from battles with other dragons was evident on his body. Strong muscles rippled from beneath the jagged thorns and scales. The shadow of his massive form dwarfed the knights below him. The other red dragons, ranging in younger age and size, circled warily above Judas and his company of men. These younger dragons looked to their battle hardened leader for guidance. Some of the warhorses screamed and their ears twitched nervously at the passing dragon and the sulfuric stench. This inspired fear amongst the men, but Judas and his mount were steadfast and stoic like a statue. Seeing the strength of their leader, the men took comfort and quieted their steeds. The knights gripped their weapons nervously as the ten dragons circled around them like buzzards. The knights and dragons took measure of each other.

"I assume that you are the leader of this rabble?" Judas challenged the massive red that flew slowly above them. "I thought the Blood Queen promised an alliance! You have no right to torch our fields and demand treasure and food!"

The massive red leader landed with a thunderous boom. Ash and dust shot up at the knights. Their horses shuffled nervously and some of the men were bucked off their mounts. Three horses lost their nerve and fled before the stench of the red dragon. The fleeing horses were quickly snatched up by the passing dragon and quickly devoured. One horse ignited into flames, shrieking and kicking, the poor animal exploded when the fire struck a black powder keg that was tied to its saddle. The red dragons became more cautious and nervous after witnessing the exploding horse. The dismounted men drew their weapons and shouted in anger. Judas remained stoic at the expected result of cowardice. The reds were looking to break his men! If they ran, they would be slaughtered like the horses that fled. Judas hardened himself, preparing himself to face the aggressive beasts that surrounded them.

"It would be wise not to follow your horse's lead," the red leader grumbled. "The stench of alchemy is in the air. It is sulfur, charcoal, and saltpeter and that is the ingredient for bombarder powder. The hairless apes have been busy with their machines of war." His words were thick, like a rock slide. The other red dragons chuckled at their leader's jest. They knew that fear was the mind-slayer, which ruled them all.

"We agreed that the city would provide logistical support to your clan," Judas stated evenly. "You are taking advantage of my people's hospitality!"

The leader raised a questioning eyebrow. This little human wasn't afraid of him? The lesser race would dare speak to him? "I will not be denied," warned the red dragon. "The beasts you ride, give them to me! We shall take them as payment for your impudence. You will be spared if you give them to me freely." The massive red dragon leaned forth, its maw ready to take Judas's horse. With a flash of steel, Judas drew his sword and, in one fluid movement, sliced the dragon's jaw. The red dragon roared and recoiled in pain. The knights unsheathed their weapons and prepared for the dragons to strike.

"How dare you?" the red dragon growled as he withdrew. The dragon narrowed his eyes dangerously at the lesser creature that dared to strike him. The human wielded elven crafted weapons. That was why the blade bit so easily. He snorted and a jet of flame and smoke burst from his snout.

"If it is a fight you want, then that is what you shall get!" Judas scowled. "You come to my land! Burn our fields and demanded tribute! How dare you!"

The red dragon smiled at the human's tenacity. "You must be the human, the Inquisitor Judas. Your fellow ape-things would pay good gold for your head."

"I am," he announced boldly. "My titles are knight and councilor of the city of Ravenshaven, witch lover, and dragon friend."

"Witch lover?" the red dragon had an amused tone. "I thought the Inquisitors killed what they do not understand. Witches, dragons, magi, and wizards have no place in the world of men. They lack imagination, natural, and magical empathy. No wonder why they are so reckless in their destruction. They wonder about this world in ignorant bliss."

"I'm not afraid," Judas declared boldly. "The Inquisition is our true enemy. We shouldn't fight ourselves. We are brothers in arms."

"You would place us as equals?" the red dragon asked. "We are not here for some pathetic ideology of equality and friendship. We are here to destroy those who have stolen from us!"

"Your enemy is the Inquisition," Judas warned.

"We have many enemies," the red dragon let out a quick snort of fire. "The Blood Queen believes that this silver dragon can deliver a one sided victory over them. Unlikely words of endorsement. The Queen does not praise those who are undeserving. By order of the Blood Queen, we serve the silver dragon and no others!"

"Lukhan is currently indisposed," Judas replied.

"I do not care if he is dead," the red leader warned. "Allow me access to his corpse. I must see this silver or we will burn your city to the ground."

Judas raised his sword in a threatening manner. "If you dare come close to my city, I will personally cut out your burning heart!"

"How poetic!" the red leader and the circling dragons above chuckled at the thought. "You are brave, little man. That is our fault. The Red Clan has been too lenient with the lesser races. With every passing generation, the weak have forgotten their place in this world."

"We have learned from our past," Judas rebuked. "We request to be equals before we surpass dragons as betters."

This brought growls and threats from the circling dragons. Smoke bellowed out of the circling dragons' nostrils and mouths. "Betters," the red leader stated. "That is a dangerous mouth you have." The red leader lunged, mouth spread wide, in a vain attempt to swallow Judas and his warhorse whole. Judas struck the red dragon's bottom jaw. The dragon recoiled like a struck snake, blood dribbled from the side of the red's mouth. The red dragon winced in pain, but then smiled and licked the blood from the corner of his mouth.

"A well placed blow!" Judas warned. His fellow knights cheered at the successful blow. "I could have cut your tongue! Stay back! If you wish to continue-!"

"Fool!" the red leader snarled. "You would dare show me pity! I will teach you to show mercy!" He struck with a flurry of bites and blows from his claws. Judas was sent flying by the red dragon's multiple blows. His warhorse shrieked and fell silent as the animal was ripped to shreds. Judas stuck the ground and rolled, avoiding the dragon's multiple blows.

"Damn you!" Judas cursed.

The blood covered dragon smirked at the prone man. "Blood for blood," he replied. With an outstretched claw, he severed his horse's head and threw it at him. "That was for being mouthy to your betters. Know your place!"

Judas slowly stood up, blade still in hand. His sword quivered in anger. His eyes knitted together in a look of pure hatred. "Now I know why the Inquisition killed the sacred herd!" he huffed. "To prove that dragons are nothing more than scavengers, preying upon the weak to strengthen their positions of power and feed their own maniacal idea of superiority."

"Bullying?" the red leader asked as he licked his bloody lip. "Is that what you call it? Does the lion bully the lamb? No, it does not. It simply eats it. You are nothing more than a lamb to me, little human. A source of food and nothing more. Know this as I devour you." This brought a round of laughter from the surround dragons that circled in the air.

"You'll find that we humans are not as helpless as you think we are!" Judas declared. His raised his weapon and his fellow knights cheered at their leader's bravado. This simple act brought frowns to their tormentor's features. Feral snarls and bared teeth were the dragon's reply.

"What is your clan doing here?" a strong feminine voice roared from above. A shadow dove out of the sun. The sudden movement and flash of gold scattered the flying circling red dragons. The red leader attempted to dodge out from under the surprise attack, but the gold dragon smashed into him like a hawk snatching a rabbit. The red leader was pinned to the ground, his snout and jaws buried into the charred earth.

"Vatara!" Judas cheered. Other gold dragons dove at the circling reds. Burst of white and red flames exploded from around the knights. The thunderous boom of dragons smashing into each other echoed over the plains. The earth shook as the gold dragons drove their red counterparts to the ground, knocking the massive creatures into the charred earth. The red dragons were quickly subdued and restrained by the gold dragons.

"What is this?" the red leader demanded. His words were muffled due to Vatara shoving his snout into the dirt. "Is this a declaration of war? How dare you place your claws on me? Damn coward! Attacking from the sun-!"

"Havoc, you thieving piece of shit," Vatara growled in his ear. "I have dealt with you before! What are you doing here? The Red Clan should not be here. Leave at once!"

"We are here to full fill the blood oath to the Blood Queen," Havoc snarled with a mouth pull of dirt. "We are here because of her!"

"The Queen?" Vatara gasped in bewilderment. "Who is that?" She looked around the grappled dragons.

"The Blood Queen," Havoc corrected. "She is our clan's new leader."

Vatara stared at him in confusion. Why wasn't the new leader leading this group? Something was out of place. The position of dragon's leadership was designed to deal with foreign affairs. Why was this thief here? Then Judas stepped forward and presented himself before her with a grateful bow. She turned to the human that stood before them. The tiny man seemed to know what was going on.

"They are here on invitation," Judas explained. "The city sent an emissary to the Red Clan-"

With a mighty heave, Havoc lifted his shoulder and raised his wings. Vatara struggled to remain on top of the red leader. Havoc's brute strength overpowered her and she was quickly tossed off. Havoc chuckled at the gold dragon's effort. "I did not realize how injured you were," he chuckled in amusement, "until I smelt the blood on you. You should not be threatening anyone in your condition."

Barely able to hold a defensive stance, Vatara struggled to back away from Havoc. The other red dragons flipped off the gold dragons. Some of the gold dragons remained where they had been tossed down, too exhausted to hold the red dragons. Judas could not believe how easily the gold dragons were defeated. It was as if they had no strength to fight the invaders.

"Vatara?" Judas asked in confusion. The gold leader turned to the side. Her wings and scales were riddled with bullet holes and feathery shafts of bolts and arrows. She appeared more like a shot up practice target than the beautiful gold creature that Judas remembered. On further investigation, Vatara had fared better than the rest of her clan. They were tarnished and bloody from the strife's of conflict.

"You are half dead," Havoc sneered as he splat out the dirt his mouth. He turned his attention to Judas. "How amusing, you defend these humans; however, I am certain that it was they who did that to you." Vatara glared at him, her golden orbs did not betray the truth in Havoc's accusations. "This is tragically comical; I remember when my great grandfather spoke of days when the lesser races served as slaves and defended the dragon races. How times have changed. Dragons have become the pets and the lesser have become the masters. The roles have reversed. The humans are now the masters and you are their trained dogs."

"Vatara-," Judas gasped.

Although defiance was in her eyes, she backed away like a cowering dog. "You know nothing," she warned. Vatara winced in pain and limped further away from the towering red leader.

Judas sprang to action. "Stay away from her!" he warned. "Defend the Gold Clan!" The knights broke rank and raced to the nearest gold dragons. The red dragons roared in fury and sprang away from the charging knights and their deadly weapons. Havoc remained where he stood and used his massive tail to knock horse and rider away like matchsticks. Judas raced to defend Vatara from the approaching red leader.

"What is this?" Havoc growled in frustration of the trivial nuisances. "Get out of my way, hairless ape! Do you wish to die?"

"What are you doing? Get out of here!" Vatara warned. "You cannot win this fight!"

"No! I came here to defend our home." Judas stated. "You've risked your life for me! I shall do the same. I will die by your side! I will die defending my home!"

"We're with you!" his men replied. Both mounted and dismounted knights raced to their leader's side. A wall of shields, spears, and swords were brought to bear against Havoc.

Frustrated scowl past over the Havoc's face. The massive red dragon stared at the forces that gathered around him and then looked for his fleeing support. The reds that followed him flew off in full flight. The unseasoned youngster used the distraction to escape the Gold Clan and knights. Havoc growled at the cowards! He understood and returned his attention to the humans and dragons. The two races were protecting each other. Dragons were not subservient to the lesser races, but the two shared a common goal. This union between the two races is what made them strong. He could easily slaughter the hairless apes and perhaps, kill Vatara, but the price of would be his own life. All it would take would be a lucky strike or an enraged gold dragon to finish him. As a veteran of many battles, Havoc was greedy, but not stupid. His death would be pointless if he died in the desert. The gold and food would have to wait. This battle couldn't be won by either side. Havoc twisted his neck from side to side, relieving the stress that had gathered upon his shoulders. His nostrils flared in frustration.

"Fair enough," Havoc admitted. "I have not come to speak with anything like you. I seek the silver dragon, the one that my Queen told me I was indebted to."

"Do you yield?" Judas demanded.

"I would never yield," Havoc warned. Smoke bellowed from his mouth at the human's accusation. "Think of this as a momentary truce or a respite. Make no mistake, your city's value is little more than meat to me. Never think that I would surrender to lesser creatures" He had hoped to subjugate the lesser races and feed on them. Havoc's plans were for not, at least not while the Gold Clan was here.

"Your followers have abandoned you," Vatara warned. She stood up shakily; the full extent of her injuries was revealed. Havoc inhaled the sweet blood of the gold dragon. How her body would taste over an open flame. His eyes narrowed at her, she was weaker than he expected. His eyes glowed with the taint of magical energy.

"I would not do that if I were you," a young voice interrupted from above and behind him. A green and silver dragon no older than hatchlings hovered behind him. "Who are you? Why do you burn these fields?"

Havoc turned his attention to the smell of death that flew above him. "You must be the silver dragon that the Queen swore an alliance with," Havoc growled. "Lukhan, if I am not mistaken."

"I am," Lukhan replied.

"Then I am here to full fill the Blood Queen's oath," Havoc announced.

Chapter 40

"Behold, Havoc, the Blood Queen's favored toy," Con'ra sneered. Lukhan and Con'ra landed behind Havoc, dividing his defenses in two different directions.

"Green backbiter, I should have killed you when you first arrived in my territory," Havoc snarled. His eyes narrowed dangerously at Con'ra. The green dragon smiled mischievously at the massive maroon dragon.

"I exposed you for what you really are," Con'ra replied snidely. "Thief." The single word enraged Havoc, cutting him deeper than any sword. Plumes of pitch black smoke bellowed from his nostrils.

"Enough," Lukhan warned. "This troubles me. I awaken to see my territory being burned by the Red Clan and the Gold Clan is injured. By the five elements, someone tell me what is going on? I have slept for too long!"

The smell of ash, blood, and gore was thick in the air. The entrails of dead horses was scattered across the charred landscape. Havoc was covered in horse blood, and the smell of fresh dragon's blood mixed with that of the surrounding smells. Judas was not mounted like the rest of his knights. The silver dragon assumed that Havoc and Judas had fought. Lukhan looked to Vatara for answers but she barely blinked at him in exhaustion. She looked terrible; her normally beautiful sleek scales appeared riddled with bullet holes and arrow shafts. The small multiple wounds seem minor and artificial. This troubled Lukhan even more. The appearance of his injured godmother angered him; his focus returned to the red dragon before him.

Judas steps forth with answers. "Havoc seeks blood and treasure!" he accused. "He killed my horse and many of my men's steeds!" He waved his sword in the air angrily. The blade sliced through the air.

Lukhan raised a questioning eyebrow at Havoc. The red dragon had not only burnt his city's fields, but butchered his friend's animal. The foolish red dragon was trying to start a war. He had pointlessly destroyed city property! The city would never trust the Red Clan after this. The damage had already planted the seeds of mistrust.

"I should kill you," Lukhan threatened. His eyebrows knitted together and his lips pulled back revealing his sharp teeth. His black claw twitched in craving anticipation. He stepped forward eager to engage Havoc.

The bellowing smoke from the red dragon's nostrils stopped. Whiffs of heat continued to swirl out of his mouth and nose. His hard eyes slowly softened. "I am no fool," Havoc stated. "I am aware that a silver dragon, no older than a hatchling, killed the infamous Orelac and the impulsive Rohad. Both dragons were of no small standing within the Blood Queen's ranks. I demanded your attention and focus. I was instructed to meet only with you. This is a display of my powers."

"Your actions were design to get my attention?" Lukhan growled. "You have it now."

"It was designed to test the lesser race's defenses," Havoc added with an evil sneer. "If we are going be allies, I must know if they are willing to fight and die."

"You killed our horses to test us!" Judas demanded.

"Silence," Havoc stated flatly. "You may have lost a horse, but you have gained my support. You were willing to fight and die; therefore, I shall keep the Blood Queen's promise. Your beast was the price you had to pay."

"I do not believe you," Lukhan stated sourly.

"Red dragons are not known to repay debts," Vatara added. She looked at Havoc with distain and suspicion. She had dealt with the troublesome red worm before.

"I agree," Judas crossed his arms defiantly. "You did large amount damage for a test or to get Lukhan's attention! You own us!"

"I do not need to explain my actions," Havoc replied. "Humans killed the sacred herd and your people will pay for that debt with their lives."

"No, I think you need to explain," Con'ra teased. "Such crude and barbaric ways are unseemly for a dragon."

"Shut up-," Havoc began. Before he could finish his sentence Lukhan jumped at him. Surprised the massive red dragon jumped away from the feint.

"Never insult her," Lukhan warned. His teeth were bared and rage flashed within the silver dragon's eyes.

A confused expression crossed the red dragon's face. He looked from Con'ra to Lukhan, uncertain of how to measure their relationship. A smile from Con'ra's lips answered the red dragon's suspicions. He eyed Con'ra's protector with distain. There was something wrong about the silver dragon, death covered his true scent. Havoc's instincts screamed at him that something was not right. He was not eager to engage an enemy he knew nothing about and the Blood Queen feared.

"Clever snake," Havoc growled. "First, the Blood Queen and now this silver dragon. You seem to worm into positions of power so easily. It must be that silver tongue that he likes." He ran his tongue across his jaws in a sexually implied gesture. A test to see how close the green and silver dragons' relationship truly was.

"Careful what you say about my godchild," Vatara warned.

Havoc grinned at the gold dragon that lied prone. "Yes, you and the silver dragon are related," he sneered. "Is this a joke? The lines between the dragon races seem to have been blurred. See what the lesser races have done to you? The bloodlines will never mingle. As a leader, Vatara, you are aware of this."

"What are you implying?" Judas demanded. He did not understand why Havoc was changing subjects. His face was still red with anger at the butchery of his horse. He slashed the air in front of him to draw the red dragon's attention.

Havoc ignored the tiny man and his metal toothpick. "The dragon clans will never mix," he warned. "Vatara, even you know this more than most. Why would you allow these two hatchlings to be together?"

"Together?" Lukhan injected. "What do you mean?"

"I know nothing of this," Vatara replied stoically. "Besides, they are too young to mate."

"Wait-what?" Con'ra stuttered. "We are not mated."

"The silver defends you as if you were," Havoc was disgusted. His eyes narrowed at the protective silver dragon that was still in an aggressive stance. His body was tense like an arrow notched in a fully pulled bow.

"Wait! What? How is this any concern to a red dragon?" Judas demanded. "We've more important issues to deal with! Like how are you going to repair the damage you have cause to my people! If we're going to kill you!"

Havoc chuckled sounded like deep thunder and he shrugged his shoulders at the temporary distraction. The tension in the silver dragon's body dispersed.

Havoc continued to eye Lukhan with caution. The silver dragon was insane and he decided to address the human's concern. He stated bluntly. "Once the humans are dead, this pathetic band of misfits will fall apart, like the fabled alliance during the plague. I can barely stand being here while my treasure is being unguarded." Havoc's attention turned to Vatara. The gold dragon turned away from his accusing eyes. The war between the green and black dragons was inevitable, despite the Gold Clan's failed attempts to prevent it. The other dragon clans viewed the weak Gold Clan's intervention as a pointless attempt to exert its power. Vatara lowered her head, but warily kept her eyes open.

"There will be plenty of blood and treasure," Con'ra promised.

"We do not need you," Lukhan finally spoke.

"Oh?" Havoc chuckled. "Then simply give me the order to disband, I will gladly depart. I am only here because of my Queen."

"All right-," Lukhan began.

"Lukhan, wait a moment," Con'ra warned in a low whisper. "Look at her. Vatara and the Gold Clan members are injured. We do not know what else is happening. We may need the Red Clan to help protect the city."

"You would have me put up with this numbskull?" Lukhan demanded.

"Havoc is not known for his manners or social graces," Con'ra admitted. "Yet the Blood Queen would not have sent him if she thought of him as an incapable tool."

"You suggest that I use him?" Lukhan growled.

"How does the human proverb go?" Con'ra pondered out loud. "Do not look a gift horse in the mouth? Havoc is that horse."

"I am not a horse!" Havoc snarled.

"Then a jackass, if you prefer," Con'ra giggled. "You may not serve the lesser races, but you are in debt to your Queen. You must obey her wishes."

"I know my terms!" Havoc grumbled.

"Good," Con'ra smiled. "Then you must follow her command and I know that she instructed you to follow Lukhan's command as if it was her own."

Havoc's face twisted into a look of pure hatred. The little bitch knew of the Blood Queen's hold over him! How could she have known! Only the Blood Queen herself knew about it! Con'ra must have been a close cohort to the Queen! Was that why the green lizard was here? To keep an eye on him? This infuriated him even more. The red dragon's massive body shook in uncontainable rage.

"Is that true?" Lukhan asked in surprise. He had heard of dragons dominating others of their kind to do their bidding, but he had never seen it. The Blood Queen must have some control over the proud Havoc.

"Yes," Havoc groaned. The single word coming out like the growl of a dog. His nose flared and plumes of smoke bellowed for his nostrils. Sparks of rage dance between his gritted teeth. An interior fire burned within the fuming dragon.

Lukhan considered this but he couldn't thrust Havoc or the Red Clan. His only dealings with red dragons were with Orelac and the Fienicks. Lukhan looked to his godmother for guidance, but Vatara seemed barely aware of their conversation. He then turned to Con'ra for guidance. She had dealt with them more successfully in the past than he had. The green dragon's attitude toward him had changed. Perhaps he should learn from her and take her advice.

"Then you shall follow my lead," Lukhan announced. "Since you like tests so much, let us run an experiment on you." The silver dragon paused in consideration of the Havoc's task. A thought came to him and a brief smile crossed his strained face.

"I am not some beast of burden that you can order-," Havoc began.

"Rub your stomach and pat the top of your head," Lukhan ordered.

"What?" Havoc growled. "What kind of command is-?"

"I am ordering you to rub your stomach and pat the top of your head!" Lukhan demanded.

"It's a task!" Judas interrupted. "Now do it!"

Grumbling under his breath, Havoc attempt to do the not so simple a task. The struggling red dragon rubbed both his head and chest with his wings. He cursed and continued to struggle with the task. After several attempts, he finally completed the task. Judas and Con'ra laughed at the absurd looking massive dragon. The knights and gold dragons stopped tending their wounds and watched the red dragon's display of self-humiliation. Havoc stared at him with a promise of death in his eyes, but he was forced to obey the silver dragon's commands.

"Now reverse the two motions," Lukhan did not join his companion's laughter. "Havoc, I wish to speak with you alone." The word alone sliced through the air and the laughter died as quickly as it had begun. Lukhan didn't like this control. The humans and Gold Clan looked to him for judgment. The sense of command and control had fallen to him and, although, he felt that he did not deserve it. Dragons were selfishly independent and Havoc was no different. The arrogant red dragon must truly be too bound to the Blood Queen for her to allow a silver dragon to exert such control over her subject.

Havoc followed his command and humbled himself before them. Lukhan had to know where this sense of obligation came from and where Havoc's true loyalties lie.

"My knights and I will not leave your side," Judas growled. "I don't trust him! He must be punished! He owes me a-!"

"Do as he says," Vatara warned. "Lukhan, when you are done, come speak to me. We have important matters to discuss. The situation in the South is dire." She slowly stood up warily and struggled to take flight. The other gold dragons followed their leader to the city. Judas and his knights watched the gold dragons depart and looked at each other with hesitant concern. Vatara's words made Lukhan uncomfortable.

"Judas, please follow her," Lukhan added. "You have my word that Havoc will be punished."

"What? I want to see-," Judas began.

"Do as he says," Con'ra was not concerned for Lukhan and she did not feel pity for the massive red dragon before them.

Judas looked at the green dragon in surprise. She was following his lead? A confused expression passed over his face. Something must have happen between the two dragons, but what it was he couldn't say. He looked to Lukhan for guidance.

"Go," Lukhan commanded.

"We can do little more," a knight called. "Let the dragons speak. We have no place among them!"

Judas frowned at his knight's reply and glanced back at the towering dragons. "That's where you are wrong. Men, move out!" he instructed. One of his knights reached down and grabbed their leader. Judas rode side saddle back to the city.

"Well, only I-," Con'ra began.

"Con'ra, see to my godmother," Lukhan added.

Con'ra snorted in reply. "As you wish and a word of caution when dealing with reds." She took to the air, but her yellow eyes continued to linger on them. The red and silver dragon watched as she flew down and disappeared behind the city's walls.

"Are you going to kill me?" Havoc demanded.

"No, I have a better idea," Lukhan muttered.

Chapter 41

"**H**elp! Help! Owen is dying!" Bar screamed in panic. Ambrosia and Owen's personal guards were already present. Within Owen's estate, a bed chamber had been made, for Owen lay in his deathbed. The white knoll's health deteriorated rapidly. Bar could only watch as Owen's breath failed him. His eyes had become distance and his tongue hung loosely out of his mouth. Tears of pain fell from his fading eyes. Many had gathered in the room to witness the fascination of death. Despite the bright sunlight outside, the room's curtains were closed. The shadow's gloom darkened the corners room.

"There must be something you can do!" Bar begged.

Ambrosia looked at him with hopelessness in her eyes. "I have done all that I can and I must be honest, his heart is failing him. He is going to die." She rested her hands on her showing belly. A profound silence embraced the room.

Human and knoll guards stood in the corner, watching Ambrosia passively. Some hardened their expressions; others covered their tearful eyes and faces, while others stared off at paintings, wishing they were someplace else. Bar shook his head in mournful denial.

"No," Bar howled. The one word pierced the emptiness of the crowded room. "He can't die! Without him, the council, city, and alliances will fall apart. We need you! Please, get up! You must live." He looked at white hair knoll. Everyone was starting to come together to battle the Inquisition, but, without Owen's leadership, the fractions within the alliance would split apart, race issues would flare up, and the power struggle between the Merchant's Guild and City Council would begin anew. This would place more strain on the fragile political climate. On a chess board, Owen would be the king. The war was lost before it even began.

"What about your alchemy?" Bar asked. "Have you tried everything?"

"I have done everything within my power to help him," Ambrosia spoke softly. "I have given him a sedative to help ease the pain." She placed a wash cloth in a bowl and place in on Owen's neck. The aged knoll didn't acknowledge her movement but stare painfully up at the ceiling. His mouth opened and closed like a fish out of water. His eyes, nose, and gums were dry. The blood vessels in the corners of his eyes bulged out. Ambrosia grabbed his arm and stroked his hand. Owen did not show any signs of recognition.

"What can we do?" Bar demanded.

"Make way! Shaman coming through!" Sacul grunted. The boarelf's grunts could be heard in the other room. Sacul pushed through the crowd of guards that encircled the room. "Get out of the way! I am part of the council! This is Judas's house! By the spirits I swear that I'll fart in your face! Part ways! What is going on?" The stout boarelf pushed his way into the room, the human and knoll guards clung to him trying to stop his stubborn advancement. The shaman's pet toad bit at the grasping guards. Sacul stopped and the guards tumbled off him.

"Bug off," Sacul grunted. "Owen, get up you lazy bum! It's the middle of the day! Still asleep I see."

"He is dying you idiot!" Bar growled. Sacul stopped in his tracks and his eyes went wide in shock.

"Let him through," Ambrosia intervened.

The guards paused and released Sacul. The boarelf grunted at them. "Thanks! I live here, you know!" he snorted at them. He walk to the side of Owen's bed and examined his condition.

"Sacul! Can you doing anything?" Bar begged. "Call on the spirits or something?"

Sacul lifted Owen's arm and released it with a flop. "Yeah, he looks like a goner," he grunted. Bar looked at him in horror. The boarelf was so callous about the situation.

"How can you be so cruel?" Bar demanded.

"Cruel?" Sacul asked. "He will be going into the spirit world! I am envious of him. He will throw off his mortal bindings and enter the home of his ancestors. Owen has lived a good life. He has brought our people together, brought down a tyrannical leader, and gave our people hope. My race is not afraid of death, as long as we have lived the best we could. I know Owen; he has lived a good life." Bar shook his head. He was not comforted by his friend's words. Sacul grunted at Bar's denial of the situation. The turn of events did not surprise Ambrosia or Sacul. They knew that their leader's health had been failing. Bar had stayed by Lukhan and Con'ra's side, so he was caught unaware. Grunting in displeasure, Sacul grabbed his toad and placed it upon Owen's chest. The small creature remained perfectly still as if listening to the dying knoll's inconsistent heart beat and breathing.

Avoiding the transfixed toad, Ambrosia retrieved the wash cloth. "He looks like he is in pain," she frowned at the thought and dabbed Owen's forehead and ears with the wet cloth. The old knoll gasped in pain at her tender touch. She let the damp cloth rest on the old knoll's throat. Owen's tongue rolled back into his mouth and choking him.

The toad's comatose state broke and it chirped. Sacul reached down and picked it up. With a quick lick of the toad and an unsatisfied grunt. "There is nothing that the spirits can do," he announced and his shoulder's slumped.

The room fell quiet with the impending doom. Some of the guards wept, others remained stoic. "We should begin funeral preparations," Ambrosia whispered to one of the guards. The man looked at her and slowly nodded in reply leaving to make preparations.

"I wish there was something we could do," Bar muttered. "I feel so helpless."

"Dragons! Dragons!" the guard who had left yelled. The man was so eager that he was out of breath. The other guards ran to the windows to see the dragons circling above.

"Who is it?" Bar asked in fear. "Is it the Red Clan?"

"No, sir! It's the Gold Clan!" the guard. "They have returned!"

There was a long pause in the room. Everyone was aware of the red dragons, but why was the Gold Clan there? Did they drive off the red dragons? Several questions arose from the guard's surprising words.

Bar realized it suddenly! "There is still hope!" he gasped. "Hurry, fetch me a stretcher!" The guards nodded their heads in understanding. The Gold Clan's mastery of life magic was legendary. Stories of gold dragons healing the sick and dying were common. This was a hopeful sign that their leader would not perish. Many guards muttered a prayer of thanks to the Holy Master or the elements for sending such a miracle.

"No, what are you doing? He can't be moved in his condition!" Ambrosia warned. "You will kill him if you take him outside!"

"They can save him!" Bar shouted eagerly. "We must take him outside.

They must see them!" He began to throw off the covers on Owen's bed. Bar's erratic behavior was driven on by an alternative motive. Ambrosia looked to Sacul, for help but the shaman watched Bar with pity in his eyes. Bar would not give up, even with his toad as reassurance. Ambrosia grabbed Bar's wrist.

"Please stop this," Ambrosia whispered. "I understand you wanting to help, but-"

"Good then let me take him outside," Bar growled. He jerked his hand away from her and bared his teeth. "I can save him." With both his good and bad arm he reached down and snatched Owen from his death bed. He held the white knoll close to him like a child. The task was easy because Owen had lost a great deal of weight. Although he could not save his pack, Bar would save Owen. This statement rang true within Bar's mind, yet the reality of the situation told him otherwise.

"Wait for the stretcher-," Ambrosia began. He shoved pass her with Owen held firmly in his hands. Desperation was written on Bar's face. The guards opened doors and moved out of the way of the two knolls. Ambrosia and Sacul gave chase.

"Ambrosia, let him go," Sacul grunted. "Bar is in one of his moods."

"Shut up!" Bar snapped. "You'll see."

"What do you think the gold dragons can do for him?" Ambrosia demanded. "Bar! Please stop and listen to me." They stepped outside into the daylight. Owen cried and winced in pain at the sudden change in lighting and temperature. His faded eyes looked past Bar and focused on the sky above. Bar joined his leader and turned his attention to the sky.

"Bar would you- oh, my," Ambrosia gasped.

The Gold Clan circled slowly above, looking for a safe place to land. Hope faded from Bar's eye when he saw the condition that the dragons were in. The low flying dragons appeared to have been through war. Their injuries evident for all to see. The Gold Clan circled slowly around the city. Some recognized friendly homes and businesses and descended on them. Sacul recognized Vatara and waved to her. The leader of the Gold Clan flew down to them and landed her elegantly massive body within the courtyard.

"Hello friends," Vatara mumbled.

"Enough with the greetings," Bar demanded. "Owen is of need of healing! Can you cure him?" Vatara looked at him with her soft glowing golden eyes. She sniffed the air and coiled up her body like a cat.

"I need food and shelter," Vatara muttered. "I must recover my strength before I examine him."

"Of course," Ambrosia offered. "Owen's condition has not improved, but has steadily gotten worse. I fear that this might be the end-"

"He doesn't have much time!" Bar pressed. "I will not give up on him!"

Vatara remained where she was, unmoved by the knoll's demands. "I do not have the will or the strength to heal your friend," she stated bluntly. "Owen has been ill for a long time. He is well past his prime. I am aware of his condition."

"You must do something!" Bar demanded. "He is our leader! Use your magic! I know you can do it! You saved me once! Do it again!"

"I never saved you," Vatara admitted. "It was a combination of herbal medicine and your own constitution that kept you alive. There was no magic involved in your recovery. You mistake me with miracles."

"What if you used magic?" Bar begged.

"Yes, I could use magic to save him," Vatara stated flatly.

"Then do it!" Bar demanded.

Vatara's eyes knitted together in anger. "Careful on what you demand from me," she warned.

"Bar, please take him inside!" Ambrosia urged. "He should not be out here!"

"No!" Bar growled. He brought Owen before Vatara and placed him before her. "This is the knoll that gave your clan a home! How can you forget his generosity to you?"

"You are mistaken," Vatara growled. "My clan bought your city. How do you think your walls and fortifications were built? It was my clan's treasure that built those walls. Your council is in debt to us."

"What?" Bar gasped. "Why does everyone else know what is going on around here? No one tells me anything! Owen's failing health and our city is in debt to the Gold Clan? What else is going on that I don't know?"

"Perhaps you should attend more council meetings," Sacul suggested with a halfhearted smile.

"Owen's condition has been kept a secret," Ambrosia revealed. "His health has been a private issue. Besides the occasional fit, his condition didn't seem to bother him. Owen has accepted this for a long time. No one blames you for not being there for your fellow knoll. I understand-"

"You know nothing!" Bar growled. "I swore to protect him!"

"You can't protect him from death," Sacul grunted. "In time, the black flame will come for us all. Where is this coming from anyway? I knew that you two were friends, but why such devotion?"

Bar knelt down beside Owen. The white haired knoll appeared too shiny in the bright sunlight. Bar could only look on as death slowly took his leader. When Owen was in command, he led the city in success. Bar believed that he had led his pack to their doom and that guilt had never left him. Once Owen was in charge, the position of authority was finally released off Bar's shoulders. Bar looked to Owen for leadership. The younger knoll was worthy of such a position because the city thrived under his guidance. While Bar had fail at keeping his small pack alive, Owen had the skills to keep a whole city in check, a rare knoll that was to be admired. Owen knew the interconnections of the city, how to make the hard choices and how to work with the different races.

"I can't give up on him," Bar choked. He looked up at Vatara; the gold dragon still had a displeased look on her face. "Please do something."

"If I was to use magic, the cost would be great," Vatara warned. "The act of infusing life into a dying body could prove to be dangerous, if not fatal."

"So there is a way!" Bar gasped. He knelt beside Owen and looked pleadingly at Vatara. The gold dragon's scowl didn't leave her face.

"Bar, let him go," Sacul warned. He walked up and placed a comforting hand on his friend's shoulder. "Please, let him go." Tears began to fall from Bar's eyes. As he clutched on to Owen's failing body, the sense of mortality surrounded him.

"He deserves a better death than this," Bar wept. "I want him to be remembered, and not fade away into the lost pages of history."

"We'll remember him," Ambrosia promised.

"A good life is a simple one," Sacul agreed. His toad chirped in agreement. Sacul smiled at the toad and place it on his shoulder. The amphibian fell silent to respect the dying.

"What about my life?" Bar asked. He looked up at Vatara. The gold dragon raised a questioning eyebrow. "Can you replace his heart with mine?"

"Bar!" Ambrosia gasped. Sacul grunted and grabbed the toad from his should. He licked his pet in nervous comfort.

"Replacing a heart is no simple task," Vatara warned. "The transfer is not difficult; the necessary parts would be there, a knoll's white flame and your heart. However, I know how important you are to my godchild. I would never do this-" She stopped mid sentences and curled her lips back. A shadow fell on the group as a heavy wind built up.

"What is going on?" Con'ra asked. The green dragon landed before them.

"What is a green dragon doing here?" Vatara demanded. Her wings shifted in an uncomfortable gesture.

"I am here because of the Blood Queen-," Con'ra began.

"Con'ra, can you help Owen?" Bar begged. "You know magic! He is dying! Please help me save him!"

Con'ra's eyes went wide at the sudden change in Bar's personality. Vatara growled in warning at the begging knoll. The green dragon backed away from the massive gold dragon's threatening growl. "Save whom?" she asked in confusion.

"This is Owen, he is our Imperator," Bar explained quickly. "You've met him before. He was there when you helped Luke."

Con'ra raised a questioning eyebrow. "What? I do not know anything about him," she asked. "Did he do anything for me? Why would I heal him?"

"He is our leader!" Bar continued. "The food that you eat! The water you drink! You owe it all to this knoll."

"I am in the service of the Blood Queen," Con'ra corrected. "I owe your *Imperator*, nothing. No plant, magic, or command can save the dying or dead."

"This Blood Queen seems to be exerting her powers," Vatara was clearly displeased.

"Her wishes were for me to accompany Lukhan and to follow his lead," Con'ra explained.

"The power shifts to Lukhan twice," Vatara muttered sourly. "I have a bad feeling about this situation. Why are older dragons submitting to Lukhan? A dragon, which is barely past his hatchling years."

"My reasons are my own," Con'ra admitted coyly.

"Keep your secrets," Vatara growled. "My only concern is that my godchild is not betraying-!" She paused in mid sentences. The alliance's power had shifted three times. Loyalty and fidelity, whether earned or deserved, had been given to the young dragon. There was something inherently wrong, for power corrupts, and absolute power corrupts absolutely.

"We have to save him!" Bar shouted.

Vatara's eyes went wide in realization. "Who is going to take over after Owen?" she asked.

"The council will," Sacul concluded.

"No," Bar mumbled. "Have you forgotten that Lukhan was appointed second Imperator? When Owen dies, the title and position will fall to him."

Vatara snorted, Owen was a wise fool. He had shifted the city's debt and responsibility to her godchild. Now the Gold Clan investment was entangled within the plot. In one move, Lukhan had obtained both Ravenshaven's and Gold Clan's allegiance. Vatara focused on the white knoll before her. She growled at the dying fool. She let her eyes fade into night vision. There was no magical aura that had caused Owen's death, no curse or magical drain on his white flame. Her eyes returned to normal. She leaned down and inhaled the knoll's breath and odor. There was no poison in his system. Vatara had suspected foul play, but there was no physical or magic evidence. She knew that death came in more than one form.

Chapter 42

"You will be our vanguard when we attack the Inquisition," Lukhan explained. "With our combined strength, we shall strike their heart! Killing the Holy Master. Without their god, the Inquisition will be destroyed in one fatal assault!"

Havoc sinister smiled at the silver dragon's murderous words. "Bold, bloody, and violent. If I did not know any better, I would say that you have the bloodlust of a red dragon. You are different from many silver dragons I have met in the past. However, you must know that there are flaws in your plan. The Gold Clan is in no condition to fight; the hairless apes out number us a thousand to one."

"Yes, I need to know what happened to them," Lukhan admitted. "For the moment, they can secure our supplies and guard our flanks."

"The life lovers are nothing but healers," Havoc sneered. "What of your hairless apes? Do you think they will join forces with a god slayer? They will abandon your cause if you speak one word against their demigod."

"You should not judge them so harshly," Lukhan muttered coldly. "Your followers abandon you when they arrived. For being healers and hairless apes, they drove your clan away."

Havoc's sneer faded into a look of despise, both for his fellow dragons and the blunt statement. A flume of smoke bellow from his seething nostrils. "They were unseasoned and untested," he stated. "Many have never seen a gold dragon before. The cowards are older than you, but unskilled when it comes to combat. I will make sure that the weaklings are ready for war."

"There is no shame in fleeing a fight you know you are going to lose," Lukhan suggested.

"Not for my clan," Havoc growled.

"So why do you fight?" Lukhan asked. "I am aware that the humans killed the sacred herd. Why?"

"The sacred herd was our clan's main food source," Havoc snarled. "Without the bison, we have been living off the desert, scouring the deserts and plains for food. Eating boarelves and giant pest to survive."

"Not that you would have a problem with that," Lukhan stated sourly.

The brutal fact made Havoc smile. "It is true that we have always fed on the lesser races," he stated. "They are meat to us, the apex predators of this world. Do knolls worry about the deer they hunt? The humans butchering the sacred herd? No. Of course not. Why should the dragon clans hold back when it comes to the lesser races? They are nothing more than common animals."

"They have thoughts and feelings," Lukhan replied. "We have more in common than you think. I have lived among them and know that should never underestimate the common races."

"Do they accept you?" Havoc asked.

"Yes," Lukhan respond confidently.

"They may now, what about their hatchlings-?" Havoc demanded.

"I believe they have children, piglets, or pups-," Lukhan began.

"It does not matter what they call their young!" Havoc snarled. "This is war and I do not care. The point is that this generation might be accepting of you, but their hatchlings will not be as tolerant."

"I do not understand," Lukhan growled.

"The other dragon clans have relied on the lesser races for important roles within their clan but only the Red Clan has stayed true to what it means to be a dragon," Havoc boast. "We have remained true to ourselves. The Red Clan created the boarelves so they could provide us food, while the other dragon clans taught them how to use magic and metal against their betters. The lesser races are little more than meat! Dragons have forgotten their place on the food chain and we turned our food into slaves and soldiers! That weakened the dragon clans and made us depend on them. This form of thought is fundamentally wrong. Strength is independence! Strength is self-reliance! Strength is the ability to do whatever you wish!"

"That is why you are in the service of the Blood Queen?" Lukhan asked.

"I serve because I fear her," Havoc warned. "I respect fear. It keeps you alive and your mind sharp. I am sure you have witnessed her powers. She views you as one of her many subjects, and if you were chosen to lead, then I shall fear you as well."

"Fascinating," Lukhan mocked. He thought that the Blood Queen viewed him as an equal elemental. Lukhan realized something then. Havoc did not know that his leader was an elemental! He had forgotten that the knowledge about the elementals was not well known. Fienicks was an elemental, a being of the fire element, and her knowledge of fire was more than impressive. Was it possible that her clan was ignorant of her status? Did they view her power and strength as nothing more than a persona? The Blood Queen was more akin to a volcano than any flesh and blood dragon. She was completely in tune with their natural element, for she was nothing but a husk fueled by the fire element. She must have told the other red dragons that Lukhan was dominated like Havoc. The Blood Queen gave him a simple task: destroy the Inquisition. A task difficult to complete and this new information placed Havoc and Con'ra into context for him.

"So I am to destroy the Holy Master because your Queen commands it?" he asked.

"That is why she released you," Havoc stated. "She views you as a powerful asset to completing her goals."

"What objective is that?" Lukhan asked.

"To make the Red Clan supreme," Havoc stated. He raised a questioning eyebrow and shook his massive wings. "Is that not every clan's motivation? To put the lesser races in their place and become the dominate dragon clan? We are to return to our natural existence."

"I have heard this philosophy before," Lukhan stated sourly. "Orelac was like minded."

"All dragons have an innate feeling of self-worth," Havoc boasted. "The Red Clan accepts this fact. Dragons are the superior race. Of the dragon races, the Red Clan is superior."

"Then why would you follow me?" Lukhan asked.

"I do not," Havoc snarled. "I am in the service of the Blood Queen. It is only her command that places my skills at your command. So long as the conditions are correct."

"Conditions?" Lukhan asked.

"My terms of bondage do not need to be explained," Havoc snarled. "My affairs are none of your concern."

"As you wish," Lukhan asked. "One more question?"

"Do I have a choice?" Havoc growled.

Lukhan thought the question over for a moment. The red dragon was bound to serve. He could demand that Havoc answer his questions. The thought was fleeting, since the red dragon despised him, there was no need to instigate more hatred. "Yes, you have a choice."

Havoc began to chuckle in amusement. "Your acts of kindness are wasted on me and I thought you had potential. You should take advantage of your opponent's weakness."

"I do not view you as an enemy," Lukhan admitted.

"Then you are a fool," Havoc snorted. "If I did not serve the Blood Queen or was unaware of you killing my brother and our past leader, I would kill you and burn this city. If I was stronger than you-"

"Then I am glad that you are not," Lukhan replied.

"For now," Havoc stated in a grumbling voice. "I shall do as you ask. Summon me when you have need of my forces."

"Thank you," Lukhan acknowledged.

"The weaker must never be thanked," Havoc growled. "The strong must never be grateful to the weak and take advantage of them."

"I feel sorry for you and your blind faith in a false philosophy," Lukhan muttered. "Now I understand the Inquisition's faith in the Holy Master. It seems that the weak are stronger than you think."

"We shall see," Havoc raised his massive wings and brought them down throwing ash and soot into the air, slowly ascending into the air. Lukhan watched as the older red dragon flew away. Lukhan looked down at the scorched earth. He noticed that the black claw was camouflaged with the charred ground. Its expanded black flesh crawled up his forearm like roots or tentacles. It didn't move or react to red dragon's presence, but remained eerily silent.

The wind changed suddenly, replaced by the harsh arid breeze of the Endless Desert. Lukhan inhaled the smoky parched air. There was little comfort in the unfamiliar breeze. The Red Clan would prove to be powerful allies against the Inquisition, but like the air around him, his thoughts were muddled. The role of leadership was dangerous in his position. He shook his head at the absurd notion; everything was going to be all right. He smiled at the possibilities of bringing the allied fractions together. He looked to the distant city. There was still hope. His friends were evidence of that, or so he believed. Yet doubt still lingered within his mind, gnawing at the bonds of fragile friendships. Would Judas's child view him as a hero or a murder for killing the Holy Master? How would Judas view his demigod being slain?

Would he be viewed as a hero? Villain? His friend still continued to pray to an unworthy god. The answer eluded him. He had to believe friendship and not war that brought the different races together. Ash blew into his magically scarred eyes, clouding his vision.

⎯⎯⬥⎯⎯

"Get out of my sight!" Vatara warned. "You are not welcomed within this city."

"Oh, shit," Sacul squealed as he ran for cover in the courtyard. Bar and Ambrosia stood in silent confusion. The gold and green dragons stared at each other. Vatara promised death in her eyes while Con'ra looked wide eyed and confused.

"What did I do to offend you?" Con'ra asked in fear. "I am here because of Lukhan. I mean you no harm. Please listen to me-" Vatara towered over the smaller green dragon. The gold dragon had grown increasingly intolerant of her. Bar, Ambrosia, and Sacul could only look on in bewilderment. Vatara's normal calm demeanor was that of insanity.

"No more lies," Vatara snarled.

"I do not know what you mean-," Con'ra began. Vatara sprang at her, but her injuries caused her to move slowly. The green dragon easily avoided the clumsy charge and took to the air.

"Vatara stop this!" Ambrosia cried. "What are you doing?"

Vatara ignored the woman's demand for explanation and focused on the hovering dragon above her. She opened her mouth and released several controlled bursts of white flame. Con'ra tucked in her wings and spun to avoid the blasts of dragon's breath.

"Stop, Vatara!" Bar growled. "You nearly stepped on us!" He protected Owen's sleeping form with his own body. Vatara's reckless charge had nearly killed them both! Con'ra fled before Vatara's attacks, the gold dragon roared in frustration at missing her target. Steam and smoke bellowed out of the thwarted gold dragon's nostrils.

"Why did you drive her away?" Sacul called from a safe distance away.

Vatara cursed and raved at the fleeing green dragon. "She must be one of the conspirators," she announced.

"What do you mean? That doesn't explain your reckless behavior! Explain!" Bar snapped.

Vatara huffed and turned on the knoll. "We have been betrayed," she stated. "The Inquisition has conquered the Kingdom of Omikse!"

Bar, Sacul, and Ambrosia fell in silent shock. Vatara's injuries were evident of the claim. Ambrosia was first to recover from the unexpected news. "What? The elves have been conquered?" she asked. "How is that possible? It would take months, if not years to-!"

"The Inquisition moves to conquer the Silver Mountains before moving against this city," Vatara warned.

"What about the middle kingdom?" Bar asked. "Is Eldora all right?"

"The Kingdom of Sedna continues its fight against the Inquisition," Vatara stated. "When the clan and I passed through, the elves were divided and considering surrendering."

"Wait, I thought elves were our allies!" Sacul gasped. "They need our help!"

"The Magi are with us; however, there are many that no longer respect their rule," Vatara explained. Those around her looked deeply confused. The elves had been trading with Ravenshaven for the past six years. Vatara decided to explain further. "When I was leading the clan to attack passing Alkaline ships, we gave part of the loot to the elves. The treasure, weapons, and prisoners we captured were turned over to the magi for safe keeping. The city accepted the agreement and we lead a successful pirating campaign against the Inquisition. Due to our raids, the humans learned quickly to avoid the elven coastline."

"What were they shipping?" Ambrosia asked.

"Shipments included food, weapons, and personnel," Vatara replied.

"How did you know you were attacking warships?" Ambrosia inquired.

Vatara tapped the side of her nose, indicating that she first smelled them out. "Ships filled with bombarder powder, men, and supplies are easy to locate," she stated.

"What about Owen!" Bar demanded with an interrupting snarl. His teeth were bared and his lips pulled back in disgust at how quickly his so called friends forgot about their dying leader!

"He is going to die," Vatara stated bluntly. "I do not need to repeat my earlier words. Nothing can help him."

"Bar, please take him back inside-," Ambrosia began.

"Luke will!" Bar spat. "He will not standby because he will save him-"

"Enough," Vatara warned. "My godchild cannot help your leader. Have you forgotten the ten laws of magic? Magic always comes at a price. Do you believe that Lukhan can save him from death?"

"Yes!" Bar cried.

"Foolish pup," Vatara growled. "For that is all you are if you believe that Lukhan will sacrifice you to save Owen. How greedy are you? You would make Lukhan suffer? You would make him choose between saving your leader and killing a friend? Do you wish to die so quickly after everything Lukhan has given you?" Sacul and Ambrosia fell silent at the gold dragon's lecture. The human and boarelf looked down, ashamed at the ignorance of their friend's grief. Yet, Vatara remained indifferent as she downplayed Bar's thoughts of saving Owen. The dying white knoll remained clutched within Bar's trembling arms. Tears welled up in the corner of Bar's eyes.

"I don't know what to say-," Bar choked.

"Then say nothing," Vatara growled. "Lukhan has been through enough as it is. I will not use his or my white flame to save someone from a natural death. Owen's time has come and you must accept this."

"I can't," Bar wept.

"Death is a natural part of life-," Vatara began.

"He must be saved!" Bar pressed. He rocked back and forth. Tears streamed down his face at the emotional torture. He truly wanted Owen to awaken and resume his leadership.

"Stop it! Right now! You are a hunter! You have been around death enough to know that it can strike at any time! Pull yourself together! Let him go-," she exclaimed.

"Is that what you are going to tell me when it is Luke's time?" Bar sobbed. "No, I will continue to fight! So long as there is hope!"

"Bar, stop it!" Vatara snarled. "So help me, if you do not go inside-"

"What? What will you do?" Bar challenged. Tears of pain and agony continued to race down his face. "Are you going to kill me? You said that death comes at any time!"

"You are being irrational and foolhardy," Vatara muttered.

"He is trying to save his friend," Sacul grunted in defense. "None of us want Owen to die. Bar has recently come into knowledge of Owen's condition. Please forgive him for his-"

"Don't apologies for me!" Bar snapped. "What good is life magic if you can't save anyone? It seems that death wins no matter what! What is the point of your element if it doesn't do anything? You are useless!"

Silence fell over the courtyard, even the guards, who had station themselves around the courtyard's perimeter, fell oddly silent. Sacul and Ambrosia winced at the knoll's insolences. Bar was challenging not only the leader of the Gold Clan, but her belief system. The dragon was showing incredible restraint when it came to Bar's attacks and accusations. Vatara knitted eyebrows twitched as she took a deep breath.

"Place Owen in front of me," Vatara instructed. Bar's face lighten and his tail wagged. "Then get out of my sight." The knoll's face darken and his tail coward between his legs.

"What are you planning to do-," Ambrosia began.

"All of you," Vatara warned. "Get out of my sight."

Chapter 43

"Lukhan come quickly!" Con'ra called. "Vatara has gone mad!"

"What?" Lukhan asked. The solitude of his contemplation was interrupted by the agitated green dragon. She flew above him in a flustered circle. "What do you mean?"

"She attacked me!" Con'ra flew above his head. "I do not know what I did to provoke her."

A confused expression passed over his face. What was his godmother doing? Why would she attack her? Vatara was injured and no doubt in a foul mood, but she would never hurt anyone! Would she? "What about my friends?" he asked.

"She was focused on me at the time," Con'ra explained. "They were talking about the white knoll. I think something is wrong with him. They called him their Imperator and claimed that he was dying."

"White knoll? Owen?" Lukhan asked.

"Yes, I think that is what they called him," Con'ra guessed.

"Does Vatara blame you?" Lukhan gasped. That line of thought was impossible! He was by Con'ra's side all the while, perhaps, when he was under Shen's curse? No, Con'ra didn't know anything about Owen. How could she have made him ill? He knew that Vatara had no fondness of green dragons. Perhaps it was her prejudice against the greens? He knew that his godmother had hard feelings against the Green Clan when they had first met. Did that bias somehow relate to Vatara turning against Con'ra? The more he thought about it the less sense it made.

"I do not know," Con'ra replied. "She grew angry and told me to leave."

There was a brief moment of hesitation. Lukhan stared hard at her, trying to discern the truth in the matter. "I will investigate, please wait for my return. I wish to speak to my godmother alone."

"About me?" Con'ra demanded.

"No, I trust you," Lukhan stated. "Not only that but I would also call you friend. Yet, I wish to hear what Vatara has to say-"

"I have nothing to hide," Con'ra defended. "She is mistaken! I am not to blame if your pets die. Let me come with you to defend myself-"

"There is no need," Lukhan muttered. "You being there will only sour her mood. First, I must find out why she is here and in such terrible condition."

Con'ra asked with a surprising stutter. "Y-You trust me?" she asked.

"Of course," Lukhan whispered. "You know my secret."

Con'ra hesitated for a moment. "Is that the only reason why you trust me?" she asked. Tears swell up in her eyes as she looked at him. She turned away quickly, least the silver dragon notice her emotion.

Lukhan opened his mouth to speak, but fell oddly mute; it was a foolish notion to believe that she could love him. They were too different, like the sky above and the ground beneath their feet. This was a strange notion, a fleeting and fantastic illusion that they could be together. Deep and troublesome thoughts of lust and love ran through his mind. His heart skipped a beat when he looked into her yellow eyes. Those eyes were both beautiful and dangerous. These thoughts clouded his mind and he held his tongue. No one knew him like she did; they looked into each other's souls. She looked into his abyss and did not reject him. Like a moth to flame, he was poisonous for her; and yet, to confess feelings for her and tell her that he could love her. His heart stopped at the thought and a feeling of empty hunger crept into his mind. That horrible dream, the nightmare that they shared together. He looked down at the twitching black claw, the black flesh that crawled up his forearm constricted and caused aching pain but the pain in his heart was worse.

"What is the matter?" Con'ra asked.

With cold and distant eyes he looked at her. "I am a monster," he whispered. What could he offer her? Nothing but death. It didn't matter that she loved or even liked him. He was cursed and she was nothing more than a dream. A seed that could never grow.

"What did you say?" Con'ra asked tenderly.

"I trust you because you know my fears," he announced coldly. "You trust me because I know yours. We are friends because of this and-" There was a brief pause before he spoke. "There is nothing more."

Con'ra's bright expression of hope melted before him. Replaced by expression of pain, confusion, and hurt. Her bottom lip trembled and her nostrils flared, but then stopped. Not wanting her emotions get the better of her; she closed her bright yellow eyes. She took a deep breath and exhaled. She reopened her eyes and looked at him directly in the face, her expression became hard. "Of course, Imperator Lukhan," her bottom lip continued to tremble. "Forgive me for saying anything, I did not mean to offend."

Her fake bravo broke Lukhan's heart and his eyes soften. "Con'ra, I did not mean-," he began.

"There is no need to explain because I was out of line," Con'ra interrupted with a fake sneer. She blew it off as if the silver dragon's words didn't mean anything to her. "You should go see your godmother. I should leave and return to the Blood Queen-"

"No," Lukhan growled in frustration and dug his black claw into the charred earth. "You will stay right here and you will not leave my side. I forbid it!" Lukhan looked down, ashamed that he had made such a demand from her. His godmother could be right about her accusations and to force her to stay by his side; it was a greedy, selfish, and perverse command. She was her own dragon and he knew that she must be respected. He cursed for saying such a thing.

A surprised expression replaced Con'ra's fake bravado. "Lukhan," she whispered fondly. "I will not leave you, if that is your wish?"

"It is," Lukhan spoke without thinking. He continued to stare at the ground, fearing that he would be scorned or worse.

"My obligation is to the Blood Queen," Con'ra gave him a joyful smile. "I am to follow your command until her grace relieves me of my duties. Please know that if I did not have to serve, I would follow you."

Lukhan looked up, surprised at her confession. She smiled at him and he smiled back. All hard feelings evaporated as they looked into each other's eyes. Con'ra's irises were clear except for the speckled glitter from yellow scarring. Lukhan's eyes were mercury clouded and did not have pupils, evidence of abusive magical scarring.

"I still know so little about you," Con'ra whispered. "Yet it seems that I know your greatest dreams and darkest nightmare. I have never been so close to anyone."

"Is that a bad thing?" he asked.

"Only time will tell," Con'ra smiled. "I do not know what it means."

Lukhan nervously scratched the side of his head. "It means that we are friends," he gave her an awkward smile.

"You are correct," Con'ra giggled and snorted at the extreme mixture of emotions that raced through her head. "Do you view your pets in the same manner as me?"

"Err, sure!" Lukhan gave an award grin and a shrug of his shoulders. "Well, a little different-" Con'ra laugh at him and he blushed. She was different from his friends, she was something totally different and yet familiarly the same. Perhaps, it was because she was beautiful and clever. She smiled at him and he stupidly grinned back.

"This is where I nearly killed you and your pets," she smiled.

"What?" Lukhan asked in confusion.

"Remember? I thought that you were a black dragon," she giggled. "I attacked your city's caravan-"

"Oh yeah," Lukhan recalled with a harsh snorted. "What is your point?" He glanced around the charred landscape, he hardly recognized it.

"I am remembering how much our relationship has changed and I am pleased that you view me as a friend. It is a pleasant feeling. I truly wish to know more about you. Maybe, when this war is over, we can discuss the matter?"

"I would like that very much, wait here, I will return for you. Trust me, no matter what Vatara says; I will believe you."

"Thank you and, please, be careful." A friendly smile passed between the two different but understanding dragons. With a mighty leap, Lukhan sprang into the air and flew to the city.

"What is wrong with Owen?" Lukhan demanded. The gold dragon and white knoll lay in the middle of Judas's courtyard. His godmother seemed disinterested in the tiny knoll that was before her.

"What of the Red Clan?" Vatara asked in an unconcerned tone. Her eyebrows were knitted together in a stern look. The gold dragon's mood had only soured since they had last met. Lukhan grew nervous as Vatara coiled around Owen with her long seek body. His godmother seemed tired and displeased.

"I have good news," Lukhan began. "They have pledged themselves to our cause. Their leader is Havoc, but he is in the service of the Blood Queen."

"You mean dominated by her," Vatara corrected. Her scowl turn into a brief grin, the thief was under control of another. This Blood Queen must truly be powerful. "Despite her powers of brutal persuasion, I do not know who this Blood Queen is; your friends have claimed that they have met her."

"Yes, she was once called Fienicks but she no longer goes by that name," Lukhan explained. "She did not harm me or my friends."

"Orelac's mate?" Vatara thought out loud. She considered this information carefully.

"Do you know her?" Lukhan asked.

"No," Vatara warned. "Not really, I do not know much about her. The reds do not come out of the Mountains of Fire, other than to hunt and raid. If what you say is true, then she would be an enemy to whoever killed Orelac."

Lukhan shook his head no and looked around to see if anyone was listening. "Yes, she would have killed me had it not been for the intervention of Con'ra."

"You enjoy the green's company?" she asked in a venomous tone.

"Yes, I do," Lukhan stated boldly.

"You keep terrible company," Vatara warned.

"You disapprove?" he asked.

"I have always heard the ancient phrase: keep your friends close, and your enemies closer," Vatara muttered. "I understand your desire to build up a strong resistant force against the Inquisition, but allying with the Green and Red Clans is not an option."

"Why is that?" Lukhan asked.

"The Red Clan is of a violent nature," Vatara explained. "They will not stop until the human race is destroyed."

"Is that a bad thing?" Lukhan asked.

Vatara raised a surprising eyebrow at him. "You are aware of this?" she asked. "Of course, you are aware of this Blood Queen's goals."

"Yes," Lukhan stated.

"Then you must be unaware of the dire consequences," Vatara warned. "Humans live within the city you are trying to protect. Because this city hosts many of the common races, do you believe that the Red Clan will simply overlook the humans dwelling inside?"

"The Red Clan seeks to destroy the Inquisition," Lukhan added.

"I know from experience that wars are easy to start, but difficult to end,"

Vatara warned. "Releasing the Red Clan's wrath on the Inquisition will only bring others against us. They will bring total war and the guilty and innocent will be put to the flame. The human's race will be destroyed."

"That happens during war," Lukhan replied boldly. "I have accepted this."

Vatara's barbels flared out in disapproval. "You have changed much."

"Isolation causes one to reflect on their life," Lukhan rebuked.

"Yet you ignore my suggestion to retreat back into the Endless Ice," Vatara growled. "Until I was able to find a cure for your black claw."

"It has been over six years," Lukhan muttered. "With no word from the outside. I can understand that you wanted to keep me safe, but hiding me away is not a plan. I know now that I cannot hide from my problems."

"Despite you looking like an adult, you still have the mind of a hatchling," Vatara scold in disapproval. "Have you not notice? Look at your arm and body. The cursed black flesh is accelerating its growth. Your time in the Endless Ice was designed to slow down its corruption and influence."

"I have come to terms with this," Lukhan growled.

"Really?" Vatara growled. "You have accepted the curse that Vilesath has placed upon you?"

"Have you ever heard of a being called an elemental?" he asked.

"Elementals? Where did you hear that word?" Vatara asked. "Mythical creatures made of the dragon elements. They are nothing more than legends. Stories to scare dragons from using the corruption of magic."

"Fienicks, the Blood Queen, is an elemental," Lukhan warned.

"What?" Vatara's face twitched in extreme displeasure. "That is not possible; no dragon would follow such a creature. Could it have been an illusion? A trick of the mind? Elementals do not exist."

"I believe in myths," Lukhan replied.

Vatara considered his words carefully. "Your encounter with the Betrayer was a mishap and a rarity," she warned. "Relics from the past have a bad habit of reemerging. The giants, common races, and impure dragons are examples of this. The legend of the elemental is before even theses relics."

"You are contradicting yourself," Lukhan stated evenly.

"There are many strange and wondrous things in this world that even I do not understand," Vatara admitted. "Even magic and alchemy cannot explain everything in this world."

"Therefore, it is possible that I am becoming an elemental," Lukhan concluded.

"I-I do not know," Vatara began. "I always thought of the black claw as a curse. A remnant of Vilesath's magic. I never considered-"

"Me becoming an elemental?" Lukhan asked.

Vatara snorted at the smug reply. "Listen to me," she warned. "Your spiteful attitude does not help your current situation. The alliances you have made in haste have placed this city at risk. The burnt crops and dead horses are evidence of the violence to come."

"I am aware of the risks," Lukhan muttered.

"If you do this then you will not be able to keep the lesser races complacent," Vatara warned. "The common races will demand retribution for their burnt fields."

"The Red Clan will pay for itself in due time," Lukhan growled. "The city will have to suffer for the loss."

"A decree that you have no right to demand on its citizens," Vatara stated.

"I can and I will," Lukhan declared. "I am part of the city's council and I was given the title second Imperator by Owen. The council witnessed this fact."

"Owen will die," Vatara stated. "Where does that leave your position?"

There was a brief moment that past between them. "Can you save him?" Lukhan asked. "You have the power."

"I will not," Vatara replied stoically. "I have no right to stop him from a natural death."

"You are choosing not to save him!" Lukhan accused. "The city needs Owen! What did my friends say about this?"

"Bar wishes for me to save him and I refused him; just like I am refusing you now. You have magical powers. Why not use them?" Vatara asked.

"I will!" Lukhan stepped forward eager to prove his godmother wrong. Owen was before him, the knoll's breaths shallow, his eyes shut; mouth open and his gums were white. He thought carefully, but was struck dumbfounded at the lack of knowledge; he didn't know the magical words to save Owen. He didn't even know what was wrong with the knoll. He knew a thousand ways to kill him, but knew of no way to save him. The thought unnerved him. He glanced at Vatara, who waited patiently for him to act.

Several long moments past as Lukhan search through his vast knowledge and experiences he had felt through others. Those souls he had absorbed were evil. Their knowledge was not based on healing and protection, but of violence and brutality. "I do not know the words," Lukhan admitted in frustration. "Give them to me!"

"There is no form of magic that can stop death," Vatara offered. "There are only ways to post pone it. Those ways are unnatural to the extreme. The plague is an example of this."

"To say that is to say that I am unnatural!" Lukhan growled.

"It is," Vatara muttered. "The claw that you bare now is part of magic and it is unnatural. You know the ten laws of magic. Your white flame was consumed by the spell that destroyed the plague. Therefore you have become a parasite, a dependent on consuming the souls of others to sustain yourself."

"I did not choose that!" Lukhan defended.

"You were innocent when it came to that," Vatara agreed. "It is the duty of the Gold Clan to protect the white flame. Even from those who are innocent."

"What are you saying?" Lukhan asked.

"I am not accusing you," Vatara sighed heavily. "Remember that power corrupts even the best intensions. Evil is incapable of kindness and vice versa. Understanding this fact will make you a true leader."

"I do not care about that," Lukhan proclaimed. "Tell me the magic spell that will save Owen."

"The magic required to save Owen is beyond white flame," Vatara announced.

"That does not make sense," Lukhan huffed.

"I promised to teach you about life magic," Vatara recalled. "Do you remember this? Then this will be your first lesson. Life is precious and must be protected. However, it is important that life must be lost if the next generation is to advance. Nothing, not dragons, common races, or beasts should be immortal."

"So that is why you are going to allow Owen to die?" Lukhan demanded. "So that the next generation- you mean me?" His eyes flew wide in realization. Vatara wanted him to take control of Ravenshaven. "You want me to take leadership!"

"Is that not what you wanted?" Vatara asked. "Our goals are the same, it is a practical replacement. Is that not why you returned with your friends? To accept the power placed within your claws? To fulfill your rightful place?"

"I do not know. I thought it was a good idea at the time," Lukhan began. "It was Owen's idea first and he asked me to become his second in command. Although he did not teach me anything in the ways of governing."

"It is no wonder," Vatara stated stoically. "The city's debts have passed on to you."

"What do you mean?" Lukhan asked.

"It is time for you to know how this city was rebuilt," she chuckled. "The new public constructions, the new fortifications, the new sewer systems."

"I thought that the city built them. It would cost a dragon's hoard to-Vatara! This is your gold?" Lukhan asked in surprise.

"Mine and many others," Vatara warned. "It is an investment that I placed on this city and a debt that you have inherited. I warned you about returning to these lands, and I warned you to hide away. Have you forgotten everything your elders told you? You are cursed. I thought we agreed that you would leave the Silver Mountains and stay in the Endless Ice until I sought you out. Instead, I find that you have foolishly left and unwittingly become indebted to my clan. Not only this, but you have made a poor choice in allies with the Red Clan and you are fraternizing with a green dragon."

"I did what I thought was best," Lukhan muttered. "You may not like the choices I have made, but they are mine! I have no regrets."

"No," Vatara replied stoically. "You did what others wanted you to do and damned the conscious. You forgot the reasons why you were exiled and now look at you."

"Then would you have done in my place?" Lukhan challenged. "Stayed in the Endless Ice?"

"Yes," Vatara said evenly. There was no pause or hesitation in her words. Lukhan suddenly felt disheartened, discredited, and disillusioned. It had been over six years since he had seen his godmother; he had hope for a happier reunion. "You want to be an adult? Make decisions on your own? Then I shall treat you as one."

"Why are you so venomous to me?" Lukhan demanded. "I am trying to do the best I can!"

"I shall begin with your return to Ravenshaven," Vatara explained in a grave tone. "The city that the Gold Clan has paid for is in the incapable claws of a hatchling. Second, you bring unwanted dragons into this city's territory, promising gifts that you cannot deliver. Third, you claim that you are a legend from the past, an elemental. Not only must this but you be a death elemental! A creature of black flames! You are a silver dragon and would never be able to transform into such a myth. Fourth, you disobey the wisdom of your elders by not staying in the Endless Ice. You have forced the Inquisition to take action against you. The purge of the elves and soon this city. Fifth-"

"You blame this all on me!" Lukhan interrupted. "That is not fair! For six years I have withered away in that frozen waste-"

"Fifth is that magic flows through you freely and without hesitation," Vatara continued. "Your scarred eyes are evidences of this. Your exploits in saving the Ravenshaven's council have reached even my ears. Look at your body. You wither and decay before me because magic is taking its toll on you. Magic must be a last resort, yet you use it freely." His godmother saw him for what he really was. The comical illusions of the black claw could not hide his withered and decayed form from Vatara's magically attuned eyes. There was no magic that she could not see within eyesight. This genetic trait, the ability to see magical auras, was rare among dragons, and it was shared between Vatara and Lukhan.

"What about you?" Lukhan growled. "Your eyes are scarred like mine!"

"I am over a thousand years old," Vatara growled. "Over that time, I have learned to suppress the addiction and sooth its demands. It has taken me centuries to develop the scarring on my eyes. Yet your progression is advanced and you are barely past being a hatchling! You are burning your white flame from both ends. Always remember the ten laws of magic: magic masters you, you will never master magic."

"I am aware!" Lukhan scowled. "You have never had the pressure that has been forced on me! I have never use magic lightly! I have only used it in the dangerous of circumstances. I sacrificed my white flame! My soul! For this land to be free of the plague! That is why I am diminished and my eyes are scarred."

"Your sacrifice is one reason why I respect and cherish you," Vatara admitted. "I have been trying to figure out a way to release you from your curse. I have asked for time, but you have sped up its progression. I am trying to help you, but first you must help yourself! Stop throwing your life away!"

"Then why do you belittle me?" Lukhan demanded. His bottom lip quivered at the upsetting notion that his godmother didn't valued his efforts. He was trying to change the world for the better.

"Despite your good intentions and effort to preserve this world," Vatara began. "I cannot help but think that you are not ready for it. This world is cruel and unforgiving place and this curse will only make it harder for you."

"What do you mean?" he asked.

"The Betrayer gave you a great deal of magical power," Vatara warned. "Dragons are motivated by self-interest and I cannot help but feel that you are part of Vilesath's ultimate goal."

"I no longer feel his presences," Lukhan explained.

"Shadows must never be taken lightly," Vatara warned. "Shadows lurk in the blackest of night and brightest of days. You must never seek out power. Otherwise, you are doomed to fulfill the Betrayer's prophecy."

"You are worried about me or him?" Lukhan asked.

"Both," Vatara explained. "You are my godchild, but you are also something unnatural. The black flesh growing up your arm is evident of the black flame's growing influence. There may come a time when you must be destroyed."

Lukhan's eyes widen in fear. He refused to believe that! The Betrayer would not use him to cause the next cataclysm. He would forge his own path, a path that was promised to him! He would master the magic that was consuming his body or die trying! His face hardened at that comforting thought. Yet he could not escape the deep hunger within his body. The same hunger that drove him to be a mindless slave.

"I will not resign my position!" Lukhan announced. "It was foolish to believe that this city could continue to exist without me. This place does not belong to dragons; it belongs to the common races. Those who believe in independence from a tyrannical religion. The alliance with the Red Clan will not be dissolved and I shall become Imperator. I belong here! Among my friends and allies."

"It is the wrong decision," Vatara warned. "Before you announce such a declaration, you should see what Owen wanted?"

Lukhan glanced up at her with a surprised expression. "He is unconscious, how could I ask-," his words trailed off, he gasped in realization. "You want me to take his white flame!" The black claw twitched at the urge to kill both the knoll and gold dragon. The suppressed hunger that lurked in the back of his mind sprang to the forefront.

Vatara sensed a sudden changed in Lukhan aura. "He is going to die," she stated. "His death is unavoidable. Is that not what you want? Leadership over this city?"

"No-," he paused with a horrible gulp before continuing. "-and yes." His stomach growled at the tiny morsel before him. Despite his wavering words, he hungrily approached the dying knoll and warily gold dragon.

"Are you afraid?" Vatara asked. "Who do you fear? Is it death? The black flame always conquers the white flame and you must accept this."

Lukhan watched the dying knoll with fear in his eyes.

"Your bond with the common race is strong," Vatara warned. "You must learn to let them go. Death is not easy to accept, it never is. This is your first true test."

Lukhan's lip trembled in fear and hunger. "A test?" he muttered.

"Accepting death," Vatara explained. "If you refuse it, then what? How far will you go? Would you raise Owen from the dead? Use magic to make him your puppet? Use your black claw to experience his life? Each path to Owen's revival is as unnatural as the next. Let him die in peace. You must learn this for yourself. Weep for him, but do not make him suffer."

"I can save him!" Lukhan declared. "I saved this world! I can save a single knoll! His body is failing him but his spirit is strong. My friends and I need him! The city still needs Owen!"

"No," Vatara warned. "Let him die because you cannot save all those who are dying. Not this time."

"I cannot do everything on my own!" A tear of madness fell from the corner of Lukhan's eye. "I must learn what he knows about this city. The backbiting and corruption of the common races. Maybe he is not the ideal leader that you think he is? He means something to this city and my friends. His knowledge is rightfully mine!" The demand was not out of place. Dragons would often take over hoards of other dragons. Those who were too weak to fend for themselves. Owen did not leave him any gold or jewels, the true gift was his life and Lukhan could take it.

"Nothing is free!" Vatara warned. "His soul is not yours to take! You must learn new life experiences for yourself, without the biases of stolen knowledge."

"Why should I?" Lukhan asked hungrily. "His knowledge will be lost!" Drool dribbled from his mouth. Owen was helpless and was going to die. The knoll couldn't move or scream. He wasn't even aware of his surroundings. All of his knowledge would be lost when his body died and his spirit left. The more he thought about it the better it sound. There was a sick justification in Lukhan's reasoning.

"No, you should not," Vatara warned. "There is no other way to save him or his knowledge. You will have no respect for Owen's stolen experience. You will forget the years of hard work to build personal relationships. Stolen knowledge that is not earned will never be respected. Remember that power corrupts and absolute power will corrupt absolutely."

The silver dragon stared at Owen's limp body, thick drool dripped from his mouth. Lukhan did not look at Owen as a friend, but as a piece of meat. A piece of meat that could make him more powerful! He needed but to stick out his claw and take it! He slowly stretched forth with his trembling claw.

He knew that it was wrong: to take another's soul, its white flame, its being. Yet his endless hunger compelled him.

"Do not give in," Vatara whispered. "You are stronger than this." She observed the intense struggle, this was Lukhan's test. Fearing for her own life, she backed away from Lukhan and Owen.

Vatara needed to see how far her ward had changed. How the years of isolation and sudden change in surroundings had affected his mental state. She had to know who the true master was and to see if Lukhan was the slave to the power that was within him. What she was witnessing was not between some strange external force on the young dragon, but the radical metamorphosis in personality. The silver dragon was fighting not only his own desires, but those of the black claw.

Lukhan was losing himself and the knoll was doomed.

The corrupted dragon sprang forth like a wild animal, with feral eyes and drooling jaws, Owen's body was snatch up. The black claw did not devour Owen; instead Lukhan opened his jaws and devoured the old knoll himself. Bones and flesh were ripped off as Lukhan quickly stripped the body down with his sharp teeth. The black claw absorbed some of the flesh that it grasped, but the silver dragon's mighty jaws stole the meat away from it. Owen's body was gone.

Vatara's eyes flew wide in fear.

Chapter 44

Lukhan's mind was filled with Owen's memories. Life as a pup was pleasant and blissful saves for the children and pups that picked on him for being white. His memories of his parents were caring and nurturing. The emotions were different from the murderous thoughts of assassins and evil creatures he had absorbed in the past. Instead of feelings of hatred and malevolence, there was a strong sense of duty to the city. The emotions felt good, like the first rays of a morning sun. Owen's thoughts on individual people were listed like neat categories within his mind. Owen was no fool, he knew everything within the city, he trusted only a few, but kept this fact to himself. He liked Judas and Sacul; they helped strengthen his image to the humans and boarelves who lived within the city. Bar was a threat to his power base because he often questioned him at inopportune times. Ambrosia was a useful witch, her alchemy helped to ease his pain. They were like common recipes to an old cook. He took them at face value and judged them as such. Owen knew Lukhan followed his companions around like a mother bear. The deep scent of warm blood passed through his emotions. He inhaled the savory sensation of righteous authority and power. The silver dragon would remain passive and easy to control as long has Owen kept those he cared about safe.

Owen had plans, big plans; yet the fate of being an outcast knoll made him desperate to extend his life. He learned that he had a weak heart, a birth defect, and Lukhan felt Owen's desperation to experience every day like it was his last. That was why the knoll was so bold and daring, the urgent need to complete his self-appointed tasks drove his existence. He had visions of a more peaceful, better world. That was why he took over Ravenshaven and sought to make it a better place for all people. Owen was pupless and looked to the people as his progeny. So focused and driven was the old knoll, that he swore an oath of chaste. Many from his pack frowned upon this and demanded that another knoll be placed as Imperator. Owen considered returning to a simpler life as a farmer, but he had grown accustom to the perks of leadership.

Although Owen sought to bring the common races together in a united front, there were many who thought they could do a better job. The council of Ravenshaven was born out of an essential pivotal point to balance Owen's leadership. Lukhan witness Owen's underhanded dealing with the city council, bribes and threats were common place. Despite Owen's best intentions and highest hopes, he was a realist and those who were unwilling to move would be persuaded through coin or bloodshed. It was difficult to move people to action. There was always someone willing to challenge his authority, even with the best intentions.

Lukhan suddenly realized that Owen was not the perfect leader and struggled daily to keep the different fractions together. As a leader, he had doubts and blood on his hands. He used his popularity as a way to get what he needed and there were few that could deny him. Owen's leadership was based on majority rule and those who were against him were often subject to street justice. Owen placed spies within every major guild within the city. Most were controlled by Owen, himself, as shadows organizations. He ostracized minor rebelling to weed out potential opposition and infiltrations from the Inquisition. The old knoll knew about the assassination on his life and had planned to die at the blades of assassins. To unite the city against the Inquisition, his death would strengthen the bonds between the different groups to fight against the Inquisition.

The plot would have worked, had Lukhan and his friends not interfered. It was then that Owen realized Lukhan's potential. How the crowds blamed one another, but failed to see those who saved them. The dragon race seemed to be above the bloodshed and blame. The common race was quick to anger and quicker to action. Few dared challenge Owen and his network of spies, but with a dragon to guard his political position and legacy, he thought he would be immortalized. Owen's deceptions worked and the well-meaning fool had tricked them all. The hopes of a dying knoll to end his life in glorious martyrdom.

The silver dragon froze at the sudden acknowledgement of what he had done. Owen did not deserve to suffer this fate. He wanted to die for his cause, not in bed or as dragon food. The last of Owen's flesh was absorbed into his black jaw. The knoll's blood was still slick in his mouth and the taste of knoll made him sick to his stomach. Lukhan's body trembled and felt distantly cold. Something took over him; it didn't feel like he lost control. With regret in his eyes he looked up at his godmother. The golden eyes and facial expression gave no hint on what she was thinking. Owen was not evil and his intensions were good. The memories were not of evil acts and wrong doings, but of a visionary knoll who longed to be remembered. Immortalized in the thoughts and actions of the people that would looked to their past for guidance.

Owen was gone.

"What have I done," Lukhan whispered. He stared down at his trembling blood soaked claws. "I killed him." He had hoped to kill Owen before the knoll's white flame was absorbed, but the transfer was quicker than he had anticipated.

Vatara did not say anything because her mind raced in both fear and awe. He appeared to be in control and even showing remorse. She allowed her eyes to fade into night vision. The silver dragon's unnatural aura was pulsating inward, focusing on his center mass. The pulse had a rhythm akin to a dying heartbeat.

"I killed him," Lukhan gasped with barely a whisper. "I couldn't stop the black claw from taking his soul and his memories race through my mind even now."

Vatara's eyes returned to normal. "You seem to be in full control of your actions and it is sad and ironic."

"W-what? That is all that you have to say?" he choked. "I murdered-!"

"Yes, you did," she declared. "Never believe that you are the only one who has killed before. I have killed many common races, although never for power and authority, and I do not make it a habit in devouring them. Yet the slaughter of the sacred herd has forced us to act out of character. The act is general a taboo within our clans, but since you belong to neither, it does not matter. Still, I understand your hunger and I have heard of knoll packs and human merchants who eat each other when they are trapped in a snowstorm or avalanche. Yet, I am in a state of conflicted. If you are a death elemental, as you claim, then you are a threat to everything my clans protects. Despite your curse, I am certain that what you did was not an act of desperation, but an opportunity to grasp for power and you must be destroyed."

"What?" Lukhan growled. "I could kill you!"

"Yes, in my exhausted and injured state, you could easily take my life and absorb my white flame," Vatara stated. "If you truly seek power, why not take my soul? I will not fight you and then you can take command of both the Gold and Red Clans. You would expand your ever growing appetite for power."

The black claw shook in excitement at her words. Lukhan's eyes widen at the growing sense of endless hunger. He felt horrible for taking Owen's life; a tear fell from the corner of his eye. "No! Never!" he snarled. "I feel guilty and remorseful! This feeling inside me, it is horrible; my actions are not justified. You must stay away from me!"

"No, you are foremost my godchild," Vatara stated. "Even I cannot escape death." She glanced down at her battle worn scales. She picked out the tiny needles of shrapnel that pieced her scales and ignored his warnings. She took a deep breath before continuing. "I swore an oath to protect you. An oath that I will never dismiss lightly. I will uphold it even if it costs me my life."

"An oath?" Lukhan asked.

"I owe it to your father," Vatara's eyes were tired as she looked at him. "I am not a good teacher or protector and I blame myself for your current condition. My responsibilities to my clan have been taxing and waning. Worse is that I have led my clan to ruin. For the past six years, I have failed at many things and I could not cause peace. Even through the threat of force."

"You must not blame anyone," Lukhan comforted. "Least of yourself and I know that threats never secure lasting peace. You have done the best you could and so have I. But I need your help if I am-!"

'You are wrong," she declared. "I grow weary of the endless feuds between common races and dragon clans. I have seen enough of their deaths that it no longer disturbs me. As one of the few leaders of the remaining dragon clans, I should have more authority in what occurs within this world. My words must be listened to, yet the servants of the white flame do not seem to be important. The endless bickering and infighting grows evermore pointless. Leadership and authority are like magic, they are illusions of control."

"Magic?"

"The element of death seems to be more important to those who seek control. The unbalanced scales seem to continue to tip in the favor of death despite my attempt to correct the situation. I have failed because a leader must take credit for both the successes and failures of their guidance. I am not worthy of being a leader of the Gold Clan nor being your teacher. I feel that it has been an error on my part not to teach you the importance of life magic and alchemy and to engage in combat with the Inquisition. I have hesitated at each turn, fearing that you would become something more dangerous. It appears that I have failed in everything that I have set out to do. Perhaps, it would have been better to let you destroy these lands and start the world anew. Then those who survived would have an appreciation for life."

"Now? What will you do?"

"I am torn between life and death," Vatara admitted. "If I teach you and you become the danger that I fear, then I may have to destroy you. It would not surprise me because I have failed at everything else."

"Why?" Lukhan asked. "I must make amends!"

"You are a dragon," Vatara stated. "It is in our nature to want more. More of everything including treasure, land, and magic. This is the cruel natural bane of our species and to ask you to become something that you are not is an even crueler fate. The blood of the innocent is on your claws and you have done nothing against the Inquisition. If I helped you, it would cause only more death and destruction."

"I never sought out those things and I have only the Staff of Selgae as my treasure and magic! This city is my only land and home! I have claimed so little!"

"It is within your power to claim and demand more," Vatara warned. "You have more wealth than you will ever know. The greed that you have does not come from any material wealth; instead it is more akin to the greed of friendship, seeking the approval of others. Friends willing to die at your command. Loyalty of others is worth more than any treasure. You are not poor when it comes to material wealth. A piece of the Staff of Selgae, the ancient artifact that you have embedded within your left forearm, enhances its wielder's natural abilities a thousand fold. That is why you are capable of defeating dragons that are older and more powerful than you. There are many, dragon and common race alike, which would kill to possess such a renowned treasure. That single artifact is worth its weight in the purest platinum. For it carries a piece of the white flame from past Grand Magi since Selgae himself created the artifact. It is priceless to the elves because it holds their ancestors' souls and they will kill you to get it back."

"You said that the elves were under assault by the Inquisition?" Lukhan asked.

"The magi are under attack by the Inquisition," Vatara warned. "My clan's pirating activities and healing missions ended when the Inquisition laid siege on the southern elf kingdom. We abandon their cities once we heard that their southern western front was crushed. It will only be a matter of time before the middle kingdom will suffer the same crushing defeat."

"The elves are lost?" he gasped. "What about Eldora? No, how?"

"Can you not see my body?" Vatara asked. "Elven magic and skill cannot compete against the human's numbers and alchemy. Not even the ancient forests provide protection. Most of the elves' defenses were crushed during the plague and they were never rebuilt."

"The Inquisition wants me?" Lukhan admitted. "Why go after the elves? They have done nothing-!"

"This war was never about you," Vatara explained. "You may be a dangerous threat but they view you as they do any other dragon. The Inquisition is not ruled by the material wealth or the trading of goods. They are after more than simple world dominance. They seek to purify all that are nonhumans and subjugate them into animals."

"That is madness! Humans were once elves; why do they do this now?"

"Any past kinship of the two peoples is now lost to paranoia and antiquity," Vatara stated. "There are few in the common races that now believe in the connecting relationship between elf and man. Instead, the two races focus on their differences than their commonalty. The differences between them are few, but it is enough for the humans to kill their ancient kin."

"What of the Holy Master? What does he say about this?" Lukhan asked.

"Attempts to communicate with the Iron Throne have failed," Vatara sighed as she laid down her head. "As so many other things have and it appears that the humans will destroy the elves."

"Judas still believes in the Holy Master?" Lukhan asked. "Is it possible that the Inquisition is acting outside of their god's will?"

"Unlikely, the Inquisition is known for its creative interpretation of the Holy Master's teachings. What is said in places of peace and worship only apply to men, not to the other common races or the dragon clans."

Lukhan's mind raced, this new information scared him. "Why this senseless bloodshed? Elves and humans have worked together in the past? Why attack now?"

"War is difficult to justify and dragons cannot judge the common race for their genocide. We murder our own kin within our own clans. That is why we have grown weak and the common races now rule vast kingdoms. Perhaps the Inquisition fears the elves more than they do you."

"The elves are closest to them," Lukhan agreed. "The humans fear magic, the magi are called heretics."

"True and we also have wings," Vatara stated. "That no land bound creature can keep up with. In addition, this city's new fortification proves to be a great deterrent for attackers. That is why my clan escaped the vulnerable elf lands and came here."

"We cannot flee forever; therefore, we must stand and fight. We must help the elves because they are our friend and a major supplier and trade partner to this city!"

"What would you do?" Vatara asked. "Send Ravenshaven's army to aid them? Leave the city defenseless? The Inquisition would take advantage of such a misstep. Men are not fools and this could be a trap to goad you into reckless action."

"You are saying they are expecting that?" Lukhan asked.

"Yes, there are warships that line the shores of the Hollylyassa River. These were not the flammable galleys the humans or the dromon of the elves, but these ships were something entirely new."

"New warships?" he asked.

"They appeared to be barges that are covered in iron plates and metal spikes, big and flat, like a turtle, the ships appear to be designed to withstand assaults from bombarders. The fire from my breath did not set them ablaze and while, I retreated from the constant barrage of enemy fire, the crews sang songs. They called their ships *gwiseon* while they slowly gave chase. Gwiseon mean turtle ship in the foreign tongue."

"They were slow?" Lukhan asked. "Could you not dodge them?"

"Yes, but they had shallow hulls and were quickly turned," she added. "These ships have been under construction for some time. I could smell the sea on them despite the river being fresh water. The Inquisition has been planning this attack and the distractions of the internal fighting must have made them more militarized."

"They control the waterways?" Lukhan asked. "The Hollylyassa River is under the Inquisitions control?"

"They control more than that and I fear that there is little that can be done to save the elves. There is no way that we can get to the southern and middle kingdoms without crossing at least one river."

"What if we attacked from the North?" Lukhan asked.

"You would enter the elves' northern kingdom?" Vatara chuckled. "The same area that was destroyed by the plague? Not even the Inquisition goes near there."

"Why not? I thought the plague was destroyed?" Lukhan asked.

"Yes, but the magi unleashed terrible magic on the plagued creatures and cursed the land," Vatara warned. "There are worse things now than feral dire wolves and scarred tree spirits. Even I would rather face in Inquisition's bombarders than enter that accursed place."

"What happened?" Lukhan asked. Vatara shook her head no in reply. "Please you must tell me!"

"In his final hour," she began. "The Grand Magus Louis was slain by Orelac while he stood on the white tower. It was rumored that he was casting a spell that could have destroy the plague that had invaded his city. Instead of completing the spell, it was interrupted and the ritual went astray. As Louis lied dying on top of his tower, a curse fell upon the dying homeland. Orelac captured the Staff of Selgae and would have moved on to the other elf lands had it not been for Louis's efforts."

"Louis, I only knew him in passing."

"Dragons and magi must keep to themselves," Vatara warned. "Never forget the bloodshed during the Elves' Rebellion. Never trust them blindly."

Lukhan nodded his head in understanding. "So what is the curse?" he asked.

"Not sure," Vatara began. "It is not wise to move an army through-" The sound of horses and the clatter of armor echoed through the street outside the courtyard's wall. Judas and his accompany knights entered through the gate. Judas jumped down from the knight he rode with.

"Thank you," Judas praised. "Take the men and- Lukhan, why are you covered in blood?"

The silver dragon glanced down at his blood soak chest and claws. His bottom jaw was smothered in knoll blood. Lukhan was speechless; he couldn't tell them what he had done. Judas and the other knights would turn on him! He recalled the violent nature of the crowds, who loved Owen; they would burn down the city if they found out that he had been devoured by him. The truth would destroy the city and his friendships. Lukhan opened his mouth to speak.

"Owen is dead," Vatara interrupted. "Lukhan killed him."

Chapter 45

There was a long silence. Judas stood dumbfounded with his mouth wide open in a bewildered expression stuck on his face. He didn't want to understand the reality of those words that Vatara said. He chose not to comprehend the meaning of those words despite the reality of the blood covered silver dragon.

Vatara took measure the human's face. "What will you do now?" she asked. Her eyes narrowed at her godson. "No more secrets or lies because it is time for them learn the truth." There were two ways they would react to her words. Both sides would accept this or they would destroy each another. They needed each other more now than ever.

"I don't-," Judas began. "Was it an accident? What happen-?"

"You know that Owen's death was no accident," Vatara warned.

"K-Kill it!" a knight demanded from Judas's ranks. There was another long pause after the declaration. "The dragon is a rabid dog, we must put it down! He slew our leader and it's as the Inquisition foretold, the dragons are our doom!" The other men grew nervous at the sudden loss of authority and leadership. Both men and horses were nervous at the sight and smell of blood.

"Shut up!" Judas snarled. "Get back in line! Who cares about lies and rumors? Have faith in the Holy Master, not in the false words of mortal prophets. No one do anything! Not until I figure out what is going on. There must be an explanation for-"

"Judas! Isn't it obvious!" the same knight began. "We'll become slaves to them. The dragons are taking control of our city! First, the Red Clan burns our fields and now the Gold Clan is taking over our government! It's a conspiracy! It's a coup d'état! We must fight and get our city back-"

"Shut up!" Judas snapped. He took off his gauntlet and threw it at the questioning man. The surprised missile struck the man's breast plate and he fell mute. "Have you forgotten that it was this silver dragon that save Owen from the assassination attempt? Owen trusted this dragon and named him his successor! I personally know this dragon, and I'll not have you threaten him! Now shut up and return to the barracks and I will investigate the matter!"

"Is that wise?" Vatara asked. "I believe that an explanation would be first. Rumors of Owen's death will spread fires of discontent among the populace. It would be better if Lukhan stated the reasons for his actions. The truth must be revealed and acceptance is required."

"What do you mean?" Lukhan gasped.

Vatara looked down at him. "You are correct. No more hiding and no more excuses. You are an adult now and it is time to take responsibility for your actions. By your own words, it is time to fulfill your destiny."

Lukhan's eyes widen as he looked up at the gold dragon leader. In the past he had counted on his family and friends to lead him. He possessed the stolen wisdom of Owen's leadership. The knoll's experience and knowledge was passed on to him. A smile passed his godmother's lips as if she could read the doubt within his mind. "Forge you own fate," she whispered. "Focus on the present and live in the present or die with the past."

Lukhan's expression harden, his outlook changed by her words. He couldn't say if it was Owen's white flame or the surprising support of his godmother. There was something different about his personality, inspired by both fear and reason, he would gain control over this city.

"What Vatara says is true," the silver dragon announced and a mummer spread throughout the men. "I murdered him."

"What?" Judas gasped. "No, you c-wouldn't!"

"You are wrong," Lukhan announced boldly. "I wanted his life. He died with honor and will be remembered as a martyr."

"With honor?" a knight bellowed. "Clarify your statement dragon! What do you know of Owen! We never saw you with him!"

Lukhan held himself in a proud pose. "What I did was an act of mercy because he was going to die and I gave him an honorable death."

"An act of murder!" another knight accused.

"Owen was diseased at birth," Vatara added. "You leader had the misfortune of having a bad heart."

The men looked at each other in surprise. Owen's health was not publicly known to them, but Judas and Ambrosia knew. His wife had been Owen's caretaker. "Knights of Ravenshaven hear me," Judas declared. "You carry a weapon, a dagger called the misericord. What is that weapon forged for?"

There was a long pause among the men, some reach down and unsheathed the long blade. Judas produced his own weapon. "This dagger is designed to end the suffering of both honored friend and enemy. A bane to knights, a sliver of death, the last pain, and the heart stopper. It is forged to kill a doomed man."

"Do you understand?" Lukhan asked.

"I understand nothing-," the knight began.

"Wait!" Judas interrupted. "Owen spoke of having a condition that troubled his heart. It doesn't surprise me that his heart failed him, but it is different to kill someone in middle of battle than it is in the safety of his city. So I must ask that were all options exhausted? Could your magic not save him?"

"Owen's natural life was over and nothing in nature or alchemy could save him," Vatara announced.

"Lies!" the doubting knight challenged. "It's well known that gold dragons are masters of life magic! You could've saved him if you wanted to! You didn't! I'll tell you why. It is because the gold and silver dragons are in league with each other! The noble gesture between men of honor, declared as coup de grace, doesn't apply to this- murderer!"

"You are mistaken," Lukhan whispered.

"Shut up," Judas roared. Everyone fell silent at his booming voice. "There will be an investigation on what has occurred. Lukhan is a citizen and has full rights to a trial."

"He has our leader's blood on him!" the knight roared. "He doesn't deserve it!" The knight spurred his horse forward, breaking ranks. Judas moved to intercept the angry knight, but was knocked aside by the charger. Lukhan bared his teeth and spread his wings. The stench of death washed over both beast and man. The knight was bucked off his horse.

"That's enough!" Judas snarled. "Get back in line! Insubordination will not be tolerated! You'll be punished for-!"

"For Owen!" the knight screamed. The man jump up and charged with sword drawn. Lukhan held up his black claw. The knight thrust his blade deep into the deformed digit and the claw bit down on the blade. The sword shattered under the might of the black flame. A sharp pain pieced his claw and blood flowed from the dragon's wound. A sudden transfer of dark energy shattered the sword's blade and brought the knight to his knees.

"I would not do that again," Lukhan growled. He examined the painful wound on his claw, the black flesh that was sliced open quickly regenerated. The black claw twitched in angry frustration. Owen's soul was nothing but a raindrop in a desert of thirst.

The knight held his trembling blackened hand and glared at the dragon that disarmed him and destroyed his weapon. "Murderer!" he spat. He clutched his injured arm to his chest.

"Yes," Lukhan announced. "I am that and by the time this war is over, so will you. There will be many more deaths, including your own, if you do not control yourself. I am not to be trifled with and I will not be placed on trial for my actions. I am your leader and you will obey me."

"I'll never follow you!" the cringing knight declared. He continued to clutch his arm and held it like a baby.

"Then what will you do?" Lukhan asked. "Leave? Run to the Inquisition? Perhaps start a new life in your own city?"

"You can't exile me!" the knight growled. "Only the Imperator can do that!"

"A title which both Owen and the city council gave to me," Lukhan flexed his black claw. Yes, everything was falling into place. He already had the support of his friends. The council would fear him. The city was already afraid of him. He glanced to the side to look at his godmother. She had a sad face, her expression that made his heart stop.

A momentary thought struck him that made his stomach turn. The sudden and unexpected pain played with his emotions. His thoughts were still jumbled with that of Owen's experiences. He shook his head in growing confusion.

"Fool!" Judas snarled. "You shame the knights of Ravenshaven! We stand for justice, not revenge. A true warrior doesn't strike at the innocent." He grabbed his subordinate and smacked him across the face. "I understand your anger but we will not give into it. Lukhan, I demand that you stand trial."

Lukhan's eyes narrowed at his friend's demands. It was true, even as Imperator, he was a subject of the city's law. Owen's vast knowledge of the justice system was often vague. If he was convicted of murder, there would be no leniency within the law. What little he knew about the justice system was if he was convicted, he would be put to death. He knew that there was no doubt of his guilt and he would not hide it. Owen's knowledge of the city council told him that he would be stripped of his title and then executed. Owen's knowledge also told him that without a strong leader, murderer or no, the city's fractions would split apart. The city would be weakening, if not destroyed, by the sudden vacuum of power. The Inquisition would learn of this and conquer the city with ease. Owen's dreams would be shattered.

"No, I would be found guilty because it is true and I will not lie. I killed Owen."

"See, the dragon admits it!" the black-eyed knight roared.

"Shut up!" Judas snarled at the prone man. He slowly looked up at the silver dragon. His friend. He slowly unsheathed his sword. "My dearest friend, please, I beseech you to surrender and stand trial. Otherwise, I swore an oath to protect this city and you killed our leader! I may have to kill-" His voice wavered and struggled to keep a steady tone.

"Correct," Lukhan stated. "Have you forgotten our oath to each other?"

"Oath?" Judas asked. He squint his eyes trying to recall the distant memory. His eyes widen in realization, of course their shared a goal. That common goal was to destroy the Inquisition.

"Owen has done nothing to further our purpose, but I will correct Owen's constant lack in aggression against the Inquisition. Vatara has told me that the elves are under assault and Eldora is in danger."

Judas looked at Vatara's damaged body and nodded his head in agreement. "The elves? Eldora?" Judas whispered with a long pause. "We must do something."

"I am the city's new leader," Lukhan announced. "This is what Owen wanted. He wrote a will supporting this claim! Speak to the council before-"

"As an Inquisitor, I murdered innocents," Judas whispered. "Blood brother, we are same. You will not stand trial."

"Lying worm," the knight snarled. "I'll see you both dead-!" Judas grabbed the prone man's hair and pulled his head to his chest. The knight's protests fade into a bloody gurgle. The knight looked down to see Judas's dagger pierced his chainmail beneath the armpit. The man looked up at Judas' haunt eyes. "Wasn't I loyal? Didn't I serve Owen and his ideas of peace, freedom, and equality-?" His words faded, as did the light in his eyes. Judas pulled out his blade and released his hair, the man fell face first into the ground.

Judas stared at the dead man for a long time. He turned to his men who sat silently on their horses. "This man spoke treason against the true Imperator," he announced. He hardened his voice and stared down his dismayed men.

"He was an infiltrator, a spy within our own ranks. His loyalty wasn't to the city or this knighthood, but to Owen." He looked up at Lukhan and nodded. "Hail Imperator Lukhan!"

"What do we do?" the knight mumbled.

"Listen to me," Judas began. "Now I'm a murderer. If you do not wish to serve under my command or that of new Imperator, walk away now, return to your families and friends. You may abandon our company and city if you wish, and no harm or punishment will befall you. Speak of what you have seen here today and think about what has been done. If you return to me, always remember that I will not tolerate disloyalty to myself or the Imperator. My loyalty has always been with Lukhan; it always will be!"

The knights seemed uncertain because the laws of their city and chivalric order no longer seemed to be followed. The knight's loyalty divided between the past and future. It was a hostile takeover, anyone could see that. Bewildered by what had transpired, the knights of Ravenshaven did not run or flee but simply turned their horses around and left Owen's estate. They were confused and uncertain of the sudden and unexpected transfer of loyalty and leadership.

"Life is no longer valued during times of conflict," Vatara muttered in disgust. She shook her tired head at Ravenshaven's leadership revolution.

"Thank you for your support and Owen would have been pleased that he would forever be remembered as the knoll that had the position envied by a dragon," Lukhan gave them a weak smile.

"Did you think that you could get away with it?" Judas warned. "You are still the cause of Owen's death and you've sown the seeds of discontent."

"From you?" Lukhan asked.

"Yes, damn you! Discontent from me and many others," Judas snarled. "I once believed I had escaped the dangerous politics of the Inquisition. What you did- what I did. I feel that we are turning into our enemy and this is not what Owen wanted-"

"No one wants this."

Judas looked at him with disenchanted eyes. "I know what you really are," he growled. "When this war ends, you will return the powers of Imperator back to the people. The council will accept this and fall into line behind you."

"Most of the common races only understand what is told to them," Vatara replied. "They will not understand the larger danger."

"The Inquisition," Judas concluded.

"I must warn you," Lukhan added. "Your god may be the driving force behind the Inquisition's action. Vatara has attempted to speak to the Iron Throne."

"Faith in the Holy Master," Judas stated with wholehearted conviction. "Despite his silences, I still believe in him. The Master must know the reason behind this madness."

"We must have faith in ourselves," Lukhan declared.

"Pray," Vatara advised. "Your god will not save you now. War is coming and I do not think we will win."

"Of course we will," Judas wiped the blood off of his dagger on the dead man and sheathed the weapon. "With Lukhan as our Imperator, we can't lose. Not while he has that black claw."

"We shall see," Vatara stated. She looked at Lukhan with tired eyes. "I need rest and the smell of blood makes me ill."

"Of course, Lady Vatara," Judas grumbled. He struggled to pick up the dead man and drag him out of his courtyard. "It wasn't like I had a choice. Anything that-"

Vatara didn't listen to the man's grumbles, but laid her head down. The smell of blood had soaked into the ground and lingered in the air. She looked to Lukhan; the silver dragon stared off into the distant sky. She slowly shut her eyes.

"Was it a test?" Lukhan asked. He turned to look back at his godmother, but the gold dragon had already fallen asleep. Her eyes fluttered with the nightmare of what she had witnessed. An evil thought crept into Lukhan's mind. He had learned much from Owen and he could learn a great deal more from his godmother. The black claw gripped the cold earth. Owen's memories were not unpleasant; on the contrary, they were wonderful compared to the evil souls he devoured. The fleeting notion disappeared when Judas returned. "Back so soon?"

Judas paused and considered the silver dragon's question. "I didn't enjoy killing him," he explained. "Take that sneer off your face. Not like you did with Owen. That man was a good knight and served Owen well. If he had any family, they will be compensated. It was a necessary loss if you are going to succeed Owen's place."

"Did you know his name?" Lukhan asked.

"No," Judas lied. "It doesn't matter now because he attacked you. Now he is dead and we are not. He wasn't going to accept you no matter what. His loyalty to Owen was clouding his reasoning. I'm surprised that you didn't kill him."

There was a long pause between, dragon and man. "I wanted to kill," Lukhan's hungry eyes strayed over to his godmother's sleeping form. "The hunger is always there."

"Have you told the others?" Judas asked.

"I'm certain that they were watching," Lukhan glance over at the house, a curtain moved. Lukhan watched the dark forms in the house move about nervously. He turned his attention back to the human before him. "Go inside, tell them the truth that I killed Owen. I am sorry."

"Why don't you?" Judas asked. "I am still not sure what is going on. An explanation would be-"

"I am leaving," Lukhan interrupted. "I do not know how the city will react to my betrayal."

"Running away?" Judas asked. His voice was strained at the thought of Lukhan leaving again. "What are you afraid of? What is done is done and you can't change the past. You're still in control, aren't you?"

"Yes," Lukhan admitted. "That is what scares me more is that I am in control."

Chapter 46

"Wait! Don't leave," Bar called. The silver dragon was already in the air, several leagues away from his friends. Judas sat down in his trampled courtyard, the grass and garden had been crushed by the recent actively. He rested his head against his hands, hiding his face from the knoll. Fresh blood smeared off his gauntlet onto his face.

"Did you see?" Judas asked. His voice was harsh and unforgiving. Bar nodded his head but couldn't remove his eyes away from the distant silver dragon.

"Yes, we saw Luke kill Owen from the windows." There was a long pause between them. Bar glanced over at Vatara's sleep form. "She could have stopped him. So why didn't she? Why did she send us inside?"

"I don't need the details," Judas's hard voice wavered at the statement. He continued to rub his temples with his hand. "Please, tell me that Owen sick and dying and that he was going to die."

"Yes, according to Sacul and Ambrosia," Bar added. "Vatara said that she wouldn't prolong or save his life. I offered my heart in exchange for Owen's life."

"Fool," Judas's hands trembled at Bar's offer of self-sacrifice to Owen. A tear fell from Judas's hidden face; he couldn't believe what he had done. His heart pounded in his chest and the armor he wore seems a thousand times heavier. He lied to Lukhan, to put distance between them. He acted like he didn't care, like his men's lives meant nothing to him. That was what he was taught in the Inquisition. Never let your men see weakness or allow insubordination go unpunished. He knew the man's name. James was a promising young man that Judas had trained. Like the rest of his men, he knew a great deal about each individual. The guilt of James' death lingered and darkened his thoughts.

"Lukhan has changed," Bar added.

Judas wiped his eyes and nose. He fortified his thoughts and hardened his face. "The Imperator shouldn't be questioned," he whispered. He slowly reached down and grabbed his dagger. The blade trembled in his hand as he placed it against his thigh

"Judas," Bar whispered. "We have to stop him."

"What are you saying?" Judas demanded. "Are you saying that Lukhan should be killed?"

"Luke has betrayed the city's trust in the worst most possible way," Bar warned. "He is an oath breaker to the council. As council members, our responsibilities do not end with Owen's death. Is he a traitor?"

Judas took a deep breath and drew out his dagger. "If Lukhan is a traitor, then so am I. What do you suggest?" he asked in a wavering tone. The blade felt heavy in his hand and Judas didn't have the strength to kill again. Lukhan was the new Imperator and the dice had been cast. Treason to the new Imperator would not be tolerated. Not even from close friends.

"I-I don't know," Bar stuttered.

"It's the way the world works," Judas couldn't look at his friend and the world seemed so much heavier now.

"Why does it have to be?" Bar asked. "We both know what Luke is and I heard Vatara talking about killing him. What should we do?" He looked at Judas for the first time. The human sat with a tear stain face and a wavering dagger at his hip. "Perhaps I should ask: what will you do?"

Judas glanced down at his dagger. "I-I shall serve Lukhan until his promise is fulfilled," he stuttered. "Only then I will kill-." He could not complete his sentence.

"After destroying the Inquisition?" Bar recalled. He glanced over at Vatara, the sleeping dragon's injuries were still apparent. "If Vatara was brought low by the Inquisition's weapons, then what chance does Luke have?"

"I think that is what he is hoping for," Judas choked. "I looked into his eyes, they were strange and unfamiliar. I don't think he is the savior that we wanted him to be."

"What was that?" Bar whispered.

"I wanted Luke to be our savior," Judas replied without hesitation. "A rallying point for all that is just and good! I wanted his kindness, tolerance, and mercy to spread and be a standard for the world. I wanted him to be the paragon of the goodness that Ravenshaven embody."

"Is he a hero or a villain?" Bar asked.

"They are the same," Judas growled. "It depends on whose ox is getting gored." His face hardened at his own weakness. "My hopes and dreams died with Owen and I will no longer hold my eyes shut like a child. We cannot change the world with kind words and hopeful thoughts. Change requires bloodshed. Have we forgotten that blood is power. It must be spilled-"

"You sound like the dragon council. Must we stoop to that level? That we must make our enemies fear us?" Bar asked.

Judas growled in frustration. "Then what do you think? Let the Inquisition win and give up on Lukhan? Do nothing or run away?" he demanded. "It takes a warrior, not a philosopher, to change the world." He sheath his blade, Bar didn't have any answers, but was quick to criticize.

"No," Bar refused. "I understand what you're saying. It's- I wish it didn't have to be that way."

"I agree," Judas whispered.

There was a long pause between knoll and man. They didn't look at each other. Bar's words carried more weight than he knew and Judas was envious of the knoll's wishful vision. To imagine a world where people worked together instead of killing each other. The blood on his gauntlet was the truth of the reality. The common races were different and conflicts would rise and fall.

"You know the sad thing about it," Judas chuckled. "Even if the Inquisition wins and all the non-human races are destroyed, the humans that survive will find another reason to hate. They will continue to fight, even over something foolish such as the color of eyes or the way someone dresses. My people will never be happy."

"It will never come to that," Bar hoped.

"I thought the sacred herd would never end," Judas scoffed. "Yet, I've not seen the buffalo since the slaughter."

"Nor I," Bar agreed.

"We mustn't lose hope," a familiar female voice called. They turned to see Ambrosia standing in the doorway of the house. Her eyes were soft and sad. A strained smile was on her face. "What matters now is that we are united. Yes, we have differences, but that is what makes us great-"

"She is right," Sacul grunted. He pushed past Ambrosia to investigate the destroyed courtyard. He brought out his pet toad and placed it on his shoulder.

"Like always, the coward is late," Judas huffed. "Where were you?"

"Sorry, but I was protecting your wife," Sacul puffed up his chest and pound on it. The wide eyed toad glanced at the abnormally eager shaman. "You should've been there, taking care of her!" The toad glared at him in suspended disbelief.

"Hush, Sacul! Your nose was face deep raiding our kitchen cabinets! You didn't even see what happened!" Bar accused.

"So! You were breathing so hard that you fogged up the glass on the window!" Sacul retorted. "What were you watching, weirdo?"

"Luke killed Owen!" Bar growled.

"Oh," Sacul grunted. The shaman smiled at the thought. "At least his memories are not lost."

"Lukhan murdered Owen and that's all you can say?" Judas growled.

"Well, it's true," Sacul grunted. "According to the toad, Owen's soul is part of Lukhan's whole. With Owen's knowledge and experiences, Lukhan will lead us; it's a victory for all." The toad chirp in agreement. "Save for Owen's soul that has been rendered by the black claw." The toad frowned at his fat master.

"According to your toad," Judas mocked sarcastically.

"The spirits don't lie," Sacul grunted with a boorish grin. "Neither do my visions."

"Take your toad induced visions and shove them!" Judas growled. "This is a serious situation, a matter more important than politics and power. It's about life and death and it's about our friend!"

"Judas, please," Ambrosia begged. "Sacul is trying to-"

"It is not a joking matter!" Judas snapped. "Our crimes are against the people we are trying to protect! We have failed in protecting our leader! Lukhan and I are both murderers-"

"No!" Ambrosia cried. "You are my husband; you are a knight of Ravenshaven, a noble and honorable man. You did what you had to, like the silver dragon!" The knoll, human, and boarelf looked at each other in hesitant pause. "Well, isn't he? Are all those stories you told me about him lies?"

Her question caused everyone to hesitate. Lukhan had change, and they didn't know if it was for the better. A gruff cough to clear his throat broke the silence that befell them. "She is right, you know," Sacul grunted. He licked his toad for comfort and the tiny creature chirped in gloomy reply.

Bar nodded his head at the thought; he had forgotten everything Lukhan had done for him. He knew that he wasn't a monster. He began to laugh at himself. It wasn't like him to think of such terrible thoughts. Judas and Sacul looked at him strangely. "Ambrosia, my dear, you are correct," he chuckled. "Even if Lukhan struck me down dead, I wouldn't blame him. I owe him my life a thousand times over."

Ambrosia smiled at the knoll. "Regardless, of what we have done in the past, we must forgive each other. Else we truly are our worst enemy."

"She speaks the truth," Bar agreed. "We owe Lukhan our lives and much more. If he is to become what we fear, should we fight him? Should we join forces with him, even though we think that his actions are wrong?"

"You fear the worse," Sacul added. "Yet he has shown great restrain with the black claw. When he killed Owen, he could have killed Vatara and then turned on us."

"That's right; why didn't he kill James when he struck Lukhan with his sword," Judas added.

"So why did you kill him?" Sacul asked.

"It was because he attacked Lukhan," Judas muttered. He felt ashamed for killing the defeated man and his face grew red at the question. "I acted on impulse, my brain was on fire and I could only see red. The man wouldn't listen to reason. What I did was wrong, but James forced my hand. If I was going to have to choose a side between James and Lukhan. It was going to be-" His words were cut short by a gasp of air.

"Luke," Bar completed the struggling man's sentence. He looked at Judas with compassion. Man and knoll understood each other. The conflict between their social obligations and friendships had been decided.

"Then we shall support Lukhan until the end!" Sacul cheered. The group looked at each other. The shaman was correct. Lukhan wasn't the perfect leader and they were willing to accept this. They had no clue how the city would react to their beloved hero, Owen, being murdered by the dragon they placed their future hopes in.

<hr>

Murderer, villain, and monster. This is what Lukhan was; the truth was evident, as evident as the black flesh that clung to him. Owen's blood stained him like a marked murderer. He flew away from the city and the damage he had caused, away from the destruction and devastation he had sown. The city would fall into chaos and blood would fill the city's sewers. He was the cause of all that would follow.

He had thrown it all away and the world saw him for what he really was. He hardened himself with the guilt of Owen's murder. He was a death elemental, as greedy and uncaring as the black flame. He left his emotions, his care, and his love behind. He was different now, much more accepting of his prophesied fate. This is what he chose and it had not been forced on him. The power he would obtain would be from those who were closest to him.

The city fell behind him. He flew over the charred landscape that the Red Clan had left behind. Among the scorched earth a single green figure stood out. Con'ra looked up at him and his fast pace slowed. Her cat-like eyes shown in the blackened surroundings. She beckoned to him, although she seemed tiny from his aerial position. Her proud statue and demeanor made him feel small.

"Lukhan!" Con'ra cried. "Is everything all right?" Her eyes grew wide when she realized he was covered in blood. "Did you get hurt? Is that your blood? What happened?" He slowly landed before her, his magically scarred eyes were distant and dead. She sniffed his scent and became watchful of any pursuer. "Knoll blood? Lukhan, are you all right? Please say something!" Her pleading words didn't reach him. A distant and stoic expression covered the silver dragon's face.

"Lukhan?" Con'ra asked. Her voice wavered as she looked at him. Something terrible had happened and her eyes flew wide in realization. It was his nightmare made into a reality! The vision they had shared together! The lesser races that he placed so much value in. Her memory of the nightmare had begun to fade, but, with Lukhan standing before her, she recalled the gruesome vision. Tears came to her eyes and the evil he had shared. "You killed them?"

"No," Lukhan stated. "Do not cry, not for me."

She choked at his words. "Why?" she cried. "You seem to be dying!"

"Is it that obvious," Lukhan muttered stoically. "I am already dead."

"That cannot be true! You stand before me now!" she cried.

"As a shell," he stated flatly. "An empty vessel, the last reminisce of the plague. My single purpose now is to fulfill my obligations to everyone I have committed myself to."

"Obligations? You are not making any sense!" Con'ra gasped.

"I am death," Lukhan stated. "I cannot heal or create because I have only the power to destroy."

"That is not true," Con'ra whispered. "I will prove it to you." She looked around in desperation, the charred earth around them needed healing. The plants that had been sown could be regenerated. She dug her claw into the earth and drew out a chunk of charred earth. The dry dirt crumbled in her palm.

"Do you remember?" Con'ra asked. "This is the first place we met."

"Yes." There was no joy or happiness in Lukhan's voice, his tone flat and cold, like the wind over an ice covered lake.

She looked at him with sadness in her eyes. She should have gone with him despite his godmother's command. Guilt pulled at her heart as she looked at the silver dragon that had changed so quickly. A tear fell down her cheek. "I will not let this place die. It may be burnt and scarred, but I will repair it."

"How?" he asked. The land was dead, as dead as he felt inside.

"There is always hope," As she said this, her tears fell on the chunk of earth that she grasped within her claw. A single tear fell into the burnt soil. Several moments passed and nothing happened.

"Nothing will ever grow here," Lukhan muttered. "The soil is charred and there is too much brimstone in the soil."

"Sulfur can be used as a fertilizer," she licked the dirt in her claws. "Even in the desert, there is life. *Sulfur adficio.*" A sudden yellow flash from her eyes was the only hint of magic. Yellow dust sprang from the dirt she held like tiny lights trying to escape the charred earth. "I need help to replant the field and I cannot do it alone. Please, it needs water. You can help it to grow." She held out the dirt clump for him to hold.

Lukhan looked at it for a brief moment, and then cast his eyes downward. She wanted him to preform magic. "I cannot," he replied.

"Why?" Con'ra asked. "Magic is not always evil and you can use it to do good."

"Magic is unnatural," Lukhan muttered.

"Then what does that make us?" Con'ra asked. "Both you and I are magical beings. Does that make us evil?"

"Magic is an illusion," Lukhan stated.

"Yes, but this seed is here and now held within my palm," Con'ra explained. "My mother told me that a plant only needs five things to grow. They are: sufficient sunlight, suitable temperatures, good soil, protection, and water. The desert will provide the sunlight and I have given this seed good soil. It was protected from the flames by the soil. Now it is your turn, silver."

"My turn?" Lukhan asked. "I have the power to make it rain."

"I do not need it to rain," Con'ra replied. "I have seen your immense power. I do not need a flood, I need this dirt sprinkled."

"I do not understand," Lukhan muttered. "Are you mocking me?"

"You never learned to use your magic properly," Con'ra warned. "You go to such extremes. Using all of your magical energy or never using it."

"Is that so wrong?" Lukhan asked.

"You should be more fluid like the wind," Con'ra gave him a warm smile. "You are acting like a raging volcano, exploding with all of its frenzy. This must cause horrible strain on your white flame, like when the earth groans when a volcano erupts. Your power in unstable and fluctuates radically."

"It does not matter," Lukhan replied. "Why are you telling me this?"

"I saw your soul," Con'ra recalled. "When I travelled into the spirit world."

"It must have been an ugly dead thing," Lukhan stated in disgust.

"Yes," Con'ra chuckled. "It was like a moonless night, but there was a flicker of hope."

"That flicker is the Staff of Selgae," Lukhan stated. "The light you saw was the white flames I have collected. I have no soul; it was burnt away seven years ago."

"I refuse to believe that," Con'ra dismissed.

"Believe what you will," Lukhan stated. "I am bound to my failed duties. I will end my destructive existence when I have completed them."

"Duties?" Con'ra asked. "What duties do you have to complete before you-?"

"To kill until I am dead," Lukhan clarified. "The promises to my family and friends. Such as I promised to you: I shall take your father's life."

"Kill my father?" Con'ra asked. She took offense to the silver dragon's assumptions. "My father will die by my claws, not yours! My problems are none of your concern! Do not give into your darker nature. It is in us all."

"I know," Lukhan replied. "Still, a promise must be kept."

"What if I asked you for something different?" she asked. "Something that has nothing to do with killing. What if I asked you to help me heal this field?"

"I-I do not think I can," he wavered.

"Please try," Con'ra begged. "Use your head and do not use magic. All that it needed is water for the soil."

Lukhan looked at her in confusion. He relied on illusions and dreams, trapped in a nightmare of his own creation. Blinded by his ambitions and greed. He glanced down at the black claw, it could not help him complete Con'ra's task. He wouldn't use magic because she requested it.

"You have other methods," Con'ra prompted. "Remember when we first met? With your mother, we had a silly competition." The thought brought a smile to her face.

Lukhan's eyes widen in realization. His breath! His natural element. He held his claws out in front of him and slowly blew ice in his claw. The air condensed and gathered around his outstretched limb. The ice burned as it gathered, but he ignored the pain. The frozen water accumulated and, when a thick enough layer gathered, he stopped. The ice began to melt soon after, and Lukhan let the water dribble on Con'ra's seeded clod.

"I knew you could do it," Con'ra smiled and small leaves began to spring to life at her command. The soil and water provided and accelerated the growth of the seeds. When the plants had taken root, Con'ra gently placed the seeds on the ground. The revitalized growth of plants began in earnest and quickly spread to charred field.

"How did you-?" Lukhan asked.

"We," Con'ra corrected. "We healed this land."

"So we did," he stated. The sea of green flourished around the two dragons. Lukhan's stoic fortitude shattered as the plants around him grew. Tears came to his eyes and Con'ra had given him a gift in his hour of need. There was still hope for him. He couldn't save Owen by magic or alchemy, but he would help the city he loved as best as he could. He had failed them once, but he would not do so again. He was capable of so much more than the darkness within him.

Con'ra crept close to the weeping silver dragon and placed a comforting wing over him. "No more tears," she whispered. "I will protect you."

Chapter 47

The city of Ravenshaven didn't riot or burn like Lukhan feared. Instead, the city mourned the loss of their leader. Public and private ceremonies were held within Ravenshaven. The Gold Clan was dispersed within the city and few openly challenged Lukhan's right to succession. The truth was that Owen's death was not a surprise, knolls aged faster than the other common races and his death not unexpected. Yet, the people were still angry. Owen's body had gone missing and several conspiracy theories arose. Some thought the illusive leader was still alive since there was no body. Others believed that the tricky leader had disappeared into the night with the city's treasury in tow, but there were also rumors that the dragons and the Inquisition were to be blamed for Owen's death.

Yet, the truth was not believed, everyone knew that silver dragon saved the council. The council was disturbed by the fact that they no longer had a leader. Owen's last will and testament was read and his property was distributed amongst his strong supporter. Thus, the council's loyalty was bought by Owen's last wishes and payment. The council stood in orderly confusion, awaiting their new Imperator. Bar, Judas, and Sacul kept the rumors of Owen's death as nothing more than rumors. No public announcement was made by the council. The mystery of Owen's death took on a life of its own.

Justice did not disappear with Owen; charges of James's murder were brought against Judas. A military tribunal was held and Judas lost his rank of commander of the Ravenshaven's knights. However, his position as a council member of the city made him immune to any further punishment. Such was mysterious power of Owen's death. The Ravenshaven's Knights were consolidated as part of the city guards under the direct control of the council.

The trial was nothing more than a brief distraction to the news-starved public. Bigger things than conspiracy murder were happening in the South.

War was already upon the elves, and trade with them came to an abrupt end. Rumors of massive armies clashing and woods burning reached the council's ears. Decisions were going to be made. The debate was heavy within the council. More questions than answers were raised. The doors to the council chamber were locked for fear of spies and assassins in the city.

"We must do something!" Bar demanded. His words rang true within the chamber. The merchant's guild was behind the knoll and they mumbled their agreement. The council was indecisively split between a defensive or offensive tactic.

"Yet we should not stretch our forces too thin," Sacul warned. "Exercising caution is more important now than ever. We don't know anything about the Inquisition's movements." Of all the races, the boarelves had the least to lose. Trade was still new to them and they were not good at it. They were far more self-sufficient and more accustom to hiding than fighting. The boarelves valued blood more than gold. Trade was a commodity for them, and they could easily do without. Sacul had become the leader in opposition to march to war. Smaller groups and organizations rallied behind the well-meaning shaman.

"We know where they are going," Bar stated. "Up the Hollylyassa River, conquering all opposition along the way. We are their final target!"

"You do not know that," Sacul grunted.

"Then what do you suggest?" Bar challenged.

The shaman brought out his toad and licked it a couple of times. "The humans are conquering all of this land, yes?" Sacul asked. The council agreed. "Well, they are going to try to control it. This will stretch out their armies and make them vulnerable."

"The humans outnumber the elves," Bar warned. "Do you think we can withstand a direct assault against the whole might of the Inquisition?"

"I don't know," Sacul grunted. "You would have to ask Judas that."

Judas slumped in his chair, away from his fellow council members. The loss of his knighthood undermined his confidence, and James's murder still weighed heavily on his mind. "What?" he whispered.

"Speak up," Sacul prompted.

Judas cleared his throat and sat up in his chair. "What was the question?" he asked.

"Stay with us," Sacul grunted. "Pay attention, commander dumb ass."

"What are you doing?" Bar growled. "Shut up!"

The boarelf grunted at the knoll's scolding. "As you wish," he snorted. "However, the seriousness of this topic cannot be avoided. The boarelves are scattered across the Endless Desert. It will take time for them to gather."

"The same goes for the knoll packs," Bar agreed. "Those in the Silver Mountains are likely fighting along with the elves, but I have no proof to back that claim. They might not be helping at all."

"Then what should we do?" Sacul asked. "We are in no position to fight and our forces are scattered."

"Don't you see what is happening," Judas muttered.

"What was that?" Sacul demanded. "Speak up!"

"The Inquisition is attacking the only force capable of mobilizing against them in a short period," Judas yelled in a loud and angry tone. "The elves are the only organized force capable of withstanding their assault. If the elves fall, we'll be next!"

"So what do you suggest?" Sacul challenged. "Take a small force and assist the elves? Would a small force be capable of turning the tide of war?"

"No, but it should give the city time to gather our forces," Judas concluded. "We can't- no- we must not abandon our friends. Never forget Eldora."

The council considered his words carefully. "If we send this small force to the elves it would weaken our position here," Bar added. "Our armory is full, but our troop command structure is off."

"Then we must have a supreme command," Sacul announced. "This is a time of war, and we must have someone lead us into battle."

"Who do you purpose?" Bar asked.

"Judas. He knows the Inquisitions better-," Sacul was interrupted by members of the council. Cries of outrage and disbelief echoed within the chamber. The notion was quickly shot down from any further discussion.

"What about Luke?" Bar asked. The council fell silent at the suggestion. The silver dragon seemed like a logical choice, he was their Imperator.

"I second the notion, put forth by Councilor Bar," Sacul agreed. "We shall give Lukhan a new title."

"I third the notion," Judas spoke up. "His new title will be Emperor." The council agreed and emergency power and the measure were passed on to a dragon that was not even there.

"Council members," a guard announced. "The Inquisition has sent an ambassador to speak with you."

There was a long pause in the chamber before anyone acknowledged the city guard.

"The Inquisition?" Bar asked. "Guard, this is a closed session. Who does this man belong to? No one is to be allowed in or out!"

"An ambassador?" Sacul grunted. "How could he know of this? How could the Inquisition know of our meetings? I issued the orders last night-" He looked around the chamber. Every member was a suspect. No one recognized the strange members of the guard.

"Let us hear him out!" Judas grunted. "Who is it?"

There was a defiant grumble in the council chamber. No representative of the Inquisition had stepped forward to speak with them. The members had only seen assassin blades, bold letters of threats, economic sanctions, and foreign currency. The chamber fell silent and the guard returned with the ambassador at his side.

The man was a spindly figure dressed in silk robes. He leaned heavily on his walking stick. A cloak hid the aged man's face, but a thin stringy long goatee fell out of the cloak's shadows.

"Who are you?" Bar demanded.

"Thank you for your help," the figure whispered to the guard. "You may return." The escorting guard folded in on himself like a piece of paper and disappeared in a pool of magical residue.

"Magic!" Judas snarled. "Defend yourselves!" Daggers and hidden weapons were drawn from beneath cloaks and hidden areas around the chamber. The council members pounced from the seat and grasped the blind man. The old man's hood was pulled back, revealing the man's aged features. He was blind, cataracts had taken his eyesight. His hair was white and thin, his skin was wrinkled by age, and slightly oblique eyes were even narrower. The old man's worn garments stank of garbage and sewage.

"Who are you?" Sacul demanded.

"Do you not recognize me?" the man asked. He smiled at him revealing decayed yellow teeth.

"I don't know who you are-," Bar began.

"Perhaps, this will speak louder than my words," the mysterious man reached down and revealed the clothing he wore under his cloak.

"An Inquisitor Lord!" Judas gasped. He recognized the fine clothing and the emblem of the Iron Throne embroider on his chest.

"Awe, you must be Judas," the man glanced over in Judas's direction. "My name is Shen Tianxiang."

"You!" Bar growled. "You must be the one behind the assassination plot! The wizard's magical attack on Luke! Why are you here? Give us one good reason not to cut off your head!"

"Don't forget the missing children and pups," Shen teased. "I needed them for my experiments. A fuel source for my alchemy and wards."

"Bastard!" Judas snarled. "You would dare admit that!" He punched the blind man's face.

Shen's face contorted into rage, but quickly faded. "Regardless, you killed my men and I killed your children. A fair trade, wouldn't you agree?"

"You-," Judas held up his fist, but Sacul grabbed his arm before he could strike the prisoner.

"Where have you been hiding?" Sacul grunted. "How do you know about this meeting? What did you do with the children's bodies?"

"Down in the sewer," Shen explained. "How else do you cover one's scent from dragons and knolls?"

"An Inquisitor Lord living in shit," Judas scoffed. "Not much different from what comes out of his mouth. Kill him quickly and be done with this matter!"

"I wouldn't do that if I were you," the blind man gave them a yellow smile. "To kill me would be signing your own death. The paper that you have been writing on, those notes, declarations, and laws, the papers were enchanted and warded." Shen pointed around the chamber, documents and paperwork was everywhere. The paper seemed harmless enough, the council gave pause. The Inquisitor Lord had done something or else he would not have been so bold.

"So what," Sacul grunted. "Who cares about what you did to the paper."

"Those children you were wondering about," Shen paused and gave them a yellow smile. "What do you think your ink is made of?"

The boarelf's eyes flew wide in realization. "Monster!" he grunted. "You used the blood and souls of the children to enchant the ink! What else have you done? What is your purpose? Answer me!"

"I am not the monster here, but I know who is," Shen sneered. "I will not speak to a witless thrall. Where is your new Emperor, pig? I wish to speak to him. The fallen silver dragon you call Lukhan?"

"You cannot use magic," Con'ra explained. "You rely too heavily on it."

"I should crush the cursed things!" Lukhan growled in growing frustration. The task that Con'ra set before him was a simple one: create and harvest a garden. Con'ra selected an Oasis in the middle of the Endless Desert for him to practice on. He had plenty of good soil and water, but he didn't know how plants grew. Con'ra had forbidden any kind of magic.

"If you crush the seeds, they will not grow," she warned. The silver dragon was more impatient than she was. Con'ra assumed that it was because he was with the common races all the time. "Sometimes you have to relax and allow nature to occur."

"The birds and rodents have eaten the helpless seeds!" Lukhan growled in annoyance. Water in the Endless Desert attracted the local wildlife to their location. Lukhan guarded his crops the best he could. Yet the crafty creatures of the desert seemed to easily slip past his defenses.

"It is all right," Con'ra giggled. "The birds and mice need to eat too. Everything eats."

Her laughter only irritated him more. His success in replanting the burnt fields of Ravenshaven had given him hope. Con'ra proved that he didn't need magic or the black claw to create and help things grow. He thought his single purpose in life was nothing more than a warrior. His naive air element seemed so far removed that he had forgotten his breath. Con'ra's words didn't heal his guilt, but it did patch it momentarily. He understood what she was trying to do. She was trying to comfort him.

He was grateful.

"Why are you looking at me like that?" Con'ra demanded. To her, the silver dragon's mood was erratic. His glowing mercury eyes gave no insight into what he was thinking. Only a twitch of an eyebrow or a faint smile gave her any sign that he was enjoying the frustrating moments.

"Oh, no reason," Lukhan gave them a faint smile.

"Did you smile?" Con'ra teased in a playful accusing tone. His expression changed and became expressionless. "I did see a smile."

"What of it," he demanded with a frustrated huff.

"I am glad that you are smiling again, you had me worried."

Lukhan glanced down at the tiny seeds in his normal claw. The ruddy-like seeds refused to grow for him, despite the oasis's abundant plant life. No matter how much he took care of them, watering and protecting them, they showed no signs of life. Con'ra had originally given him one hundred pomegranate seeds. She had plucked the last fruit from the bushes. Now he only had ten seeds left and they seemed to be afraid of their owner.

"Are you afraid of me?" Lukhan asked.

Con'ra cocked her head to the side. "I have spent time with the Blood Queen and survived my father's cruel capture. I have been stung, bitten, burnt, clawed, and everything in between. Why would I be afraid of you?"

"I never explained to you what I am."

"You are a death elemental."

Lukhan was taken aback by her reply. This scared him more than anything else.

"You look surprised," she giggled. "The Blood Queen told me about you."

"What else did she tell you?" he asked nervously.

"Well, that is it," Con'ra stated. "She said that you were a death elemental and that was about it."

"Do you know what that means?" Lukhan pressed.

"No," Con'ra laughed. "I thought that it had something to do with the smell of death around you, and the black flesh growing up your arm, and the lack white flame. Your metamorphosis is not as hidden as you would like it to be."

Lukhan nodded his head in confirmation. "What you say is true," he stated. He opened his mouth to speak, but feared how she would react. Even after he had killed Owen, she was not afraid of him. Nonetheless, there was a great deal of hesitation.

"I know who you are," Con'ra whispered. "I have seen your withered soul, gazed into your nightmares, and witnessed your terrible rage. I think I know you, or at least, what you are becoming."

"That does not frighten you?" he asked.

"No," she stated honestly.

"I killed Owen," Lukhan warned. "I could turn on you, my friends, anyone."

"So you say," Con'ra shrugged. "I did not know this Owen, but he must have meant something to you. You place a great deal of fate and love into such fragile creatures and I am not surprised at what happened. A human does not weep for a chicken he had for supper. You must change the way you think if you are to defeat the Inquisition and its god."

"How can you say this?" he asked.

"Do I have to remind you that these pets you care so much about are going age and die?" Con'ra asked.

"What does that have to do with anything?" Lukhan growled.

"Everything," Con'ra comforted. "You place too much value on them-"

"Enough," Lukhan let out a cold snorted as he turned away from her.

"You must listen to me," she warned. "Otherwise, you are killing yourself! Look at the seeds within your claws. How many of them have survived? You have done your best to protect them and nurture them. You started with more seeds than you could keep track of, and now those are all gone, eaten by the smallest of pests, lost in the sands, or crushed within your claw. You, with all of your strength, could not stop it from happening. Some things are destined to happen, no matter how much you wished that they never did."

"Stop speaking in riddles! I am in no mood for such games," Lukhan snapped. "Are you implying that there is a correlation between these seeds and my friends? You are saying that they will not survive?" He began to tremble in anger and frustration. Was this a game to her? Was she trying to protect him from what was to come?

Con'ra remained silence. The silver dragon's mood changed rapidly; at times he appeared normal and in control, but certain events triggered his aggression. He was an easy read, but his breaking points appeared to be growing more frequently. He was easily agitated and quicker to anger. He had lost something when he killed Owen. The question still remained on what that was.

"Stop staring at me," Lukhan growled. He could feel her yellow eyes staring at him. The tiny seeds trembled in his hand. She was correct. He could not save his friends. They would die in war or fall victim to the decay of time. Worse yet, he would devour their white flames. Either way, he would lose them.

"It is the way of the earth element," Con'ra explained. "We are born from dust and we must return to it. Nothing, not even the sand and stone beneath our feet, lasts forever."

"You are wrong, death lasts forever."

"True," she conceded. "Everything has an ultimate end."

Lukhan stopped trembling. Those seeds that he held in his claw were tiny lives. He could sense the tiny white flames inside each of them. Should he leave the seeds to their fate? Protect them? Crush them? Even take their white flames? Did it really matter? These seeds were capable of feeding this oasis, but it seemed like the place they were created was trying to destroy them. It was a cruel fate, unfair and unjust. Even if the seeds took root he could not stay and protect them. He had other obligations.

"I do not know what to do," he whispered.

Con'ra waited for him to continue, to explain what he meant. When no answer came forth she broke the silence. "I was like you," she explained. "When my mother died and when I was captured by my father, I was lost. My anger and rage at my father was unfathomable. It has been an obsession of mine and this obsession nearly cost my life. Yet, by fortune or chance, my life was spared. I think my father was trying to teach me my place in this world, to teach me that I have limitations and I dare not approach him. He takes great pleasure from my suffering."

"I do not understand," Lukhan still remembered her painful vision like it was his own.

"My point is that you cannot protect your pets," Con'ra warned. "No matter how much power you obtain or how big an army you raise, you will not be able to save them from the inevitable."

"Then what do you suggest?" Lukhan asked. "If death is so inevitable, than why do you care what I think?"

"I cannot make your decision and I can only make mine," she whispered.

"What is that?" he asked.

"I have my obsession," she stated plainly. "That gives me propose and a reason to keep living. I expect it is the same for you. It is based on realistic goals and plausible achievements."

"What if you were free of your obsession?" he asked

"You mean the day my father is dead and I have taken his place?" Con'ra let out a snorting chuckle. Lukhan nodded his head in all seriousness. "You asked me this once before. At first, I was not sure what you were asking. During the nightmarish curse, you told me that there were other reasons to live and you told me to live for love."

"Yes?" Lukhan asked with a hopeful expression.

"I am too proud to devote myself to another," Con'ra giggled. "Love is not enough. This emotion that you have for me is a silly and fleeting notion. It is silly that you have feelings for your pets." His shoulders and wings sank at her cold words. "Listen, I enjoy your company, I truly do. The emotion of hate is easy, but love takes courage. How do I explain this, you and me, we it could never be? We are too different, like the earth and sky."

"Why is that?" Lukhan asked. He turned to look at her, his scarred eyes were hurt.

She looked away from him. "You have important thing to do and so do

I," she had a regretful tone. "Our lives are complicated and it does not need to be harder than it already is."

"So then why do you comfort me?" Lukhan asked. "By the five elements, why do you linger? You should leave before you get hurt!"

"I have a task I must complete," she muttered. "It will make me strong for what is to come."

"What is that?" Lukhan demanded.

Con'ra looked him straight in the eye. "Do you want to know the truth?" she asked. Her normally polite and joyful voice dropped into a threatening tone. He nodded his head yes. "The Blood Queen assigned me the task; to kill you when you become a death elemental."

Lukhan's jaw dropped open at her confession.

Chapter 48

"I have the Blood Queen's blessing!" Lukhan eyes flew wide in sudden realization, Fienicks wanted him dead! He wasn't surprised but how close Con'ra had gotten to him emotionally. He was going to confess his love to her and she was closer to him now than his best friends. She had reassured him and spoke to him as if they were equals. How could this have happened? He was a fool to fall in love with her. His feelings were nothing to her! The enigma that was Con'ra was beginning to fit. The illusion and hopes began to fade. He was a death elemental, how could she love the black flame? Con'ra wasn't the Blood Queen's slave or servant.

"You are the Queen's assassin," Lukhan concluded.

"I have many talents," Con'ra whispered.

Lukhan frowned at the thought. She did love death, but not him. Who better to trick him and his friends than a green dragon? His godmother warned him about her. Both cunning and manipulative, she was the prefect assassin. Her attacks on Ravenshaven were to draw him out. The Blood Queen must have realized what he was before they even met. That was why the brood mother, Sessess, and the Green Clan leader, Krain, wanted her dead. She was a traitor to the Green Clan.

"Was everything you told me a lie?" Lukhan asked. His voice was surprisingly calm, but a deep undertone stated that he was everything but calm. "Our conversations, the time we spent together, you are-were my friend. Was it all an act so you could get close to me?"

"Yes," Con'ra stated simply. Her eyebrow twitched at the necessary lie. Lukhan waited for her to continue, wanting for a detailed explanation. They simply stared at each other.

"Well?" he demanded in a sharp growl. He broke the awkward silences that fell over them.

"What?" Con'ra challenged. "You are a death elemental and you did not tell me."

"Your Queen knew," Lukhan roared angrily. "I should have known that you were sent here to kill me." His nose flared in growing frustration. He should have listened to his friends and godmother. She wasn't to be trusted! They warned him and he didn't listen. The endless hunger flared up its ugly head within his mind. The black claw twitched in growing anticipation. Perhaps he should kill her and learn the absolute extent of her lies, maybe then he would know the truth.

"You do not thrust me now?" Con'ra asked. "I have told you the truth. No matter how painful it is for me to say."

"How-?" Lukhan growled. "Why should I believe you now? I doubt everything you say!" His eyebrows knitted together at the thought of being tricked into sharing personal moments with someone who was plotting to kill him. A sharp pain in his chest began to throb. Lukhan's emotions were in a whirlwind and he dropped the pomegranate seeds he held in his claw. They meant nothing to him now. This could all be a trick or another lie. He began to pace back and forth in tormented frustration. "I should not be surprised because it seems that everyone wants something from me."

"That is not true," Con'ra scowled.

"Oh?" Lukhan snarled. "Your Queen seeks to use me to spearhead the assault on the Inquisition. While I risk my life for her cause, she plots my assassination!"

"Yes," Con'ra agreed. "It seems you have taken her cause under your own banner."

Lukhan continued to pace back and forth like a caged animal. Con'ra sat politely, waiting to see what the silver dragon would do next. "Why did you tell me this?" he demanded. He was angry at himself for not seeing the obvious signs.

"I speak now because I care about you," Con'ra sighed. "I have never told you a lie if I could help it. I am protecting my own interests now."

Lukhan paused his pacing and stared at her. His dumbfounded expression quickly turned to anger. "You would dare say that now?" he roared. "After stating that you have no feelings for me! You lie even now!" He sprang forward and raised his claw to strike her. He should kill her before she killed him! Every muscle in his body told him to take the skinny lying worm's life! His mind ached and broken heart pounded in his chest. Fury and rage swelled up inside of him. He loved her.

She didn't scream or cry out in fear. No words of magic passed her lips. No wards had been placed on the ground. She stared at him with sad yellow eyes. Lukhan's anger did not subside as the black claw trembled against her throat. He could feel the blood pumping through her veins. A strong and constant pulse, the beating of her heart. He could end it. Squeeze his claw shut. The conflict of emotions within him focused his anger and rage, yet there were still deeper feelings. He still loved her!

"You are not going to do it," she stated.

"You don't think so!" he snarled.

"No," Con'ra said coldly.

White froth dripped out of Lukhan's trembling mouth. His body shook between his broken heart and his resisting mind. She could not deny him! He would devour her! Body and soul! He was a death elemental! He could have whatever he wanted because no one could challenge him! The world! An eternal life! Power! Wealth! All would be his if he but claimed it! He could take her life! End her suffering! Her soul would be his forever! It didn't matter that she did not love him!

"No!" he gasped. "Not that!" He withdrew his claw from her throat. He wouldn't take her life like he had taken Owen's.

Con'ra rubbed her neck and continued to stare at him. "You are not a death elemental yet," she whispered. "I was afraid that you would not stop."

Lukhan's eyes flashes in anger. "It is foolish to tease me," he warned.

"The Blood Queen's only desire is for me to kill the death elemental," she replied. "Not the dragon. I will wait until the end. Before you become an unstoppable force, I will end your life."

"Do you think you could stop me?" Lukhan demanded. "I could crush the life out of you!"

"I cannot stop death," she warned. "None of us can; however, I can stop the black flame from taking you. I will make certain of that. I will keep your mind intact while your body decays."

"Then you should fear me," he snarled and turned away. "As the Blood Queen does."

"Is that what you believe?" she asked. "As I recall, it was she who defeated you. I could do the same."

"That was only because we fought in the Mountains of Fire," Lukhan snarled. "I was at a disadvantage! I could defeat her!"

Con'ra smiled at the bait, but she didn't take it. "So when you fight the Holy Master, upon his Throne of Iron, you will not be at a disadvantage?" she asked. Lukhan snorted in reply. "The Blood Queen believes that the Inquisition will kill you before you get to Holy Master. Saving me the effort in killing you and giving the Blood Queen the reason to allow you to exist. I suggest that you save you strength and threats for a common enemy. Focus on the end goal, not on foolish pride or prejudice."

"I do not have to explain myself!" he snarled.

"Of course you do not, but I believe that it is luck that has kept you alive for this long," she warned. "You sense of moral conduct and pride will kill you. The Blood Queen believes that you will die on this campaign, and it is my job to keep you alive until the humans are destroyed. Only then will the Red Clan find peace, perhaps, you might find it also."

"So she sent you to protect me?" he scoffed. "Only to kill me later? How twisted and perverse she must be."

"I have been that way for some time now," she replied. "My actions are not always honorable or worthy of praise, but I get my task done, completely and efficiently. You could learn a thing or two from me."

"So what did the Blood Queen do to earn such loyalty?" Lukhan challenged.

"It has nothing to do with loyalty," she offered. "I have earned my place amongst the red dragons and took a position as the second strongest dragon. I work for the Blood Queen because it serves my interests. I was unscrupulous in killing those who stood in my way."

"What interest is that?" Lukhan challenged. "Your sovereign pits you against me and, in the same breath, tell you to protect me. I believe that she wants you dead."

"Does it matter?" Con'ra asked. "I know my place in this world. The Green Clan wants me dead and I have done what I must do to survive. I am a renegade, like you. We are at the mercy of the foreign powers."

"Only because we choose to serve," Lukhan growled. "I would rather die on the wing, than kneel in slavery."

"Yet you submitted to the Blood Queen's will," Con'ra replied. "Like me."

"I have submitted to no one," he announced. "The Red Clan bows to my will."

"Are you referring to the ragtag group of browbeaten reds who are led by Havoc?" Con'ra asked. "They will only serve until the easy gold and plunder ends. When real battle happens, they will make loud boasts. Until Havoc is dead, then they will flee with their tails between their legs."

"That may be, but we need them-," he began.

"The same will happen to your pets," Con'ra interrupted. "The Inquisition is more advanced in weapon forging. Your pets will be defeated without the dragon's aid."

"I am aware of this," Lukhan declared. "That is why I help them."

"That is why the Blood Queen thinks that you are doomed," she replied.

"What about you?" he asked.

Con'ra considered the question for a brief moment. "I hope that you do whatever makes you happy," she replied. "These are your final moments."

Lukhan's jaw dropped at her words. Was she mocking him or wishing him the best? "Explain!" he demanded.

"I hope you remain the dragon you hope to be," she clarified. "I wish you the best."

"Says my would-be murderer," Lukhan growled.

"You are gravely mistaken," Con'ra scoffed. "When you become a death elemental you will become little more than a brutal beast. The Lukhan that I know will be gone and the bonds that hold us together will disappear with your madness. I am to kill your dark nature; nothing personal against you-"

"The Blood Queen is an elemental," Lukhan countered.

"Yes, but she is a fire elemental," she explained. "A creature of fire, her internal organs gone replaced by the infernal blaze of her natural element. You saw her spirit, yes?"

"The giant bird made out of lava," he concluded.

"Correct," she continued. "Every so often the Blood Queen must shed her mortal body and cast her soul into the burning earth. This regenerates her soul and mends her mortal body from the brutality of the raw fire element. When you become a death elemental, you will do the same."

"Is that how you will kill me?" Lukhan asked. "By destroying my body?"

"Yes," Con'ra admitted. "The Blood Queen shared this secret with me and now I have told you."

"What if I continue to stay in my body?" Lukhan asked.

"I do not know," she admitted. "It was difficult for the Queen to speak of this to me and I dare not press my luck with her. Perhaps she told me this, so I could destroy her body. Maybe it was the final test to prove my loyalty to her. Who can truly say what is in the mind of an elemental? Her skull is full of lava."

"Does she suffer?" Lukhan asked. "I mean, when her soul leaves her body?"

"She never spoke of the transition to me," Con'ra admitted. "I can only see how her body grows cold without her burning spirit. The ruby in her chest does not glitter and the rumbling of the volcanos become more active. When her spirit leaves her body, it was like a water skin. When her soul was in her body, it filled the sack but when the soul was gone, she became limp."

"A surge in the fire element," he guessed. "That was why she was so powerful! I did not destroy the ruby and she was being fed by the lava! She is like me! She is invincible!" His eyes widen in realization. Fienicks couldn't leave the Mountains of Fire because she was trapped! She couldn't challenge the Holy Master or lead the Red Clan into battle. She couldn't travel unless there was a fire that she could feed on! That was her life spark, the element in its natural form. Like humans needed water, an elemental required its element! That was the only way they could survive, to feed. That was what Vilesath was warning him about! That was why he needed souls of others! He needed their deaths! Was the Blood Queen was trying to keep him alive by focusing his destruction on the Inquisition?

"You have come to a revelation?" Con'ra asked. She shrugged at her companion's sudden excitement. "I tell you this, not because I wish to hurt the Blood Queen, but to warn you. When the time comes, I do not want you to question my motives."

Lukhan closed his eyes and thought for a moment. His mind swirled around the idea that the Fienicks was trying to help him. He quickly dismissed the idea. The Blood Queen was using him, and now he knew her weakness.

"A word of caution," Con'ra warned as if reading his thought. "Killing the Blood Queen would not be an easy task."

"What makes you think-?" Lukhan began.

"You may be a silver dragon, but you are also a death elemental," she replied. "It is in your nature to want to kill someone who plots your death."

"Does this plot include you?" Lukhan asked.

"Of course," Con'ra smiled weakly.

He laughed at the thought and her smile disappeared. Lukhan glanced down for the seeds he had dropped, but they were lost to him.

"Vatara, please wake up," Ambrosia begged. The massive gold dragon continued her slumber in Owen's courtyard. "You must be hungry and thirsty. It seems like you haven't eaten for weeks. You must regain your strength." The gold dragon did not stir at the woman's request. Her minor injuries had scabbed over and her damaged wings where on the mend. Herb soaked bandages covered the wounds as best they could. "This can't be good for you. You must move or do something. Lying around all day, you should be ashamed of your laziness." Ambrosia walked around her self-appointed patient. The gold dragon was not in any physical danger, but the woman sensed that something else troubled the golden creature.

The gold dragon did not move at the tiny human's command.

"I have heard rumors and legends about your clan," Ambrosia smiled. "My husband told me about your magnificence, a paragon of what it meant to be a dragon. Your clan is kind, forgiving, and thoughtful of those who are weaker than you. You are servants of the life element and protect it as best as you can. I admire this! Few dragons can claim this! You are beauty and splendor! The stories and legends about you do not give you justice. Those who gaze upon your glory must be envious of you wealth. Even your scales shine like polished gold coins."

Vatara opened a lazy eye and looked at the pestering woman. "Flattery and false ignorance will get you nowhere with me, little one," she mumbled. "I remember. Ambrosia, I can hear the child rolling around in your belly, the sound resemblance of an egg that is about to hatch. You must be proud. You must be Judas's spouse."

"Yes," Ambrosia replied. She gave the dragon a deep and respectful curtsey.

The gold dragon chuckled at the silly notion. It was the humans who gave her the injuries, yet it was a human that was helping her. The common race was full of hypocrisy. Vatara examined her injures and turned her attention to Ambrosia. "You have been treating my wounds with alchemy. I am impressed. The wounds are dressed correctly. You are a skilled healer."

"Yes, I'm an apothecary and herbalist of sorts," Ambrosia admitted. "I learned by trade while traveling in my parent's caravan. My knowledge of the natural world flourished under my families' care. I took care of Owen before he passed away." She took a long pause and fall strangely quiet.

"Before my godson took his life," Vatara corrected. "You were there, inside the house and I could smell your fear. You witnessed his murderous act." She closed her eyes and shook her head at the horrible memory. Her godson had become something different from what she had expected of him. She blamed herself for his faltering condition. Why didn't he listen to her? Stubborn and foolish silver dragon. He refused to see what he really was.

"The truth is rarely pure and never simple," Ambrosia replied. "Owen was a visionary and he will be remembered. He must have had his reasons for Lukhan to take his place. I'm sure it was done for a reason. Owen was strategic when it came to politics. Everything he did served a greater purpose." She crossed her hands over her showing belly.

"Tell me," Vatara asked. "How is it that you are an Inquisitor's spouse? Those who served in the Inquisition are not known for their tolerance or their understanding."

"Judas is different," Ambrosia explained. "At first he was painfully shy, almost fearful of me. Could you imagine? A knight who helped defeat the plague was afraid of me. We began to talk. Our relationship almost never happened had it not been for fate bringing us together. It was by happy circumstance that our love was allowed to blossom. He, being the leader of the knights and me, the girl everyone loved to fear."

"How is that?" Vatara asked.

"That is a silly question," Ambrosia gave her a heartwarming smile. "Have you been in love?"

"Once, a lifetime time ago," Vatara replied with great sadness.

"Oh?" Ambrosia asked in growing curiosity. "You must have many children."

"Hatchlings," Vatara corrected. "No, I have no hatchlings to call my own. There are few of us left, and I am the closest blood relations to my clan's surviving members. Therefore, I will never have a gold dragon as a mate. My kin and I are too closely related."

"I thought that Lukhan was your-," Ambrosia began.

"Godson, we are of no blood relations. The Gold and Silver Clan cannot produce hatchlings," Vatara eyes faded in reflection and then she closed her eyes at the painful thoughts.

"Yet you look after Lukhan as if he was your own?" Ambrosia asked. "Why is that? I thought the Gold and Silver Clans went their separate ways."

"I promised his mother and father that I would look after him as if he was my own," Vatara muttered. "I have failed my duty to them."

"How is that?" Ambrosia asked.

Vatara snorted at the tiny human before her. "You must truly be a witch," she let out a halfhearted chuckle. "Who else could heal a healer? A master of life alchemy? I must be in a sorry state to be unable to heal my own wounds.

Not only this, but a human questions me about my personal life and actions. I, a gold dragon, who has lived thousands of years compared to your few decades. Tell me, who are you to ask me of my troubles?"

"I'm a friend," Ambrosia smiled. "I'm a good listener."

"Friend," Vatara repeated. "A word sorely missed in a time of war. It feels like I have dealt with nothing but enemies lately. War has become the norm while peace and friendship is a distant memory. Even my own godson seems to be turning against me and my best wishes for him. The world, it seems, no longer needs friends."

"That is not true," Ambrosia offered. "It's during our darkest moments when we find out who is truly our friend."

Vatara's eyes widened at the truth of the human's word. "How old are you?" she asked.

"I'm twenty-two," Ambrosia replied.

"You have the wisdom of a dragon," the gold dragon replied. She stood up reenergized by the woman's kind words. "There is still hope. I know that Lukhan is not gone and this war is not lost. It is hard to justify his action, even within my own mind. Tell me, as his physician, you personally knew Owen?" Ambrosia nodded her head in reply. "I am a protector of life and I failed to save Owen. The knoll was dying and there was nothing I could do to save him naturally. Does that make me evil? To make the question blunter: is it evil to allow Lukhan to continue to live?"

"I knew Owen, the leader," Ambrosia stated with grave hesitation. "I knew Owen's multiple personas. Owen knew his heart was failing him. When his persona was the leader, he was bold, daring, and wise. I also knew Owen, the ailing, when he was uncertain, afraid, and scared. When he was the leader, that news didn't seem to bother him, but when his heart troubled him he was afraid of dying."

"Do you think that is what Lukhan is doing?" Vatara asked. "Putting up a persona and being in denial?"

"I barely know him," Ambrosia admitted. "It would be unfair for me to make a serious judgment on a dragon I barely know."

"An honest assessment," the gold dragon agreed. "I can see why Judas loves you so much."

Ambrosia blushed at her complement. "Thank you, for your kind words," she replied. "I do not mean to pry, but what did you mean when you said *is it evil to allow your godson to die*? He is a silver dragon, isn't he?"

"He is something else," Vatara warned. "According to what Lukhan said, he is a death elemental. According to clan tradition and elven lore is the great destroyer of life, a living nightmare of black flame that consumes all other elements into nonexistence. He is the beginning of the end. He is a death elemental."

"Your godson doesn't appear to be that," Ambrosia considered. "He acts strange and distant at times, but I doubt that he is the nightmare you claim. If death elementals were so evil and powerful, then why is there still life? What keeps him from going on a rampage and consuming everything in his path? I don't think you should put distance between each other, let alone kill him. It sounds like he needs you more now than ever!"

"I forgot that you are unaware of the seriousness of his condition," Vatara growled. "There are more important things than personal feelings. I do not take the responsibility of killing my godchild lightly."

"You are correct, I do not understand," Ambrosia replied. "What could warrant the death of someone you love? Please tell me. You would destroy your godson's life to save the world?"

"Yes," Vatara sigh at the terrible thought. She could speak the words, but doing the deed was something else.

"I do not believe you," Ambrosia smiled.

The gold dragon looked up sharply a sour expression on her face. "I have done many things in the past that were necessary for the survival of the life element," Vatara growled. "Did your mate tell you that I was part of the dragons that were going to sacrifice him to destroy the plague?"

"Yes," Ambrosia stated. "Judas also said that Lukhan sacrificed his white flame so that his friends could survive."

Vatara considered what the human said. She had spoken to Lukhan about compassion for others. She set placed standards and unrealistic expectations on her godson, but she didn't apply them to herself, what example was she setting? It was a farce to believe that she could kill him. She could never denounce the hatchling she swore to protect.

"What are you thinking about?" Ambrosia asked.

"You are correct," Vatara laughed. "Absolutely and indefinitely correct. My leadership has taken a toll on how I interact with others. I have forgotten that the best things in life are the smallest and simplest; like friends, family, laughter, love, and good memories. I have become callus to the living world around me. I have spent too much time being leader and I have forgotten those who are important. It does not matter if Lukhan becomes a death elemental. He is my godson and I will protect him."

"It sounds like your mind is made up," Ambrosia smiled.

"I do not fear for my fate or yours," Vatara warned. "I fear for the future of the child you carry in your womb."

Chapter 49

The disrupted council disbanded and they placed the intruding Inquisitor Lord in prison beneath the council chamber. Shen was placed into interrogation to gather information about his operations within the city. Surprisingly, the odd man was willing, if not eager, to answer their questions. The bold blind man spoke freely and at ease with his captives.

"What was your mission here?" Judas demanded. "How did you know about the meeting?"

"A simple trick," Shen mocked. "You see, the paper that your council wrote on was specially designed and magically warded by me. Every word you scribbled was transferred to the Iron Throne's interpreters. Whatever was written, my people know, your battle plans, laws, personal messages, even everything your council ordered for lunch. You've already seen many of my missions carried out. They know everything."

"Is that your task?" Bar demanded.

"I had to gather intelligence, but that was only a side job," Shen admitted.

"So what is your true goal?" Judas demanded.

"Well," Shen recalled with a superior grin. "At first, it was to weaken your city's political system. Everything was going well, but I thought that I would step it up."

"The assassination attempt," Bar concluded.

"Attempts," Shen clarified. "I knew something was odd about the open party. Yet my counterparts thought it was a perfect opportunity to wipe out the council, including you Judas. You were a special target."

"Me?" Judas scoffed.

"The Inquisition does not look fondly on traitors and deserters," Shen chucked. "You are a mockery of what it means to be an Inquisitor."

"You know my name, yet I don't remember seeing you before," Judas muttered. "You have the look of a foreigner. I thought only those born within the kingdom served the Inquisition. One of your station and status would never be out in the field, let alone turn themselves over to an enemy. Is that why your lips are so loose? What game are you playing? What is your true purpose here?"

"Oh no," Shen mockingly laughed. "I've been found out by the enemy! Whatever should I do? What is the worse you could do to me? Hang me? Cut off my head? Torture me?"

"Yes," Sacul grunted. "Your body is covered in strange markings and tattoos. What are those about?"

"Ask me anything but that," Shen replied. "That shall be my parting gift."

"Strange gift," Bar growled. "Fair enough, why are you blind? You seem to have magical powers. Why don't you heal your blindness?"

"It is your dragon's fault," Shen hissed. "He did this to me!"

"You blame the dragons?" Sacul spoke in a rhetorical tone. "This human is blind because of the taint of magic. His white flame has been abused to the breaking point. He is a dead man on borrowed time."

"He does look like Kale when we last saw him," Bar added.

"Humans should never use magic," Judas growled. "That goes against the Holy Master's teachings. Only wizards and heretics seek out the use of magic. So how is it that you come to possess theses dangerous powers?"

"True, I am a dead man and magic is dangerous," Shen cried in frustration. "I was not casting the spells. Instead, I *influenced* the heretics that were. That is the only way war can be won! In the service of our Master, I used evil to destroy evil."

"You were using magic," Judas growled.

"No, never! I was the catalyst! I'd never go against my Master's word! How dare you accuse me of such?" Shen snarled. Judas fell silent at the blind man's growing frustration. "I use my enemies' weapons against them! I made prisoners use their condemned souls. In the name of the Holy Master, I damn you and your kind to the-!"

"You dare use *his* name to damn others!" Judas growled. "You would go against the master's teachings and stand upon a pillar of lies. One of the few strict laws enforced by the Inquisition is the absolute resolve to never use magic! Your world is built on sand and I will see it fall! What you say and do! Our Master is not a being of death and judgment but a god of kindness and forgiving! His old teachings tell us-!"

"What does a heretic know of our god's will?" Shen spat. "You abandon your people and forsake our god! For what? These dogs, serpents, and pigs? Even going so far from the divine that you'd marry a witch, a whore that even your own people fear! You worship a dragon that will be the death of us all! Fall on your knees and repent-!"

"You know nothing about Luke!" Bar snarled. "You are ignorant of everything! You've caused more death and destruction than he ever has! You kill our children and accuse a dragon of worse?"

The Inquisitor Lord cringed at the sudden compassion and support of a creature he knew to be evil. "No man is without fault," he mumbled. "Even a god is capable of such simple acts of sin. The children's deaths were payment for the hardships yet to come. You follow the doom of this world. Remember that those children died so that others can live!"

"Explain!" Judas demanded.

"The Holy Master is god," Shen stated as matter of fact. "He seeks to protect those who love him from the appending darkness. As his servant, it's my sworn duty to stop the evil that is rising! Even if it costs me my life!"

Judas raised a questioning eyebrow. "What darkness!" he snarled. "You're delusional!"

"You are already in league with the destroyer of this world," Shen stated. "Your souls can't be saved. Mortals cannot know what the Master has predicted over the centuries. This war is to stop the death element and its minions from killing all life! I have seen it in your dragon's dreams. As was foretold by the Holy Master! Praise him! Blessed be the faithful! Eternally, I shall bathe in his light!" He looked up at the ceiling and fell to his knees. He began chanting wildly to his god, praising and worshipping the empty air above him.

"Is he referring to Luke?" Bar whispered to Sacul. The boarelf could only shrug at the knoll's question. "If it is, does that make us his minions? Is that what they are trying to stop?"

"That would explain the Inquisition's attacks and actions," Sacul whispered back. "The Blood Queen said something about Lukhan being a death elemental. Could the Holy Master be aware of this?" The shaman and hunter were confused by the new information.

Shen stopped chanting and began mumbling a few prayers and he stared up with his dead eyes. "I digress. Have you spoken to the Holy Master?"

"No, I've never sat down and spoken to the Holy Master," Judas growled. "It is forbidden to speak to *him* save for the Inquisitor Lords."

"I'm glad that you haven't forgotten your place, heretic," Shen gave them a yellow smile. "I'm one of his true servants, chosen by him." His yellow smile shown all the more from his boast. His eyes widened at the thought of seeing his god, but his happy expression soon faded.

"Yet you have failed your mission and surrendered?" Bar asked.

"I would have you execute me," Shen admitted. "My task is complete. I'm ready for my reward."

"What? Why?" Sacul gasped.

"He seeks martyrdom," Judas growled. "Among the Inquisition, it is believed that if you die for the Holy Master, then you shall be rewarded by serving again. He wants to die to in the name in the Holy Master."

"Correct," Shen replied. "So that I may be reborn! This body no longer serves *him* and I've been tainted by elf magic, and I can never return to the Iron Throne. The last Inquisitor Lord is aware of my activities and the usage of magic. I fear they will place me on trial and strip me of my rightful place."

"As a heretic should be," Judas mocked.

"My actions are for my god to judge, not you! Nor are they for an Inquisitorial tribunal," Shen growled. "In the end, all will be forgiven. My actions have turned the tide of war. This war is over before it has even begun."

"How is that?" Bar demanded. "We haven't even begun to fight!"

"Yes, but the Inquisition knows everything!" Shen chuckled. "About the loss in leadership! About the Red Clan's impending assault! We know everything-!"

"So you believe," Judas interrupted. "The written word does not state the conviction against the Inquisition or the resolve in our hearts."

Shen began to laugh at his fellow citizen. "Do you think we care?" he asked. "Yes, fight! Struggle! Do everything you can! Yet you cannot defeat a god! Man will have dominion of this world because of our god! The Holy Master has said so! It doesn't matter how much the knoll bites, the boarelves hide, or the dragons burn! It's our people's destiny to control you animals. It's our god's will manifested into a new world order. We are created in his image! This is our destiny! It's our world!"

"We will fight you to the end!" Bar snarled.

"You will try," Shen replied simply. "You will all die."

"How does someone argue against such zealotry and conviction?" Sacul asked. "Humans are such strange creatures, willing to give their lives up for blind faith and to become corpses. Truly it's madness that drives them."

"Faith, pig, is something a shaman would never understand," Shen snarled. "Boarelves never believed in the holiness of the Mixed Kingdom and the given right for men to lead this world. They look to trees and rocks and worship them."

"My people were never equals in the eyes of a god that was never theirs to begin with!" Sacul grunted. "One time humanity was kind and defenders of all, but now they have become the tyrants of the world. As the dragons once were! My people will not trade one master for another. Your Inquisition will rise and fall and this time my people will not run away."

"We grew stronger without your tainted magic," Shen laughed. "Spirits do not care about the living! They will not fight or defend you!"

"Yes, I see how you refuse to use magic," Sacul mocked. "You believe in a demigod, but not in spirits, the white flame that exists within your being."

"The Holy Master is the heart and soul of the Inquisition!" Shen snarled. "The Inquisition is the body of the divine. We live and die, but the Holy Master is eternal! Judas, you were once a man of the cloth! The Master's teachings haven't been given to theses damn beasts?"

"I didn't think there was a point since you were going to kill them anyway," Judas stated in a sarcastic tone. "I think it would be a moot point."

"I suppose you are correct," Shen conceded. "Even as a fallen servant, I would have you inflict the fatal blow. Better to be executed by a man rather than some strange evil brute."

"Gladly," Judas unsheathed his sword and prepared to use it.

"Wait," Bar growled. "Why not turn him over to the Inquisition, if he wants to die by human hands. He is not everything he claims to be and is tainted by magic. He is a wizard and would not be viewed as a hero. I suggest that we allow his peers decide his fate."

"What?" Shen whispered. The blind man's eyes widen in fear and his face turned pale white at the sudden suggestion. Sweat began to appear on his brow and he gulped nervously at Bar's suggestion.

"Turn him over to the Inquisition?" Sacul asked in consideration. "Why would we do that? Wouldn't they free him? He still holds the title of Inquisitor Lord."

"It depends on who we turned him over to," Judas smirked. "The Inquisitors are always trying to eliminate a rival faction. The last Inquisitor Lord would be no different from his subjects. Though Inquisition plots are done through saboteurs and assassinations rather than out in opened challenges."

"Was that why you were chosen?" Bar demanded. "You were the sacrificial lamb?" He grabbed Shen by the scruff of his robes. He had heard of religious fanatics chosen at random to do the Inquisitor Lords' decree.

"What are you saying?" Sacul asked.

"He is a tool," Judas gasped. "He never held any power or authority. That was why he was chosen."

"No, I was chosen by the Holy Master himself!" Shen voice wavered in desperation and fear. "I spoke with him!"

"What does the Holy Master look like?" Judas asked.

"I-I don't know," Shen confessed. "How does one explain a god?"

"You said you saw him!" Judas pressed. "During the ceremony, what did you see?"

"It is forbidden to speak of it!" Shen growled. "It is forbidden to speak of his glory. No image can portray a god's divinity! Mortal eyes and skills fall short to his glory! Humans can't fathom the beauty and splendor that is the Holy Master. I will not have my faith questioned! I know what I saw! To a nonbeliever, it doesn't matter!"

"You don't know because you were drugged! Part of your white flame was stolen by-" Judas began.

"Shut up!" Shen snarled. "Nothing was taken! It was offered willingly! Have you forgotten your pact with the Master? Your service to the Inquisition? Your service to humanity and the world you were born? You are in league with pigs, wolves, and dragons. Your soul will be forsaken and damned for all time-!"

"Shut up!" Judas snarled. "I haven't forgotten my humanity! It's those who would wear the false robes of Holy Master who will drive this world to war and ruin! It is men who has betrayed the Master's grace and cursed this world with war. I shall free my god from your tyranny!"

Shen gawked at him with blind eyes. The white of his eyes bugged out, giving him a wild and crazy appearance. His lips pulled back and a boisterous laughter erupted from his mouth. "I thought that I was mad," he laughed. "You think the Holy Master a prisoner? That we are the cause of this? A human hating his own people? How moronic and who would you have lead this new world?"

"Hey! What about us!" Sacul grunted.

"The knolls," Bar added.

"Wolves and pigs," Shen scoffed. "Both are no better than the beast they were spawned from."

"So says the hairless ape!" Bar countered.

"Face it, dog!" Shen gave them a victorious grin. "My people are superior in every way! We're smarter, stronger, and more cunning! This world belongs to the Inquisition!"

"I would not dismiss the dragons or elves so quickly," Judas warned.

"The death throes of a bye gone age," Shen dismissed. "It is time for humanity to rise!"

"Let us kill him and be done with it!" Judas sword quivered within his restless hand. This is what he fought against. The blind prejudice, the self-righteous pompous, and the pointless destruction. This religious man believed in a god that didn't belong to the Inquisition. The Holy Master's teachings belonged to all, not to the top hierarchy of the Inquisitor Lords.

"No," Sacul grunted.

"What? Why?" Judas demanded.

"This human wants to speak with our leader, I'd let him." Sacul smiled boorishly.

"Yes," Shen agreed. "Now we are getting somewhere."

"May I speak with you all in private," Bar whispered. "Let us leave Master Shen in his own ignorance and self-inflicted darkness. I feel that this conversation is getting us nowhere" They left the jail cell with the blind man struggling to follow them out. Shen's breathing became heavy as the isolation and silence crept in on him.

"Do we dare trust his word?" Bar asked. "It would be foolish not to use this opportunity to bring a murderer to trial."

"Of course not," Judas huffed. "Shen is no fool and he couldn't have become an Inquisitor Lord by doing such stupid and reckless actions. Something else must be happening, hidden behind a veil of deceit. He could be an anomaly or delusional. Driven insane by magic."

"Are you justifying his actions?" Bar asked. "That human is a dangerous fanatic! We should knife him and be done with this business!"

"Poison him," Sacul offered his toad.

"Such bloodlust from my peers," Judas complained. "He knows something! I feel it and we can't kill him. I say let him rot in a cell."

"We should give him to Luke," Bar barely whispered.

"What are you saying?" Sacul asked.

"That is a good idea," Judas sudden realization. "He could figure out what Shen is up to!"

"No, it's not a good idea," Sacul warned in grave hesitation. "The human has strange tattoos and markings on his body. Don't you find it strange that he desires to speak to Lukhan?"

"Should we deal with this matter without Luke?" Bar asked. "He is our Imperator and he has not returned!"

"We can handle this situation on our own," Judas offered. Bar and Sacul glanced at each other and nodded their heads in agreement. They had served the interest of the people of Ravenshaven before Lukhan. They would do so again.

"We should use your toad," Bar replied with an evil smirk.

Chapter 50

Within the Endless Desert, Lukhan continued to look for his lost pomegranate seeds. He had recklessly thrown them aside when he grew angry at Con'ra. Now he was angrier at himself for losing them and hoped they survived his foolish wrath. Though the tiny lives had disappeared from his sight, he did not stop searching.

"What are you doing?" Con'ra asked.

Lukhan glanced up to see Con'ra's head bobbing out of the oasis's spring fed water. "I am looking for the seeds you gave me," he replied. He could help, but notice that her yellow eyes reflected beautifully with the blue water. He shook his head in denial of such thoughts and returned his focus on the task at hand.

"Stop what you are doing and come swim with me," Con'ra dove in and out of the water.

"You look silly," Lukhan grunted dismissively.

"No more than you rooting in the dirt," Con'ra replied.

Lukhan chuckled at her sharp wit and biting tongue. "For the life of me, I cannot figure you out. One moment you promise to protect me, the next you are going to kill me, and now you are asking me to swim with you."

"I am asking you to swim," she huffed. "Oh, I get it. You think I have an ulterior motive."

"Yes," he stated flatly.

Con'ra thought it over for a moment. "Now that I think about it, yes, I do," she giggled.

"Oh? What is that? Are you going to drown me?" Lukhan demanded.

"The perfect assassin strikes!"

"No. You simply stink and you need a bath!" she replied in a mocking tone. Lukhan rolled his eyes; he didn't find the tease amusing. "Oh there, there. I thought you had thicker skin than that. I thought you did not care what I said!"

"That is not true," Lukhan valued her opinion, despite his better judgment. She was younger than him. Why did he listen to her? Did he really love her or was it him wanting something normal in his life? He couldn't have her. She was too proud and he was doomed.

"There you go again," Con'ra teased.

"What?" Lukhan snarled.

"Thinking," Con'ra replied in a coyly manner. "You always frown like it hurts."

"More teasing," Lukhan grunted. "I thought we are going be honest with each other." \

"I am," Con'ra game him a mischievous smile. "You do smell and you look like you are in pain when you think."

Lukhan lifted up his wings and sniffed under his wing pits. Perhaps he was a little pungent. He frowned and rolled his eyes.

"You are making that face again," Con'ra called. "Are you thinking?"

Lukhan's face lightened at her jest. "You have wisdom in your words," he conceded with an evil smile. "You are correct. I smell and I make faces when I think about something that troubles me. You are good at reading my body language." An evil grin spread across his face.

"What are you thinking-," Con'ra began. Her eyes widened in sudden and terrifying realization!

Lukhan jump into the air and cannonballed into the water. The resulting explosion scattered both green dragon and fish into the air. After the wave settled and the water returned to the pool, Lukhan emerged from the water in a chuckling dazzle.

"The water feels fine!" Lukhan winced at his sore reddening wings. They had suffered at the brunt of the giant dive.

"You little shit!" Con'ra gasped. She was still gathering her wits about her. "At least you are swimming."

"A small price to pay," Lukhan chuckled. He swam around her an evil grin still on his face.

"You smelly evil silver turd," she laughed. "At least, you are not making that ugly face anymore." She cupped her claw and splashed him in the face. Lukhan snorted as water splashed into his eyes and nose.

"Hey!" Lukhan growled. Then the splash war began! Water was thrown everywhere. No tactics, only dodging, diving, and wing blocking, despite them both being soaked down to the scale. The water splashing raged on and finally broke down into fits of laughter.

"You are all washed up!" Lukhan chuckled.

"You smell like a wet boarelf!" Con'ra teased.

"What does a wet boarelf smell like?" he asked.

She paused at the strange question. "Hmm. I do not really know," she replied. "Probably smells like you!" The quick insult brought a scowl from Lukhan and then the water war was on again but this time it included dunking each other under water. Lukhan was at a slight disadvantage; he held his black claw in check, but Con'ra took advantage of the silver's self-imposed crippling. In the end, Lukhan was dunked more times that she was, but it was she that came out gasping for air. The two quickly grew exhausted from their struggles and lounged upon the shore in the warm sands.

"You are silly," Lukhan gasped for air.

"You stink," Con'ra giggled. "Not as bad."

"Thanks," Lukhan chuckled. They looked up at the blue sky above them. Light wispy clouds passed over them. They fell silent as they stared up in peaceful wonder. The wind blew over them and the insects of the oasis began to sing their melodies. "It is quite peaceful here."

Con'ra shifted her yellow eyes at the silver dragon that lie next to her. His eyes were fixed upon the sky above them. "Yes, it is. This is a special place to me because this was where I was banished from the Jade Rainforest. This was the first place that I truly found shelter and safety. It was a sanctuary from a dangerous world. Protected by a hundred leagues of desert."

"You brought me here for sanctuary?" he asked.

"You looked like you needed a safe place to go," she replied. "So I lead you here."

Lukhan sighed and closed his eyes. She understood him, but she was still a puzzle to him. He took a deep breath and, for the first time in a long time, relaxed. This was a peaceful and surreal place. The simple place reminded him of his isolation in the Endless Ice. Open, clean, and clear. He took a deep breath; the sweet smell of life was strong here. The solitude helped him to forget his troubles. The landscapes were both beautiful and harsh, the reality of their predicament.

"What are you thinking about now?" Con'ra asked.

So she did care about him.

"I do not like that smile," she added. "It is too mischievous for my taste."

"I am thinking about how beautiful and peaceful it is here," Lukhan replied. "It reminds me of simpler times, when no one was trying to kill me."

"That must have been pleasant," Con'ra stated thoughtfully. "I feel like my life has been nothing more than a battle. A fight to struggle and survive. Kill or be killed."

"For me, it has not always been that way," he opened his eyes and looked at clouds above. "It seemed like centuries ago when I was protected by my family. Sheltered from the harsh realities of this ever changing and violent world. I miss that time. They shielded me from the danger of this world."

"It sounds like a dream," she awed. "I wonder, if my mother had lived, would she have sheltered me the same? Would she have been as cruel and demanding as my father? I will never know."

"If she was anything like you, she would have been a good, protective mother."

"You think so?" she whispered.

"I know so," he replied.

No one had compared her to her beloved mother before. A stream of emotions filled her eyes. She turned away from him so he could not see how his words had touched her, but a muffled sniff gave her emotions away.

"Are you all right?" Lukhan asked in sudden fear and confusion. He didn't mean to make her cry, he had hoped for a smile!

"I am fine," she replied.

"I did not mean to hurt you," he continued to explain. "I think that under your hard scales you are a good dragon-"

"No, I am fine," Con'ra explained. "Your kind words moved me and I am unfamiliar to such acts of kindness."

Lukhan turned to his side and looked at her. He wanted to say something comforting and intelligent, something to tell her that she wasn't alone, that he understood her and how it felt to be isolated, even from their kind. He reached out to her.

The black claw reached out to her.

He recoiled from such a horrifying embrace. Who was he joking? Even amongst outcasts he would be a stranger. He shook his head at the thought and she was here to complete a task. Nothing more. Like she said, love was a foolish emotion.

She turned to look at him with her beautiful yellow eyes. All of his hardened resolve melted away. His heart pounded in his chest and his mouth went dry. There was a different hunger in him now, not like the endless droning desire to consume life, but the longing desire to create. Maybe she felt the same way, but she was imprisoned by circumstance like he was.

"Lukhan?" Con'ra asked.

"Yes," Lukhan whispered.

"Has anyone told you that you have beautiful eyes?" she asked.

His mouth gave her a warm smile. "No, I was thinking about how alluring yours are."

Her eyes fluttered at the complement and smiled at the goofy expression on the silver dragon's face. She liked him. He was loyal and kind almost to a fault. She couldn't believe that this dragon could be as horrible and terrifying as the Blood Queen made him appear. She knew that he was powerful! She shuttered at the thought on how powerful he could become. Lukhan was a proud and flighty silver dragon and, despite the smell of death that accompanied him, in her eyes he was a normal dragon. He was like her. Scared, alone, and afraid of the future.

"Do you think of me as a cripple?" Lukhan asked.

Leave it to him to spoil the mood, she thought. "No," she sighed in slight frustration. "You are not a cripple and you seem capable to me. It seems to me you are more powerful than you let on."

"I was told that power comes at a price," he whispered as he raised his blackened arm.

"As one with little power, I would not know," she admitted. She glanced at him flirtatiously. Fluttering her eyebrows and smilingly mischievously. "Although, I have heard that those with power attract others in more than one way."

Lukhan turned his focus away from his ugly appendage and stared at the beautiful creature that lied next to him. "Is that why you are loyal to the Blood Queen?" he asked. "It is because she is powerful?"

"Yes, and no," Con'ra let out a coy giggle. She lean closer to him and smiled seductively. She lowered her voice to a low whisper. "Let us not talk about unpleasant things; I want to talk about here and now." She leaned in closer to him and parted her lips seductively.

Lukhan gulped nervously at her sudden closeness. "Then what should we talk about?" he voice cracked in growing stupidity. She giggled as he grew dumber.

"What do you dream of?" she teased. The world seemed to fade away as the two grew closer. Their breaths became deeper as they inhaled each other's scents.

The silver dragon considered the question. "A peaceful world," he whispered nervously. "Released from this curse so I could live a normal life."

Con'ra giggled and battered her eyes at him. "How about something closer? Something within reach."

Lukhan gulped as the green dragon drew closer. His eyes widened as he grew dizzy staring into her beautiful eyes. Her scent was intoxicating, something akin to jasmine. She was truly a wonder to Lukhan's senses.

"My daughter is a whore," a cold voice pierced the mood of their sanctuary. Lukhan and Con'ra woke up from the shattered dream and stared into a nightmare. An ancient green dragon surrounded by hundreds of wyverns stared down at them from on top of a dune. A burst of hissing laughter came from the creatures surrounding them. The Green Clan leader towered above the loathsome creatures.

"F-Father?" she gasped. She tried to move, but couldn't. She looked down in fear.

"Krain!" Lukhan growled. He recognized the ancient green dragon instantly. He tried to flip over, but the soft sand clung to him like glue. His eyes widened in realization! They were stuck in quicksand!

"First my daughter plots against me," Krain announced in a rather amused tone. "Then she runs away. Now I find her in the Endless Desert whoring herself out. What a disappointment. I had hoped that you would be able to challenge me one day."

"Murderous fiend!" Con'ra growled. She struggled against the grasping sands. "Foul trickster! I will kill you!"

"See my slaves," Krain announced boldly. "She would kill your god." A fake disappointed expression passed over the ancient dragon's face. The wyverns' silence broke into furious fits of raging screams and hisses. They grew into a throng of thrashing and screaming creatures, biting and snarling at each other in growing fury.

"Silence," Krain snarled. The howling creatures fell mute at their master's command. So trained were theses brutes that they had no mind of their own. Their bodies and spirits were broken by a mortal god that knew no tolerance or mercy. Scars of punishment were evident on the craven beasts.

"What are you doing here?" Lukhan demanded.

"I should be asking you the same thing," Krain muttered. "What are you doing here with my daughter?"

"What concern is it of yours?" Con'ra snarled. "I claim no relations you! I reject you! I despise your grotesque presence! You disgust me!"

"Such harsh words and criticism," Krain stated in an uncaring tone. "From a traitorous slut."

"Shut up!" Lukhan snarled. "*Glacialis terra!*" His eyes flashed in rage and the ground around them frozen. Although ice clung to their scale, Lukhan and Con'ra were able to escape the grasping earth. They sprang to their feet prepared to fight the oncoming waves of wyvern.

The creatures did not move, but remained aggressively nervous at their master's side. "Magic is such a dangerous tool," Krain mocked. "I never really relied upon it. What is the point on using something that will eventually kill you?" He shrugged at the passing thought.

"If you looking for a fight," Lukhan crouched into a defensive stance. "Then you found one!"

"Really?" Krain replied harshly. "To be honest, I am traveling through this dead land on my way to conduct business with the Inquisition. They are interested in forming an alliance-"

"Die!" Con'ra screamed. "*Silicis lorcatus!*" She sprang forward, eager to engage her evil father. The sudden appearance of her mother's murderer sent Con'ra into a furious rage. Vines coiled around Con'ra like living armor. Wyverns moved to intercept her charge, stingers held ready to strike at the passing dragon. Their barbs could not pierce her living defense. The wyverns scattered and those that didn't were run over and crushed by the larger green dragon. The wyverns scattered and broke as the gathering thorny vines engulfed her in a protective casing. She moved like poison ivy, defying gravity and entangling all who opposed her.

"Such a foolish gamble!" Krain snarled in delight. "*Adhuc lapis!*" The spell had no effect on his daughter, but on the vines that shielded her. The creepers expanded and interlocked, creating a prison of petrified wood. Con'ra gasped for air as the skintight stone covered her mouth and face. The uphill momentum Con'ra carried with her slowed and reversed direction.

"Con'ra!" Lukhan gasped. He sprang up the dune and grabbed Con'ra's encased body before it shattered. The wyvern sprang at the silver dragon, but a quick blast of ice breath stopped their assault. They retreated quickly, fearing the icy pain that clung to them. The maneuver cost Lukhan his balance, he growled and struggled to keep the statue from rolling on top of him. He angled her rock-encased body to the side so that they would slide down the sand.

"How touching," Krain watched the struggling silver dragon. "Now I am truly curious! Any other dragon would have allowed my daughter's body to shatter! Who are you? You seem strangely familiar to me."

"She is your daughter! Release her!" Lukhan demanded.

"Oh? Making demands are we?" the green leader called. Krain crossed the top of the dune and watching Lukhan struggle under Con'ra's stone weight. "I do not take kindly to commands."

"She will suffocate!" Lukhan growled. "She does not have much time!"

"If I was you, I would worry about yourself," Krain chuckled. "*Syrtis!*" The sand beneath Lukhan and Con'ra's petrified body shivered and became quicksand. They began to sink rapidly. Lukhan grabbed Con'ra's encased body and held her next to him. Lukhan struggled to keep his head above the liquid sand and extended his wings to slow their descent to a painful crawl.

"Oh! This is enjoyable!" Krain called with renewed excitement. "Tell me your name, silver. I would love to know!"

"Why?" Lukhan growled. "I will be your death if we are not released!" He grunted under the struggled to maintain Con'ra's added weight and his extended wings. He kicked with his hind legs and thrashed his tail in a vain attempt to find the edge of the quicksand.

"A riddle and a challenge!" Krain was amused and bored. "I will make a deal with you silver! I have not had a stimulating dialogue in a couple of weeks. Wyverns are such horrible conversationalist, you know-"

"*Glacialis terra!*" Lukhan snarled. The quicksand around them solidified into frozen sand. Con'ra's encased body was stuck under the frozen sand while Lukhan's head was above the surface.

"Splendid!" Krain cheered. "You are proving to be more entertaining than my daughter. The game can last longer! I was about to send my wyverns in to save you! Now, that would have been boring."

"Do you find this entertaining," Lukhan growled. He had stopped one problem, but caused another. He felt incredibly vulnerable with his body encased and his head exposed.

"Yes," the ancient green dragon agreed. "I have always found it entertaining how creatures will react when they are on the verge of death. On their last moments, I see the truth of their character before the ground swallows them."

"Once I get out of here, I will show you the true meaning of death!" Lukhan promised. He twisted and struggled against his spell. The more he moved, the quicker the ice broke around him.

Krain smiled at the empty and meaningless threat. "It has been a long journey, and you would be dead if I was not starved for amusement!" He laughed at his own weakness and sadistic behavior. "This is how the game works. I get three guesses to determine who you are. If I get all three guesses wrong, then I will release you! However, if I guess your name correctly, I leave you in the sun and ants."

"What about Con'ra?" Lukhan snarled.

"I would-but I think that would kill her," Krain taunted. "Oh, why not! I will release you both! Do we have a deal?" An evil expression passed over his cruel lips.

Lukhan's eyebrows knitted together. He realized something that he had seen before. His eyes widened in realization! Krain didn't kill anyone; he set up situations where they would kill themselves! Krain was never the aggressor! He saw it in Con'ra's nightmare! That was how his daughter escaped! Krain played with her like he was doing to him! He was a master manipulator! That is what he did to Con'ra and her mother! The Green Clan leader toyed with his victims by using their strength against them! He controlled the earth element. It was the perfect defense! The perfect shield! He never attacked, but goaded others into attacking him and thus killing themselves!

"My daughter is correct," Krain chuckled in amusement. "You do make a stupid face when you think."

Chapter 51

"How long were you watching?" Lukhan demanded.

"Listening," Krain corrected. "I am not that depraved." He examined his claws as if he was bored. His bright yellow eyes showed no evidence of magical scarring or corruption. They didn't even turn to a different color! Lukhan was confused at this strange phenomenon. How could a dragon use magic and not fall to its dangerous side effects! It was impossible! The ten laws of magic forbid it! Lukhan allowed his eyes to fall into night vision. Krain's power appeared to be absorbed from the ground itself. The earth fueled his magical energy! How was he able to tap into the land itself?

"The ground picks up vibrations as the air carries a voice," Krain explained. "Despite you having sex with my misguided daughter, you know so little about the Green Clan. How shameful."

"What? I care about her!" Lukhan stumbled. "We have not done anything! Never insult her!"

"Oh really?" Krain snickered. "Do you not find her appealing? You want her because of her smell, graceful and beautiful body, ample hips, and wings. I would say she is worthy of egg laying. A rare flower that needs a bee to come along and pollinate her."

"She is beautiful-," Lukhan began.

"She is my daughter!" Krain snarled. The brief glimpse of anger revealed something more sinister within the green leader's mind. His voice softened and he regained his composure. "I own her. I created her. You are not part of the Green Clan! Like her mother before her, she is mine, to do with as I please. Idealistic and foolish silver worm. Believing your morals and ethics are the only ones that are correct. I remember who you are."

Lukhan eyes widened in disgust. What was he planning for his daughter? He shivered at the thought. Did Krain love her incestuously? No, it was about control, manipulation, and dominance. It had nothing to do with love, fatherly or otherwise.

"Back to the game. Your name is Loco," Krain guessed.

"That is not my name!" Lukhan snarled. He struggled against the frozen earth, but the ice barely gave way.

"Vibrations are difficult to interpret," Krain considered. "I am sure Lu or Lo was the beginning and it had a hard sound at the end." He began to mumble all the hard vowels and consonants that came to mind.

"Leave us!" Lukhan demand. "You have no business here!"

Krain stopped his mumbling. "You are correct; neither does the Silver Clan have any rights here. After all, we are deep in Red Clan territory. I would dare say we are out of our clan's rightful boundaries. I suppose this would be considered contested land."

"Which does not tell me why you are here?" Lukhan snarled. He felt his black claw slowly slice its way through the thick ice. He could no longer feel Con'ra's body. The stone and ice felt the same temperature. He cut to himself keeping Con'ra's statue protected.

"Luxon?" Krain guessed. "I love this game! Getting to know you! What is that human proverb? Oh, yes! Know thy enemy."

"What? That is not my name!" Lukhan snarled in growing frustration. "Answer me!"

"Then this name will have to take some serious consideration," Krain stated. "Killing you would be so boring and anticlimactic! Furthermore, I would not have any fun!"

"So you are going to talk me to death!" Lukhan challenged.

"Impudent worm!" Krain was amused and he turned to his closest slave. "Punish him!" The wicked creature jumped up and down in excitement, it swooped down like a giant bat and latched onto Lukhan's face. A quick blast of ice breath froze and shattered the stupid and eager creature.

The dead wyvern's wing still clung to his face. "What is the matter, Krain?" Lukhan taunted. "To afraid you might get hurt! Why not come down here and finish me off?" He shook his head and the frozen body parts fell off his face.

Krain appeared unbothered with the loss of his slave. "I am no fool, silver;

my daughter would not lay with any dragon. I know Con'ra, she is greedy and selfish! She lusts for power and I can assume that you are powerful. I do not know who or what you are. I plan to know exactly what you are capable before I soil my claws with your blood. Sessess! Where is Sessess?"

The wyverns screamed and hissed in growling excitement and fear. A creature, more hideous and mutilated than those next to her, stepped forth from the throngs of wings, teeth, and barb tails. Her sun burnt flesh had been ravaged and torn a thousand fold. One of brood mother's eyes was put out; filling the gapping black hole was madness. Her teeth and lips had been removed and so had her barb stringer. The ugly creature that resembled the brood mother no more. She appeared to be a scarred withered blob of flesh with wings. She was declawed, toothless, and broken. She was no threat to her towering god.

"Sessess?" Lukhan gasped in horror. The creature's one good eye looked at the silver dragon encased in ice and sand. A hint of distant recognition lit her eyes.

"You know him," Krain demanded. "Well, answer me!" He backhanded the tortured creature. The ancient green dragon towered over the tormented creature. "Answer me! Yes, I can see it in your eye." He grabbed her by the throat and held her up. "Answer me-Oh, I forgot you could not speak. Your tongue has been removed." Sessess went limp in her god's cruel clutches. The creature clawed and groveled before him in mute silence.

Unnerved by such cruel evidence, Lukhan's voice wavered. "W-what did you do to her?" he demanded.

"I did nothing to her," Krain swore. "I swear by the earth element that I did not touch her." He smiled and held out his claw to the crazed wyverns that surrounded him. "However, her peers might have. You feel for this worthless slave? It is almost like you care for it. How touching! You must-," His eyes flew wide with sudden realization. "By the five element! Lukhan! That is your name! You were the son of Stratos and Crystal! The vanquisher of the plague! We have met before! Your mother was there! You survived the combat with the wyverns. When I swore my oath to The Betrayer." He recalled the distant and faded memories.

"You spoke to Vilesath!" Lukhan remembered that the two had struck a bargain.

"I made a deal with the evil spirit!" Krain chuckled. "He promised to give me whatever I wanted as long as I taught a silver hatchling everything I know.

Do you know what I asked for? Do you?" Lukhan shook his head no and Krain smiled at the hatching before him. "So, I asked for the impossible."

"Impossible?" Lukhan asked in bewilderment.

"I wanted the prefect body forged from the earth itself," Krain announced proudly. "The Betrayer kept true to his word. Look at my body. It is indestructible, and has unlimited magical power."

"Power comes at a price!" Lukhan challenged. "What was your toll?"

"I am power!" Krain declared. He stuck his claw into the ground, the land cracked and groaned in protest, and a sudden surge of magical energy poured up and out of the earth. The ground rumbled and quaked at Krain's will. The wyverns around him screamed in fear and flew into the sky. Krain spread his wing and flapped; the ground leaped up and followed him into the sky. The frozen earth around Lukhan shattered under the heave and spat him out, tossing him down the growing mountain's side. Jagged rock emerged out of the sand like the hidden reefs of an ocean. Unnatural vertical layers of stone crawl up each other, matching Krain's ascension by turning and twisting. Their oasis sanctuary disappeared under the gasping and growing sand mountain. Con'ra's encased body resurface and spiraled down. Lukhan dove after her and shielded her petrified body from the surfacing rock formations. He smashed against them in a turbulent sea of sand.

Suddenly the world stopped shifting and became still. Lukhan and Con'ra came to an abrupt stop at the base of the newly created plateau. The silver dragon glanced up to see a giant bust of Krain's likeness. Krain stood upon of his own nose.

"See," Krain called. "This world is mine and it will be shaped in my likeness! I am entitled to this world's wealth and those beneath me will be lucky enough to serve me!"

"Such vile conceit!" Lukhan snarled. "You destroyed the natural beauty that was here! You destroyed everything, all in the name of vanity."

"I think it looks better," Krain called from his monument. "Such a place is a stain on my family's name and must be erased from the world's memory. Starting with her!" He point down at the statue of Con'ra. His daughter remained in her petrified state.

"You will not touch her!" Lukhan warned.

"She is already dead," Krain sneered. "She has been turned to stone. Why protect a rock? She meant nothing to you. She is a green dragon after all. There is no bond of kinship or blood. You confuse me. I can understand wanting to protect those slaves that belonged to you. She is my property and you have no kinship to my whorish daughter."

"You're wrong; she is not a piece of meat!" Lukhan confessed. "I love her!"

Krain's head cocked to the side with an expression of both horror and amusement. "Love?" he balked at the silver dragon's confession. "You sad and disillusion hatchling. I feel sorry for you. You do not know what love is!"

"Release her! I know you have the power to do so!" Lukhan demanded.

"By the earth element, this has gotten more delightful!" Krain said in growing excitement. "A silver dragon falling in love with green dragon! Hilarious! Laughable! Above all: irrelevant. Your desires mean nothing."

"Release her!" Lukhan growled in growing rage.

"Do you know why you are irrelevant?" Krain continued. He didn't wait for the silver dragon to reply. "No, I thought not. You are a hatchling, one who has not even seen his first century, and you claim that you have fallen in love! You do not even know what love is! You claim to have feelings for her, but they are only sexual urges and desires. You are no better than a bitch in heat! Do you even know what you are saying? Have you ever noticed that there are no half breeds? Even with dragon clans that live next to one another?"

Lukhan's sprang into the air, flew up the plateau bust to where Krain stood. "It does not matter! Release her-!"

"Your naiveté is foolish," Krain said. Lukhan reached for the ancient dragon's perch but the green dragon did not give him any space. The rock snaked around him like the roots of a tree. It was difficult for Lukhan to distinguish where Krain's body began and the rocks ended. "Like father like son! Stupidity must run in your family!"

"Die!" Lukhan roared. He opened his mouth and released a blast of frozen death. Krain held his ground. Once Lukhan had reached his, limit, he gasped for air. The ice created a thick mist around the blast area, concealing the green dragon leader.

"The wind breaks against the mountain no matter how hard it blows," Krain said. Shards of ice clung onto Krain's rock covered body. The green dragon shook, and the ice sickles tumbled off his impenetrable frame. "Wonderful, you seem to grow in strength whenever you are protecting something. Was that your deal with the betrayer? Power? Love? Strength? What is it that you asked for?"

"Shut up!" Lukhan snarled as he gasped from exhausting his breath.

"It does not matter. You should thank me for killing her," Krain continued in a dismissive tone. "She would not have to suffer the reality of a silver dragon's lies and false hopes, promises that could never be kept! Future hatchlings that can never be."

"Lies! Deceptions!" Lukhan growled. "You know nothing about our future!"

"Oh no," Krain smiled wickedly. "The truth is much more painful than any falsehood I could invent."

"I never promised her anything!" Lukhan paused a moment to consider what Krain was saying. Did her father know what was best? He was over a thousand years old. Lukhan had never seen or heard of half breeds. What did he mean like father like son? What did Con'ra have to do with his family? Krain knew something that he didn't! What was it? His head spun at the questions that this ancient dragon seemed to know.

"Yes, a promise of nothing," Krain chuckled. "You have such a bright future."

"Shut up!" Lukhan growled.

"I wonder if my daughter even knows," Krain said. "She has always been a clever girl. I am sure she does. Perhaps it is you, Lukhan, who has been deceived into believing her. Did she promise to stay with you? Whisper sweet nothings in your ear?"

"Explain!" Lukhan growled.

"Which part?" Krain said with fiendish grin. "Like father like son? Con'ra's deception? The attempts to make half-breeds?"

"Father? Deception? Half-breeds?" Lukhan asked in bewilderment. Stratos, his father, was in love with another dragon before his mother? No, that wasn't possible!

"Stratos and Vatara," Krain stated flatly as if reading his mind. "A long time ago, they were lovers."

Lukhan's mouth dropped in realization. His godmother! So that was why she cared so much about him! She was his father's lover! He realized the truth of the situation! Why his mother and father kept their distance from each other! He became disheartened by this plainly hidden truth.

"No one told you?" Krain asked. His eyes widen in growing victory. "How sad and disgraceful." He fed off of Lukhan's suffering and confusion.

"More lies!" Lukhan began. "It cannot be-!" He gritted his teeth, his eyes flashed with growing rage and anger. He had killed Con'ra! This green dragon had insulted his family name and his godmother! He would make Krain suffer for his slander! The rage built up inside of him like a festering wound. The claw prompted him to kill the arrogant dragon before him.

"Yes," Krain smirked. "I can read you like a scroll! You never knew! Your godmother would not give two shits about you if you were not her ex-lover's mate. You use your feelings as a catalyst for your power. How foolish! Emotions are fleeting and temporary! Yes, let your hatred grow and consume you! Attack me, but know this: the earth element is forever! This battle is over before it began!" Lukhan snapped and he charged eager for the taunting dragon's blood.

"*Calx partis!*" Krain goaded. The stone beneath Lukhan twisted and warped into piercing pikes. The stone stalagmite pierced the silver dragon's scales and flesh. Lukhan screamed in agony as the rocks drove into in chest and abdomen. He thrashed about, breaking the stones off in his gut. His eyes flashed in furious rage. He charged again and was driven back by the pike-like rock. The rocks pieced several vital organs, but within Lukhan's rage, he felt no pain.

"Such fury!" Krain awed. "You would kill yourself to get to me. I think it is time for you to wake up. *Silicis contego!*" The rocks beneath Lukhan opened like a bear trap and snapped down on him. Lukhan sliced off one of the many teeth and shattered one side of the rock formation with his body. The blow knocked him senseless and snapped him out of him blood frenzied state. Pain shot through his body and he collapsed from the agony.

Krain waited patiently for the Lukhan to stop writhing in agony. "Does it hurt?" he teased.

"You wanted me to attack!" Lukhan gasped as he snarled through the pain. His life blood poured out of him. He began to regenerate, but the rocks remain embedded in him. The wounds retracted and expand, Lukhan writhed in pain. He felt foolish because he knew something like this would happen. Black flesh grew over the stones stemming the loss of blood. "You may have the prefect defense; however, I have the prefect offense!" He attacked the ground at his feet, shattering the stone beneath him. His claw dug deep into the stone. Krain screamed at the unexpected and surprising effect.

"What is this?" Krain gasped. The scales on top his head began to break and fracture. As if he was made of stone. He reached up and touched his crumbling head.

"You are not the only one who has power," Lukhan snarled. He lifted his black claw and smiled at his opponent. His injuries began to slowly regenerate.

"That black claw!" Krain gasped in realization. "The power! He gave you that!"

"Now you understand," Lukhan declared. "Vilesath chose you to give me all of your knowledge. Your white flame will belong to me! I will enjoy taking your white flame!"

Krain snarled at the silver dragon's new found strength. "Come at me then!" he challenged.

"You never attack the prefect defense," Lukhan sneered in growing victory. "You attack the ground the defender stands upon!" He struck the stone monument again, cracking the massive stone structure.

"Bastard!" Krain cursed. He grasped the top of his head, tiny diamonds oozed out of the tiny wound like blood. "Stop it! Stop it!"

Fueled by the memory of Con'ra's nightmares, Lukhan hacked at the stone, digging massive chunks of stone. Krain grabbed his crumbling head and skull. Lukhan broke through the stone surface of the statue. Thick iron veins that resembled muscle were revealed.

"I found you!" Lukhan cheered in victory. Diamond sand poured down the side of Krain face, reflecting the statue's damage. The green leader stood by, unable to counterattack Lukhan's assault.

"Protect me!" Krain commanded. "Kill this troublesome worm! Make him suffer!" Wyverns dropped from the sky and dove at the digging silver dragon. Lukhan turned to face his new attacker.

"*Aer inritus!*" Lukhan bellowed. His mercury eyes flashed with magical energy. The air froze and became a breathless void. With no wind for lift and no air to breathe the wyvern fell out of the sky and became easy prey. "This is no challenge!"

"Oh?" Krain gasped. He seized the giant statue and the damage Lukhan had caused disappeared in a great earthquake. New rock layers covered the damaged surface and stopped Krain's diamond bleeding. Lukhan lost his grip and was tossed down the monument. The sudden jarring caused him to lose his concentration and the air returned to the magical void. The confused wyverns recovered quickly and tumbled after the silver dragon.

"What will you do now?" Krain called from on top of his monument. Lukhan landed in a sea of quicksand. The ground itself became his enemy. Wyverns assaulted him from above while the sea of sand threatened to swallow him. "Like I said! You cannot defeat the earth element! I shall enjoy watching you drown!"

Lukhan looked around for a way to escape! The wyvern drove at him with their poisonous stinger poised to strike. The quicksand kept him from jumping out of the grasping earth. Lukhan latched onto the stone statue. He couldn't attack while defending against the wyverns. They kept him off balance and unable to focus his attacks against the monument. Lukhan fended off another wyvern's assault with a quick snap of his jaws. The creature's wing was damaged and it crashed into the quicksand. The poor wyvern was sucked beneath the sand in a nightmarish gurgle. The many wyverns above ignored their doomed companion and continued to focus their attacks against him. They circled above him like a murder of crows against a trapped tormented hare. Lukhan roared, but that drove the wyverns into an even greater frenzy.

"Amazing," Krain called. "If only you had slaves like mine, you might have been able to defeat me. Yet now, at the end, you sink alone!"

Lukhan looked around for aid, but there was none to be found. He had two fates before him. Allow the sand to shallow him or allow the wyverns to poison and devour him. Where was his rage? Why couldn't he defeat Krain! He needed help! He couldn't do this alone!

"Help!" Lukhan roared.

Silence filled the air at the silver dragon's cry for help. Krain broke the silence with a chuckle that turned into a rolling laughter. The wyverns joined in their leader with hissing laughter, which resembled crude sniggering.

"Finally admitted that you need me," a coy female voice called. "About time! I have been waiting for you to say something." Lukhan looked to see Con'ra emerge from the quicksand. Stone still clung to her, but she was able to move.

"Con'ra!" Lukhan gasped.

"Do you think I would die that easily?" Con'ra gave him a sly smile. "Do not let my father get under your scales. That is what he likes to do, mess with your head."

"Awe, my wonderful daughter," Krain growled in annoyance. "A bit slow getting out of my little trap."

"I am going to kill you," Con'ra promised. "Thanks to Lukhan, you showed me how to do it. First, by killing your mindless slaves! Lukhan cast your spell now!" She latched on to the monument and stood side by side with him. Silver and green dragon smiled at each other.

"Right," he nodded. "*Aer inritus!*" The wyverns crashed into the quicksand and were devoured by the gasping earth.

"Behold my father's digestive system!" Con'ra explained. "The ground is consuming them! The earth is the source of his power."

"Sly worm," Krain growled. "You should have known better than to arise from your protective barrier. Now. I will have to damage that beautiful body of yours."

"Worry about yourself!" Con'ra roared. "*Fracturis lapidem!*" The monument cracked and shuttered under her will. Plant roots dug into the statue, fracturing it in multiple areas. Krain's scales cracked as his defense began to tear asunder by the plant roots. The monument groaned and shook violently.

"Attack him, while I fracture the stature!" Con'ra instructed. "The fractures cause his stone sense to become incoherent! His defense will be broken down. Make use of the distraction! Hurry! Attack him directly!"

"Right," Lukhan released his spell and jump into the air. He landed on top of the massive structure. Krain's body was crumbling, but the green dragon leader still had a look of superiority on his face.

"I am done playing with you," Krain growled. "Time for you to die."

"You should have never shown yourself," Lukhan snarled. Another blast of magical energy shook the monument, vines shot out of the massive stone structure, and Lukhan charged. "Prepare to die!"

Chapter 52

Krain accepted Lukhan's charge, his rock pikes crumbled because of his daughter's seismic vibrations. His defensives weakened, Krain braced himself by digging his claws deep into the stone, rooting him in place. Lukhan led with his black claw shattering Krain's frame and stone defense. Krain's body fragmented into mud and solidified around Lukhan's outstretched claw.

"Did you really believe that was my only defense?" Krain asked in amusement. His mud body solidified and clung to Lukhan. slowing the silver dragon's movements. Krain reformed his shattered body out of the loosing stones gathered around them.

"Coward!" Lukhan roared. "Fight me!"

"As you wish," Krain gave them an evil sneer. His crumbling scales became jagged spiked rocks, his limbs sharped stones held together by unnatural magic. As Krain's defenses crumbled, his body became jagged stone. Krain, freed by the earthen chains that bound him to act defensively, was able to move against the muddy silver dragon. His ruptured body became a weapon of jagged spikes. Lukhan's scales were shredded under the stony assault.

The monument below them shook violently, throwing both combatants off balance. Lukhan seized the opportunity and released his icy breath on Krain. The green dragon's rock formation froze together at the rock joints. Lukhan used his tail to shatter a frozen leg. Chunks of stone flew everywhere. Krain screamed in pain and tumbled to the side. The rocks tumbled into the quicksand below.

"You cannot destroy me!" Krain snarled. "No matter how many times you break me. You cannot stop the earth element! I am immortal!" His missing arm was made whole by the stone beneath their feet. The monument of Krain's body was fractured, his stone form seemed to thrive and become more dangerous.

Lukhan fell back and allowed his eyes night vision. Magic flow up Krain's legs and dispersed within his rock body. Lukhan realized that Krain's unlimited magical resource was his weakness. "So, as long as you are connected to the earth element you can regenerate," he concluded. "Clever, but I know your tricks."

Krain struggled to stand. "I have killed you multiple times," he growled. "Your scales are peeled like an orange and you think that you will be victorious. How foolish of you. Even if you defeat me, it will only be a matter of time before I regenerate."

"Nothing is immortal," Lukhan declared. "I know your weakness. Even if I broke your body up into dust you would be able to regenerate."

"That is why I am immortal," Krain chuckled. "You will never defeat me."

"So long as you are touching the ground!" Lukhan bellowed.

Mountainous booms resonate within the structure of the monument and a deep crack split it in half. Thorny vines coiled and snaked through the broken structure. Krain's body crumbled apart at the middle, reflecting the damage Con'ra had done. The ancient green dragon screamed in agony and continued to crumble apart. She emerged from the crack like a budding plant. "You need to destroy the dust or take his white flame," Con'ra interrupted. "I have altered this monument's stone and weakened his defense. We can shatter his body into tiny grains of sand and scatter it across the Endless Desert."

"A fate worse than death," Lukhan declared. "I like that idea. I never knew you had such cruelness inside of you."

"I have my moments," Con'ra smiled wickedly. "If we are going to do this, we need to do it right now."

"Together?" Con'ra asked.

"Together," Lukhan agreed with a nod.

Con'ra focused her attention to her crumbling father. "Farewell, father, *fracturis terra!*" The monument beneath them turned to soil and sand. The dragons fell into a brief momentary free fall. The illusionary structure disappeared and Krain's earthen body became real and substantial. The dragons spread out their wings to slow their descent. The ancient green dragon dove to the ground.

"Quick," Con'ra commanded. Her eyes grew bright yellow with

magical energy. "Do not let him touch the ground or else this will all be for naught!"

"*Ventus vortex!*" Lukhan bellowed. A funnel cloud suddenly formed in the sky above them. A sudden upward draft sucked all three combatants into the air. The sky darkened as funnel heads of multiple tornados appeared in the skies above them.

"Such raw unnatural power!" Krain growled. "Where is this coming from? The staff! The Staff of Selgae!" The upward drafts denied him his perfect defense, disconnected and out of reach of his element. The larger green dragon was at a disadvantage in the powerful howling winds.

"You will die by my claws!" Con'ra swore. She drove at him, attacking his flank and back. The dragons spun around each other. Krain dodged and dove away from his daughter's lightning quick assault. Lukhan kept his distance and focused his magical energy to Krain's ever changing position. The winds worked against the ancient dragon.

"Such a wonderful daughter you have become!" Krain announced. "You will become a great leader! Such deception, fury, and power! I am proud that I am the stem of your hatred. I hope you are strong clever enough to survive!"

"I will turn you into dust!" Con'ra screamed. She ripped at his tail and flanks causing deep gashes. Krain angled up and put distance between them. Con'ra remained on him, biting and slashing whenever she saw an opening.

"Yes, become stronger," Krain declared. "Prove to me that your mother's lost was worth the effort! It is only through the strength of another that you are able to challenge me! You are capable of anything! What a powerful deceiver you have become!"

"It does not matter who or what helps me to kill you!" Con'ra snarled. "You fall today!" She tore his wing, causing the ancient dragon to go into a wild spin. Yet the blowing winds kept him from tumbling to the earth. The green dragon turned his full attention to his daughter.

"You wound me!" Krain acknowledged in an unimpressive tone. "How annoying." Diamond blood dribbled from his wing and hind legs. "I have not had to fight fair in a long time. Let me see if I can remember how it is done." He opened his mouth and spewed forth a blast of acid. Con'ra spun out of the way of the oncoming blast and returned fire of her own. Krain's injuries prevented him from dodging out of the way. Acid splatter across his frame, eating away at his thick skin and weakening his rocky armor.

"Your time has come!" Con'ra cried in growing sense of victory and excitement. "Die!"

"Do you think I can be so easily defeated," Krain began. "I will make you suffer-!" A frozen blast of energy interrupted the ancient dragon's boast. Lukhan flanked him and interrupted his magical spell. Con'ra screamed in rage and latch on to her father's throat. Lukhan struck from behind penning the ancient dragon's wings while the blowing wind kept them in a midair spin. Krain dug with his claws into his daughter's side but she ignored the pain.

"Do you remember?" Con'ra whispered in her father's ear. "When I was little? You wanted me to kill. I was afraid back then, but not anymore." She drove her sharp claws deep into her father's chest. Krain opened his mouth to speak, but only a bloody gurgle came out. The ancient green dragon gasped for air and smiled at his daughter. He turned his attention to Lukhan.

"No, you will not!" Con'ra screamed. "I am your enemy!" She began to claw and thrash at her father's chest.

He drew close to her and whispered. "I will make you suffer," Krain gurgled. "One last time."

Krain ignored his daughter's bloody rampage and focused on the silver dragon behind him. He held out his closed claw and opened it suddenly. The stalagmites that were inside of Lukhan erupted with violent force, Lukhan's chest and guts were ripped open. Lukhan's body went limp, the tornados and wind disappeared as quickly as they arrived. The stone fragments within Lukhan were absorbed by Krain's dying body. With unnatural dying instinct, Lukhan drove his black claw into the ancient dragon's back. The collected stone was not enough to shield Krain from his daughter's wrath and the deadly effects of the black claw. The wind fell silent and all three dragons tumbled to earth. Con'ra abandoned her father's copse and sprang over him to Lukhan's limp body. She grasped the silver dragon's lifeless body and beat her wings desperately tried to slow their descent.

Krain's body crumbled into diamond dust and vaporized before touching the ground. Without the ancient dragon's magic influence, the ground returned to normal sand dunes. Lukhan and Con'ra spiraled into a nearby sandbank. Con'ra recovered quickly and limped to Lukhan's bloody form.

"Lukhan!" she screamed in fear. The silver dragon's blood covered her, his tongue hung loosely out of his mouth. Her father had ended his life! The stench of death and gore was overwhelming. She stepped away from her friend's body. She wanted victory and her father to pay, but not at the cost of Lukhan. She felt sick and her head swoon at the sight his bloodied body.

Silence filled the air as if the breeze in her life had disappeared. The sudden sense of truly being alone was overwhelming.

"I am so sorry," Con'ra wept. "Forgive me. I did not mean-"

Lukhan trembled under some strange and unseen force. He rose from the sand like a terrible ragged creature. His alien silver eyes were distant and dead, overtaken by endless hunger and the promise of death to come. Nothing about him seemed real. His guts and smashed internal organs were exposed and bloody sand clung to them. His mouth opened and closed like a fish out of water. He limped his way towards her. A dark magical aura surrounded his damaged body. The sand around him melted away as if eaten by some otherworldly force.

"Lukhan? Is this your elemental form?" Con'ra asked in disgusted horror. "You are undead! A death elemental! He defeated you! How is that possible? What are you?"

Lukhan did not answer, but continued to stalk her. He then suddenly stopped. New flesh and organs sprung forth like entangled snakes in a cocoon. The tainted black flesh worked feverishly to contain and repair Lukhan's damaged body. He fell on all fours and wailed like an injured animal. His body shook and his black claw respond with the white flame of the ancient green dragon. Sand crawled up his skin and swirled around his horrendous wounds. His body absorbed the elements around him and became hardened and solidified. Lukhan gasped at the sudden painful manifestation of regenerated lungs. His newly formed black heart began to pump blood. He fell over in raving pain as nerve endings reconnect. His body trembled and his long mute scream fell silent.

"Lukhan?" Con'ra asked. "What is-?" She reached out to him. The silver dragon stirred and arose. Sand swirled around him as if shielding his newly repaired body. Black flesh and sand mixed together to form a thick layer of unnatural scales.

"You absorbed by father's soul!" she gasped.

Lukhan stood passively, his hunger satisfied by the years of knowledge provided by the ancient green dragon. His stomach muscles and chest knitted together, yet his eyes remained distant and dead.

The memories and experiences of over a thousand years overwhelmed his conscious. Lukhan stood silent as he relived the ancient dragon's past. Never lifting a claw, Krain had caused the deaths, murders, and sabotages of hundreds of thousands dragons and common races alike. He spoke true about his father and godmother. Having personally witnessed their subtle hints and sexual innuendo. He despised them for that! Krain loved Con'ra's mothers; she had once been his daughter. Krain was sickly obsessed with keeping his bloodline pure. Krain sought to insure his likeness would be bred into the core of the Green Clan forcing all the females within his clan to raise at least one of his eggs. Then he would force his progeny to kill each other to gain his favor. Within Krain's mind of twisted thoughts and evil manipulation, he was making his clan stronger. However, he was immortal now and he no longer needed his offspring! Secrets of earth alchemy were revealed to him. Hidden secrets of the Green Clan's wealth, power, and prestige.

Lukhan's mind snapped back to reality. Con'ra stood over him with a concerned expression on her face. "Snap out of it!" her voice sounded like it was in the distance. Her voice wavered with doubt and relief. His mind still was muddled with thoughts of another's past. "Return to me!"

His body and head ached all over. He struggled to move but he remained stiff and distant. Con'ra hovered over him in weary caution and fear. She examined his eyes. He blinked a couple of times and his mercury eyes returned to their soft glow.

"You have suffered a concussion, internal bleeding, and broken bones! Death!" she declared. "Among other things, I thought my father had killed you!"

"What?" Lukhan whispered. He looked down at his disfigured chest and stomach. Black scales and bits of rock fortified his newly regenerated body. "What happened to me?" He looked around in confusion. The last thing he remembered was attacking Krain's flank. He didn't even see the fatal blow. Who and what he was slowly returned to him. The wyverns, drowned in dust and sand, littered the barren landscape of the Endless Desert. The world seemed to change; their paradise reduced to a battlefield.

"We won," Con'ra gasped in disbelief. "We defeated my father!" Tears of joy, relief, and sadness filled her eyes. She jumped on him and gave a tight hug. The silver dragon was too weak and confused to hug her back.

"He was an elemental," Lukhan gasped. "An earth elemental! That was what Vilesath promised him. That was why he thought he was unbeatable. The betrayer planned this from the beginning! He wanted me to take Krain's soul, to gain all of his knowledge!"

"What?" Con'ra asked in a skeptical tone.

"The memories are so jumbled together," Lukhan struggled to sort through the ancient dragon's life. "Krain was going to meet with the Inquisition! The Inquisition sent ships to the Jade Rainforest seeking him out. They seek to buy time by negotiating with the dragon leaders or keep some of the dragon clans out of the coming war."

"The Green Clan would never ally themselves with the humans, it is beneath them," Con'ra declared.

Lukhan shook his head no in reply. "That was why your father was here," he continued. "He was passing through the Endless Desert when he stumbled upon us!"

"He was going to join them?" Con'ra asked in shock.

"No, but he was going to requisition gold!" Lukhan continued. "Krain knew about the human and elf war and took advantage of negotiations. He demanded gold during the war so that once both sides had exhausted their resources; Krain would pick up the pieces."

"Sounds like my father," Con'ra grumbled. "Tell me, how is the Green Clan?"

"Your father's tyranny and proxy war with the Black Clan has taken its toll," he muttered. "The Green Clan is in no shape to help or hinder the Inquisition. He was going to set up a false bravado with the wyvern he subjugated. I believe that no one trusts your father. Krain was a truly unbeatable tyrant."

"What about my brothers and sisters?" she asked.

"Many of your siblings were murdered by wyverns," Lukhan mumbled. "At your father's command." He struggled with Krain's horrible memories of suppressive and malice to his own kin. He shivered at the madness that made up the ancient dragon's conscience. He growled with the growing frustration and aggression that he felt. A shadow reflected what Krain felt about his daughter. "My head throbs like its being smashed by a boulder."

"Feel no pity for his death," Con'ra soothed and drew closer to him. "I was scared of losing you."

Lukhan's mind cleared at her words. Krain's evil memories and doubt faded away like midday shadows. He looked at her. She somehow suppressed his endless hunger and the evil that clouded his thoughts. The rage inside him was not there. Even in the cold grips of death, he remembered her.

Con'ra laughed at him and his stupid expression. "You know," she smiled. "I heard everything you said to my father."

Lukhan's wings blushed at the thought. He couldn't remember, did he say what was in his heart? How could she over hear their conversation? She was entrapped within a stone prison. The more he thought about it, the more nervous he became.

"You are making that face," she teased.

"Face? I am not!" Lukhan grumbled. His eyes darted away from hers. He fell mute as he recognized one of the wyvern bodies. The death around him brought him back to his senses. "Sessess." The brood mother had served her master to the end. Such loyalty could not be dismissed.

Con'ra glanced coldly at to her old pet, those who had betrayed her at Krain's command. "So it seems."

Lukhan walked towards the brood mother. She had suffocated on the quicksand like the others. The silver dragon had unexplainable feelings of pity. She had followed a dragon-god that was cruel to her. Despite this, she had always been loyal to Krain. Lukhan couldn't tell if it was his emotions that were tormenting him or that of the ancient green dragon. A spell came to mind that could save the wyverns! Krain's knowledge of earth alchemy was so deep that he could pull the sand out of each wyvern's lungs.

"I can save them!" Lukhan gasped.

"What? Save Sessess?" Con'ra asked. "Why?"

"No, I cannot, but I can use Krain's memories," Lukhan explained. "I have to try."

"Stop," Con'ra interrupted. "These creatures were slaves to my father. Do you want another fight? You suffered a terrible injury! You do not have to do this."

"I have seen enough death," Lukhan muttered. "They are victims, as you are and I must save them."

"This is foolish," Con'ra warned. "If you do this, it will not matter. Remember? I tried to save them from my father's rule, but they turned against me! The same thing will happen to you."

"You may be right," Lukhan admitted. "Their god is dead and I have to believe that they can be saved."

"Such foolishness," Con'ra scowled.

"Please," Lukhan begged. "I am not familiar with the earth element. I will need your help."

She gritted her teeth and grew angry. "Fine!" she huffed. "Do not expect them to wake up and be grateful!"

"Thank you," Lukhan whispered.

"Give me you claws," she instructed.

"What?" Lukhan gulped.

"We have to hold each other," Con'ra stated. "The closer the better. The earth element is based on physical contact. You must feel the stone sense."

"Really?" he asked. He nervously stretched out his claws to her in a warming embrace.

Con'ra stared at his black claw. She had witnessed its terrible power and saw Lukhan rise from an undead state. The grotesque withered skin spread across his body like the cruel roots of a tree. There was a brief moment of fear that warned her to stay away. There was only the cold embrace of death within his arms.

"Please," he asked. Her morbid attention turned to his strange mercury eyes. They were dead once, the shine lost its luster and only contained an endless void. It seemed like a nightmare, but his eyes returned to their resplendent state. A haunting reflection of what he would ultimately become. With uncertainty, she reached out to him.

"Thank you for trusting me."

She narrowed her eyes at him, uncertain of what the horribly disfigured silver dragon was planning. She held on to him tighter. Lukhan closed his eyes and focused on the sand around him. The sand shivered as Lukhan's magical energy passed over them. Con'ra's white flame began to vibrate in the same frequency with Lukhan's magic. The ground rumbled and the sand within the wyverns' throat and lungs dislodged. The sand escaped and spun around the two dragons. Lukhan released his magic power while Con'ra directed it. Pomegranate sprouts began to shoot out of the sand around them. His lost seeds had found them.

The wyverns began to stir as the spell finished. The two dragons realized that they could accomplish anything, even save the dying from death, together.

Chapter 53

"We seek your guidance," Bar pleaded. "Since Lukhan has abandoned us." The gold dragon remained coiled within Owen's courtyard. Judas, Sacul, and Bar stood together in passive reserve, respecting the leader's slumber. Ambrosia worked on changing the gold dragon's wounds. Vatara lied with her eyes closed and allowed the herbalist to complete her work.

The gold dragon shifted uncomfortably and opened her eyes. "I smell blood and ink," Vatara grumbled. She focused on the paper they held in their hands. "Strangely, I see magic."

"You can sense the magic," Sacul grunted. "Yet none of us are able to detect it. Leave it to a dragon to sense these matters. Not even the spirits were aware of the great wrong that has occurred. Curious that Lukhan did not sense the plot."

"What has happen?" Vatara asked.

"A man named Shen Tianxiang," Bar explained. "He claims to be an Inquisitor Lord. However, Judas has never seen him before and he uses magic. He is also a foreigner who claims to worship the Holy Master. We do not know if we can trust this man and his claims of magic."

"Thaumaturgy," Vatara opened her eyes and stared at the three before her. "I know the human called Shen Tianxiang and he is an Inquisitor Lord. The man is a foreigner from across the Azure Ocean and uses *miracles* to complete physical tasks. This is similar, but different to our magic and alchemy. It is a hybrid between the physical world and the white flame, according to foreign scholars."

"Meaning?" Bar asked.

"Using others to cast spells," Vatara stated bluntly. "In an over simplistic way, using another's white flame as a charge to power something else. This is call thaumaturgy."

"Like when you were going to sacrifice us to destroy the plague?" Judas demanded.

"Somewhat," Vatara exampled. "While our magic and alchemy is often volatile and explosive, thaumaturgy is far more stable and consistent. You have seen it before."

"Oh, so it's like burning hay compared to burning coal," Ambrosia explained.

Vatara lifted her head and looked at the woman on her back. "Correct, grass burns hot and fast while coal burns slower and then smolders. The fuel source and result is the same, but the outcome is different. The comparison is a fair analogy, but in truth, magic is far more complicated."

"Shen killed many children and then used magic to curse this paper?" Sacul grunted. "I thought the Inquisition thought magic was evil."

"Miracles are not magic," Judas sighed. "That is how the Inquisitor Lords justified it. They call upon foreign magic and call it a miracle. Now I understand. Shen used his foreign tricks to gain his position and title."

"I doubt that the Holy Master was misled," Vatara warned. "He would be aware of such simple devises. However, I feel that we have all been played as fools and the damage has already been done."

"Not so," Bar muttered. "It depends on how much information was given to the Inquisition and how they understood it."

"According to our captive, they know everything," Sacul grunted. He scratched his head. "We must assume the worse and prepare for siege."

"Behind strong walls we will endure," Judas agreed.

"You will not withstand the Inquisition's bombarders," Vatara warned. "Their weapons have grown in size, power, and range. The elven kingdoms' falling should be warning enough."

"If the elves lost against the Inquisition, what hope do we have?" Sacul demanded. His words were somber and stoic. The elves and their ancient woods were not to be taken lightly. He licked his toad for comfort. The tiny creature chirped in sad reply.

"I thought the middle kingdom still stands," Ambrosia stated. "Have we forgotten our allies so quickly?"

"Fair enough," Vatara conceded. "A question worthy of investigation. My clan is in no condition to fight. I am injured and so are many of my kin. We fled the elf lands to regroup and regain our strength. If the Inquisition struck this city now, we would have no choice but to flee into the Endless Desert."

"Is the Inquisition so powerful?" Bar asked.

"No," Judas declared. "We're fighting men and they are nothing more than humans. We have two dragon clans backing our city and an arsenal of weapons and supplies. We must fight them, stop their momentary success. They fought the elves who are still reeling from devastation of the plague. They simply took advantage of their weakened state."

"What do you suggest?" Sacul asked. "Take the war to them?"

"Yes! Our passive nature has cost the elves too much," Judas added. "We must do something unexpected!"

"They know all of our plans!" Bar said.

"Then we will make new ones!" Judas announced. "While the Inquisition's army is spread out it cannot defend the capital! Let us strike at the city of Alkaline!"

Silence filled the courtyard. Judas line of thought was not off track. The Inquisition is plotting a lengthy siege, not a preemptive strike. The humans would have to recall their divided forces and end their assault on the elven kingdoms. The plan will work.

"It would be an all-out assault if we did this," Bar warned.

"No foreign army has taken the city of Alkaline," Judas warned. "The city is on the coast and has several ports. We need ships, men, and weapons. Sadly, we have none of those. The city is guarded by more than men, and was engineered for a single purpose: to protect the Holy Master."

"I have seen the Iron Citadel," Vatara warned. "It is as impressive iconic structure. Unlike the bulwark of this crude town, the human city and citadel have been around long before I was hatched."

"Age doesn't count for anything," Judas stated. "We can use bombarder powder to blow a hole in it!"

"What of the next interior wall?" Vatara asked. "The fortress is layered like an onion. The logistics required to get enough bombarder powder to blast our way into the Iron Throne is impractical. Time is of the essence. We need someone on the inside to get us in."

"Not one of the Inquisitor Lords would betray the Holy Master," Judas warned.

"Could you request an audience?" Ambrosia asked.

"I attempted that," Vatara warned. "Even under the pretense of announcing my arrival to the Inquisitor Lord Shen. They would have killed me, given the chance."

"Shen?" Bar asked. "The man we now hold prisoner! He could get us inside!"

There was a long moment of silence while the group considered the option. The Inquisitor Lord be could get them inside the Iron Throne.

"It is an option and must be considered," Vatara announced. "Bring the Inquisitor Lord before me. I would like to see how this little man reacts when he is under interrogation."

———◆◆◆———

"I will not betray my God," Shen hissed. "I would rather burn out my eyes with hot iron than serve you!"

"That can be arranged," Bar growled.

"Lady Vatara, the man is blind," Judas stated. "Would it not be better to castrate him?"

"Hang me and be done with it!" Shen growled. "Do what you will with me! Stop playing games! I will never be a tool! I serve the Holy Master! I shall die in his serve-!"

"Is that what you want?" Vatara asked. "Do you not wish to see your god one last time?"

"Not from you!" Shen cursed. "Nothing you tempt me with will ever change my mind! However, I could be persuaded by your newly leader."

"Lukhan," Vatara muttered. "This is the second time we have met and you still seek my godson-"

"You are part of his relations!" Shen gasped in realization. "Now I understand why would did not speak of him. Other dragons talk about him with repulse and disgust! Why are you protecting such an abomination?"

"Strip him," Vatara commanded. "Let me see theses markings you warned me of." The blind man was held and his clothing was cut off. His naked flesh and tattoos were exposed to the air and her scrutinizing eyes. Vatara recognized the symbols right away. "You are right to be concern. He has been turned into a weapon. How clever of you. You wish to blow yourself up. However, I do not think your bone or flesh will pierce dragon scales."

"Do what you will with me!" Shen laughed. "You will never conquer my spirit! My soul will not break! The Inquisition's dragons will hunt you down!"

"What dragons?" Vatara asked. Shen's blind eyes went wide in fear. He had revealed a secret. Vatara's eyes widen in realization. "So the Inquisition has sought allies among the dragon clans. How foolish. No clan would serve under the Inquisition."

"The Silver Clan," Shen declared. "Would." He smiled revealing his yellow and disgusting teeth.

"More lies," Bar growled.

"I was told that the Silver Clan was vital in conquering the elves," Shen explained. "I was sent messages! How else do you think we defeated the elves in their ancient woodlands?"

"I don't believe you," Sacul grunted. "Your people destroyed the sacred herd! The dragon clans' main food source-!"

"Yes," the naked man laughed. "You hear me, Lukhan! The Silver Clan is an ally of the Inquisition! Come out here! Face me, Coward! I am ready to die!"

"He is not here, little man," Vatara snorted in frustration. "Be glad that he is not here. Otherwise you would be suffering and horrible fate."

"Then finish me off," Shen bellowed. "You talk too much! Kill me-!" Vatara stretch out her claw and snatched the tiny human, letting out an ear deafening roar. Those around her dropped to their knees and held their ears. Vatara allowed everyone to recover before continuing. Other gold dragons around the city took flight and circled above their leader. Vatara waved them away.

"You do not realize how much restraint it takes for me not to crush you," she growled. "I lost many of my kin fighting the Inquisition. You place so little value on your life! I have destroyed many who have threatened my family-"

"You believe Lukhan is your family?" Shen choked. He gasped for air as the gold dragon's grip tightened. "He is everything that your clan hates! The Silver Clan views him as an enemy. Why don't you? Turn him over to the Inquisition and let us be done with this threat. Join the Holy Master and his servants; let us end the death element conclusively!"

"Under a false banner of peace, you conquer the elves and invade Ravenshaven!" Vatara snarled. "Now you speak of peace? All we could hope from you is betrayal! Would you buy the silver dragons only to slaughter them later?"

"You know more than anyone what Lukhan will become," Shen continued. "We can still correct the situation. No more have to die! We can save more lives by destroying him than allowing him to exist! Leave the Holy Master in peace, without the fear of death."

"You have caused this war, not my godson," Vatara snarled. "Lukhan's death would not stop your people's conquest. There has been too much blood spilt to be ignored. Too many wrongs have been committed. This war will not end until either dragons or humans have dominion over Lemuria. I grow weary of your lies."

Shen laughed in growing hysteria. "Dragons couldn't stop human destiny. The slaughter of their precious sacred herd is proof of this claim. The dragon race is old and feeble. You are already defeated! While dragons fight and kill each other, humanity is united. You will become nothing more than legend, a bed time story to frighten little children."

Vatara's eyes narrowed at Shen's boast. He was correct. Her clan was incapable of defeating the Inquisition. The dragon clans were too divided and scattered to defeat them. She'd seen over a million soldiers fighting under the flag of the Holy Master. Knights, men-at-arms, bombarders, warships, and hulks were only the figures of the Inquisition's long reach. If the Silver Clan joined forces with the Inquisition, then what could she do? A sense of dread and doubt filled their hearts.

"You know this," Shen stated. "Don't you."

Anger flashed in her golden eyes. "The blind are the least likely to see the future," she growled. She turned her attention to Bar. "Return this fool to his cage. Let him spread his lies among the rats and cockroaches. Perhaps they will listen to him." She released the old man back to his captives.

"Of course!" Bar agreed.

"I may not be able to see but I know that you are all doomed," Shen spat. "You are doomed! All of you! May the Holy Master take pity on your souls! May he-!"

Bar gagged and restrained him. "That's enough out of you," Bar growled. Sacul grunted and helped his friend subdue the blind man. "It's time to go back to your cage."

"Thank you for your time," Judas offered. "I didn't mean to disturb your slumber with his deranged ranting."

"Judas, please stay. The rest of you may go," Vatara instructed.

"Of course," Bar nodded quickly. "We shall seal him always as you have instructed. Should we alter his markings?"

"Yes," Vatara said. "His tattoos must be changed and disrupting the patterns and adjusting the ink's depth. That should change its function."

"It will be done!" Sacul grinned boorishly. "I know many young shamans that need to test their skills with dyes and inks."

"He is not to be tormented or tortured," Vatara warned. "Make the adjustments."

Sacul grunted in sour displeasure, his toad chirped in protest. "I'll see to it," Bar patted the boarelf on the head and led them out of the courtyard.

"May I stay, Lady Vatara?" Ambrosia asked.

"Judas is your husband and my request is not to be taken lightly," Vatara turned her attention to the fallen knight. "Your wife has told me you have fallen from grace and favor with the council. I should speak to them. A favor for a favor? With Shen choosing not to help us, the task falls to you. Can you get to the Iron Throne?"

"No," Judas warned. "The Iron Citadel is not like a normal castle or house where anyone can walk into it. The Iron Throne is protected by a moving labyrinth and ever changing passageways. The Holy Master grants access to the Inquisitor Lords to enter the main chamber-"

"That is not true," Vatara interrupted. "I have spoken with the Holy Master, centuries ago."

"You have seen him?" Judas gasped. "What did he look like?"

"Like a sickly mortal man," Vatara replied simply. "With the Inquisitor Lord being uncooperative, our only option is for you to get us inside."

"I'm no longer an Inquisitor and I'm a wanted man," Judas grew frustrated at her excessively sarcastic and simplistic response.

"What will they do if you are captured?" Vatara asked.

"I'd be killed on the spot," Judas crossed his arms defiantly.

"Then our only course of action is to break their armies," Vatara concluded. "A task that we cannot complete."

"Not an easy feat when we are at a disadvantage in every way," Ambrosia added. Vatara nodded her head in agreement with the woman's conclusion.

"We must act before they lay siege to this town," Judas warned. "Else we'll be stuck-"

"Vatara!" a gold dragon called from above. The gold dragon circled above them in a slow circle.

"What is it?" Vatara asked.

"There is a massive dust cloud on the horizon," the gold dragon called. "The Inquisition's army is here!"

Vatara looked at the humans before her. "We are too late; they have already made their move."

Chapter 54

Ravenshaven was surrounded by the Inquisition's poorly prepared military. Legions of knights lined the outside encircled perimeter. The summer's heat had taken its toll on the hard driven army. Their forced marched appeared ill advised because they were tired and ill equipped to handle the desert's summer sun, their banners and colors hung in shameful disarray. Armor was thrown aside and tents were hastily built for shade. The thin lines of men were weak in multiple areas and could be easily broken from an organized assault.

"What do you make of it?" Bar asked. The city's populace gathered on rooftops and walls in a vain attempt to see the oncoming army. Soldiers, women, and child of all races stood in fear upon the battlement. An awkward silence filled the air as the distant army encircled them, cutting off their city from the rest of the world.

Judas squint his eyes at the desperately aggressive army. It appeared to be what it was. The men were road weary soldiers. They appeared tired, fatigued, and low on morale, not the dangerous and threatening army the defenders had expected to invade. "It could be a trap," Judas announced. "I'm surprised how quickly they arrived. I'm curious what their goal is."

"We should take advantage of their weakened position and kill them," Sacul grunted. His pet toad chirped from inside his pocket. He took it out and began to lick it. "You should ride out and face them. I will stay here and protect the city."

"Sacul, brave as always," Bar muttered.

"They're light cavalry," Judas ignored his two companions. "I assume

428

they are the vanguard of a larger force. They could be here to test our defenses before the main force or survey our perimeter. I don't know."

"We must do something," Bar growled. "We can't allow men to set up camp. Let's drive them off. A pack must defend their territory when it is invaded! We should attack them!"

"Wait a moment," Judas paused. "Where is the Red Clan? They promised to serve under Lukhan and they should have destroyed this small band of men. Where are they? Something is not right."

"Could they have gone around them," Bar offered.

"Anything is likely," Sacul grunted. "Red dragons have an excellent sense of smell. Yet, anything is possible."

Vatara shifted her body nervously and considered what was possible. "I assume that they are defeated, as we were."

"You think they are captured?" Judas asked.

"Dead," Vatara corrected. "It is time for my clan to leave."

"Leave!" Ambrosia gasped. "Do you fear the Inquisition?"

"Yes," Vatara stated stoically. "You should fear them. Never underestimate your enemies. My clan is few and we cannot risk another defeat. What you see here is all that is left of the gold dragons."

"I understand," Judas frown in disappointment. "We must prepare for battle. Vatara, if you do not wish to stay, we are ready to make our stand here. If this is goodbye-"

"Where is Lukhan?" Vatara interrupted. "Where is my godson? Was he not entrusted by your people to take command? My clan will not abandon their investment."

"Yes, the council approved him by Owen's will-" Bar began.

"He should be here," Sacul grunted.

"I agree," Vatara sighed. "Yet, he is not. I fear that your leader ran into trouble. I doubt that it was human, but there are many dangers in the Endless Desert and the company he keeps is questionable. Who does leadership fall to?"

"The council must chose," Judas announced.

"This is no time for politics," Bar growled. "We need Luke! Where is the damn fool?"

The sound of bombarder fire thundered in the East. Two dragons and an angry brood of wyverns descended upon the armed riders. Screams filled the empty silence that the bombarder fire had previously filled. Unarmored men were plucked from the ground and ripped apart in midair by the murderous swarm. The plants swallowed man and horse alike. The invaders broke ranks and fled before the onslaught.

"It's him!" Bar cheered. A flash of silver and flat black signaled who it was. "It's Luke!" A cheer arose from the Ravenshaven's guard and civilians.

"More dragons!" Ambrosia gasped.

"No. Those are wyverns," Judas warned. "Slaves of the Green Clan. Prepare to fire!"

Lukhan and Con'ra broke off from the main attack group and flew toward the city. The wyverns were slower to adjust course, but followed the two dragons all the same. The two dragons appeared to be in control of the fowl creatures. They couldn't tell if the dragons were leading or being chased by the massive brood.

"Hold your fire! The wyverns are under Luke's command?" Bar asked. "How is that possible?"

"I doubt that he is in command," Vatara growled. She narrowed her eyes in suspicion.

Lukhan and Con'ra flew over the cheering cowards. "Forgive me," Con'ra called. "I must attend to the pets and make sure that they do not do anything foolish."

"Are you avoiding my godmother?" Lukhan asked.

"I am," Con'ra gave them a quick wink. "Better to avoid an argument than a fight." She broke off from their flight path and returned to her servants. The green dragon had quickly asserted her authority over them. With the death of her father, she had become their new *goddesssss*.

Lukhan approached his friends' position. His damaged body drew horrifying gasps from them. Vatara moved to block his landing path. The silver dragon angled off and circled above them.

"What are you doing?" Bar demanded. The gold dragon didn't acknowledge the knoll's question. Her full attention was focused on godson, scrutinizing his damaged body, his blackened flesh.

"Why do you stop me?" Lukhan asked in bewilderment.

"What happened to you?" Vatara demanded. "Your body glows with dark magic. The flesh has covered most of your body! The corruption has spread beyond your arm. Your body was damaged beyond-"

"Who cares?" Judas warned. He placed his hand on his sword hilt. "Let him land. He is our leader, leave him be."

Vatara raised a questioning eyebrow at the human who was threatening her. The chant of *Lukhan* rose in response to her mute silences. The common races were clearly blind to his damaged body, or they were ignorant of the threat. She couldn't blame them. Her godson inspired hope in the shadow of the Inquisition's troops. She step aside and allowed their leader to land.

"What is the matter?" Lukhan asked. His words were muffled by the roar of the crowds and the chants of his name.

"It is time for my clan to depart," Vatara muttered.

"You are leaving?" Lukhan asked. "Wait! I thought you were going to teach me the ways of the life alchemy! You made a promise to me!"

"You have others to look after," his godmother spoke in a regretful tone. "I do too."

"Vatara?" Lukhan whispered.

"You are in command," she announced. Her tone was hard and sharp. "These people look to you now. I look to you to protect my clan's investment. I will return once my clan is secure and safe."

Lukhan gulped at the thought of losing his godmother. Was she judging him, or was she abandoning him to his fate? He hoped to learn more from her. "Krain is dead. We killed him and I took his white flame. Through his memories, I saw my father and you-," He shook his head at the passing thought. "Krain sought to speak with the Inquisition and form a partnership."

Vatara raised a questioning eyebrow. She turned her attention to the distant green dragon who led the wyverns against the disorganized cavalrymen. "Krain's loss is not a terrible one to the dragon council and I will not morn his memory." Her eyes followed the young green dragon. "I hope she is worth it."

"Con'ra has proven more reliable than some," Lukhan muttered.

"The burdened of leadership is a heavy responsibility," Vatara warned. "You will not enjoy the burden." She turned her attention to those who had healed her wounds and provided safety. "Nonetheless, my clan and I are in your city's debt. For your people's hospitality and providing us shelter, I shall grant you a single boon. If it is in my power, ask what you will of me and you shall have it."

Lukhan looked at his friends. They seemed disappointed that the Gold Clan was leaving. That was when he noticed that the city had fallen silent in passive observation. It seemed that the Gold Clan and the people had found a bond while he was away. No doubt the gold dragons healed the injured and cured the sick. Now the relationship was concluding.

"I have something to ask you," Lukhan said. "The wyverns have suffered under Krain's rule. Can you heal them?"

Vatara snorted with laughter. "You could have asked me for anything. Crush your enemies, call a dragon council, or teach you about life's magic. Instead, you ask a simple task: to heal wyverns."

"Do you think me foolish?" Lukhan asked. "Or wise?"

"It is yet to be proven either way, but I am honored to call you are my godson," she smile. "A promise is a promise and I will comply with your request."

"Thank you," Lukhan bowed deeply.

"Yet I have done nothing for you," Vatara stated in sorrow. "Once this world has fallen quiet of war and the yoke of leadership has weakened, I will teach you everything I know. I promise you will be released from your curse."

"I look forward to it because I have many questions to ask you," Lukhan muttered.

"A word of caution," Vatara added. "It is easier to forgive an enemy than it is a friend."

"Mysterious as always," Lukhan smiled. He stopped guessing what his godmother meant. Her words seemed to lead to more headaches than answers, so he didn't question it.

"Does Con'ra have control of the brood?" Judas asked. "I'll not have wyverns running wild all over the city!"

"I agree," Bar said. Sacul grunted his approval with his companions. They had dealt with the troublesome winged creatures before.

"Decide for yourselves," Lukhan signaled Con'ra and the green dragon and her ravenous brood moved away from the retreating invaders and approached the city. Con'ra roared commands to the wyverns and they fell in line behind her. Some of the people cried out in fear while others dropped low, fearing the wyverns' renowned poisonous stringers. Hundreds of wyverns perched high on rooftops and battlements. Con'ra landed before them with Sessess at her side.

Con'ra boldly marched up to Vatara and bowed before her. "Thank you for healing my servants."

"I do this for my godson," Vatara growled. "Not for you. Remember your place."

"I hope to prove myself to you-," Con'ra began.

"Only time will tell," Vatara interrupted. "You, wyvern, come close. What happened to you? Such a miserable existence you come from." Sessess crawled forward in an awkward gait.

"Forgive her, she cannot speak," Con'ra said. "She was declawed, blinded, and had her tongue removed by my father's command. Can you heal her?"

"The wounds are old," Vatara said. She bent down and touched Sessess with her barbels. The brood mother cowered before the ancient gold dragon. "I will not be able to regrow the lost teeth and claws, but the flesh and tongue can be easily mended. *Carne carnis sanguis sanguini.*" A flash of bright light passed through Vatara's barbels into Sessess. The effects were not sudden or violent. Sessess's missing eye bloomed forth like the bud of a flower. Her severed tongue popped out of her scar like a vine seeking sunlight. Her dead skin and scars melted away and yielded to newly grown flesh. Her skin pigmentation turned green like a new spring's leaf.

Sessess looked down at her regenerated body. A gummy smile spread across her face. The brood mother spoke with a heavy edentulous voice. "ank goo, eiry muk." she muttered. "Die goes arr goo."

"You will have to forge her teeth and set new claws in her joints if you want her to be viable in this war," the ancient gold dragon stated. "I will tell the rest of my clan to do the same to all others who are willing."

"Wait! Why not heal Lukhan?" Con'ra demanded.

"His scars go deeper than the flesh and bone," Vatara muttered. "Those are easily repaired."

"He has no white flame," Con'ra whispered.

"What did you say?" Vatara asked as she narrowed her eyes. The green dragon knew much about her godson. This troubled her even more.

"Nothing," the green dragon was nervous. "There are others that are in need of healing. Many of them suffered from lung damage and past scarring."

While Vatara and Con'ra attended the wyverns, Lukhan's companions gather around him asking about his damaged body and if he was in any pain. Lukhan reassure his friend that he was all right and that Con'ra and her wyverns were there to help protect the city. News of Krain's death and Shen's sabotage passed quickly between dragon and common race. This put most of the gathered populace at ease, while others turned their attention to the horizon.

The Inquisition cavalry reorganized and became more conservative in positioning. They took command of a small rocky outcrop in the middle of one of the planted fields. The slight elevation provided little comfort to their vulnerable position.

"The Inquisition is obsessed with locating you," Bar said. "Even going so far as to buy the Silver Clan's loyalty."

"When did the humans get here?" Lukhan asked. He dismissed the idea of the Silver Clan serving any human master. He had no doubt that it was a plot designed to provoke him into reckless action and investigate the false claims.

"The cavalry arrived today," Judas said. "I fear that all of our strategies have been foiled. We must assume that they are aware of everything, defenses, troop numbers, supplies, everything!"

"Then I will do something unexpected," Lukhan said. "I will speak to them. See why they are here."

"You attack and now you open dialogue?" Bar asked.

"Always negotiate from a position of strength," Lukhan said with a wicked smile. Krain and Fienicks taught him that.

"How will you approach them, my Imperator?" Judas asked.

The silver dragon liked that title. Imperator Lukhan. He had fought and killed for it. The experience of the ancient green dragon and the political genius knoll was behind him. Pride and cruelty was tempted by wisdom and ambition. Leadership was no longer a question of doubt. Those around him loved him and worshiped him as a savior. They all belonged to him! The city was his treasure and the people were his jewels. He was motivated by greed! No one would ever steal his dragon's hoard!

"Luke?" Bar asked. "What is the matter?"

Lukhan looked down at his precious friend. "Today I make an oath," he announced. "I will never abandon you again. I am your leader, your protector, and your friend! My loyalty belongs to this city and its people. I shall be your sword, if you will be my shield, and together we shall be rid of the Inquisition."

The declaration brought a cheer and fear from the gathered populace. Lukhan still noticed that there were those few that didn't view him as their leader. Those that didn't cheer would soon learn to respect him out of fear and awe. He would show the doubters and dreamers the true meaning of power. He would subdue humanity, conquer a religion, and destroy a god.

They would learn to fear him.

Epilogue

"What are you doing here?" Lukhan demanded. With their bombarder ammunition expended the Inquisition invaders cowered before him. While on the ground his body turned to stone, same as Krain's body did. Some of the men jumped on horseback and fled, their commander screamed promises of traitorous executions. Other men unsheathed their swords, determined to face the single threat head on. They didn't understand what they faced.

A white flag of truce was held up at the end of a spear. A sun burnt man with the holy symbol of the Iron Throne, establishing his rank as an Inquisitor, stepped forward. He appeared to be in his mid-forties, but his bright eyes suggested that he was younger. No doubt aged beyond his years by the sacrifice of his white flame to the Holy Master.

"Hold beast!" the brave man announced. "I'm the Inquisitor Herbert, charged with the sacred duty in bring back the Inquisitor Lord Shen to the city of Alkaline-"

"So you encircle my city and attack?" Lukhan asked. "Poor choice in tactic. I would consider it an absolute failure." Saliva dribbled from the corner of his open jaws.

The knights appeared nervous at the scarred dragon's appearance. They didn't expect such a dangerous threat. "My orders are to ensure that he doesn't escape. He is a criminal and traitor and we encircled your town because-"

"Your Inquisitor Lord is safe within the city's dungeon," Lukhan sneered. "He is awaiting trial and execution."

"What is his charge?" Herbert demanded. "What is the meaning of holding a-?"

"I am sure that you were not told everything," Lukhan said. "So I will make this simple. Take your men and leave my territory or you will die."

"That is an act of war," Herbert said. "You would dare speak to me-?"

"War?" Lukhan scoffed. "The slaughter of the Sacred Herd was the first declaration! The attacks against the elves? The assassination attempt on Ravenshaven's council? These are not acts of war?"

"I have no knowledge of those actions," Herbert declared. "Those were carried out by other men. You have no grounds to hold an Inquisition Lord. The Silver Clan recognized our actions as necessary and forgave us! As a silver dragon, you will make peace with us-"

"Oh?" Lukhan said. "By whose command?"

"The Silver Clan leader," Herbert explained. "Kronus."

"An Inquisitor invoking the name of a dragon?" Lukhan asked. "Now, I have seen and heard it all."

"No, Kronus has been an ally to the Inquisition for a long time," Herbert said. "Before the tragedy of the plague. If you harm us, you will feel his wrath and that of the Silver Clan! Beware those who you look down upon, for we have enlisted powerful allies that will-"

"Then you are aware that I am no silver dragon," he growled. He lifted up his deformed claw. Its necrotic flesh rooted throughout his arm down the middle of his chest and burrowed into his belly. "I am the exiled, Lukhan, I do not recognize-!" He fell mute and his eyes widen in realization. Kronus! He was with the Inquisition before the plague? So what Shen said was true. Impossible! No silver dragon would dare-could he slay his own betrayed kin? Did the Inquisition buy the Silver Council's loyalty so easily? He knew his homeland had suffered, but to sell out to the Inquisition was horrible.

He paused in reconsideration. He was no longer part of the Silver Clan. He was an outcast to them. Other than his mother, his relationship with his clan was all but dead. He had not seen his mother since he spoke with Cirrus. They would never recognize him as one of their own.

His body shook with a terrible rage. "I now understand," he snarled. He was blind to world events; the ignorance of a hatchling was gone. No wonder his parents were trying to protect him! There was division within his clan. The relationship between Vatara and Stratos would make them an outcast in all but name.

Kronus and the Silver Council must have always sought to undermine his father's leadership! His father's majesty was built on sand. Kronus sought to rule the Silver Clan and sold out to the Inquisition!

"U-Understand?" Herbert asked.

"You were sent as a sacrifice," Lukhan said. "To start the war with Ravenshaven. Your master is cunning. It is sad that you will die for your ignorance."

"We are here-," Herbert began.

"More lies," Lukhan said. "I will see the truth, through your eyes."

The ground beneath him rippled like water, knocking the men off their feet. He pounced on them; reloaded bombarders fired their single round piercing his rocky protection but not his scales. Inquisitor Herbert was first to die, absorbed by the black claw. The man's memories were transfer instantly; he was a tool and nothing more. His masters didn't even have the decency to tell him the truth.

His mind suppressed and cleared of the human memories. The few led balls and spears that had pierced his scales were pushed out by black flesh. Lukhan smiled at the satisfying morsels. With their leader dead, those knights who remained ran in fear.

Hunger drove his remorseless killing spree. He had held hunger in check for too long. It was always there! The smell of blood was intoxicating. The thrill of murder, a joyous event. There was nothing out here that forced him to keep his rage in check. The lines between beast and man blurred until there was nothing left. His endless hunger drove him on, even though a hundred lay dead at his feet.

Nothing could stop him! No man, machine, or beast could kill him. A sense of immortality arose in his chest as he cut down another invader. They were like pigs to the slaughter. Each soul gave him the strength to continue on and confirm his suspicions. Each death meant less. It no longer matters that theses humans had loved ones that would never see them again. They were souls and flesh to consume.

It was his destiny, his fate; he would become the embodiment of death.

———◆◆◆———

The single dragon routed the small army. This glutinous murder brought cheers from the gathered populace. The siege ended before it truly began. Bar, Sacul, and Judas stood silent as they watched their leader continue his berserker feast.

"He is our leader," Bar said. He words were empty and hollow. He couldn't believe how much his friend had changed. From exile to leader.

"I should take my people and go," Sacul grunted. "Follow the Gold Clan into the Endless Desert. I can see no good come out of this." He looked at the boarelves who were among the gathered crowds. They cheered for the death of the Inquisition. They seemed to enjoy their enemies' bloodshed. They held up boomerangs and spears, grunting war cries and beat on their chest.

"I don't think they will want to leave," Bar said dryly. "They like what they see." The citizenry seemed to rally at their dragon leader's blood frenzy.

"Is this what you wanted?" Ambrosia asked her husband. She couldn't stand the sight of blood. Even from this distance, crimson soaked their fields. "To kill your fellow Inquisitors? Have you no pity for them?"

"I have seen many battles," Judas said. He hugged his wife and held her close, blocking her view of the massacre. "It's difficult for me to watch." He stood silent and focused on his wife. They took comfort in each other's arms. Judas didn't have the answers, his only desire was to protect his wife and save the Holy Master. He was convinced that the Inquisition threatened both of these goals. What type of god would need men to fight for him? When it came down to the Holy Master and Lukhan, who would he chose? The choice was not an easily one, but it would be made.

The city watched on in glorious pleasure.

"Why are you really here?" Vatara asked. She ignored the violence that her godson was committing. This was war and Lukhan was the city's only hope in defeating the Inquisition. The cries of distant slaughter did not disturb her.

Con'ra thought carefully on how to answer that question. Her yellow eyes were focused on the distant silver dragon. She had seen his rage before and a deep desire to stop him swelled in her chest. For a brief moment she felt powerless and fearful. Comfort came when she realized that she wasn't alone. She was surrounded by her regenerated wyvern brood. She cleared her throat before speaking. She opened her mouth, but was interrupted.

"Do not lie to me or twist the truth," Vatara warned. "Never underestimate my insight."

"I will not lie," Con'ra promised. "I am here to kill him, your godson."

Vatara blinked at the bold green dragon. "He knows this?" she asked. "Then you know what he claims to be and he believes what he will become? A death elemental?"

"Yes," she stated unwaveringly.

"Do you care about him?" Vatara asked.

"I-I do not know," Con'ra stuttered in wavering uncertainly.

"A lie," Vatara warned. "I may be old, but I am not blind. Do not fall in love with him or it will make your task all the more impossible."

"What?" Con'ra asked in confusion. "You do not defend him?"

"To kill Lukhan, you must remove the Staff of Selgae from his upper left forearm," the ancient dragon instructed. "The ancient artifact is embedded in his body. Destroy that limb and it will sever the last barrier that protects Lukhan's fading mind and spirit. Strengthen your resolve. Find something you hate about him and use it to protect your heart. He is a silver dragon; it should not be difficult to find differences."

"You sound as if you have given up on him," Con'ra said.

"No, I will never give up on him," Vatara said. "I do not have the heart to kill him. However, you must do what I cannot."

——◆——

"Inquisitor Lord Michael," a canoness said. The beautiful sun kissed woman sat on a brown gelding and pushed her black hair out of her veiled face. The niqab and hijab matched her simple but elegant robed clothing. When the man didn't reply immediately, she sat in silent attention behind the Inquisitor Lord. "It appears that the Master Shen's redeemers have failed in their task. What are your orders?"

"They were a necessary loss and the monster took the bait," Michael announced. He peered through his monocular and watched the last of Shen's guards be slaughtered. The traitors served their purpose; they were nothing more than expendable soldiers. "The city of Ravenshaven attacked Alkaline's troops. It's an act of war against the Holy Master. Prepare to move against them." The announcement didn't come as a surprise to his generals and advisors, who stared at the distant city on the horizon. An army of over a hundred thousand strong stood behind them.

A large knoll, cloaked in shadows, knelt before the Inquisitor Lord.

"My Lord, the main artillery is ready to be moved into position," the knoll whispered. A spiked collar was wrapped around his cloak and neck, but this device didn't stop his voice from cutting through the air like a knife. "The dragon heads have been strapped to the mouth of the bombarders according to your instruction."

Michael turned to investigate his chief assassin's claim. Severed red dragons' heads were placed over the end of the muzzle of the massive bombarder artillery. Each bombarder varied in size and shape, some appearing like long metal tubes while others akin to a witch's cauldron. The massive artillery was pulled by teamsters and their beasts.

Soldiers from every rank of human society stood at the ready. Michael smiled at the sight. They had come together under his leadership. It was the Holy Master's will that led them to him, his men's eyes were bright and their code of arms and war banners shined with proud loyalty and dedication to the Holy Master. They were servants of god, righteous weapons of humanity.

Yet, this was not his proudest achievement. Towering above these massive weapons and legions of men stood the Fist of the Master. An iron golem forged by the Holy Master himself, known as the left hand of Iron Throne. Imbued with magical wards beyond count, the golem had been the key to his successful campaign against the troublesome elves. The elite guard of the Holy Master stood at attention. The steel giant was the perfect soldier. It didn't have to eat, rest, or feel. It had no flesh to cut and no soul to give it pause. True perfection, a weapon built by a god.

Michael, the last Inquisitor Lord, smiled.

Definitions:

Alchemy – to the modern age it is chemistry and physics. Alchemy is a mixture of different natural ingredients. Alchemists are surrounded by mystery and myth. To the uneducated and unknowledgeable, alchemist are considered to be wizards or witches. See the study of dragons and elves as five elements; humans as four elements.

Air Element – it is a shared element by both humans and dragons. Air in alchemy is for the natural elements found in the wind itself. It is one of the common elements. *Elemental*: powerful beings who dwell in and control Lemurian skies.

Ambrosia - [am-broh-zhuh] – is a Ravenshaven native that has family connections to the powerful merchant's guild. She is the wife of Judas and a powerful alchemist in her own right. She is kind, but somewhat naive when it comes to dragons and other nonhuman races.

Azure Ocean – is known for both its beauty and dangers. Mythical sea monsters are said to roam freely devouring ships and sailors alike, other than its coastal shorelines little is known about its deep depths.

Bar - [bahr] – was once a leader of a knoll pack and is a loyal character. He has a deep history with Lukhan. He is knowledgeable about nature and wilderness survival. He is a member of the Ravenshaven's Council and seeks to find his missing pack.

Black Dragons – are known for their ebony scales. Black dragons are considered evil by most of the common race. Black dragons are opportunist to the extreme; this is why the common race believes that they are evil. Black dragons are known to attack defenseless areas and back bite other dragon clans. They use their sound tactical judgment to win battles and do not prefer balanced or equal fights. Black dragons are master of the element of death, and use death magic and alchemy. Their numbers were drastically reduced when the plague spread out of control.

Black Flame – is one of the five Dragon Elements, also known as darkness, negative energy, abyss, emptiness, and void. The Black Flame is usually associated with the ultimate evil. In alchemy it is symbolized as the ending of a reaction. Once the Black Flame was equally worshiped as the White Flame, but after the fall of the Mixed Kingdoms and the rise of the Inquisition, few of the common races worship Black Flame viewing it as evil. Only the dragons and elves do not view the Black Flame as evil. The Black Flame is also known as Death Element.

Black Kingdom – After the fall of the Gold Kingdom and Elves Rebellion, the Black Clan led a successful campaign against the elves. Using magic they warped their enslaved elves into knolls and trolls. With the aid of theses creations the Black Kingdom rose to power. Their power was unrivaled until their advancement was stopped by the united forces of the Silver Mountains.

Black Marshes – is a relic from the fall of the Black Kingdom. The Black Clan retreated to their original homelands. This is where the Black Clan lives; it is a harsh climate that consists of everything deadly. The land is nothing more than salt marshes, swamplands, and bogs combine into one territory.

Blood Queen – is the title known to the current leader of the Red Clan. She is a powerful combatant and holds untold fury for the dragon that killed her beloved mate, Orelac. She holds vast amount of knowledge and secrets.

Blue Dragons – are Leviathans are the masters of the depths of the oceans and seas. They are considered one of the few surviving impure dragon clans. They have been despised and hated ever since the Dragon Wars. Despite the other dragon's land dominates the Blue Clan has been able to survive for centuries under the world's oceans and seas.

Boarelves - [bohr-elvz] – is a race of swine humanoids. The boarelves are barbaric and tough because they live in the Endless Desert. Although considered crude by others, boarelves can eat most things that could kill the other common races. Despite their small stature they are physically strong and resilient. Boarelves are concerted prime fair to many of the dragon races.

Box - [boks] – is the twin brother of Brick. Box fled with the females and children before death of the Bar's tribe.

Brick - [brik] – is the twin brother of Box. He is the warrior of the two brothers and youngest knoll known to become hunter. He was part of Bar's tribe before it was destroyed by trolls.

Cirrus - [sir-uhs] – was an ancient silver dragon who has been corrupted by the addictive powers of magic. He was once the mentor to Stratos and Vatara. Cirrus was a powerful member of the Silver Council. He exiled Lukhan because of the corruption of the black claw and his impure blood.

Con'ra - [kuhn-rah] – is a green dragon approximately the same age as Lukhan. Her father is Krain, leader of the Green Clan. Con'ra is incredibly charismatic and self-righteous leader; this has helped her in the past with double dealing and back biting. She is slightly younger than Lukhan. Con'ra has a scar that appears to be vines going down the side of her neck, a curse placed by her father.

Common Race – referred to by dragons as the "lesser" races. They are named so because they are so common. They were once viewed as a food source by many of the dragon clans. However, this changed during the third Council of Dragons, when the council allowed elves and humans to speak openly among them. The common race includes Elves, Humans, Knolls, Boarelves, Trolls, and Wyverns.

Council of Dragons – There have only been four times in history that the council has come together to discuss major events. Generally, the continent of Lemuria seems to change and shift in concert whenever there are these unnatural meetings. War and world changing events occur soon after the council meets. Many of the common races are apprehension whenever this council gathers; this fear has caused the lesser races to hate dragon kind.

Death Element – These creatures have intense power over death and are the rarest of the elements. Few dragons have attempted to raise such a powerful creation. These powerful beings actively seek out life to destroy it to feed. *Elemental:* are rare creatures that have laid cities to waste to feed its endless hunger before disappearing into a black mist.

Dire Wolf – an animal that was created and lived side by side with the elves. Dire wolves and elves have a long and peaceful history together. They are an endangered race because of their large size and the loss of food supply caused by the aggressive expansion of humans. Humans and wolves are in competition over territory on the Golden Plains. This has caused tensions between man and elf.

Dragon – is the lords and masters of the world's elements. Many clans are isolationist and xenophobic. They are considered masters of the Dragon's Five Elements. They are the oldest known creatures in Lemuria. Although they can live to be over four thousand years, dragons rarely live past their three-thousandth year because of their over use of magic. There are few dragons left after the Dragon Wars, but their power is unrivaled. Dragons control the elements and magical abilities, which give them the appearance to have god-like powers. They can shape and craft the lands that they live in to suites their clan's needs. Few of the common races, let alone individuals, can come into power without the aid or favor of at least one clan of dragons. The worst enemy to a dragon is another individual from its own clan.

Dragon's Five Elements – After the Dragon War, there were only five major dragon clans left. The five clans developed a mastered form of the five elements. The elements include Life, Death, Earth, Fire, and Air. The human alchemist disagrees with the dragon's five elements. *Elemental-* are living embody of the five dragon elements.

Dragon Wars – an ancient world wide civil war that helped spur on the creation of the elves. Many elements, giants, and animals were created and destroy during this time. The wars lasted for eons and almost caused the dragons to become extinct. The dragons destroyed one another until only five "pure" clans dominated vast tracks of territory. Outcasts or "impure" dragons fled to the ends of the world to escape the five major clans. The war ended with the rise of the Gold Kingdom and the creation of their elves.

Fienicks - [fee-niks] – is a fire elemental enslaved to the Red Clan. The element resembles the legendary firebird and phoenix. A being of fire element, this creature is much more than it seems.

Earth Element – It is a shared element by both humans and dragons. Earth in alchemy is for the natural elements found in the ground itself. It is one of the common elements being found everywhere. Earth Elements are the most common lost relic of the Dragon Wars. *Elemental-* is powerful beings live within the earth and is sometimes unearthed by accident.

Eldora De'Saurma - [el-dohr-uh] [duh-sawr-mah] – is a middle age female elf from the city of Angakok. She is master archer and is a friend to Lukhan. Her age and experiences have made her both deadly and wise.

Elementals – are living creatures of the Dragon's Five Elements. Most are considered symbolic entities by alchemists, ancient dragons, and magic users. These creatures predate the dragons and their vast history. Such beings have no known civilianization or languages and are considered myths and legends.

Elves – known as the first creations by the dragons. They are blessed with long life by the Gold Clan. Elves have a deep and troubled history with the dragon clans. The elven race has served and fought the dragons. After the Elves Rebellion the elven people became shadows of their former selves. Only three kingdoms exist today.

Elves Kingdom – after the fall of the Gold Kingdom, elves created their own kingdom in the wake of the destruction of the Gold Kingdom. With the combined war effort of the Red, Green, and Black Clans attacked and ultimately subdued the Elves Kingdom. Many surviving refugees fled to the Silver Mountains. Meanwhile the red, green, and black dragons punished and destroyed the elves within their dominion. Ultimately, it was the Black Clan that conquered and ended the Elves Kingdom. Today the elves live in three smaller realms near the Silver Mountains.

Fire Element – is a shared element by both humans and dragons. Fire in alchemy is for the natural elements found in natural infernos. *Elemental-* are beings made of pure survive within and around fire.

Fortaleza - [fawr-tl-ey-zuh] – was the last elven city and fortress that stood against the onslaught of the Black Kingdom. The ruined city and elven fortress is a symbolic tombstone to the Gold and Elves Kingdoms. The current ruins are nothing but a degraded trophy for the Black Clan. The fall of the mighty fortress announced the end of the Elves Rebellion and the birth place of the magical disease known as the plague. Within the city, stand a great elven temple, where Lukhan and his friend helped to vanquish the threat of the Plague.

Giants - [jahy-uhnt] – are a race of oversized animals and elves. Giants are a broad term used to explain abnormally large creatures. The humanoid giants and animals are rare. Giants require vast amounts of resources and space. Many surviving giants are relics from the Dragon Wars.

Gold Dragons – The most caring race of dragons to the common races. They take an active role in the troubles of others; this is considered weakness by the other dragon clans. This dragon clan once had their own kingdom; however it was destroyed by the elves during the Elves Rebellion. Gold dragons are from the element of life, and control both life magic and alchemy.

Gold Kingdom – the largest and most successful dragon kingdom in recorded history. As the name suggests, the Gold Clan were the masters of this once ancient kingdom. The Gold Clan success was due to their elf servants. The five dragon clan shared and trade knowledge. Together the clans kept the peace with their elf servants and the dragons prospered. The elves grew tired of their dragon masters and rebelled. The Gold Clan was defeated and they fled to the Silver Mountains. The elves took over the Gold Kingdom and turned it into the Elves Kingdom.

Golems - [goh-luhm] – are constructs made from the earth. Powerful magic and alchemy is required to animate these lifeless creatures. Such automatons are not given birth to, but are constructed. They serve their masters until their destruction or are dismantle. Golems are slow and mindless.

Grand Magus – is a title given to magi with learned magical abilities. The position is usually persevered for the oldest magus within the city-state's school. They are considered high lords and headmasters of the elven cities and schools.

Green Dragons – are the smallest and quickest of the dragon races. Unlike the other larger dragons the Green Clan lives together in small groups for most of their lives. These groups are much more powerful than a single large dragon. Green dragons are social only within their own families. They are from the earth element, which means they control earth magic and alchemy.

Havoc - [hav-uhk] – is an adult red dragon, who is proud but not foolish. He cautious and seeks to grow in power. His past dealings with the Gold Clan had earned him a title of being a thief. He looks forward to the approaching war. More food, gold, and a chance to gain more power.

Hollylyassa River - [hol-ee-lahy-as-uh] – is a major landmark which splits the Kingdom of Alkaline and the three smaller elf kingdoms. It is a major geographical boarder for the humans and elves. The humans that have river locks and forts along the massive river control trade. Several elf and human cities exist along the major trade route.

Holy Master – is a demigod among humans. A mortal man bound to an Iron Throne, forever unable to move and never die. The real name of the Holy Master has been lost to history. Dragon kind views his existence as an abomination and a self-inflicted curse. It is unclear if the Inquisitors are simply abusing their power or the Holy Master has gone insane.

Horrus'ra River - [hawr-uhs-rah] – is a major geographical river in the Green Clan's territory. The river flows through the Green and Jade rainforest. The river levels change yearly due to the constant rains. It is untamed by all the lesser races, because of its dragon owners.

Human – is a race of masculine elves. The Silver Clan punished them for turning on the Gold Kingdom. Humans are more aggressive and larger than normal elves. Individual's attitudes vary from village to village. They are intelligent warriors for the most part. They are a short-lived race, caused by the loss of the gold dragon's blessings, which the Silver Clan took away as punishment for rebelling. Humans are a distrustful race and do not care to spend time with other races that they consider different.

Human's Elements – Humans worship the four elements. The human elements are air, earth, fire, and water. Humans focus on the more violent elements, such as earth and fire. Dragons and elves recognize the Dragon's Five Elements as the "true" elements.

Inquisition – is the ruling elite of humans with a divine connection with the Holy Master. They are the officials that rule in the name of the Holy Master, only Inquisitor Lords are allowed to look upon his holy presence. One of the few empowered organization ruled by the human race. Despite their divine connections, economic influence, and racist superiority there is an underground resistance against the ruling class.

Judas - [joo-duhs] – is a human male that serves as an Inquisitor to the Holy Master. He is a human "religious" leader that has high ideals and morals. When he was twenty-two, Judas had willingly sacrificed half of his white flame to gain favor within the Inquisition. He has slowly giving up his hatred and ignorance for a more peaceful outlook.

Kale - [keyl] – was once the Grand Magus of Angakok, the elf who became corrupted by magic. He had control of one of three parts of the Staff of Selgae.

Kingdom of Alkaline - [al-kuh-lahyn] – is also known as the human's kingdom. After the destructive fall of the Mixed Kingdoms, the city of Alkaline ruled the Golden Plains. It is the major economic power of the common races. The religious order of the Holy Master, the Inquisition, rules over the kingdom. It is the Inquisitors that carry out the divine will of the Holy Master to the kingdom's subjects.

Kingdom of Angakok - [ang-guh-kok] – is the most northern city-state of the three elf kingdoms. It is known for its magus tower and its vast redwood forest. It is a place of learning and many of the elves go to study inside the Magus Tower. There is a one piece of the legendary artifact Staff of Selgae. The Grand Magus carries the powerful artifact. This kingdom was destroyed during the plague.

Kingdom of Omikse - [oh-mee-ksey] – is also known as the lower elf kingdom. It has a close connection with the Human Kingdom of Alkaline. It is the economic vain to the other city-state Sedna. The city of Omikse lies within a hundred leagues of the fortress port city of Alkaline. Due to its location, the ports at the Hollylyassa River and the ocean give it rich economic opportunities. Human traders are warmly welcomed within the kingdom. This city holds the dagger artifact that belongs to the Staff of Selgae.

Kingdom of Sedna - [sed-nah] – is also known as the middle elf kingdom. The elf city-state is known to be the main elves defense. The Kingdom of Sedna is the oldest known elf kingdom. This city holds the yellow diamond artifact that belongs to the Staff of Selgae.

Knoll - [nohl] – a race of short-lived canine humanoids that is prolific. The race is considered evil by most of the common race. This is a misconception because knolls vary greatly from pack to pack. Humans actively hunt them down because of the betrayal of the Mixed Kingdoms. Elves tolerate them unless they become violent or rebellious. Knolls are smaller in stature than humans and elves and have a greater endurance. They are considered primitive by the other races. Knolls have no known permanent cities or kingdoms, preferring a tribal life style instead.

Krain - [kreyn] – is the leader of the Green Clan. Wise and cruel behind his years, Krain looks to gain the upper hand during the recent events. He is not afraid to take risks to insure that his clan rules and dominates the land. Father of Con'ra.

Kronus - [kroh-nuhs] – is the Silver Council's champion and ascetic politician. He is a rival of Vatara and Stratos. Kronus has taken the recent events and has turned the Silver Council against the wishes of Vatara and Stratos. Although the Silver Council views the Gold Clan as neighbors and friends, there is division within the council about what to do with their peaceful dragon neighbors. A divided rift, Kronus is willing to use for his own benefit.

Lemuria - [le-myoor-ee-uh] – is the major continent and has vast geographical diversity. It is part of the "old" world where kingdoms and territory are already established within the five dragon clans and the common races. Although there have always been established kingdoms, borders continually change depending on the strength of an individual groups.

Lesser Races – see common race. It is generally an insult or muttered in distain by dragons. Dragons often refer to their creations as lesser, mostly because it is true. Few other creatures can match the strength and intelligence of a fully grown dragon. This has caused some dragons to have a superiority complex over the "lesser" creatures. The common race often enjoys taking advantage of the dragon's overconfidence, which has led to the downfall of several powerful dragons.

Life Element – also referred to white flame and five dragon elements. It is one of the rarest elements in the world. Only through the creation of life are these beings created. *Elemental-* Unlike other elements, life elemental can live forever once they have been given life. They require no external resources to remain alive and simply live.

Lukhan - [loo-kahn] – is the protagonist, a young silver dragon, the son of Stratos and Crystal. Godchild to the Gold Clan leader, Vatara. He is known as the Defender of the Common Races, Destroyer of the plague, and Silver Lord. The common races believe that Lukhan is a symbol of virtue, sacrifice, and honor. While dragon kind view him with begrudging respect for his defeat of the plague and his rising popularity with the common races. He has fallen and disgraceful in the Silver Council's eyes.

Louis - [loo-eez] – After the fall of Kale, the elf named Louis took the position of Grand Magus of Angakok. When the plague's invade the Silver Mountains, Louis was slain by the infected Orelac. Louis cursed the Kingdom of Angakok with his final breath.

Michael - [mahy-kuh] – is an Inquisitor Lord, a red haired robust man who is a fighter. He is considered an extremist within the Inquisition. Michael seeks human supremacy and genocide for those creatures he views as less than human.

Onekyh - [wuhn-key] – was an ancient life giant, protector, and guardian of the Vilesath. The Gold Clan bound him into the form a life golem shape as a suit of golden armor and placed him as the jailor of the Betrayer. When Vilesath was released he turned on Onekyh.

Oracle – see black dragon named Vilesath. The Oracle has the gift of foresight and has foretold many things. Including the fall of many kingdoms and the plague that once ravaged the land.

Orelac - [ohr-lak] – was once the leader of the plague, destroyer of the city of Angakok, murderer of the Silver Clan leader Stratos, and mate to Fienicks. Orelac unwittingly becomes the sacrifice require to destroy the Plague. He was slain by the silver dragon named Lukhan.

Owen - [oh-uhn] – is the ruling council member of Ravenshaven. A white knoll, which is uncommon among the knoll tribes, is the leader of the council and is skilled at working the difficult relationships with the multiple fractions and special interests groups within Ravenshaven.

Ravenshaven - [rey-vuhns-hey-vuhn] – is an outcast city that resides in the outskirts of the human Kingdom of Alkaline. The silver dragon Stratos once fought to protect this city from the Inquisition, but departed so after to allow the common race to rule their city. This left a power vacuum in which merchant guilds, thieves, and slaver traders gathered and did business. The town is transitional point between the Golden Plains and Endless Desert. After a successful coup d'état, a knoll named Owen is now the leader of the perfidious fortress city. With the aid of Judas and the Gold Clan, the city was rebuilt and flourished. The symbol upon the flag was a three prong raven that looked similar to a dragon's claw.

Red Dragons – Are the most violent tempered of dragon kind. Red dragons value strength above all else, this philosophy has caused the Red Clan to grow larger and physically stronger than other dragons. They are the archetypical dragon and are best known to the world. Red dragons actively steal treasure from dragons and common race alike. They have made the common race fear the dragons because of their lust for battle and treasure. Red dragons are from the element of fire, which means that they control fire magic and alchemy.

Shen Tianxiang - [shuhn] [tee-ahn-hsiang] – is an Inquisitor Lord, who is both a foreigner to the lands of Lemuria and the Inquisition order. Shen is loyal to the Holy Master but is despised by his follow Inquisitor Lords. Being a foreigner gives him the advantage of a worldly view and knowledge of strange magic, but is contained by his faith to the Iron Throne.

Silver Council – Within the Silver Clan, there are ancient dragons that form the council. The title of ancient and membership are gained to those silver dragons that have reached the three-thousandth year of their age. Silver Dragons like to keep to themselves and are slow to react, however the older the dragon gets they begin to isolate themselves from the rest of the world. After living for three thousand years there is not much in the world that an ancient silver dragon has not seen or motivates them into action.

Silver Dragon – The most commonly isolated dragons, who prefer to let events happen as they watch from afar. Silver dragons are kind but uncaring. Like other dragons they are furiously territorial. They do not take an active role until a problem is at their door step; in the past this has served them well when dealing with other dragon clans. Silver dragons are from the element of air, meaning they control air alchemy and magic.

Staff of Selgae - [sel-eyj] – is a legendary artifact of the elves. The artifact was created by Selgae the First Grand Magus during the Elves Rebellion. When Selgae created the staff he was completely drained of his immense magical power. So powerful and dangerous the staff had become that it had to be split into three parts. The staff's three parts: a golden staff, yellow diamond, and a dagger. One piece of the legendary artifact can gain a boost to the wielder's magical abilities. When the artifact was completely combined, the whole staff will increase the wielder's natural magical abilities by one thousand fold.

Strait of Dracon - [drey-koh] – is a geographical boarder between the Silver Mountains and the Black Marshes. The strait is known to have violent storms because of the clashing cool and warm fronts of the Gulf of Dracaena.

Stratos - [strat-taws] – was once the Leader of the Silver Clan, a beloved father to Lukhan, and loyal mate to Crystal. He is known by the elves as the Hero of the Eastern Woods. He died fighting the plague corrupted Orelac on the rim of a volcano in the Mountains of Fire.

Thaumaturgy - [thaw-muh-tur-jee] – the working of wonders or miracles; magic. A rarely acceptable use of foreign magic within the Inquisition. The Inquisitors do not use magic; instead they used condemned prisoners or slaves. By using binding rituals and tattooing wards on prisoners, the Inquisition can force others to use their "evil" magic against their enemies.

The Ten Laws of Magic – The dragons created ten laws of magic. These rules are laws and cannot be bent or broken. Many have tried to find ways to get past this laws.1. Casting magic always cost greater and is never equal to or lesser than.2. No race can master magic, magic always masters you.3. Magic is always unnatural in a natural world.4. Magic that feeds or combines with the white flame is not as costly as attempting to extinguish it.5. Every race can cast magic, but only dragons and elves can survive its deadly consequences.6. Magic can be created or destroyed.7. Magic is unnatural; natural elements can help or hinder the white flame and its effects.8. Magic can and will become addictive.9. Magic cannot be stopped once it is cast.10. If one learns how to use magic, they will die from the stain on their white flame.

Three Kingdoms of Elves – Three city-states that share equal power among the Grand Magi. Each city is ruled over by a single Grand Magus. The three major kingdoms are called Angakok, Omikse, and Sedna. Each of these cities holds a piece of the legendary artifact called the Staff of Selgae. During the Plague the city of Angakok was destroyed.

The Plague – was a pandemic event that effected both common and dragon races alike. The magical disease appears to be a living green substance that was created by the black dragon named Vilesath and was destroyed by silver dragon called Lukhan. The diseased infects the blood stream and brain causing the infected individual to become aggressive and mad, until the event of their death when they become the undead. Highly contagious and aggressive, this magical disease spread rapidly and caused massive amounts of destruction and loss of lives. The Black Marshes and Silver Mountains were places under siege. The elf city of Angakok was destroyed by the plague's rampage.

Troll - [trohl] – The Black Clan created these creatures from the scales of the dead gold dragons and the captured elves after the fall of the Gold Kingdom and Elves Rebellion. Trolls are the physically largest of the common race. They can be slow witted, but with proper training trolls can become powerful warriors. Wild troll brutes are common in the Black Marshes where the Black Clan lives. Trolls are trained and used as personal bodyguards for some of the evil dragon clans.

Undead – is caused by the plague. Once a creature is infected by the plague it has unnatural strength and resistance to pain. However, when the afflicted dies, the victim become an undead mockery of its former self. Only the basic needs and desires of the green substance are left to control the body. Undead slowly decay over time and body complete falls apart. The afflicted creature may take off decayed or destroyed body parts and replace them with another's limb. Only with the complete destruction of the body can the undead be defeated.

Vatara - [vah-tahr-rah] – is a powerful gold dragon and a charismatic leader. She was appointed by Stratos to be Lukhan's godmother. Once leader of both the Silver Clan and Gold Clan during the Plague, she has been forced out of the Silver Mountains by Kronus. As a female gold dragon, she is not always accepted, but her wisdom and healing capabilities are always welcomed.

Vilesath - [vahyl-sath] – is also known as the Oracle, the Betrayer, Death Lord, Shadow Dragon, etc. He was the creator of the knolls, trolls, and the plague. Once a powerful black dragon and mastermind, Vilesath is a forgotten legend even among dragon kind. He was the one who gave Lukhan the Black Claw in an attempt to save the world from his own creation, the plague.

Water Element – is an element that is in disagreement between the human and dragon alchemists. This element is unique only to man because it is so important to them. Dragons and elves have tried to convince man that water is a combination of the air elements. Humans view the water element important to their existence and trade. *Elemental-* nonexistent.

White Flame – is one of Five Dragon Elements. Also known as the spirit, Ki, soul, essences, Ka, light, positive energy, and qi. The white flame is usually associated with the ultimate good. In alchemy the White Flame is the beginning of a reaction. Different common race religions give it different names. Dragons and elves are the only ones that live long enough to become one with their white flame. Occasionally, the other races tap into this force but they do not live long enough to continue to summon it. Every race has a limited amount of white flame; however it is difficult to measure an individual's limits.

Wyvern - [wahy-vern] – is the youngest of the common races. These creatures serve the Green Clan as warrior slaves and guard dogs, using poisonous stingers as their main weapons. They are an elusive race much like their dragon masters. Within their rainforest wyverns serve under the watchful eyes of their dragon masters.